Full Circle

I can feel it now, magick threading through the trees like a scent. These vibrations are strange to me—is this good magick being worked? What if it's not? But surely I would pick up on it if it's dark magick. For a moment I hesitate. What if . . . But I press on. Just ahead of me the greenish light filtering through the trees' crowns grows brighter: there's a clearing ahead. I swallow and try to press forward, crashing clumsily through the trees and bushes, slapping the vines aside. This is it—soon, soon I will see the magick worker. Soon I will compare myself to her—she will be more trained and more knowledgeable, but I will be stronger. My throat is tight with excitement. Soon, soon, just another step . . . and then my foot catches on a tree root, throwing me off balance.

As I feel myself falling, my muscles tense and I fling out my arms. My wrist hits something hard with a startling smack. Wild-eyed, I jerk to a sitting position, not able to make sense of what I am seeing. Did I faint? Did the witch put some kind of spell on me?

. . .

SWEEP

SWEEP

Cate Tiernan

Volume V

Reckoning

Full Circle

Night's Child

speak

An Imprint of Penguin Group (USA) Inc.

Book Thirteen

SWEEP
Reckoning

Reckoning

SPEAK

Published by the Penguin Group
Penguin Group (USA) Inc., 345 Hudson Street, New York, New York 10014, U.S.A.
Penguin Group (Canada), 90 Eglinton Avenue East, Suite 700, Toronto, Ontario, Canada M4P 2Y3
(a division of Pearson Penguin Canada Inc.)
Penguin Books Ltd, 80 Strand, London WC2R 0RL, England
Penguin Ireland, 25 St Stephen's Green, Dublin 2, Ireland (a division of Penguin Books Ltd)
Penguin Group (Australia), 250 Camberwell Road, Camberwell, Victoria 3124, Australia
(a division of Pearson Australia Group Pty Ltd)
Penguin Books India Pvt Ltd, 11 Community Centre, Panchsheel Park, New Delhi - 110 017, India
Penguin Group (NZ), 67 Apollo Drive, Rosedale, Auckland 0632, New Zealand
(a division of Pearson New Zealand Ltd)
Penguin Books (South Africa) (Pty) Ltd, 24 Sturdee Avenue, Rosebank, Johannesburg 2196, South Africa

Registered Offices: Penguin Books Ltd, 80 Strand, London WC2R 0RL, England

Published by Puffin Books, a division of Penguin Young Readers Group, 2002
Published by Speak, an imprint of Penguin Group (USA) Inc., 2009
This omnibus edition published by Speak, an imprint of Penguin Group (USA) Inc., 2011

1 3 5 7 9 10 8 6 4 2

 Produced by 17th Street Productions,
an Alloy company
151 West 26th Street
New York, NY 10001

17th Street Productions and associated logos ,
are trademarks and/or registered trademarks of Alloy, Inc.

ISBN 978-0-14-241028-8
This omnibus ISBN 978-0-14-242011-9

Printed in the United States of America

RECKONING

Prologue

Two days have passed since Mother died. The neighbors do not come by to pay their respects. I watch them hurry past our house and shiver, as if the misery here were like a cold hand pressing them away from our front gate.

My thoughts remain entirely on that fatal night. It sticks in my mind like a nightmare too horrible for any detail to be forgotten.

The house was quiet. It was so still and peaceful that I could feel the gentle pulsing of the waves on the shoreline almost a quarter of a mile away. The cats were sleeping by the fire. Then Mother came rushing in. She was naked, and her hair was wild.

"Máirín," she cried, her eyes glistening, "it is done."

I had experienced far too many strange nights since Mother had been ill to be completely shocked. Calmly, so as not to frighten her away, I crossed the room to cover her. When I got close, however, I saw that her hands were covered in blood. She had pricked both of her thumbs, and there were smears of blood all over her body. To be skyclad and to show signs of letting one's own blood—these are signs of the darkest magick. This was not something I had encountered before.

"What have you done?" I gasped.

She reached up and began gently stroking my face in reply. As I tried to put the blanket over her shoulders, she ran away from me, up the stairs. She moved with unnatural power and speed. As she ran, I heard her yelling out. She was spelling, that I knew, but her voice was crazed and unintelligible.

I had no time to take a lamp to guide me, and I stumbled up the dark steps after her. I found her on the widow's walk, on her knees, calling out to the moon in words I could not recognize. She went limp as I approached and seemed to lose interest in whatever it was she was doing, and I had a terrible feeling that she had just had time to complete whatever it was. Again I begged her to tell me what she had done.

"Soon," she said, "soon you'll know."

She allowed me to lead her back downstairs, where I washed away the blood and dressed her in a nightgown. She kept calling her own name over and over again, "Oona . . . Oona . . ." dragging the words along in a pitiful moan until the act of repetition exhausted her.

When I came back to the parlor, I passed by the glass and saw myself. On my face, sketched out in blood, were hexing signs—

that's what she had been doing when she touched me. Horrified, I ran to the basin of seawater that I kept in the kitchen for scrying and washed them away as quickly as I could. I stayed up half the night, trying to dispel whatever it was that she had done. I burned rosemary and uttered every purification and deflection spell I'd ever learned.

The next morning her bed was empty.

A fisherman found her yesterday. She was about half a mile from the house, washed up on the shore. She had gone out during the night and walked into the water. She still wore her nightgown.

Now the house shudders. This morning the windows broke for no reason. The mirror in the parlor cracked from side to side.

Mighty Goddess, guide her spirit and have mercy on me, her daughter. May I break my voice, lose it forever from my lamentations and weeping. My mother, Oona Doyle of Ròiseal, is gone, and something dark has come in her stead.

—Màirín

1

Omens

June 14, 1942

The ghosts are angry today. They smashed a vase in the front room, and they knocked over a lamp. The lamp almost hit our cat, Tady. He ran and hid under the sofa. Mother told us to be brave and not to cry, so I have been trying very hard. I have not cried once, even though the ghosts started banging the door of my room open and shut. My little sister, Tioma, is not as brave as I am. She hid in her closet and sobbed. She does not understand that we must prove to the ghosts that we are not afraid. That is the only way we can get them to leave.

—Aoibheann

Finally, some peace and quiet.

Hilary, my father's girlfriend, is pregnant. Since she'd moved in a few weeks before, I had been more or less treated like a pet or a piece of furniture, just something to be dealt with or moved around while they were getting ready for the "real" child to come.

Among her many awful ideas, Hilary had major redecoration plans. These included taking up a lot of the carpet, painting all the walls in a color called "aubergine dream" (also known as "scary purple"), and putting our sofa into some kind of big white bag. My father was letting her redecorate to her heart's content, and I had to stand back and watch as everything familiar to me vanished. Despite my protests, she'd recruited me to help. All of my free time seemed to be spent helping Hilary with her painting, her relentless scrapbooking, and the wedding plans. It was like being forced to dig my own grave.

But tonight—a reprieve. They'd decided to go out and see a movie. I *lived* for nights like this one, when they were out of the house. I was supposed to be doing my homework, but I had to savor the time I had on my own. It was far too precious to waste. So instead of doing math, I watched reruns of *Buffy the Vampire Slayer*. When I heard the car pull into the driveway, I switched off the TV and pulled my algebra book into my lap—the classic I've-been-studying-all-night trick. No one falls for it, but everyone tries it, anyway.

The door opened, and my dad came in making faces and talking *baby talk* to Hilary, and of course she was baby talking right back. It was probably the most awful thing I'd ever seen in my entire life, and let me tell you, I'd seen some bad stuff recently. When they turned and saw me gaping in horror, they looked genuinely surprised.

"You're home . . ." my dad said, suddenly looking embarrassed. "You're up."

Well, hello? It was nine o'clock on a Wednesday. Where did he think I'd be?

"Yeah," I said, reaching for a pencil, which I was considering using to poke out my eyes so I wouldn't have to witness any more of this unbearable cuteness. "Just doing my homework."

"Have you cleaned out your room yet?" Hilary asked.

"No."

"You know we have to get it ready," she said, dropping her spreading butt onto the bagged couch and picking through her crocheting.

Another sore point. Because it was next to my dad's—or *their* room—Hilary had set her sights on turning my bedroom into a nursery. She wanted to move me to the little room at the end of the hall.

"I'll do it when I have time," I said, suddenly finding my factoring exercises totally engrossing. "I have a quiz tomorrow."

"I know you don't want to switch rooms, Alisa," Hilary said with a sigh, "but when the baby comes, I'll need to be able to get to him or her quickly in the middle of the night. This is as much for you as it is for me. The room at the end of the hall will be less noisy."

She had to be kidding. The room at the end of the hall was a glorified closet. In fact, it wasn't even glorified. It was pure, plain closet. It had a tiny window, too small for normal blinds or curtains. It was more like a vent. I looked to my dad for support, but he just folded his arms over his chest.

"Hilary's been asking you about this for over a week now," he said, getting into his stern voice.

"I said that I'll do it," I replied, trying to keep the anger out of my voice. Algebra never looked more appealing.

"You'll do it after school tomorrow," he said, "or you're in all weekend."

I definitely wasn't going to let myself get stuck in the house with Hilary. Rather than say something I would later regret, I nodded, grabbed my things, and got out of there as quickly as I could. At that moment Hilary's pregnancy scrapbook tumbled off the table, scattering photos and papers everywhere.

"Oh, no!" Hilary said, bending over to pick up the scattered contents. My dad swooped down to help her, and I left the room. Fortunately they had no idea I had anything to do with it. I hadn't meant to do it, either. These things just kind of happen to me. Objects fall off walls, fly across rooms, and tumble off tables when I'm around.

See, I'm half witch.

A few months ago I didn't know real witches existed. Even a month or so ago I had been terrified of magick, of Wicca, and of anyone who had anything to do with it. But everything had changed in the last couple of weeks, after I discovered my mother's Book of Shadows at Morgan Rowlands's house. I read it and realized that my mother had been a Rowanwand witch from Gloucester, Massachusetts. She was as afraid of her power as I was—so much so that she actually stripped herself of her magick in order to lead a normal life. She died when I was three, so she never had a chance to tell me this herself.

A blood witch is the child of two witches, descendants of the Seven Great Clans of Wicca. Since my father was a non-witch, I was only a half. Technically this meant that I wasn't supposed to have power. For some reason, I did—in abundance. To top it off, I had a whopping bad case of uncontrollable telekinesis. Even in witch terms, I was really strange. Because I was such an odd case, I was able to withstand the more serious effects of a dark wave spell that had been cast against our coven, Kithic, a few days before. While all of the other blood witches became incredibly ill, I got only a slight headache. I was strong enough to perform the spell that defeated the wave that would have killed all of the members of our coven and their families.

My father didn't know about any of this, and he certainly wouldn't have believed me if I had told him. He probably would have sent me to a therapist, claiming that I was making a really weird cry for attention.

Once safely in my room, I switched on my computer to check my e-mail. There was a note waiting for me from Mary K., Morgan's younger sister and my good friend.

> Hi, A.,
>
> What have you been up to? You seem kind of out of it lately. Anything wrong? We should hang out. Gimme a call or send me a note.
>
> —M. K.

I'd been wondering for a while what to do about Mary K. She's Catholic and completely turned off by Wicca. Just a couple of weeks before, I'd been trying to help her persuade Morgan to give up magick. Everything was different now. I was a witch; I had powers. And I'd seen the good that magick could do, how it could be used to fight evil.

I knew I'd have to tell her the truth at some point—that I was back in Kithic, that I was a Wiccan, that I was a blood witch. Mary K. was going to freak, there was no question about that. I was going to have to do it, anyway. I sent her off a note, suggesting that we meet after school at her house the next day to hang out. It was a ruse, of course. Devious me. I would have to think of some way to break the truth to her once I got there.

I switched off the computer and climbed into bed. I took out my mother's Book of Shadows and the collection of letters written to her by her brother, Sam. I paged through these every single night before going to sleep. It was reassuring. Here was her entry about Sam putting her bike up on the widow's walk of the house. Here was the one about looking at the lilacs in the window of the flower shop and the one about passing her driver's exam. Except for the magick parts, my mom's life sounded so nice and normal, so fun . . . until the later parts of the book, when her brother performed a spell that accidentally produced a deadly storm. I usually didn't read that far in. I stayed near the beginning.

Sighing, I put the book and the letters in a big pile by the side of my bed and turned over to go to sleep. A strange dream overtook me instantly.

The sky was yellowish green, pulsing with the energy of a storm about to break loose. I was on a rocky shore. There were buildings just behind me. This was a town, not a desolate stretch along the water. Somehow I understood at once that this was Gloucester, Massachusetts, my mother's hometown.

The weather had whipped the ocean into a frenzy. High, dangerous waves were crashing down just a few feet from where I stood. Any one of them could have snapped me up and taken me out to sea, killing me in a moment. Instead of running for cover, though, I was looking at something far down the beach—a woman, sitting calmly on a large rock, waving to me. I started to walk closer to her, and I could tell as I approached that she was not an ordinary woman. The top half of her body was normal, though unclothed. The bottom half of her body was a steel gray finned tail, which flicked and twitched whenever the water lapped against it. She was a mermaid.

The distance between us sometimes grew when I should have been getting closer. Finally I was just close enough to be able to see her face, but she spun around to hide herself with her long hair and dove straight into the water, vanishing from my sight. At the same moment a wave hung above my head, poised to crash down on me.

And I woke up. My alarm was going off.

Shivering, I crawled to the bathroom for a shower. The water reminded me of the rain shower on the beach, and I swore I could still feel the cool sand under my toes. I'd heard that witches' dreams could sometimes be very powerful. Sometimes they were signs, visions. I started to think about this.

I'd stumbled onto my mother's Book of Shadows: The chances were one in a million that it would turn up at Morgan's house, yet it had found its way to me. I'd discovered my uncle's letters that had been hidden for years in the trap compartment of my mother's old jewelry box. And now I was dreaming of Gloucester—and dreaming so vividly that I could taste the salty breeze. Sky Eventide, one of the blood witches in Kithic, always says that there are no coincidences. What if that was true? The things that had been happening to me were so strange, so unlikely. What if this was all a series of signs, telling me to do something?

Like what?

Well, there was my uncle, Sam Curtis, for a start. I hadn't even known I had an uncle. But now I'd found the letters, and now I knew he existed. I also knew he loved my mother. Maybe he would want to know about me. Maybe I could write to him. Unfortunately my mother kept only the letters, not the envelopes with the return address. There was a mention of a post office box, but that had been set up in the early seventies. I doubted that Sam had kept it after my mother's death.

E-mail. Maybe he had an e-mail address.

By the time I had finished drying myself off, I had a plan. I went straight back to my room and switched on my computer. I knew that my mother's coven's name was Ròiseal, so I did a search. To my amazement, something popped right up. It was a Web page for a magick shop called Bell, Book, and Candle, in Salem, Massachusetts. The person who made the page listed himself as a member of Ròiseal. At the bottom was a link to contact the Web master. I clicked on it, and a blank e-mail popped up. What would I say? I had no idea who this person was or how well he or she knew my uncle. I had little to say, so I had to keep it very simple.

Dear Sir or Madam,

I'm trying to get in touch with my uncle, Sam Curtis. If he is still a member of Ròiseal, could you forward this note to him? I would really like to meet him or speak to him, but I do not have his address or phone number. This means a lot to me, so I would really appreciate the help.

Many thanks,
Alisa Soto

Turning off the computer, I had a huge sense of satisfaction, a deep feeling of release. It was really strange, since all I'd done was act on an impulse. Of course, this pleasant feeling was going to evaporate quickly if I didn't get to school in the next eighteen minutes. I pulled on my clothes and ran for the door.

2

Contact

December 17, 1944

The ghosts have been getting more and more wild. They break things regularly. Mother and Father wrote to some specialists from Boston who came last night to examine the house for signs of haunting. They did seem to detect a strange energy, but they couldn't pinpoint anything that could help us identify or deal with our poltergeist. Some experts!

When I am initiated in a few months, I will have access to the family library. Right now I don't even know where it is—it's carefully protected by layers of spells. Our store of knowledge is said to be one of the most impressive of any coven in the area. Surely we must have something there that would help guide us and solve this problem. I feel strongly that this is so . . . I can barely explain it. My anticipation grows every day.

—Aoibheann

Once Mary K. and I had settled ourselves in her bedroom after school (with a huge assortment of snacks, of course), she gave me all the latest on Mark, the current object of her affection. She'd finally worked up the courage to ask him out, and of course he had said yes. Mary K. is perky and adorable, and she drives the menfolk crazy, unlike myself. They had a date set for Friday. I listened distractedly as she ran through all the possible options for the location of the big event.

"So," she concluded, "what do you think?"

Oh, man. I hadn't been paying attention. I vaguely remembered hearing something about going to Colonel Green's, the new theme restaurant that had just opened near the mall. It was supposed to look like an old sportsmen's club, and it had a handful of little secluded tables with curtains around them, perfect for a first date.

"Dinner," I said, grabbing a handful of chips. "Good idea. Colonel Green's."

"You were completely tuned out," she said, but not angrily. "Weren't you?"

"Kind of," I admitted. I took a deep breath. "I need to talk to you about something."

"What's up?" she said, concerned.

"You asked me what's been going on recently, why I've been so distant."

"I've been worried about you," she replied, popping the top of a bottle of iced tea and setting the cap on the ground for Dagda, Morgan's kitten, to bat around.

Okay. Just come out and say it.

"I'm a witch," I blurted. "Just like Morgan."

Mary K. flinched just a bit, then seemed to try to ignore what I was saying by going through the contents of her bag. "I know you were in that thing she goes to . . . that Kithic thing."

"It's more than that," I explained. "My mother was a witch. I'm a blood witch."

She looked up at me, frozen.

"What do you mean, your mother was a witch? What's a blood witch?"

"Do you remember that book Morgan had here the other week?" I asked. "The one I kept staring at? That book was my mother's Book of . . . her diary."

"How could Morgan get your mother's diary?" she asked shortly. "That's ridiculous. Do you hear what you're saying?"

"I know what I'm saying," I said with a sigh, "and I know how it sounds. But it's true. My mother was a blood witch. I can . . . do things. . . ."

"You're trying to tell me that you have magical powers?" she said. "Is that it?"

Oh, God.

"You've been sick," she said, agitatedly shaking out the entire contents of her bag onto the floor. "You're stressed out about what's happening with your dad."

"I wish that was it," I said. "I wish I was just imagining all of this. But I'm not. This stuff is real. It's not some dumb high school trend or some kind of Ren Faire spin-off club. Witches are real. I have the book here. I'll show you."

I reached into my bag to get my mom's Book of Shadows. I always carry it with me. She held up her hand, indicating that I shouldn't bother.

"I don't understand," she said, her brown eyes blazing. "We were going to write that letter to the paper. Now you're telling me that you're back into this witch stuff, just like that, and that somehow Morgan had some book that said your mother was a witch?"

"Look, I didn't mean to upset you." I hung my head. "I would give anything for this not to be true. It's not a choice."

We were both silent for a few minutes. The only noise came from Dagda trying to chomp on the bottle cap.

"Alisa," she said sadly. "I'm sorry, but I don't know what to do with this."

"Neither do I," I replied, running my finger along the seams of her lemon-colored comforter. She took a pretzel out of the bag and dropped it to the floor. Dagda pounced on it in excitement. "I should probably go," I said quietly.

Mary K. looked unhappy, but I think we both realized that our conversation was over. There was just a lot of dead air between us, and it was making both of us uncomfortable.

"My parents aren't home yet," she said. "Neither is Morgan."

"It's nice out," I said. "I'll walk home."

We looked at each other; then she turned her attention to her books, her face drawn. I quietly let myself out.

Morgan drives the weirdest car I have ever seen in my life, some kind of monster from the early seventies. It's huge and unbearably ugly, with a white body and a blue hood, and she treats it as if it were her very own child. She was docking this scary ship in the driveway when I came out her front door. I stopped, and she stepped out of the car and looked at me.

"What's wrong, Alisa?" she said, eyeing my slumped shoulders.

"I just told Mary K. the truth," I said flatly. "That I'm a blood witch like you."

She exhaled loudly and leaned back against the car.

"How'd that go?" she asked.

"It sucked."

She frowned. At least she understood what it was like for me. I knew that when she'd told her family, it had ended up being a royal mess. Things had improved for her, though . . . maybe they would for me, too.

"How about a ride home?" she asked. I nodded my thanks. She climbed back into the car, and I got in on the passenger's side.

"Mary K. will come around," she said, trying her best to cheer me up.

"No, she won't," I said, playing with the window crank. "You know that as well as I do. This isn't something that people come around to."

"Want to have an informal circle?" she asked. "It might clear your mind a bit. How about we go to Hunter's?"

Morgan's boyfriend is Hunter Niall, the leader of Kithic. Hunter had really intimidated me until very recently. He's an imposing guy—very good-looking and tall, with chiseled features and piercing green eyes. He's always, always serious. To top it all off, he's British, with this exacting accent. But I had gotten to know Hunter a bit better recently, and I'd seen that he wasn't so scary after all. Even if I'd wanted to go and have a circle with them, though, I couldn't.

"It's all right," I said wearily. "I have to pack up my room or I'll be grounded until I'm twenty."

"Pack up your room?"

I explained Hilary's master house-arranging plan, and Morgan gave me a sympathetic look.

"This hasn't been a great month for you," she said.

"For you, either."

"No," she agreed. In the process of dealing with the dark wave, Morgan had confronted her father—a very powerful, and apparently evil, witch named Ciaran. Morgan had assisted Hunter and some of the others in catching him and stripping him of his magickal powers. From what I'd heard, that had been pretty awful. "I guess not," she said with a sigh. "Maybe it's never easy to find out you're a blood witch. That's something that Hunter and the other witches can't quite understand. They don't know what it's like to have regular family members and witch blood. We're unique."

How about that? Morgan and I, two of a kind.

"So," she said, pulling up to my house, "see you on Saturday for the circle? I can pick you up at seven-thirty if you want."

"That would be great," I said. "Thanks."

I ran through the door and straight to my room, trying to avoid contact with the Hiliminator. While I didn't see the woman herself, she had left a stack of folded boxes, tape, and markers by my door as a sign of her presence. How very kind it was of my stepmonster-to-be to provide me with moving supplies. It made me feel warm all over. I pushed the pile through the door and shut it behind me.

My first thought was to check my e-mail. I expected nothing, but there was a little envelope on the corner of my screen when I logged on. I quickly opened the note. It read:

Alisa,

    Sam Curtis is indeed a member of Ròiseal. I forwarded your note on to him. He seemed very excited to hear from you. You should be getting a response soon.

        Blessed be,

        Charlie Findgoll

At last, one single piece of good news.

That night I dreamed of the mermaid again. The dream was almost identical to the one the night before. This only increased my conviction that there was something going on in Gloucester that I needed to find out about.

At school on Friday, Mary K. seemed standoffish, so I ended up eating lunch alone and going home by myself. When I got there, I found that Hilary had bought rattan boxes for diapers, new sets of shelves, and a lamp shaped like a baby giraffe. I noticed there was nothing new planned for the closet down the hall—no swatches, no carpet samples, no new pieces of furniture. She had gotten me some more folded boxes, though.

After taking these to my room, I hurried to my computer and got online. There was another note. I saw that the sender was Sam Curtis. I couldn't even open it for a moment, and I just sat there, staring at the name. Then, my hand shaking slightly, I clicked on the note.

Alisa,

    I could barely believe it when Charlie sent me your note. I usually don't like e-mail, but this was a major exception! I am so happy to hear from you! I think about you often, and I want to know all about you.

I only have a computer at work, so here is my phone number and address. Write, call, visit . . . or all three.

—Sam

I didn't know quite how to respond. I'd acted so quickly in sending the note that I hadn't really come up with a complete plan about what to do if Sam actually wrote back. If I called him, my father would question the long-distance charge. Visiting—that sounded great, but how was I going to go to Gloucester, especially without my father knowing?

Quickly, hands shaking, I printed out the note and tucked it into my mom's book. Then I trashed the note from my inbox. I didn't want anyone finding the letter by accident when they were going online. My father didn't know anything about my mother's heritage, and Hilary certainly didn't, either. This was private, between my uncle and me.

At dinner (a pregnancy blue plate special: cold soba noodles and baked lentil burgers) Hilary actually looked worried about me when I left my plate untouched. She offered to get me whatever I wanted—pizza, burgers, anything. It was my father who said that he wasn't going to give in to my "moods." When he ordered me to stay in for the night and work on my room, I went along with it quietly. I was too preoccupied, and too afraid of being grounded, to argue.

The next morning, the beginning of spring break week, I was still fully engaged in this process. Admittedly, I spent most of my time unearthing old magazines and reading them, sorting out old piles of letters and birthday cards, sifting through clothes and shoes that I didn't wear much and moving them around. The boxes sat in the corner, still folded.

I could tell Hilary had no idea what to say to me. She was starting to lose her patience, and she made frequent passes by my door. On the one hand, every time she looked, I was working. She saw me shuffling things around. On the other hand, nothing was really being accomplished. All of my posters and pictures were still on the walls, and the contents of the drawers were spread all around. In fact, my cleaning had only resulted in a huge mess. By six o'clock that night all I had managed to do was put my socks into a laundry bag and move them to the other room. I was dressed and ready for Kithic's weekly circle a half hour early, though.

"You know," said Hilary, leaning in my door and staring at the massive pile of magazines and loose papers at the foot of my bed, "we're going to need to start moving this furniture on Monday. Things don't quite look ready."

"Oh," I said, thanking God as I heard Das Boot's engine, signifying Morgan's approach. I grabbed my purse and headed for the door. "They will be. I just had a lot of junk to go through. It will all be in boxes tomorrow. You'll see."

3

Flood

April 14, 1945

Today is my fourteenth birthday, and I will be initiated tonight. I've worked hard, and I've studied all my lessons. I know I am ready. Still, it's hard to sit and wait until evening comes. I guess I am a little more nervous than I would like to admit.

I spent the morning arranging all of my books perfectly on my shelves, but the ghosts came and pulled them all down when I stepped out of my room. They must know I am looking for a spell to make them go away. They do things to me because they know I will succeed. It makes them angry.

Tonight after the ceremony Mother has promised to show me the location of the library. Finally! Everything I've prepared for and dreamed of . . . Goddess, be with me today!

—Aoibheann

Every time I see Hunter Niall, I'm struck by his amazing good looks. There's no way not to notice them. It's like getting hit in the eye with a baseball—you just can't help but be aware of something striking like that. I was aware of them as he greeted us at the door of his house. He's really tall and very lean, all muscle. His hair is a golden blond. I don't think he goes to much trouble to get it cut well, and I'm absolutely sure he doesn't style it. It just always looks good naturally, all tousled. On top of it all, there's the sexy British thing. Enough said.

"Da's out tonight," he said, opening the rickety screen door for us. He smiled at Morgan and gave her a welcoming kiss. "He won't be back until well after the circle is over."

I flushed. Must be nice to have a love life. I assumed that Hunter noticed my reaction or read my mind because he laughed.

"My father doesn't go out much," he explained. "He's not very social, as you might have noticed. This is a big step for him. He's having dinner with Alyce Fernbrake, then they're going to do some research on medicinal uses of milk thistle."

"I didn't think anything," I said, immediately implicating myself. I backed into the hallway. "I'll, uh, go in. . . ."

Candles were burning in every corner of the living room, giving it a romantic glow. Everybody looked comfortable, but it seemed like I was surrounded by couples. There were Robbie Gurevitch and Bree Warren, Ethan Sharp and Sharon Goodfine, and Jenna Ruiz and Simon Bakehouse. Then there was Raven Meltzer, decked out in a black shirt so sheer that there was no point in wearing it. She was sitting cross-legged on the floor, examining the design on a tarot card, then looking at her arm. I had a feeling she was considering another tattoo and wondering how much biceps real estate this particular picture would take up. Raven, while she had no current significant other, was never really single. Matt Adler was sitting next to her at the moment. I knew they had fooled around at some point.

So there I was. Painfully alone Alisa. I felt like I had wandered through the wrong door, into some kind of couples' encounter session instead of the coven meeting I was supposed to be at.

"I think we have everyone for this evening," Hunter said as he and Morgan walked in side by side. "Thalia is under the weather, so there will be eleven of us."

He drew the circle in salt. We blessed the four elements—fire, earth, water, and air—and performed a power chant to bring energy to our circle. Hunter sat us all down and started the ritual for that week.

"Some of us haven't been feeling well lately," he said. I thought he must be referring to the dark wave that had almost engulfed Widow's Vale just days before. As it approached, it had made all of the blood witches incredibly sick. Morgan and Hunter had recovered. My head was still sore from where I'd hit it on a gravestone while we were in the old cemetery, fighting the dark wave. Hunter's father, Mr. Niall, was still weak.

"It's true," said Bree. "This is a really bad time for allergies and the flu."

I almost laughed, but I was able to hold it in.

"Actually," Hunter said, "the purpose of this exercise is to clear our minds of things that have been troubling us. It's designed to purge us of negative feelings that we may be holding back, feelings that may inhibit our personal progress.

Sometimes illnesses are related to emotions, and when we release some of the bad ones, we can experience improved well-being."

He had placed a little cauldron in the middle of the circle. This was full of twigs and bunches of herbs. Next to it was a small pile of handmade papers and a box of pencils.

"Clear your mind for a moment," he said, "and concentrate on finding something that's blocking you. Then I'd like everyone to take a piece of paper from the center," he went on, pointing at the papers. "Write down what you've come up with. Something that causes you pain. Be as clear and concise as possible. When you're finished, fold the paper and put it into the cauldron."

Those little papers weren't going to do the trick for me. I needed something a bit more sizable, like a three-subject notebook. Everyone else seemed fine with it, though. Raven scribbled just one word, then flicked hers into the cauldron. Other people took more time, carefully choosing a few words. I did my best to cram as much as I could onto the slip. When we had all completed this, Hunter took out his bolline and carved something into a dark blue candle, which he then turned and showed to us. There were two runes sliced into the wax.

"Yr," he said. "Death, the end. Then Dag, the dawn. Clarity. May the spark of this flame purify us and lift these weights from our souls and minds."

He touched the candle to the cauldron contents, and they sputtered into flames.

"Alisa," Hunter said, looking at me with a smile, "would you mind leading the chant? Just repeat the following as we go around: Goddess, I turn myself over to you. With this smoke, so goes my care."

I knew Hunter was making a special effort to include me in the ritual. After all, aside from him and Morgan, I was the only other blood witch present. This was something the others didn't know. We joined hands and began walking deasil, and I started the chant. My voice sounded squeaky and thin next to Hunter's, but I did my best to speak as clearly and boldly as I could.

At first all I felt was a kind of nice lightness, as if I was taking a brisk shower and washing off layers of emotional grime. I could actually see it coming from my skin, like a slight vapor. I sometimes saw things like that now—colors, auras—things that had been invisible to me before.

"Goddess, I turn myself over to you," I repeated. "With this smoke, so goes my care."

Some of the others had their eyes closed, but mine were open. I was fascinated by what I was seeing. The substance was coming from everyone now. Around some people it was a fine mist, but Morgan, Hunter, and I appeared to be smoldering. It was as if the fire was burning the emotion up just like the slip of paper and pushing the smoke through our pores.

"Goddess, I turn myself over to you. . . ."

We circled around and around, the energy mounting higher and higher. I felt a force rising up from me—something welling up, wanting to get out of me, jump out of my mouth or break out of my skin. It was such a powerful feeling that I had to push it down in order to keep speaking and moving, but my voice started to crack under the strain.

"With this smoke ... so goes my care."

I had written too much on the slip, I realized. I had brought up too much. The smoke was obscuring my vision, tightening my throat. It's not real smoke, I told myself. It's magick. Focus. You can breathe, Alisa. You can speak. But my voice was still crumbling to pieces. Control it! I thought.

I noticed that some of the others were acting a little strangely, looking all around and falling out of step. Then I suddenly realized why. It was just a little sound at first, and I'm not even sure when I became aware of it. All the pipes in the house were rumbling. The sink in the kitchen had turned itself on. The toilets began to flush themselves.

"It's all right," Hunter said. "Keep going, everyone." But he, too, looked around in surprise. His gaze fell on me. By this point I could barely speak or see. The force of the spell was dragging things up from every corner of my mind, every cell of my being, and I just had to keep shoving them down to keep going.

"Goddess, I . . ." Every word was hard. ". . . turn my . . . self ... o ... ver ..."

The hiss of water could be heard coming from every corner of the entire house. The shower had come on.

"What the hell *is* that?" said Raven, breaking the circle. Everyone stopped moving.

"Stay within the circle," Hunter said firmly. But it was no use. The others had already broken away in confusion. The sounds only got louder. Now the pipes thumped in the walls, trying to hold back the swell. Then they gave up the effort, and the running water took on a raging, fearsome quality. The faucets were no longer just running, they were gushing. Water could be heard hitting the floor of the bathroom above.

It was me, I realized through the haze. I was doing this with my telekinesis. I was wrecking this whole house, and I couldn't even stop myself. It was this emotion—this smoke coming out of me. Force it down! I told myself. Force it down! I gave up the chant and started slapping my body, as if it was covered in real fire that I could extinguish. But it didn't work. Hunter quickly stepped over to me and put his hand to my forehead. A strange warmth came from him, which dribbled down over me. The smoke began to subside, and my mind began to clear. I could see everyone standing there, looking at me.

"What's she doing?" Raven asked, pointing at me. "Why was she hitting herself?"

"I'm fine," I lied, my voice hoarse.

"Perhaps it would be best to call it a night," Hunter said quickly. The others looked at one another and silently started reaching for their jackets. I felt my stomach sink. My only thought now was that if I had turned on the water, maybe I could turn it off. I lurched into the kitchen. Water came out of the faucet with such force that it actually bobbed up and down in waves. The stopper must have been plugging the drain in the sink because the whole thing was full and water was pouring out, covering that part of the floor. I reached for the knobs, but they were useless.

"Turn off," I said out loud, thinking that might work. It didn't. The water continued to gush, flooding the countertops and soaking the kitchen rug. I put my face in my hands. This was too embarrassing. I wanted to cry.

"Alisa, are you okay?"

Morgan was standing behind me.

"Fine," I said, backing away. "I'm fine. I just need to clean up this massive mess I'm making."

"What are you talking about?" she asked. "Mess *you're* making?"

"Hunter knows," I said, staggering over to open up what looked like a broom closet to look for a mop.

"Hunter knows what?"

It wasn't a broom closet I had entered; it was a pantry cupboard. Since I couldn't clean the floor with crackers and cans of soup, I shut the door and hung my head.

"About me. About my problem. I was going to get help...."

"Help with what?"

"My . . ." Ugh. I was in no condition to explain. I didn't even have the energy to say the word *telekinesis*. It had too many syllables.

"Why don't you go sit down by the fireplace?" she said, taking me by the shoulders and leading me toward the door. "This is nothing. I'll get it."

I nodded and stumbled into the empty room where the circle had just been. Everybody else was gone. Suddenly feeling exhausted, I slumped down in a corner of the room between the sofa and the wall and closed my eyes. Everything in me hurt. It all passed through my mind, everything I'd written on the slip of paper, everything that had been eating at me. Hilary. My father. My mother. My insane powers. The dark wave. And now all the water flooding Hunter's house. The images just kept on coming, smacking into my mind like it was a punching bag.

Someone was approaching me. Without opening my eyes, I knew it was Hunter—it wasn't witch power: He was just one of the only two people left, and I heard Morgan moving in the kitchen. I felt him slide down and sit on the floor next to me. Whatever he had to say to me, I clearly deserved it. I was a freak. I was flooding his house. I was a danger to myself and others. I braced myself for the lecture I was sure he was about to give. He was going to kick me out of Kithic, I thought, just when I had realized that was the only place I found any peace. I pulled my knees into my chest to steady myself.

Instead of giving me the berating I was expecting, I felt Hunter put his long arm over my shoulders.

"Alisa?" he asked, trying to get me to open my eyes and look at him. I couldn't. He put his other hand on the back of my head, guiding it down so that it rested on his shoulder. I felt the whole wave of emotion coming to the surface. It was so powerful, it almost made me shake.

"Let it out," he said, his voice soft.

Much to my embarrassment, his words opened up another floodgate—this time in me. I started to sob. And just as with the plumbing, I couldn't control the flow.

In the distance, over my sobs, I heard the sound of the kitchen drain releasing and the water gurgling as it was sucked down into the pipes.

4

Uncontrollable

September 2, 1946

Goddess, merciful Goddess. What is happening in this house?

The event that started it all seems so trivial now, it nauseates me. Tioma had taken my favorite sweater, my pink angora one, from my room without asking, only to get ink on the sleeve. I found it in a ball at the back of the drawer. Furious, I went off to find her. She was in the living room, shrinking behind a book, as if she knew what was coming.

Of course, I was trying to control myself, but I was enraged. She stood up and tried to deny what she had done, which only made me angrier — so angry that I couldn't speak. Just as I turned to stalk back to my room, the heavy, glass-doored bookcase tipped over and slowly fell — right onto Tioma. I heard the glass shatter as it fell against her, knocking her to the ground and landing on her back. She made no sound. For a minute I thought she was dead — then I saw her fingers move.

Mother and Father weren't in the house, so it was up to me to help her. A spell came from the back of my mind, something I'd read in an old Book of Shadows—a spell for making things lightweight. Without another moment's thought I quickly performed it, and I was able to lift the bookcase off my sister's back. She looked broken. There was blood coming from all parts of her body where the glass had punctured her, but she was alive. I called out to all members of the coven, asking them to run and help. Then I started reciting every healing spell I had ever learned to stop the bleeding. Within minutes my parents and various members of Roiseal were running through the door. They rushed her off to the hospital.

Tioma is still there and is still insensible, but the doctors say she will recover. Mother and Father praised me endlessly, telling me that my quick thinking and composure saved her life. But all I can think of is my rage—my stupid rage over a sweater—and the sight of the massive cabinet coming down on my sister.

Why do these ghosts want to harm us?
—Aoibheann

I don't know exactly how long we sat there like that, but it had to be a while. It seemed like every drop of water in my entire body was being sucked out through my eyes. Hunter just sat through it all, rocking me back and forth, like you do with crying children. I was a mess.

Finally my breakdown slowed, and he let go so that I could sit up and wipe off my face with my hands. I saw that I had completely soaked through the shoulder of his gray T-shirt. Very fitting. I was dousing everything else—why not Hunter, too?

"I'm sorry," I sputtered, my breath still jagged. "I'm so sorry. I did this. All this damage . . ."

"What happened?" he asked softly.

"I don't know." I sniffled.

"Could you feel anything physically?" he asked. "Could you sense anything happening?"

"You mean aside from the sound of the exploding pipes and the stampede of people out the door?" I said, much more sharply than I intended.

"Maybe some tea," he said, backing off the subject. He looked up at Morgan, who I suddenly realized was standing right by us. She handed me some Kleenex, which I desperately needed. "Morgan, would you mind?"

"I'm on it," she said, standing upright and heading for the kitchen.

"Use the blue canister," he said. "It's in the back."

I just sat for a few minutes after that, saying nothing, staring at the floor and wiping at my eyes whenever they teared up again. He set his arm back over my shoulders and let me lean against him. I finally worked up the will to say something.

"I didn't mean to. . . ." I waved my hand around, trying to indicate the flooding, my crying . . . basically everything that had happened that night.

"Do you think I haven't seen tears before?" he said softly. "And after the dark wave, do you think some water on the floor is really going to bother me?"

That did put it into perspective a bit.

"What's wrong with me, Hunter?" I said, unable to keep my voice from breaking.

Morgan returned with a tray full of steaming earthenware mugs and a small chocolate chip cake that must have been intended as an after-circle snack before I made everyone scatter. Hunter released me, and I pulled myself into one of the chairs in front of the fireplace. Morgan handed me a mug of the tea and sat down on the floor next to us. It was scalding hot to the touch, and I must have winced. She reached over and circled her hand above it, and immediately it cooled to the perfect temperature. I looked down at her in amazement.

"How did you . . . ?" Duh, I thought. This is Morgan. Cooling some tea wasn't exactly a big deal for her. "Never mind," I added. "Dumb question."

Hunter sat down across from me and leaned forward. He took a mug and then reached for my hand.

"It's a simple spell," he said. "A little transferal of energy. Just focus your energy. Tell yourself that the tea will cool. Know it."

I did my best to focus. He rotated my hand once over the cup, and I felt a little warmth, like I'd grabbed a hot potato and let it go. He took a sip of the tea.

"Very nice," he said with a smile. "Well done." Hunter doesn't smile too often, but when he does, he could melt a stone. He really could have been a model.

"Drink that," Morgan said, pointing at my cup. "Believe me, it works."

"Better than Diet Coke?" I croaked, rubbing the last of the moisture from my eyes.

"Almost," she said. Hunter rolled his eyes good-naturedly.

I tried a sip of the tea. It was sweet and tasted like a whole garden of herbs, nothing like the nasty concoctions Hilary bought at the health food store. This was powerful stuff, and I could feel it all through my body, spreading calm.

"Do you feel up to talking about it now?" Hunter asked, watching me as I drained the cup. I nodded. Morgan poured me some more from the pot and mixed in the honey.

"Right," said Hunter, his tone turning professional. "The exercise we did tonight was designed to help bring out and release negative emotions. A lot has happened to you recently, to say the least. You have a lot of new information. Morgan has told me that there have been some things going on in your family, too. All of that was shaken loose, and it seems to have triggered an attack."

"An attack?" said Morgan. Hunter turned to her.

"Alisa is telekinetic," he explained. "We said that we would look into the problem after the dark wave had been dealt with, and now we are."

"Telekinesis," Morgan repeated. "Is that what that was? I thought I felt something weird in the *tàth meànma brach*." Just before the dark wave had come, Morgan and I had joined minds in a ritual called a *tàth meànma brach* to fight it. She had seen everything inside my mind, and I had seen everything inside hers.

"No doubt you did," he agreed. "Could you get a clear idea of what was going on?"

"No," she said. "It was a strange sensation, but I didn't really know what to make of it. It felt like an electric shock, but a mental one. I thought it was coming from the dark wave."

"All that stuff that happened to you—the shelves in the library, the butter dish in the kitchen—that was all me," I said, looking down at her. I was referring to various instances of things falling over or flying around in the last few weeks. Several had ended up heading for Morgan, and she'd seemed really upset by them. "I didn't mean to do those things. In fact, at the time I didn't even know it was me."

"So the deflection spell . . ." she started to say, turning pale. "It put you in the hospital. Oh, Goddess."

I wasn't sure what she was talking about, but Hunter nodded to her. "It wasn't Ciaran at all," he said. "But to get back to the problem at hand," Hunter went on thoughtfully, "aside from helping to release your emotions, the spell obviously triggered something. It would be very hard to tell what exactly that was. It's a general release spell with a broad range. How did you feel when we were performing it?"

"It was so strong," I said, remembering it with a shiver. "These feelings . . . I felt like a volcano. I kept trying to push the emotions down. I didn't even know what was going on until I saw everyone panicking."

He drummed his fingers on his knee and looked thoughtfully into the fire for a moment.

"Judging from what I've seen so far," he said, "I'd guess the phenomenon is somehow connected to your emotional state. I remember that objects would fall when you became frustrated with learning the dark wave spell. Tonight the flooding stopped when you started to cry."

"That's it?" I said hopefully. "So how do I stop it?"

"Its exact mechanism will be bit more complicated to determine, I'm afraid," he explained. "These things are rarely easy. You may react to certain substances or elements more than others, or you might be attuned to certain magnetic or magickal forces. In order to draw up that much power, you're tapping into something fairly deep—probably a whole web of energies."

Wrong answer. He was supposed to say that this was a cake problem and that he had a book that would fix it *right here.*

"How long have you had this condition?" he asked.

"My whole life, I guess," I said, picking at the flecks of herbs that floated to the top of my cup. "Weird little things have always happened to me. I just used to think that I was very unlucky and clumsy. But it's gotten a lot worse recently. My mother had it, too. She talks about it in her Book of Shadows."

"That's very significant," Hunter said, furrowing his brow. "Very significant. I didn't know that. Is there anything else you've noticed about these episodes? Do they have anything in common? Anything at all?"

"Not really," I said. "Nothing I can think of."

Hunter got up and started to pace a bit. He seemed to be thinking the problem out. I noticed that the cuffs of his jeans were soaked, as were his boots. "I know a man in London named Ardán Rourke," he said. "This kind of thing is his specialty."

"What kind of thing?" Morgan asked. "Telekinesis?"

"Uncontrollable magick, in any form. It's too late to ring him now—it's after two o'clock in the morning there. I'll try tomorrow. There's also Jon Vorwald, a Burnhide who works out of Amsterdam. He might be able to tell if it's a magickal reaction to certain metals or other substances, which it very well might be. I'll contact him, too. In the meantime I'll talk to Bethany Malone. In fact, let's see if she's home now."

He went into the kitchen for the phone. Morgan reached up and took my hand. I felt a warm flow of energy coming from her, soothing some of my frayed nerves.

"I wish I'd known," she said.

"I just figured it out a little while ago," I said. "It was news to me, too. I never meant to do anything to you. You know that, right?"

"Of course," she said.

"No answer," Hunter said, coming back in and breaking himself off a handful of the cake.

"Do you want me to scry for her?" asked Morgan.

"No." Hunter shook his head. "I'll try again tomorrow, after I talk to Ardán and Jon."

"I need to wash my face," I said, wanting to get up and be alone for a moment. I suddenly felt like some kind of leper. All this talk of phenomena and metals and bringing in specialists from London and Amsterdam was too much. Was my problem so bad that it required a *global effort* to fix?

Hunter shifted uncomfortably. "I'd use the upstairs one. The downstairs is still ... very damp."

In the upstairs bathroom there was a thin film of water covering the black-and-white-tiled floor. Hunter had thrown down a few towels. They were strewn around the various puddles, swollen and heavy, like enormous slugs. Water had pooled into a kind of lake under the claw-foot tub. If this was the drier of the two bathrooms, I really didn't want to know what the downstairs one looked like.

Though I had soaked the place, I could see that it was otherwise spotlessly clean, even austere. Soon it would smell like mildew, thanks to me. I picked up the towels and wrung them out as best I could into the tub, then hung them from the shower rod.

My face was also a damp wreck. My huge eyes were completely bloodshot, and the lids were puffy. I looked gross, froglike. I splashed cold water on my face until it seemed less swollen, then dried it on one of the hemp washcloths that hung from the towel bar.

When I came back into the living room, Hunter and Morgan were huddled together in discussion. They separated as I entered.

"Are you feeling any better?" Hunter asked, rising to give me his chair.

"I think I should go home," I said.

"I don't think that's advisable, Alisa," he said. "You've just been strongly affected by a spell. I think you should stay here until it wears off a bit."

"I'd really like to go," I said quietly.

Hunter studied me for a moment, and I felt a weird sensation come over me, as if someone was trying to climb inside my skin.

"What's that?" I asked.

They both raised their eyebrows.

"You felt that?" said Hunter.

"Yeah," I said, running my hands over my arms. "It was creepy. What was it?"

"That was us," he said. "We were casting our senses out to you, trying to get information about how you felt."

So they were witch-spying on me. At least he was honest.

"Have you ever felt it before?" he asked.

"No," I said. "Why? Have you done it before?"

"Very strange," Hunter said, not answering my question. He rubbed at his chin, then nodded to himself. "Right, then. I'll take you, if you really want to go. Morgan, you might want to have a look at those books on pyromancy while I'm gone."

A minute later I slid into the passenger's seat of Hunter's old Honda and stared into my lap. Seeing that I wasn't in the mood to talk much, he turned on the radio, but it didn't work very well. All he could get was a static-ridden country station. After a few minutes of trying to get something else, he grimaced and switched it off.

"Unbelievable," he commented, shaking his head. "We witches can tap into the power of the universe. We can rip holes between life and death. But we still can't get an old radio with a bent aerial to pick up anything besides crackly country and western."

I couldn't help but smile at that.

As we pulled up in front of my house, Hunter turned to look at me.

"I'll try to have some answers by the morning," he said. "For now, just get some rest."

"Okay," I said, reaching for the door release. As I was getting out, he reached up for my arm. I turned to see him stretching over the passenger's seat to look at me.

"Ring me if you have any more problems tonight," he said. "I don't care what time it is."

He waited until I was inside before pulling away. I could hear my dad and Hilary in the kitchen, talking about their plans for converting my room into the Hilspawn habitat. I took from what they were saying that they had just gone out to order a crib and a dresser. Now they were making a list of objects to put on the gift registry—the monitor, a sliding rocker, a Diaper Genie. . . .

In their excitement they didn't even notice that I had come home, which was fine with me. I headed off to my room. I wanted to enjoy it while it was still mine.

5

Explosion

October 29, 1948

A strange thing happened today. I was down in the library, looking through some old books on the elder futhark alphabet. These particular books are rarely used, so they're kept well in the back. As I pulled the book from the shelf, I noticed another book wedged behind it.

To my amazement, it turned out to be a Book of Shadows that belonged to my great-great-grandmother, Máirín Quinn. How it had gotten lost like that for so many years is beyond me. Our family has always taken great care with its books, especially the Books of Shadows. Stranger still, some of the pages have been violently torn out. It's not like a Rowanwand to mar a book in any way. I wonder what happened. I'm going to read the book tonight, then I'll make sure it's filed away in the proper place.

—Aoibheann

Even before I turned on the light to my room, I knew that something was wrong. Things were different. There should have been shoes by the door for me to trip over. Somebody had changed things in here. Had my attack done something to my room as well? I flicked on the light and discovered the worst.

My belongings were in boxes. Clothes. Shoes. Posters and pictures from my walls. One box was full of books, including my mother's Book of Shadows and mine. It took me a frantic minute even to find Sam's letters—they were packed in with a bunch of old papers from the floor. They were bundled together and retied in ribbon. I felt my stomach clench.

This had to be the work of Hilary. For her to have gone through my stuff was bad enough, but she had been handling *my mother's personal property*. Had she read the letters? My book?

My brain couldn't even put those thoughts together. Insane, raging, I blew open the door and tore through the house. This was it—I couldn't hold it back any longer. I found them still sitting in the kitchen, giggling over something.

"What's the matter, honey?" my dad asked.

I must have looked like something from an alien movie. I felt my eyes bulging and my heart racing. My hands were clenching and unclenching.

"What did you do?" I hissed.

"Oh," Hilary said, as if just remembering, "I did some cleaning in your room."

"*Cleaning?*" I spat. "You didn't clean—you went through everything I own, everything personal. . . . You went through my mother's things. . . ."

They fell silent and looked at each other.

"I didn't go through them, sweetie," she said. "I just put

them in boxes."

"First of all," I said, my energy on the rise, "I'm not your sweetie. My name is Alisa. And I'm sorry that I've been inconveniencing you with my presence, but I live here, too. You can't just wish me away. I know you're in a big rush to move me down to the storage spot at the end of the hall, but that gives you—"

"*Alisa!*" my father yelled. "Watch your mouth! I know you're upset, but Hilary's pregnant. Think of what she's going through!"

"What *Hilary's* going through?" I yelled in disbelief. "What about me? You let Hilary come in here, take over the house, order me around. You barely even know I'm alive. I have to eat her horrible food, and move all my things, and listen to her puke."

"How dare you talk about her that way!" my father said, barely able to control himself. "This is the woman who is going to be your stepmother. You have to show her respect!"

"*Please!*" I groaned. "She's practically my age! What, couldn't you find anyone *younger?* Why didn't you just ask me? I could have introduced you to some freshmen at my school."

I knew I had entered uncharted, dangerous territory, but I couldn't seem to stop myself. It was like my jaw had become unhinged or something, and every terrible thought I'd ever had was spilling out. I wondered if the spell was still affecting me, allowing me to let fly with all my thoughts and emotions. I knew I was digging myself into a very deep hole.

"You're just marrying her because you got her pregnant," I hissed, all control gone. "Because you were *stupid.* You were both stupid. And I've got to suffer because the two of you don't know how to control yourselves."

Hilary began to cry, and my father's face turned purple. He turned to me with more rage than I have ever seen him show anyone. All at once it hit me what I'd done. I'd told them everything I'd been thinking—everything I hadn't wanted to say. On top of it all, the spice rack fell off the wall.

Oh, God. Oh God oh God oh God.

Before he could even retort, I decided to get the hell out of there. I didn't ever want to know what he was going to say to that. I ran back to my room and slammed and locked the door. This was bad. This was very bad. My life was about to take an abrupt turn for the worse, if such a thing was possible.

A thought suddenly flashed into my mind. *Gloucester.* I would go to Gloucester. *Now.*

It was an insane idea, but not much more insane than the thought of going back into the kitchen after that conversation. Really, there was no better time to go. Besides, didn't my mother's family have a right to have me if my own father couldn't be bothered? Something had been telling me to go there. Now I would listen to it.

Impulsively I grabbed my duffel bag. I put in my mother's Book of Shadows, the printout of Sam's e-mail, some random clothes and things from my dresser. What else would I need? I looked around and took my warmest sweater, a hairbrush, and my own Book of Shadows and stuffed my purse right on top. That was it. The bag was full, and I felt that I needed to move quickly before my father recovered enough to come after me.

I peeked out into the hall. No one was there. I could hear

fevered talking in the kitchen. As silently as possible, I crept down the stairs. Fortunately you can't see our front door from the kitchen, so I was able to slip out. I ran, as quickly as I could, across our neighbors' yard and down the street. I knew it wouldn't be long before my dad figured out that I had given them the slip, and then he would be out on the street, looking for me.

Once I was away from the house, I realized that I didn't have a second move planned out. When I slowed down to a walk, I saw that I had been going in the direction of the Rowlandses' house. It was probably right around Morgan's curfew. She would have to pass the local playground on her way home from Hunter's. I headed for it and tucked myself in behind the spiral slide so that I wouldn't be easily seen but I would still be able to scan the road. About ten minutes later the distinctive shape of Morgan's car made its way around the corner. I came out from where I had been hiding and waved her over. She slowed, looked out the window in surprise, then came to a stop.

"Alisa," she said, "what are you doing?"

"I need help," I said, not quite sure how to explain myself. That statement seemed to cover a wide range of options. She looked at me, with new tear trails running down my face and an overnight bag in my grip.

"Get in," she said, reaching over and unlocking the door.

I got into the passenger's side. She pointed to the bag.

"What's going on? Did you just run away?"

"Something like that," I said, slouching low in the seat in case my dad passed by. "Would you mind driving around a little?" I asked sheepishly. She started down the street, torn between looking at the road and looking at me.

"Alisa," she said, her voice serious, "nothing that happened tonight was that big of a deal. You know we've been through a lot worse. And Hunter will have some information in the morning to help you."

"This isn't about what happened at the circle tonight," I said. "Not entirely."

"Fight with your parents?"

"Uh-huh."

"Was it about magick? Did you have another problem with the telekinesis?"

"No," I answered, shaking my head. "It's a lot more complicated than that."

"Do they know you're gone?"

"I don't know," I said, playing with the zipper on my bag. "Maybe. If not by now, soon."

She glanced at me. I felt my body tingle, and I guessed that she was looking me over in some magickal way, trying to figure out what I was thinking. She'd seen me flood a house and then sob on her boyfriend's shoulder for half an hour. Now she'd just found me hiding by a swing set at midnight with my clothes in a bag. The evidence would suggest that I wasn't entirely stable.

"Come on," she said, "I'm taking you back to Hunter's." She started heading for Valley Road, which led to Hunter's house. I was surprised she didn't speed me to the closest mental hospital. "I'd take you to my house," she continued, "but between my parents and Mary K., that would just cause you a whole new set of problems. You can stay with Hunter for a few hours, and then he can take you home."

"No," I said, clutching my overnight bag to my stomach.

"Please. No."

She pulled over to the side of the road and put the car into park.

"Why not?" she asked.

I shook my head, willing back the new storm of tears that was welling up inside.

"Look," she said gently, "you don't have to be embarrassed because he saw you so upset. Hunter can handle that. Trust me, I've turned to him enough times."

"I know what I have to do," I said, my voice wobbling.

"What's that?"

"I need to go to the bus station," I said. "I have to go somewhere."

"No way," Morgan replied, reaching for the shift. "It's Hunter's or it's home. Which will it be?"

"I have to go see my mother's family, Morgan."

That stopped her for a moment, so I jumped right in.

"It was instinct that made me take my mother's Book of Shadows from your house," I said, the words coming quickly now. "Then my telekinesis made my jewelry box fall over and break—that's how I found my uncle's letters. And I've been having these dreams, visions of my mother's hometown. I've been in touch with my uncle. He told me I can come anytime I want."

Morgan stared out in front of her and drummed her fingers on the steering wheel, deep in thought. Along with her witch skills, Morgan had a powerful big-sister vibe. Right now I could see the two were in conflict.

"Come on," I said, "how am I going to explain this to my father? How am I going to tell him that my mother was a witch, that she stripped herself of her powers, and that I've been having visions and problems with telekinesis? When you and I say that our parents don't understand us, we're not just angsting."

She couldn't deny anything I'd said.

"I still think we should go to Hunter's first," she said slowly. "You can talk it over with him."

"It's not that I don't want to talk to Hunter," I said, "but I need to get out of here. If I wait until morning, my dad will have the police after me."

Absolute silence for about two minutes.

"Tell me where you're going," she finally said.

"Gloucester, Massachusetts. To my uncle Sam Curtis's house."

"Do you have enough money?"

I reached into my purse and fished out my wallet. "I have my bank card and six dollars in cash."

"How much do you have in your account?"

"Just over three hundred," I said, "from babysitting."

Without another word, she put the car back into drive and turned it around, back toward the bus station. I could tell the internal battle was still raging on, though.

"I don't like it," she said, breaking the long silence, "but I guess I understand."

There were no cars in the bus station parking lot, and I saw no one through the plate-glass windows. It was empty, except for the plastic seats and a few ticket machines. Morgan hunched down to look at the place through my window, then she groaned loudly.

"I can't believe I'm letting you do this," she said, her voice low. She lifted herself from her seat, pressed her hand into the pocket of her jeans, and produced a few crumpled notes.

"Here," she said, pressing them into my hand, "take this, too. It's, um . . ." She smoothed out the bills and counted them. "Twelve bucks."

"Thanks," I said as she pressed the wrinkled money into my hand. "I'll pay you back."

Strangely, in response she reached over, pulled back my collar, and started tickling my neck. At least, that's what she appeared to be doing.

"Is this what they mean when they talk to kids about 'bad touching'?" I asked.

"Call either me or Hunter," she warned, drawing back her hand. "I'm serious. If we haven't heard from you within twenty-four hours, we're coming after you. I just put a watch sigil on you, so we'll be able to find you anywhere."

"Thanks," I repeated, somewhat uncertainly. I didn't actually know what it meant to have a watch sigil burned into your flesh. It sounded kind of ominous.

"I guess that's all I can really do." She sighed.

"You've done a lot," I said, stepping out and leaning in through the window. "Don't worry. I know what I'm doing."

"I have to get home," she said, obviously annoyed by the limitations of her curfew. "Be careful. And remember, call within twenty-four hours."

With that, she slowly pulled away. I watched Das Boot vanish into the night, and then I stepped inside the dingy, fluorescent glow of the bus station.

6

The Runaway

October 30, 1948

Máirín's book has opened up a whole new world to me. Goddess, how was it that I never knew this horrific story?

Máirín's mother was named Oona Doyle. She and her husband came over from Ireland in 1865 with a small group of other witches. They built this house and started Róiseal that year.

According to Máirín, a hideous influenza outbreak spread through Gloucester in 1886. The whole coven worked as hard as they could to combat the sickness. Young Máirín describes long nights of visiting sickbeds and working on spells. In their attempts to cure others, some of the members of the coven were infected and weakened. The sickness claimed the lives of Máirín's father and her two younger brothers, leaving the two women alone. Máirín was, of course, devastated—but her mother's reaction was even worse. She lost control of her mind. For two years Oona lived in this condition, and Máirín watched over her at all times.

Máirín describes a horrible night during which her mother ran skyclad through the house, casting hexing spells in her own blood. Two days later Oona's body washed up on the shore. Oona, unable to overcome her sadness, must have wandered out to the ocean and just kept going, allowing the waves to overtake her. Máirín then describes the beginning of a long series of hauntings that went on for years. She made several attempts to control the phenomena.

The last few pages of the book are missing. What Rowanwand destroys a book—much less a Book of Shadows? What was written there? I need to study this book more closely. I've told Mother what I found, and she seemed very interested. Could it be that we have some kind of an answer to our haunting problem at last?

—Aoibheann

When I told Morgan that I knew what I was doing, I'd probably been overstating my case just a little bit. I knew that I was running away, that I was going to Gloucester, and that I was going immediately. The details—well, I hadn't quite worked them out.

I was the only person waiting at the bus station for the midnight ride to New York. I used my bank card to buy a ticket and sat down to wait. I felt like I was in a cheesy movie of the week—teen leaves home, gets on bus to the big city. Things like this weren't supposed to happen to me. But this was real, and I was alone, seething, and nearly numb with anticipation. Fortunately I'd timed it well, and I only had to wait a few more minutes before the bus arrived.

About three hours later I saw the lights of New York in

the distance. Though I love the city, the Port Authority Bus Terminal, where we eventually stopped, is probably the last place I would normally want to be at three A.M. on a Sunday. Though it was less crowded than usual, there were still a lot of people wandering around. Many of these people had hollow gazes; several mumbled to themselves. Everyone seemed to be eyeing me—this squeaky-clean teen with her fat duffel bag.

According to the video monitor, the next bus for Boston left at four A.M., so I had an hour to kill. I used my bank card again to buy my ticket, taking care to have it out of my bag for the least amount of time possible. I also really needed to go to the bathroom, but there was no way I was venturing into one of those desolate ladies' rooms.

My adrenaline rush was fading. I was shivering. I passed a phone, and I thought about picking it up. I wasn't quite ready to call my father. Morgan? Mary K.? Too late. Their parents would freak. I could call Hunter. His dad wouldn't mind that I called so late (an advantage to letting your father live in your house and not vice versa). But I figured Hunter probably wouldn't be too happy about my running away, and I didn't really want to get a lecture.

No. I had decided to go, and now I was going to deal with it. So it was a little scary—I would be in Gloucester soon. I sat down and watched a screen with the weather forecast refresh itself about two hundred times before it was time to board the bus.

The bus to Boston was also almost empty, so I had two seats to myself, nice and close to the driver. This made me feel a little more secure. He didn't seem to notice anything strange about my being there alone. I guessed this was pretty much standard runaway procedure, something he'd seen before—something just like what my mother had done over thirty years before. Shoving my bag behind my head, I closed my eyes and fell right to sleep.

I dreamed of the mermaid again. It was night this time, and we were both on the shore. The sea was calm now. The mermaid hid herself under a green veil, and she pointed up to the moon, which was a hook hanging low over the water—a waxing moon. We sat in silence for a long time; then a wave lapped up on the sand. As it pulled away, the beach was glowing with runes and Gaelic words. All the space between us was filled up by this mysterious writing. Another wave came and washed it all away, leaving the beach bare and sandy. And when I looked up for the mermaid, she was gone. I woke up just as the bus was pulling into Boston's South Station, the biggest train and bus depot in the city.

I discovered by reading a few rainbow-colored folding transit maps and asking a few commuters that I needed to take two subway lines to get to North Station, where I would be able to get on a train to Gloucester at seven-thirty. From there, the ride to Gloucester would take about an hour. My brain was waxy and numb from too much emotion and too little sleep. The color-coded routes on the map seemed like they would be impossible to navigate. But I pulled up some hidden reserve of energy and brainpower and managed to get myself on the subway and across town. For the third time in only a few hours I was waiting on another platform. If only I had a car, I thought. Life would be a lot easier.

I thought of my bed back in Widow's Vale, all made, ready

to be climbed into and enjoyed. Of course, there was nothing else left in my room, but my bed was there. My dad was probably pacing. I was sure he'd been up all night. . . .

There was a phone behind me. Impulsively I picked it up and called the house collect. Someone snatched the phone off the hook on the first ring. It was my dad, who frantically accepted the charges.

"Hello? Alisa?"

"It's me, Dad," I replied, frightened by the urgency in his voice.

"Alisa, where are you?"

"It's okay, Dad," I said, keeping my eye on the track for any sign of the train. "I'm fine. I just need . . . some time."

"Time? What are you talking about?"

"It's just been too much for me to take in." I sighed.

"Alisa . . ." he said. He sounded confused, like he didn't know which would be more effective: being angry or pleading.

"I'm not just running off," I said. "I'm going to see Mom's family."

He had *no* idea what to say to that. I might as well have just told him that I'd hopped on a slow boat to China. My mother never talked about her family, so my dad always assumed that they must have been pretty bad to make her run away when she was eighteen. From what he'd told me, my mom wasn't exactly a rebel.

"There's a lot you don't know about them," I added. Understatement of the year. "They know I'm coming. They wanted to see me. I have to go."

"I've had enough of this, Alisa," he said, opting for the angry approach.

"I'm just telling you," I continued, "so you won't worry. I'm in safe hands, not out on the street somewhere. I'm going to a house, to stay with Mom's brother. There's no need to call the police or anything."

"Your mother didn't even have a brother!" he said, his voice breaking.

"She did," I said. "He lives in a nice place. It's fine. I'm fine. I just need to think. I promise that I'll stay there, where it's safe—just please don't call the police. I promise that I'll call."

He didn't know what to say. I heard his breath coming fast.

"Do I have a choice?" he finally said.

"Not really," I admitted.

"I love you, Alisa. You know that, don't you? I know you've been . . ."

The train was coming.

"I love you, Dad." I felt myself choke up on that. "I have to go. Please don't worry about me."

I think he was calling my name again when I hung up. My hands shook, and my eyes stung. Onward, I thought. No turning back now.

I crashed again on the commuter train, with my head resting against the window. No dreams this time. I woke with a jolt and a crick in my neck as I heard the conductor announcing that we were pulling into Gloucester.

No one was around on the platform. Only a few people were out walking on the street—it was still early on an overcast Sunday morning, after all. I didn't know where I was or how to find Sam's house, so I just headed out and started walking in the direction that seemed most promising. I don't know how to describe it, but the town felt right to me. I could sense the heavy pull of the ocean. Lobster traps and fishing gear turned up everywhere—in signs and displays, on people's lawns. It seemed like a modest place, a functioning fishing town, very old and not very fancy. While I definitely wasn't giddy with delight, I felt a sense of calm after the chaotic night. Whatever it was that had been calling me—it was here.

A half hour later a lonely cab happened to go past me, and I frantically waved it down. The driver looked at me a bit hesitantly—I guess high school kids don't usually hail cabs off the street in Gloucester—then took me in. I gave him the printout of the e-mail with Sam's address on it and settled back in the seat. We wound up and down the tight streets filled with old colonial-style houses, many marked with plaques commemorating the people who had lived there hundreds of years ago. The cab slowed at a neat little cape house, tucked tightly in a row of similar houses on one of the town's center streets. We stopped, and the driver turned to me.

"It's all right," he said, eyeing me and my bag. "No charge."

"Are you sure?" I said, reaching into my pocket for my eighteen dollars. "I have money."

"Don't worry about it," he said. "I'm going off duty."

I must look lost, I thought. Or just really pathetic. Still, it was nice of the driver. I thanked him profusely and slid out of the car.

So there I was, standing on my uncle's doorstep at just before ten in the morning on a Sunday. I looked up above his door and saw a pentacle there—a little one, imprinted into a clay plate and carefully hung above the entrance. This was definitely the right place.

It should have felt very strange and very scary. My uncle and I were strangers to each other. But I knew that it was going to be all right. There was something about his relationship with my mother, the tone of his note, and my dreams that told me he would welcome me. With a deep breath, I rang the bell.

Meowing from inside. Lots of it. I tightened my grip on the handle of my bag as I heard footsteps coming toward the door.

"It's all right," a man's voice was saying. "Calm down, it's just the doorbell."

More frantic meowing.

"What, do you think it's a fish delivery for you guys?" he said. "Just calm down. Let me through."

The door opened.

The man who stood before me looked very boyish, though I knew he was in his forties. His hair was light brown, streaked through with golden blond and a few shots of gray. His blue eyes were framed by a stylish pair of wire-rimmed glasses. Obviously he had just been relaxing on a lazy Sunday morning, and he was comfortably dressed in a Boston University T-shirt and a pair of running pants.

"Sam Curtis?" I asked.

"Yes?" he said, looking at me strangely. He became very still and seemingly tense as he studied me. It was as if he had found a mysterious ticking package on his front step and was trying to figure out if it was a clock or a bomb.

"I'm Alisa," I said, "Alisa Soto. Sarah's daughter."

"Goddess!" said Sam, gripping the door frame. I could tell he wasn't sure if he should hug me or shake my hand. As a compromise, he decided to grab my shoulder.

"I can't believe it!" he almost whispered, looking me over. "Alisa!"

I nodded shyly.

"How did you get here? It's what, ten in the morning?"

"I got your note," I said quickly, evading his question, "and I thought it would be okay."

"Of course!" he said. "Of course! Let's get you inside."

7

Sam

Máirín's Book of Shadows is missing. I was reading it all last night before going to sleep, and I left it on my desk. When I woke up, it was gone. I immediately ran to tell Mother. I was wild with excitement and fear, but she was very subdued when I told her it was missing. She told me not to worry, that there was nothing that could be done. Control, she reminded me. Witches must always be master of themselves. Only clear thought can produce strong magick.

Still, I feel as though I had the answer in my hands, only to have it snatched away! Oh, Goddess, what can I do?

—Aoibheann

Inside Sam's house, I was met by the comforting witchy smell of lingering herbs and incense, particularly sage. Everything was made of wood and brick, and there was a fireplace with a little fire to take off the morning chill. Two Siamese cats padded up to me, chattering their greetings.

"Meet Astrophe and Mandu," he said, picking up one of the cats and handing him to me. The cat purred loudly and pushed his head under my chin in affection. "That's Mandu," Sam said. "He's a baby, loves to be picked up. Astrophe will get you when you sit down. He thinks every lap is his."

"Astrophe and Mandu?" I asked as the cat gave me little kisses with his wet nose. "Are those magickal names?"

"No." Sam laughed. "Cat-astrophe. Cat-mandu."

I groaned, remembering my mom's description of her brother in her Book of Shadows. She'd said he was a real joker. Actually, she'd said he was asinine. I knew they'd played practical jokes on each other all the time.

"It's so early," he said. "When did you leave to get here?"

He cast a slightly strange look over his shoulder at me, but I kept my focus on Mandu, who was swatting at my hair.

"Sorry," I said. "I thought I'd take the earliest train. You know. Get a jump on things."

Lame. Obvious. But what was I going to say?

"Wait a minute," he said, "let me change into some proper clothes, and I'll make us some breakfast. I'll be right back. Make yourself at home."

With one cat in my arms and another wrapped around my ankles, I took a walk through Sam's living room. The wood floor was covered with a large Turkish rug colored in browns and oranges. On one side of the room there was a small altar, with some candles, seashells, fresh flowers, a cup, and a beautiful black-handled athame. He seemed to have about a million representations of the moon, in pictures, tiles, and masks.

Bookshelves took up most of the wall space. Rowanwands

are famous for collecting, and sometimes hoarding, knowledge. (I wasn't sure if I'd gotten much of that particular family trait.) Sam's collection covered an incredible array of subjects, from physics to literature to art. There were volumes on herbs, magick, Wiccan history, divination, Celtic gods and goddesses, tarot, and a hundred other witch-related subjects. Two shelves were devoted to volumes on astronomy. Three more were occupied by books on yoga, meditation, chakras, and Indian religion.

I noticed a few shelves that were devoted to the history of homosexuality and some current books on gay politics and culture. I was paused on these when I realized that Sam was back. He was casually dressed in a maroon short-sleeved shirt and tan pants.

"I have a lot of books, I know," he said. "Such a Rowanwand. This is nothing. You should see the family library. I think we have more books than the town library."

He noticed what shelf I was looking at and smiled.

"Oh," he said, nodding. "I'm gay."

I didn't know much about my uncle, so the fact that he was gay was just one item on a very long list. I liked his ease with the fact. I figured it had something to do with being Wiccan. I supposed they were a lot more open and well adjusted when it came to that subject. So I had a gay uncle. That was kind of cool.

"Okay," he said, directing me into the kitchen, "let's get some food for you. I can tell you're starved."

There's no use hiding anything from witches. They always seem to know. I set Mandu down on the ground and followed Sam into the kitchen.

"Do you drink coffee?" he asked.

I nodded. I was dying for coffee, actually. I hadn't slept much.

"How do you like it?"

"Sweet," I said, sitting down at the table. Astrophe, as promised, hopped right into my lap and curled into a ball. "And milky, please."

"Sweet and milky coffee." Sam nodded approvingly. "You are definitely my niece! We're going to get along well." He cheerfully put down two huge mugs and filled them up. Then he loaded in sugar and milk and pushed a cup in my direction. I took it, thanking him. It was incredible. Uncle Sam didn't fool around in the coffee department. This was the good stuff.

"All right," he said, opening the refrigerator. "Let's see. How about an omelet? I have some cheddar cheese and bacon. That might taste good."

He couldn't have known that I'd been living on mashed tofu and organic leeks for weeks now, could he? A bacon-and-cheese omelet sounded like heaven on a plate. I tried not to drool when I nodded my appreciation. For appetizers, he put some chocolate croissants, macaroons, orange slices, and strawberries on a plate for me to munch on as he worked. Munch I did. I could barely control myself. I noticed that he kept glancing back at me as he set some brown eggs, hickory-smoked bacon, and a big piece of cheese wrapped in paper out on the counter.

"I'm sorry that I keep staring," he finally said, whisking together the eggs. "It's just that you look so much like your mom."

This stopped me cold.

"I do?" I asked.

"It's kind of amazing," he said.

I had a few photos of my mom, and while I'd seen a little resemblance, I didn't think I really looked a lot like her. My father's family is from Buenos Aires, so I'm half Latina. Half witch, half Latina . . . half everything. My eyes are brown, and my hair is dark but streaked with a honey color. My skin has a warm, olive tone—not at all like the alabaster face that I saw in the pictures.

"Mom was very blond, right?" I said. "Kind of pale?"

"That's true," Sam admitted. "The Curtises come from England, and we all tend to be fair. Your coloring is darker, but there's so much of your mother in you. It's in your expression. Your face. Your height, the way you stand. Even your voice. You could be her twin."

"I'd like to know more about her," I said. "That's why I'm here."

He nodded, as if I'd just said something he'd expected to hear. Then he turned to the stove and poured the egg mixture into the pan where the bacon was cooking.

"I'm glad," he said. "I've wondered what your life must be like. I assume you weren't raised practicing Wicca?"

"No," I said, grabbing another strawberry. "I didn't know about any of this until a few months ago. I kind of stumbled into a coven at school. I saw people do things that I'd never known were possible. I've seen a lot, actually. Not all good."

He turned in surprise, then had to go back and do a little fancy pan-shaking. A minute later he presented me with the largest omelet ever made.

"Aren't you going to eat something?" I asked as he sat down.

"I will." He smiled. "Later. I'd rather talk now. You eat up."

I didn't need to be told twice. Between mouthfuls, I told Sam a little about Widow's Vale, Kithic, my dad and Hilary. This left the door open for him to start talking.

"About your mom," he said. "There's a lot to tell."

"I know part of the story," I said, accepting more coffee. "I have her Book of Shadows."

"How did you get that?" he asked, shocked.

"Through a friend, actually." I shrugged. "It just kind of turned up at her house. It seemed to have a pull on me. I actually stole it from her. She didn't mind after I told her why."

"It just turned up at your friend's house?" I nodded. Sam looked at me for a second, then laughed and shook his head. "Well, the Goddess certainly does work in mysterious ways. So you must know that your mother stripped herself of her powers. Do you know why?"

"I know about the storm," I said, feeling that was what he was getting at.

When he was young, Sam had used a book of dark magick to try to bring a little much-needed rain to the town. Instead, he accidentally produced a storm that raged out of control and killed several sailors. This was one of the events that had caused my mother to give up her magick, but not the only one. She had been pushed to the brink by her own telekinesis, which had frightened her as much as mine frightened me. The final thing that caused her to strip herself was a telekinetic incident after she argued with Sam. A table lurched away from a wall and pushed him down the stairs, nearly killing him. Sam didn't know anything about my mom's telekinesis. I could see that he thought she'd left because of his actions, and it was clear that the guilt had never left him.

"I was a really stupid kid," he said. "Beyond stupid. I had good intentions, but I produced really bad results. Horrific results."

"It wasn't just that," I said, trying to make him feel better. "She was afraid in general. She thought that her own powers were dangerous. She—"

I cut myself off. Did I want to get into the whole story of her telekinesis and mine? I would eventually, but maybe not at this very moment.

"It was a lot of things," I said. "She wrote about it. It wasn't just the storm, honestly."

He looked up, and his eyes had a glint of hope in them. He'd obviously been carrying a very heavy weight around with him for years. I felt for him.

"You know," he said, nervously shifting his coffee cup, "we know Sarah—your mom—is gone. We could sense that much—but we really don't know...."

"She died in 1991," I explained, "right before I turned four. She had breast cancer."

"Breast cancer," he repeated, taking it in. Maybe to witches that seems really mundane. For all I know, we can cure that with magick. That thought made me a bit sick to my stomach—maybe my mother could have lived....

But I was jumping to conclusions.

"Was she ill for very long?" he asked quietly.

"No," I said. "My dad told me that by the time they found

it, it was too late. She only lived for about another two months."

Sam looked stunned, shaky. For me this was old news—horrible, but something I had long accepted. He took off his glasses and rubbed at his brow.

"I'm so sorry, Alisa," he said. "I didn't know. If I had, I would have come there. I promise you."

"You didn't know," I said. "It's not your fault."

"I kept in touch with Sarah for the first few years," he explained. "But I had mixed feelings. I didn't understand why she had done the things she did. And then I went to college, got my first boyfriend—I got caught up in my life and my own dramas with our parents. I let things slide, and years went by. Pretty soon I didn't have her address, and she didn't have mine."

He saw my coffee cup was empty, and he jumped up to the stove for the pot, as if keeping me well fed and full of java helped to ease his guilt.

"So, how many people are in the family?" I asked, changing the subject. "I mean, who lives here, in Gloucester?"

"Let's see," said Sam. "There's my mother, your grandmother. Her name is Evelyn. My father died a number of years ago, as did my mother's sister. But there's Ruth, her daughter. And Ruth has a daughter your age, named Brigid. Plus there's the coven—Ròiseal. We're all family, even though we're not related. There are eight of us in all. My mother is the leader."

"Can I meet her—I mean, my grandmother?" I asked eagerly. My mother's mother. I could barely imagine it.

Sam seemed to pull back a little, though he continued to

smile. "Of course," he said, "I can take you over there as soon as you're done eating."

I shoveled in my breakfast, wanting to finish it as quickly as possible. Sam looked genuinely pleased at how much I enjoyed his cooking.

"I'll get the dishes," he said. "If you want to freshen up, there's a bathroom right by the stairs."

"That would be good," I said, wondering what I must look like after the crying jags of last night and all the lost sleep. Surprisingly, the damage wasn't too bad. I brushed my teeth and fixed my hair, pulling a thick strand of it back away from my face and off to the side, securing it with a clip I found in the pocket of my bag. Ten minutes later we were in Sam's ancient Dodge, driving up the avenue that ran along the water. We veered off, up a slight incline, into an area of dense trees. Then the trees thinned out, and I could see that we were on a high road above a rocky beach.

"This is it," Sam said, pulling over.

The house was large and imposing. It faced the water and was painted soft gray with black shutters. I saw the widow's walk my mother had written about so many times and the front porch with at least half a dozen stone steps leading up to it. There was the porch swing that she used to sit on and look out over the water. A row of thick trees and bushes bordered the property, and other tall trees dotted the front yard and lined the walk, making a shady grove.

Two cars were already parked in the driveway, so we had to park on the street. Sam unclicked his seat belt but waited a moment before getting out of the car.

"Listen," he said, "my mother is a little touchy about the

subject of Sarah. She didn't take the whole thing well. She hasn't really talked about Sarah since she left. Mother has also been under a lot of stress recently. We've had a lot going on here. So she might need a minute to get over the shock."

"Don't worry," I said. "It will be fine. I can't wait to meet her."

Sam nodded, but his brow remained furrowed. As I stepped out of the car, I felt the strong, clean breezes coming up off the water, and in the distance I could see fishing boats heading out from the harbor. It was a beautiful sight. My mother must have loved growing up here.

A splintering noise drew my attention. Sam had stepped ahead to pick up a rolled newspaper from the walk to take inside. A branch from the tree right above his head had split off and was falling—and it was huge, big enough to cause serious harm. I screamed. Sam straightened, glanced up, and jumped aside. The massive piece of wood made a sickening smack on the stone walkway and cracked in two.

"Goddess," he said, his voice full of awe. He looked from the branch to the tree, then reached down and picked up one of the broken pieces of wood.

"Are you all right?" I asked, rushing to him.

"Fine," he said, examining the branch closely. "But it's a good thing you yelled."

With one last wide-eyed look at the tree, he took me by the shoulders and hurried me to the front door. Branches fall out of trees all the time, I thought. Then again, it seemed like less of a coincidence when you considered a telekinetic girl was passing by when it happened.

Had I just done that? Had I almost killed Sam?

8

Homecoming

August 15, 1950

I've been spending more and more time with Hugh recently. He's a good man, very suitable, from a coven in Boston called Salldair. Although he is ten years older than I am, we do seem to make a fine match.

Hugh is a professor of Germanic languages at Simmons College in Boston, and he's written several textbooks. This makes him, more or less, an ideal Rowanwand husband. I know that's what Mother and Father are thinking, at any rate. They're very fond of him.

I don't really feel ready for marriage, but I know I must marry. I did fight when they first suggested it, but now I see that I was selfish and foolish. I am nineteen years old. I must accept my responsibilities. Of course, it's unthinkable that I should leave Gloucester. Our family is the head of Ròiseal. As the oldest child, I will take over the coven when Mother and Father are gone. That's the way it has always been done.

—Aoibheann

Unlike my friendly reception at Sam's door, my entrance into the Curtis house was spooky from the get-go. The woman who answered the door bore only a passing resemblance to Sam. She was about the same age, and her short hair was completely blond. She seemed taken aback by my presence, as if I was standing there naked.

"This is Sarah's daughter, Alisa," Sam said quietly, forgetting any greetings.

"Goddess," she whispered, drawing back, "it's like looking at a ghost."

"This is Ruth," Sam explained to me, indicating the stricken-looking woman. "Ruth and I are cousins."

Ruth regained her composure, but her stare was still a little buggy.

"Nice to meet you, Alisa," she said.

"Is my mother home?" Sam asked, showing me inside.

"In the study . . ." Ruth replied. Her eyes were full of silent questions. Sam nodded, as if to say that he would explain as soon as he could.

Inside the house, everything was alarmingly clean. The dark, heavy wood furniture glistened. The wood floors glowed. There was nothing out of place—no piles of magazines, nothing on the steps, no stacks of mail. Just cool breezes skimming along the austere hallway, looking fruitlessly for some dust bunnies to blow around.

Sam indicated that I should wait for a moment, and then he took Ruth by the elbow and ushered her back into what looked like a colonial kitchen. I saw a brick fireplace there, along with a large wooden worktable. I could hear them talking in low, urgent voices. When they returned, Ruth looked even jumpier than before. With a final look at Sam, she knocked on the wall. I thought this was really weird, but then she reached out and grabbed two little notches in the old paneling. These turned out to be handles to a pair of ancient sliding wooden parlor doors. In opening them, Ruth revealed another room, this one small and intimate, packed closely with antique furniture. She ushered me inside.

There was an older woman working at a large desk. Even though it was a Sunday morning, she was perfectly dressed in a crisp blue blouse and black pants. Her hair was steel gray with a heavy streak of white at the front. It was cut to just above the shoulder and feathered elegantly away from her face. She had silver rings on four of her long fingers. She tapped one of these on the desk as she worked.

"Sam," she said, without looking up, "I need you to . . ."

She stopped, and I saw her become aware of my presence. It hit her physically, as if her chair had shifted slightly under her, causing her to jolt. She looked straight up at me. Her pale eyes were narrow. She didn't look a lot older than my dad, but I knew she had to be about seventy. This was Evelyn Curtis, my grandmother.

A cordless phone fell from one of the tables, causing everyone but Evelyn to jump. Sam reached for it and put it back in its cradle. She seemed totally unaware of its falling. She was aware only of me now.

"Sarah?" she said, color draining from her face.

"No, Aunt Evelyn," Ruth said softly. "This is Sarah's daughter, Alisa."

Either they owned the loudest clock in the world, or it got really quiet in the study. All I heard was the ticking. This, I thought, is my grandmother. Grandmothers are supposed to want to see you all the time, to run and hug you, to give you presents. Mine scrutinized me, taking me in, head to foot.

"I see," she finally said, her eyes squinting at the corners. "Perhaps you should sit down. Ruth, could you bring in some tea?"

Ruth vanished back the way we had come. Evelyn peered at me.

"How did you get here?" she asked. "Are you with your father?"

"No," I explained, feeling my skin grow cold all over. "I came on my own. I wanted to meet my mother's—my —family."

She gave Sam a meaningful, and not entirely friendly, look.

"Alisa contacted me a few days ago," Sam said, reaching over and taking my hand. "She took it upon herself to find me. She wants to learn about us."

Evelyn stiffened and drew herself up even straighter. I was quickly grasping what Sam had been saying to me out in the car and realizing that I wasn't nearly as prepared for this as I'd thought I was. Sam gave my hand a squeeze, as if he could feel my confidence dropping.

"I see," Evelyn said again. "Perhaps we could talk for just a moment, Sam."

Sam shifted his jaw, but he nodded.

"We'll just be a minute," he said, turning to me. "Why don't you go have a look at your mother's old room?"

"Sure." I nodded dumbly.

"Turn right at the top of the stairs," he said. "It's at the end of the hall."

I excused myself and slid the study doors behind me. As I

walked up the steps, strange feelings started to flow through me—broken, choppy signals, pieces of emotions—leaving me a quivering mess. My mother's house. Here it was, just like she'd described it. The four-paneled doors with the old sliding bolts. The stairs that Sam had tumbled down. I even bent down and saw the thick chip that she had taken out of one of the banisters while she was carrying her bicycle down after Sam had stashed it on the widow's walk. It had been painted over, but the mark was still there.

This was my mother's home.

I found the room at the end of the hall and cautiously opened the door. In my imagination, I was about to be swept back to the early 1970s. My mother had described her bedroom in her Book of Shadows. The walls were blue, and she had painted yellow stars on them. There was a braided carpet on the hardwood floor. She had bamboo blinds on the windows and paper lantern lights. Her bed was covered in an old family crazy quilt. She had a portable record player and a desk with a typewriter. There were pictures of her favorite rock stars on her closet doors.

The room I found myself in was narrow and sterile, painted a plain off-white, all traces of my mother's handiwork gone. The floor was covered in a plush coffee-colored carpet. There were a neat worktable by the window, a bookcase, and a large cabinet filled with various Wiccan and household supplies. None of the furniture my mother had described remained—not even the old bed. Nothing. It was all gone, all traces of my mother ripped away. I couldn't help but think of what was still going on at my own house, with Hilary and her plans for total home domination.

For the first time on this insane trip, the weight of it all hit me. I was lost. It seemed as if my grandmother wasn't exactly overjoyed to see me. And something just didn't feel right. Everybody was on edge. I had thought that I would find my mother here somehow, or at least some loving relatives or warm memories. But this sterile room made it obvious that there was nothing here for me.

Voices. I looked around. I could hear voices. Was I going crazy now? No, I realized. There was a heat vent in the corner. I was hearing the conversation coming up from below.

" . . . and it just came down?" Ruth was asking.

"Right down. No warning . . . well, except for Alisa. It's a good thing she was there."

"How big was it?"

"Big enough," Sam said. "It would have knocked me out or worse."

"Aunt Evelyn," Ruth said, her voice full of fear, "we can't let this go on. It's worse each time. Remember what happened with Brigid and the oven. And now this. They both could have been killed."

What was this? What were they talking about? This was more than just the branch.

"The council," Sam added, his voice firm. "Mom, it's time we called them. This is really a matter for them. They have the resources, and they have specialists—"

"I have worked with specialists," Evelyn cut in. "They did nothing. I am dealing with this. . . ."

The sound of breaking glass caused me to jump, and I turned to see what had formerly been a lamp. Now it was a pile of glass pieces sitting under a cockeyed shade on the floor. I rushed to pick them up. Oh, God. Another telekinetic hiccup. The lamp was clearly unfixable. I was so desperate that I tried to spell it back together, but the truth was, I didn't know many spells and certainly not any for lamp repair. There was nothing I could do. The branch, the phone —now I'd gone and broken my grandmother's lamp.

As I fought off tears, a blond girl around my age peeked in the doorway. She had some of Evelyn's regal bearing, but her eyes were more soulful, like Sam's. Her golden hair was coiled on top of her head.

"Who are you?" she asked, looking at me as I stood there, caught red-handed with the lamp fragments. I quickly set them on the nearby bookcase.

"I'm Alisa," I said, wiping my eyes. "Sarah Curtis's daughter."

The girl looked confused, then amazed.

"I know who Sarah is," she said. "She had a daughter?"

I nodded. There I was. Proof.

"Goddess," she said brightly. "That means we're cousins, sort of. I'm Brigid. Ruth is my mom. Aunt Evelyn is my great-aunt." She stopped and cocked her head. "Are you all right?"

I wasn't sure what she was talking about for a second, then I realized that my eyes were probably still a bit teary. And there was the lamp, of course.

"Oh." I stepped away from the broken bits of green glass. "Sorry about the lamp. I, uh . . . I'm fine. I was just looking at my mother's bedroom, but I'm done now."

"This was your mom's bedroom?" Brigid said, looking around. "I didn't know that. I thought it had always been a workroom."

Brigid, at least, seemed kind of interested in me—this strange new cousin who'd shown up out of the blue, busted a few things, and seemed to know the history of her house. I guessed I'd be curious about someone like me, too.

"Are you staying here?" she asked, shifting a stack of beaded bracelets up and down her arm.

"No," I said, "I'm staying with Sam. We just came over to say hi. I don't know what we're doing now. Sam is busy talking to ... my grandmother."

"Big conference talk, huh?" she said with a smile. "Aunt Evelyn can be kind of intense. It takes a while to get to know her. You look a little freaked out."

I laughed nervously, incredibly thankful that someone seemed to understand something about my situation. "I am," I admitted. "Just a little."

"I'm about to go out," she said. "I'm going to meet my boyfriend, Charlie, for lunch. You're more than welcome to come with me. I promise I'm not as scary."

Charlie, I thought. That must be the guy from the e-mail.

"Is that Charlie Findgoll?" I asked. "I found the Web site for his shop. I wrote to him. That's how I got in touch with my uncle."

"Oh, right." She nodded. "He told me about that. You made his day. He's always complaining that no one looks at his Web site. You should come with me and meet him."

That really sounded good. Anything to get out of here.

Brigid escorted me back downstairs and boldly slid open the parlor doors. Evelyn, Sam, and Ruth were huddled together by the desk. They stopped talking the moment we walked in, which made me queasy.

"I'm going to go meet Charlie," Brigid said, unaffected by the oppressive air in the room. "I thought I'd take Alisa. You guys look busy."

"Great," Sam said, seeming very distracted. "That seems like a good idea."

Much as I wanted to avoid the topic, I had to tell them about the lamp.

"I kind of . . . broke a lamp. I don't know how. It fell off the shelf."

Ruth and Sam exchanged looks.

"What? That old green one?" Sam said. "It's fine. Don't worry about it."

Evelyn was twisting her lips into a thoughtful grimace and rearranging the alignment of her desk blotter.

"You're welcome to join us for dinner, Alisa," she said crisply. "If you would like to come back."

If this had been a movie, thunder would have cracked overhead and a horse would have whinnied. I'd never heard such an ominous invitation in my life.

"Thank you," I said, my voice a near whisper.

"We'll call," Brigid said cheerfully, leading me out.

"Six o'clock!" Ruth called to us.

That meant I would have to have to go back—unless, of course, I was prepared to run away for the second time in twenty-four hours.

9

Attraction

March 21, 1951

Mother and I have been hard at work on my wedding robe all day, and my fingers are so sore from the sewing that I can hardly hold this pen. The robe will be the most beautiful garment ever created when it is complete! We're making it from the most delicate white linen. The hard part, of course, is all of the embroidery—we're stitching in runes and symbols in oyster-colored thread, spelling each stitch. It is this work that has given me the sore fingers. And this won't be the last time. It will take us until June to finish.

Hugh has settled on getting a house here in Gloucester. He loves it here, and it's close enough to Boston. He's also decided to take time away from his teaching to write another book. Naturally I'm pleased that all is going so well. I have been a bit concerned about other things recently—Father has been looking ill. Good to know that our wedding plans are coming together without incident.

—Aoibheann

"Don't worry about the lamp," Brigid said, backing her little Toyota out onto the street. "That was just the ghost."

"Ghost?" I said. She was kidding, right?

"We have a poltergeist problem," she said, as if she was casually telling me that the house was full of termites. "Always have—it's just been getting worse recently. That's why everyone is so tense."

That did explain Sam's reaction to the branch. He had seemed concerned, more than he should have been by just a freak accident. At least he didn't suspect me, his creepy telekinetic niece who had just popped up out of nowhere—he just thought it was the house ghost. Of course. Nothing weird about that.

"It's a long story," Brigid went on. "We'll explain over lunch."

"Right," I said, eyeing a church as we passed. Poltergeists and witches, dark waves and telekinesis. What the hell was happening to me? What had I gotten myself into?

At that moment I noticed I was in a very speedy car. Brigid drove through the streets at Mach 3, squealing around corners as she felt around the console, looking for something. I gripped the seat.

"Sarah's daughter," Brigid remarked with a shake of her head. "Who knew?" She successfully came up with a CD, which she slipped into the stereo.

"You know about my mom?" I asked.

Brigid nodded. "No one talks about her, really, but everyone *knows*."

Her tone told me everything. My mother was the scandal of the century. The unmentionable. The dark blot on the family name.

At the rate Brigid was going, it took only about two minutes to drive to the town center. She pulled into a small seafood place called Take a Chowda.

"It looks cheesy," she said with a smile, "but it's good. We'll have lunch, then I'll show you around the town."

"Perfect," I said, getting out. "That sounds great."

Once inside, we seated ourselves. The place was an old diner, full of booths with Formica tables. We started looking over the menu, which consisted mainly (as I might have guessed) of different kinds of chowder, served in all different sizes and manners. If you weren't a chowder fan, this would have been a bad place to come. Brigid recommended that I get something called chowda 'n' cheddar, which came in a bread bowl.

Over the top of the menu, I saw the door open. A guy came into the restaurant and scanned the people at the tables. He was tall, even taller than Hunter, which was why I could see him. I lowered the menu to get a better look. His hair was a dark reddish brown with finger-length curled strands. He wore a pair of corduroys, a gray T-shirt with a pentagram design, and some kind of vintage tweed jacket. What really caught my attention, though, was his face. It was so expressive, with a full mouth and deep laugh lines that blossomed as he smiled. Something shot through me as he entered. It was an emotion, but it had an electric charge. There was something I immediately liked about him.

He was also just a little clumsy. As he passed through the door, he managed to get his jacket caught, which caused him to trip as he approached us. As he steadied himself, he caught my eye and smiled. I was amazed as he continued right toward us. I could see now that he had light freckles high on his cheeks and over his nose, and small peaks in his eyebrows. When he sat down with us, I knew it could mean only one thing—he was Charlie, Brigid's boyfriend. He gave Brigid a light kiss. I tried to convince myself that I wasn't disappointed.

"This is Alisa," Brigid said, pointing at me.

"Hi," he said, confirming my suspicions, "I'm Charlie."

"I wrote you the e-mail," I said quietly. "The one to Sam Curtis."

"That was you?" he asked brightly in recognition. "I was so excited! No one ever looks at my site."

"Here we go," said Brigid, rolling her eyes. "Charlie's obsessed with his site."

"Just trying to get some more business for the shop," he said with a grin. "That's why my boss loves me."

"And how many people have looked at it?" Brigid asked, egging him on.

"Seven," he said, "but I'm waiting for the big rush. It's coming any day now."

Even as he was speaking, Charlie looked me over, as if fascinated. While it would have been nice if he was doing so because he had fallen instantaneously in love with me, I knew the real reason: I give off a weird half-witch vibe. It must be like some high pitch that only full witches can hear. Brigid, though, didn't seem to notice anything odd about me, which was kind of strange in itself.

I'm so terrible at small talk. I searched my mind for something else to say. "Do you guys, um, go to the same school?"

"Charlie doesn't have to go to school anymore," Brigid chimed in. "He finished after the fall semester. He'd taken the highest levels of everything. There was nothing left for him to do."

She folded her arms and looked at him with pride, as if he was her blue-ribbon-winning entry in the state fair. He looked embarrassed.

"I'm taking some classes at the community college," he explained. "It's not like I'm just free to do what I want. But my schedule is a bit more open. I have a job at Bell, Book, and Candle in the hours between class times. It works out pretty well. I might even be able to transfer some credits when I start college in the fall."

"Wow," I said, impressed.

"It's just that, you know, we're Rowanwand." He shrugged. "Academics is what we do best."

"Speak for yourself," said Brigid, flagging down the waitress.

"So," he said, changing the subject. "You're Sam's niece? You got up here quickly. You just sent that note."

"Right ..." I said. "You know, why wait?"

Fortunately the waitress came at that moment, preventing me from having to explain any further. Brigid and I ordered up our chowda 'n' cheddars. Charlie ordered something called a superchowda power hour.

"Sam and Alisa had an Oona moment when they came up to the house," Brigid said. "A branch almost fell on Sam's head."

Charlie turned to me in concern. "Is he all right?" he asked.

"He's okay." I nodded. "But what's an Oona moment?"

"I guess you wouldn't know about Oona," he said. "Have you explained, Brig?"

"I'd just started," said Brigid. "I didn't get that far. You can explain."

"Oona," Charlie said, slipping off his jacket, "is a relative of yours. I guess she would be your G5 grandmother."

"G5?"

"Great-great-great-great-grandmother. That's her relationship to Brigid, so it would be the same to you. It's her ghost that they're talking about."

Ghosts. Uh-huh. What next? Did they have vampires in the cellar? Unicorns in the yard?

"You're telling me that ghosts are real?" I said incredulously. "I'm still getting used to the witches."

"She's an energy," he explained, popping the wrapper off a straw. "A force. She's been around for years, causing all kinds of little problems. She used to swat things off tables, break an occasional window, rip the curtains. That sort of thing. Now objects aren't just moving or breaking—they seem to be attacking people."

"Attacking people?" Huh. The good part of this story was that it didn't sound like I was the one responsible for what had happened to Sam. At least, I didn't think so. The bad part was that I seemed to be walking into another in a series of scary situations. The fun never stopped.

"The story goes like this," he explained. "Oona's husband, your G5 grandfather, and their two sons died in a flu epidemic in the mid- to late 1800s. Oona lost her mind. It's bad when anyone loses his or her mind, but when it happens to a witch, it's really bad. If the person can't be healed, the person's coven will perform a reining spell to protect everyone, including the afflicted. In really bad cases, the person will be stripped of power. That's a horrible process. Máirín, her daughter, must not have been able to stand the thought of her mother going through it, so she tried to keep the illness hidden. It was a huge mistake. Oona ended up committing suicide."

"Oh my God," I said.

"No one knows what spells Oona cast after she lost her mind," he continued, "but it seems that one of them must have ended up lodging her energy in the house. Máirín describes all kinds of problems that started the minute Oona died."

"How do you know all of this?" I asked, feeling the hairs on my neck starting to rise.

"Aunt Evelyn found Máirín's Book of Shadows years ago," said Brigid. "But it disappeared from her room a day later. Maybe Oona took it."

"From what Evelyn's said," Charlie chimed in, "there were problems when Evelyn was a child. Then they quieted down for years and started again . . . in the, um, early seventies. After the other family problems."

He was saying that they had started around the time my mother left home. During the awkward pause that followed, the waitress brought our food. I had to admit that though the menu was a bit much, the chowder was amazing.

"What happened after my mother left?" I asked, taking a big spoonful and nodding for Charlie to continue.

"It was bad at first, I think," Charlie answered, reaching for the bowl of crackers. "I think there was a small fire and definitely some broken windows. Then the problem quieted down again. I think it only popped up occasionally during the late seventies and eighties. But in the last few months it's gone off the charts. One of the walls developed a crack. Some banisters tumbled down from the widow's walk. Two weeks ago the gas line to the oven was punctured when Brigid was alone in the house. It could have been really serious, but fortunately she smelled the gas and got out."

"We've done just about every kind of spell we can think of," Brigid added. "Now Mom's even trying to talk Aunt Evelyn into selling the house. But Aunt Evelyn won't do that. We've owned the house for over a hundred years, and she's way too stubborn to give up trying to solve the problem. She's sure that with our combined powers, we can do it. Oh, but . . ." She looked at me with what I thought was slightly exaggerated pity. "You wouldn't know anything about that. You don't have any powers."

It wasn't a bad assumption since I *shouldn't* have had any powers. It just turned out that I did. I could have told her, but somehow, "I just squashed a dark wave" wasn't going to slide right into the conversation.

"It must be *terrible* for you," Brigid went on. "How long have you known that your mom was a witch?"

"Just a couple of weeks," I said, dragging into my chowder. "I joined a coven, and then I found out later. It was a surprise."

"Well," she said, "I think it's great that you've decided to join a coven. I mean, considering that you can't do what we can do. But even though you're not a real witch, you can definitely be a part of Wicca. It's open to everyone."

Charlie started rocking his spoon on the table and stared at the wall next to us. I don't think he liked the patronizing tone that Brigid was using but didn't really want to intervene.

"I'll show you something, Alisa," she said. "Want to see me work with the rhythm of the waves?"

"Brig," Charlie said, his eyebrows shooting up, "are you, um . . . ?"

"Don't worry," she said. "This is a new spell I've worked out. Sending the energy out to the water. It's a really mild version of a return-to-me spell. I'd just like to show Alisa some magick. She's probably never seen any."

Since I'd just been through enough terrifying magickal phenomena to last a lifetime, it was all I could do not to laugh out loud. And considering that my uncle had acciden-tally killed several people while trying to help with the rain, this seemed like the worst kind of arrogant, foolish magick in the world. A party trick using the ocean? I wasn't a trained witch, but I had enough sense to know that this was a bad, bad idea.

Charlie blanched. Apparently he didn't think much of this idea, either.

Hunter had taught me a few basic deflections while I was learning the dark wave spell. I tried to find them in the back of my memory, where they were stuck together. *Nal nithrac, tar ais di cair na, clab saoil* . . . which were the right words? It was as if I was grabbing at hundreds of jars of exotic unmarked spices, each tantalizing and overwhelmingly pun-gent, and trying to figure out how best to combine them.

Suddenly I heard Morgan's voice somewhere in my mind, just as I had when we'd joined our minds, giving me words to a spell I'd never heard before. They ran through my head, like an old song: *Sguir bhur ire, cunnartach sgeò, car fàilidh, agus eirmis tèarainte sgot.* I had no idea what the words meant, but

I understood how they worked. I was to look for a safe place to redirect the energy that Brigid was sending to the waves. I happened to be looking at the salt, so I put it there.

The saltshaker began to bounce. Brigid, who had been focusing on the waves lapping at the seawall outside the window, looked down at the noise. The shaker wobbled down the table and hit the floor. From there it rolled unsteadily to the wall near the window and stopped, unable to go any farther.

When I looked up, Charlie's amber eyes met mine and didn't flinch. His expression was unreadable, not unfriendly, but definitely serious. I felt a wave of electricity ripple through me, giving me goose pimples. He had power, lots of it, and he was sending some of it my way, casting out his senses like Morgan and Hunter had. I suddenly felt very self-conscious.

Within a second the event had passed. Brigid was flushed with embarrassment.

"Well, that didn't work right," she said.

"It was fine," Charlie said graciously. "The salt was trying to reconnect with the seawater—it was affected because it was lighter and closer to you. Working with the ocean is tricky."

"It was good." I nodded in agreement. "It was cool." Anything to make her stop.

Brigid started moving everything on her place mat around, seeming uncomfortable. Conveniently her cell phone rang. I wondered if she'd managed to spell it, too.

"Damn," she said, hanging up after a quick conversation. "That was Karen, my boss. She needs me at the shop. Sorry,

Alisa. I guess I can't show you around after all. Can you do it, Charlie?"

"Sure." He smiled at me. "I'm off today."

"Good," Brigid said, stuffing her phone back into her purse. "Alisa's coming back for dinner, six o'clock."

"Is this okay with you?" he asked, pulling out his keys.

"Sure," I said, hoping I didn't sound too eager. "Let's go."

10

Charlie

June 23, 1951

    I woke up this morning to the sound of a great tearing.

    When I opened my eyes, I saw that Oona had torn the front of my bridal robe—right from the collar down to within six inches of the bottom hem. My beautiful robe!

    I couldn't help myself. I started weeping uncontrollably. Mother ran upstairs and came right into my room. I felt so hopeless, but she knew just what to do. She sewed up the great, jagged rip with a basting stitch. It looked like a Frankenstein robe, with ugly scars. Then she put me in a hot bath filled with rosemary and lavender and instructed me to stay there for one hour, repeating the wedding day blessing. When I emerged and returned to my room, the gown was as good as new. In fact, it looked more beautiful than before. Mother had cast a glamor that concealed the tear. I am ready now, and we will be leaving soon. There is no more time for me to write.

    —Aoibheann

I instantly figured out which car was Charlie's. It was a small green Volkswagen, obviously a few years old. There was a neat line of stickers on the back for different Irish and Celtic bands, including the Fianna. The thing that really gave it away, though, was the one that read, $2 + 2 = 5$ . . . for Extremely Large Values of 2. I just knew that was his. Don't ask me why.

We drove around the harbor, looking at the fishing boats and the activity on the docks. He told me all about Ròiseal, how they worked a lot with the energy of the sea, and how they often had circles on the beach in the moonlight. He also explained how the coven was set up and how they worked. Because they were all experienced blood witches, they did a lot more complicated things than we did at Kithic circles. I began to wonder if Hunter found it frustrating to work with us. In comparison, running Kithic must be like watching over a bunch of kindergarteners, trying to make sure they don't eat the crayons.

"We each have a general background in magick," Charlie explained, "and we each have an area of expertise to help balance out the coven. We're all lifelong students, of course, because we're Rowanwand. This way we split up the burden of studying. Ruth does a lot of healing work. Brigid is being trained to do the same. Evelyn works in divination. Kate and James work with defensive and deflective magick."

"What about you?"

"Spellcraft," he said. "How they're written, how they're broken, how they're restricted. My dad works in the same area but on a less practical level than I do. I usually work with everyday magick. He works with the mathematical stuff relating to astronomy, sigil drawing, the Key of Solomon, things like that—right into the realm of abstract math, where numbers turn into sounds and colors and shapes ... really hard stuff, and he also studies some very dark stuff for reference. Academic magick."

He parked the car, and we walked down Western Avenue, along the water, then up into the shopping area. As we walked, I saw that I was passing by many of the places my mother had described in her Book of Shadows. There was the chocolate shop, where she used to get chocolate turtles and peanut-butter fudge. There was the town hall, with the library across the street where Sam had found Harris Stoughton's book. I smelled the delicious aroma coming from Rocconi's Pizzeria on Middle Street, where she used to meet her friends after school. And at the old floral shop on Main Street, the window was filled with lilacs—her favorite flower. It was all so strange, so unreal. I felt so close to her. For the first time in a long while, I missed her with a physical ache.

It began to rain again, catching us completely off guard. It wasn't a warning trickle that led to a bigger downpour—it was like thousands of buckets had been kicked over at once, sudden and freezing. Charlie grabbed my elbow and steered me down the street through the rain into a nearby coffee bar. We squished up to the counter and surveyed the offerings. When I reached for my purse, Charlie held up his hand.

"Please," he said. "It's on me. What do you like?"

"Thanks," I said. "Just coffee. Lots of milk and sugar."

"Got it," he said.

I snagged a cozy table by the window with two plush seats and sat down to consider the significance of his action. No guy I knew had ever just bought things for me. I didn't even know that many people who were bought things on dates. What was *this* about? You don't buy coffees for someone you don't like, right? Charlie must like me. Not *like me,* like me—but he could tolerate me. Or so it seemed.

I occupied myself with this stupid internal dialogue until he came over a few minutes later with two grotesquely large mugs of frothy something and two biscotti wrapped in a napkin.

"What are these?" I said, accepting one of the heaping cups with a smile of thanks.

"I have no idea," he said, poking suspiciously at the foam, as if he was testing to see if it was alive. "Grande cappu-frappes or something. I told them to make something big and steamy, with lots of milk. They gave me these. I'm assuming they're coffees."

He held up his foamy stirrer and grimaced theatrically. I had to laugh.

We sat in the coffee shop for hours, talking. Usually I'm not great around people I don't know very well. I'm that shy girl, the one who goes through a crisis every time she even has to ask someone where the ladies' room is in a restaurant. So my ease around Charlie was odd. For some reason, I felt like I could talk to him about anything. I loved the way he could be so serious, and then something funny would occur to him, and he'd half jump from his seat and lean forward in excitement, his whole face bursting. During one story he became so animated that he knocked the sugar canister off the table three times.

"So," I said, continuing our conversation from the walk, "your dad's some kind of genius?"

"More or less," he said. "He's a number theorist. He's

your classic absentminded professor. Brilliant beyond belief, but he literally forgets to feed himself."

"And you ended up finishing high school early? You must be pretty smart yourself."

"It's not a big deal," he said, stirring what was left of his coffee. "I did well, but it was nothing exciting. And my dad's been a really, really good math tutor."

"What about your mom?" I asked.

"Oh"—he shrugged uncomfortably—"she died a few years ago."

"Sorry," I said, understanding his reaction. "My mom died, too, and I hate having to explain to people. They always give you the *look*. It's kind of sympathetic, but mostly it's really nervous. It's like they think they've torn open a wound, and you're going to start screaming or something."

"That's the one," he said, grinning thankfully.

"So you must spend a lot of time alone, then," I said.

"No." He shook his head. "I spend a lot of time with Brigid and her family. I have a standing invitation to dinner every single night, which is nice."

He put his feet up on the empty chair at our table and leaned back to look at me.

"So," he said, "what about you? Your dad doesn't know anything about Wicca at all?"

"He knows that it freaks him out," I said. "That's about it. I'm sure he just thinks it's some kind of phase I'm going through. A better-Wicca-than-drugs kind of a thing, I guess."

"If he doesn't like Wicca, why did he let you come here?"

"Um . . . my dad doesn't exactly know where I am," I confessed.

"What does that mean?" he asked, one eyebrow arching.

"It means I ran away."

Okay. There. Someone knew. I twirled my biscotti in the dregs of my coffee foam as nonchalantly as I could, wondering if Charlie was going to jump up and start yelling for the cops. Instead, he exhaled and leaned back into the red velvet seat.

"Why?" he asked calmly.

"A lot of reasons. Mostly because things were happening to me—I was having dreams about this place. My mother's Book of Shadows appeared out of nowhere. Sam's letters fell out of a broken box. So I wrote to you, and I made contact. It all felt like it was meant to be."

"And, of course, you couldn't tell your dad about any of it."

"Right," I said, running my hands through my hair. "There were other reasons, too. . . ."

"Like what?"

"I have powers," I said. "They came on all of a sudden and kind of freaked me out."

He dropped his feet down to the floor and leaned in to me.

"How's that possible?" he said, his eyes glowing with wonder. "Your father's not a witch, and your mother . . ." He stopped himself and shook his head. "Wow. I'm an *ass*. I can't believe I just said that. Sorry."

"It's all right," I said, waving my hand dismissively. "I know it's weird. My coven leader's father thinks it might be that since my mother stripped herself of her powers, they were all somehow concentrated in me. I definitely have more than I can handle. They tend to do things on their own. The last thing I did before running away was cause some kind of water explosion in my coven leader's house. We were doing a release spell to get rid of negative emotions, and . . ."

I hung my head. Charlie was so experienced—I was a moron. Still, he was listening attentively, and I knew I could tell him what had happened to me. Again, don't ask me why.

". . . I almost flooded his house. It was awful. It was the most embarrassing moment of my life, and that's saying something. I just started crying, and I couldn't stop."

He was quiet for a minute. I couldn't raise my head. I just stared into the table.

"Trust me," he said, "I know how difficult and embarrassing it can be when you're first trying to use your power. Everyone screws up. All witches know this."

"I can't imagine the people who run my coven screwing up," I replied, envisioning all of the experienced blood witches I knew—Hunter, Sky, Mr. Niall. They were probably born cool, calm, and talented. And sure, Morgan was erratic, but she was also superpowerful, and I'd seen some of the wonders she was capable of when we'd put our minds together. I was just regular and inept.

"They did," he said with conviction. "I promise you. I know I was a master at it."

He could see I doubted him.

"I'll give you an example," he offered. "A lot of covens get together to hold circles and lessons for preinitiates. Our assignment one week was a simple nochd. A nochd is a revealing spell. Our teachers would hide something, and we would each use the spell to find it. When I was a kid, I always used to try to prove to everyone how smart I was. I wanted to do the most amazing and complicated nochd in the group. I searched through all of our books for a whole week. I finally found one that was hundreds of years old that I was sure no one else would have. I can still remember it. It was very long and involved. Everyone was impressed. Unfortunately, what I didn't realize is that not all nochds are alike. The term has many meanings, and the spells have many purposes. I wasn't smart enough to figure that out until it was too late."

"What happened?" I asked, looking up with interest.

"Just as I came to the end, silence. Everyone just stared at me. I mean, *stared*. And then they all started to laugh. Then I realized that the room had gotten really cold."

"Did you do some kind of weather spell?" I asked.

"A nochd," he said with a grin, "is also a spell for nakedness, a complete revealing of self."

I gasped with sudden laughter and put my hand over my mouth.

"Well," Charlie went on, "because I was young and dumb, I didn't realize right away that I was standing in front of my friends completely naked. I was so busy looking around to see what I had revealed that it took me a second to look down at myself to see what people were staring at."

"But aren't Wiccans okay with that?" I asked, still laughing. "I mean, being naked?"

"Sure," he said. "It won't get you in trouble. But we were still just a bunch of thirteen-year-olds. And being thirteen and naked in front of all your friends, both male and female—that's the same for everyone."

"What did you do?" I asked.

"I froze," he said. "I had *no idea* what to do. One of the teachers quickly undid the spell, but I was standing there long enough for everyone to get a nice long look at me. There I was: brilliant, naked Charlie."

He didn't seem to mind that I was rolling with laughter over stories of his childhood traumas. He even took a little bow.

"So messing up is one thing. The real trouble comes when you're just trying to impress people with magick you don't know how to control. Like what Brigid was trying to do back at the restaurant," he said, looking directly into my eyes, "before you stopped her."

I almost fell out of my chair. Even though it happened again and again, sometimes I just couldn't get used to the fact that other witches always seemed to know what you were doing and thinking.

"I—I didn't . . ." I stammered. "I mean, I did, but I wasn't trying to embarrass her. . . ."

"No," he said, waving his hand. "It's all right. It was a good thing that you did. It could have been dangerous."

"How did you know?" I said.

"I felt your energy coming out. I could sense it redirecting hers."

Funny. He and I could both sense energy, but Brigid didn't appear to be able to. I wondered if something was wrong with her powers. Maybe they were weak. Maybe that was why she was trying to prove herself so much.

"How did you do it, exactly?" Charlie asked. "What spell was that?"

"I don't know," I replied, shaking my head. "It just kind of came to me. I did this thing about a week ago . . . a tàth meànma . . . something. . . . I kind of locked minds with someone, a very powerful witch."

"A tàth meànma brach?" he said, his eyes wide.

"That was it. I didn't realize it at the time, but I just kind of . . . learned things, I guess. When I saw what Brigid was doing, I was afraid, and I wanted to stop her. Suddenly it was as if I heard my friend's voice somewhere deep in my mind. I just knew what to do."

Charlie was staring at me as if I had just sprouted wings and a beak.

"What?" I asked anxiously, looking myself over. "What did I do?"

"You did a *brach?*" he repeated.

"Is that weird?" I asked, feeling myself hunch down in my chair.

"No . . ." he said, pulling absently at a handful of his loopy curls. "Well, not in a bad way. It's rare. And difficult. And dangerous. Why did you do a *brach?*"

"Oh. It wasn't my idea—it was my coven leader's, and he's crazy careful. He's a Seeker."

"Your coven leader is a Seeker?"

"Yeah." I nodded vigorously. "He's the youngest Seeker. He's nineteen."

Charlie stopped speaking. His mouth just hung open slightly. He waited for me to go on.

"There was an emergency," I said. "Something really bad had happened, and they needed me to help with a spell. The only way I could do it was by getting information from my friend. So we did a *tàth meànma brach.*"

Charlie sat and silently contemplated this for a moment. I glanced up at the clock. It was six-ten.

"We're late," I said, alarmed. "It's after six."

He nodded, still deep in thought, and we grabbed our

things and ran out toward his car. The rain was coming down hard, and the streets were full of foggy mist. After we slithered, soaking, disgusting wet into the car, I turned to him. His hair was dark, and one or two of the curls clung to his face very attractively. I wanted to ask him something, but the sight of him made my tongue go all numb.

"What's up?" he said, immediately sensing my question. He brushed some of the water from his face and rummaged around in the glove compartment. He produced a handful of tissues, which we used to dry off.

"Are you coming tonight, or are you just dropping me off?" I asked quickly. He looked up with interest.

"I could come," he said. "Why? Can't get enough of my amazing company?"

"Sort of." I laughed. "It's just that Evelyn . . . my grand-mother . . . she doesn't seem to like me. She seems angry that I'm here. It would be nice to have a friendly face."

This didn't seem to shock Charlie.

"Sure," he said. "I'd be happy to come. I'll help you get through it."

Though I must have looked like hell, I felt about a million times better as we headed back toward the house.

11

Shatter

July 30, 1951

Father died of a heart attack five days ago. It came on suddenly, and no one was at home. Nothing could be done.

Hugh and I have stopped looking for a house. We will live here. Mother will need support and help with Tioma. To make matters worse, this has stirred up Oona. She shredded the curtains in the living room and broke the panes of glass in our front door. Mother and I watched as it happened. She wept endlessly. I need to be strong.

Goddess, I know you give, and I know you must take. I revere you, though my heart is broken.

—Aoibheann

"I came along," Charlie said, peeling off his sopping jacket as we stepped into the foyer. "I hope that's all right."

"Of course," Ruth said with a smile. "Always. I'll set another place."

"I'll get it," he said, slipping back toward the kitchen. "Don't worry about it, Ruth."

Ruth nodded, looking at me kindly. "Alisa, the bathroom is right by the front door. You can wash your hands and dry off a bit in there."

"Thanks," I said. Ruth returned to the kitchen, and I found the powder room, which was just big enough to fit a toilet and a very small sink. I looked like a drowned rat. My hair was completely soaked, and it clung to my head. My clothes were getting really swampy. There were beeswax soap and a jar of salt crystals for washing hands. I used both, rubbing the crystals into my skin anxiously, as if I could impress my grandmother by having the cleanest hands of anyone she'd ever met. By the time I came out, I'd turned my hands red from the effort, and everyone was gathered in the dining room, waiting for me.

The room was filled by a long oval-shaped table and a massive sideboard, both of which looked like they were probably well over a century old. The table was heavy with food, served up on delicate pieces of blue-and-white china. There was an incredible-smelling roast, with big bowls of fluffy potatoes, asparagus, and roasted carrots. The gravy was so thick and aromatic that it had to be completely homemade, and the soft biscuits were already dripping with butter. From what I'd seen so far, the Curtises were very good cooks.

We all sat down. I had been put next to Sam. Charlie set his place next to Brigid. Evelyn and Ruth had the opposite ends. With a snap of her fingers Evelyn lit the two tall taper candles in silver candlesticks. I had a feeling that little trick was for my benefit.

"When are you returning home, Alisa?" Evelyn asked me, rather properly, as she passed Ruth the potatoes. Nice. I'd just gotten here, and she wanted to know when I was leaving.

"In . . . a few days," I said. "It's my spring break."

"Well," said Sam, "I hope you can stay for our circle on Wednesday. It's our annual celebration of the founding of Ròiseal. We're getting together the night before as well, for Ruth's birthday. It's a big week."

"Yeah," Brigid agreed. "You have to come."

"I'd like that," I said, not really sure if that was true. Sam, Charlie, Brigid, and Ruth were great—but Evelyn was so seriously scary that I had to wonder how long I really wanted to stay here. Well, at least the circle on Wednesday gave me something to plan around.

Evelyn said nothing, just eyed the progress of the food around the table. When everyone had filled their plates, she nodded, and I saw the others take up their silverware. I followed suit. My mother hadn't mentioned how formal the family dinners were. She probably hadn't noticed. Unlike me, she'd had no Hilary leaving the table to barf every fifteen minutes. She had no basis for comparison.

Evelyn started talking again but to everyone but me. She asked Charlie about school, his job, his father, and his plans for college. She asked Brigid if anything interesting had happened at the shop and how her training was going.

"Brigid has been training with a healer," Sam explained to me, attempting to include me in the conversation.

"That's great," I said to Brigid, who smiled proudly. "Do you need to do a lot of studying?"

"Some," she said. "A lot of it is exercises in channeling energy. Then you add the herbs and the oils, but only after you learn to feel out the problem or the injury."

"You wouldn't understand, Alisa," Evelyn said, turning to me. "It involves magick."

Charlie looked over at me meaningfully. I could tell he was wondering if one of us should tell them about my powers. I shook my head quickly. I really didn't want to get into it with them. He got the message and opted to change the course of the conversation.

"So," he said, "you're from Texas, right?" I'd just told him that this afternoon.

"That's right," I said, breaking open a steamy biscuit. "That's where I was born. We lived there until recently."

"How do you like the winters up here?" Sam asked cheerfully.

"I don't," I said with a smile, "except for the snow. I like snow, but my father can't drive in it. He never learned how. So if it even flurries, my future stepmonst—mother has to drive. If she's not home, we're stuck."

A polite chuckle from everyone but Evelyn, who was communing with her roasted carrots. Sam, Ruth, Charlie, and Brigid continued to ask me questions about my life. For the most part they were just making polite conversation, not going into anything too deeply. Evelyn pointedly said nothing. I noticed all of the others giving her sideways glances, but these didn't seem to penetrate her steely exterior. She wasn't interested in talking to me. Period.

I had just finished telling them a little about my dad's job and my grandparents in Buenos Aires when Evelyn suddenly lifted her head and focused on me, hard and fast.

"How does your father feel about the craft?" she said.

"The craft?" I repeated. "You mean Wicca?"

"I do."

"I don't think he's happy about my involvement with it," I answered honestly. "But he doesn't really know that much about it. I think he assumes it's a fad at our high school."

"A *fad* at your high school?"

"A lot of my friends are in my coven," I explained, gripping my silverware fearfully. "He just knows that's where I go on Saturdays. We rotate hosting the circle, although I probably won't be hosting one. I bring snacks, though."

"Snacks are good," Sam said with a nod. "Witches love snacks, especially sweets."

"So you contribute snacks at Wicca circles," she said.

This was a blatant twisting of my words, designed to make me look like a fool. I couldn't believe it. It was so unnecessary, this quietly vicious behavior. She was so composed, passing around her roast and her gravy and just stinging the hell out of her granddaughter. Around me I felt these little tendrils of emotion as the others reached out to me. That was nice of them, but it didn't really take away the painful reality of the situation.

Then, in with those gestures of sympathy, something else came along. It wasn't in words, and it wasn't in sound—but somehow it was as clear as if someone was shouting into my ear.

Something's wrong.

What the hell was that? A vicious chill ran all through my body, as if someone had just plugged an IV of ice water into my veins. There was a creaking sound and a snap of wind. Before I knew what was happening, Charlie jumped up and pushed Brigid away from the table.

"Ruth!" he shouted, throwing out his hand and pointing at her. A bolt of energy, pale white, came from his hand and threw Ruth back toward the wall. In the same second all the lights in the room went out in a cloud of electric sparks as the chandelier above us broke free and crashed down onto the table, shattering glass and splintering wood. The snapped wires danced above our heads like angry snakes, still pulsing with current. Evelyn, already on her feet, held up her hand and made them still. With another flash of movement she deadened the sparks that still came from the chandelier. Now all was dark, and acrid burning smells hung in the air.

"Is everyone all right?" Charlie called.

"I am," I said, my voice shaking. "Sam is."

Evelyn snapped to light some candles on the sideboard. I could see that Ruth had been thrown far enough to spare her head, but her arms had still been too close. The thing had come down on them, pinning her to the table. Brigid was by her mother's side, crying, mumbling spells that had no visible effect. Ruth looked like she was in too much pain to speak. Her face was covered in tiny bloody trails, probably slices from the flying glass.

Sam joined Charlie, who had uttered a quick spell that seemed to make the heavy, tinkling fixture a little easier to lift. They gingerly moved it away from Ruth, taking great pains not to further her injury. Brigid started running her hands over Ruth, obviously trying to do some healing work, but Evelyn came and took her shoulder.

"Go start the car, Brigid," she said. "She needs to go to the hospital. Charlie, can you carry her?"

Charlie nodded and ran for his jacket.

"I think we should call the council," Sam said. "This has gone far enough."

"I know a Seeker," I found myself saying. "If I called him, he could be here in a few hours."

Evelyn looked up at Sam and looked in my direction.

"I think you'd better leave," she said. "We'll take her to the hospital."

Charlie came back in just in time to catch the tail end of this conversation. His eyebrows rose, and his naturally cheerful expression faded into one of surprised disgust. I had a feeling that if the situation hadn't been so dire, he might have even spoken up on my behalf. But this wasn't the time. He bent down and picked Ruth up in a cradle lift. She quietly wept in pain and fear, and I heard him reassuring her as he took her through the hall to the door.

Sam, thunderstruck at our dismissal, stood there staring at his mother. She turned on her heel and followed Charlie down the hall. Sam put his arm around my shoulders and led me through the front door. We stood on the porch and watched as Brigid pulled out and sped the car down the street and out of sight. Sam quietly pulled a key from his pocket and locked the door.

"Are you sure you're all right?" he said.

"I'm fine," I assured him. "What about you?"

"It could have killed her," he said, instead of answering what I had asked. "Thank the Goddess Charlie's quick."

We got into his car. For a moment Sam just sat in the driver's seat, hands on the steering wheel, looking too tense to put the key in the ignition.

"Evelyn seemed so angry when I mentioned calling a Seeker," I said. "Why?"

"Not everyone likes the council," he answered, his expression dark. I got the feeling this was a regular bone of contention. "Some people are offended that one group of witches should take it upon themselves to govern other witches, to pass judgment. I think the council has done some very good work. We could use their help."

He sighed, beat a little rhythm onto the steering wheel,

then started the car. I looked out at the people walking along the beach path and heading to the pubs for the evening. Apparently some people in this town had normal lives.

"Charlie and Brigid told me about Oona," I said. Sam glanced over at me.

"They did?" he said. "Good. I was wondering how to explain what just happened."

"Stuff like that has happened before?" I asked.

"This was the worst so far," he replied. "But the phenomena have been getting more serious just lately. It certainly seems like my mother wants to wait until someone gets killed before she'll ask for help."

His undercurrent of rage was palpable, so I fell silent and let him have a few minutes to think things over.

"I'm sorry, Alisa," he said just as we pulled into his driveway. "I'm sorry about the way your grandmother treated you. I don't even know what to say about it."

"It's like you said, I guess," I answered, trying to be diplomatic. "It's just strange to have me show up."

"Still, she has no right to behave like that. I just want you to know that she and I feel very differently about your being here. You can stay with me as long as you like—and as long as your dad lets you."

This triggered my memory. Twenty-four hours . . . the watch sigil on my neck. I had to call Morgan.

"Oh," I said, as casually as I could, "would it be all right if I used your phone? I just need to check in. It's long distance, but I'll be quick."

"Take your time," Sam said. "I'm sure your dad would like an update."

A strange expression crossed his face, but I decided not to

try to read into it too much. For all I knew, Sam had been onto me from the first.

"I leave for work pretty early in the morning," he said. "Sleep in. I'll leave you keys so you can come and go as you please. I'll be home around five. We'll do something different tomorrow night, like see a movie."

"Thanks," I said. "That would be great."

Astrophe and Mandu pounced on us the moment we stepped in the door. Sam fed them, then went upstairs. I took the phone into the kitchen for privacy. I got lucky. Morgan answered, not Mary K.

"It's me," I said. "Alisa. I know I'm almost out of time, but I made it."

"Oh, hi . . ." she said casually. I heard her quickly moving into a quieter place and shutting a door. "Alisa," she said in a low voice, "how are you? Is everything okay?"

"Um," I said hesitantly. "A little weird, actually. My uncle is great. My grandmother looks at me like I'm an escaped convict that's hiding in her house. And there's some kind of killer ghost on the loose. . . ."

"What?"

I told her the grim tale as it had unfolded so far.

"You were right," she said. "Something weird was definitely going on up there. Do you think this is what the dreams were about?"

"I don't know," I said as Astrophe leaped into my lap. "I'm going to have to stay here a few more days to find out. I figure I have spring-break week, at least. So, how bad is it down there?"

"Well," she said with a sigh, "your dad is upset. Frantic,

actually. He called here about an hour after I got back." My stomach turned. "I also told Hunter what happened," she continued. "He understands what you're doing, but he's really worried, too. He'll be glad to know you called."

I had to promise to call back soon before she let me get off the phone. You can always get out of something your parents try to make you do, but when a powerful witch puts a sigil on your neck, you're pretty much stuck.

A while later, after I had settled down for the night on Sam's couch and was flipping through my mother's Book of Shadows in preparation for going to sleep, the phone rang. After a minute Sam called down for me to pick up the phone.

"Hey," said a voice. "Sorry to be calling so late."

It was Charlie. He sounded tired, and I could hear him climbing into bed as he spoke. Thank God he couldn't see me—I was grinning like an idiot. Charlie was calling for me!

"I just thought you might like to know," he went on, "Ruth's arm is broken, but she's okay otherwise. Banged up and upset, of course, but intact."

"I—I'm glad," I said, stuttering in my excitement. "I mean, I'm glad that she'll be all right."

"What about you?" he asked.

"What about me? It didn't land on me."

"The chandelier didn't, no," he said. "But that whole dinner was kind of rough."

"Oh. I'm fine," I said, pretty unconvincingly. "No problem."

"I guess you haven't realized yet that it's pretty much useless to lie to witches," he said.

Actually, that much I had figured out on my own. I knew that most other witches could read me like a book. But what surprised me was that I could read him as well, and his concern amazed me—it was deep. Deep to the point that I could feel it all the way across the town, physically, as if a warm embrace could travel down a telephone line. "It wasn't the welcome I wanted," I confessed. "But it was nice that you were there. Thanks for coming."

He let the line go quiet for a moment. He didn't try to tell me that it would all be fine, because it didn't appear that it would be.

"What are you doing tomorrow?" he asked.

"Sam's working," I said, throwing my legs over the top of the couch and hanging upside down. "I don't know. Staying here, I guess. I don't think Evelyn wants to have me over again anytime soon."

"Want some company? We're on spring break, too, and I have the day off from the shop."

A *whole day* with Charlie? I couldn't think of anything I wanted more. But was that weird? This was my cousin's boyfriend. Should I be spending that much time with him?

"What about Brigid?" I asked. "Doesn't she have off from school, too?"

"She does," he said, "but she's working." When I didn't answer right away, he came back a little nervously. "We don't have to," he said. "I just thought . . ."

What the hell was wrong with me? Just because Charlie made me weak at the knees didn't mean that he was going to ditch my cousin to run off with me.

"No, no," I backpedaled quickly. "I want to. I mean, I'd like to. Actually, I'd like to do some research on my background. There's a lot of stuff I have questions about, family stuff. There's a library my mom keeps talking about in her Book of Shadows. It's in the house. That would be perfect, but it sounds like it's secret."

"Research!" he said. "That I can help you with. As for the library, I've never seen it, but I'm sure there is one. All Rowanwands have a collection of books somewhere, and as head of the coven, I'm sure Evelyn has thousands of books. The door is probably spelled, so you can't see it unless someone shows you where it is. I'll bet we can find it. It might take a while, but it can be done."

"How?"

"Spells leave traces. There'll be runes or sigils to mark the doorway. We'll just need to narrow down the area of the house where to look because it can take a long time to find them. Does she say anything about where it might be?"

By now I knew the book almost by heart, and I automatically flipped through to the pages that mentioned the family library.

"Well," I said, finding a page, "she says one time that she was writing in the study, and then she went down to the library."

"So it's in the basement," he said. "Great. That's where we'll start."

"Start?"

"We're going to go in there and find it," he said matter-of-factly. "If Evelyn's not willing to help you, I am. I'll pick you up first thing in the morning."

12

Revealing

Mabon, 1952

Five years of scrying for Oona have been fruitless. Every spell has been tried and retried. There is only one other option: I must open a bith dearc, an opening to the land of the dead. This is a difficult and dangerous procedure, but it is the only option left that I can see. I have been researching this process for over a year, and I feel that it is time to proceed.

Tioma wants me to ask the council's permission. The council? Who are the council but a bunch of busybodies with nothing better to do than to pry into the business of others? Their time would be better spent honing their own craft. As a witch and as a Rowanwand, I take responsibility for my own decisions and actions.

The need is real. Oona is trapped here, and she must be released, for all of our sakes. By opening the dearc, we may be able to provide her with a channel through which she can return to the spirit world. The ceremony will take place in two days' time, *when the moon is full. Great care has been taken to restrict the spell, so it must be written with absolute precision. Claire Findgoll has been assisting me in this task. Her collection of books on lunar spellcraft and spell restrictions is unparalleled.*

I had planned on telling Mother about the dearc, but she has not been well recently, and I do not want to worry her. Better that she remain unaware.

—Aoibheann

I woke up to the sound of the door shutting. I heard a car engine start and the sound of the car pulling off down the street. Sam was gone, off to work. Astrophe and Mandu were tangled together and sleeping in the space between my back and the sofa. Carefully, so as not to disturb them, I slipped out from under the afghan.

I wanted to be completely ready whenever Charlie showed up, and I had no idea when that would be. I rushed into the tiny bathroom and took a shower. It was obvious when I went through my bag that I had been pretty distracted when I packed. Eight pairs of underwear, three sets of pajamas, three bras, and one T-shirt. No clean socks or pants. Good job, Alisa. I pulled on the T-shirt and grabbed the socks, jeans, and hooded sweater that I'd been wearing for the last thirty-six hours and did my best to fix myself up a bit.

Dressing complete, I headed to the kitchen. On the table I found the keys, a neat list of local points of interest, a small hand-drawn map, and a note with Sam's work number. I made myself some scrambled eggs and toast and turned on a morning talk show. I was just coming to the exciting con-clusion of a discussion on new trends in lighting fixtures when the doorbell rang. Through the curtain I could see the little green Volkswagen out on the street.

Panic. Did I have jam on my face? Would he notice that I was basically wearing the same outfit, which was still kind of nasty from the day before? No time to do anything about that now. I opened the door.

Charlie had on a well-worn fisherman's sweater, and his hair was still slightly shower damp, which brought out the curls. He was waiting on the step, holding out two paper cups from the shop that we'd stopped at yesterday.

"Coffee," he said, smiling and holding one out to me. "Four sugars. Extra milk."

"Perfect, thanks." I eagerly accepted the cup. "What happens now?" I asked after I'd had a sip. "How do we know when everyone at Evelyn's house will be out?"

"They're out now," he said. "I checked. Ruth and Brigid are both working. Evelyn went to Boston for the day. She meets with other witches there once a week to study new divination spells. We can leave whenever you're ready."

"Are you sure about this?" I asked, suddenly feeling a little nervous.

"Completely," he said.

We headed out to his car. Operation Find the Library was under way.

We parked well down the street from the house and walked back. Charlie casually did these little spells he called see-me-nots, which he assured me would keep us from being noticed by anyone.

"So," I said with a nervous grin as we stood on the porch of Evelyn's house, "how do we get in? Magick?"

"Yup." He smiled back, reaching into his pocket. He fished around for a moment and produced a key. "Ta da!"

I shook my head in mock disgust.

"This is my key," he admitted. "I'm pretty much allowed to come and go as I like. I fix the computer, shovel the snow, get herbs from the garden. I pretty much live here half the time. Getting in won't be quite as exciting as I might have made it sound."

"Please," I said as he unlocked the door. "Give me boring any day. I have enough excitement in my life."

Just as a precaution, Charlie called into the house to see if anyone was home. When there was no reply, we slipped inside and locked the door behind us. The house was still and sunny. We hurried to the basement door, which was in the kitchen. A narrow, steep flight of stairs led into the unfinished basement. The low-ceilinged space was full of snow shovels, sleds, old boots, and a few well-organized sets of shelves holding ordinary household items like flowerpots and bags of potting soil. There was a rickety old toboggan in the corner and a small box with a badminton set.

I was tingling from the moment we entered this part of the house. It seemed as if my mother's presence hadn't been washed clean from here. Some of these things, I knew, were hers. Even though it was rather strange and painful, I felt my senses expanding, as if I was growing stronger with her energy. There was something down here that seemed to be screaming out to me.

"It's here," I said suddenly.

He looked back at me.

"You feel it?" he said.

"Yeah," I replied, looking around for some sign of a door-way. Unless they were keeping it in an old box under the lawn darts, I didn't see anywhere they could be hiding a library in this place.

"Okay," he said, glancing around, too. "We've got to move all of this away from the walls."

With a quick motion he pulled off his sweater. Underneath he was wearing a dark blue T-shirt printed with just one word: FRED. I noticed that his arms were covered in very light freckles as well and that they were surprisingly well defined. I guessed he did more than just work on math problems, or else he had some really heavy pencils. Then I decided to stop gawking at his arms and look like I was actually there to help. I pulled off my sweater as well and threw it down with his.

Together we shifted everything away from the wall by at least a foot or two. When we were done, Charlie pulled his athame out of his messenger bag. It was entirely made of highly polished silver, with a Celtic engraving around the handle and a round piece of black onyx set at the very top. Slowly, working right under the ceiling, he ran the athame around the walls, moving down a bit every time he made a complete pass. He had to go around about two dozen times to cover the whole area.

When that revealed nothing, he started on the floor, passing the athame carefully over every inch. He had to stop every few minutes so that we could rearrange the furniture. Again nothing. He straightened up and stared down at the floor, puzzled. Then he slouched against the wall and squinted around with an intent expression, tapping his athame in his palm.

"I have an idea," he finally said. "But it involves both of us. It's possible that because you're a blood relative, the door will be revealed to you more easily. So together we're going to do a nochd."

"Should I close my eyes?" I said, keeping a very straight face.

"I expected that," he replied with a wry grin. "Here." He held out the athame to me, handle first.

I pointed to the athame. "Can I . . . hold that? I mean, is it *sacred* or something?"

"Well," he said, "it's a magickal tool—so, yes. It's sacred. But it belongs to me, and I have no problem with you using it. Whether or not it works pretty much depends on you. Magickal tools function when the user brings their magick to them."

"You mean, like the toaster only works when you plug it in? Then it can use its bread-charring powers."

"Exactly." He nodded with a smile. "The tool is the toaster. You're the socket."

I accepted the athame, and he fished through his bag and removed a white candle and a piece of chalk.

"I'll cast the spell," he said. "We're going to see if your energy can guide us. I'll lead you as we go, so don't worry."

"Okay," I agreed, feeling weird with the heavy athame in my hand. "How do I hold it? Up, or down, or out . . ."

"Just let your arm fall naturally by your side," he said, expertly drawing a circle around us. Then he placed the candle in the middle, between us, and drew a series of runes around it in chalk. Standing, he lightly took hold of my right wrist, gripping just below the handle of the athame. He flashed me a look to see if I was ready, and I nodded.

"*Aingeal*," he intoned.

The candle snapped to life. I guess I shouldn't have been so startled. I'd seen both Morgan and Evelyn do that. Still, to see Charlie do it surprised me.

"*Sinn sir ni keillit*," he continued. The metal of the athame grew warm. He tightened his grip on my wrist—not enough to hurt me, but enough to have a firm grasp. "*Tar er ash, seòl heen.*"

I saw now why he had tightened his hold. My arm began to quake, and for a moment I thought I might drop the athame. He locked his hand around mine and looked down at me. Magick was flowing through us, between us. I could feel his strength as he controlled its flow. I'm not sure if it was the magick or simply being so close to him, but my heart started beating like crazy. It seemed so loud that I actually thought he would be able to hear it.

In one movement our arms rose together—mine started to come forward, pushing his back. I was pointing the athame to a spot on the floor. He couldn't see it because it was behind him, but a square appeared in that spot. It was made of symbols, very finely drawn in a bluish light. I wanted to say something, but I thought it might ruin the spell. As it was, he seemed aware that something was happening, even though he couldn't see what I saw.

Giving thanks to the Goddess and the God, he ended the spell, but he held on to my hand for a moment. We said nothing—just stood there, looking at each other. I felt the warmth of his body and could smell the faint smell of laundry detergent, some kind of spicy men's deodorant, and faint traces of sage smoke. Charlie smell. So nice. As he gazed down at me, I realized that he was the only person who could really stare at me like that without my wanting to turn away or hide my face. I could actually look him right in the eye and not flinch. Even though his expression was serious and intent, his mouth still retained its wide, happy curve. It was as if he was born to smile and to make others smile. Such a nice mouth.

Such a *what?* What was I thinking?

Unintentionally I pulled away. He backed up, as though I'd startled him. His face was flushed, and he didn't seem to know where to look for a moment.

"There's a . . . thing on the floor," I mumbled, pointing.

"Good!" he said, quickly kneeling down and snapping out the candle flame with his fingers. "That's what was supposed to happen. We did it. Good work."

I brushed the chalk circle away as Charlie sprawled flat on the floor to examine the symbols up close. I saw him working his way all around the square. By now my mind was everywhere it shouldn't be. I could see only the length of his body, the way the sleeves of his T-shirt tightened around his upper arms, the speed of his movements.

Cousin's boyfriend, I kept saying to myself over and over and over.

"Okay," he said, getting up to his knees, "this shouldn't be too bad. Finding it was the hard part. The seal itself isn't a tremendous piece of work." He reached back for his bag and started rooting through it again, producing a handful of runes.

"Have you got a whole magick shop in there?" I asked.

"No, ma'am," he said. "Just the basics. Some candles, chalk, athame, runes. All the things witches should never travel without, especially when they're trying to break into other witches' private libraries."

I gulped, feeling a pang of guilt as he set a rune in each corner of the box, then put the white candle in the center. He muttered a spell quietly to himself. The candle winked to life again, and over the next few minutes, as he spelled and tapped his athame around its perimeter, the dusty patch of floor revealed itself to be a wooden door with a round handle.

"Voilà," he said, looking up in satisfaction. "One trapdoor."

"That was amazing," I told him, completely awed. "You're like a safecracker." He didn't reply, just gave a nervous little laugh.

When we opened the wooden door, we found a switch that turned on a set of overhead lights. They revealed a set of tiny steps that dropped almost straight down into a darker room. Charlie went down first, then offered up his hand to help me down. He had to bend down, as the low ceiling didn't give him much clearance.

You'd think a room under a house like this would be musty and dirty, but it was spotlessly clean. The walls and floor were made of smooth stone. There were an air filter and a dehumidifier. Every inch of space was carefully utilized. The walls were completely set with shelves, and several freestanding floor-to-ceiling bookcases sat back to back in eight rows. The pathways between the rows of books were narrow, just large enough for a person to pass through with a step stool. In one corner there was a small antique reading table with a lamp and two chairs.

"This place is *great*," he said, his expression melting into one of amazement at the sight of all the books. It was like watching a little kid at an amusement park, so deliriously excited that they don't know where to head first. In his enthusiasm he stumbled but caught himself on one of the bookcases.

"It's my ballet training coming through," he said with a smile as his face turned charmingly pink. Then he bounded off into the stacks.

As Charlie devoured the titles on the shelves, I walked around quietly, taking in the magnitude and splendor of the collection. Many of the books, though ancient, weren't particularly frail. They'd been so well taken care of that age had affected them only slightly. There were books in strange blocky print, dating well back into the 1600s. There were books in all kinds of languages, in mysterious prints and symbols. Some sections were full of dry, academic-sounding titles. Others were filled with books so exotic looking that I was actually frightened to touch them.

As I turned down one aisle, it was as if the books were whispering to me. I glanced over their titles. I couldn't read any of them. They looked like German to me, lots of huge words starting with *das* or *der.* Still, even though I couldn't understand them, I wanted to touch them. I wanted to pull them from the shelves. I wanted—this one—*Edelsteine und Metalle,* whatever that meant. I *needed* this book. Gently I slipped it from the shelf. It seemed warm to the touch, as if I'd been holding it for a long time. Surprisingly there was nothing on the front cover. It was a plain green book, covered in cloth, obviously very old. I flipped it back and looked at the spine again, but I now saw nothing written there.

I almost dropped the book in shock.

"Charlie!" I called, my voice husky.

He came right around from the row behind. I explained

what I had seen and offered the book to him. He took it, examined it all over.

"Edelsteine und Metalle," he said, holding the spine out for me to see. "Something and metals."

I looked at the spine again. There was the title, in gold letters on the greenish black cloth. It hadn't been there a second ago. I was shaking a bit now, and he put his hand on my shoulder to steady me.

"It must have been spelled with some kind of glamor or concealment spell," he said. "That's all. You're not going crazy. Let's have a look at it and find out why it was being hidden. This is a private family library, so it's kind of strange for a Rowanwand to hide a book from a relative."

We took it over to the reading table and switched on the light. Charlie began to page through the book. In the first moment we could see that it was definitely not a German textbook on something and metals. It was handwritten, in English. It looked like a Book of Shadows, with dates at the tops of the pages. Charlie's eyes grew wider with every page.

"This is Máirín's book," he said, looking up, his eyes full of awe. "Oona's daughter. No one's seen this book in years. How the hell . . ."

Máirín's book. That was what I had found. The story of the family witch, down here, in the secret Curtis family library. This was where my mother had experienced a frightening telekinetic episode. There was too much magick, too many feelings tied into this house. I chose this moment to become completely overwhelmed. Even though I tried to will them back, I felt tears well up behind my eyes. Charlie looked up in alarm and saw my eyes glistening.

"What is it?" he said, setting his hand back on my shoulder.

"All these weird feelings," I answered, rubbing my eyes. "All of these strange things I don't understand."

As much as I knew he was dying to look in that book, he slid it aside and turned all of his attention to me.

"It must be really hard to have to deal with so much magick at once," he said. "Just try to relax. I'm right here. Nothing that's happened is too out of the ordinary."

"Everything is out of my ordinary," I moaned.

Instead of reading, we sat there for a while, talking. I found myself telling him about the dark wave and how frightened I had been. I told him about Hilary and all the things that had led up to my running away—all of the really personal things that I'd left out of my first explanation. I finally explained that I had a problem with telekinesis and that that what I was trying to find out more about.

"The newest thing," I explained, feeling my defenses collapse under the calming weight of his hand on my shoulder, "is that I can feel other witches around me. I can sense their feelings. I can sense my mother here, even though she's gone. I like the feeling of connection, but it also scares me. Everything comes so fast now. I'm never expecting any of it."

Then he leaned in, and his look took on a new level of seriousness.

"Can you feel my senses right now?" he said.

My body seemed to freeze in time. My heart stopped. I didn't breathe, didn't move. Everything was anticipation. I *could* feel him. He was going to . . . what?

He came in close, took my face in one of his soft hands, and kissed me.

I'd never been kissed before, and I'd been kind of worried that I wouldn't know what to do when and if it ever happened. Luckily I didn't freak out or accidentally bite him or anything. I pressed into his mouth and responded naturally. He slipped his hands behind my neck and pulled me closer. Warmth . . . so much warmth. A universe of warmth. As he pulled away, he looked at me in happy surprise.

"I . . ." He seemed to catch himself speaking but didn't know what to say. "I've been wanting to do that since I saw you yesterday."

Could I speak? Did my mouth still work? Was my voice going to come out all funny? Only one way to find out.

"Me too," I said. "I mean, not kissing myself. You know. You."

Smooth, Soto. Smooth.

Fleeting concerns zapped through my brain. What about Brigid? What did this mean? Those feelings were numbed when I felt the sensation again. He wanted to pull me into him, and I wanted him to wrap his arms around me. But the flow cooled quickly, like we'd blown a fuse, and all the power went down. We must have become aware of it at the same moment. We sat very still and listened.

Someone was upstairs.

13

Attack

September 24, 1952

Goddess, Goddess, where have I been? I'm only just now getting the strength to get out of bed and resume my daily activities.

We opened the bith dearc two nights ago, Claire Findgoll and I, down on the shore below the house. It is a terrible yet fascinating thing, this small hole that rips through the fabric of the universe and seems to go on eternally. I maintained the dearc while Claire conducted the spell to try to draw Oona from the house into the opening. I am glad that Claire stood away from it, as it possesses a devastating force. It actually drains you of life energy. I feel as though I've been poisoned.

We haven't had any visitations since we performed the spell, but only time will tell if we've been successful.

Oh, I must go to sleep again. There is nothing left in me. No energy at all.

—Aoibheann

"Hello?" called a female voice. "Mom?"

"It's Brigid," Charlie whispered, all color draining from his face. "She's home early."

"Should I . . . hide down here while you go up?" I offered. Good one, Alisa. The sitcom solution always works so well in real life.

"No," he answered, shaking his head. "She knows we're here."

Brigid, I had figured, wasn't a powerful witch—but she was still a witch. Feeling another person's presence in the house seemed like something she would very well be able to do. We heard her walking through the kitchen and then opening the basement door.

"Okay," Charlie admitted, "this is kind of bad."

"What do we do?" I asked.

He squeezed my hand quickly, as a kind of apology for what was probably going to happen next. "I have no idea," he said.

"Hello?" Brigid called again. She approached the door to the library, which was still open behind us. "Aunt Evelyn?" Brigid said. She came down the steps and looked at the two of us, first in confusion and then with a growing flurry of emotion.

"Charlie? Alisa?" she said, her voice wavering. "What are you two doing here?"

"Researching," Charlie said simply.

"Researching?" she said. "You came in when we weren't here . . . *both* of you?"

Whether through magick or regular female intuition (which might also be magick, I don't know), Brigid seemed to know at once that there was a problem. She sat down on the bottom step, blocking our way out. Did kissing a witch leave a mark on your mouth? Did my lips glow? Could she see some kind of imprint?

"Alisa needed help," Charlie said. "She's trying to find out about her ancestors, and Evelyn definitely wasn't going to give her a hand. Sorry. We had to come in when Evelyn wasn't here."

"You could have told me," she said. "I would have helped you."

Oh. If we didn't feel bad before . . .

"So," she said, staring hard at me, "did you find anything?"

"A book," I said, immediately realizing how stupid that answer was. I went to a library and found . . . a book. Not for the first time in my life, I wished the floor would open under me and swallow me whole.

After a few moments of silence it finally dawned on me that I should leave them alone. I didn't want to leave Charlie to the wolves or anything, but I had no place here. They needed to talk. And I had a feeling Charlie was going to come clean about what had just occurred.

"I should probably go," I said, "before Evelyn gets home, like you said. She'd be furious to find me here."

"That might be a good idea." Charlie nodded. We probably realized at the same moment that he had driven me there.

"I'll walk back," I added. "I could use some fresh air." I tucked the book into my messenger bag. "I'll return this to Sam," I said to Brigid. "He'll put it back in the library." Then I did my walk of shame, crossing the room and heading to where she was perched.

Brigid slid aside to let me pass. She said nothing. She wouldn't—or couldn't—even look at me. As I stepped past, my leg brushed against her. I almost jumped as a surge went through that whole half of my body. I felt a wave of pure raw emotion coming off her. She might look furious, but inside, everything in her was weeping.

It was a long walk home through the mist and the wet, with my brain clanging around between elation and guilt.

I mean, *he* kissed *me*. What was I supposed to do? Slap him, like they do in old movies? Call him a cad? I hadn't done anything wrong. . . . It wasn't my fault. . . .

But then I examined my motives. Did I want Charlie to kiss me? Yes. Had I kissed him back? Yes. Was he my cousin's boyfriend? Yes.

Guilty.

I sucked. I sucked, I sucked, I sucked.

But it still had been the best moment of my life. I had touched his face and felt the tiny, soft curls at the back of his head, down near his neck. It had been good, so good, too good. I still felt like I was walking through an incredible dream.

Yet Brigid's feelings were still so close, so strong. She loved Charlie—who wouldn't? He was adorable and funny and smart. Tall. Powerful. She had turned her back for a moment—to be responsible and go to work, no less—and then her weird new out-of-town cousin appeared, broke into her house, and made out with her boyfriend.

I trudged along, seagulls screaming overhead, my hair slowly collecting dampness from the air. It took me about forty-five minutes to get back to Sam's. When I got there, Enya was playing and delicious smells of garlic, fish, and cooking tomatoes were coming from the kitchen. Sam had obviously gone to the trouble to make sure I came back to a nice welcome—and I returned, the other woman, the coven wrecker. . . .

"Did you have a good day?" Sam asked, putting a salad bowl out on the table.

"Great!" I said, with forced enthusiasm.

"What did you do?"

"Oh," I said, picking up Mandu and letting him climb up on my shoulder, "just hung out with Charlie."

"Charlie's a great guy." Sam nodded. "A fantastic witch, too."

You have no idea, I thought. . . . Sam looked up at me strangely, and I banished all thoughts of Charlie from my mind and set a straight and steady expression on my face.

"Before I forget," he said, "I found some pictures of your mother I want to show you. Could you watch the stove for a second? And feel free to start the salad."

"Sure," I said, setting the cat on the floor. As Sam headed for the stairs, I started making the salad, dumping the mesclun into the salad bowl and replaying the kiss again and again in my mind. I set it against the music, felt the surge of bliss thrumming through my body. Charlie was so handsome, so tall, so funny, so nice, so smart, so . . .

Taken. By my cousin. What was I thinking?

I tossed some vinaigrette into the greens a little more aggressively than was really necessary. The cats cocked their heads at me.

Just as I had the night before, I suddenly felt something in the pit of my stomach telling me that something was wrong, very wrong. I looked up, all senses alert. Something was here. A presence. Something very foul. I let go of the salad tongs and looked around the kitchen.

And then it happened.

The first blow was on my left arm, and it sent me reeling backward, pain jagging all the way down into my hand. I heard glass shattering behind me. I whirled around to see all of the dishes flying out of the open rack under the cabinets, and they all came at me, one after the other. I didn't have time to move or to think. Something broke against my head. Glass fell onto my eyelids. I pulled up my arms to guard my face and head as best I could, but the blows were coming harder, pushing me back against the wall.

Something in me stirred, ready to do battle. I felt every fiber of my being tingling. I could stop this. I could . . .

I concentrated hard. Some of the dishes started to pop and splinter in midair, before they got to me. It was as if they were smashing against an invisible wall, and I knew I was doing it. No idea how—but I was doing it. Some still made it through. There were so many. The drawers were rattling, coming loose, coming at me. I dropped to the ground and started crawling for the table, elbowing my way through the shards.

I could see Sam trying to get to me, but I felt myself growing weak. Everything went to black and white, and there was a ringing in my ears that drowned out every other sound. I was fainting, I realized.

The next thing I knew, Sam was putting me down on the sofa. My clothes sparkled with bits of plate and drinking glass.

"I'm all glassy," I said, tears welling in my eyes. "Sam, I'm all glassy."

"I know," he said, checking over my head, my face, my eyes. "Look at me, Alisa. Look at me."

It was hard, but I focused on his face. He studied me.

"I'm going to take off my clothes," I said, standing uncertainly and wobbling from foot to foot. For some reason, the glass on my clothes was really preoccupying me. "I have to get this stuff away from me."

"Steady now, sweetheart." He looked over the shards that dangled like icicles from my clothes. He yanked a pair of pajamas from the top of my bag and set them down. "Get changed. I'll be back in a second."

I heard him run upstairs, heard the bang of a cabinet door. I pulled off my pants and T-shirt and dumped them in the center of the room. Then I put on some soothing fleece pants and the camisole pajama top. That was better. So much better.

I looked down and saw that my forearms were dripping blood.

The sofa loomed up at me, and I grabbed for it, holding tightly to the cushions for balance. And then everything went black again.

The lights in the room were dim. I was waking up. I was under a blanket. Was it morning? I didn't think so.

Where was I?

Sam's, I realized after a moment. The dishes. I remembered now. I looked up to see Ruth sitting next to me, holding an ice pack to my forehead with her uncasted arm. I tried to sit up, but she put a gentle hand on my shoulder.

"Stay down, Alisa," she said.

"What happened?" I asked.

"We don't know." Ruth smoothed my hair. "We're trying to figure it out."

"We?" I asked.

"Charlie was here when you were out," she said. "He put a ring of protection spells around the house."

"While I was out?"

"You've been unconscious for hours," she explained. "It's almost ten. Kate Giles is here now. She's another member of Ròiseal. She works in defensive magick."

"Where's Sam?" I asked, trying to lift my head to look around.

"Doing a divination spell to see if he can find out what caused this," she answered, indicating that I should rest again. "He's fine."

I took an inventory of myself. Both of my arms were wrapped in gauze from my palms to my elbows. I felt something on my head as well. I had no shirt on—that was probably why I was under the blanket. There were soft little things resting on various points of my stomach and chest—they felt like little cloth bags. I guessed they were full of herbs or witch ointments. I was generally a bit sore, but nothing felt broken.

I'd done a lot of strange telekinetic things in the last few weeks, but I'd never attacked myself. Also, what I'd felt right before the dishes started flying hadn't come from inside me. I'd felt something coming in from the outside, like a magickal draft. This time it hadn't been me. What was happening? I thought of calling Hunter. He would know what to do. This kind of thing was his job.

There was the sound of loud heels on the steps. A young woman, maybe just around Hilary's age, came into the room.

"She's awake," Ruth said. "Come on over."

The woman approached. She was striking—definitely shades of Raven. Her hair was long and auburn with a dramatic streak of blond in the front. She had a powerful body, with sleek, defined arms and a Celtic tattoo up near her right shoulder. The whole effect was set off by the form-fitting black pants, sleeveless shirt, and black boots she wore. This was Kate, I guessed. She looked really tough, but also feminine. Pretty much exactly how you think a female defensive magick expert should look—kick-ass and cool.

"Alisa, this is Kate," Ruth said, confirming my suspicion.

"Hi, Alisa," Kate said, sitting down on the floor next to me. "How do you feel?"

"Like I've just been hit on the head with a lot of plates."

She smiled. "Well, at least your sense of humor is still intact. That's a good sign." She looked up at Ruth. "Sam get anything?"

"Not yet." Ruth shook her head. "So, what do you think?"

"Well," Kate said, twisting one of her many silver rings, "it looks a little like Oona. I'm finding the same residual energy disturbance that I usually see after she graces us with her presence. It's not exactly the same, but it's close enough."

"But how can Oona be here?" Ruth asked, putting her hand to her head in concern.

"Beats me," Kate replied. "She's never transferred her energy like this before. This is totally new. Charlie covered this place well, but I'll add another layer of protection spells before I go. It's all I can think to do."

"Goddess," Ruth groaned, panic in her voice. "Oh, Goddess. It's spreading."

Sam came in from the kitchen. He looked to Kate, and she repeated what she had just said to Ruth. Then he came over to me.

"Hey, kiddo," he said, squatting down.

"Sorry about your dishes," I said.

He broke into a boyish grin and stroked my hair.

"Okay," Kate said, "I'd better get back. Don't worry, Alisa. We've been spelling this house for hours. Rest easy tonight. If you have any more trouble, Sam, I'm a phone call away."

Kate gave Ruth a gentle pat on the shoulder, pulled on a black leather jacket and a pair of gloves, and headed out.

"Do you want me to stay?" Ruth asked. "Or I'm sure Aunt Evelyn's home by now. We can call her . . ."

"No," Sam said, standing up. "Let's not. We've done all we can do. Alisa just has to be able to rest. There's nothing left here. I don't see any immediate threat."

She and Sam shared a long look, as if they were communicating telepathically. (Which they may have been able to do. I had no idea.) Ruth finally nodded.

"Leave these packs on for another half hour," she told Sam. "Also, put some marigold tisane and apple cider vinegar on a washcloth. You can apply that to the bruises tomorrow. But I'll check in and see how things are going."

After Ruth had gone, Sam and I sat down at the kitchen table and drank tea out of some paper cups he had left over from a picnic. Sam lent me a snuggly bathrobe to wear since I couldn't put my shirt back on over the packs that Ruth had attached to my chest with medical tape. The kitchen looked more or less normal, just with piles of broken glass swept into the corners.

"Tomorrow," he said, "I'm taking the day off. How about we go to Salem? You know, get out of here for a little while."

"Sounds great," I said, holding out a bandaged hand to accept a cookie he passed over to me from the counter. He looked like he wanted to say something but didn't quite know how to put it.

"What is it?" I asked, cracking the cookie in two.

"Some of those dishes," he said, his big blue eyes fixing on me hard. "I saw them burst in midair. They were being deflected."

"I have powers," I said quietly. Though there was nothing wrong with this fact, I treated it like it was my dirty secret. It still felt foreign.

"That's not possible," he answered, shaking his head.

"I don't know why or how, but I do," I said. "Honest."

"Goddess," he said. "So all this time, you've been fully capable of doing magick?"

"Yep," I said, biting my cookie. "Poorly, but I can."

Now that I thought of it, Sam would be the perfect person to teach me how to scry. Scrying seemed like a perfect way to get some information—maybe find out something about why I was supposed to come to Gloucester.

"You work in divination, right?" I said.

"Mostly," he replied.

"Can you teach me how to scry?"

"Scry?" He shrugged. "Sure. I can try. Not all witches can scry successfully. It's a personal thing, and there are lots of different methods. You have to find out which one is right for you. We'll try my method first. We're related, so we might use the same element."

He got up and went into the living room and returned with a large black bowl. He filled this from the contents of a jar he pulled from one of the kitchen cabinets.

"It's seawater," he said, setting the bowl down on the table. "I gather up a jar a week. A major rule of Wicca—never take more natural resources than you need, even from something as huge as the ocean."

Sam lectured me on the basics. I was impressed with the depth of his knowledge. Part of me always saw Sam as the goofy kid my mother had described in her book. Now I saw what he really was: a mature and incredibly responsible witch with years of training. He placed five white candles around the bowl, elevating them on stacks of books so that they sat just above the rim. After lighting them with a match, he turned off the overhead light.

"All right," he said, taking my hands. "Relax. Breathe deep. Focus on the water."

I did. At first nothing happened. It was just us, sitting in the dark, staring into a bowl of water for about twenty minutes. Then I realized that I was looking down through a square form, as if I was peering into a box. There was a flash of purple, then we were back to the water. I'd been hoping to see people, to hear them say clever, cryptic things. All I got was a box full of purple.

"I think I've had enough, Sam," I said, sighing.

"Did you see something?" he asked.

"I don't think it was anything," I said. "Just a flash of color."

"You're probably exhausted." He got up and turned on the light. "We'll try again when you're feeling better. For now, I think we both need some rest."

14

Witch Trials

March 21, 1953

Ostara already. I've been so busy the past few months, I've barely noticed how much time has gone by since the dearc. No visits from Oona, thank the Goddess. We seem to have been completely successful.

In the meantime the little child inside me grows and grows. She is a girl, of this I am certain. I never knew what utter joy motherhood would bring. I have become even more aware of the turning of the wheel and the phases of the moon. I feel her movement when the moon is full. She tends to be sleepy when it wanes.

—Aoibheann

Salem was only a short drive away, and Sam took a scenic route along the water. The sky was finally clear, and it was breezy. Aside from a few little aches and the cuts and bruises, I was fine. It was nice to get out alone with Sam.

Pulling into the town, I was amazed by all the Wiccans I

saw on the streets. Everyone seemed to have a pentacle necklace, or a tattoo, or something kind of witchy. In fact, the witch thing seemed to be done to death. Every store window seemed to feature a picture of a little figure in a black pointed hat, riding a broom. Sam parked in a lot near the visitors' center.

"Come on," he said. "There's something I want to show you."

Tucked behind some buildings next to the lot was an ancient cemetery, with thin, frail headstones—some sunk halfway into the ground. Next to this was a square sectioned off by a low stone wall. Heavy slabs of stone jutted out from the wall at equal intervals, forming benches.

"This is a weird park," I said as we entered the square.

"Have a better look," Sam told me, pointing to the first bench. I went over to it. There was writing there. It read: Bridget Bishop, Hanged, June 10, 1692. I continued around, looking at each bench. Sam followed along behind me. Sarah Wildes, hanged. Elizabeth Howe, hanged. Susannah Martin, Sarah Good, Rebecca Nurse, George Burroughs, Martha Carrier—all hanged. Giles Corey, pressed to death. There were more still, their names carved roughly into the stones. It was so stark, so disturbing.

"This is the Witch Trial Memorial," Sam explained. "These are the names of the people who were executed."

I knew a bit about the witch trials from school and from some reading I'd done on my own. Two young girls had made claims that they were bewitched. From there, accusations flew and a court was set up. People were dragged in to testify. The girls convulsed and seemed to go crazy. More people came forward, claiming that they too had been attacked. In the end, twenty people were executed and dozens more accused or affected. The whole thing was over in a few months; then the people who ran the court were forced to close it and apologize for what they'd done.

With a shiver I thought of my own behavior, how I'd wanted to write a letter to the local Widow's Vale paper and "expose" Wicca. While no one would have been tried or executed, I could have caused a lot of trouble for Morgan, Hunter, Mr. Niall . . . so many others. Thank God Mary K. and I hadn't actually done anything.

"You know what the weird thing is?" Sam said, looking down at the closest slab. "These people weren't witches at all. Some of them were outsiders, just a little weird in society's eyes. Some were prominent citizens. No rhyme or reason to it."

"Then what happened?" I asked. "Does anyone really understand?"

"Not really," he said, carefully brushing some dead leaves that obscured the name on the bench below us. "It was hysteria. People pointed to anyone in sight, claimed anything the judges asked them to claim—if only they would be allowed to live. People admitted to things they didn't do. If you didn't confess, they executed you. These people"—he indicated the benches around the square— "they wouldn't confess to things they hadn't done. They were very unlucky, and very brave."

"But now the town is full of witches," I said. "Why come here when the people who were killed weren't even Wiccans?"

"The idea still remains that witchcraft is evil and dark. I

guess we feel the need to come here and set the record straight."

"All this," I said, shivering as I looked over the bleak stone benches, "just because some girls made up stories about witches."

"It was more insidious than that," Sam said. "People were ready to rush to judgment, even to kill, just to exorcise their own dark thoughts and fears. Now everyone looks back on this, not understanding how it ever could have happened. But people still persecute and hurt one another over things they can't personally understand."

"I guess maybe you know something about that," I said.

He nodded, understanding my meaning. "I guess so. I've always been out as a witch, and I came out with my sexuality early as well. I refuse to lie."

"My mom never mentioned that you were gay. Did she know?"

"Well"—he exhaled and tucked his hands into the pockets of his jeans—"I came out when I was eighteen, a few years after your mother left. But she always knew. I could tell. She was incredibly empathetic. She probably didn't think it was a big deal; I guess that's why she didn't mention it."

My mother was empathetic. She could feel other people, sense their emotions—just like I had been doing more and more since I'd been here. I liked that part of being a witch. But the mention of my mother also brought my attention back to the graveyard with its decaying grave markers. We quietly walked away from the memorial.

"So," I said, "do you have a boyfriend, or . . . ?"

"I did," he said. "We separated about two months ago."

"Oh." I pushed some leaves around with my foot. "Sorry."

"Don't be," he said genuinely. "Shawn and I decided that we needed to be apart for a while."

"Shawn . . . was he a witch?" I asked.

"Yes." Sam nodded, staring out at the street. "He lives in Holyoke. It's nearby." He snapped back to his normal, sunny demeanor. "Okay," he said, "we're getting way too serious. Let me show you the cool stuff."

I followed Sam along, and he pointed out favorite restaurants, shops, and houses. We passed Bell, Book, and Candle—the shop where Charlie worked. We stepped in, but he wasn't there. I had to hide my profound disappointment. It wasn't like the blows to my head had given me amnesia. The incident in the library had been on my mind more or less nonstop from the moment I woke up. I wondered what had happened between Charlie and Brigid. It couldn't have been good. Maybe, I thought, cringing with guilt—maybe he was breaking up with her at this very moment. Maybe that's why he wasn't at work.

Not likely.

Uggggh. Too much to think about. I still felt guilty. Maybe it was a good thing the plates had knocked me senseless last night. I probably would be a basket case otherwise.

After picking up a birthday gift for Ruth, Sam took me to an old hotel for lunch. He told me stories about my mother, all kinds of brother-sister high jinks. As we were talking and enjoying ourselves, I realized how good Sam was being to me. He'd put me up and cared for me with no advance warning at all. He'd stood up to his family to defend me. I owed him my honesty. There was a convenient lull in the conversation as Sam was eating. I decided to use it.

"My dad doesn't know where I am," I said, not looking up. "I ran away."

Sam stopped eating, set down his fork, and waited for me to continue. He didn't look all that surprised. With that stunning introduction, I proceeded to tell him the whole story—and I mean the *whole* story. Everything from the dark wave to Hilary to the night I ran away. The entire Alisa Soto soap opera.

"I've been calling someone from my coven," I said, coming to the end. "She put a watch sigil on me so that she'd be able to find me if I wasn't in touch."

"That's something, I guess," he said, processing the information for a moment. Then he dug into the pocket of his brown suede jacket, pulled out a tiny cell phone, and plunked it down on the table.

I got the hint.

When the first sound I heard was Hilary's voice, I readied myself to snap the phone closed again but then thought better of it. Sam was trusting me to call my family—and Hilary, like it or not, was family now.

"Hi, Hilary," I said, trying to sound cheerful, as if this was the most normal call in the world.

"Alisa? Is that you?" She sounded breathy, really alarmed.

"It's me. Hi."

"Where are you?"

"Safe," I said firmly. "Fine. Staying in a nice warm house, eating three meals a day. Nothing to worry about."

"Nothing to worry about? Alisa, your father's about to

have a heart attack, and . . ." I heard her stop and steady her-self. She must have known I could be spooked away.

"I just called to tell you guys that I was okay," I said. "That's all. Is Dad around?"

"No, he's at work, sweet— Alisa."

She caught herself so abruptly, I actually felt bad, like I'd been way too rough on her. I knew she wasn't all bad.

"How are you feeling?" I asked.

"How am *I* feeling?" She was surprised. "Oh, I'm fine. Good. A little jumpy the last few days."

We actually made some small talk over the next few min-utes. I think I was even able to convince her that I really was fine. I didn't sound crazy or strung out. In fact, I was about a million times calmer than I usually was at home. She told me that they'd stopped doing any planning or moving during the time I'd been gone, but that she'd had an ultrasound done. I was going to have a little brother. This news didn't nauseate me as much I would have imagined, and I even congratulated her with some real excitement. As I said good-bye, I felt like a changed woman. She would probably recommend to my dad that I be allowed to run away more often.

I'd asked Sam if I could make one more quick call, and he'd agreed. I dialed Hunter's number.

Hunter, I noticed, sounded even more adult and more British on the phone. His voice was deeper, and I could almost feel him pacing.

"Alisa!" he said, exhaling loudly.

I filled him in on the situation so far, and he hmm-ed and ah-ed in typical Hunter fashion. He'd gotten most of the story from Morgan, so I didn't have to start from the very beginning.

"Have you spoken to your father?" he asked, with just a slightly parental edge to his voice. "Morgan tells me he's very upset, understandably."

"I just spoke to Hilary for a few minutes," I said. "Everything's fine."

"Well," he said, clearly not sure if he believed that last statement of mine, "I have some news as well, and it fits in rather neatly with what you've just told me. I spoke to both Ardán Rourke and Jon Vorwald. Jon said that it's possible that you have a trigger element, but he'll have to test you in person to figure out what that might be. He also said that he'd heard of one case, back in the fifties, of a telekinetic power that seemed to be passed down via firstborn female children."

"Firstborn females?" I frowned. Actually, that would explain why my mother and I had telekinesis, but not Sam or Ruth. But if it was passed down to my mother . . . then Evelyn . . .

"That's right." Hunter's crisp voice interrupted my thoughts. "Also, and this is very interesting, Ardán knew of at least one case of a witch in the 1800s who had telekinesis. What's interesting about her is that when she got older, maybe sixty or seventy, her telekinetic incidents became more violent, harder to control. He thinks that it's possible that as witches get older, they lose some of their inhibitions. Their emotions become stronger and harder to rein in."

"I don't understand," I said. "What does that have to do with me? I'm fifteen."

"Think about it," he said. "You have telekinesis. Your mother had it. It's quite possible, then, that your *grandmother* has it. You just said that the incidents were getting worse with time and that they also flared up during times of family crisis."

Evelyn. I sucked in my breath. This could be Evelyn. It made complete sense—to me, anyway. When Evelyn was upset or under stress, that was when Oona was at her worst. But what could I do with this information? If she didn't already hate me, Evelyn would really lose it if I came forward and suggested that she was responsible for all of the horrible things that had happened to her family. Besides that, I didn't have enough proof to be sure that it was true.

"Hello?" Hunter drew me back to reality. "Alisa?"

"Still here," I said, gripping the lobby wall. "God, Hunter. What do I do now?"

"I wouldn't do anything yet. We can't be sure that this is actually what's going on. It's just a theory. Ardán's looking into the matter some more. Your case really interested him, and he wants to come over and meet you."

"What can I say?" I said. "I'm fascinating."

"So," he said, "when can we expect to see you?"

"Uh . . ." I shifted from foot to foot. "Soon. I promise. Spring break is almost over. I just need a little more time."

In the end, I had to promise to call him the next night, after the Ròiseal circle. Reeling from what I'd just heard, I headed back into the dining room. Should I tell Sam? No. Hunter had said to wait until he had more information. Waiting. Not my strong suit.

As I came into the dining room, the waitress approached our table with the biggest brownie sundae I had ever seen.

I sighed. Sam was *the best*.

15

Ròiseal

February 3, 1955

The baby will be coming any day now. At the Imbolc celebration last night, all of Ròiseal performed a ritual to ensure a safe birth.

Just as I knew Sorcha was a girl, I know this is a boy—a rascally little boy, at that. From the way he kicks, I tend to think that he will give his sister no peace! He's feisty! We have decided to name him Somhairle.

Sorcha seems to know that something is going on. I can tell by the look in her eye. She likes to run up and touch my stomach, then she giggles and runs away. She'll sometimes drag Hugh over and point it out to him, her eyes full of wonder. My little girl—she's so full of the Goddess!

—Aoibheann

"Looks like we're the last ones here," Sam said as we parked between Charlie's Volkswagen and a red motorcycle.

Just the sight of Charlie's car turned me into jellyfish woman, with wobbly legs and a googly stare, but I managed to pull myself together enough to be able to walk to the front door like a normal human.

Sam let us right in and headed for the living room, where everyone was already gathered. A fire was going strong in the fireplace. In the middle of the room there was a cauldron filled with cool water and flower blossoms. Ruth's birthday cake was set on a small table, uncut.

It wasn't exactly a rocking party. Brigid, Ruth, and Evelyn sat together on a long sofa, all looking uncomfortable. Ruth's heavy cast was obviously itching. Brigid looked tired and pensive. Evelyn was her usual sparkling self. The three of them were having a quiet conversation with Kate Giles. Ruth and Kate each gave me a hug when they saw me. Brigid and Evelyn each gave me a thousand-yard stare.

After giving Ruth her gift, Sam settled down across the room, where Charlie was sitting with an older man. I tried to look as casual as possible as I joined him there—my mind, however, was constantly replaying our kiss. I had the DVD version going, with multiple angles, the trailer with the highlights, and the full director's cut. Charlie eyed the bruise near my eye, and I nodded to indicate that I really was all right.

The man next to Charlie was dressed kind of formally in a neat gray suit with a light cream-colored sweater underneath the jacket. He was just as tall, but heavier. He looked like Charlie, with the same kind face and the mischievous peaked eyebrows, and though his hair was shot through with silver gray, it curled defiantly. I knew instantly that this was Charlie's father.

"You're Alisa!" the man boomed, looking straight at me. He spoke so loudly that it startled some of the others. No drawn-out introductions needed here. Everyone should have a weird witch vibe. It makes things so much easier.

"My dad," Charlie said.

"I understand you were raised by nonwitches, Alisa! I'd love to know what that was like," his dad added. Charlie's eyes went wide, then rolled back into his head in comic grief.

"My dad," Charlie repeated, containing an exasperated sigh. "Right to the point."

"Did I say something wrong?" his father asked innocently. From Charlie's description of his father, I could easily see that he might have some strange people skills.

"It's okay." I laughed. "If you have a few days to spare, I can tell you the whole story."

"I'm not sure if I have a few entire days," he said, sipping his tea and honestly thinking it over, "but I'll check my schedule. Perhaps we can do a few blocks of time over the course of a week."

Okay. He was very literal, too, but he seemed nice enough. I couldn't imagine Charlie coming from a family that wasn't nice.

"I was just going to get something to drink," Charlie said, standing up. "Would anyone like anything?"

He ended up getting orders from almost everyone in the room, so I immediately sprang up and offered to help, praying that I didn't look too obvious and scheming. However, I did notice Brigid slipping me a steely glare as I left.

I followed Charlie into the kitchen. He was at the counter, setting down the glasses. He looked so good, just simply dressed in a dark blue button-down shirt and jeans. He seemed extra tall, so much more adult looking than me. There was no way I could have kissed him. I must have been delusional.

"Hi," I finally said. That was the best I could do. Words were failing me.

"Hey," he said, giving me a little smile—not his usual light-up-the-room beam. "How are you? Are you okay?" I thought I saw his hand moving, as if he was going to reach out to me, but he pulled it back and moved the glasses around instead.

"I'm fine." I nodded. "Thanks for coming last night. I felt a lot safer knowing that you protected the house. Sorry I was, um . . . unconscious."

"Don't worry about it," he said. "I guess it was that whole getting-hit-on-the-head-with-everything-in-the-kitchen thing."

"Something like that," I agreed.

I could see the coppery freckles under his eyes in the warm glow of the kitchen light. I felt warmth coming from him but also something else—pain, maybe. Definitely stress. It made me want to . . . I don't know, give him a big hug or something. He wasn't himself.

"Maybe we could talk?" I said.

"This isn't really a good time," he said, opening the refrigerator and pulling out some drinks. His smooth brow furrowed, as if he really, really had to concentrate on sorting out the beverages.

"Is everything okay?" I asked.

"Everything's fine."

That wasn't true. I could see that. "You're not supposed to lie to witches," I said. "Remember? You're not even supposed to tell half-truths to half witches."

"Right." He sighed, putting the drinks on the counter and leaning against the refrigerator. "Good point. Sorry."

"So," I said, "what's up?"

"Look," he said, as if he was searching for the words, "I can't talk right now."

"Okay," I said uncertainly. "Do you want to give me a call later?"

"I'm going to be busy tonight." He sighed again. "Maybe tomorrow, okay?"

With Brigid. That's what he wasn't saying. He was going to be talking to Brigid. His girlfriend. The person he was supposed to be talking to.

"Oh, sure," I said. Though I tried to keep smiling, I felt my face fall. I was rapidly coming to my senses. Why had I followed him? What had I been expecting him to say? Did I think he was going to jump up and down with joy and tell me that he'd ditched Brigid? At best, our kiss caused major problems. At worst, he was regretting that he'd ever met me. Although who could say? Maybe there was something even worse than that.

I turned and started filling the glasses quickly.

"Alisa . . ." he said. Again I saw his hand moving, as if he wanted take hold of me. Again he held himself back. There was a rush of frustration coming from him.

"It's okay," I told him, fixing the limp smile back on my face. "Tomorrow or whenever you have a chance. Just give me a call."

I saw that he was about to reply, but I scooped up some of the glasses and headed out. One more word and I knew I would be bawling. I couldn't risk it.

Back in the living room, I passed around the drinks and sat down next to Sam, who gave me a strange look. I knew he must have realized I was upset about something, but he probably assumed that it was related to Evelyn. He inched closer to me, and I felt a little better having him by my side. Charlie followed a moment later and gave out the other cups.

"It's a little chilly in here," Ruth observed, pulling her sweater around her uncasted arm.

Since Charlie was next to the fireplace, he reached down to put another log on the fire. I was sitting next to the fireplace, and he glanced up and caught my eye for a moment. I couldn't meet his gaze, so I threw my attention across the room. Of course, I looked right up at Evelyn. She was staring at me. The room *was* cold. Very cold. And the force of her stare made me even colder.

Suddenly Ruth screamed, and I felt a rush of extreme heat cutting the chill. As if it had been stirred by some unnatural breeze, the fire in the fireplace leaped out, blue with heat. It reached for Charlie, licking at his clothes, his skin. I felt a fear rising up through me. Charlie was going to be hurt—badly.

No. I could not let this happen.

Water . . . I thought, my body standing itself up and my hand raising without my willing either to do so. I pointed at the caldron, and it lifted itself from its resting place. Time was slow now—I was unaffected by it. The water would do what I needed it to do; I had only to ask it. Once again words came to me from the recesses of my mind, in an echo of a woman's voice, a voice I couldn't quite place.

"*Cuir as a srad,*" I said, moving my pointed finger to indicate Charlie. "*Doirt air.*"

The caldron sailed through the room, past Charlie, and smashed itself against the smoky brick of the fireplace, spilling all of the flowers and water onto him. He stumbled back as it thundered to the floor and rolled back and forth before the fire.

The crash brought me back in step with everything else, and I lurched forward, as if I was in a car that had skidded to a halt. Charlie quickly rolled away from the fireplace and looked down at himself in shock. He was soaking wet and covered in soggy flower pieces. His hands were singed, but the water had protected him somewhat, keeping his clothing from igniting.

"I'm okay," he said, patting his body down and checking for injuries. "I'm okay." Brigid and Ruth descended on him, dragging him off to the kitchen to attend to the burns. The whole thing had happened in less than a minute.

"Goddess," said Kate once they had gone, "did everyone just see that?"

I became aware of the fact that everyone left in the room was staring at me. My hand was still outstretched. I jammed it behind my back.

Charlie's father was next to me. All traces of cosmic goofiness were gone from his face.

"Thank you," he said, reaching out to squeeze my arm. His face was pale with shock. "I've never seen anyone do a deflection that quickly before."

"You're welcome," I mumbled. "I mean . . . I just did it."

Sometimes I just blow myself away with my fancy talk.

"You do know," he said seriously, "that you moved the

cauldron almost *simultaneously* with the flame, killing its progress—don't you?"

"I did?" I said, feeling very dull-witted.

"You gave a command spell," Charlie's father said. "Very simple. The energy was channeled through the water. The Gaelic charge was basic. But it was very, very fast, and you brought up a lot of energy within a moment."

I wobbled, and Sam gently helped me to sit down. Evelyn, I noticed, had returned and was looking at me up, down, and sideways.

"You have powers," she said.

She didn't sound happy, or amazed, or impressed, or grateful. She sounded suspicious.

"She not only has powers," Charlie's father added, "she's strong. Quite strong. And fast. And she has a rather shocking command of spell language."

"Have you been studying with someone?" Kate asked, pulling up an ottoman and sitting close to me.

"A Seeker," I said, looking around nervously.

"A Seeker?" she said. "Goddess. For how long?"

"A few weeks. On and off over the last few months."

"A few *weeks?*" she repeated after me again. "That's it?"

"So," Evelyn said, "you have powers—somehow—and you've been studying with someone from the council."

Evelyn hadn't exactly been sending valentines to the council. I realized that I'd just made another huge mistake in her eyes.

"He's from the council," I said, trying to defend myself, "but he's not teaching me as a representative of the council. I mean, he's just my coven leader...."

Ruth looked in through the doorway.

"Charlie's fine," she said. "The burns on his hands are minor. I treated him with some aloe. We'll add a preparation of calendula and cantharis. Brigid is mixing it up now."

There was a murmur of relief from everyone. I felt like I needed air. I was on emotional overdrive. I tugged on Sam's sleeve, hoping he would understand the can-we-go message. Fortunately, Sam is perceptive.

"I think," he said, standing and pulling his keys from his pocket, "that we should call it a night. Alisa's still kind of worn out from last night, and this has been a long day."

I nodded in confirmation. It was an awkward and hasty exit, but then, this was the House of Strange Happenings. Sam said nothing—just took me home and let me spend some time with my thoughts. I certainly had enough of those.

After Sam had gone to bed, I found that I was still wide awake. I stared at the phone for a while, trying to will it to ring. I thought about calling Charlie, even though he'd indicated pretty clearly that he didn't want to talk to me tonight. Bad idea.

I was going to go crazy if I didn't think of something to do.

First I tried scrying again, but I was even less successful than I'd been the night before. Giving that up, I went for my bag and pulled out Máirín's book. I set it down next to the scrying bowl and started to read. As I did so, Astrophe jumped into my lap, causing me to flinch. My elbow struck the bowl, causing it to splash water on the pages.

The ink began to run. I almost screamed.

I scrambled around, grabbing for paper towels, anything to blot the water. I couldn't find anything. Everything must have been used up in the cleanup the night before. Frantic, I ran back to the book to try to brush the water from the page with my hands, only to make an amazing discovery: Something was there that hadn't been there before.

It came into clearer focus as the water ran out over it. There was writing there, scribbled all over the margins, squeezed into every available inch of space. There were combinations of runes, symbols, bits of Gaelic, and words in English—*uncontrollable magick*—*Rowanwand*—*stabilization of energies, provided that the* . . .

The water was bringing it out. If I wanted to fill out the passages, my only choice would be to drip on more. Using a spoon, I tried this very carefully, working drop by drop. By doing this, one passage became clear enough to read:

. . . *this plague of uncontrollable magick, the roots of which are all too human, forged by the dark spell of our poor tortured ancestor. Being Rowanwand, we pride ourselves on our ability to master knowledge and control our destiny. Pride, of course, is well known to be one of the deadliest vices. Fear is another. Both were at work when I destroyed the pages in a fit of terrified rage. I was fifteen years old at the time. I hope now to rectify my mistakes and to add to our store of knowledge.* . . .

It went into the Gaelic and symbols. I saw the occasional word in English here or there, but no passage was entirely clear, and I was worried about actually destroying the book in my attempts to extract the information.

Even though I felt guilty about making a long-distance call without asking Sam first, I knew I had to tell someone about this right away. This was *huge*. Besides, it was after nine. The rates were cheaper. I called Hunter. Much to my irritation, though, he wasn't home, and neither was his father. I left a garbled message for him, frantically trying to explain what I had seen.

Now what? I knew that this was important. Someone had to see this. Maybe even . . . Evelyn?

Sam kept a bike on the side of the house. If I used that, I could be to Evelyn's and back in no time. The hills would be a pain going up, but I'd get back really quickly. Since this seemed to be my big week for impulsive behavior, I decided to go for it. Compared to what I'd done so far, taking a bike for a midnight ride was nothing. I put the book into my messenger bag and let myself out.

The town was beautiful at night. I rode along the water. There was plenty of light from the ships and reflections of the moon on the harbor. The breeze was moist and heavy, cold but not biting. I couldn't help but notice that the view looked a lot like my last dream, with the dark, calm sea and the waxing moon hanging in the sky. Of course, there was no mermaid.

The last hill up to Evelyn's was horrible—I would feel it in the morning—but I needed the exercise, anyway. The house was completely dark. I walked the bike up to the porch, looking above me for falling branches or tiles or posts. I carefully put the book between the screen and the door and hurried back to the bike and rode away, trying to get back as quickly as possible.

I woke up at eight in the morning to the sound of the phone ringing. Sam called down from his room to tell me that the call was for me. There was a strange note in his voice. Cautiously I picked up the phone.

"Alisa."

It was Evelyn. Yikes.

"Yes?

"I want to talk to you. This morning. Can you be here at ten?"

"Sure," I said, quaking.

"Fine. Good-bye."

And that was that. I was left staring at the phone.

16

Bloodline

October 3, 1971

There was an incident today in the kitchen.

Sorcha came to me, extremely upset. She was speaking wildly about the craft, saying that it was dangerous and that we shouldn't be allowed to wield as much power as we do. I attributed the remarks to an emotional reaction to the storm. Both Somhairle and Sorcha seem to have been very affected by it.

As we were speaking, one of the drawers pulled itself out and flew across the room, right at Sorcha. She stepped aside, and it fell to the ground. In the same moment, the cabinets started to open up and the dishes came at us. We had to throw ourselves to the ground.

This can mean only one thing—Oona has returned.

I have already called Claire Findgoll and Patience Stamp. They are coming to help me cast spells of protection this afternoon. Patience has no one to watch her little daughter Kate, so I will be able to distract Somhairle and Sorcha with babysitting. My mind

*is racing, though. Will I be forced to reopen the dearc? And how
is it possible that Oona would come back after so long, and why
after this horrible storm?*

I have a terrible feeling in the pit of my stomach.

—Aoibheann

Sam was quiet as he drove me to Evelyn's. I could see
that he was baffled by this sudden morning visit, and my
brain was too addled for me to be able to explain. Evelyn
met me at the door and took me directly to her study without saying a word. She indicated that I should sit.

"You left something very interesting for me to read," she
said. "We need to discuss it."

I nodded stiffly. I wasn't even going to ask how she knew
it was me. She crossed around to her desk and carefully
picked up Máirín's Book of Shadows and her athame. She
ran the athame over the cover and the spine of the book,
and it took on a faint phosphorescent quality.

"I've examined this closely through the morning," she
said, turning it over in her hands, covering every inch with
the athame. "I see that there are quite a number of spells on
this book. One of them is an attraction spell, designed to
help those of us looking for an answer to our family difficulty find it. I'm sure it helped you. Where was it?"

"In your library," I said sheepishly. She didn't seem
surprised that I'd been there, even though it meant that I'd
broken into her house and snooped around. She nodded
thoughtfully.

"Was it hidden?" she asked.

"Well"—I shook my head—"sort of. It was misfiled and

mislabeled. That's all." I looked at the spine. The German writing was gone. "It had German on the spine," I said, confused. "It would appear and disappear."

That didn't seem to surprise her, either. "There are quite a few glamors on this book," she said. I was waiting for her to start explaining the green writing, but she kept examining the cover, as if it was the most interesting thing imaginable.

"I found this book when I was a girl," she said, a trace of a strange smile appearing on her thin lips. "It vanished from my room before I had a chance to look it over thoroughly."

"What happened?" I asked.

"In all likelihood," she said, "my mother took it. She could see how agitated it had made me, so she decided it was best for me not to read it. But aside from Oona's story, which is very tragic, there's nothing in here worth hiding. The fact that someone has torn out some of the pages, however, suggests a very serious problem. No Rowanwand destroys a book—especially not the Book of Shadows of an ancestor."

"Who do you think tore out the pages?" I said.

"I don't know," Evelyn replied. "The pages were torn when I located the book. It seems to be the same witch who wrote the spell in secret writing, but I don't know her identity. I see that the ink is smudged now. It wasn't when I first found it. Someone else was trying to make the book unreadable."

"No." I shook my head. "That was me, and it was an accident. Couldn't you see it?"

Her eyes narrowed in on me.

"See what?" she asked.

"The writing," I said. "The green writing."

She looked like I'd just given her a shock of static electricity.

"What green writing?"

I got up and took the book from her, quickly flipping through the pages.

"It's gone," I said, speeding through. "It was here, and now it's gone."

She looked at me, demanding further explanation, and I told her about the water spilling onto the book and the mysterious writing that blossomed like creeping vines all over the page.

"I saw it," I promised her. "It's gone now."

"The spell could be old," she said, her eyes flashing. "It could be fragile. Or the spells may be counteracting one another. That could account for the fading. I'd say we should try dampening it again, but we might destroy it."

"That's what I was afraid of." I nodded.

"Did you get a good look at the pages?" she asked.

"Pretty good. But I didn't understand all of the words. Some of them were written in another language."

"Then I have an idea. Have you ever heard of a ritual called a *tàth meànma*?"

"I've done one of those," I said. "I did a *tàth meànma brach*."

Evelyn looked up at me with knitted brows.

"Somehow I doubt that," she said. From Charlie's reaction, I knew that this probably did seem unlikely. But I guessed she would find out that I was telling the truth soon enough. "It's a very intense connection spell that can only be performed by . . ."

"I know what it is," I said, starting to feel a little annoyed. "I did one."

She looked a bit surprised, but she seemed to like the fact that I showed I actually had bits and pieces of spine every once in a while.

"All right," she replied, still skeptical, "how do you feel about doing a regular *tàth meànma* so that I can have a look at the pages?"

The idea of having Evelyn in my mind was more than a little scary, but I knew this was the only way we were going to get to the bottom of the story.

"Okay," I said.

Evelyn instructed me to sit down and meditate for a few minutes while she prepared some ritual tea. I sat cross-legged on the floor and did some breathing exercises that we'd been taught in circle. I would show her. *Tàth meànma* . . . bring it on!

She returned for me a few minutes later and indicated that I should come to the kitchen. I got up and followed her.

"Drink it all," she said, pointing at a huge cup of tea.

This stuff was nasty. Seriously nasty. It tasted like I was licking a slimy, insect-infested tree. But I gulped it back, determined to show no signs of weakness. She drank one herself, and I saw her grimace slightly. When we had gotten this down, we sat cross-legged on the polished wood floor, took each other's hands, and put our foreheads together.

"Relax," she said. "Just breathe."

At first I just felt my butt getting sore and heard the hum of the refrigerator.

I became gradually aware that I wasn't in the kitchen

anymore. I wasn't sure where we were. It might have been on the shore because I thought I could hear the sound of the ocean. The ground was soft, like cool, damp sand.

"Come, Alisa." Evelyn's voice was somewhere in my mind—not in sound. I could feel the words. I started walking along, not sure where to go. Then I saw that Evelyn was beside me. I could tell that she was somehow in control of the experience, that she was the guide.

What came next was a weird mix of images—a falling piece of furniture, the sound of splintering wood and ripping fabric. A storm. A baby. Evelyn—or both of us—was holding a baby. Sorcha was her name—Sorcha . . . Sarah . . . my mother. Evelyn led me away from this image. There was an overwhelming love of the Goddess. I could feel her power all around me, especially in the ocean. And I felt walls—anger, sadness, terrible loss—a father, a mother, a sister named Tioma, also named Jessica, killed in a car accident, a husband dying quietly in his sleep, a daughter gone forever . . . unbearable sadness . . .

We were leaving Evelyn, and Evelyn was coming into me. Evelyn drank up my life, taking in everything. She saw me, at three years old, trying to understand my father's explanation that my mother was gone and that she was never coming back. She saw my life in Texas—the long flatness of the land and the constant warmth of the sun. Then New York State, Widow's Vale, so cold and bleak and lonely.

I felt her close attention to the whirlwind of events that followed—discovering Wicca, my fears at seeing what magick could do, my hospitalization. Finding my mother's Book of Shadows and realizing I was a blood witch. As we came to the point where I was standing alone as the dark wave approached, linked to Morgan through the *brach*, I felt her speeding, falling through my mind. This she couldn't take in enough of, and she could hardly believe what she was seeing. She couldn't get to everything I had learned through Morgan, but the power she saw there was unlike anything she had ever encountered. She saw me finish the spell as the dark wave closed in, and I felt her pride.

There was an interested pause as she caught a flash of my strange dreams about Gloucester and the mermaid. I felt her mind hooking onto the images and processing them in some way. And I was *telekinetic?* Sparks of surprise as she saw objects falling, flying, breaking ...

After that, her emotions changed, softened. I came to something raw within her. She felt for me as I returned to the house where no one understood what I had seen or been through. She was with me on the floor at Hunter's as I wept, full of frustration and pain. Then she saw me running away, coming to her, and how rejected I felt. Her guilt was thick, smothering. Images of my mother flickered through our minds.

She was moving faster now, through the events of the last few days. We came to Charlie—my ripple of excitement at meeting him, our kiss in the library. I cringed—how embarrassing!

The book. That was what she wanted to see. Finally we faced the book with its strange green print. She pulled in close to it and read the pages. What was odd was that now I could see even more writing that had been invisible before, along with the passages I had been able to uncover. Telekinesis ... she was thinking again ... uncontrollable magick

. . . uncontrollable . . . The word was making her uncomfortable.

Then she saw what I had concluded—what I had asked Hunter to look into—what Ardán Rourke had suggested . . . that she also suffered from telekinesis. There was no ghost. No Oona. No . . .

Everything was rushing back at me, a rush of gravity, pressing on my head, making my stomach churn. I wanted to get up—to move around, to stretch and feel the blood flowing through my veins. But she put a hand on my shoulder.

"Sit," she said. "It catches up with you."

I sat. It caught up with me. I wondered if I was going to barf.

"You," she said, "you're telekinetic?"

I nodded and steadied myself.

"And the Seeker is trying to find out if it is hereditary?"

I nodded again. "He thinks it may be passed down by firstborn females. Like my mother, me . . . and you." I looked at Evelyn. "Think about it," I said softly. "When did you have the most problems with Oona? When something bad happened? When you were upset or confused? That's when it happens to me."

No answer. She stared at some tiny birds that had come to eat at a bird feeder outside her window.

"What you saw in the book," Evelyn said, "I understood what it was saying. The passage suggests that Oona performed a spell—probably a bit of dark magick. The result brought telekinesis into our family, starting with Máirín."

"What else did it say?" I asked, my voice hoarse.

"There is no cure—at least, not that the writer knows of. The attacks are caused by repressing emotions, so the only solution is to try not to bottle them up. The more they are kept under pressure, the greater the explosions."

"What about the missing pages?"

"The spellwriter admits to ripping out any pages relating to a description of telekinesis. Later in life she regretted it. She spent many years investigating the problem, with only some success."

"But why did she destroy them?" I asked, shaking my head. "I don't get it."

"All good witches pride themselves on control." Evelyn sighed. "Rowanwands especially. We rely on the power that our knowledge gives us and the control we have over it. When a witch's control is in question, his or her power may be reined in. Most of us will do anything to avoid that fate, even lie when we are ill or weak. The woman who wrote these words was smart enough to know that if her own fear and pride could actually cause her to tear out pages in a book that described a family affliction, there was a good chance that one of her descendants might do the same. So she hid her writing and spelled the book so that it could be found by the right people—people ready to face the truth, to admit that they didn't have the control that they thought they had."

She leaned her back against the refrigerator, legs akimbo, looking more like a stunned teenager than the imposing, matronly woman I had known. "That's why I couldn't see this book for years," she added. "I was open to ideas the first time I found it. When my mind closed up, the book became invisible to me. All these years . . ." She shook her head as realization lit her eyes. "I could have done something about these problems. Oh, Goddess, Sorcha . . ."

Suddenly Evelyn's composure completely abandoned her, and her face crumpled into a sob. "Sarah, your mother," she whimpered as her age finally seemed to show, "she had it, too. She stripped herself because she was frightened by her powers. Her telekinesis." Evelyn closed her eyes and sobbed again. "Oh, Goddess, I could have saved her. . . ."

I shook my head, reaching out to take her hand. "You didn't know," I said.

"I should have," she whispered. "It was all there for me to put together. If I had been honest with her, if I had told her about what was happening to me instead of just pushing her away . . ."

"You couldn't have known what she was planning," I said, squeezing her hand. "She was frightened, and she didn't tell you how deep her fears went."

Evelyn sighed wearily. "I could see how frightened she was. I thought I could take care of Oona on my own." She looked me in the eye. "I pushed my daughter away," she concluded, wiping her eyes with the back of her hand. "And I lost her."

She looked over at me, slowly regaining her composure. I opened my mouth to say something, but nothing came out. I was suddenly profoundly aware that I could pass on telekinesis to *my* daughter, if I ever had one. Looking at Evelyn's tearstained face, I swore to myself that I would always be honest with my children. And open.

"I'll have to tell them the truth," she said, sitting up straight again. "There is no Oona."

"No," I said. "You were right. She was real, and she cast the spell that's affecting us."

"I suppose," she replied. "All these years, I thought it was something entirely outside myself, something I could eventually control. But it was coming through me. It was always me."

I could tell it was more than she could bear.

"The Seeker," she said, "he's working with a chaos specialist in London to find a remedy?"

"A chaos specialist?"

"That's what someone who specializes in uncontrollable magick is called." She smiled wryly.

"Yes," I answered, slightly chilled by the term *chaos specialist*. That had a really bad sound to it. Hunter had obviously been trying to be delicate. "He is."

"Well, then," she said. "I suppose we'll have to see what he comes up with." She pulled herself off the floor, moving stiffly.

"I'm not going to tell anyone up here about this," I said as I watched her. "I'm only going to tell some people in my coven and that man Ardán. This can just be between us. We'll tell them that we found something to bring Oona partially under control."

Evelyn's eyes looked pale and red rimmed in the sunlight from the window. She turned to me. For the first time I felt something coming from her, something warm.

"Thank you," she said simply.

"I should go," I said, gathering up my things. "I mean . . . I should rest before the circle."

Evelyn nodded and put her hand on my shoulder as she walked me to the front door. "Have a good rest, Alisa. And thank you." She looked me in the eye. "I am very lucky that you chose to visit."

"You're welcome," I whispered, and walked slowly down the front steps and along the roads to Sam's house. I wasn't very tired. I just thought Evelyn needed some time alone. She'd just learned some serious things about my mother and her leaving, and I knew it would take her a long time to come to terms with them.

If she ever did.

17

The Mermaid

November 14, 1971

Sorcha has been gone for one month. Hugh and I have decided that we will not scry for her anymore. She is gone.

Somhairle raged when we told him of our decision. He screamed. He threatened to leave as well, to go and find her himself. Then he stormed out of the house to walk off some of his anger. Soon, I think, his emotions will regulate themselves and he will understand. Sorcha has willingly given up her power. She has refused the blessing of the Goddess and turned her back on her heritage. When a witch is stripped, it is understood: No longer shall that witch be one of us. Sorcha made it easier for everyone by taking herself away.

While I know what I must do, and while I know I am right, my heart is broken. I feel hollow, as if a hole has been drilled in me and all feeling has gone forever. Hugh looks gray, and I worry about his health. This has taken a great toll on him.

After Somhairle left, we heard a noise upstairs in Sorcha's room. We found her quilt in shreds, her books on the ground, and her bedroom window broken. Hugh and I stood there, looking at each other, unable to express the blackness that has taken over our lives.

—Aoibheann

We met at Evelyn's at eight o'clock. Kate and Charlie's dad were in the hallway talking, waiting for the bathroom so that they could change into their robes.

Evelyn swished down the hall from the direction of the kitchen, elegant in a long purple robe with wide, sweeping sleeves. She had a beautiful silver pentacle around her neck. She came right for me, her face serene, and kissed my forehead. I noticed that stopped the conversation Kate and Sam had started. I don't think Charlie's dad noticed anything.

"Come with me for a minute, Alisa," Evelyn said, drawing me into the study and shutting the doors behind us.

On her desk there was a large, dusty old box. She walked around to it and opened the limp flaps at the top.

"It's time these saw the light of day again," she said, looking down into the contents. She seemed lost in whatever it was she was looking at; then she waved me over and pushed the box toward me.

"These are for you," she said.

Inside, there was a bundle of purple cloth. I had scried this! A box, something purple! Eagerly I opened the bundle. As I dipped my hand into the folds, I got a sharp spark of electricity and drew my hand back. Evelyn nodded for me to continue, so I reached in again. My hand hit something smooth and flat. I pulled it out. It was a ceramic plate, hand-made—very seventies, crafty looking, with a pentagram thickly drawn into the surface. I reached in again and produced a chalice, silver, with a stem made of figures of the moon and stars. A chunk of quartz wrapped in yellow silk. A bolline—the white-handled work knife used to prepare herbs and other magickal elements. Many of these items sat in the small cauldron, which I had to pull out with both hands.

These were my mother's things. They warmed my hands as I touched them.

I looked up at Evelyn, unable to speak.

"There's something else," she said, nodding for me to reach in once again. At the bottom of the bundle there was a pale green linen robe, finely embroidered with runes.

"She made this by hand," said Evelyn, running her fingers over the embroidery. "Every stitch is sacred."

I picked it up, but it was surprisingly heavy. Something was wrapped inside. As I unfolded it, I saw a glint of metal. I drew in my breath in surprise.

"Does it look familiar?" Evelyn said, watching me with glistening eyes.

It was an athame with a bright silver blade. But my eyes were stuck on the handle. It was cast in the shape of a mermaid—a steel gray mermaid.

I ran my hand over the sculpted handle, tears welling up behind my eyes. The mermaid—this was what had been calling me here, and now I had it. The athame was beautiful, and it was my mother's. I imagined her holding it in her hand, wearing her light green robe as she worked some beautiful magick. Before the storm. Before everything changed for her. I looked back at Evelyn as a few tears began to slip down my face. "I can't believe it," I whispered.

"The Goddess often speaks to us in our dreams," she said.

*   *   *

Evelyn had instructed me to remove all of my clothing, even my underwear, before putting on the robe. I thought this would make me very cold, especially with those seaside breezes blowing all over the place, but I was comfortable in the fine linen. The fit was perfect—my mother and I must have been the exact same height. Standing there in my robe and holding the athame, my bare feet on the cool nighttime grass, I felt so witchy ... and so natural.

The house had a large backyard, which I hadn't seen before. It was surrounded on all sides by trees, so we were in a safe little grotto for the circle. White lights had been strung around, making the scene romantic. The large cauldron contained a sweet-smelling fire, laced with herbs and fragrant woods. I took my place in the opening of the group, beside Sam, who looked quite dashing in his crimson silk robe. Charlie stood just opposite me, looking amazing in a pale yellow robe. He nodded slightly but approvingly in my direction.

Evelyn stepped forward and presented the four elements—the candle, the incense, the bowl of water, and the dish of sea salt.

"Alisa," she said, "if you would please bring out your athame, I would like you to cast the circle."

She held out the bowl of water and indicated that I should dip my athame in it. When I had done so, she placed the elements in their respective quarters and nodded for me to begin.

I'd never actually done this before, so I was a bit nervous. You're supposed to try to make the circle as perfectly round as possible. Using my right hand, I held the athame out in front of me. Walking deasil around the group, I concentrated on feeling its power, and I visualized the wall of energy that I was drawing. Automatically I started to speak, not really knowing where I had found the invocation. I supposed maybe I'd read it somewhere, but it came out of me naturally, as if I was saying my own name: "I conjure you, circle, to be a protected space, boring down through the earth and rising into the sky. I cast out from you all that is impure. Within your protective embrace, may we honor the Goddess and the God."

Evelyn smiled, and I took my place. I saw quite a number of surprised glances ping-ponging between Evelyn and me. The circle was very peaceful—no busted pipes, no floods. When it was over, everyone headed for a table that had been set up next to the house. There were cookies, brownies, and little bowls of milk and rosewater pudding decorated with rose petals. Someone switched on some Celtic music. I stayed with Sam most of the time, chatting with Kate—but I was really scanning the yard for Charlie. He had vanished into thin air the moment the circle was over.

When I was alone for a moment by the table, Brigid approached me, reaching past me for an oatcake. I felt a chilly, brittle energy coming from her.

"Hi," I said. "This circle—it was great. It was beautiful."

She picked through all of the cakes very deliberately before choosing one. At last she looked up at me. "You saved Charlie last night. Thank you."

I opened my mouth to respond but quickly realized that I had no idea what to say. I didn't feel like I should be accepting thanks for something like that. Finally I just nodded.

"I'm not happy about what's happened," she said, real sadness tearing at her voice, "but what you did was good."

Having said her piece, she walked off. I saw her go into the house.

"What happened?" I said out loud to no one in particular. I desperately wanted to find Charlie and ask, but his dad came up to me at that very moment.

"I've checked my schedule," he said. "I didn't have a few full days."

I had no idea what he was talking about. "I'm sorry?" I said.

"You asked me if I had a few days to listen to your story," he explained. "I do, but not until June. Maybe we could speak on the phone instead. I'd very much like to hear all about your experiences. Charlie's told me some, and I am absolutely fascinated."

"Oh." I laughed. "Right. Sure."

"Wonderful," he said, taking a dish of pudding. "Does Charlie have your phone number?"

"I'll give it to him," I replied. "Have you seen him?"

"Oh, yes," he said, peering around the yard. "He's on one of the benches in the back."

Far in the back of the yard, there was a small clump of four tall shrubs. In the middle of these was a tiny white stone bench, and on this bench was Charlie. As usual, my stomach twisted around completely.

"You found me," he said, sounding kind of pleased.

"I'm supposed to give you my phone number," I said, joining him on the bench.

"Oh, yeah?" he said, arching his brows.

"Your dad wants it."

"My dad's been asking for your number?" He laughed. "Is there something going on I should know about?"

I felt myself blushing. "Um, listen, I'm sorry about yesterday," I said. "I didn't mean . . ."

"No." He shook his head quickly. "No! Don't apologize." He looked around and then checked his watch. "Let me explain, but not here. Can I give you a ride back to Sam's? Things are wrapping up here, anyway."

My ride arrangements were fine with Sam, so I went back inside to change into my clothes, and I carefully folded the robe and put it in with my mother's tools. Evelyn gave me a warm hug and another kiss on the forehead as I left.

"We have a lot of work to do," she said to me quietly. "We need to put these tools back to good use."

"Thank you . . ." I said, not even sure how to express my gratitude.

"Call me Grandmother," she said with a smile. "That is my name. Or Grandmom. Gran. Whatever you like."

I'd only ever had one grandmother, and she was from Buenos Aires. I called her Lita Soto.

"How about Lita?" I asked. "It's a nickname for grandmother in Spanish."

"I like it," she said with a satisfied nod. "I like it a lot."

18

The Castle

February 13, 1991

I sat straight up in bed at three o'clock this morning and screamed.

Poor Ruth, I think I scared her half to death. I woke little Brigid as well. They both turned up at my door. While I assured them that I had just had a bad dream, I knew it was more. My heart ached as though it were broken. It's difficult to explain, but it felt as though a candle that always burned inside me had been snuffed out. I felt an emptiness, an indescribable loss.

After Ruth and Brigid had gone back to bed, I walked all through the house, trying to convince myself that there was some reasonable explanation for my disturbance. I walked through the basement, the kitchen, and the study, praying to the Goddess that I would find some mundane solution. But in my heart I knew there would not be, and my heart was right.

In my workroom, Sorcha's old bedroom, I found everything in

a shambles. The shelves had collapsed, and everything I was storing had tumbled down. The carpet was shredded where the bed once stood. I knew then that my worst suspicions were true.

My daughter, my lost Sorcha, is dead.

—Aoibheann

Charlie guided the car through the streets of Gloucester, past the huge neon Gorton's fisherman and the crowded pubs along the waterfront. He didn't say anything at first— he just played with the windshield wipers, flicking them on and off, as if they could help him clear his thoughts. I couldn't get a good read on what he was feeling. It felt like a whole soup of emotions.

"On Monday," he finally said, "in the basement, I told Brigid what happened."

I remembered the wave of emotion I'd felt coming from Brigid as I passed—that whole nasty mix of panic, anger, and sadness. It made me nauseous just to think of it.

"You mean what happened in the library," I said.

"Right." He nodded. "And it was really bad. She was so upset. I've never done anything like that."

"I'm sorry," I said. "I've caused a mess...."

"No!" he said, accidentally jerking the wheel a bit as he turned to look at me. "It's not that I regret it. I'm sorry I was so quiet yesterday. I was just trying to take care of things."

"Take care of things?" I asked.

"I spent yesterday thinking it all over," he continued. "Today I told her that I needed a little time to think things over."

"You ... broke up with her?"

He stopped for a red light and turned to me. "Yes," he said. "I think so."

I nodded, unsure of what to say. I didn't think, "Great!" would be appropriate, but by now it was clear that we had some kind of bond, however strange and undefined.

"It's for the best," he said. "We've been together for two years, since she was fourteen. Now she's sixteen and I'm seventeen. I care about her a lot, but we've both grown and changed. I don't think we're the best match for each other." The light turned green, and he drove through the intersection. "I'm going off to college in the fall. I'm going to be leaving Gloucester." His tone was pained, as if he was trying to convince me and convince himself that he had done the right thing. He fell silent for a minute, obviously not sure what to say next.

"Evelyn and I had a talk, too," I said.

He pulled into a small parking lot and killed the engine.

"About what?" he said, unsnapping his seat belt and turning to me. "I mean, everything seemed good at the circle tonight. I was wondering what was going on."

While I didn't explain what had transpired in detail, I told him that Evelyn and I had reconciled, and I explained what had been in the box in the back.

"Alisa." He broke into a smile and took my hands. "That's great. I can't believe I didn't notice. . . . I'm sorry."

"It's all right," I said, smiling, too. "You had a lot on your mind. How do you feel?"

"Well," he said, "I feel like a jerk for what I've done to Brigid, even though I think it's for the best. And I feel incredibly happy that you're here."

He watched me to see what effect his words were

having. I'll tell you what effect they had—I almost melted. Kissing energy was on the rise.

"I wanted to show you this place," he said, pointing out into the shadows. "Take a look."

I leaned forward and glanced up through the windshield. Then I rubbed my eyes and looked again. It was a medieval castle—complete with turrets, drawbridge, the works. I wondered if he had spelled some kind of illusion.

"It's called Hammond Castle. It's real," Charlie said, answering my unspoken question. "Well, it's a real fake. It was built in the 1920s by a rich inventor. He wanted a nice place for his art collection."

"This is really strange," I said, "but cool." And absurdly romantic, of course.

"Over there," he said, pointing out into the inky darkness of the water, just past the castle, "is one of the most famous places along the shoreline. It's a rock called Norman's Woe, the site of many shipwrecks and the inspiration for the poem 'The Wreck of the Hesperus,' which I will now recite to you."

He drew himself up, as if he was about to give a big speech. I stared blankly.

"Just kidding," he said quickly, breaking into a grin. "But the force of the sea and the spirits of the sailors give this place tons of energy. It's our local power sink. I've performed some amazing magick here."

We got out of the car and sat down on a bench in a small stone bell tower, where we could hear the roar of the ocean just below. The floodlights illuminated the towers above us and threw strange shadows on the ground.

"Hold on," he said. He went back to his car and came back with his messenger bag.

"Want to learn a little spell?" he asked.

"As long as it doesn't make anything fall over or break," I said. "Or make my clothes disappear!"

"No." He laughed. "Nothing like that. This one brings back something that made you happy once, a good experience. Sometimes just something you like to eat or a beautiful sunset. It's a small spell, but it's a nice one. It reminds you of a joy in your life."

"That sounds nice," I said. "Sure. Show me."

He penciled the Gaelic on a slip of paper and went over the pronunciations with me. I practiced it a few times. After the dark wave spell this little three liner was nothing. Then he poured about a half cup of coarse sea salt into my hand.

"Okay," he said, "I'll draw the circle. You walk it deasil three times. Say one line each time you go around. After you recite the spell, close your eyes and throw this straight up in the air, right above your head. Get it all up there in one strong, fast throw. Keep facing up, letting it fall back down to you."

Taking some more of the salt, he drew a circle on the asphalt, leaving me a space to step inside. He closed it behind me. Then he drew sigils in the air, signifying the four elements. He nodded at me to begin. I made my three circles, reciting one line each time:

"Ar iobairt ar miann
an sòlas goit faod till
tromhad tràth-sa."

I closed my eyes, and with one swift stroke I threw the salt into the air. I was expecting it to rain back down on my head, but it never came. Instead, the snapping ocean breezes seemed to stop. I couldn't hear the waves hitting the shore, and I couldn't smell the salty air.

"What is this?" I said, suddenly panicking.

"Relax," I heard him say. "Just let it come. Close your eyes and breathe slowly."

Now the air felt warm to me, like a heady summer breeze or like every day in Texas, where I had been born. There were chirping cicadas. There was grass, soft grass high around my ankles. I felt unsteady, but a pair of strong hands were holding mine, stretching my arms above my head.

I smelled lilacs.

My mother. My mother was teaching me how to walk. She was taking me over to a pot of flowers. I started to run to them and lost my balance, but the hands caught me. I heard laughter. She was encouraging me.

"You've got it, Alisa," the voice was saying. Her voice. "Good girl. You did it."

I looked up, and I saw her. Her face was like mine.

"You did it," she repeated.

Encouraged, I took off again toward the flowers, but they faded from my view.

In a moment the sound of the ocean returned, and the wind kicked back up. The fragrance rose like a lifting fog and dissipated. I kept trying to breathe in more deeply, just to get one last breath. Different hands held me. Larger hands, with cooler skin and longer fingers that could grip my arms all the way around.

"Alisa!"

I opened my eyes. I had tipped forward, and Charlie had caught me before I went facedown on the ground. He said a blessing to close the circle and helped me over to the stone bench. As I watched him brush away the salt, my vision grew mistier. No magick this time—I was crying. He looked over in alarm.

"What did you see?" he asked, coming over and squatting down in front of me. I shook my head. I couldn't describe it.

"Was it something bad?" he said, his brow furrowed. "This is such a gentle spell. What . . . ?"

"It was my mother," I said.

He exhaled sharply and shook his head.

"Alisa," he said, "I'm sorry. We're at Norman's Woe. I should have realized that the spell would intensify. I'm an idiot."

"No," I said, wiping my eyes. "No. It was . . . good."

He sat down and took me in his arms. We listened to the waves hitting the shore just below us. Normally I would have been a complete wreck sitting there, wondering if he was going to kiss me again, worrying about what I should do or say. But my thoughts were on bigger matters, and Charlie seemed to understand that.

It was all clear to me now, what all of this had been about. I'd reconciled with my grandmother. I'd gotten the mermaid-handled athame and the rest of my mother's tools. I'd come to grips with my heritage. These were all the things my mother had been trying to show me.

Now, I realized, I could go home.

19

Full Circle

February 16, 1991

I haven't explained to anyone yet what I know to be true: Sorcha is indeed gone. I have performed multiple divination rituals, and the result is always the same.

Somhairle will take it very hard. He has never stopped grieving for his lost sister, and I think he has always felt that they would be reunited one day. It was not to be.

Some time ago Somhairle told me that he had received word that Sorcha had a child, a baby girl named Alisa. The poor child is without a mother now, only three years old. She will never know the joy of magick, the indescribable feeling of being with the Goddess. If only Sorcha had never left us, if only she had never turned her back on her family or denied the beautiful powers given her by the Goddess. Now this poor child will never know us and will never discover the great richness of her Rowanwand heritage. I might have had a beautiful, powerful granddaughter.

Now that is never to be.

—Aoibheann

"Sorry it's so late," I said sheepishly when I called Hunter. "You weren't in bed, were you?"

"No, not for hours yet," Hunter said. "How was the circle tonight?"

I'd arrived back at Sam's just moments before, and I had immediately picked up the phone. Not only did I owe Hunter a call, but I figured that once I told Hunter I was coming home, I couldn't back out. I had to move quickly before I lost my nerve.

"It was good," I said. "Different. My grandmother, she gave me my mother's tools. The athame . . . it has a mermaid handle."

Hunter gave a low whistle. He'd heard about my dream from Morgan.

"Oh," he said. "I *see.*"

"At least I know I wasn't crazy," I said.

"I never thought you were crazy," he said matter-of-factly.

"I did," I said with a laugh. "Plenty of times. But Hunter . . . I . . ."

"Yes?"

"I know I need to come home, as soon as possible."

"That would probably be for the best," Hunter said, his voice immediately getting very calm. "The longer you wait, the more problems you may have."

"Maybe there's a bus leaving tonight," I replied, looking around the room as if I thought Sam would have a huge bus schedule on the wall.

"No, not the bus. I'll come get you," he said, in a tone that didn't suggest I had an option.

I thought of what was probably a four-hour trip each way.

"Hunter, it's far. You don't have to . . ."

"I know I don't have to. I want to. I'll leave soon. Tell me exactly where you are."

After listening to me make rambling guesses about the driving directions for about five minutes, Hunter cleared his throat and politely interrupted me. "That's all right," he said. "I'll find the best route to Gloucester on a map. The sigil will guide me from there."

"How will I know when you're coming?" I said. "Should I set an alarm?"

"No need," he said. "You'll know. The sigil will warn you."

"Hunter . . . um, thanks. For everything. For what you did the other night—for this. There was a lot I needed to deal with."

He didn't reply for a second.

"I'm pleased to help," he said, his voice softening. "And Alisa, I'm glad you found what you were looking for."

We got off soon after. There would be plenty of time for me to tell him everything on the long car ride home. I readied myself for a second call. Sam had Charlie's number in his little phone book on the counter. When he answered, I could hear music in the background. He seemed excited that I had called so soon after he dropped me off. But then he seemed to pick up on something, maybe the tone of my voice.

"Something's up," he said.

"Yeah," I said sadly.

"It's not great news," he said, "is it?"

"I have to go home. I have to go back to my family."

"When?"

"Tomorrow morning."

I heard the springs as he sat down quickly on his bed.

"Do I smell or something?" he said, trying to make his voice sound light. "Because I'll shower ..."

"I'm sorry. I'd really like to stay, but I have to go before the situation at home gets worse than it already is. My dad is really upset."

"A runaway." He sighed. "A fugitive. I fell for a dangerous type."

Fell for. Charlie had fallen for me. No one fell for me. I fell—into things, over things. I caused things to fall over. But no one had fallen for me, until now. I sank into one of the kitchen chairs, fighting the urge to call Hunter back and tell him not to come.

"But," Charlie went on, "it makes sense. You don't want to mess up your life. As much as I hate the thought of your leaving, it's better that you should go. I don't want you to end up locked in your house until you're ninety-five."

"If that happens," I replied, "you'll come and bust me out, right?"

"Of course!" he said. "But for now, I'll drive you home. I could get the day off, no problem."

I'd always thought it was a cliché, but I actually got butterflies in my stomach at the thought of being alone with Charlie in a car for four hours. But my head knew that it wasn't a great idea. "Um, well, my coven leader is going to pick me up," I said reluctantly. "Believe me, it's better that way. It'll be difficult when I get home. That's not the way I'd like you to meet my dad."

The music in the background was the only noise I heard for a minute.

"You'll be in touch," he said, "right?"

"I'll annoy you with e-mail," I said. "I promise. You'll be *so* sick of me."

"I'd better be," he said. I could hear that he had smiled as he said that. "I want full reports on the whole Hilary situation."

"Oh," I said, "don't worry about that. You'll get those. The big wedding is coming up all too soon."

Neither one of us could figure out how to get off the phone, so we talked for a few more minutes, both of us trying to sound casual. Being Charlie, he had to crack a few jokes about how he had chased me away. Being me, I had to sniffle a lot. He promised to come and visit New York as soon as he could.

Just one more gut-wrenching conversation to go.

Sam was sitting up in his bed, reading, when I knocked. He welcomed me in. His bedroom was gorgeous. Very Sam. The furniture was huge and antique, with dragonfly-patterned stained-glass lamps on either side of the bed. The cats were contentedly nuzzling each other. I sat down on his down comforter near the foot of the bed.

"I have to go home," I said, stroking Mandu as he came up and stood on my lap. "My coven leader is coming for me. He'll be here in the morning, probably pretty early."

Sam set down his book and took off his glasses.

"Tomorrow morning?" he repeated.

I nodded.

"Good luck, Alisa," he said gently, reaching over to take my hand. "I'm not going to say good-bye, because I know you'll be back. The door is always open here."

"Thanks," I said, going all misty once again. These good-byes were rough. I could see that his eyes were getting red as well. I sat there for a few moments, petting the cats, just taking in the moment with Sam.

"You're tired," he finally said, looking me in the eye. "It's time you got some sleep."

He was right. I was exhausted, but I was also too edgy to rest. Sam got up and walked me back downstairs, his arm over my shoulders. After he had securely tucked me into my bed on the couch, he put his hand to my forehead, and I felt a slow, blissful relaxation take me over. It felt like I was lying on a raft in a pool, the lulling bump of the water pushing me along inch by inch. I was asleep within seconds. I don't even remember Sam turning out the light or going back upstairs, so I have no idea how long he sat there.

I had another dream that night, but it wasn't like the one about the mermaid. I was back in the yard with my mother, walking toward the pot of flowers. Once again I looked up, but this time I could see her clearly. I saw the almond shape of her eyes, so much like mine. Her pale skin was flushed by the Texas sun.

"You did it," she said again.

Then I realized—I wasn't a toddler. It was me, just as I am now, standing across from her and holding her hands.

"You showed me," I managed to say.

She shook her head and said no more. But her smile told me everything.

Book Fourteen

SWEEP
Full Circle

Full Circle

SPEAK

Published by the Penguin Group
Penguin Group (USA) Inc., 345 Hudson Street, New York, New York 10014, U.S.A.
Penguin Group (Canada), 90 Eglinton Avenue East, Suite 700, Toronto, Ontario, Canada M4P 2Y3
(a division of Pearson Penguin Canada Inc.)
Penguin Books Ltd, 80 Strand, London WC2R 0RL, England
Penguin Ireland, 25 St Stephen's Green, Dublin 2, Ireland (a division of Penguin Books Ltd)
Penguin Group (Australia), 250 Camberwell Road, Camberwell, Victoria 3124, Australia
(a division of Pearson Australia Group Pty Ltd)
Penguin Books India Pvt Ltd, 11 Community Centre, Panchsheel Park, New Delhi - 110 017, India
Penguin Group (NZ), 67 Apollo Drive, Rosedale, Auckland 0632, New Zealand
(a division of Pearson New Zealand Ltd)
Penguin Books (South Africa) (Pty) Ltd, 24 Sturdee Avenue, Rosebank, Johannesburg 2196, South Africa

Registered Offices: Penguin Books Ltd, 80 Strand, London WC2R 0RL, England

Published by Puffin Books, a division of Penguin Young Readers Group, 2002
Published by Speak, an imprint of Penguin Group (USA) Inc., 2009
This omnibus edition published by Speak, an imprint of Penguin Group (USA) Inc., 2011

1   3   5   7   9   10   8   6   4   2

Produced by 17th Street Productions,
an Alloy company
151 West 26th Street
New York, NY 10001

17th Street Productions and associated logos
are trademarks and/or registered trademarks of Alloy, Inc.

Speak ISBN 978-0-14-241029-5
This omnibus ISBN 978-0-14-242011-9

Printed in the United States of America

To those who struggled to keep Sweep *alive*

1

Morgan

Goddess, how did I get here?

I'm barefoot on a narrow, rocky shore, and the sharp pebbles are biting into the bottoms of my feet. I stumble left and right, struggling to walk. The wind picks up, blowing hard, tangling my hair around my face so that it's almost impossible to see. The air smells faintly of brackish water, algae, and fish.

Where am I? How did I get here?

I realize that I'm afraid. I'm incredibly afraid of being here. Every cell in my body is begging to leave this beach. I could take off into the lake or head into the woods that border the water. Anything to get off this rocky shore, where I feel so vulnerable, so alone. Where am I? What lake is this? It's completely unfamiliar. I glance over at the woods, and then a dark shadow appears over me.

Cold. Black. And getting bigger.

My whole body goes rigid. Everything in me knows that this shadow means danger. Looking up, I'm shocked at how close it is, and I reflexively crouch down on the stony shore. Now I can see its source: a huge, dark-feathered hawk, flying just overhead, its vicious, golden eyes glowering. Who are you? my mind screams. What do you want with me? But the hawk has caught sight of something else.

As I watch, consumed with panic, the raptor tucks its wings to its sides and shoots down like an arrow. Ten feet above the water it swings powerful legs forward and slashes at the choppy surface with curved razor claws. A moment later it spreads its wide, dark wings and beats the air, bringing itself upward slowly at first and then with increasing speed. In its talons a large, speckled rainbow trout is twisting frantically, arching back like a bow in an attempt to drop free. As the hawk surges upward, soon to become a small spot against the sky, I see the fish's eyes go blank with death.

The fear I feel is overwhelming, even though the hawk is gone. My whole body feels shaky, numb, as though I had just avoided death myself. Without understanding it, I know the hawk was after me. Is after me.

I have to get off this beach!

I run for the trees, the pebbles flaying my feet. Soon I'm limping, stumbling, looking back over my shoulder, desperate to make the line of trees before the hawk returns. Then, just as quickly as the hawk appeared, I'm at the entrance to the woods, and I plunge into darkness. It's cooler. It takes a minute for my eyes to adjust to the shaded light. The ground is covered with pine needles, ground-hugging vines, weathered bits of leaves, all dry and crackly. I look around but can't see any kind of path, any destination. There's a fallen log nearby, and on it is a cluster of pale, spindly mushrooms sprouting up like a tiny Dr. Seuss forest. Large black ants swarm over the log, moving fast in a wavering line.

Oh, Goddess, where am I? Without knowing that, I feel so alone and scared. What woods are these? One thing is clear: I have to find my way out. I'll have to make my own path. A quick glance finds a slightly less overgrown section, and I head for it. I hold slim *branches aside as I pass through, heading deeper into the woods.*

Then I stand quiet and unmoving in the woods and realize that all of my senses are prickling. Magick. There is magick here. More than the constant low hum of energy that most blood witches pick up on and then ignore as background noise. This is magick being worked, being created, brought into being by design and effort and thought. My skin is tingling, my breathing faster.

Closing my eyes, I cast out my senses, searching for the magick's source. I concentrate, slow my heartbeat, remain perfectly still . . . there. My eyes pop open and automatically search ahead of me at eleven o'clock, north and slightly west. I ease my way through closely grown trees, step over fallen logs and thigh-high vines blocking the way. I get ever closer to that elusive, irresistible vibration, the vibration of a blood witch pulling power out of air. Now the woods' smell of humus, dry bark, fungus, and insects is overlain with crisscrossing ribbons of smoke from burning herbs. Somehow I know, without a doubt, that a powerful blood witch is working this magick, and that she is a stranger to me, and that I could learn from her. My fingers begin to itch with anticipation—what can she teach me? What can I show her of my own powers? My chest fills with both pride and uncertainty: I know I am strong, unusually strong, and have impressed witches much more educated than I. I also know that my successes are sometimes flukes—that my abilities are unpredictable because I am untrained, uninitiated.

I can feel it now, magick threading through the trees like a scent. These vibrations are strange to me—is this good magick being worked? What if it's not? But surely I would pick up on it if it's dark magick. For a moment I hesitate. What if . . . But I press on. Just ahead of me the greenish light filtering through the trees' crowns grows brighter: there's a clearing ahead. I swallow and try to press forward, crashing clumsily through the trees and bushes, slapping the vines aside. This is it—soon, soon I will see the *magick worker. Soon I will compare myself to her—she will be more trained and more knowledgeable, but I will be stronger. My throat is tight with excitement. Soon, soon, just another step . . . and then my foot catches on a tree root, throwing me off balance.*

As I feel myself falling, my muscles tense and I fling out my arms. My wrist hits something hard with a startling smack. Wild-eyed, I jerk to a sitting position, not able to make sense of what I am seeing. Did I faint? Did the witch put some kind of spell on me?

No. I was in my bedroom, at home. It was quite dark—not yet dawn, it seemed. My bed felt soft and weirdly smooth beneath me since I was expecting the crunchy edges of leaves and twigs. Blinking, I looked around. It had been a dream.

My heart was still racing. In the strange half-light of my bedroom I could still see the hawk above me, still see the glint of its razor-sharp claws as it grabbed the fish. I pushed my damp hair off my face and reassured myself that none of that was real, that everything in my room was just as I had left it the night before. Of course it was. It had just been a dream, that's all. An incredibly realistic, visceral, strong dream.

Slowly I lay back down and flipped my pillow over to the cooler side. I lay blinking up at my ceiling, then glanced at my clock. 5:27. I never wake up that early. It was Saturday. No school. I could go back to sleep for hours if I wanted to. I tried to calm down, but I still felt anxious and headachy. I closed my eyes and deliberately relaxed, willing myself to release all tension and enter into a light meditation. Very quietly I whispered, "Everything is fine and bright. Day must follow every night. My power keeps me safe from harm. The Goddess holds me in her arms."

It was a simple soothing spell, something to help me banish the leftover weirdness from my dream. It hadn't been a *nightmare,* exactly—not all of it. But strange, with some frightening parts that I could hardly remember anymore.

When I opened my eyes again, I felt better, calmer. All the same, I wasn't able to fall back asleep. Instead, I lay on my bed and watched as my room slowly filled with the ever-brightening pink glow of dawn. By six it was definitely light out, and I heard birds chattering and the sounds of the occasional car going by our house. Though my eyes drifted shut, I didn't sleep until I heard my parents get up around seven-thirty. The sounds of them going downstairs, talking softly, the rush of water as Mom filled the coffeemaker—it was the lullaby that finally eased me back to sleep. I had no more dreams and didn't reawaken for another two hours. I heard my younger sister, Mary K., turning on the shower in the bathroom we shared, and I smiled as she started singing a song that had been all over the radio lately.

Everything is fine, I told myself, stretching and yawning loudly. My family was all around me. I was safe in my bed. Later on I would see Hunter, and as usual, just the thought of my boyfriend—his short, white-blond hair, his fathomless green eyes, his intensely attractive English accent—made me shiver pleasantly. Everything was calm and normal, an incredibly nice change when I considered what the past several weeks had been like.

Everything was okay. I was Morgan Rowlands, a blood witch of the Woodbane clan. Tonight I would meet with my coven for our regular Saturday night circle. But now I was going to go downstairs and see if we had any Pop-Tarts.

2

Hunter

"Right," I said. "But why you would use the *second* form of limitations here? This spell is all about place, about where you are, where you want the spell to ignite."

My da nodded. "Aye. But what's its purpose?"

"To make a barrier that would stop something or slow it down," I replied. It was Saturday morning, and Da and I each had about an hour before we had to leave: me for my part-time job at Practical Magick, one of the few very good occult bookstores nearby, and Da for a lecture in a town two hours away. Ever since he had crafted the spell that dismantled a dark wave, he'd been in high demand as a speaker at coven meetings. Witches everywhere were eager to know how to dispel this massive threat, and Da seemed happy to teach them.

Right now, he was teaching me.

"You're right there," said Da. "But is the place in which you set the spell its most important aspect?"

"Of *course*," I said. "If you set this barrier in the wrong place, it's useless."

Da gave me his even look, the one that made me feel like I was particularly slow-witted. He was an incredibly gifted spellcrafter, and I was lucky to have the chance to learn from him. As a Seeker, I had been well trained in many areas but had gotten only the most basic training in spellcraft.

What was he was getting at? I waited, telling myself to stay calm, not to get my hackles up. It wasn't easy: Da and I had had a lot to argue about in the past few months.

"What level of a starr is this?" Da asked, flipping through his Book of Shadows, hardly paying attention.

"What level? This is a . . . a . . . ." Oh, *bloody hell!* my brain screamed, recognizing too late the trap I had fallen into. Damn! I *hate* it when I do something stupid. Especially, most especially, in front of my father. I tried to keep burning embarrassment from reddening my face. I had two conflicting feelings: humiliation, over making a mistake in front of my father, and annoyance, about the lecture I knew I was about to receive.

But to my surprise he said, "It's not easy, lad. You could study spellcraft for years and still make mistakes like that. And who knows? There could conceivably be a situation where the exact location of a starr *is* more important than its strength."

I nodded, surprised at this unprecedented display of mercy. "Mum was a great spellcrafter, wasn't she?" I asked the question gently, still feeling the pain myself and knowing how heavily my mother's death, only four months before, had affected my father.

Da's eyes instantly narrowed, as if he had suddenly stepped into sunlight. I saw his jaw muscles tighten, then relax. "Yes," he said, sounding older than he had a moment ago. "She was that." A wistful half smile crossed his face for a moment. "Watching your mother craft spells was like watching a master wood-carver cut complicated figures out of a simple block of wood. It was an amazing thing. My parents and teachers taught me the Woodbane basics when I was a lad, but it was your mother, with her thousand-year Wyndenkell heritage, who taught me the beauty of pure spellcraft."

"I would like to become a master spellcrafter someday," I said. "Like Mum."

Da gave me one of his rare smiles, and it transformed his thin, ravaged face into that of the father I had known so long ago. "That would be a worthy gift, son," he said. "But you have a lot of work ahead of you."

"I know," I said, sighing. I glanced over at the clock and saw that I had about half an hour till I had to leave. It would be midafternoon in England. I had a phone call to make. "Ah, I think I'll ring Kennet now, while I have the chance," I said offhandedly.

The truth was, I was dreading this phone call. A few weeks ago, following our battle with the dark wave, I had decided that I was quitting my position as a Seeker for the International Council of Witches. At seventeen I had become the youngest Seeker in history, and for a time I'd had complete faith in the ICOW's judgment. I had taken great pride in my work, in making the world a safer place for good witches. But that was before the council had failed me in several key areas: neglecting to tell me that they'd found my parents, for one, a decision that resulted in my mum dying before I had the chance to see her and say good-bye. Also, they had failed to warn Morgan and me that her father, Ciaran MacEwan, the leader of a dark coven called Amyranth, had escaped from captivity and might be coming to Widow's Vale to harm us (or to send the dark wave after us, as turned out to be the case).

Da was quiet for a moment. I knew he had his reservations about my quitting the council, but I also knew that I couldn't continue serving a system I no longer trusted. Kennet Muir had once been my mentor and my friend, but he wasn't any longer as far as I was concerned. "Are you quite sure?" Da asked.

"Yes."

"It's not too late to change your mind, you know," he said. "Working at Practical Magick is fine for now, but in the long run, you'll be hurting for a career with more fulfillment. Even if you no longer want to be a Seeker, surely you could find something to challenge you a bit more. I just hope you've thought this through."

"I know, Da. And I have. I just need some time to figure out what the right new career is." Nobody was more frustrated by my lack of direction than I, but you can't spend years dedicated to being a good Seeker and then find something just as fulfilling overnight.

"Perhaps I could help you," Da said, organizing the books we had been using for reference into a clean stack. "I do speak to a wide variety of witches in my spellcrafting lectures. Perhaps one of them . . ."

"No, Da." I shook my head and tried to give him a reassuring smile. "I'll be fine. I just need some time."

He looked like he wanted to say more, but then he nodded and headed to the kitchen. I heard the tap turn on and the sound of water filling the kettle. I fetched Kennet's number and dialed it quickly, before I lost my nerve, even though

I knew it was going to cost a fortune, calling England in the middle of the day. After five rings Kennet's voice-mail system picked up. I grimaced and left a brief message, giving him my mobile number and the number at Practical Magick.

Soon Da headed off to his lecture, not sure if he would be back that night, and I set off for Practical Magick. It was in Red Kill, about twenty minutes north of Widow's Vale, the town in midstate New York where I lived. As I drove, I thought about what Da had said. It was funny. For the last eleven years of my life I'd had no father. Now, at the age of nineteen, I had to get used to having a da to take an interest in me. But he was right about one thing: I did need a new life plan. All around me everyone had a purpose, goals—except me.

The doorbell jingled lightly when I entered Practical Magick. Its owner, Alyce Fernbrake, smiled a greeting at me as she rang up a purchase for a customer. I smiled and waved, then headed through a new doorway that had been cut into the right-hand wall of the store. The room next door was divided in two: a larger room that would stock store items and books, and a smaller room in back that people would be able to use privately. It was in this room that I worked, imbuing objects with low-level magickal properties.

For example, I might spell a small bottle of evening primrose oil so that it would be even more effective in easing menstrual cramps. Or I might spell different candles to increase their individual auras, make them more effective in rites or meditation. Alyce kept a small supply of spelled objects in a locked cupboard in the back room, to be bought and used only by witches she trusted. They didn't have to be blood witches, but she had to know them and be sure these things would be used only in the way they were intended.

For the first couple of days this had been amusing, even relaxing work. It allowed me to trot out all my basic second-year spells, brush up on my technique, my focus, and in general stay in tune with magickal energy. But now I was growing bored and restless. I still enjoyed being at Practical Magick, working with Alyce, but the repetition, the predictability of this job was starting to make me impatient. Da was right—I needed to find a vocation that would challenge me.

I was putting a light worry-not spell on a pale blue candle when my mobile rang, making me jump. I yanked it out of my pocket, then checked the number. It was Kennet, calling me back. I took a deep breath and answered it.

"Kennet. Thanks for calling me back."

"Hunter, how are you? No problems there, I hope?"

Not in the last week, I thought. It seemed that ever since I'd come to Widow's Vale, my life had been a roller coaster of huge events—not the least of which was meeting Morgan Rowlands, who's—well, she's more than my girlfriend. She's my *mùirn beatha dàn*—my soul mate.

I decided to dive right in. "Kennet—you've had trust in me and put enormous effort into my training, and I've always appreciated it. I hope I've never let you down." *Like you've let me down,* I added silently.

"Why do I feel you're about to?" he asked.

I took another breath. "I've decided to leave the council," I said. "I can't be a Seeker anymore."

There was silence on his end. I waited.

"I know you've been growing more and more dissatisfied, Gìomanach," he said, using my coven name. "And I know you were very upset at how the council handled telling you about your parents."

To put it mildly. Just thinking about it made my body tense. "Certainly that's part of it," I said, feeling anger rise up in my chest. "But there have been other problems, Kennet, other disappointments." I let my words hang there in the air for a moment. "The truth is, I feel I can't continue with the council in good faith. Not when I don't believe in it."

More silence. "Gìomanach, you know it's almost unheard of for *anyone* to quit the council, especially a Seeker." His voice was soft, but I sensed some anger behind his words.

"I know," I said. "But I have no choice. So I'm telling you officially—I'm leaving. I can't accept any more assignments. I'm sorry."

"How about a leave of absence?" Kennet asked carefully. "I could certainly okay that."

"No."

"Gìomanach," Kennet said with more authority, "this seems an extreme reaction. Surely it doesn't have to be all or nothing. Would you prefer a different assignment? Or to go to a different place? Perhaps your compensation—"

"No," I said. "It really isn't about any of that. It's just—the council itself."

"Would you like me to come there, to talk to you? Perhaps the two of us could come up with a more moderate decision."

"You can come if you'd like, but I don't feel it would change things," I said.

Kennet sighed. "I would be remiss not to tell you that this is not a wise move politically. I have no idea what the council's reaction will be, but I can't imagine that it will be positive."

"I understand," I said. Bugger the council and their reaction. My back ached with tension.

"As your adviser, I must caution you that you have surely made enemies during your time as a Seeker. The council will no longer be able to offer you protection should any of these people seek revenge."

I considered his words. It was true that making enemies was part of being a Seeker. Witches themselves, their friends and families—hardly anyone was glad when a Seeker came to call. But what kind of protection was the council able to provide? The council leaders were at odds with one another, working at cross-purposes. The council kept bungling things, kept making the easiest decision instead of the best one. I shook my head silently. There was no way I could rely on their protection anymore, anyway.

"I'll take my chances," I told Kennet.

"Gìomanach, as your mentor, I'm asking you to reconsider," he said cajolingly. "You are my protégé, the youngest Seeker the council has ever had. Please tell me you'll at least think more about this decision."

"No, Kennet," I said. "This is my final answer. I can no longer take part in what the council has become." It was very difficult for me, having to say this. In his day, before the council had started to slip out of hand, Kennet really had been an excellent mentor. I had relied on him a great deal during my first months as a Seeker. But things were different now.

"I can't tell you how disappointing this is to me personally, as it will be to the rest of the council," he said, the warmth in his voice leaching away. He didn't sound angry now so much as regretful and hurt.

"I realize that. But I know this is the right thing for me to do."

"I hope you'll give this further thought," he said, sounding stiff.

"Good-bye, Kennet."

Click. I looked at the phone in wonder. He'd hung up without saying good-bye. I hung up and pressed my eyes with the heels of my hands, trying to dispel tension. The conversation had been difficult—every bit as difficult as I'd feared, perhaps worse. But it was done. I had quit the council. I rolled my shoulders, feeling like a huge weight had been removed. I felt relieved but also frightened: I wasn't trained to do anything else.

Automatically I picked up my phone and rang Morgan. She'd been through the whole decision-making process with me. I knew talking to her now would definitely help. Talking to her always helped.

"Hello?" Not Morgan.

"Hi, Mrs. Rowlands," I said to Morgan's mother. "It's Hunter. Is Morgan there, please?"

"I'm sorry, Hunter—Morgan's taken her sister to a friend's house. Can I have her call you?"

"Yes, thanks—or I can catch her later. Good-bye, Mrs. Rowlands."

"Bye, Hunter."

I hung up and sighed. No immediate Morgan. I rubbed the back of my neck and settled down again, this time to gift some dried lavender with extra soothing properties.

"Hunter?"

I looked up to see Alyce, followed by two middle-aged women. One looked slightly older than the other, I'd guess in her late fifties. She was lean and muscled like a former dancer, with crisp silver hair cut in a simple style that just skimmed her jawline. She was wearing off-white canvas pants, loose but not sloppy, a trim T-shirt, and an unconstructed canvas jacket over that. Everything about her showed confidence, maturity, self-control, an acceptance of self.

The younger woman was a striking contrast. She was perhaps in her early forties but as surrounded by layers of agitation as the first seemed pared down to the essentials. Her layered, wispy skirt and top flowed around her in batiked shades of olive green and soft brown. She was slightly plump. Her heavy makeup was almost like icing.

Without thinking, I cast out my senses: Alyce was curious but not disturbed. The two women were blood witches. From them I got uncertainty, mistrust, even an edge of fear.

"Hunter, these women were asking for you," Alyce supplied. She turned to them and gestured to me. "Celia and Robin, this is Hunter Niall."

The two women exchanged glances, and then, as if making a decision, the older woman nodded. "Thank you, Alyce," she said. It was a gentle dismissal, and Alyce raised her eyebrows at me when they couldn't see her, then left.

I took a moment to examine them with ingrained Seeker thoroughness. They both had relatively weak energy patterns—they were blood witches, but not powerhouses.

The older woman stepped forward. "I'm Celia Evans," she said in a smooth, modulated voice. She held out her hand, and I rose to shake it. Her grip was firm but not aggressive. "And this is Robin Goodacre." She gestured to her companion, who then stepped forward. Where Celia projected calm and confidence, Robin projected a fluttery distraction that I instinctively felt came from insecurity, or nonacceptance of herself.

I shook Robin's hand. "Hello," she said, in a nervous, breathless voice. I wondered what her relationship was to Celia.

"Hello," I said. There were a couple of unmatched chairs in the corner, and I pulled them over, then sat down again at my table. I gestured for the two women to sit, and they did. "Can I help you with something?"

"Well, we've heard about you as a . . . uh . . ." Robin began, then seemed to get stymied by self-consciousness.

Celia took over. "We've come to see you because we've heard that you're—experienced with good magick and with . . . dark magick."

Hmmm. I nodded and waited for her to go on.

"Like the dark wave, for instance," Celia continued, beginning to seem slightly uncomfortable. "Or perhaps other kinds of dark magick."

Oh. Of course. "You need a Seeker?" I asked, and Robin visibly pulled back.

Celia looked alarmed. "We need . . . someone to help us. Someone who would recognize what might be dark magick. And maybe know what to do about it."

"Well, I'm sorry, but I no longer work for the council. I could put you in touch with someone, though."

"Actually," Celia said slowly, "we hadn't realized you were a Seeker. We wouldn't have come if we'd known. It's much better for us that you're *not* a Seeker, not part of the council.

Honestly, we need help, and we don't know where to find it."

Robin's plump hands fluttered around her skirt, playing with its folds. "It has to be the right kind of help," she said earnestly. "We can't make matters worse. But we don't know what to do." She twisted her hands together, her chunky rings clicking. "We heard you had experience with all kinds of things. We heard . . . you could be trusted."

That was interesting. I looked from Robin's round, earnest face, the distress in her brown eyes, to Celia's barely concealed tension.

"Can I ask who referred you to me?"

"Joanna Silversmith," said Celia. "Of Knotworthy. We went to school together."

Her name sounded familiar, but I didn't think I knew her personally. Knotworthy was a coven back in England, so maybe I had run across her there.

"Can you tell me a few more specifics about your problem?" I asked gently. "Then if I can't help you, maybe I'll know someone who can."

"It's our coven leader," Celia said, and took a deep breath. "We think she may be involved with dark magick."

3

Morgan

As I had done hundreds of times before, I parked my beloved Valiant, Das Boot, at the curb by my best friend Bree Warren's house and walked up the stone path to the double front doors. I rang the bell, and the door was opened almost instantly by Thalia Cutter, one of the other coven members. Our coven, Kithic, had the ideal number of members, thirteen: our leader and my boyfriend, Hunter Niall, Bree, Robbie Gurevitch, Sharon Goodfine, Ethan Sharp, Simon Bakehouse, Thalia, Jenna Ruiz, Raven Meltzer, Alisa Soto (our youngest member), Hunter's cousin, Sky, who was in England right now, Matt Adler, and me. I had known most of these people my whole life. Bree and Robbie had been my best friends since first grade. Sharon, Jenna, Matt, Ethan, and Alisa all went to my high school. Thalia and Simon went to the other high school in town.

"Hi," said Thalia. Her long, wavy hair hung almost to her waist, and her oval face was smooth and serene. "Come on in. Bree's in the kitchen. We're setting up in the pool house."

"Okay." From experience we'd found that at Bree's, the slate patio in her pool's enclosure was best for channeling energy. I headed for the kitchen and passed Ethan carrying a tall pillar candle. Bree called after him, "Wait—take a paper plate to put it on. If we get wax on the slate, we'll never get it off."

Ethan took the plate from her, smiled a greeting at me, and went out.

"Hi," I called, walking into the Warrens' huge kitchen. Bree, looking beautiful as usual, was arranging some cut fruit on a plate. Her fine, mink-dark hair had grown out a bit and fell in feathery layers past her shoulders. I sighed. It wasn't easy being best friends with someone who looked like a model. We're talking high cheekbones, fabulous body, the works. Always impossibly, sophisticatedly hip, she was wearing an Indian-print cotton skirt that hung several inches below her belly button and a white peasant top that showed perfect, ivory skin both above and below.

I tried not to look down at my own lame ensemble of jeans and T-shirt. I was just about to start feeling bummed when I remembered Hunter—incredibly hot and irresistible Hunter—and the fact that he didn't seem able to keep his hands off me.

"Look—Bree's making food from scratch," said Robbie, cutting up fresh pineapple at one end of the Corian counter.

"Oh, so *witty*," said Bree, but she smiled at him, and he smiled back. It was obvious how strongly they felt about each other. She went back to artistically placing strawberries on the platter.

"That looks great," I said, inhaling the tropical scent of pineapple, heavy in the air. Now that spring had finally sprung, I was relishing the lighter clothes, the warmer weather, the longer days. It had been a long, dark winter, in more ways than one. I was looking forward to being in the light again.

"Hi," said Alisa, entering the kitchen. Her wavy, caramel-streaked hair was pulled back off her face, emphasizing her huge dark eyes. "Can I help with anything?"

"Thanks, I think we're about ready," Bree said. "As soon as everyone's here, we can start."

Alisa and I trailed out of the kitchen. We'd had kind of an up-and-down relationship in the months since Kithic had formed. Things had been difficult for Alisa lately. She had recently found out that she was half blood witch on her mother's side, which had really freaked her out. A few weeks ago she'd run away, partly to find her late mother's family in Gloucester, a family of full blood witches. The trip had wreaked havoc on her home life—her dad had had a fit—but in some way it seemed that she had found what she was looking for. These days she seemed happier, more centered. I don't know whether she was doing dances of joy over being a blood witch, but she seemed to have accepted it.

"How's it going?" I asked her in the hallway. The last circle that Alisa had attended had been a little strange. She had been stressed out, and since she had trouble controlling her powers, that stress had made all of the faucets in Hunter's house spew uncontrollably. Eventually his house had practically flooded. She had been really upset.

"Not too bad," she said. "Things are a tiny bit better at home—Hilary's stopped barfing, so that's good. And get this—she's quit calling me the flower girl. I'm now a real bridesmaid."

"Way to go," I said, and we both grinned. Her father was marrying his pregnant girlfriend soon. Hilary was only about ten years older than Alisa, and they'd had a really rocky start. But it sounded like her stepmother-to-be was getting more sensitive.

"At least she's trying," Alisa said, "and I've been trying, too. Not that it's easy. But she agreed to alter my dress so I won't have that huge bow across my butt anymore."

"Excellent," I said. We'd stopped beneath a weird abstract oil painting right outside Mr. Warren's home office. "What about your room?"

"Dad's buying me a new bed for my new room," Alisa reported. Hilary had made her move out of her old room so she could be closer to the baby. "Oh, you know, Dad said I could invite a guest to the wedding."

"Hmmm, like Charlie of Gloucester?" I said, raising my eyebrows suggestively. Alisa smiled and looked a little embarrassed. One of the people Alisa had met in Gloucester was Charlie, a member of her mother's family's coven and a cute, funny, attractive blood witch. He and Alisa kept up through e-mail.

"No," Alisa whispered. "I'm sure Charlie wouldn't be able to come all this way. But I want Mary K. to come—I've called her twice, but she's never home."

And she obviously hadn't returned Alisa's calls. My sister was still pretty uncomfortable with the whole Wicca/blood witch thing, though she seemed to have accepted it as far as I was concerned. Maybe finding out that her best friend was some kind of weird, witchy creature, in addition to her sister, was just too much for her. Mary K.'d been really upset when Alisa had discovered her heritage. I hoped she wouldn't give up on their friendship.

"She's been seeing Mark Chambers a lot lately," I said neutrally. "But I'll remind her."

"Thanks."

Matt passed us on the way to the pool house and said hey, and then Raven stomped down the hallway in her Doc Martens. She was wearing a vintage rayon dress with huge gaps held together by safety pins. This, her cornrowed black hair, and her clunky shoes added up to a picture that was totally Raven.

Then the back of my neck tingled, and a whole cascade of responses, emotional and physical, burst through me like sparks. My head was already swiveling as Hunter said, "Morgan?"

He was standing at the foyer entrance to the hall. Alisa melted away toward the pool, and I tried not to run and fling myself into Hunter's arms. I'd spoken to him just before dinner, and he'd told me that he'd finally truly quit the council. I was dying to talk to him. Among other things.

"Hi," I said, walking toward him, admiring my incredible self-restraint. He came to meet me halfway, and then my restraint broke loose. I put my arms around him, backed down the hallway, and drew him into Mr. Warren's office. With the door shut behind us, I let my huge, goofy smile show. He drew me closer, smiling also, and then he bent down and I went on tiptoe to meet his kiss. I pressed closer to him, molding myself against his lean body, feeling the strength of his arms as he held me tightly. My hand reached up to touch the short, light blond hair at the back of his neck, and my fingers traced the smoothness of the skin there. Hunter. Everything about him spoke to me. The timbre of his voice, the scent of his skin, the depth of his green eyes. The way his jaw tight-ened and his eyes narrowed when he was angry. The sound of his breathing when we were making out on his bed. The pressure of his hand as he splayed his fingers across my back, urging me closer. His quirky, dry sense of humor. His incredi-ble intelligence. His strong and controlled magick. I admired and respected him. I felt incredibly tender love and incredibly strong desire for him. I trusted him implicitly. I shivered as Hunter pushed his knee between my legs. I coiled one leg around his as we kept kissing each other over and over, as if we'd been separated for a year instead of a day. I wanted to drink him in, imprint him on my skin, be warmed by his touch.

Eventually we slowed and came up for air. My lips felt swollen, and I was breathing hard. Hunter's eyes glittered down at me.

"Well, hello to you, too," he said in his soft English accent. "Did you miss me?"

I grinned and nodded slowly. "Just a little. But enough about me. Tell me everything that happened with Kennet."

Hunter shook his head and let out a breath. "I told him I was quitting. He said witches don't quit the council. I said I did. He asked if I'd consider it a leave of absence. I said I quit. He said I would no longer have the council's protec-tion and that I had made a lot of enemies, being a Seeker."

"Nice," I said with a grimace. "Glad he was so under-standing and supportive."

He shrugged. "He wasn't bad, really. I suppose he didn't know what to do."

I stood close to him and rested my head against his chest. I heard the strong, steady beat of his heart. "I'm sorry," I said. "But how do you feel about it? Are you glad you did it?"

"I don't think I should reconsider," Hunter said, stroking my back. "I gave quitting a lot of thought. I know it's right for me."

I leaned up and kissed his cheek. "We should probably get back to the others, but if you want to talk about this more later, we should, okay?" I asked.

He nodded, his chin against the top of my head. His fingers trailed smoothly down my shirt.

"Where's Morgan?" I heard Sharon say out in the hall. "Didn't you say she was here? Isn't Hunter coming?"

We waited until the hallway was quiet, then slipped out. I ducked into the powder room, and Hunter headed to the pool house as if he'd just gotten here. Quickly I splashed water on my face, seeing the flush of Hunter's kisses there. Then I pushed my brown hair off my shoulders and went to join the others.

"Welcome, everyone," Hunter was saying as I walked out onto the enclosed patio that surrounded Bree's pool. Dim stars shone overherad through the tinted glass ceiling, and Bree, with her usual flair, had arranged perhaps fifty pillar candles of various heights all along one edge of the pool. Their flames were reflected in the dark water and provided our only light. The effect was beautiful and mysterious.

Several people turned to greet me silently, and I smiled and nodded, then took a place between Jenna and Raven.

"Bree, thanks for hosting," Hunter said. "It's always nice to be here."

"No problem," said Bree.

"Now, before we cast our circle tonight, does anyone have any announcements or questions?" Hunter asked. "Where are we meeting next time?"

"It can be at my house," Simon offered.

"Right, cheers," said Hunter. "Since we're coming up on Beltane, the next official circle won't be for a while. But in the meantime, we have one of our most festive celebrations to look forward to. Have you guys read about it?"

"Yes," said Thalia. "It's a fire festival, and with Samhain, it's one of the most important Sabbats."

"Right," said Hunter. "Like Samhain, Beltane takes place when the veils between the worlds are the thinnest. At Samhain we celebrate and honor death and endings, the closing of a circle, the end of a cycle. Beltane, the last of all the spring fertility festivals, is all about birth, new beginnings, life. Traditionally people make bonfires, have maypoles, and celebrate all night. It's when the Goddess, ripe with fertility after the long winter, joins again with the God, who has now grown into manhood."

There were a few somewhat embarrassed giggles at this, and Hunter acknowledged them with a grin. "This is when the Goddess conceives the next God and so propagates the life cycle once again. Does anyone know the symbols of Beltane?"

I did, but I didn't say anything. My covenmates knew that Hunter and I were going out. I usually stayed pretty quiet at circles—I didn't want to be seen as the teacher's pet. When Hunter was in Canada and Bethany Malone had led our circles, I had been more outspoken.

"The maypole," said Robbie, and Bree raised her eyebrows suggestively, making people laugh.

"Doesn't it have some of the same symbols as Ostara?" asked Sharon. "Like bunnies and eggs?"

Hunter nodded. "Symbols of fertility."

"I read where people actually have sex outside, to bless their fields or their animals," Raven said.

Hunter laughed. "Well, that's one tradition we don't have to feel obliged to perform."

I saw Bree and Robbie exchange glances, Sharon and Ethan making faces at each other, Jenna and Simon smiling quietly and looking at their feet. Jeez, had all of them already done it? Was I the only seventeen-year-old virgin left in Widow's Vale? Hunter and I had planned to make love a couple of times, but something had always happened to keep us from going through with it. Now we both knew that we were ready—we were just waiting for the time to be right. I hoped it would be right very soon.

"Before our next circle," Hunter went on, "I'd like all of you to do some more reading about Beltane." He listed some useful sources, then said, "Now, if there's nothing else, we can cast our circle."

We stepped forward. Hunter quickly and expertly drew a perfect circle on the slates with a piece of chalk. We went in through the opening he'd left in it, and then he closed it behind us. We'd set up four bowls, one each at east, north, west, and south. They held dirt, to symbolize earth, a smoldering incense cone to symbolize air, a candle for fire, and water. With the four elements represented, our energy would be balanced.

The twelve of us joined hands, and Hunter said, "I invoke the Goddess. I invoke the God. I invite them to join us at this our circle. Tonight we celebrate being together, being at the threshold of spring. As we raise the Goddess's energy, we'll think about our own renewals, rebirths. Now, everyone can join in when they're ready." We began to move our circle deasil, or clockwise, as Hunter began singing a familiar power chant.

One by one we blended our voices with his, letting the words weave together. I waited for just a few moments, and then it happened, as it always did: I felt a burst of happiness, of joy. I knew who I was, I knew what I was doing. I was joining my energy with that of others, and it was an incredible experience.

As we moved more quickly, our feet keeping pace with the complex, ancient rhythm, I gradually began to be aware of another thread of sound underneath the one we were singing. It was inside my head, coming from within, and I followed it like a colored string, trying to untangle it. It was elusive, not complete, and I couldn't seem to get closer to it. Sometimes it seemed vaguely familiar, but I just couldn't place where I'd ever heard it. Still, I moved with the others in a circle, one part of my mind focused on the thread. Vague images came to me: when my half brother Killian had used a hawk's true name to force it to earth and also, weirdly, when my biological father, Ciaran MacEwan, had initiated me into the racking pains and heady pleasures of shape-shifting. But these thoughts drifted away like clouds, and soon my mind was full of the excitement of our raised energy. My heart felt both full and light, my vision seemed exceptionally clear—I could see the faint, colorful auras shimmering around my friends' heads. Being part of a circle was like plugging myself into a higher consciousness, a higher reality. It was completely fulfilling.

Our pace quickened, and our chanting swelled to bursting.

Our joined energy rose and crested, and at the peak of its crescendo we flung our hands apart and stopped where we were. Smiles on our faces, our hands floating downward, we looked around to enjoy the looks of transport on one another's faces.

My gaze locked on Hunter, on his angular, fair-skinned face, his sharp cheekbones, the amazing depth of his eyes. His cheeks were flushed with a pale pink, like dawn breaking. His eyes met mine, and between us there flashed an instant understanding, an immediate message of love sent and received. I smiled, and he returned it.

"That was a great circle, everyone," he said, assuming his leadership role again. "I can see a definite improvement in your focus and concentration."

I remembered the elusive tune and the strange images I'd seen in the circle. Why had I thought of shape-shifting again? Was the Goddess trying to tell me something? Or was it just that now that we were out of immediate danger, my mind was really beginning to deal with those images? Probably the latter, I decided. There had been no new or scary information in the images.

"I've got some food and stuff in the kitchen," Bree said, brushing her fine hair off her face. "Robbie and I will get it."

Hunter drifted over to me as they left, and automatically our arms went around each other's waist. He kissed the top of my head, and I shivered. All thoughts of the elusive tune I'd heard had disappeared. I'd meant to mention the strange dream I'd had to Hunter but decided not to. Everyone has weird dreams sometimes.

4

Hunter

"What about here?" I asked. "No rocks, a mixture of sun and shade, nice view." The picnic basket was starting to feel heavy—I was ready to sit and eat and lie in the sun.

"This looks good," Morgan agreed, nodding.

"Okay by me," said Robbie.

For a moment it looked like Bree might object, but then she followed majority rule. She and Morgan unfolded an old blanket and shook it out.

"Goddess, what a beautiful day," Morgan said, immediately lying down on the blanket in a way that made me wish Robbie and Bree weren't there. I wanted to touch her, feel the smooth skin of her stomach. Well, nothing I could do about it yet.

By unspoken agreement the four of us ended up on our backs, looking up at the intensely blue spring sky and the puffy white clouds slipping past.

"This is great," Robbie said.

"Mmm," Bree murmured in agreement. "Oh, Morgan, did

I tell you? That B and B on Martha's Vineyard worked out."

"Hey, great," Morgan said. "When are you guys going?"

"The end of June," Robbie said. "Just for a week. I don't think I'll be able to get more time off from the shop." Robbie had gotten a summer job at Widow's Vale's tiny used-book store.

Using my lightning-fast former Seeker intuition, I deduced that Bree and Robbie were going to Martha's Vineyard together for a week later in the summer. A quiet envy settled across me. I would *kill* to have that kind of time alone with Morgan. Sometimes I wished her father were more like Bree's father—rather absent and not entirely aware of what she did. I knew that Morgan's intensely caring and involved parents were, in general, a much better thing. But sometimes . . .

"That sounds so great," Morgan said. "I'm probably going to be working at my mom's office all summer. Data entry, filing, et cetera. Making coffee. Yawn." Her mom was a real estate agent, and I knew Morgan often worked for her when she needed money.

"At least you'll be in air-conditioning," Bree pointed out. "Which reminds me—speaking of being chilly—I was reading about Beltane online this morning, and it seems that many covens feel the Beltane rites are best done skyclad. Like the fertility rites, the dances. The maypole."

"Skyclad?" Robbie asked. "What does that—*oh.*"

Bree giggled and crossed one of her legs over Robbie's.

"I'm so sure," Morgan said, rolling her eyes. "Count me out."

Trying not to laugh, I said, "I don't know, Morgan. I believe that if we're going to be historically accurate, Kithic should celebrate Beltane authentically. I imagine it would be all right if not *everyone* has sex under the moon, but the nudity . . . pfaw!" I stopped to spit some grass, which Morgan had been flinging at me, out of my mouth and held up my hands to ward off any further attacks.

"Very funny," said Morgan, throwing more grass. I half sat up to brush it off and saw that her face was flushed with self-consciousness. I grinned at her. In public she was fairly reserved, and she certainly didn't dress to show off her body. But in private . . . we had been together enough for me to know that her physical desire and innate sensuality ran as strong in her as her magickal powers did. And I had been the lucky recipient of those feelings. I hoped that soon we would be ready to take those feelings to their natural conclusion.

"Right, then," I said, lying back down and grabbing Morgan's hand. I held her hand on my chest and felt her relax against me, her foot resting against my ankle. "So I'll go ahead and inform the coven that nudity and public sex are optional."

Robbie snorted with laughter, and Bree told him, "You can strip down first."

I was happy, lying there in the sun and dappled shade. It felt normal, natural, light. I hoped that the rest of the year would be more like this and that the darkness we'd been facing had finally gone for good.

After a while we sat up and ate our sandwiches. Everything tasted better because we were outside in the cool spring sun and we were together. I lay on my back with Morgan and her friends and watched the clouds. I couldn't remember the last time I'd felt this calm.

Not long after that, Bree and Robbie took their leave to make a foreign-film matinee in Taunton. Bree left the dessert with us, and soon we heard the distinctive sound of her BMW driving off. Leaving me alone with Morgan at last.

I turned on my side and gathered her to me, pushing her down on the blanket with my weight, feeling her slenderness beneath me, her leg automatically bending to curve around mine. Her arms came around me and I began kissing her all over, touching her everywhere. I felt intensely alive, curious, excited about our future. My body responded to hers so strongly that I knew if we waited much longer to make love, both of us would lose our minds. It wasn't until I felt her hand on mine that I realized I was at her waist and I had undone the button on her jeans.

Feeling foggy, I blinked and looked at her flushed face. I looked down at my hand and at her hand holding it. She smiled at me with slow amusement.

"Right here? Wouldn't we scare the chipmunks?"

I was too far gone to make a coherent response right away. Everything in me was telling me to charge ahead, and the fact that we had stopped and she was talking was taking a while to imprint on my lust-clouded brain.

"Mommy, what are those huge ugly animals doing?" Morgan said in a high, squeaky chipmunk voice. "Don't look, sweetie," she answered in a concerned mother chipmunk voice. "Just go back in the tree."

For a moment I just stared at her, then I started laughing hard. Morgan grinned at me while I guffawed, and it was only with effort that I got my wits about me. Leaning down, I kissed her on the nose. "You are incredibly odd," I said tenderly. "Really, incredibly odd. I'm sure that's the first time in the history of human sexuality that someone has imitated a chipmunk as part of foreplay."

We laughed together then, sitting up and holding on to each other, cackling like maniacs. She rebuttoned her jeans, and when we lay back down again, it was just to cuddle and talk. In the back of my mind I remembered my upcoming meeting with Celia Evans and Robin Goodacre. All they'd told me was that they were concerned about their coven leader possibly working dark magick. They weren't sure what to do but needed help in deciding if there was anything they *could* do. Later tonight we were going to meet again, and they'd promised to give me the whole story.

I had wanted to talk to Morgan about them, get her impressions on what she thought might be going on. But I didn't have their permission to talk to anyone, and while I would have felt all right about telling another Wiccan "professional," like my da, telling Morgan seemed like a breach of confidence.

"What are you going to do this summer?" Morgan asked me, snuggling close, and I heard the wistfulness in her voice. She was thinking of Bree and Robbie's trip, no doubt.

"Well, I'm hoping to earn enough money to go home for a while," I told her honestly. "I want to see everyone, eat some decent fish and chips, fill up on England." She was quiet, playing thoughtfully with one of my shirt buttons, and I went on. "Is there any way you could go with me? What about if you promise to visit historical sites and write a report?"

She smiled, looking sad. "I'll ask my parents, but don't hold your breath."

I cuddled her closer again. We both knew, without saying it, that there was no way her parents would let her go to Europe with a guy. Not when she was only seventeen. I nuzzled her beneath one ear and felt her shiver. "We need time alone." Morgan nodded. "Then maybe we could get around to certain things we've been thinking about," I said meaningfully. Her hazel eyes, the color of stones seen through clear water, brightened with amusement, and she gave an instinctive wiggle against me. I kissed her gently, not wanting us to get all worked up again. Soon we were lying still again, our arms around each other, looking up at the sky.

As my eyes drifted lazily closed, I heard an odd cry above me. My eyes fluttered open and my gaze fastened on a red-tailed hawk, shooting groundward incredibly fast. It dropped below the level of the trees but almost instantly shot upward, each strong beat of its powerful wings taking it farther into the sky. In its talons was a writhing black snake.

"Lunch," I said, admiring the bird's almost perfect predatory ability. I looked down to see Morgan frowning.

"That's weird," she said, squinting to watch the bird disappear high above us.

"Why? Hawks hunt all the time. This place is full of red-tailed hawks." I stroked her hair, loving the way the sunlight played across it.

"Yeah, I guess," Morgan said slowly. "It's nothing."

"I have to tell you," I said, gently easing her head up onto my shoulder, "I'm not thrilled about working at Practical Magick."

"No?"

I shook my head. "I know I can't be a Seeker anymore, but putting little spells on herbs isn't my life's calling, either. If only—it would be so great if the council weren't the only show in town."

"What do you mean?" Morgan asked, rolling over on her side and tucking one arm under her head so she could look at me.

"Well, if there were an alternate council, say," I said. "One that held more closely to the Wiccan Rede."

Morgan was quiet for a moment, and I wondered if she understood what I was feeling. "Maybe you should start your own council," she said.

I laughed, then saw that she looked solemn and thoughtful. "You're not serious." The idea of me creating a whole new council, single-handedly, was laughable. "Are you?"

"How serious are *you?*" she asked me, and I had no answer.

I was almost out the front door that evening when the phone rang. I debated not answering it—I had only ten minutes to get to the coffee shop where I was meeting Celia and Robin—but then I picked up on the fact that it was Sky calling. I lunged for the phone.

"Hello-ello," I said, and she snorted. "How's jolly olde England?"

"Still repressed as ever," Sky said dryly. "Even English witches are more restrained than American ones."

"You say that like it's a bad thing," I said, and she allowed herself an amused heh-heh.

"I guess it *is* a bit of a relief not to have everyone's emotions hanging out all over," she said. "On the other hand, Americans seem simpler to deal with. They say what they feel or think, and you never have to guess what's going on behind the silence."

I thought for a moment, and it came to me. "How's Uncle Beck?"

Sky sighed loudly into the phone, which told me I'd hit my mark. As light and beautiful and loving as my mum had been, her brother, Beck, Sky's father, was dark and hard hewn and almost forcefully introverted. He'd raised me, my younger brother, Linden, and my sister, Alwyn, from the time I was eight, and though I'd always felt physically safe and taken care of, I'd also always felt wary, distanced, and on thin ice emotionally. Sky and her four sisters hadn't fared much better, though they were his own daughters.

"Anyway, I think I'm ready to come back to Widow's Vale," she said.

"Good news," I said sincerely. "It's not the same without you."

"Right. So I think I'm getting a standby flight, probably on Tuesday. Think you can give me a lift home if I tell you when?"

"Absolutely," I said. "Why standby?"

"It'll be cheaper," she said, "and I can't see waiting another two weeks for a discounted flight."

So the family was definitely getting on her nerves. She'd stuck it out for a long while, though. "Just give me some advance notice and I'll be there," I promised.

"Cheers. Anything happening?"

"Yeah, Da is more in demand—" I broke off as I caught sight of the clock. "Damn! I'm sorry, Sky—I'm late for a meeting. I'll talk to you later, all right?"

"Sure. 'Bye."

I hung up the phone and raced out the door.

"Sorry I'm late," I said as I arrived at the coffee shop almost fifteen minutes later. Celia looked up at me, then glanced at her watch. I got the message. She was dressed as though she'd come from an office, in neat, tailored navy pants and jacket that looked professional yet not too formal or uncomfortable.

"I had an international phone call just as I was leaving the house," I explained truthfully, sliding into the remaining seat at our small table.

Robin glanced at Celia, and when I focused my senses, I picked up on feelings of nervousness, fear, and guilt. Once again I found myself intrigued. What was it they wanted, exactly?

"Why don't you get something to drink and then we'll talk," Celia suggested. I nodded and went to the counter. While I waited for my tea, I looked around the small café. Only one other table was occupied. Celia and Robin had chosen a table in the far corner, and each of them was sitting with her back to a wall.

I carried my huge cup over and sat down. I stirred in two packets of sugar and waited for one of the witches to speak. They kept glancing at each other, as if communicating telepathically, but they weren't, I didn't think. I waited, trying to look unconcerned. People want to talk. I'd found that out as a Seeker. Simply waiting was often a far more effective means of getting information than a hard-edged interrogation.

"Thank you for coming," Celia said at last. "When you were late, we wondered if you'd changed your mind."

"No," I said mildly, talking a sip of tea. "I would have called."

"We need you to promise you won't do anything without our permission," Robin blurted, an anxious look on her round face.

I met her gaze calmly. "Why don't you just explain what's going on?"

Celia leaned forward, the smooth planes of her face taut with tension. "Can we *trust* you?" she asked, her voice low and intent.

"Do you practice dark magick?" I asked, and she drew back.

"No," she said in surprise.

"Then you can trust me." I took another big sip.

"It isn't *us*," Robin said. There was so much anxiety coming off her that I was starting to feel jumpy myself. I kept casting out my senses to be aware of any possible danger nearby. But there was nothing.

"You said it was your coven leader," I said.

"Yes, and we need you to promise that you won't . . . harm her," Robin went on. Celia gave her a sharp glance, and Robin looked down and began twisting her hands together in her lap.

"I would never harm anyone," I said. "Unless they posed a threat." I couldn't figure out what these two were getting at. Of course, if I found a witch practicing dark magick that might hurt someone, I had an obligation to turn them in to the council to have their power stripped. As little faith as I had in the council these days, I still knew how important it was to prevent anyone from causing harm.

Robin glanced at Celia nervously, and the two of them seemed to be considering my reply. Finally Celia looked around as if to make sure we were alone. Then her clear brown eyes met mine. "We're both members of Willowbrook, a mixed coven up in Thornton."

Thornton was a town about forty minutes away, north and east from Widow's Vale. A mixed coven meant that not only was it blood witches and nonblood witches, but also blood witches of different clans. I was sure Willowbrook had been mentioned casually by people I'd talked to, but nothing in my memory triggered any negative reaction.

I nodded. "Go on."

Celia continued in a low tone. "For the last seventeen years Willowbrook has been led by a gifted Brightendale named Patrice Pearson."

"How long have you each been in the coven?" I asked. I had been around them enough now to realize that though they seemed to know each other well, there was a distance between them. They were covenmates but not best friends, and they certainly weren't lovers.

"Eighteen years," Celia answered.

"Twelve," said Robin.

"And there's a problem?" I asked.

"Patrice is wonderful," Robin said earnestly, leaning closer to me. Her round brown eyes were once again surrounded by complicated makeup.

"But . . ." I said leadingly, and Celia looked annoyed.

"But nothing," she said shortly. "Patrice *is* wonderful. She's so . . . warm. Giving, helpful, caring, full of joy and life." She paused. "I went through a very difficult personal situation a few years ago, and I don't know what I would have done without Patrice."

"We all just love her so much," Robin said. "We're all so close as a coven. Most of us have been together for at least ten years or more. Patrice just brings us closer and makes us all feel—" She looked for the word. "Loved. Even— About six years ago Patrice went through an ugly divorce. We were all so surprised. But even through all that, she came to circle each week without fail. Every week. And led our circle with generosity and joy."

"She's an exceptional leader," Celia said simply. "She has exceptional clarity and focus." I was starting to get a bad feeling about the perfect Patrice.

"But lately," Celia said, and she and Robin exchanged glances one more time. "Lately she's been different."

I relaxed in my chair. Now that the dam had been breached, everything else would follow. I projected feelings of calm, of being nonjudgmental.

"She's unchanged in most ways, but sometimes—it's almost as if someone else is looking out through her eyes."

All my senses went on alert.

"Circles are different, too," said Robin. "They've always been the high point of my week. Energizing. Life affirming."

"But lately several of us have noticed that after circles, we feel unusually drained," Celia said, looking at her long, slim fingers wrapped around her mug. "Sometimes some of us have to lie down afterward. One night a few weeks ago Robin and I finally mentioned it to each other and found we were feeling the same things. So we decided to try to find help. *Discreet* help. We can't say what's wrong or even *if* anything's wrong. But it doesn't feel completely right anymore, either."

"Of course, Patrice has been under an awful lot of pressure," Robin said. "Joshua—her son, he's eleven now—was diagnosed last year with leukemia. He underwent a bone-marrow transplant about eight months ago."

"Now he has host-versus-graft disease," Celia went on.

"What's that?" I asked.

"Well, they matched Joshua up with a donor," Celia said. "Then they did massive chemo and radiation to kill all the can-cer-causing cells. It killed all of Joshua's own bone marrow, too.

Then the donor's cancer-free marrow was implanted in him. It's working, in that it's producing white blood cells and boosting his immune system. Unfortunately, this marrow's white blood cells have identified Joshua himself as being foreign, and the marrow is attacking virtually every system in his body."

Her voice was tight with pain, and I reflected on the fact that both of these women must have known Patrice when Joshua was first born and had probably known about or been involved in his upbringing for the last eleven years. Now he was deathly ill. It wasn't only Patrice who was feeling the strain.

"It's a different kind of sickness from the cancer," Celia said. "But still awful. It could kill him."

"He's in such pain, such misery," Robin said, her voice wavering. "But even with all this, Patrice has missed only two or three circles in the past year."

"I offered to take over leading the circles for a while, to give her a break," said Celia. "I'm the most senior member of the coven. But she refused."

"That's how loyal she is, how dedicated," Robin said.

"What do the other coven members say?" I asked.

"I know some of them feel something's wrong," said Celia. "No one's said anything to me outright. The thing is, every once in a while it seems fine. It almost made me wonder if I was just imagining things or coming down with the flu myself."

"But I felt all the same things," Robin said. "And last week I heard someone else whisper a concern about it."

"If something negative is affecting all the coven members . . . we have to figure out what," Celia said firmly.

"We know Patrice is a good person," Robin put in quickly. "We just think she needs help, maybe."

I frowned, sipping my tea. This did not sound good. Of course, there might be some benign, rational explanation. And it would be wonderful if that were true. But instinctively I felt there was more to this.

"What is it you want me to do?" I asked carefully.

"We want you to . . . figure out what's going on," Celia said, and Robin nodded. "As a former Seeker, you would have investigative skills, knowledge about the different paths witches take, ideas about how to confront Patrice if it's necessary."

"If she's strayed a little, we can help her get back on the right path," Robin said.

"Or maybe just figure out how to protect her from herself," Celia suggested. "Or protect us from her. We don't know, really. We just know we need help."

"And we need to keep this very, very quiet," Robin said urgently. "We don't want you to go to the council, even if you have affiliations. Patrice is a good person. She just needs help."

I rubbed my chin while I thought. "I don't know whether I can promise that. If I discover that Patrice is involved in something dangerous . . . I'm no longer a Seeker, but I still have an obligation, as a blood witch with a conscience." I leaned back, and Celia and Robin both seemed to deflate a bit.

"Well . . ." Robin glanced at Celia hesitantly.

"We don't . . . we don't want anyone to be hurt," Celia assured me. "Perhaps . . . what if you make no promises, except that you won't harm anybody unnecessarily and you won't let anyone else be harmed?"

I sighed and considered her words. Well, at the very least, I could certainly track down more answers than they had now. "That goes without saying. Maybe I can look into it," I agreed. "See what I can come up with. But if Patrice is mixed up in something dangerous—I simply can't let her continue."

Celia nodded tightly. "Of course. We just—"

"If there's another option other than calling in the council, we want to explore it," Robin said, nervously picking at a loose thread on her sleeve. "You know, we don't want to see her . . . hurt."

"Nobody wants to see anyone hurt," I assured her.

The two women sat back, relief emanating from them like perfume.

Blimey, I thought. What kind of mess have I gotten myself into?

5

Morgan

I'm in a huge house, huge like the palace of Versailles. I keep running down corridors, sure I know the way out, but no matter where I go, I only end up in more corridors, more halls, more rooms that lead nowhere. I feel like something's after me—I'm running away from something, but I don't know what or who. I'm cold, and my bare feet make no sound on the smooth floors. Several times I stop to look out a window, to try to get my bearings, maybe see someone who could help me. Each time I see dream walls floating outside, like stage scenery. They're scrawled over with runes, sigils, words, and magickal drawings, drawings that frighten me, even though I don't know what they are. Then I look out a window and see a hawk swooping down to attack. I don't know why, but this sight chills me to the very bone.

I begin to run down the corridors again. As I pass each enormous window, curtains burst into flames behind me. Is this house going to burn down with me in it? I need to get out of here, to escape. I'm so alone, so cold, so scared. Why can't I find my way out? What's after me? What's that dark, horrible shadow? The fire *is crackling behind me, more shadows flickering on the walls ahead of me. I'm going to burn.*

I woke myself up yelling something like, *Goddess, help me!* I was in my bed, sweating and clammy and icy all at the same time. I wondered if I had shouted out loud, but no one came to check, so I guessed I hadn't. I felt panicky and kept looking at my windows to make sure my shades weren't on fire. I drank some water in the bathroom and lay back down on my bed. I stared at the ceiling until the sun came up, and then I went back to sleep until it was time to meet everyone for the day's picnic.

That was last night. I had considered telling Hunter about it at our picnic, but suddenly it seemed so silly. Obviously I've been through a lot of stress lately. Who wouldn't have weird dreams?

This night will be different, I promised myself. I was trying to quiet whatever demons I was carrying around in my mind. I had taken a relaxing bath. I was trying to think good thoughts, to concentrate on positive things.

It was ten-thirty. I had reviewed some of my history notes in preparation for finals, figuring if that didn't put me to a sound sleep, nothing would.

"Good night, honey," Mom said, poking her head in my open door.

"Night, Mom," I said. I heard Mary K. brushing her teeth in the bathroom we shared, and I turned off my light, taking comfort in the familiar sounds. I thrashed around until I was comfortable and in the perfect Morgan sleeping position. *Now for good thoughts.*

The day had been so great. I'd gone on a picnic with

Hunter, Bree, and Robbie—my three favorite people. Bree and I had never been able to double-date before; though she'd always had boyfriends, I hadn't. And Bree and Robbie's relationship seemed to be going well. I'd never seen either of them so happy.

Okay, I thought. Good thoughts. The picnic had been perfect. And it had gotten only better after Bree and Robbie had taken off. I smiled to myself, thinking about Hunter and me. Goddess, he made me crazy. When, *when* could we be alone together the way we wanted—when would we finally make love?

Sometimes I felt so much love for Hunter that it overwhelmed me and I felt like I was going to cry. He was such a good person, such an ethical person. Such an incredibly talented, knowledgeable witch. I was totally fascinated by everything about him.

I was getting sleepy, and I felt warm and calm. I consciously relaxed every muscle in my body, starting from my toes and working my way up to the top of my head. I repeated my simple little soothing spell: Everything is fine and bright. Day must follow every night. My power keeps me safe from harm, and the Goddess holds me in her arms.

Then I fell asleep.

Frowning, I look down at the map spread out on the bench seat next to me. I squint, but all the names and roads and markings are blurred. Frustrated, I look through the windshield at the tree-lined road, hoping that some feature of it will become familiar. I shift into third gear, as if moving faster will help me feel less lost. I don't know where I am or where I'm going. I feel sure that I did know when I set out—but the reasoning escapes me now.

Das Boot feels familiar and comforting, moving heavily down the narrow road, but that's the only thing that feels okay. There are gray clouds ahead of me, low and malevolent in the sky, as if a storm is coming. I want to turn and go home but don't know which direction to turn in. And there are no cross streets, any-way—nowhere to turn.

Dammit. I look down at my map again, trying to force some of the symbols into focus. They're in Gaelic. I recognize a few letters, but none of them make sense. I feel so frustrated, I want to cry. What's wrong with me? I feel so stupid. The seconds slide by and I become more and more anxious, almost panicky. How can I fix this situation?

A sudden hard tap on my back windshield startles me. Carefully, trying not to drive off the road, I turn around to look—and almost scream. A huge, horrible, dark-feathered hawk is on the trunk of my car, its talons scraping paint as it holds on. Its hard golden eyes seem to laser right through me. It looks fierce and hateful and without pity.

I spin around again, ready to stomp on the gas to try to dis-lodge it, but instead find that I'm now a passenger in the car. Someone else is driving, and I keep trying to see who, but for some reason, whenever I try to look, I can never quite see all the way to the driver's side. Again and again I try, and my gaze keeps sliding away from where the driver is sitting. I can see in front of it and in back of it but not actually the driver's seat itself. Who is this? Am I being kidnapped? A burst of anxiety closes my throat.

A dim gray figure up ahead catches my eye, and I peer at it through my window. Can I signal this person for help? Huge, fat raindrops begin to pelt the windshield like tiny bullets, smacking forcefully against the glass. I lean forward to see who the shape is. I gasp in shock—it's Hunter! Stop! I cry, stop! but the car doesn't even slow down. I see Hunter's face, his eyes locking onto mine, his surprise and concern as we whiz by.

I bang on my window and turn around to yell back at him—I want to stop! I want to come get you, I can't! Tears of fear and anguish roll down my cheeks. I'm trapped in this car. I need to escape, need to get back to Hunter. Goddess, now I feel awful. I'm angry and in tears and so confused and powerless. I keep thinking, I want to stop, I want to stop, I want to stop.

Up ahead, the road begins a slow curve to the left. Das Boot slows, and impulsively I throw open my door and fling myself from the car. I hear the squeal of brakes, and then I'm rolling down a short embankment covered with sharp-thorned thistles. I tumble to a halt. My arms and legs are scratched, rain is pelting my face and hair, and cautiously I begin to climb toward the road, both hoping Das Boot and its mystery driver are gone and feeling upset that my car might be missing.

But there's something—I feel a warmth on my back. I feel back there with my hand, and I jump back—fire! I look behind me, and there are wings made of fire flowing from my back! Who am I? What am I?

No car is on the road. Evening is sweeping in like a cape, flowing over the land. I make it to the road and begin to run back toward where I saw Hunter. I have to see him, to explain. I don't care what happens to me as long as I'm with him. I have to tell him that I wanted to stop, that I never would have passed him if I'd had a choice. I've abandoned my car in order to come tell him.

Soon my lungs burn for oxygen, and my running slows. I look behind me, and my fire wings are gone. I can't find Hunter, even though I'm screaming for him! I'm sure I've passed by where I saw him. I've gone back and forth a half dozen times, looking for *him, calling his name. I'm soaked through and shivering, my skin rough with goose bumps. My feet hurt. I look down, and then the sharp, dark outline of a hawk overshadows the dusky gray of twilight. I feel a sudden, instantaneous terror—the bird is coming for me. I'm its prey! Wildly I look up, my arms already raised to protect myself from its attack—*

—and I woke up in my bed, shaking and flooded with adrenaline. I glanced around in panic, but I immediately realized I was in my room. Confused and terrified, I burst into tears, grabbing my pillow and holding it against me. I'd had another nightmare. I braced myself, trying to remember its terrifying details, but found all that remained was a foggy miasma of fear, of panic. But why? What had it been about? I couldn't remember. The memory was slipping away from me. I punched my pillow in frustration, fresh sobs erupting. I muffled them in my pillow, then flopped down on my bed, crying harder. I don't know how long I cried, but eventually I choked to a watery stop and lay there, exhausted.

I had to get to the bottom of this. This was my third night of frightening dreams. What were they about? What was going on with me? Tomorrow after school I would tell Hunter and Alyce and Bethany about them. They were starting to affect my state of mind. I needed help.

And a drink of water. I pushed back the covers, barely noticing that my legs seemed to sting slightly. Then, as I was standing, I glanced down—and froze with horror. My feet and legs were *wet*! They had bits of wet grass clinging to them, as if I had just run across a lawn! And my legs were *scratched* all over, with dozens of tiny scratches, like I had— *Oh, Goddess!* My heart stopped and my blood turned to ice. *Like I had rolled down a thorny embankment.* I had been *outside*. I had been outside while I was *asleep*. Oh, Goddess, what was happening to me?

Shaking, I walked across the room, noting the faint outlines of damp footprints on my sisal rug. My throat was closed with fear, but desperately I cast my senses. I felt nothing out of the ordinary—just my sleeping family. And Dagda? I looked around for my kitten. He always slept with me, often under the covers. I went back and looked on my bed, patting the covers. No Dagda. I made little kissing sounds, calling him. Then I tiptoed out onto the landing and started down the stairs. I saw the barest trace of wet footprints on the stairs and a few pieces of grass. Goddess, Goddess.

Then, at the bottom of the stairs, I saw Dagda's glowing green eyes. He was hunched in front of the front door, his back arched, ears back. He was snarling, showing his teeth. I stared at him, then glanced behind me. There was nothing.

"Dagda, what's wrong?" I asked softly, padding down to get him. He drew back as I reached him, flattening himself against the door, his claws out, looking manic. Low growls came from his throat, along with a sibilant, teakettle hiss.

"Dagda!" I stopped and pulled back my outstretched hand in shock. He was hissing at *me*.

My parents were so surprised to see me the next morning that they stopped talking. Everyone in my family is an early bird, except me. It was a running joke that Mary K. sometimes had to resort to throwing water on my face to get me out of bed in time to get to school.

"Are you okay?" my mom asked, looking at my face. "Did you not sleep well?"

I hadn't further depressed myself by looking in a mirror this morning, but I had a good idea of what I must look like. I moved zombielike to the refrigerator and pawed around inside until I found a Diet Coke. I managed to drink some, hoping the caffeine would help jump-start some brain cells.

"I did not sleep well," I confirmed in an understatement. Automatically I looked around for Dagda and saw him hunched over his bowl, wolfing down kibble. Last night had been so strange—he had never come back into my room.

"Are you sick?" my father asked.

"I don't think so," I said, bracing myself against the kitchen counter. At least not physically, I amended silently. Maybe mentally. I drank some more soda and sat down at my place at the table. "I just haven't been sleeping much."

"Studying," my mom theorized, nodding and clearing her place. "It won't be long till finals. Honey, I'm glad that your schoolwork is getting back up to par, but I don't want you to ruin your health staying up till all hours, studying."

"It's paying off, though," my dad said encouragingly. "You've been bringing home terrific grades, and your mom and I are really pleased."

I gave him a little smile. My grades had nose-dived earlier in the year, in part because of the time and energy I was putting into studying Wicca. My parents had gone ballistic and lowered the boom on me. Now I was studying more, careful to maintain a decent average.

I glanced over at Dagda—he was gone, and as I gazed blankly around the kitchen, I suddenly felt something warm and soft brush against my legs. Cautiously I looked down. My kitten—almost a cat now—was rubbing against me, purring, as he usually did. I tentatively reached down one hand, and he butted his little triangular head against it, demanding ear scratching. Almost weeping with relief—my cat didn't hate me!—I scratched his favorite spots until he flopped limply on the floor in a surfeit of pleasure.

"Morning!" Mary K. said brightly, coming into the kitchen. She looked fabulous, as always, with her clear skin, shining, bouncy hair, and bright brown eyes framed by long lashes.

"Morning, sweetie," Mom answered, and Dad gave Mary K. a fond smile.

My sister pulled a lemon yogurt out of the fridge and sat down at the table. She glanced across at me, taking in my appearance. "Are you sick? What are you doing up?"

"Couldn't sleep," I mumbled, sucking down more caffeine. Several brain cells sprang into action, and it occurred to me that I needed to get dressed for school. Picking up my soda, I headed upstairs to face this new challenge.

I already had Das Boot's motor running when Mary K. climbed in, russet hair swinging forward into her face, Mark Chambers's letter jacket slung around her shoulders. She'd been dating him for a couple of weeks.

"I assume the jacket means things with the beloved Mark are chugging right along?" I asked as I pulled out of our driveway. Mary K.'s face dimpled in a happy smile.

"He's so, so nice," she said, dropping her book bag onto the floor.

"Good. Because if he's a jerk, I'm going to gouge his eyes out."

Mary K. giggled, but her face was shadowed slightly by the meaning and the memory behind my words. "I don't think you'll have to."

What Alisa had said to me on Saturday night suddenly came back to me. "So, have you thought about what to wear to Alisa's dad's wedding?" This had all the subtlety and finesse of a sledgehammer, since I'm notoriously fashion-challenged.

Mary K. looked at me. She wasn't a fool, and I could see she was trying to figure out my angle. "I'm not sure if I'm going to go," she said cautiously.

"Why not? Weddings are fun. And you get cake," I pointed out.

"I don't know," Mary K. said, looking out the car window. "I don't know if Alisa and I have that much in common anymore."

"Because she's half witch," I said, stating the obvious. My sister shrugged.

"Well, I know how you feel about Wicca and the whole blood witch thing," I said. "I know you would feel better if I didn't have anything to do with it and if Alisa didn't have anything to do with it."

Mary K. didn't look at me.

"The thing is," I went on, "no one chooses to be what they are. They just *are*. It's like the color of your eyes or hair or how tall you are. I was born with blood witch genes because my biological parents were blood witches. Alisa is half and half, and there's nothing she can do about it."

My sister sighed.

"In fact," I said, "Alisa herself was really freaked out when she realized she was half witch. I mean, the girl ran away just a few weeks ago because being half witch wasn't something she wanted to sign up for."

Mary K. bit her lip and looked out the window some more.

I had only a few blocks till school. "Do you think Alisa's bitchy?" I asked.

Mary K. turned startled eyes to me. "No."

"Does she lie? Cheat? Steal? Has she moved in on Mark Chambers? Does she say bad stuff about you behind your back?"

"No, of course not," said Mary K. "She's really cool—"

"Exactly. You guys like the same books, movies, clothes. You have similar and incredibly lame senses of humor. You both inexplicably have a crush on Terrence Hagen, the most insipid boy actor ever."

Mary K. was giggling by now. Then her face sobered. I fired my last shot.

"Mary K., you can be friends with whoever you want. If I didn't think that you really cared about Alisa, I would shut up. But you do care about her. And right now Alisa's dad is getting married. She's about to get a new half sibling. She has no real mom. I just think she could use some friends. And between you and me, I think she wouldn't mind it if those friends *didn't* have anything to do with Wicca."

I parked my car in the school lot, the wheels crunching on the small white shells that covered the ground.

"You're right," Mary K. said softly, hauling up her book bag. "I do care about Alisa. I do want to be friends with her."

"Good," I said cheerfully. "And just think, if you're really, really, *really* persistent, you might be able to win her over to Catholicism. Ouch." I rubbed my thigh where Mary K. had just punched me.

"Later, 'gator," she said, just like she used to do when we were little. I smiled at her.

"In a while, crocodile," was my original response.

6

Hunter

I spent most of Tuesday at Practical Magick, helping Alyce sort the books properly. The bookcases in the new room of the store were almost finished. Alyce and I had gone through most of the stock, keeping long, detailed lists of each category. Within each category there were many sub-categories, and of course most books had to be cross-referenced. It was engrossing and renewed my interest in reading or rereading some important Wiccan texts, but as with the herb imbuing, it wasn't exactly fulfilling.

I was up on a ladder, calling down titles to Alyce, when I sensed someone coming. The bell over the door jangled in the next moment—Morgan. I glanced at my watch. It was four o'clock already.

"Teatime," I said, starting to climb down the ladder. My hands were filthy with dust, and I wiped them on my jeans. "Hello, my love," I said, meeting Morgan halfway. I held her shoulders lightly and kissed her. "Couldn't stay away from me, I see. I missed you, too."

Her mouth quirked in a nervous smile, then she looked past me to Alyce. "Actually," she said softly, "I need to talk to both of you. Can you spare a couple of minutes?"

"Certainly, dear," said Alyce. She walked to the back of the store and called out to her other employee. "Finn, could you mind the shop for me for a bit?" He nodded and walked to the cash register.

Alyce gestured to the tattered orange curtain that led to the employees' lounge/storage room/lunchroom. Already I was picking up on Morgan's tension, overlain with fatigue, and I wondered what was going on—she hadn't mentioned anything. I rubbed her back as we walked in and sat down. She gave me a strained smile and put her hand on my knee. I tried to read her eyes, but they seemed shuttered, and I went on alert. If something was bothering Morgan, how had I not sensed it before? Or was she hiding something from me?

Within minutes Alyce put three mugs of tea on the table, projecting, as usual, an air of calm, maternal empathy. "What's going on, Morgan? You look very upset."

Morgan nodded and swallowed. I let my arm rest across the back of her chair so she would feel my support. "I've been having . . . dreams," she said. "Nightmares, actually. Scary ones."

I began rubbing her back again with one hand. "These must be somewhat out of the ordinary for you to want to talk to us both about them," I said.

Morgan gave a short, dry laugh. "They're out of the ordinary," she agreed. "They've been going on for three nights now." I put my head to one side, curious, and she turned to me to explain. "I just thought they were ordinary dreams.

Everyone has nightmares sometimes. And nothing that explicitly bad ever happens in them—I'm not seeing murders or anything. They're just really strong, disturbing images. I thought maybe it was stress—finals coming up, that kind of thing. But last night . . ."

She paused to sip her tea, and beneath my hand I felt a fine tremble shake her. "What happened last night?" I asked.

"I had another dream," she said. "I can't even remember most of it. I feel like I keep seeing hawks, dark hawks, in the dreams, but I'm not sure."

I remembered Morgan's response to the hawk we had seen the day of the picnic, and I felt irritated with myself that I hadn't picked up on it. I must be getting thick.

"Last night's dream felt like the worst, but I can't say why," Morgan went on. "All I remember is—I think I was in a car, my car. I wasn't driving, and I had to get out. But it wouldn't stop. I think I jumped out. And when I did, I realized I had bird's wings, but they were made of fire."

Instantly Alyce's eyes met mine. That had to be a symbol for something.

Morgan shook her head, frustrated by not being able to recall more details. "I fell in a ditch, I think. Then I was running on a road, looking for something or someone, and my wings were gone." She shivered again, though it was warm in the room, and hunched her shoulders as if to protect herself. "But that's not the worst part," she said in a small voice. "The worst part is that when I woke up, my legs and feet were wet. And there were little bits of dried grass stuck to me."

"Oh, Morgan." My muscles tensed. Goddess. This was incredibly serious.

"And I had these," Morgan said, pulling up the sleeve of her shirt. Her arm was crisscrossed with many fine scratches. "My legs are scratched, too." She sounded afraid but was trying not to show it. "So I was *sleepwalking*. I went downstairs and saw wet footprints all the way to the front door. And Dagda—" Her voice broke off, and she gripped her mug in both hands. "I saw Dagda and went to him, and he hunched up like a Halloween kitty and *hissed* at me. Like I scared him." Her voice wavered. She was obviously fighting back tears. I scooted my chair closer to her and tried to wrap my arm around her protectively.

Alyce's kind, round face showed some of the concern I was feeling, though she still looked calm.

"Have you ever sleepwalked before?" I asked.

Morgan shook her head. "Never."

"The other two nights you had these dreams . . . do you think you were sleepwalking then?"

Morgan frowned, trying to remember. She shook her head, and her hair brushed back and forth against my arm. "Not that I know of."

Alyce sat back, looking at Morgan thoughtfully. "Goodness," she said. "You must feel very frightened, dear."

Morgan nodded, not looking at her. Alyce reached out and covered Morgan's hand with her own. "I don't blame you. I would be upset, too. What else do you remember about the dreams? Any kind of detail, anything at all. What about the first dream?"

Morgan sighed. "I remember waking up and knowing I'd had a bad dream and that I was kind of upset, but I just put it out of my mind. All I could remember about it was my feet hurting."

I smiled at her in encouragement.

"The next dream I remember better," Morgan said, "because I was determined not to repeat it again last night. I remember running through huge halls, like in a mansion. I kept getting lost. I looked through the window to get my bearings, and outside there were more walls, floating there. They were covered with writing, but I don't remember any of it. I remember running past the windows, and when I passed them, their curtains caught on fire. And there was a hawk, I think." Her forehead wrinkled as she tried to remember anything else. Then she shook her head. "That's all I remember."

"Was there a fire in the first dream?" I asked, looking for common threads.

"I don't remember. I don't think so. But maybe? Maybe I smelled smoke?" Morgan looked frustrated and confused.

"Okay," said Alyce, patting her hand reassuringly. "Let's look at what we have. You said that hawks were a part of your dreams. Do you remember what they were doing, how they looked?"

Morgan slowly shook her head. "I don't remember. I just *feel* like they've been in all of my dreams."

"All right," said Alyce. "Usually dreaming about birds symbolizes freedom or happiness."

"Yes, but she's dreaming about raptors, birds of prey," I pointed out. "That could indicate greed or a power struggle. Having a dark-feathered hawk to me seems more ominous: sensing danger or threat." I didn't know all that much about dream interpretation. I had learned just enough to pass my initiation, but I remembered a few of the common symbols.

"What about me having wings with flames on them?" Morgan asked.

Alyce shot me a hesitant glance.

"Well, fire usually symbolizes purification, cleansing," I said.

"Or sometimes metamorphosis, something changing from one form to another," Alyce added. "But you also have personal connections to it."

Morgan nodded solemnly. She had shown a special affinity for fire ever since she'd first learned she was a blood witch. She was one of the few blood witches I'd ever known who could successfully scry with fire. There was also family history with fire. Apparently her birth mother, Maeve Riordan, had also shown an affinity for it. Until she'd been burned to death.

"There's something else," Alyce said, looking thoughtful. "A bird with wings of fire . . . It's ringing a bell, but I can't quite place my finger on it. I feel like I've heard of that somewhere before." She thought for another few moments, then shook her head briskly. "Well, we'll need to do research on that one and on the curtains catching fire. Now, the car. Cars often represent the path you're taking through life, the path you're taking to achieve goals."

I frowned, trying to recall old lessons. "And being a passenger symbolizes someone having control over you, dictating your path."

"Walls can represent either safety or confinement. The halls you ran down were also a life path. The symbols you couldn't understand represented your literal confusion about something, that there's something going on you don't understand." Alyce leaned forward, thinking.

"I'm hearing a lot about life paths, sensed danger, and also confusion, hidden stuff," I said uncomfortably. "These symbols seem to keep repeating themselves."

"Yes," Alyce agreed. She looked at Morgan. "You need to do some deep thinking, dear. Some meditation might help make some of this clear. To me it feels like there's something hanging over your head, symbolically if not literally. The fact that these dreams are so strong, strong enough to make you actually sleepwalk, means we must take them very seriously. Your psyche is sending you a powerful message. It's important that we figure out what it is."

Morgan looked troubled. "There's something else that I just thought of," she said. "The walls with the writing on them, the symbols and runes—they remind me of Cal's *seòmar*—his secret room where he worked all that dark magick."

And where he had tried to kill her. My stomach knotted, and fury boiled up in me like lava. My half brother, Cal, was dead, yet it seemed Morgan would never be free of his influence, his corruption. He'd nearly seduced her, manipulated her, and tried to steal her power. For a minute I was so angry, my teeth clenched so tightly, that I couldn't speak. Then I spit out the obvious. "But Cal is dead."

"I know," Morgan said in frustration. "I don't understand any of it. All I know is that it's making me crazy, and now I'm actually *sleepwalking*. That's just too much for me to deal with." She put her elbows on the table and dropped her face into her hands.

"We have to sort this out quickly," I said to Alyce, surprising myself with the harshness of my voice. "Morgan's obviously in danger. We have to figure out where the threat is coming from and eliminate it."

"I agree," Alyce said, regarding me calmly. "But the 'threat' could be coming from Morgan herself. Her psyche could simply be using strong means to get a message across. The sooner we figure out that message, the sooner it can stop trying to make an impression on her."

"I don't believe that," I said, looking at Alyce evenly. "I know Morgan. I don't think her psyche would cause her to sleepwalk in the middle of the night to get its point across. I believe these dreams are magickal."

"I hate this," Morgan muttered, shaking her head. I stroked her hair down her back, smoothing the heavy strands.

"I know," Alyce said, patting Morgan's hand again. "I don't blame you. It's hard to sort out. But one thing is clear: These dreams might be serious, and we need to take action."

"On the chance that these dreams could be influenced or caused by an outside source, I'm going to research how one would do that," I said. "Maybe I can suss out some examples of cases where it was found that outside forces were influencing a person's dreams. And perhaps I'll talk to my father about otherworld influences acting in this world."

Like dead people, coming back to terrorize Morgan. Like Cal. Or maybe a living person, someone from Amyranth, someone who was possibly doing Ciaran's bidding. I nodded at Alyce, already considering how to go about it.

"Morgan, I'd like you to do some self-examination," Alyce said. "Meditate, think, work revealing spells—anything you can think of that might help explain what these dreams are about."

"You might want to do this when you feel safe, like when your parents are home or with me," I suggested. "Any other details that come to you, any snatches of memory or insights or fragments, write down. Keep a record of everything."

"Okay," Morgan said, sounding glum.

"As for myself, I'll do more research into dream symbolism," Alyce said.

"I'm curious about what the fire-winged hawk might mean," I said, and she agreed.

"Also," Alyce said, "I'll make you a tisane today—a simple drink that will help you sleep and prevent you from dreaming further until we can get a handle on what's going on."

"That would be great," Morgan said in relief. "I'm afraid to go back to sleep after all of this."

Alyce clucked sympathetically, then got up and filled the copper teakettle with fresh water. "I'll fix you something that will help, at least for the next night or two. Just be sure to drink it at least ten hours before you have to get up the next day. If you have to get up at seven-thirty for school, drink it no later than nine-thirty the night before. Or else you'll be slow and sleepy at school."

"We don't want *that*," Morgan said dryly, and I laughed, despite my concern. A morning person, she wasn't.

"All right, then," Alyce said, bustling about, opening cupboards and taking out different herbs and oils. She put valerian, kava kava, and ginseng on the counter. "Morgan, why don't you and Hunter visit while I get this ready? It should take me about half an hour, forty minutes."

"Good idea," I said, standing and tugging on Morgan's hand. She got up.

"Thanks, Alyce," she said.

Alyce smiled at her. "My pleasure. We're both here for you—I'm really glad you came to us. You don't have to fight these battles alone. Not anymore."

Morgan smiled a bit, then we left the back room and headed

to the new half of the store. Inside my little work area I closed the door and pulled Morgan onto my lap. She rested her head against my shoulder, and I felt her comfortable weight settle closer. I threw a quick "delay" spell at the door. It wouldn't actually keep anyone out, but it would slow them down for a few seconds.

"Morgan, I wish you had told me," I murmured against her hair.

"I thought they were just ordinary dreams," she said. "But this morning when I realized I'd been *outside*—" Her fear was plain in her voice, and I held her closer.

"We'll take care of it," I promised her. "We'll figure it out, and you'll be fine again. At least tonight you know you're going to sleep really well."

"Mmm-hmm," she said.

For long minutes I held her on my lap, stroking her hair and gradually feeling the tension in her slender body uncoil. She relaxed so completely against me that I almost thought she had fallen asleep.

"Hunter?" she said.

"Hmm?"

"I'm tired of being afraid," she said. Her voice was very calm, almost matter-of-fact, but it struck a chord deep within me. Ever since she had realized she was a blood witch, her life had been a cascade of incredible highs and wretched lows. We both felt ready to have some smooth sailing for a while.

"I know, my love," I said, kissing her temple.

"I wish I could get out of here."

I'd never heard her say anything like that before. "You mean, like come to England with me this summer?"

I felt her smile. "I wish. No, I just feel like I need to get out of here for a while. Like I keep getting layers of bad emotions. All through the autumn and winter. Now through the spring. I need to go someplace else and start over. At least for a while."

"Let's think about it," I said. "Let's try to come up with a way to make that happen for you."

"Okay." She stifled a yawn.

It wasn't long before we felt Alyce approaching, and Morgan stood up to lean against my worktable. I heard Alyce reach for the doorknob a couple of times, apparently missing it, and I wondered if she sensed the delay spell. If she did, she didn't make any mention of it.

"Here you go," she said, coming into the room. She held out a small brown bottle with a screw-on lid and put it into a Practical Magick shopping bag. "Drink half of it tonight and save half for tomorrow. Don't mix it with anything else, and don't drink or eat anything else for two hours before or after you drink it."

"Okay," said Morgan, taking the bag. "And this will really keep me from sleepwalking?"

"It will," Alyce promised.

"Thanks," Morgan said. "Thanks so much. You don't know how much I've been dreading going back to sleep."

"Take care, and we'll talk tomorrow." Alyce gave Morgan one last smile and headed back to the shop.

"Do you think you'll be all right tonight?" I asked.

Morgan nodded. Her beautiful eyes were dark with worry and fatigue. "I'll be okay."

7

Morgan

Alyce's tisane didn't taste quite as bad as I thought it would. At nine that night I managed to get it down by holding my nose and swallowing it in two gulps.

Now it was ten, and I was distinctly woozy. I got off my mom's bed—we'd been watching her favorite cop show together—and told everyone good night. I got into a big T-shirt and brushed my teeth and fell into bed. Almost immediately, using his superkitty senses, Dagda knew it was bedtime and came trotting through the bathroom. Sleepily I patted the bed and he leaped up, making no sound and hardly any vibration.

With Dagda purring hard next to me, I went through some guided relaxation exercises, affirming that I felt safe, that I would sleep well, that everything was fine, that my subconscious would reveal anything I needed to know. I pictured myself sleeping like a log until morning. I pictured myself safe and surrounded by protective white light. I pictured all my worries and fears floating away from me like helium balloons.

I got sleepier and sleepier until I realized I wasn't even thinking straight. Then I let go of the day and embraced sleep.

Why are you trying to avoid me? The words clawed their way into my brain as I struggled to wake up. Dimly I knew I was floating upward toward consciousness and felt a tinge of panic, as if I shouldn't be leaving this soon. *Why are you trying to avoid me? Come join me.* The words were white slashes against the dark backdrop of my sleep.

Suddenly, just as I was beginning to sense the sheet gripped in my hands, an image flashed: a dark-feathered hawk, streaking away. It was being chased by another hawk, rust colored and cruel eyed, who seemed terrible and strong and whose powerful wings were edged with flames.

I looked down, as if I were one of the hawks, and saw the ground far beneath me, grids of gold and green. With frighteningly clear hawk sight I saw a lone person standing in a field of wheat. Like a laser, my eyes zoomed in on the figure, and as I swooped closer, the person looked up and smiled.

At that moment I woke up and sat bolt upright in bed, my heart racing, clutching the sheet to my chest with fingers like claws.

It had been Cal.

"Will you *stop?*"

Robbie quit drumming his fingers on the lunch table and looked at me in hurt surprise. My heart sank. I was being a total bitch.

"I'm sorry," I said stiffly. "I'm having a bad day."

Understatement of the year. Ever since I had seen Cal in

my dream last night, I'd felt like my whole world had shifted. Cal is dead. Cal is dead. That was what I'd been telling myself for the past five months. But now he was trying to contact me when I was most vulnerable—while I slept. What did he *want*? Where, who, or what was he? I couldn't make sense of any of it. I was frightened, confused, horrified—and a small, terrible part of me was flattered. Maybe even happy. Cal had done horrible things, but he'd loved me, in his own twisted way. I loved Hunter now, but the thought that Cal might be trying to contact me from the *dead* was a sick kind of ego boost.

"You've been kind of off all week," Bree said, with typical best-friend frankness. "Are you and Hunter okay?"

I pushed my school lunch of clumpy mac and cheese away and grimaced. "Hunter's fine. School's fine. Folks are fine."

"Sister's fiiiiine," sang Mary K., dipping quickly to get that in as she passed by on her way to the Mary K. fan club table.

Bree giggled, watching Mary K. weave through the cafeteria, brown lunch bag swinging at her side. "So what isn't fine?" she asked, turning back to me.

I sighed heavily. How to put this? "I think my dead ex-boyfriend's spirit is trying to terrorize or even physically hurt me"? Why didn't I just call Jerry Springer *now*? "I've been having bad dreams," I said inadequately. "They've been keeping me up."

Bree and Robbie both looked unimpressed. I saw them glance quickly at each other and make a decision: Let's just walk on eggshells until she chills out.

As soon as I had cleared my tray, I called Hunter and asked him to pick me up after school.

*   *   *

Seeing a six-foot-plus length of blond, handsome witch leaning against his car and grinning did a lot to calm me down.

"Hi," I said, knowing I sounded pathetic. Hunter folded me in his arms, and I let my head sink against his chest. My whole life, I had been strong and self-sufficient. I'd always thought of those as good qualities. Now I was experimenting with relying on someone else. So far, it was going pretty well.

"I'm glad you called," Hunter said. "I was going to send you a message. I have to go and collect Sky at the airport. Can you go with me?"

"I think so. Let me call my mom." I borrowed Hunter's cell phone and dialed my mom's office number. She said it was okay. With relief I made sure that Mary K. got a ride home, then I left Das Boot all by its lonesome in the parking lot and climbed into Hunter's anonymous green Honda.

"I'm so glad to see you," I said, turning to him and scooting as close as I could.

He leaned over and gave me a lingering kiss, then started the engine. "How did it go last night? I wanted to call you this morning to see but didn't know if it would be a good idea."

"I had a dream," I said, looking out the window.

"No," he said, frowning. "Even after taking Alyce's potion?"

I nodded. "I followed all her directions. I think for the most part, I didn't dream that much. But right before dawn I heard a voice."

Hunter looked at me, then pulled onto the entrance to the highway. "What did it say?"

"It said, 'Why are you trying to avoid me?'" I repeated,

trying not to let my remembered fear overcome me. "Twice."

"Goddess," Hunter said. He rubbed his chin with one hand, the way he did when he was thinking something through. "That isn't good."

"No, I didn't think so," I said wryly. "And I saw hawks again. Just for a second, but they were there. A dark hawk being chased by a fire-winged hawk. Then it looked like I was a hawk, flying overhead. I looked down and saw someone standing in a field."

"And?"

I couldn't help shuddering. "And it was Cal."

The car gave a sudden swerve, and I grabbed my door handle.

"Sorry," said Hunter. "I'm sorry, Morgan. So you saw Cal in your dream?" He was trying to sound casual, but I knew him, and his voice was tight. He had hated Cal to the very bone and still got tense at the mention of his name.

"Yes." I shook my head. "That's when I woke up. Maybe Alyce's drink wore off right before I was going to wake up, and that's why I suddenly had all these dream images."

"Maybe," said Hunter, sounding grim. "Well, we'll find out more tonight. I've arranged for us to meet with Alyce and Bethany tonight, at Bethany's apartment. Is eight o'clock okay?"

"Yeah, no problem. Did you tell Bethany what's going on?"

"Alyce did, and Bethany's concerned, like we all are."

I leaned my head against Hunter's shoulder, feeling the warmth of his skin through his thin jacket. I couldn't wait till it got really warm and Hunter would be wearing T-shirts and shorts. Thinking about that cheered me up a little.

"How did Sky sound when she called?" I asked.

"Ready to come home," Hunter said, and grinned.

We turned into the airport and Hunter pulled into the pickup spot he had arranged with Sky. We had been waiting only a few minutes when we spotted Sky's white-blond hair bobbing through the crowd. Soon her thin, black-clad body appeared, tugging a large green suitcase on wheels behind her. She spotted Hunter and waved. They were first cousins, but more important, they had grown up together, living like brother and sister since Hunter was eight.

"Sky! Over here!" Hunter called, and Sky's fine-boned face split into a grin.

"I'm back," she said, and then she and Hunter were hugging, and he lifted her off her feet. "Goddess, what did you do to your hair?" she said critically when they pulled apart. Since his hair looked exactly the same as it always had, I knew she was just teasing him.

"What?" said Hunter, running his hand over his short blond spikes. "What's wrong with it?"

Sky caught my eye and smirked, and I laughed. She swung her suitcase into the trunk with effort. "Hallo, Morgan," she said, somewhat formally but with a nod.

"Welcome back," I said, getting in the car next to Hunter. Sky got in the back. I half turned in my seat so I could see both of them at once.

"I'm looking forward to seeing Uncle Daniel," Sky said, watching Hunter carefully. "How's he been?"

"He's getting better, I think," said Hunter. "Healthier. He's giving talks about spellcrafting at covens around the area. He's not thrilled by my quitting the council."

"Have you heard from Kennet since you called to quit?"

"No."

Seeming to want to change the subject, Sky said, "Oh! I brought you some small tokens of my affection." She rummaged in her backpack and pulled out various paper and plastic bags. Hunter sat up, interested, and I hoped he was paying attention to the road.

"A jar of Marmite," Sky said, holding up a smallish brown jar.

"Yes!" Hunter said enthusiastically. I'd never heard of Marmite and wondered if it was a jam or something.

"Some PG Tips tea, tea of peers," Sky continued, tossing a large yellow box into the front seat.

"Bless you," Hunter murmured.

"A package of actual crumpets, only slightly mashed."

"Crumpets," Hunter repeated, sounding blissful.

"McVitie's." Sky dropped a couple of round cookie packages over my shoulder. From the picture on the front, they looked like round graham crackers.

"And for Morgan, a lovely new tea towel featuring the family tree of Her Royal Majesty." She tossed a folded rectangle of linen into my lap.

Hunter cackled. "Too brilliant."

"Oh," I said, surprised. "Thank you. This was really nice of you." I shook it out and grinned. "This is great."

"Every home needs one." Sky sat back against her seat. "So, any news?"

"Um, Alisa's coming to terms with being half witch."

"Good. It might be rough for a while," said Sky.

"Dagda caught a vole in the yard." I was trying to think of

more interesting things that didn't have to do with my nightmares but was running short.

"Stout lad," Sky approved. "And what news of your half
brother?"

My jaw almost dropped. Killian was the only one of my
three half siblings I had met, and I had mixed feelings about him.
On the one hand, he was charming, funny, generous, and generally well meaning. On the other, he was irreverent, thoughtless,
undependable, and somewhat amoral. One night Sky had gotten drunk and had ended up in a compromising position with
him in his room. Raven and I had found them. Sky and Raven
had just broken up. A nasty scene had ensued.

"He's doing fine. You know Killian," I said cautiously.

Sky looked nonchalantly out her window. I wondered if
she'd wanted to ask about Raven but couldn't, so she'd asked
about Killian instead. Hmmm.

"Morgan, I'm going to drop you at your car before I take
Sky home," Hunter said, and with surprise I noticed we had
already turned onto the Widow's Vale exit.

"Okay."

At school Das Boot was the only car left in the lot.
Hunter walked me over to it. "I'll see you in about an hour
and a half," he said softly, leaning down to kiss me.

"At Bethany's." Just thinking about it made me feel better.

I climbed into Das Boot and started it, watching while
Sky got into the front seat. I couldn't help being a little jealous of Sky. She got to live with Hunter, see him all the time.
It was what I wanted. Hunter waited till I had started my car
and headed off before he went in his own direction.

*　　　*　　　*

At ten after eight I hurried up the stairs at the front entrance to Bethany's apartment house. It was dark, and the streetlight shone amber on the building. A movement caught my eye, and I turned to see a large dark shadow taking off into the air. I followed its silhouette, but the streetlight shone right in my eyes, making it hard to see.

"Damn crows. They're everywhere," an older man said, coming up the steps after me. He gave me a casual smile and went past, holding the door for me.

Maybe it *had* just been a crow. Maybe. I followed him in and hustled up to Bethany's apartment.

"Morgan!" Bethany said warmly, opening the door to my knock. Her dark brown eyes shone with concern, and her short black hair was arranged haphazardly in a pixie style. "How are you? Come in, come in." Rubbing my back, she followed me into her smallish living room, where Hunter and Alyce were already waiting.

"Hi. Sorry I'm late," I said, taking off my jacket and dropping it on the floor next to a chair. I suddenly felt a little self-conscious—everyone was here because of *my* problems. I sat down and tucked my hands under my legs so they wouldn't clench nervously. These three people cared about me. They had all helped me before, and I had helped them. We were friends. I could trust them.

"I told Alyce and Bethany about last night's dream," Hunter said.

"It sounds . . . very disconcerting," Bethany said. That was an understatement. She arranged herself comfortably on the overstuffed couch.

"I did some research," she said, "after Alyce told me about this last night. But first, I know you've told Hunter and

Alyce all you remember, but I'd like to hear it again for myself, if you don't mind."

"Okay," I said. Once again I related what I could remember of the dreams I'd had but couldn't come up with any new details. Bethany jotted a few notes as I spoke, and I was aware that Hunter and Alyce were listening attentively.

"So that's it," I concluded. "But last night was the first one where I felt like I saw someone who might have something to do with the dreams."

Bethany nodded. "Alyce, do you still feel that these dreams might be coming from Morgan's subconscious? That it's trying to send her a message?"

"Not as much, not after last night's dream," Alyce admitted. "The voice asking about being avoided, actually seeing Cal. I have to say, it now sounds like these dreams are coming *to* Morgan, not coming *from* Morgan."

"Oh, Goddess," I said, feeling my stomach cave in. "It was bad enough when I thought I had something inside *me* to work out. But now I'm being attacked?" My voice sounded whiny, but I couldn't help it. I felt so afraid and frustrated and angry that it was all I could do not to jump up and start screaming.

"Assuming that it's Cal," Hunter said, "it isn't clear how he's doing this." I could see a vein in his neck standing out and knew he was controlling his anger only with difficulty. "The few times I've had any contact with the otherworld, it's been with the anam of a very powerful person. My research turned up much the same information. I would have thought Cal's powers weren't strong enough."

"What's an anam?" I asked.

"A . . . soul," Alyce said. "A spirit, an essence. The *you* that remains after your body is gone. And yes, I agree that one must be very strong to do this. Of course I didn't know him well at all."

"What's even more important is *why* he would be doing this," Bethany said. "What does he want? What's his aim?"

"Besides turning me into a screaming lunatic," I said bitterly.

"To get control of Morgan, obviously," Hunter said. "It's what he always wanted."

"But what good would I be now?" I asked. "He's gone, Selene's gone. He sacrificed himself to save me. What would he want from me now?"

Hunter looked down at his feet. I knew he still hated Cal. He'd never believed that Cal had tried to save me. I reached out and took his hand.

"I don't know, dear," Alyce said. "We need to find out. In the meantime let's compare notes and research. Maybe some of it will start to fall into place."

"I think we can't rule out that it's someone else, perhaps working through or with Cal's anam," Bethany said thoughtfully. "Right now he's our main suspect, but it would be foolish to settle on him as the answer until we know for sure."

"I can't believe this." I shook my head. Why? Why was he doing this to me? "I feel so powerless. For him—or whoever—to do this while I'm sleeping, when I'm totally helpless and at his mercy . . . I can't stand it."

"You're not totally helpless, my dear," said Alyce. "We need to talk about interactive dreaming, guided dreaming."

"Hold on," Hunter said. His voice sounded hoarse.

I looked over at him and saw a sick look on his face. He turned to me.

"That night in Selene's library—we saw Cal and Selene die. But what happened then? We got Mary K. and hustled out of there—I wanted to make sure you were both safe."

"Uh-huh," I said, hating to remember that horrible night. "What are you getting at?"

"What happened to their bodies?" Hunter asked, and I felt the blood drain from my face.

I forced my memory back, back to seeing Cal crumple under Selene's dark power, the bolt of evil meant to kill me that he had taken instead. I remembered holding Selene in a sort of magickal crystal cage. And then she had died. They had both been lying motionless on the library floor. We had left, and outside, Sky was just arriving with some council members. They had streamed into the house, and I hadn't looked back.

My gaze met Hunter's, and I felt hollow. "I don't know," I said. "We left them there. They were dead."

Hunter stood and headed for Bethany's phone. Quickly he punched in a long number, then waited, pacing in tight circles.

"Kennet?" he said after a moment. "Yes—sorry. I know it's late. I wouldn't have woken you, but this is important. Listen, I must know—what did the council do with the bodies of Cal Blaire and Selene Belltower?"

I watched him, feeling clouded by sorrow and memory.

"No, I understand, but it's important, I promise," Hunter said. He listened silently, his face becoming more and more set.

"Kennet—I appreciate that. I know I'm no longer on the council, and I know there are things that don't need to be broadcast. But this is me, and I'm asking you, as a friend. Please, can you just tell me what happened to their bodies?"

He listened for a while more, then seemed to lose his patience. "Kennet, please. Right now I don't care about the council or its protocols or what anyone is authorized to say. I need some answers—it's a matter of life and death."

His face was grim and tense. I knew Kennet had been his mentor and his friend.

"You're quite sure? Did you see it? You saw this yourself?" His head tilted to one side, and it occurred to me that he was probably analyzing Kennet's voice to determine whether he was telling the truth.

"Yes, all right. I understand. Yes, I know. Thank you, Kennet. I appreciate it. You won't regret telling me. Good-bye, then." Abruptly he hung up, then wiped his forehead, pushing his short hair up as he did. He came back and sat down next to me, taking one of my hands in his. I waited, staring into his eyes.

"Cal and Selene's bodies were taken back to England, where they were cremated. Their urns were interred in a small family mausoleum near Selene's birthplace. Kennet swears he actually saw the bodies cremated. I believe he was telling the truth, or at least the truth as he knows it."

I felt a sense of relief. "I guess it can't be them, then."

"Not necessarily," said Alyce gently. "This tells us that neither Cal nor Selene had a chance to go back into their own bodies. But it doesn't mean their anams were destroyed—just their physical beings."

"But how could they survive this long?" I asked. "How could they get to me now?"

"I don't know," Alyce admitted. "That's one of the questions we need to answer."

"Let's talk about what actions we can take now," said Bethany firmly, and for the next hour she and Alyce coached me in both interactive and guided dreaming. Before I went to sleep, I could deliberately decide to take part in my dreams, to be able to take action in them. Once there I could guide my dreams the way I wanted them to go; for example, I could *find* a door, *stop* my car, be unafraid of anything I might see or hear.

"I know this will help. I just wish I didn't have to do any of this," I said.

"I understand," said Bethany. "But for tonight we'll try to give you a reprieve. I've created a very strong sleeping draught that should really knock you out, no dreams. If you do somehow dream, use the exercises we've gone over. But I'm confident that you'll wake up tomorrow feeling better, safer. And by tomorrow evening we hope to have more solid information about how dreams can be influenced either in the real world or from the netherworld."

"Thanks," I said. "I really appreciate you all helping me like this."

"Of course," Bethany said, and smiled.

I was supposed to be home by ten, so I got my jacket, took Bethany's little bottle, and said good-bye. Hunter wanted to walk me out, and I wasn't about to discourage him.

Outside, my car glowed under the streetlight, heavy and familiar and safe. I opened the door and leaned against it for a minute.

"I'm sorry, Morgan," said Hunter, brushing my hair back. "We'll fix this somehow, I promise."

"Thanks," I said. "I just feel . . . like I'll be paying for my mistakes for the rest of my life." The mistake of trusting Cal, of loving him.

"You won't," said Hunter, and he sounded so sure that I wanted to believe him. "Listen, do you want me to stay outside your house tonight? Just in case?"

I thought about it. "No," I decided. "The only time I sleepwalked was before any of you were helping me. I feel okay about the interactive dreaming stuff. Plus I have Bethany's magick potion." I held up the small purple bottle.

"All right," said Hunter, sounding reluctant. "But call me if you need anything."

"I will." We kissed and hugged, not wanting to let go.

Then I got in my car and started the engine. Hunter got smaller and smaller in my rearview mirror until I turned the corner at the next block.

8

Hunter

I got home from Bethany's by ten-fifteen and found Sky making a pot of tea.

"I knew there was a reason that I missed you," I said, and she swatted me with a tea towel. "Put out a mug for me, will you? Is Da out? Did you two talk much?"

She nodded, putting my mug on the table.

I love Sky, I respect Sky, and I know who Sky is underneath. She can be funny and warm and thoughtful. Though sometimes I worry that someone who doesn't know her like I do might be put off by how self-contained she is.

"He's something, your da," she said, sitting down with her mug of tea. "He went out for an hour. Should be back soon. He seems quite different from the way you described him when you first saw him."

"He's night-and-day different," I assured her. "He's going to seem like my old da any day now."

Sky made a face at my cheekiness and took a sip of tea.

"How's your corner working out?" I asked. One thing

none of us had thought of was that our house had only two bedrooms. Da had immediately offered to give up his, which had once been Sky's, but she wouldn't let him. I had done the chivalrous thing and offered my room, too. But I had to admit to myself that I was relieved when she didn't take me up on it. Not when I still had hopes of getting Morgan in there someday alone. So we had rigged up a makeshift curtain across a small alcove that might have once been a pantry, off the dining room. There was just enough space for a single futon, small table, and reading lamp. Oddly, it seemed to suit Sky's somewhat spartan needs.

"Corner's fine," she said. "Very cozy. In fact, I'm heading there now. Jet lag is knocking me on my back." She stood up and automatically carried her mug to the sink.

"Good to have you back," I said, catching her hand as she went past. She gave mine a squeeze, then headed into the dining room.

Around eleven my father came home. I was waiting in the kitchen and had a mug of tea ready for him. He looked grateful, if somewhat surprised, at my thoughtfulness. He filled me in on his latest speaking dates, and I decided to let him in on Morgan's dreams. I felt a bit odd talking to him about it. Cal had been Da's son, just as much as I was. It wasn't hard for me to hate a half brother I had hardly known, but I knew that Da had much more conflicted feelings. For one thing, I knew he blamed himself for leaving Cal, his infant son, with Selene, in order to be able to marry my own mother, Fiona. He would always question whether Cal would have practiced dark magick if he'd grown up with us, in our family. We'd never know. I deliberately kept my tone as neutral as I could, but I saw a familiar weight bow his shoulders.

"That sounds bad," he said quietly, stroking his chin. "Do what you can, lad."

"What do you think of the possibility of Cal's anam coming back this way?"

"It would be extremely unusual," he said. "Despite all the fairy tales, it's incredibly difficult and rare for someone to come back from the netherworld—at least, not without a lot of help." His face was taut, and by unspoken agreement we didn't discuss how he had once supplied that help to others. "And I didn't know Cal, mind, but I wouldn't have thought he was strong enough."

"Right, that's what we think, too. And there's something else," I said, moving on quickly. I felt glad I had someone I could trust to talk about Patrice Pearson with. My father, for all his parental idiosyncrasies, could actually be very helpful at sorting out what was happening with the Willowbrook coven. I knew he could be trusted, and he was experienced in the ways of dark magick. I told him everything that Celia Evans and Robin Goodacre had told me, along with my own impressions of them. He listened attentively, giving a low whistle when I described how drained the women felt after a circle and how they sometimes felt they couldn't remember the entire evening.

"Sounds like a job for a Seeker," he said meaningfully, but I shook my head.

"I think I can do more not being a Seeker. Anyhow, I need to start investigating. I was wondering if you felt up to some spying and scrying tonight."

"Me?"

"Yes. I'm not sure how strong Patrice is—I could use someone else's powers, and then, you might also see things I would miss."

"Are you referring to breaking and entering?"

"Nooo. Strictly outside work."

He nodded, considering, then grinned. "Let me get my jacket."

Celia had given me Patrice's address, and we located it without much trouble. Forty minutes after leaving my place I drove past her house, which turned out to be a large, well-maintained Victorian in a historic section of Thornton. I parked around the corner, then made sure my mobile was on and set to vibrate. I had faith that Bethany's potion would work, but I wanted to be available if Morgan needed me.

Da and I were dressed in dark clothes, and we said a few see-me-not spells on our way to Patrice's house. We also put up some basic blocking spells: Patrice might feel the presence of other blood witches, but before she could investigate, she would be distracted by something. It was almost midnight; she was probably asleep. But just in case, we wanted to be smart.

It was a quiet, moonless night, and I was thankful for magesight as I picked my way unerringly through her neighbors' backyards. The air was still and quite chilly, but the late spring scent of newly opened flowers drifted toward me, and I inhaled appreciatively. From the very back of her property we looked up at her house. One or two windows had a slight glow to them, as if there were night-lights on. That seemed odd—night-lights were one thing you didn't often

find in a witch's house. Then I remembered her ill, uninitiated son and figured he must be the reason.

Neither Da nor I sensed any kind of activity from the
house, so we wove our way silently to her large backyard
garden. It was a real witch's garden, I saw, with neat beds,
raked paths, and green everywhere. I read the small copper
signs, seeing the familiar plants: burdock, beetroot, rosemary,
yarrow, thistle, goldenseal, mullein, nettle, skullcap. Herbs for
dyeing, herbs for tinctures, herbs for healing, soothing,
cleansing. Very appropriate.

Then I saw the neat row of foxglove at the back of one
bed. Then I looked around more and noticed Da doing the
same. Wordlessly he pointed to a plant. Even in the dark I
identified it as a young castor bean plant. By autumn it could
be up to ten feet tall, with seedpods full of attractive seeds
that people make necklaces out of. Hopefully no one would
decide to chew on their necklace because it would likely kill
them. I began walking slowly around the beds, becoming
concerned, but didn't see anything else out of the ordinary.

I signaled to my father, and we crept across the yard to
sit beneath a huge oak tree.

"Interesting," he said in a barely audible tone.

"Very."

"Of course, a great many plants are poisonous, and people still have them," I said. "Because they're pretty or useful
in a nonedible way. Laurels, rhododendrons, oleander, yew.
They're everywhere."

"But castor bean? Nightshade?" said Da skeptically.

"No. It doesn't look good." Deep in the shadows here, I
pulled out my scrying stone, a large, flat piece of obsidian that

Da had left me when I was eight. He gave a small nod of recognition. Together we placed our fingertips around the very edge of the stone, and I said the little scrying rhyme Sky and I had made up so many years ago. It had always served me well and could be adapted for any number of situations.

> Stone of jet, hue of night
> Help us as we join our sight
> Let us scry the one we seek
> She whose name we now will speak.
> Patrice Pearson.

I traced the rune of Sigel over the stone to help us achieve clarity. Then I concentrated on my heartbeat slowing down, my breathing becoming more shallow, my focus and gaze centering on the stone before me. Almost immediately a very clear image of a dark-haired woman came to me. She was in a darkened room and was lifting something in the air. I didn't realize what it was at first, but then I recognized it as an IV bag. Patrice hooked it onto some sort of metal frame. In the next instant she looked up, as if she had just felt us scrying for her. She frowned.

"Here we go," said Da, and we leaped to our feet. Within seconds the back door of Patrice's house had opened, and we heard the furious barks and snarls of a dog tearing toward us in the dark.

"Run!" I said needlessly—Da was already outpacing me by a yard. We fairly flew through the neighbors' yards, pounded down the sidewalk, and scrabbled at the door handles of my car.

As soon as he slammed the car door shut, we heard a

heavy thunk against the metal: the dog hitting the car. Outraged barks were barely muted by the closed windows.

"Goddess," Da breathed, pushing his hair off his face. "Fierce bugger."

I started the engine, planning to do a quick U-turn so I wouldn't have to pass Patrice's house. My father peered through the windows.

"What is it?" I panted, feeling adrenaline pulsing through my veins. I'd been bitten by a dog before, as a Seeker, and it had been incredibly painful. "A rottweiler? Mastiff?"

My father started chuckling—an unusual sound, coming from him. It sounded like rusty nails being shaken in a can. "It's a dachshund," he said, really starting to laugh. "It's a long-haired dachshund. Look, you can see him when he jumps up to the window."

I looked across and saw a small, elegant brown head lift into my sight for a moment, then sink down again. A moment's pause and then once more his little face appeared, teeth bared viciously, horrible-sounding snarls coming from his throat. Then he sank down, no doubt already mustering the strength for another determined leap.

I snorted with laughter, almost choking, as I pulled slowly and carefully away from the curb. "Oh, Goddess, Goddess," I wheezed. "If that dog had caught us, it would have torn us apart."

"From the knees down, anyway," Da said, and we convulsed with laughter again.

Tomorrow I would need to talk to Celia and Robin.

On Wednesday, I was jolted awake by the ringing of the phone, which I had placed right next to my bed. I grabbed it without opening my eyes. "How did it go, my love?" I asked Morgan.

"Okay, I think," she said. "Did I wake you up?"

"It's all right. I was up a bit late last night. But I want to hear what happened."

"I don't think I dreamed," she said, uncertainty in her voice. "I can't remember anything, and I don't think I sleep-walked. But I feel yucky. Weird and uneasy, as if I saw something awful but I'm blocking it out."

"Hmmm. But you remember nothing?"

"No, nothing since I fell asleep. I just feel like I have a storm cloud hanging over my head. I don't know why."

"We're going to unravel this," I promised her. "Very shortly."

"I know," she said, sounding wan. "I'd better go—Mary K. has a pep club meeting before school."

"All right. Call me after school and we'll get together," I said. "I want to see you."

"Okay," she said.

After we hung up, I lay in my bed for a while, worrying about Morgan. I didn't know for certain what was going on with her dreams, but if it was that bastard Cal, come back to haunt her, I was going to destroy him. Somehow.

"Morning, all," said Da as he entered the kitchen about an hour later. His gray hair was recently trimmed, and the more time that passed, the more his rangy frame seemed to fill in.

"Da." I nodded.

"Morning, Uncle Daniel," said Sky. "Cuppa? I've got a pot made."

"Ta, lass," said Da.

"Say, Da," I said. "I've arranged to meet Celia and Robin—those two witches I told you about—downtown in half an hour. Since you know a bit about the case now, do you want to come?" I was happy to spend time with my father again, and truthfully, his quiet, matter-of-fact nature might help keep this meeting from being ugly.

"Yes, if I'm free," he said, taking his first sip of tea. "I'll need to check my book."

It still struck me as odd that my father was becoming so in demand as a speaker and teacher. I would always have that image of him as the emaciated hermit in Canada, as he'd been when I'd first found him. It seemed like he was metamorphosing in front of my eyes.

"There they are," I said in a low tone as we entered the coffee shop half an hour later. Once again Celia and Robin had taken the corner table, but unlike last time, the place was much more crowded. My father and I both ordered herbal tea.

"Hello, Celia. Hello, Robin," I said politely as we approached their table. "I hope you don't mind—this is my father, Daniel Niall. I've told him about your case, and I think he could be helpful to us. Da, this is Celia Evans and Robin Goodacre."

They all shook hands, and I was pleased and a little surprised that they recognized his name and looked impressed: the man who wrote the spell to conquer the dark wave.

"Last night my father and I visited Patrice's house," I began, and went on to tell them of what we'd found, the couple of poisonous plants mixed in with the herbs and vegetables. Both women looked concerned.

"Many plants are ornamental," Celia said, obviously looking for a loophole.

"You're right," I agreed, "and I certainly made allowances for that. What bothered me was the placement of the plants. They were in vegetable and herb beds, right next to edible plants that looked similar. Few of them were truly ornamental. In other words, I wasn't concerned about the row of rhododendrons lining her drive. You see the difference?"

Robin nodded reluctantly, and Celia clasped her hands around her glass and frowned.

"There's been no evidence of her trying to poison anyone," she said. "None."

I took a sip of tea. "I know—I'm not suggesting that she's poisoning anyone. It just struck me as interesting."

"Well, you're on the wrong track here," Celia said shortly.

I held up my hands in a placating gesture. "Look, I don't have any definitive answers at this point. It's important that I don't rule out any possibilities—even ones that are hard or ugly or not what you want to hear. I'm either looking for the truth or I'm not. Right?"

Celia set her jaw and deliberately uncoiled her fists. "I'm saying that I feel it's *highly* unlikely that Patrice could ever poison anyone."

"Right. And it *is* highly unlikely. But the only thing we can do is look at the whole picture, not just parts of it. Do you agree?"

"Yes. But the scenario you're describing is simply incompatible with Patrice as a person."

"Good," I said. "I would love to be able to tell you that your trust is completely well placed. I hope I can, once I've done more research."

"Well, what do we do now?" asked Celia. "We have a circle in two days."

"I need to investigate some more," I told them. "We can't do anything until we know for certain what's going on. It's possible that I'm completely misinterpreting the situation. It's possible that someone or something else is causing the strange fatigue after your circles. However, if Patrice is responsible, if she really is practicing dark magick . . . well, in most cases the witches are turned in to the council and stripped of their power."

"We can't have that," Celia said, and Robin shook her head. "Absolutely not," she agreed.

"There must be other options," Celia said. "Perhaps counseling, or an intervention, or simply removing her from her source of power."

"There are always options," I said mildly. "But it may be that Patrice's own actions will cause her options to be narrowed."

Celia and Robin were silent.

I glanced across at Da, who had been quiet and watchful during this whole exchange. He gave me an almost imperceptible nod, and I felt incongruously pleased.

"We need to think about this," said Celia.

"Please, don't do anything until we contact you again," Robin added. She grabbed her purse and stood, and Celia got up as well.

"We're not trying to be difficult or obstructive," Celia assured me. "It's just a complicated situation, and it seems to be getting more complicated. But we'll talk things over and give you some definite direction as soon as we can. Okay?"

I nodded. "I understand."

"Fair winds," Celia murmured as she and Robin brushed past me to the exit.

"And to you," I made the traditional reply.

My tea was now cold. I sighed and heated it up again with a quick circle of my hand.

"If she's working dark magick, our options just went down to one," Da said finally.

"Perhaps," I said. "But perhaps Celia and Robin are right: we can come up with something else. Somehow I don't want to turn her in to the council, not now. We're smart, Da. You're a brilliant spellcrafter. I have strongly honed skills and instincts. Surely between the two of us we can find a different solution."

"Well, we don't have to decide now," my father said, sipping his tea. "If they want you to continue, we'll just concentrate on gathering as much information as we need."

"Right."

9

Morgan

"Night, honey," Mom said. "Don't stay up too late."

"I won't," I said. She smiled and closed the door behind her. I was sitting up in bed, reading the Great Depression chapter in my history textbook—a little light reading to keep my mind off things. Well, I needed to study. And the truth was, I didn't want to go to sleep tonight. Bethany's potion had worked last night, as far as I knew. But I had still felt uncomfortable this morning, like something was off. All of my instincts were telling me that sleep was a bad idea tonight.

It had been so good to see Hunter this afternoon after school. He, Mary K., and I had all gone to the diner out on the highway and had milk shakes. It had seemed so normal, so reassuring. But now I was alone, it was bedtime, and my family was going to sleep around me.

As soon as I heard the door to my parents' room close and heard Mary K. get into her own bed, I put down my book and pulled out a slim magazine: *Green Gage,* a quarterly journal of modern Wicca. I loved their articles—in this issue there were recipes for light summery drinks and how to imbue them with magickal properties. There were features on summer gardening and on various crafts, like sewing, basket weaving, and spinning your own yarn.

When I cast out my senses, I found that everyone was asleep, probably having normal dreams about forgetting to study for a test, or that one that Mom had told me about, where she dreamed she sold the perfect house for a ton of money and when she proudly threw open the door for the new owners, it was a total wreck inside. Those were the kinds of dreams I could handle.

It was eleven-fifteen. My eyelids felt a little heavy, but I wasn't about to give myself over to sleep. I padded downstairs barefoot and got a glass of juice from the fridge. I took it into the family room, where the family computer was set up. Dad had recently gotten a cable modem and now we were always online and fast, fast, fast. I loved it.

I did a search for *dream magick/Wicca,* and that turned up some useful sites. Forty minutes later my eyes felt gritty and the glare of the computer screen in the dark room was giving me a headache. I still didn't want to dream, but if I took Bethany's potion now, it would surely knock me out safely. I clicked on one more Wiccan site and found a mention of a disclosure-type spell, one to reveal who was expending energy on you: people who were thinking a lot about you, working for you or against you, people who had strong emotions about you. I shrugged. It was worth a try. It wasn't like I'd found anything else.

I printed out the page and went up to my room. After a short internal struggle—was I ready to risk another dream?—I surrendered to exhaustion and gulped down the second half of Bethany's potion. It would take almost an hour to kick in. I would probably be a mess at school the next day, but oh, well. Inside my room I did a quick delay spell on the door, then got my magick-making supplies from my closet. I set out my four element cups and drew three circles of protection before casting the final circle. Then I sat cross-legged inside the circle and lit a single candle, invoking the Goddess and the God. I also gave thanks for everything in my life that was going well. I was learning that expressing gratitude for everything I possibly could helped dispel some of the negativity I picked up without even trying.

The page with the spell was on the ground next to me, and I read the words carefully. Some of them were in Gaelic, written out phonetically so that they were easy to pronounce. At the appropriate times I drew the runes Ansur, Eolh, Daeg, and Sigel in the air above the candle. Then, facing the candle, I pressed two fingers from each hand over my eyes and tried to see with my "inner eye," the one that sees reality with no interpretation.

Soon I saw Hunter's image, and followed by that, like a page flipping in a book, I saw Alyce's image and Bethany's— they were concerned about me and trying to help me. More faintly I saw my own family, who loved me but didn't seem actively worried about me, which was good. Then they faded away, and I saw the fuzzy outline of a shadow, huge and distorted on a wall. It became slightly clearer, darker, enough so that I could tell it was a person. I kept watching and once more murmured the words of the spell. As I watched, the shadow seemed to come away from the wall, becoming more three-dimensional, as if the shadow itself was assuming a form. Reveal yourself, I breathed. Reveal yourself.

As if from a distance the shadowy form contracted and

writhed and expanded. Finally it took on a form I could recognize: a hawk. *Another hawk!* Dumbstruck, I watched it fly away, and then I slowly opened my eyes.

Why couldn't I see who it had been? Was it Cal, as everyone seemed to think? How could he do this? I had felt his cold cheek—he had truly been dead.

I dismantled the circle and put my supplies away. In my readings I had learned that most Wiccans believed when someone died, their anam went to the netherland, a kind of holding place. In the netherland their life is reviewed, and a person can then choose to come back to this world in a new incarnation, ever working toward that spiritual perfection that will allow them to join with the Goddess as one. It was a nice idea. I had grown up believing in Catholicism's idea of heaven, and I could still see the appeal of a perfect resting place. But I liked Wicca's chance to come back again and try to do better with your life.

A few sources I had found discussed the ability of an anam actually to linger in the world without immediately going to the netherland. They had suggested that for an anam to retain any of its power or coherence, it had to have another vessel to reside in. It could be a literal vessel, like a metal box or glass jar with a lid—or in extreme cases it could be another person or even an animal. Like a hawk.

As soon as I had that thought, a cold chill washed over me. A *hawk*. Was there any way—oh, Goddess, I couldn't think about this. I was really getting paranoid. As Hunter said, hawks were all over the place, everywhere. The images of hawks in my dreams were probably representative of something else, like a generalized threat of some kind.

Okay. But what if it *was* a person doing this to me? These dreams seemed so personal. It would have to be someone who knew me, even knew me well, or at least could find out a great deal of personal information about me.

Ciaran? My natural father had had his powers stripped, so it couldn't be him. But what about other witches from Amyranth? How could I find out?

Killian.

It took me a minute to find my half brother's latest phone number and go back down to the family room. When I called, I got a disconnect message. I called information and got another number for him, and amazingly, when I called it, my half brother answered. On the seventh ring.

"Morgan! How lovely to hear from you!"

I couldn't help smiling. For all of Killian's character flaws, I couldn't help responding to his good nature, his affection, his unquenchable thirst for fun. And he apparently didn't hold a grudge: the last time I'd seen him had been in the old Methodist cemetery, our local power sink. I had trapped our mutual father there, and his powers had been stripped. Ciaran MacEwan had gone from being an incredibly powerful, charismatic, forceful, and evil witch to being a shriveled, powerless husk. Because of me.

"Hi, Killian," I said. "How are you?"

"Tops, sis, just tops. On my way out—the local watering hole does a bang-up microbrewery stout. The lads are waiting for me."

"I bet. And some lasses, too, no doubt."

Killian laughed.

"Listen, Killian," I said. "I was wondering—I haven't talked to you in a while, and I was hoping you could give me some news about Ciaran."

"Ah," he said, and I had a sudden image of a glass of champagne losing its bubbles. "Our sweet da. Well, sis, I won't lie to you. He has seen better days."

My heart gave a pang of remorse and guilt. "Where is he?" I asked softly.

"A type of rest home in Ireland," said Killian. "Down in Clonakilty, by the southern coast. It's warmer there. Relaxing. I hopped over to see him a fortnight ago. He hasn't really turned a corner yet, I'm afraid."

"I'm sorry." My throat felt tight as I experienced the usual dichotomy of emotions I felt about Ciaran. He had killed my birth mother. He had been one of the leaders of an incredibly evil dark coven, Amyranth. I knew he had personally caused any number of people to be killed, and he had, in fact, tried to kill me. But in an unexplainable psychological perversity, I had loved him and respected him. I had been very drawn to him, and oddly, he had seemed to sincerely care for me, though his love for power had definitely outweighed his love for me. Something in me resonated with something in him, and while that worried me, I also couldn't deny it. I cared about him. I didn't want him to die. But I hadn't been able to let him continue to work the appalling forms of dark magick he had loved.

"Tchah, Morgan," Killian said with unexpected gentleness. "I'm sorry for him, too, but Goddess, this is the threefold law barely coming home to roost. You didn't set him in motion. You only slowed him down a lot."

"Thanks," I managed to say. The knot in my chest loosened a bit.

"Besides," he went on. "What Mum's doing to him is making your bit look like child's play."

"Oh, Goddess. What's happening?"

"She's divorcing him," Killian said, and there was amusement in his voice. "An illegitimate child, untold dark workings, several very public affairs, years of fights and barely masked hatred and betrayal—none of these were enough to make Mum take this drastic step. But now that Da has no more power than a firefly, she's running him down."

"Oh, no," I said. I had been the illegitimate child.

"Well, it's a shame, but what goes around, comes around," Killian said lightly. I knew he cared for his father, but I also knew there was a great deal of anger and resentment there, too. Ciaran hadn't been a good father to anyone. And he'd treated his wife just as badly.

"Goodness. I wonder what's happening to Amyranth without him?" I made my voice casual, but from the pause on the other end I knew Killian wasn't fooled.

"Basically I think they're running around like chickens with their heads cut off," Killian said, deciding to answer me. "I haven't had any direct news, but from gossip I've picked up, I gather that Da had held his reins of power so tightly that no one was really waiting in the wings. It would take an incredibly strong witch to assume control, and knowing Da, he probably made sure there was no one that strong near the top."

"Huh. So what happens now?"

"Someone will eventually get their act together and step in. I predict lots of infighting and backstabbing," he said cheerfully. "It should be quite the soap opera for a while."

"Wow." So it didn't sound like either Ciaran or Amyranth

was together enough to be behind my dreams, then. "Well. What are you doing for Beltane? Anything planned?"

"I've had a couple of invites. What about you?"

"Oh, we're having a celebration here," I told him. "Food, drink, maypole, dancing."

"Say, what a great idea! That sounds terrific, and we can get all caught up," said Killian.

Ack! I thought. I could just picture Killian loping into our little Beltane celebration. It was going to be tense enough, with both Raven and Sky there, but to have the third member of the disastrous love triangle there would be too much. Either this thought hadn't occurred to Killian, or it had, and he simply assumed it wouldn't be a problem. But I hadn't even *invited* him!

"Um," I said, wondering how to put this. "Okay, but wear armor?"

"Great, then, Morgan. I'll see you Beltane Eve. Thanks so much for calling! Ciao!"

The phone line went dead before I could say anything. Jeez, I thought. What horrible emotional catastrophe had I set in motion? I shook my head and hung up the phone and then was hit by an unexpected giggle. Killian was really too much. I was knotted up by stress, yet Killian was living it up. Nothing seemed to get to him. It was oddly comforting.

Still smiling, I sat down on the family room couch and pulled a throw pillow into my lap. The house was dark around me, except for the glare of the computer screen and a small lamp on a side table. I could feel my family sleeping upstairs and lamented the fact that lately it always seemed that I was the only one who was up when everyone else was asleep.

I rested my head against the back of the couch, feeling like my arms and legs weighed a ton, like I was standing on Jupiter. I closed my eyes. Of course, I couldn't actually stand on Jupiter—it was mostly made of . . .

"Morgan. I've been waiting for you."

I jump. Oh, Goddess. This can't be real.

Cal is sitting right next to me. I'm struck with different feelings; the most disturbing is an actual gladness to see him. I felt terrible when he died, and something in me won't let me forget my first love. Then I feel the fear and mistrust sink in. My muscles tense, and adrenaline starts pumping into my system. Lastly I'm hit with overwhelming guilt—that I could feel glad to see Cal when I am so completely in love with Hunter.

"It's so good to see you," Cal says, his warm golden eyes probing mine. I feel dreamy, slowed. Part of me knows what to do, how to take charge of this situation, but most of me feels like just floating along, waiting to see what will happen.

"I've missed you so much, Morgan," he says earnestly. "You're very special to me. Together you and I can do wonderful things."

Struggling with my sleep-tied tongue, I manage to spit out, "I doubt it."

"No, no, it's true." Cal takes my hand and stands, pulling me up with him. Is this a dream, so I can use my guided-dreaming techniques? Or is it real? I can't tell, and it seems so hard to think about it, to concentrate. Cal's walking along, and now we're in a beautiful rolling meadow, dotted with wildflowers. The sun feels warm on my skin; I hear the soothing drone of bees as they buzz from flower to flower. The wind blows, fresh and cool, and at this moment it seems that everything is perfect.

But when I look ahead, it's Cal holding my hand, not Hunter. I pull back and frown. "No," I say.

Cal turns around, puzzled. "It's just up here a little bit. Not far. I've got a picnic waiting."

Some small part of my brain remembers my picnic with Hunter in the woods, how in love I felt, how close to him. "I don't want to go," I say, my bare feet stopping in the cool green grass.

Oddly Cal doesn't become angry or upset. Looking sympathetic, he comes to me and gently brushes my hair off my face. "I understand," he says. "But it'll be okay. It's just a little bit farther."

Inexplicably I begin walking again, letting him lead me on through this heavenly place. Is this what the netherland is like? Oh, Goddess, am I dead? For some reason this thought strikes me as funny, and I laugh, feeling the cool breeze on my face. I can't be dead—I have finals starting in two weeks! This makes me laugh more, and Cal turns around and smiles at me.

I look around, still being led by the hand like a child. Behind me is a dark line of trees, their leaves swaying gently. We're walking down a gentle slope, and I become aware of a rippling, gurgling brook. The idea of putting my bare feet into an icy stream sounds wonderful, and I walk on. It must be close.

"Here," says Cal. He stops and gestures proudly. I look up and see not a burbling stream, but Cal's bed. It's set up in front of me, a beautiful, dark four-poster bed, hung with a filmy mosquito net. When I first saw it, I thought it was the most romantic bed I had ever seen. For one moment I flash on Hunter's bed—his mattress and box spring on the floor in his room, his unmatched sheets, his threadbare comforter. . . .

I would rather be there, my mind insists.

"I don't want to be here," I say clearly, hearing my words drift away on the breeze.

"It's okay," Cal says soothingly. "I would never make you do *anything you didn't want to do. I've missed you. I just want to be with you."*

I look at him, and his face is open, real, and as beautiful as I remembered. This face was the first to ignite desire in me, but those first sparks felt nothing like the rich, full longing I feel for Hunter. I pull my hand out of his.

"No," I say, more loudly. "This isn't what I want. I don't want to be here. I can't be with you, Cal."

His perfect brows arch downward. "I don't understand," he says. He takes my hand again and tugs me gently forward. "You love me. You want to be with me. I've always been the one you loved. I love you."

"No," I say again. "I didn't know any better then. But I do now."

He frowns, starting to look determined. "You'll never love anyone more than me," he insists. "You know we need to be together."

"That's not true," I say strongly, and pull my hand away again. I start to back away. I don't know how to get out of here. Dimly I remember something about guided dreaming? Interactive dreaming? But it doesn't make sense.

Cal comes and stands behind me, his hands on my shoulders. I feel the warmth of his touch through my long T-shirt.

Long T-shirt? What am I doing outside, dressed like this? This is what I sleep in—

"No!" I cry, wrenching my shoulders away from Cal's hands. Then suddenly the world goes black. I blink again and again, trying to focus. Where's the meadow? Why am I cold? Where am I? The sound of water is loud in my ears.

I looked down and sucked in a frozen breath. *Goddess!* I was outside, it was night, and I was standing on the rocky ledge where Cal and Hunter had fought, months ago! My toes could feel the unstable ground crumbling beneath me. This was where I had thrown an athame at Hunter, where I thought I had killed him. Now I was going to fall over the same cliff. My arms started to windmill in slow motion as I felt my weight start to shift over the ledge. Below me was a twenty-five-foot drop onto rocks, surrounded by icy mountain runoff.

I was going to die. Cal had led me here to die.

Small pebbles and dirt broke free beneath my feet, and I heard their almost imperceptible tumble down the cliff. Goddess, Goddess, help me, I thought, cold sweat breaking out on my forehead. I was going to die, right here, right now, unless I saved myself. I needed to save myself.

Holding my breath and going against every survival instinct I had, I consciously willed myself to relax every muscle. My feet were peddling against the side of the ledge. I felt my balance start to shift. Drop, I told myself, my eyes closed. Drop. Your weight will carry you backward. Just let yourself fall.

Like a building in an earthquake, my body went limp and I crashed heavily to the ground with a *thud*. Every bone in my body shook with the impact. The breath left my lungs in a whoosh, and for several seconds my mouth worked uselessly, trying to suck in air. I felt my feet dangling over the edge, and my eyes shot open. I turned over and scrabbled at the dirt and roots around me, finding one to latch onto. Holding the root, I snaked forward on my belly until I was sure I was on solid ground. There was a pine tree right there, and I crawled over to it, sitting curled up with my knees drawn up under my big T-shirt. I was filthy.

It was then that I allowed the rest of my consciousness to come to life. I shivered uncontrollably, partly because of the chill of the late-spring night and partly because it was hard to remember when I had last been so frightened. I had experienced plenty of danger in the last few months, but the reality of death, the possibility of dying without any of my loved ones understanding what had truly happened—it was terrifying. Cal had led me here in a dream. I looked around quickly, casting my senses, but didn't pick up on anything except the normal animal life of the woods.

Cal had led me here to kill me.

Suddenly my stomach roiled, and I got to my hands and knees. I dry-heaved for a minute, then curled up again, feeling the sickening crash of the adrenaline leaving my veins. I needed Hunter.

Hunter, come. Please help. Hunter! Help me!

Was he asleep? Had he heard me? Should I try Sky, or Alyce, or Bethany?

Coming.

Oh, thank the Goddess. Now I just had to keep it together until Hunter got here. Then I could turn into a shrieking, terrified banshee.

I couldn't estimate time—every minute felt like an hour—but finally I heard a car coming down the dirt road to the river's edge. When I recognized the familiar outline of Hunter's car and then felt his presence, I was too relieved to even stand up and go to him. Instead, I collapsed on the ground as he hurried over to me, and he put his arms around me.

10

Hunter

Hunter, come. Please help. Hunter! Help me! For a moment I didn't understand who was calling me, but then Morgan's voice pierced my brain, and I bolted awake. Within moments I was zipping up my jeans, pushing my feet into shoes, grabbing my jacket on the way out.

Coming, I sent back, practically leaping off the front porch. It was as black as a cave outside, and I had no idea what time it was. I looked at the moon, low on the horizon, and figured we weren't far from dawn.

Inside my car I started the engine, then remembered the message, thinking on where it had come from. I closed my eyes and recalled it. Bloody hell! The cliff by the river!

I poured on the speed, practically flying, not questioning why Morgan was there, only sure that it had been her voice. I found the old rutted road without difficulty and turned onto it. Finally, right by the cliff, my headlights illuminated Morgan's slender body, curled up in nothing but a dirty T-shirt under a tree. I threw myself out of the car and raced toward her.

"Goddess. My love, come here," I said, pulling her into my arms. I sat on the ground and held her in my lap. I wrapped my jacket around her and rubbed her arms and shoulders to warm her. She must be freezing. What the hell was she doing out here? Her bare feet were dirty, and her legs were scratched and damp. I knew I had to wait for her to calm down before I would get any answers. In the meantime I tried to keep my own panic and anger down.

"Hunter—" she began, her voice breaking on a sob.

"Shhh, shhh, my love. I'm here. You're safe now. You're completely safe." I stroked her back, sending waves of calm, soothing comfort. Finally she lay quiet and relaxed against my shoulder. I pushed her hair, damp with tears, away from her face and held her more closely.

Her voice, when it came, was so small, I could barely hear it.

"It was Cal," she said.

At that name a white-hot rage ignited in me, and I struggled to damp it down.

"What happened, my love?"

She shook her head. "I was at home. I wasn't sure I wanted to go to sleep, but finally I just got exhausted and took Bethany's potion, the other half. I went downstairs to the family room and called Killian. I thought maybe he might have heard something about Ciaran or Amyranth that could help me figure out what's happening."

I nodded.

"But he said Ciaran was a mess, in some witch rehab place in Ireland, and that Amyranth was falling apart without him. So I figured neither one of them could be doing this."

"Sounds like you're right," I said. "It was a good idea to call Killian. And what happened then? Do you remember?"

"I sat down for just a minute—I remember feeling really tired. But then I looked up, and Cal was there, right next to me."

My stomach knotted up, and I felt my jaw clench.

"He said, 'Come on,' and then we were walking through a meadow," Morgan continued. "We were outside, and it was daytime. I guess that's when I probably left the house." She gave a little shudder, and her voice sounded wobbly again. "We walked through that meadow, and it was so pretty. Cal was saying stuff to me, like he knew I loved him. . . ." She hung her head and gripped my jacket more tightly around her.

"It's all right, Morgan. It was a dream. Do you remember what happened then?"

"He . . . he wanted me to *join* him. I said no, I didn't want to be there. And he said he knew I loved him, and I said no, not anymore, or something like that. He started getting upset and trying to pull me closer, and I was trying to remember the interactive dreaming, but nothing would stay in my head." She shook her head in frustration.

"It's all right," I said again. "You did just fine."

She drew in a deep, shivery breath and went on. "Finally I think I shouted *no!* and pulled my hand away, and then every-thing went dark because I had woken up, and I was outside, and it was nighttime." She started sobbing again, and I tried to soothe her as best I could.

"When I realized where I was, I was standing at the very edge of the ledge over there." She pointed. "At the *very* edge. My feet were almost over, and I could feel myself losing my balance."

I was speechless. I had once gone over that ledge myself, and it had been a miracle that I hadn't died. As it was, I had cracked two ribs and been covered with massive bruises for weeks. The water was lower now, since the mountain snowmelt hadn't been under way for long. If Morgan had gone over, I would now be looking for her battered body. I felt like I had been punched and very slowly tried to suck in a breath.

Cal had done this.

I blinked several times, using every bit of self-control I had to not give in to my fury. It was made a thousand times worse by the gripping panic I felt at how close Morgan had come to dying.

"What happened then?" I asked, my voice raspy and dry.

"I was about to fall. I could feel the dirt breaking away under my feet. I was so tense, I was sure I was going to lose my balance and fall forward. Finally I did a calming spell to relax my body and then let myself fall backward."

I tightened my hold on her, pressing her head against my chest and hugging her with all the relief and gratitude I felt.

"*Fuh*-uh," came her voice, and I realized I was crushing her. Instantly I relaxed my hold.

"I'm sorry," I said.

"It's okay," she said, drawing a deep breath. "I'm glad you're here." She looked up at me, her hazel eyes wide and red rimmed from crying. She still looked incredibly beautiful, with that strength I always saw in her.

She gave me a watery smile. "What time is it?"

I glanced at the horizon. "Looks like the sun's about to come up."

"I've got to get home," she said, looking at me with wide eyes. "My parents will be up any second!"

I nodded.

I parked one house down from hers, and we sat for a minute, casting out our senses.

"I'm not getting much," I said. "But it's still only five till six."

"I don't feel much, either," she said, sliding out of my jacket. "I guess I'll risk it. This is one day I won't have to rush to get ready for school."

"Tell them you were getting the newspaper," I suggested, pointing at the paper on the front walk.

Morgan gave an ironic snort, glancing down at her soiled T-shirt and feet, then kissed me quickly and opened her door.

"Morgan, this will end today," I said. "No matter what. As soon as I think Alyce is up, I'll call her and Bethany. Come to Practical Magick today after school. We'll be there, and we won't leave till we have a plan."

She gave me a wan little smile, then ran up the cold front walk. She paused for a moment in front of the door, then carefully eased it open. Seconds later her hand came back outside, its thumb pointing up. Everything was fine. Her parents would soon be up, and Mary K. was awake. Reluctantly I started my engine and headed for home.

Back home I went straight to my room. For almost half an hour I just lay on my bed, staring at the ceiling. Morgan had almost died because of Cal. I had to get a grip and then get to work with a cool head and a strong will. Finally I got up and started flipping through piles of books, looking for something that I could use to stop him. It was clear Cal's anam had somehow survived. I guessed that bastard had been stronger than I thought. Obviously he just couldn't get over the idea that Morgan loved someone else and that the someone else was me, his hated half brother. But now he wanted her so badly that he was willing to *kill* her to be with her? The thought was unbearable.

At seven-thirty I called Alyce and told her everything. She was horrified and also astonished that it had happened despite Bethany's sleep potion. She agreed this was too serious to continue for another day and said she'd meet us at four that afternoon. I asked her to call Bethany and tell her what had happened, and she said she would.

Downstairs I found Sky in the kitchen, an unusually sour look on her face.

"What's wrong?" I asked, pouring myself a cup of tea.

She sighed and shook her head. "I called some members of Kithic to talk about Beltane," she said. "I thought I could get the ball rolling on the celebration. Everyone seemed gung ho. So I started making plans yesterday—thinking about fresh flowers, oatcakes with honey, where to get a maypole."

"Sounds good," I said.

"You would think so," she said tartly. "Unfortunately, what no one told me was that someone *else* had also started working on plans for Beltane."

I frowned. "I hadn't heard about that. Who?"

Sky gave me an icy stare. "Raven."

I took a drink of my tea to allow myself time to formulate a response. On the one hand, I almost felt like saying, Well, you know what? Morgan almost died this morning. But on the other hand, I knew how much Sky had been hurt by her breakup with Raven, and she was my cousin and I loved her and didn't want her to be hurt.

"Crap," I said inadequately, then realized with no small amount of horror that I had picked up that expression from Morgan.

Sky looked at me with raised eyebrows. "Raven called here last night, incensed," she continued. "I can't just waltz back into town and start messing with her plans and so on. So we barked at each other for a while, and neither of us would back down, and then we had a better-idea-than-thou contest."

"Who won?"

"Neither of us," Sky admitted. "As hard as it is to believe, she actually had one or two decent ideas."

"Hmmm. So what happens now?"

Sky gave a heartfelt sigh and stretched her arms over her head, arching her back. "Well, unfortunately, my brain tumor chose to act up just then, and I agreed to meet Raven in person to discuss ideas." She shook her head, her feathery white-blond hair flying. "I don't know what I was thinking. All I can do now is hope that I'm hit by a stomach flu."

I looked at my cousin with interest. Morgan was strong, and Sky was also strong, but in a different way. Morgan was strong like a young willow tree, able to bend with the storm. Sky was strong like a knife. It was extremely unusual for her to admit any kind of weakness whatsoever. For her to tell me that she would rather get horribly sick than see Raven was a clue as to how raw her feelings still were. Sky could be quite ruthless—all she had to do was call Raven and cancel. But she wasn't planning to do so. It was very interesting and also a little alarming.

Sky looked at me looking at her and got an irritated look on her face. "Oh, shut up," she muttered, standing and carrying her plates to the sink. I waited till she left before I groaned quietly.

Later I found my father in our circle room, hunched over an old tome that looked like it was disintegrating right before my eyes.

"You were up early, lad," he said, looking at me over the half-moon reading glasses he had recently started wearing.

I told him everything that had happened this morning with Morgan, and his face became increasingly concerned. It was hard for me to moderate what I said about Cal and his suspected involvement, but Da hid his reaction, if he had any.

"Bad news, son," he said when I was done. "Do you think Alyce and Bethany have a handle on it?"

"Yes," I said. "We're all doing research, and I think we're pulling a plan together tonight."

"I see. Is there something I could do to help?"

His voice sounded a little stiff, and I knew there was no way he could remain objective about Cal.

"No, Da, I don't think so."

"Right, then. Well, let me know." He paused. "In the meantime, I've been thinking about Patrice." He took off his glasses and tapped the book with them. "There's some interesting reading here. It talks about some variants of common limiting spells that seem to have interesting possibilities. Of course, I'm afraid Patrice is in all probability going to end up getting her powers stripped."

"I hope not," I said. "Let's just keep trying to be creative."

I told him about some of the reading I had done lately, a few histories of witches who had, by accident, been the victims of spells that had gone awry. There had been one witch who had surprised herself by losing her powers in January—only in January—but in every January after that, for the rest of her life. Things like that. Another had lost the ability to work any kind of animal magick, but only animal magick.

Da looked intrigued, and I told him I would show him my sources.

"It's an interesting problem," he said, putting on his glasses and turning back to his book. "Very interesting."

11

Morgan

When school was over, Mary K. met me by Das Boot and we headed for home. I felt foggy and distant, and I could barely remember anything that had happened that day. However, as awful as I had felt, being surrounded by hundreds of other students hadn't been a bad thing. I had felt safe, lost in the hustle and bustle of classes and lunch and more classes.

"Yoo-hoo," Mary K. said loudly, and my head snapped in her direction. "I *said*, do you think you can give me a ride to Alisa's later?"

"Sorry," I said. "Didn't hear you. Um, I don't think so. I'm going to be home for just a minute, then Hunter's coming over and we're going out. Maybe Alisa can get a ride to our house."

"Okay, I'll ask."

At home I went up to the bathroom and tried to salvage my appearance somewhat. There wasn't a heck of a lot I could do. I stood in front of the mirror, feeling depressed and wondering if Hunter was legally blind. I felt Mary K. come up and sighed.

"Yeah, you're not exactly the poster child for glowing health, are you?" she said, leaning against the door frame.

"No, guess not." I turned to go, but my sister stopped me.

"Hold on a minute." She rummaged through her bath-room drawer and then held my face in a hard grip while she dabbed and brushed and stroked and almost blinded me with a mascara brush when I blinked.

"I'm going to look like a clown," I said warningly.

"No, you're not," she said. "Look."

I turned to the mirror, and once again my sister had man-aged to somehow work with my unpromising raw materials. My cheeks looked healthily pink, my eyes larger and more distinctive, and my mouth looked natural instead of looking like I had just donated a lot of blood. Yet I didn't even look made up. I looked like me, but me on a *really* good day.

"Nice?" she asked, obviously pleased.

"You are my idol," I said, staring at myself. "This is great."

Mary K. grinned, and then the phone rang and she went to answer it. I quickly changed my shirt, since I had spilled Diet Coke on it at lunch, and then Mary K. tapped on my door. "For you," she called. "It's someone named Ee-fuh or something like that."

Eoife. That's strange, I thought, taking the phone. "Hello?"

"Morgan," said Eoife McNabb's familiar voice. Instantly I pictured her in my mind: she was small, probably not much more than five feet tall. Her eyes were a warm, light brown, and her hair was the most shocking shade of natural red I had ever seen. "Hello, how are you?"

"Okay, I guess," I said warily. I liked Eoife and respected

her, but that didn't mean I trusted her completely. She was one of the subelders of the council.

"Morgan, do you have a moment? I need to talk to you about something."

"Um," I said, glancing at my watch. Hunter should be here any minute.

"I've been talking to some of the witches at Dùbhlan Cuan, the retreat where our most talented and knowledge-able teachers are, up in northern Scotland. The short story is, they've agreed to accept you as a probationary student this summer."

She sounded incredibly excited.

"Hm!" I said.

"It would be an intensive eight-week course. You would have to pay your airfare, but everything else, room and board, would be covered. Morgan, this is the first time any American witch has been accepted for teaching, much less one as young as you and as relatively untrained, uninitiated. It's the chance of a lifetime, one that many, many witches can only dream of. You would be foolish not to take it."

"Why did they accept me?" I asked. Eoife hadn't even told me she was going to put in an application.

"Because of your power," Eoife said simply. "A witch like you comes along only once every several generations. Morgan," she said gently. "I really think these could be the most important eight weeks of your life. The summer session starts in mid-June and lasts until mid-August. Please tell me you'll come."

All kinds of thoughts were flying through my head. Bree and I had a tradition of driving over to the Jersey shore for a beach vacation. That would be out, and so would long summer evenings eating snow cones, all the dumb summer movies. It would mean I couldn't work and earn money this summer, money that I always depended on to supplement my pitiful allowance throughout the year.

On the other hand, Hunter was going to be in England during the summer. I hadn't even been able to think about the pain of that separation and how much I dreaded it. If I was up in Scotland, it would be easier to see him. And the idea of being in an all-witch environment, where everyone understood me, where no one was suspicious, sounded like heaven. I would learn so much.

"I would love to," I said at last, and immediately sensed Eoife's relief. "The problem is, I'll need to ask my parents. If I was going over there to study math, they would be packing my bags. But to study Wicca—it's not going to go over well." My heart began sinking as soon as I said that.

"I see," said Eoife. "Yes. That could be a problem. Do you think it would help if I talked to them?"

I thought about it. More likely that conversation would be an unmitigated disaster. "Um, well, let me try asking them first. I'll let you know as soon as I can—and I'll really try to get them to agree. I really, really want to go."

"I'm glad," said Eoife. "Please do try, and let me know if it will help for me to talk to them. I'll call you soon for news, all right?"

"Yes. Thanks, Eoife. I really appreciate it." We hung up and I hurried downstairs just as I sensed Hunter coming up the walk.

He smiled when he saw me, his eyes examining me for signs of my horrible ordeal last night. We said good-bye to Mary K., and I grabbed my jacket.

"So, horrible stress agrees with you," he said as we walked to his car. "You look like you just took a brisk walk in the fresh spring air."

I shrugged, feeling pleased. "Hunter, you'll never believe what just happened," I said, and on our way to Red Kill, I told him all about Eoife's amazing offer.

Hunter looked more and more astounded, and when we parked in front of Practical Magick, he leaned over and hugged me hard. "Morgan! That's brilliant! It's like winning the Nobel Prize as a teenager! Goddess, I'm so proud of you!" He looked at me, his hands on my shoulders, and I smiled some-what self-consciously. "Have you asked your parents yet?"

"No—they're not home, and Eoife just called. I'll ask them soon, when I find a really good moment."

"It would be an amazing, incredible experience," he said. "I hope they let you take it."

We got out of the car and headed into the store. "Does Mary K. know?"

"I didn't have time to tell her. You came right then, and she was headed to Alisa's house. She's agreed to go to Alisa's dad's wedding."

"Good. I'm hoping they can work things out."

Alyce came forward to meet us and took both my hands as an interested young customer watched us. "Come into the other room," she said quietly. "Bethany's already here."

Alyce had moved another table and more chairs into the back room where Hunter worked. Because the room had a door that closed, it felt more private than the little back kitchen, which had only a curtain.

Again, I told them everything I could remember about my

dream the previous night. I was already starting to forget details, and Hunter added things that I had told him when he'd first found me.

"To me, based on the things Cal was saying, it sounds like he simply can't let go of Morgan, can't accept that he's no longer part of her life," Hunter said, trying not to show how angry he was. "It's like he wants her with him."

"That could definitely be part of it," Bethany said. "But I think there's more to it than that. All the images of the fire-winged hawk—that's a common symbol for an uncommon person, a *sgiùrs dàn*."

Ciaran had called me a *sgiùrs dàn*, I remembered, but I hadn't known what to make of it.

"That's what I found out also," Hunter said. "And *sgiùrs dàn* basically means destroyer."

My eyebrows raised.

Alyce went on. "The research I've done in the last few days has turned up some interesting facts. First, the idea of the *sgiùrs dàn* seems particular only to the Woodbanes. The rough translation of the actual words is something like 'scourge of fate.' But the references to it I found made it sound more like the Indian Siva, something that destroys or wipes clean but also clears a path for new beginnings."

"And I'm one?" I asked, my voice practically squeaking.

Alyce looked at me and took a deep breath. "Possibly," she said. "I don't know why Ciaran would lie about that. In Woodbane history there are mentions of *sgiùrs dàns* every few generations. They're almost always women, and it seemed that after they've lived, or because of them, the course of Woodbane history changes."

"It could be coincidental," Hunter suggested. "A particularly charismatic or powerful witch comes along, and then they later attribute the change to her, identifying her as a *sgiùrs dàn* after the fact."

"Which doesn't explain why Morgan would be called one," said Bethany.

"I can't really find a connection to Morgan," Alyce admitted. "The last one seemed to be noted in 1902, and one source I found believes that person cleared the way for the creation of Amyranth."

"Great," I muttered, feeling a headache coming on.

"And then there was one back around 1820 or so," Alyce went on. "The *sgiùrs dàn* seems to be either light or dark, with no discernible pattern." She gave a sudden smile. "We're hoping you're light."

I made a thanks-a-lot face. "And this relates to me how?"

"We don't know," Alyce admitted. "It's just that you had dreams with images of a hawk that had wings made of fire. The only references we could find of that image were related to the *sgiùrs dàn*."

"At any rate, what's become quite clear is that these are definitely attacks against Morgan, and they're increasing in danger. They're now life-threatening, and they must be stopped," said Hunter.

"I agree," said Bethany.

"We have a plan," said Alyce, surprising me. She glanced across at Bethany. "We were working on it until late last night, and then today we think we've finished it—almost. The dreams are getting more realistic, more cohesive. I feel, and Bethany agrees, that there is a being behind this, probably

Cal Blaire, though we're not totally certain. My theory is that as the dreams become more cohesive, so does this being, or this anam. The dreams are leading up to a climax: Morgan's death. The presence, for lack of a better word, is finding that it has to keep upping its power, upping the tricks it uses on Morgan."

"A witch who wasn't strong as Morgan probably wouldn't have made it this far," Bethany said.

"What's your plan?" Hunter asked.

"A magickal trap," Alyce said. "Our idea is that as the being becomes more cohesive, it also becomes more vulnerable to being caught. If Morgan didn't take any sleeping potion and allowed herself to dream, I feel that this presence—"

"Cal," Hunter supplied.

"—would take that opportunity to launch its final attack. We three would be watching, hidden magickally. If Morgan sleepwalks, we'll follow her. If the presence shows up, we'll trap it."

"How do you catch an anam?" I asked.

"The three of us will join our powers and hold it in a binding spell," Bethany explained. "We'll adapt it for an amorphous being, but I feel that the three of us should be able to hold on to just about anything."

"At that point we'll ensnare it—"

"Cal," said Hunter.

"—in a piece of brown jasper, using a spell I've adapted from one I've read," Alyce went on, continuing to ignore Hunter's interruptions. "Then, after we question the anam, the crystal can be destroyed in any number of ways."

I thought this through. I didn't like the idea of sleeping

with no potion at all, but the idea that these three witches, whom I trusted so implicitly, would be right there, made it seem more doable.

"Okay," I said firmly, leaning forward. "I'm ready. Let's do it tonight. I appreciate all the work you've done," I said to the three of them.

"We're happy to help," Alyce assured me. "Now— we need a few hours to prepare and get set up. Morgan, I think you should just go home, have a light dinner, then come back to my apartment around eight. Will there be a problem with school?"

I frowned, then shook my head. "I'll tell my parents I'm sleeping over at Bree's. They usually don't mind."

"Fine, then. Hunter and Bethany, can you stay here so we can go over things again?"

"Let me just run Morgan home, then I'll be right back," Hunter said. They agreed, and as Hunter drove me home, I felt more optimistic than I had in days.

12

Hunter

I was on my way back to Practical Magick when Celia called me on my mobile. "We just heard—Patrice has asked us to move our usual Friday circle to this afternoon because Joshua is undergoing tests tomorrow."

"Why doesn't Patrice just ask someone to step in?" I asked pointedly.

"She never likes substitutes," Celia said, her tart tone telling me she had gotten my point. "Can you come? This would be a good chance to observe a circle."

I glanced at my watch and remembered that I had my magickal gear in a backpack in the boot of my car. "I'm in the middle of something crucial," I said, "but let me check, and I'll call you right back."

I spoke to Alyce, and she agreed that if I could get back there by eight o'clock, it should be fine. We'd have to explain the entire plan to Morgan, anyway.

"Right," I said. "If I can make it earlier, I will." Then I called Celia back. "I'm on my way," I said, and Celia gave me directions.

Many covens meet in someone's house or outdoors. It was somewhat unusual to have Kithic move from house to house, the way it did, and Willowbrook also was a little unusual in that it rented commercial space.

In Thornton, I parked my car about three blocks away from the address Celia had given me. They were starting their circle early, at five. I slipped on my backpack, then made my way toward the small, three-story building whose top floor Willowbrook rented. I made note of alleys, escape routes, which buildings connected where, which streets ran between what. By about quarter of seven I was in back of Willowbrook's building. There was a rusty fire escape ladder about two feet above my head. I gauged its condition, cast a quick see-me-not spell, and then jumped hard, catching the bottom rung and quickly clamping my other hand above that. A bit of hand-over-hand, and then my right foot caught the bottom rung.

One story up, the ladder attached to a small, rusted metal balcony that ran in front of two windows. Another staircase ran up to the third floor, and then a ladder went to the roof. I cast out my senses, then crept closer to the two windows I would have to pass. They led to a hallway with some employees starting to take off for the day. I scrambled up the staircase as fast as I could. Then a step across nothingness to the last ladder, and voilà, I was on the roof.

It felt like old days—by coincidence I was dressed all in dark gray, useful for reconnaissance, and I surrounded myself with the strongest cloaking spells I knew. No one would detect my presence. Up on the roof, I padded around until I felt I was right over Willowbrook's rooms. Robin had told me that their space included a one-room library, a tiny kitchen, one room of storage, and a larger circle room.

Inside my backpack I had all my Seeker tools—some magickal things, but also some gadgets I had gotten at mail-order spy stores. Now I opened a small, foam-lined case and took out my tiny periscope. It was basically similar to the cardboard one Sky had made to spy on me when we were little, only this one was well made and spelled.

Slowly I lowered it down over the side of the building, grateful that their circle room overlooked the back of the building rather than the front, by the street. I said a little enhancement spell as it went down and hung over the edge so I could see exactly where the periscope was going.

As soon as it was maybe half an inch below the top of one window, I stopped and fitted my eye to the eyepiece. I rotated and zoomed and soon had a stellar view of the circle room. The room was painted a deep, rich purple. Crimson curtains hung on either side of an attractive altar lined with candles, incense, and silver cups filled with fresh flowers appropriate to the season. An embroidered cloth hung down on both sides of the altar, and I could see sigils for the Goddess and God. Nothing looked pretentious or fancy or flavored by wealth or pride. There were no obvious traces of dark magick. It was a circle room I would have felt comfortable in.

Turning my scope, I was able to count seven women (including Celia and Robin) and two men so far. I knew there were seventeen witches in all in the coven, but I assumed several of them wouldn't be able to make it at this unusual time and on such short notice. A minute later a woman came in, wearing a bright yellow robe: Patrice. She smiled and greeted everyone, and though I cast my senses strongly, I couldn't pick up on anything like fear or mistrust or anger. Of course, they were mostly blood witches, and they could hide their feelings easier than most. But I got genuine warmth, affection, and caring, both to and from Patrice.

Right at five Patrice invoked the Goddess and the God and, with a simple, elegant, and heartfelt ceremony, dedicated the circle to the four elements. Then the ten present members joined hands and began some familiar chants: to raise power, to join and mingle their energies, to recognize spring, to acknowledge the Goddess. Each phrase had a wealth of meaning and a subtlety I appreciated. The members raised their linked hands above their heads and began to move deasil around the large room. The way they chanted told me that most of them had been together a long time, years, and were intimately familiar with the forms of the ceremony and with each other.

My nose wrinkled. This was an old building, and the sun of the spring day had released some acrid scent from the old-fashioned pitch that sealed crevices on the room. My knees already ached, and I shifted positions. All part of the job. I was thirsty and realized with annoyance that I had left my water bottle down in my car. Damn.

I watched Patrice in particular—she was attractive for an older woman, I saw now, something I hadn't picked up on when Da and I had scried before. She had medium brown hair streaked with lighter shades and dark blue eyes. She looked vibrant and intelligent, but also fatigued and tense.

The circle went totally normally, as far as I could tell, over the next half hour. When their chanting slowed, many coven members shared things about their lives, or asked for help with a certain thing, or asked questions they hoped others could answer. I couldn't detect any reticence or mistrust. It was odd. Patrice really felt like the warm, caring, generous woman that Celia and Robin had described. But they couldn't deny their concerns.

Once again the ten witches joined hands and began moving deasil, beginning the final power chant, the one that should leave them feeling energized and peaceful for the next couple of days. Patrice began it, and one by one the other witches joined in, their sopranos, altos, tenors, and basses all weaving together like a tapestry of sound. To my eyes, Celia and Robin and perhaps two or three others looked a tiny bit hesitant, but no one refused to participate. Everyone joined in, and like a well-rehearsed choir, their voices fitted seamlessly together in a beautiful expression of the joy of magick.

This was confusing. I just didn't see what had concerned Celia and Robin, yet I had trusted their instincts and feelings. Was this the one night Patrice was going to skip whatever it was that had made them nervous?

But wait. I frowned and angled my little scope so I could once again see the whole circle. A new note had entered the song, a thin line of meaning underlying and circling and flitting in and out among the other voices. Quickly I determined that it was Patrice's full, attractive voice—and just as quickly my eyes opened wide as I recognized her song as one of the basic forms of a "hypnotic" spell. Her dark blue eyes seemed a bit more focused on the coven members as she sang. Over the next two minutes the other witches slowly began to seem glassy-eyed. All of them, including

Celia and Robin, were smiling, moving comfortably, keeping pace with the circle, continuing their song in a kind of circular reel that often helps invoke the most energy.

Patrice wasn't even pretending now to be part of the power chant. She held hands with two members and kept moving in a circle, but she wasn't singing and her eyes were clear and intent. Her mouth had lines of tension around it, and her face looked more set than it had earlier. In the next moment I saw her lips move in an actual spell, and I cast my senses as strongly as I could to make out what she was saying.

Oh, Goddess. My mouth opened and I held my breath, training the scope on Patrice, zooming in so I could see her closely. I wasn't mistaken. Patrice was casting a spell on the coven, a spell that would gather the energy they were raising now and refocus it on her so that she would absorb all of it. Not only that, but some of the phrasing she was using indicated that this would gather not only the energy raised here and now, but also whatever energy could be pulled without too much force from each person there.

This was dark magick. If Patrice had been ill herself and had asked her covenmates to direct energy toward her, to aid in her healing, that would be fine. People did that all the time. This was deliberately taking something not offered from a living being, doing it without permission. To hypnotize an entire coven and sap their energy was completely wrong, and any initiated witch would know that.

After several minutes Patrice once again joined her voice into the power chant, and I heard her weave a spell of forgetfulness, of trust, of safety into the last round. Then voices raised to a crescendo. I looked up quickly to see that the sun was just setting at this instant, that it had gotten dark as I had sat on the roof, and my knees were completely numb from being knelt on for two hours.

My eye back on my scope, I watched as the last note was cried. Instantly each witch sank to the ground, crouching on their hands and feet, as if to ground themselves. This was unusual. I hadn't seen a coven do this before. I looked at Patrice and saw that she was hunched over, her shoulders shaking, her head bobbing. I assumed she had absorbed so much excess energy that she felt sick and needed time to assimilate it. At least four of the witches on the ground seemed to be leaning against others, as though they would fall over without support. Robin was also hunkered down on all fours, her shoulders heaving as if she felt ill.

I shook my head. Having your energy taken from you against your will is an ugly thing. No wonder Celia and Robin had forced themselves to overcome their loyalty and trust of Patrice to seek out help. Patrice had driven them to extraordinary lengths.

Slowly people began looking up, either sitting down cross-legged or trying shakily to stand. Two women walked unsteadily to the kitchen and reappeared a few minutes later with fruit, fruit juice, tea, and cake. They put these on the floor, and witches literally scooted or crawled over to them, helping themselves to the food. This was horrible. Virtually every coven has snacks after a circle—there's something about making magick that seems to deplete one's blood sugar—but to see these initiated witches on the ground, too weak to stand up, turned my stomach. The food helped them, however. After eating and resting, they began standing up, grinning sheepishly at each other, as if embarrassed to be left so weakened by a circle. Patrice was the last one to stand, and I saw Celia and Robin watching her.

When she stood up and I saw her face, I saw that she too had been transformed by the circle, but in quite a different way than her coven. She looked terrific, as if she'd just had sixteen hours' sleep. She seemed to be glowing with good health and energy, while all the others still seemed a bit wobbly and sluggish.

I had seen enough. I sat back and folded up my scope and was just putting it in its case when the back of my neck prickled.

"What are you doing up here?" a man's voice demanded.

I turned around and gave a nonchalant nod. He was obviously the janitor. "Cable guy," I said in an American accent, patting my little case. I glanced around, and bless the Goddess, there was actually a black cable running right by my feet. I took out a pair of wire strippers and picked up the cable in a professional matter. "Emergency call. It's too much to let a guy eat dinner, right?" Go away. Everything's fine. Someone on the second floor has called about a dripping sink.

"Oh," said the man. "Okay. Lock the access door when you leave."

"Will do," I said, not looking up. As soon as he closed the access door behind him, I stowed everything in my small backpack and shimmied down the ladder to the fire escape. Within seconds I was walking briskly to my car. The neighborhood was quiet and approaching twilight.

The truth was, I didn't know what I was going to do. If I were still a Seeker, I would recommend that Patrice be stripped of her powers. But I wasn't a Seeker, and I had promised Celia and Robin to try to think of some other less drastic way to stop Patrice. What Patrice was doing was egregiously wrong—no question. But Celia and Robin seemed so certain that Patrice was, in fact, a good person at heart, just someone who had been pushed to do extraordinary things because of difficult situations.

I would have to find another option.

I waited in my car until I saw Patrice's car pass mine. As soon as she did, I frowned: Robin was with her. Maybe Patrice was just giving her a ride home. But there was something about the tilt of Robin's head—I couldn't pin it down, but something felt off to me. After a minute I pulled out and followed her, keeping a good distance between us.

I followed Patrice to a state park not far from there called Highgate Woods. I hung back far enough to make sure Patrice didn't pick up on my presence, then followed her into the parking lot. There were maybe twelve other cars here, people jogging, walking dogs, but nowhere did I see Patrice's SUV. I parked and got out, strolling past every car, mentally doing reveal spells so that if Patrice had set some kind of magickal camouflage on her car, I would notice it. But though I circled the lot twice, I saw no sign of Patrice or Robin or the car.

This couldn't be—I had followed her right into the park, right past the welcome center, dammit. Had there been another turnoff there?

I sprinted back to my car and started the engine. Rookie move, Niall, I thought as I wheeled my car around and headed for the park entrance again. I went slowly this time, and there was, in fact, another turnoff. And beyond that were another two forks. I swore under my breath. I was wasting time I couldn't afford. Though I cast my senses, I couldn't detect Patrice's signature and so had to search the other two turnoffs by sight. Of course, she wasn't at the first parking lot I checked—that would have been too easy. I retraced my route again and tried the right turnoff. This time, among the few other cars parked there, I saw the SUV.

I jumped out of my car and then pawed through my backpack and took a number of things I might need. I strode quickly to the park's entrance and cast my senses for Patrice, turning up nothing. No surprise. I searched for Robin, counting on the fact that Patrice probably wouldn't have thought to cover her tracks. This time I got something and headed into the park, down one of the maintained trails.

Although it was rapidly growing dark, I soon sensed that Robin had left the trail and set off cross-country. If I hadn't had to backtrack so much, I'd have been able to see them ahead of me. As it was, I relied on my senses and realized that the deeper I got into the woods, the more I could actually pick up on a trail of magick. Of course, I expected confusion spells, misdirection spells, and so on, but just the pattern of those spells themselves, where they were placed, what area they covered, was enough for me to triangulate a location. A more experienced witch—or a witch in less of a hurry—would have done a much better job of covering her path.

Besides the lingering prickles of magick I felt around me, I also saw signs that someone—two someones—had been through here recently. And they hadn't been careful about not leaving their mark all over the vegetation. A snapped twig here, the scrape of lichen there. It was a pretty clumsy show. I quickly considered the possibility that there were fake signs, created to mislead me, but I didn't feel that they were. The whole thing felt almost amateurish.

Here in the protected part of the woods, it was almost completely without light and more thickly vegetated. Once again I felt some misdirection spells. They were like tissue paper—I was walking right through them. Good thing Patrice hadn't set up the ones my da had used in Canada— the ones where everything in you is screaming uncontrollably that you'll die a horrible, painful death if you take one more step. Though I had managed to get through those, too.

After another minute or so I stopped and concentrated on Robin's energy pattern. I had never touched Patrice and so wouldn't recognize hers, but I did pick up Robin's, a bit more strongly this time. I turned about ten degrees to the north and set off again, stepping over fallen trees, pushing through thick undergrowth that waved leafy, twiggy branches in my face.

Soon I picked up on some disturbing feelings, of being upset, of fear, of feeling lost. More spells. It was actually rather amazing that Patrice had had enough time to do all of this, considering that she didn't seem experienced in terms of dark magick—plus the fact that I was only a few minutes behind her. All this had taken time. Unless she had set it up beforehand, and I didn't think she had. I told myself it wasn't real, that my mind knew the truth, and just bashed on, regardless. It was the only way to get through.

Though the early evening air was brisk, a chill sweat trickled down the back of my shirt. The air felt stale and muggy, making it difficult to breathe. Patrice's spells were a constant irritant, making me impatient. I damped down all these emotions. Emotions only clouded things in magick.

I stopped quietly when I realized I was close. Slowly I stepped forward, a foot at a time, as silently as I knew how. I crouched down on a small patch of damp leaves that wouldn't crinkle noisily under my weight. By edging a bush's branch down, I could see about fifteen feet ahead, to a very small clearing.

Robin was propped against a young sycamore tree, looking lifeless. Her head hung awkwardly to one side, strands of untamable auburn hair falling over her face. Her eyes were mere slits and had no consciousness flickering in them. Bloody hell.

Patrice was a few feet in front of Robin, wearing her yellow robe. I'd refreshed my earlier cloaking spells, and it was clear she had no idea I was there. Leaning over, she began to trace sigils and runes in the air above Robin's head. In her left hand she held a book that looked so old, its pages were brown and crumbling. I realized Patrice was crying as she continued the spell.

I listened hard and heard Patrice saying, "I'm sorry, I'm so sorry, Robin. I don't want to do this, but I have to. I don't know any other way. Please forgive me, Goddess forgive me." Sobs distorted her words. It was the strangest sight I'd ever seen, and that was saying something. I'd never seen someone working dark magick, causing harm to another, but feeling such regret about it at the same time.

From the form of the spell I could tell that Patrice was still working the limitations. From the form of the limitations it was clear that this spell was designed to sap Robin's life energy in a very strong way—such a strong way that I doubted whether Robin would survive. Maybe an incredibly strong witch might, but not Robin.

I took fifteen seconds to settle on a plan and picked an old favorite: the element of surprise.

With no warning I burst through the bush, racing toward Patrice, the *braigh* in my hand. She whirled, stunned, but instantly threw a ball of blue witchfire at me. I swerved and it only glanced off my arm, causing a stinging, tingly feeling like an electric shock. Then she turned and took off through the woods, moving surprisingly quickly. But I was taller, faster, and more ruthless. As I gained on her, she threw another spell at me, but she simply wasn't strong enough to stop me. Within seconds I had tackled her, pinned her to the ground with my knee on her chest, and had her wrists bound in the *braigh*. There had been times when just achieving this much against a dark witch had been a life-or-death battle. Catching Patrice had been comparatively easy.

Patrice's face was rigid with fear and astonishment, her dark blue eyes wild, the irises surrounded by white. With interest I noted that the *braigh* wasn't actually burning her wrists—a good sign. The more corrupt your soul is, the more the spelled *braigh* hurts.

"Seeker?" she whispered, trying to suck in breath.

"Not exactly," I answered, pulling her to a standing position with me. She collapsed instantly, falling against me, and I brought her up sharply, wary of tricks. But she was bent double with sobs, holding her linked wrists in front of her face.

"Oh, Goddess, I'm so sorry! Take me to Robin. Is she all right? Make sure Robin's okay!" Huge, gulping sobs shook her body, and I had to help her back to the clearing.

When we got there, Patrice stumbled toward Robin. She sank to her knees and held her bound wrists out to me. "Just undo this for a minute while I take the binding spell off Robin. Please!"

I narrowed my eyes at her, thinking. Then I knelt and said

the spell that opened the lock on the *braigh*. The silver chain dropped into my hand, and Patrice instantly took one of Robin's hands and gasped out a spell I recognized. Robin blinked and moaned, starting to shift. Patrice reached out to help her, then realized how incongruous and unwelcome that would be. She drew back and like a child crawled toward me and held out her hands. I put the *braigh* back on her, and she sank down on her side, giving over to racking wails that filled the air with remorse.

I knelt by Robin and saw that she was coming around. I spoke to her softly, explaining what was happening and checking her pupils, her pulse, her breathing. She seemed more or less her usual self, though she was upset and trying not to weep. She looked past me at Patrice, and her face contorted with shared pain. Then, unbelievably, she rose and went over to Patrice and patted her shoulder. Patrice was ashamed and put her fists in front of her face, hiding her face in the ground.

It was a while before Patrice's grief subsided enough so that she was relatively coherent. I sat about ten feet away, leaning against a tree, not interfering. If I were a Seeker, I would be doing all sorts of things. But now I had the freedom to let things be, at least for a while.

Eventually Patrice blinked and looked around at Robin.

"Oh, Robin!" she said, fresh tears flowing. "Oh, I'm so sorry! Are you okay? Are you okay?"

"I'm okay," Robin said.

"There's no excuse for what I've done," Patrice said. She lay on her side, curled up in a ball, staring straight ahead. "I deserve to have my powers stripped." She squeezed her eyes tightly shut against that new pain.

"What is all this about?" Robin asked more firmly than I'd heard her speak before.

"It's Joshua," Patrice said, trying not to cry. "He's not getting better. I feel like we're losing the battle. I've tried everything I can think of, but I'm just not strong enough. I couldn't think of what to do. Then one night after a circle I felt so energized, so powerful. I went home and transferred some of my power to him. It all went on from there." She shook her head in disgust at her actions. "I've betrayed you, the coven—everything I believe in and have worked for. I betrayed Joshua—how could I have done this to him? Made him a party to my crimes? Oh, Goddess!" Once more she began crying, until it seemed there would be nothing left inside her.

"Is Joshua better after you transfer power to him?" Robin asked.

"Yes, for a bit. But it doesn't last long. He's losing weight again, he's covered with an awful rash that makes him miserable, he's all puffed up from the steroids—I don't know what to do. I've always been able to solve problems, but I can't solve this." Patrice sniffled and rubbed one wrist against her nose, then looked up at me. "How did you know?"

"Your friends were concerned about you," I said. "I followed you tonight, after the circle."

Patrice nodded, ashamed. "Things were going on, getting worse and worse. I hated myself, but I couldn't stop. The only thing that mattered was that I somehow make Joshua better. But thank the Goddess you stopped me before I went any further."

Robin seemed subdued but not at all angry or withdrawn—more tired.

"You've saved me from myself, you've saved yourself and the rest of the coven from me, you've saved Joshua from having a complete monster for a mother." Patrice seemed exhausted and resigned and full of remorse. But relieved. It was over. "I don't know what will happen to me now."

Slowly she got up, with her and Robin supporting each other. Robin seemed a bit more wobbly, and I offered her my arm.

"You should go home," Robin told Patrice. Without Celia here, Robin seemed to be taking a more active role. She seemed less flighty somehow, stronger, more authoritative. "Can you take the *braigh* off her, please?"

I hesitated. "Is that a good idea?"

The two women stared at me in astonishment.

"What do you mean?" asked Robin.

I shrugged uncomfortably. "Patrice seems to regret what she's done. I believe she's truly sorry. But what she was doing—or was about to do—wasn't shoplifting sweets. What would have happened if I hadn't followed you? Would I be looking for your body?"

"That spell wouldn't have killed Robin!" Patrice said, horrified.

"It probably would have," I said with quiet assurance. "It probably would have killed any witch who wasn't very strong. And Robin's energy had already been sapped—by you. At the very least you weren't doing her any good, were you?"

Patrice stared at Robin, mouth agape, as if realizing anew her colossal error. The idea that this spell might have actually taken Robin's life stunned her, and she wobbled on her feet, looking dazed.

"What are you proposing?" Robin asked, keeping an arm around Patrice to support her.

"I don't know, exactly," I said. "If I were a Seeker, I would turn her in to the council, and she would most likely have her powers stripped. As it is, I'm reluctant to do that. But I'm also reluctant to let Patrice go her merry way."

"We all need time to think," said Robin. "Let's just go home and think, and then we can try to decide what's best."

"What if Patrice runs off?" I didn't want to be hostile, but these two weren't facing the hard realities of the situation.

She looked at me, startled. "I can't leave. Joshua isn't strong enough to be moved—and I could never leave him."

My instincts told me she was telling the truth. I took off the silver *braigh*, and though she rubbed her wrists, her skin wasn't seared or red. "Are you all right to drive?"

She nodded, pale and wide-eyed.

"Right, then. I'll take Robin home. Everyone stay put and take it easy until we arrange to meet again."

Then the three of us picked our way back through the night-dark woods until we hit the trail again. We were each quiet and thoughtful as we got to the parking lot. Patrice climbed into her car, and Robin and I got in mine. And so ended Patrice's reign of power.

13

Morgan

When I got home from Practical Magick Thursday afternoon, I found Aunt Eileen and Paula in the living room.

"Hi!" I said, giving them hugs. "I feel like I haven't seen you in ages."

"Morgan, is that you?" Mom called, pushing through the kitchen's swinging door into the dining room. "Will you set the table?"

Wanting to visit more with my favorite aunt and her girlfriend, I glanced hopefully at Mary K. across the room.

"No way, José," she said firmly. "I already made the salad and pulled all the stringy things off the corn. I've been here since *four*."

Okay, she had a point. I got up and went to the kitchen to get silverware. A witch's work is never done.

"So I thought the family room was completely finished," said Paula as we were sitting down. "We'd been working on it after work every day for a week. It looked so great. I folded up the last drop cloth—"

"Must you tell this story?" Aunt Eileen said plaintively, but I could tell they were just teasing each other.

"Washed the brushes, hammered on the paint can lid," Paula went on, pulling her chair in next to mine. "We stand back, we look, the whole room is a soft, buttery yellow—"

"It was perfectly fine the way it was," Eileen put in.

"But when I went to hook the cable thing back up, I saw that the whole wall behind the entertainment cupboard hadn't been touched!"

"Lots of people wouldn't bother painting behind a huge, heavy piece of furniture," Eileen defended herself.

"The whole *wall*," Paula said, taking an ear of corn and passing the rest to me.

"I couldn't move that thing by myself," said Eileen, but we were all laughing at this point, and she looked sheepish. Paula winked at her across the table, and they both smiled like honeymooners.

"Why does this story not surprise me?" Mom asked, giving her younger sister a look. We all laughed more—it was fun to see adults still acting like real sisters. Mary K., on my other side, pointed her fork at me, like this was the kind of thing I would do. I gave her a big, fake smile.

"I was wondering if you'd heard from the agency," Mom said. "I remember you contacted them last week."

Aunt Eileen and Paula had been thinking about adopting a child.

Eileen nodded. "They sent us a huge packet of information."

"It was terrifying," Paula said. She speared a piece of chicken on her plate and ate it.

"We still just don't know, is what it comes down to," said

my aunt. "The idea of adopting a child in need is really compelling—a friend of mine at work recently adopted a baby girl from China. And one of our neighbors brought back a baby from Romania."

"But each of us had always assumed we'd have a baby of our own someday," Paula said. "There are just so many things to think about, issues to consider. Everything we think about seems to carry so much weight."

"We just have to keep gathering information," Eileen added. "I think the more we learn, the clearer our decision will become."

"Have one of each," said Mary K., talking through a mouthful of chicken. We all turned to look at her. She swallowed and nodded, her shiny russet hair swinging gently around her shoulders. "One of you has a baby, and then you also adopt a baby. Tons of people have two children. Isn't the average in America like 2.1 or something?"

Paula and Eileen stared at my sister as if she were a talking dog.

"We never thought of that," said Eileen, and Mary K. shrugged.

"Two children. It just never occurred to me," said Paula in bemusement. "I've been so wrapped up in trying to figure out how to have one."

"She has a point," said my mom. "If you started having your own baby now and put in the adoption papers, then two or three years from now, when the adoption comes through, they'll be the right age apart."

Just like Mary K and me.

"I've been offered a scholarship to study in Scotland this

summer." As soon as the words were spilling out of my mouth, my brain was already screaming for a shutdown. What had possessed me to blurt this out now? Five heads swiveled to look at me, five pairs of eyes opened in surprise. Morgan, shut *up*, I told myself, aeons too late.

"What?" Mom asked. "You haven't mentioned this. What scholarship?"

"I just heard about it today," I said, threatening myself with all kinds of revenge for being so stupid. "I didn't even know it existed," I added truthfully.

"What is this scholarship?" my dad asked. "Why is it in Scotland? How did you find out about it? Is it for math?"

"Um, Eoife McNabb called me today," I mumbled. I started pushing my peas around on my plate with my fork. "I don't know if you ever met her. But she's a . . . teacher. And she got me a full scholarship to go to a really exclusive, impossible-to-get-into college. I'm the only American they've ever accepted."

"Congratulations, Morgan!" said Aunt Eileen. "That's marvelous! This is really impressive!"

"Goodness, Morgan," said my mother. "I don't think I've heard you mention Eva McNabb. Is she one of the teachers at school?"

"Not exactly," I said, looking at my plate. "Um, the course is for eight weeks. I have to pay my airfare, but everything else is taken care of. It's a huge honor."

"Is this through the math department?" Dad asked again.

"Not exactly," I repeated in a small voice. There were several moments of silence.

"What is this a scholarship for, Morgan?" asked my mom in a calm, don't-give-me-any-crap voice.

Witchcraft? Magick? "Um, healing? Herbal medicine?" I said.

"You have a scholarship to go to Scotland to study *herbs?*" Mary K. asked in disbelief.

I looked down at my plate. "It's a famous place of learning," I tossed out into the deafening silence at the table. "Only the most learned and powerful . . . teachers are there. I'm the youngest person they've ever considered, and the only American. It's considered a huge honor—the chance of a lifetime. Tons of people would be ecstatic to be offered this opportunity."

I saw Eileen and Paula glance at each other—gee, they wished they'd stayed home tonight. Mary K. was looking fixedly at her plate. I could tell she wasn't thrilled about this idea. I didn't even want to look at Mom or Dad.

"It would be an education just to go to Europe," I said, starting to use my desperation tactics, none of which I'd thought through yet because I'd been *certain* I was going to *wait* until the right moment to bring this *up*. "I'd be in northern Scotland—surrounded by tons of history. Historical monuments. And then England and Ireland are just train rides away. Just visiting those would practically count for a world history credit. Think of the cities—Edinburgh, London, Dublin. Castles, gardens, moats." Okay, I was really stretching here. "And I would be working, working, working, not getting into trouble or being bored, or—"

When I finally glanced up, I saw my mom and dad looking at each other. I felt a familiar pang of guilt—I was their fish out of water, the egg some cowbird had left in their nest. When they had adopted me, seventeen years ago, nothing could have prepared them for this last year, as I was suddenly revealed as something they distrusted and feared: a witch by blood.

There was no way they would let me go, to further my study of Wicca, pushing myself one step closer to being an educated, accomplished witch. They were probably still fruitlessly hoping that something would happen to me and that I would somehow turn back into a Rowlands—go to MIT for math, get a nice engineering job or maybe teach. Get married. Have nonwitch grandchildren. Look back on my witch period the way they looked back on their flower-child years.

It wasn't going to happen.

"We need to discuss it," my mom said, her lips somewhat tight. I almost fell out of my chair. What? It wasn't an out-right no!

"Yes," Dad said, swallowing. "There's a lot to think about. We need much more information before we can even make a decision. Is there some kind of brochure or something for this place?"

I was so stunned, I felt like I'd just been hit on the head with a golf ball. "Uh, I don't know," I stammered. "I can ask Eoife. She can give you more information."

Mary K.'s large brown eyes were opened wide.

"I'll do anything you say," I put in, trying not to sound pathetic and desperate.

"Well, your grades have been acceptable lately," Mom said, not looking happy. She stabbed her fork into her salad, and I felt I could have heard the crunching from three blocks away.

"There haven't been any recent . . . incidents," my dad said, his mouth in a tight line.

I looked down. There was a lot they didn't know about. But it hadn't been my fault. Most of it. When I looked back up,

Aunt Eileen and Paula were gazing at me solemnly. It occurred to me that I had no idea what they thought about my involvement with Wicca. I was sure Mom had told Eileen about some of it at least. They were really close, despite the difference in their ages and the different paths their lives had taken.

"We realize that you feel that . . . Wicca is somehow important to you," Mom said. "While it's true we're not very happy about it, we also know that not everyone can live the same life."

"If you let me do this, I will never ask for anything again," I swore.

Mom looked at me for the first time, a smile quirking her mouth. "You said that when you wanted Rollerblades. And now look at you. Still asking for things."

That broke the tension a little bit. Mom and Dad looked at each other again.

"At any rate, we'll discuss it," said Dad, pouring himself another glass of wine. "We're not promising anything. We're only agreeing to think about it."

"Thank so much," I breathed. "That means so much to me."

"Excuse me," said Mary K. "Who's going to give me rides to the beach this summer?" Her eyebrows raised as she looked at me pointedly.

"Um, Alisa's dad?" I suggested. "The church youth group?"

"Whatever," Mary K. said with a big sigh, but I felt it was her way of letting me know this somehow wouldn't kill her.

I looked back down at my plate, suddenly starving. This was amazing. If I didn't know better, I'd swear I had put a spell on my whole family.

"Oh, my goodness," Mom said, looking up with surprise. "We never said grace tonight."

"No, you're right," Dad agreed, thinking back.

"Let say it now," I suggested. I felt an overwhelming gratitude in my life right now and wanted a chance to acknowledge it. I felt that any thanks given to any god all went to the same place, anyway, no matter what religion you were centered in.

We all held hands and bowed our heads. It was a tiny bit like a weekly circle, and I felt comfortable and relaxed. My mind was still whirling with the possibility that my parents might actually consider letting me go to Scotland.

Dad began, "Oh, heavenly father, we your children who are bowed before thee thank thee humbly for the gift of this our food tonight. Your mercy is never ending, your constancy eternal. . . ."

As Dad said the familiar words, a feeling of peace and happiness came over me. I was surrounded by my family, Scotland wasn't out of the question, and I felt safe and as far away from Cal Blaire as I could possibly be.

Dad finished, and we all said, "Amen." And my heart was full of gratitude.

Right after dinner I talked to Bree, who agreed to say that I was sleeping over at her house. She wanted to help with my nightmares, and since my parents knew that Bree and I wouldn't get wild or anything, it was okay with them.

Around eight I said good night to Aunt Eileen, Paula, and the rest of my family, packed a bag, and drove to Red Kill. Alyce's apartment over Practical Magick was like Alyce herself: comforting and appealing. She opened the door at once as soon as she sensed me on the stairs.

"Come in," she said. "Hunter isn't here, and Bethany stepped out for a minute. But come in and sit down."

I sank into her chintz sofa, and Whistle, one of her cats, jumped up on my lap, smelling Dagda. By unspoken agreement we talked about light things—the weather, our gardens—I had dug mine just recently and was starting to fill it in with herbs and flowers. It wasn't long before we felt Bethany on the stairs, and then the three of us sat and waited almost half an hour for Hunter. In the meantime I told Alyce and Bethany about my offer to go to Dùbhlan Cuan. They were really pleased for me and seemed impressed. They both really hoped I could go and offered to talk to my parents if I'd like.

Hunter finally showed up, looking stressed and a little preoccupied. He came over and gave me a quick kiss, then noticed my questioning expression. "I'll tell you about it later," he whispered, and brushed his fingers along my cheek. Then the four of us settled down with cups of herb tea—no caffeine—to go over the strategy.

"Will this thing be able to find me here?" I asked, thinking that if it couldn't, I could just move in.

Bethany nodded. "We believe so. It's your consciousness that it traces, or at least that's the theory. Tonight we're going to work on the assumption that as it's getting more insistent, it will simply need to take on a somewhat less amorphous form. But even if it's barely present, we're prepared to handle it."

I thought of Cal as he'd been when I'd met him, glowing and charismatic, a teenage Wiccan god. How had it all come to this?

Alyce showed us the chunk of brown jasper she had gotten. It was the size of a softball, and though it was shot through with interior flaws and occlusions, it was still beautiful and impressive.

"You'll be sleeping in my bed," Alyce said. "The three of us will be magickally cloaked. Your role will be to go to sleep and be as powerful as you can. Did you bring your mother's tools?"

I nodded and kicked my backpack gently.

"You'll surround yourself with protection spells that will limit anyone who attempts to bind your powers. Then you'll go to sleep and wait for Cal to come to you. Once he does, once he makes a connection with you, you will need to, in your dream, actually take hold of him. Hold him and don't let go. Our theory is that what happens in your dream will be mirrored in real life."

"So you'll just wait while this thing approaches me while I'm asleep?" My voice sounded tight with tension.

"We'll absolutely be on the alert and able to get to you in a moment," Bethany assured me. "There will be three of us, joining our powers. Once you have a hold on the thing, we'll trap it with the binding spell we created. Then we'll further encase it in the brown jasper. And I think that should be the end of it."

"And you're quite sure Morgan won't be hurt?" Hunter asked.

"We'll be right here," Alyce said. "She certainly couldn't go anywhere."

"Does this sound all right with you?" Hunter asked me. "If you're afraid, we don't have to do this. We'll think of something else." He rubbed his hand across his eyes, and I noticed the dark circles there.

"No, it sounds okay," I said. "It's frightening, but not as bad as the idea of having more dreams like this. I just have to stop them."

"Okay," said Alyce, standing up briskly and gathering our cups. "Sounds like we've got a plan, then."

I went into Alyce's bathroom and put on my mother's magickal robe. It was a deep green silk, embroidered with symbols, runes, and letters. As usual, it felt comfortable and light against my skin. When I wore it, I was never too hot or too cold—it was always perfect.

I went into Alyce's bedroom, which I'd never seen before. Once again it seemed to embody its occupant. The bed looked overstuffed and comfortable, the colors were shades of lavender and green, and there were fresh flowers, a crocheted runner across the dresser, and the scent of soothing rosemary and chamomile. Alyce, Bethany, and Hunter were performing cloaking spells on themselves.

At the head of the bed I placed one of Belwicket's silver cups, with water in it. I also placed my birth mother's wand there. Around the other three sides I placed the other three cups, to represent earth, fire, and air. I got into bed, sinking into the comforting softness, the fresh, clean-smelling linens. I had the Belwicket athame, the one engraved with generations of initials of Riordan witches. Someday, I would have my own initials engraved on it, too.

I pulled up the covers and tucked the athame at my side. Surrounded by the powerful tools that had helped women in my family work magick for hundreds of years, I felt fortified and more confident. I felt connected to the long line of witches who were my ancestors and a special connection to

Maeve, the woman who had given me up for adoption rather than allow me to be killed by Ciaran MacEwan.

Hunter came over and tucked me in. "Got your spells ready?" he asked. I nodded. "Right, then—sweet dreams. When you see me next, all this will be over." He leaned over and kissed me, then went back to Alyce and Bethany, who were opening the window and removing its screen.

Alyce came over, smiled, and patted my shoulder. "This will all be okay," she said.

"All ready?" Bethany asked. I nodded. "Good luck, then."

Alyce turned off the light. I looked at the luminous hands on my watch—it was ten-thirty. I often stayed up later than that, but at the moment I felt completely wiped. Closing my eyes, I took in a deep breath, trying to relax and concentrate. Just relax, I told myself. Relax. Everything is all right. You're safe.

"Of course you're safe," Cal says, sitting on the edge of the bed. I jump—I hadn't sensed him coming.

"Why are you doing this?" I ask. "What do you want?"

He leans over. "I want you, Morgan," he says. "I always did. You never would join with me the way I wanted. But now you will." He smiles and strokes my hair, and I can't help flinching. He doesn't seem to notice. "Tonight you'll be mine, all mine. You didn't take any of those nasty potions that kept us apart." He frowns at that. I try to think of what I'm supposed to do now. I can't remember.

Then Cal cheers up. "But tonight is different," he says, smiling again. "Tonight I'm here, and he's not. Tonight you and I will join completely."

"I don't want to." My voice comes out sounding faint, and I say it again, more strongly. "I don't want you. I want you to leave me alone."

Cal tips back his head and laughs, exposing the smooth brown skin of his neck. "Of course you don't really want to be alone," he says, sounding indulgent in a way that pisses me off. "Not when you can be with me. Didn't you have too many years of being alone? You did. But now you'll never be alone again."

"What are you talking about?"

He takes my hand, and it really feels like a person holding it. His skin is smooth and warm, and I feel the brush of the leather friendship bracelet he used to wear. When he was alive. I shiver, but again he doesn't seem to notice.

"You've been playing hard to get," he says. "I don't blame you. You're an exceptional witch—very strong. You're simply too strong not to be joined with me." His smile lights his face, and I'm struck by his physical beauty. "You know what they say—if you're not with us, you're against us."

"Who's us?" I ask. I know I'm supposed to do something, something guided or interactive—but what? Desperately I try to remember—I'm supposed to do something, for some reason. . . .

Cal shrugs casually. "With me. Tonight you're going to join with me forever."

"No."

He laughs easily. "You don't really have a choice, Morgan. Not anymore. Not tonight."

"I always have a choice." My voice comes out stronger than I intended, and it makes his golden eyes flick over at me.

"Not really. Not against me." He stands up and holds out his hand. "Now, come on. Let's get going. I've waited too long for this. You won't get away from me tonight." He remembers to smile at the last bit, but it's a horrible, almost vicious expression, and I recoil.

"No," I say, pulling farther back into the bed. What should I

do? What should I do? Isn't something supposed to happen now? Is someone supposed to help me? Where are they?

Cal reaches forward and grips my wrist in a tight, almost painful grasp. My eyes narrow a bit—I'm not a pushover. Not anymore. I'm no longer innocent Morgan, never had a boyfriend, so flattered that a demigod like Cal Blaire would want me. He thinks I'm weak, is counting on it. But I'm not weak. I'm very strong, and I know it. I'm so strong, I can protect myself in this situation. Strong enough to fight Cal all by myself. I can win. I can beat him.

"Why are you doing this? I want you to leave me alone," I say firmly. I tug on my hand, but he doesn't release it. "I don't want to be with you. I'm not going to join with you. You need to leave and never come back."

He frowns. "Morgan. Stop it. This is nonsense. Now, come on." He gives a hard yank on my hand and almost pulls me out of the bed. My shoulder feels a sharp pang, as if my arm is straining against its socket. Determinedly I pull it back.

I realize now that we're in the meadow again. I don't remember where we were just seconds ago. But we're in the meadow, and there's Cal's bed at the edge of it. The sun is warm on my hair, the bees' droning noise is mesmerizing—it's the most perfect, peaceful place in the world. Except Cal's in it.

Time to act. I reach forward and grab Cal's other hand, pulling it toward me. He smiles—playful Morgan—but I keep a death grip on it and won't let go. He frowns in puzzlement and tries to pull his own hand back. "Let go," he says.

I send every bit of power I have into the hold I have on his hand. "No," I say calmly. "I won't let go."

He suddenly gives a hard yank, and I hold on tighter, clenching my teeth. "You can't hurt me anymore," I grind out—

Then my eyes opened to darkness lit only by a glow of blue witchfire. I lurched up in bed and stifled a horrified scream—in my hand I was holding one leg of a dark-feathered hawk! The same hawk I had seen in all my dreams—the one with the cold, golden eyes. My face froze in shock as I took in the scene—the hawk's huge, powerful wings beating the air, my fist gripped around its leg tight enough to break its bone. The hawk screamed unbearably loudly, right in my face, and I squeezed my eyes shut, the horrible sound raking my eardrums.

Its beak lunged toward my face, and I ducked at the last second to avoid having my cheek ripped open. Around me I heard a commotion—moving and shouting, and then a light flashed on. Other hands were grabbing at me—I was on my knees on the bed, hanging on to the hawk's leg, avoiding its beak. Then I recognized Alyce's voice, and Hunter's and Bethany's, and it was enough to pull me back into reality. Hunter managed to grab a beating wing. Alyce grabbed the other one, holding it hard, outstretched against her body. A sudden slash made me cry out, and I saw that the hawk had managed to slice into my arm with its other taloned claw.

I let out a gasp, and then Hunter grabbed the other leg, and between the four of us we held the hawk down. It struggled fiercely, still lunging with its beak, and then Alyce reached out one hand and grabbed its neck. Her face was contorted with fierce, ruthless determination—I had never seen her look like this before.

I still held on to one leg and glanced down at the gashes on my arm, dripping blood. I stared at the hawk, at its golden eyes—they were like Cal's eyes. I looked up at Alyce to ask what should we do now, but I saw a look of horror come over her face. My head snapped back to the hawk, and then my jaw dropped in terror as the hawk's mouth opened and a wisp of thick, oily smoke emerged. In a second I remembered the last time I had seen something like that—it had been back when Selene had died, in her library. It was here now, and it was incredibly foul, this close. Just being within proximity of it made me feel like my life force was draining away, as if it was the coldness of death itself. My heart sank and my mouth went dry, and then, as the last of the smoke roiled out of the bird's mouth, it went limp and sank lifeless in our hands. It was dead.

"Quick!" Bethany shouted, dropping the bird's body on the bed and throwing herself toward the window. She slammed it down and locked it, and Alyce sprang for the door and locked that, too. I was still trying to get my bearings, but the other three witches were circling the anam, grim looks of resolve on their faces.

Then, as we watched, the nebulous smoke slowly began to achieve more form. It coiled upon itself, becoming more three-dimensional. My eyes felt like they were burning as a grisly, acid-eaten face gradually emerged from the oily fog.

It was Selene.

My mind went blank with terror. Selene! My first thought was that against Cal, we had good odds of beating him. Against Selene, who besides Ciaran was the strongest, most evil witch I'd ever come across—our odds were much worse.

Selene! How was it possible? Her anam must have been within the smoke that drifted from her mouth when she died. She must have found some other host—this hawk, or another one, or something else. Then she had decided to take revenge on me. It hadn't been Cal at all. It had never been Cal.

I felt my heart sink at this realization. The real Cal was dead—he had been dead all this time. Selene had used his image in my dreams to make me follow him. She must have known that I still had conflicting feelings about her son: anger, fear, maybe even a little fondness. But most of all, guilt. He had sacrificed his life for me. And as much as I knew he was a twisted person who had done terrible things, a small part of me still regretted that. Because he might have truly loved me, in his way. And because he never really had a chance. Not with a mother like Selene.

Her death's-head grin was becoming more apparent—in life, Selene had been as beautiful as Cal, in the same sleek, golden, feline way. She was no longer beautiful. It was as if every bit of evil she had in her had eaten away at her human form, leaving only the grimacing mockery of a challenge.

Without thinking I threw out my hand, and a jagged, neon blue bolt of energy snapped from my fingers and sliced right through the smoky form. Her slash of a mouth widened in horrible amusement.

I was stiff and stupid with fear. We hadn't prepared for this. I felt pearls of cold sweat popping fully formed on my forehead, felt the ache of adrenaline tightening my muscles, the dull pain of my stomach, tight with terror. Selene.

Alyce made an incoherent sound—she and the others had been muttering spells nonstop since the hawk had died—but now I looked down and saw that dark tendrils were spinning off from lower down, and they were beginning to curl around the legs of Hunter, Alyce, and Bethany. They each quickly tried to jump away but already seemed held. They were throwing witchfire at it, spitting spells at it, and nothing they were doing was having any effect. These three witches were all strong, quick, and knew well how to protect themselves—but not even Hunter seemed to be able to stall her attack.

The smoky tendrils were weaving themselves higher, coiling insidiously around their bodies.

"Why are you doing this?" I shouted. I was going to sit here and watch my friends—and my *mùirn beatha dàn*—die, and then I was going to die myself if I didn't figure something out. A horrible, risky idea was starting to take form in my mind. I rejected it, but it kept coming back, and now I saw it as perhaps my only hope. It would be dangerous, and I didn't know if I could pull it off. I didn't even want to try.

"If it's me you want, take me, and leave them alone!" I cried.

The horrible Selene face laughed, and I realized that she wanted to see them die, that she would enjoy it. I found my mother's athame in my hand, glowing with a white heat, and without a plan I leaped forward and plunged the blade into the middle of the smoke. To my surprise, Selene actually seemed to feel it—the smoke recoiled and the face gasped. Then her expression twisted with anger, and a dreadful, perforated voice emanated from it. "You can't stop me, Morgan," it said, every word feeling like a steel nail scraped down a blackboard. "You're not strong enough. I'll take my revenge. My kind have been waiting hundreds of years to wipe out your kind, and I'm not going to let my own death stop me. You're the last of Belwicket, the last of the

Riordans. Once you're dead, true Woodbanes can continue their work. I'm willing to martyr myself to that cause. Soon we'll be more powerful than you could possibly imagine."

Twining vines of smoke slid toward me, running up the bedspread like fire. I edged back against the wall, then looked up to see that Bethany's neck was entwined—she was choking and gagging, and her face was tinged with blue. Bethany was going to die. Alyce and Hunter had turned their energies to saving her, but Selene's march toward death seemed unstoppable.

Unless.

Fully formed, my mother's power chant, the power chant of Belwicket, came to me, as it had on so many other occasions. The ancient, beautiful, and sometimes harsh words spilled from my mouth as I kept my eyes locked on Selene's form. *"An di allaigh an di aigh an di allaigh an di ne ullah. . . ."* I kept the words flowing like lifesaving water as my hand crept across the bed to the body of the dead hawk. My half brother Killian had caught a hawk once by calling its true name. If you know the true name of something, you have ultimate control over it. I knew Ciaran's true name, but no one knew mine, including me. My fingers brushed the soft feathers, felt the absence of a life force, and I included the hawk's true name in my chant.

Selene was hardly paying attention to me—perhaps she thought it would be amusing to see what I could come up with, what puff of breath I could throw against her turbulent hurricane of power. Bethany was almost unconscious now, and the coils were moving up Alyce and Hunter. I saw hard intent in his face but no fear, and my heart felt a searing pain at the thought of what he was going through and how he was facing it.

I remembered what it felt like to be wolf-Morgan. My

birth father, Ciaran, had taught me a shape-shifting spell. I didn't remember most of it, but now I called on ancient Riordan power, the power of my mother and her mother before her, back through the generations. *Help!* I sent the message silently. *Mother, help me. Help me now.*

I closed my eyes, swaying for a moment as new words, at once unknown and familiar, streamed into my mind. I recognized the form of limitations of the shape-shifting spell, and silently I repeated them, putting everything I knew, everything I felt, every need I had into the words.

I was frightened, deathly frightened, yet felt I was pulled inexorably toward this future, this one direction. Silently I murmured the true name of the hawk. Then the pieces came together in my mind in a beautiful, dazzling, stained-glass window of magick, the three things I needed weaving themselves together in a spell so balanced and perfect and beautiful, I wanted to cry.

Bethany sagged in Selene's grasp. Alyce and Hunter were now fighting the deadly tethers around their necks. There was no more time—not one second.

"Rac bis hàn!" I shouted, throwing my arms wide. Selene whipped around to look at me. *"Nal nac hagàgh! Ben dàn!"* I had a moment to see her gaping, protruding eyes widen in shock, then I was forced double, and I was screaming in pain.

Even Alyce and Hunter stopped struggling to watch me, and I cried out, instantly regretting my decision through a thousand hours of ripping, racking pain that lasted less than a minute. My bones bent unnaturally, my skin was pricked with thousands of needles, my face was drawn forward like burning steel. There was no way of getting through this with dignity or even a show of bravery. I wailed, screamed, cried, begged for mercy, and finally ended up sputtering incoherently, lying on my side on the bed. I blinked and struggled to rise. The room was strange and hard to understand. My feet couldn't clutch the bed well, and I gave a clumsy hop so I could perch on the footboard. Hesitantly I flapped my wings, felt the latent power contained within.

I was a hawk. I had shape-shifted. I now had a hawk's laser sight, razorlike talons, and merciless, ripping beak. I sent a message to Selene: Catch me if you can. Then I gathered my wings to me, and with a brilliant burst of immense joy and an aching longing for air and freedom, I took flight, right through the closed and locked window. I felt the wood splinter, the glass shatter against my chest, but then I was soaring up, up, into openness. I heard glass raining down, and then, with a soft sound, my wings caught fire and I streaked through the sky.

A few, exhilarating moments later I sensed another hawk coming after me. It was Selene, back in the body she had usurped. However, that body had already been dead for several minutes, its systems breaking down, and as I glanced back for a millisecond, I saw that it flew with jerky, uncontrolled movements, working hard to keep up with me.

Yet right now Selene seemed unimportant. A hawk's wild joy ignited in me as I wheeled effortlessly through the dark night air. I felt incredibly light and incredibly strong. A thousand scents came to me as I soared higher—the higher I went, the thinner and cooler the air was as it filled my lungs. I heard the flames on my wings whip fiercely through the air, but I felt no pain, no heat, only a terrible, righteous anger and an increasingly strong need for revenge. As ecstatic as I was, shooting through the night, my thoughts once again turned toward Selene. She had been haunting me all this time, appearing to me in Cal's form. She wanted me dead. She wouldn't ever stop until I was dead and the dark Woodbanes were able to flourish. I couldn't let that happen.

I tucked one wing slightly in and began a huge, sweeping arc at sixty miles an hour. The dark hawk was slowly gaining on me, and even from this great distance I saw the glint of hatred in it golden eyes, the overriding lust for my death, and I knew that this could end in only one way: her death. My victory.

Once more I began saying the Riordan power chant, hearing the words unspool in my mind, feeling my power strengthen and swell.

I'm a Riordan, I thought. I'm the *sgiùrs dàn*. This will end here, and my descendants will go on to help Woodbanes be everything they can be, on the side of good.

Then, like children responding to a dare, we squared off and faced each other, hovering for a moment in the onyx-colored sky. I felt everything in me coil and hesitate, and then, like a bolt of witchfire, I hurtled through the night toward Selene, aware that she also was streaking toward me. I was both falling and soaring, my wings tucked close, feet drawn up: I was a weapon, going eighty miles an hour downward toward my enemy.

I was on Selene so fast that I didn't have time to really expect it—it was only a few seconds before we were swerving at the last second so we wouldn't just crash into each other. Quickly I circled as tightly as I could, and then I let all my raptor instincts take over—I quit thinking like a human, quit being Morgan altogether. I let go of all that and let my hawk free.

I don't know who drew blood first—Selene or me. But we attacked at the same moment, and my hard beak shot forward and seized her flesh, pulling and ripping. I tasted her blood, warm and salty, at the same instant I was aware of a searing pain in my right shoulder. The next several minutes were a blur of feathers and fire and a fine mist of blood arcing through the air. Selene's feathers were scorched by my fire, and the acrid smell of burned feathers filled my sensitive nostrils. Harsh, raucous screams filled the air, upsetting and distracting me—and then I realized I was making them. Finally with one huge surge of power I rose up just enough to be able to clamp one of my vicelike feet around Selene's thick neck. It reached around and I squeezed my grip as tightly as I could, as if Selene were a rabbit and I was about to have lunch.

In a frenzy Selene's dark wings beat the air around me, obscuring my sight. But still I hung on. It was impossible to fly and hold on at the same time, so I swung my wings when I could and concentrated on closing, closing, closing on Selene's neck.

This is for Cal, whom you destroyed with your evil, I thought grimly. This is for me, whom you haunted and terrorized. This is for all the people you've hurt or used or killed. You are going to die here and now, at my hand.

When I had been a wolf, I had been seized with an overwhelming lust for the hunt, a palpable desire to track prey down and rip into it. I had been able to stop myself at the last second when I realized my prey was Hunter. I felt no such inclination to stop now. Every tenet I had been raised with against murder, against revenge—disappeared now as I felt myself slowly pressing the life from Selene's body.

We were spinning now, falling toward earth in a death spiral. I was unable to keep myself aloft and hold on to Selene at the same time, so I allowed myself to fall. Selene was still beating her wings, but more and more weakly. My claws, holding her neck, ached with the pressure, the tension of staying tight, but I was locked onto her and there was no way I would let go. I glanced down and saw with a sickening realization that the ground was rushing up to meet us. Soon I would crash, probably breaking every bone in my body. I didn't think even a hawk could survive that kind of collision. But at least I would take Selene with me.

All at once I felt the life force of Selene's hawk blink out. One breath later I was sure of it—the hawk was dead. I was maybe fifteen feet from the ground, and I loosed my talons and let Selene drop heavily to the ground. Then I began beating my wings backward furiously—how to land? I didn't know!

I did the best I could, slowing myself as much as possible and setting my feet in front of me. I ended up crashing, anyway, my feet running against the ground, my wings outstretched, but I lost my balance and tumbled head over claw several times in what must have been the most humiliating hawk landing ever.

Still, I didn't break anything, and as soon I stopped rolling, I was up on my feet and leaping over to Selene. Just as I got there, the hawk's mouth opened, and once again the oily black smoke began to coil outward. I slammed my foot around its neck, crushing it shut, holding it ruthlessly.

It was horrible—the dead bird's battered and bloody body

flopping and struggling against me. My own blood running into my eyes and stinging them. The oily smoke of Selene's anam stopped short. This close to her, I felt her panic, her intense fury, her hatred, her venom and malice. I flapped my wings to keep my balance, hopping awkwardly on one foot while the other held on. It seemed like hours later, but at last I sensed the final, twitching, muffled death of Selene's anam. Trapped inside a dead being with no escape, she could not survive.

Selene Belltower was no more. Yet I didn't let go, not for a long time, not until the shaking of my muscles forced me to release my grip.

Then I released my hold, folded in my wings, and began the agonizing process of becoming myself.

Selene was dead, and I had killed her.

And I wasn't sorry.

14

Hunter

We got Morgan cleaned and patched up at Alyce's. She felt terrible about the broken window, and Alyce looked at her like she was insane when she offered to pay for it. Bethany didn't think any of her wounds actually needed stitches, but she did put butterfly bandages and poultices everywhere. Then I brought Morgan to Bree's house, about half an hour before the sun came up. We woke her up, and she helped me put Morgan to bed. I said we'd explain later. As soon as I was sure Morgan was asleep and safe, I took off and went home.

Once there I took a long, hot shower, getting blood and pain and evil off me. I dropped into my bed and passed out cold.

"Here, lad, have a cuppà," Da said. I heard his voice and groaned, but then the tantalizing scent of strong tea reached my nostrils and I struggled to surface.

I propped myself up on my elbows and took the hot mug. "Cheers."

"How are you? You look all worn out."

I moaned. "Don't ask. I've had better weeks. What time is it?"

"Oneish. I've been thinking about that witch, Patrice," Da went on.

"Me too," I said, and told him about everything that had happened with Patrice and Robin in the woods last night. I sighed. "I'm thinking that maybe I should ask her to turn herself in to the council. I hate the idea, but I don't know what else to do. Despite how sincere she is, now that she's done something like this, I just can't see never keeping an eye on her again. And next time she would be much more subtle, more experienced. I don't know."

I took a big gulp of tea. Ahhh. "I know that if she absolutely refuses to turn herself in, I won't make her," I went on. "I won't strip her of her powers against her will. That's a bloody awful business."

"Well, maybe you won't have to," Da said. "Look." He took out a black-and-white composition notebook. "I've been working on a translation, from Middle Gaelic. It's been very unusual, very enlightening. It seems to have been a textbook from a Wiccan center of learning, back in the 1500s. I've been finding some incredibly unusual spells, and they're almost all to do with limiting powers in some way."

"Really?"

"Yes. I mean, these spells haven't seen light of day, as far as I can tell, in hundreds of years. When I was studying for my initiation, I never even touched on this category." He flipped past pages covered with his fine, scrawly handwriting and began reading me pieces of his translation.

My brain wasn't quite up to par after the events of the last two days, nowhere near enough sleep, the trauma of having

Morgan go through what she had. I squinted up at my father.

"I'm not getting it," I said bluntly.

"Look," he said, a deliberately patient tone entering his voice. "I'm saying we take the basic form of this spell here because it does things in stages and can be broken up. Now, this spell"—he flipped through several pages—"is interesting because of how it sets out its limitations at the beginning, and the best thing is that it doesn't seem to be tied to the phase of the moon. This spell has a really good ending in how it wraps things up, seals things, in the way it controls its effects. So see? We take these parts from these three spells—plus one or two phrases from a couple of others— and create one spell from them. What do you think?"

I struggled to make sense of it. I sat up and took the notebook from him, flipping back and forth between the marked pages, reading his careful translations and margin notes. Slowly the picture began to seep into my troubled brain. My jaw dropped at its implication.

I looked up at Da. "Oh, Goddess—do you think it could work?"

He sat back on his heels, pleased. "I think it might."

"You are absolutely bloody brilliant," I said, and he laughed, tilting back his head.

"Can I get that in writing?" he said.

We took a couple of hours to carefully write out the whole, new, complete spell. The two of us went over it again and again, checking and cross-checking everything. Around four, an uncharacteristically domestic Sky brought us some tea and sandwiches, as well as some sample oatcakes from a recipe she was trying out for Beltane.

"They're great," I said, practically spitting crumbs. "Go with it."

At last we felt ready.

Da and I were very familiar with the spell; there seemed to be no loopholes in it—it was exciting, different, as if we were about to make Wiccan history. Da must have felt this way about the dark wave spell, having created something beautiful and terrible out of nothing. It was funny, when I'd first found him in Canada, he'd been a mess. Now he really seemed to be excelling. It made me proud to be his son.

We drove over to Thornton, to Patrice's house. We'd called ahead, and she was expecting us. When we got there, she was alone, which surprised me. I would have thought she would have called, if not Celia or Robin, then at least some other friend or colleague.

"Thanks for meeting with us," I said as we stood awkwardly in her foyer. She looked tired and somehow beaten, as if she was going to give up now, since her most desperate plan hadn't worked.

I introduced her to my father, and like Celia and Robin, Patrice was a bit impressed to meet the dark wave destroyer. I let Da explain what we wanted to do.

"From what I understand, you've worked magick that could almost certainly get you stripped of your powers," Da said in his forthright way.

Patrice flushed and hung her head, the edges of fear showing in her eyes. "I know," she said, barely audibly.

"However, no one in authority knows about it yet," I said. "But anyone who knows about this will never forget it. Because there's always the possibility that you'll drift back to dark magick."

Her face blanched at these stark words.

"So you seem a bit dangerous, do you see?" I asked, not meanly. "Once someone crosses the line, it seems so much easier for them to cross it again. People will be watching you, waiting for it to happen. But my father has crafted a spell that seems to address this particular situation. We believe that we can work a spell around you that will satisfy others' fears about you."

"You want to strip my powers," Patrice said dully, looking at the floor.

"No. We want to limit them, forever. But in a very specific way," Da explained.

"It's a bubble spell," I said. "A spell that affects your powers in a certain way for the rest of your life. As of today, it can't be undone. Your powers wouldn't actually be limited in strength, but in effect: if you agree to undergo this, you'll never again be able to affect any other living thing with your magick again."

Patrice gave me a quizzical look.

"You'll be able to make magick, beautiful, powerful magick. You'll be able to celebrate and take part in magickal rites. You'll be able to affect stone, mineral, air, and earth as much as you can now. But you won't be able to affect your son's health. You won't be able to rid yourself of the smallest headache. You won't be able to create a sleeping draught for a friend. You won't be able to do the peas-times-three spell on your garden."

She gave a slight smile at the mention of a very basic spell that every witch child learns.

"You won't be able to call your dog with magick; you won't be able to scry to see other humans or animals or plants. But you'll be able to learn, to teach others, to witness magick, to

participate, to feel the joy and satisfaction of creating something beautiful from nothing—just like any other witch."

"But because I can't affect any living thing, I can't harm
anyone with dark magick," she said, looking thoughtful. "And
neither could I help anyone with good magick."

"That's correct," Da said.

"I hate this," she said calmly.

"It's the best option you have right now," I said.

"You're right," she said, years of strain and fatigue in her
voice. "How long will it take? I have to give Joshua his medicine at eight."

"It will take about forty-five minutes," said Da.

Trying not to cry, Patrice led us to her small circle room,
in what used to be a butler's pantry, off her dining room.
"Let's do it, then," she said.

It took longer than forty-five minutes because neither Da
nor I had ever done it before. We also hadn't had an idea of
what effect it would have on Patrice physically, and at one
point she became so nauseated, we had to stop for a few minutes. But we followed each step carefully, as we had written it,
and by a few minutes after six we said the final ending words.

When it was over, I felt drained and hungry. Da dismantled
the circle, and I edged away and sat with my back against the
wall. Patrice simply lay down on the wooden floor, right
where she was, looking white and ill. Da also seemed very
tired, but it was he who went to the kitchen and came back
with a pitcher of iced tea and a package of cookies.

"I raided your fridge," he said cheerfully. Slowly we ate
and drank, and afterward we all felt better. I fetched a wet

washcloth for Patrice's forehead, and she seemed glad to have it.

"Do I look different?" she joked weakly, and I shook my head.

"No. I don't even know if you'll feel different or how the spell will take effect," I said. "You were the guinea pig. But if it works, it could save a great many witches from having their powers stripped in the future."

"Then it will be worth it," Patrice said. "Now I need to go tend to my son."

I went to Morgan's house after that. Mrs. Rowlands let me in, smiling pleasantly, even though I knew she wasn't thrilled with the idea of Morgan dating a witch.

"Hello, Mrs. Rowlands," I said. "I was wondering if I could see Morgan."

"I'll call her down," Mrs. Rowlands said. "You aren't going to believe what she looks like. Apparently she and Bree were trampolining in Bree's backyard this morning, and Morgan managed to bounce off and crash right through a lilac hedge. She's a mess." Tsking and shaking her head, she went to the stairs, where Morgan was already on her way down, having sensed me come in.

I looked at her solemnly. She did look like a wreck, but there was a relief in her eyes, a lack of fear, of tension, that hadn't been there in ages. For that I was glad.

"I told you that trampoline should have a safety net around it," I said.

"Hunter Niall: Wiccan smart-ass," Morgan said in disgust a few minutes later. "That will be the title of your biography."

We were out on the double glider that had recently made its spring appearance on the Rowlandses' front porch. We had some iced jasmine tea, and Morgan had also managed to supply some zucchini bread.

I gave her a little smile and put my arm across the back of the glider, resting against her shoulders. We would have to go over the events of yesterday in depth, but not tonight. "Good story, by the way." I paused. "When I was in the house, I felt Alisa upstairs."

Morgan nodded. "They're going to the nine o'clock movie downtown. Dad's taking them. I think Alisa might be sleeping over."

"Good." I hesitated before I brought up the next subject. It was an idea I'd had a couple of days before, but it had seemed impossible then. It might not be impossible now. "How strong are you feeling?" I asked.

Morgan looked up at me with curiosity and shrugged. "You mean, after yesterday?" I nodded. "Actually, though physically I feel like crap, magickally I feel pretty strong. It's like every time I go through something that should have killed me, when I come through, I just feel stronger."

I smiled. "There's something I'd like to ask you to do for me," I said. "Not tonight. But tomorrow. It involves your magick."

15

Morgan

"How's my little acrobat?" Hunter asked, kissing me and hugging me to him as we walked to his car.

"Ouch. Don't squeeze too hard."

We got into his car, and he looked at me as he started the engine. "Are your parents thinking of suing Mr. Warren?" he asked seriously, and I whacked him on the leg, remembering too late that virtually every part of my body was sore. "Ow!" I laughed, cradling my hand.

He and I hadn't talked much about what had happened with Selene and my shape-shifting. It was as if we were both too freaked out about it and needed time to process it individually before we delved into it together. For right now I wanted to pretend it had never happened.

We headed out of town. It was a beautiful Sunday. My parents, Mary K., and Alisa had gone to visit a garden. I'd wanted to go, but Hunter was more important. Dagda and I had slept in, and I was actually feeling a tiny bit better. "So what are we doing?" I asked, watching the late April sun sparkle on the new green leaves of the trees.

"I wanted you to meet Patrice, the witch I've been working with in Thornton," Hunter said. "And her son."

I gave him a questioning look. He had given me only the vaguest information about the case he was working on with his father. He'd told me the day before that they'd reached some kind of resolution, which I guess made it okay to tell me her name and where she lived, but he didn't seem inclined to say more than that, like why he wanted her to meet me and why she would want to see him again. I just tried to relax and enjoyed the ride. I had never been to Thornton but saw that it was cute and old-fashioned looking in kind of the same way Red Kill is. Hunter drove through the town and into a residential section. He stopped in front of a large, beautiful Victorian home.

"Whoa," I said. "I love this house."

The door opened as we approached the porch. I hadn't really formed much of a mental picture of Patrice Pearson, but she was more normal looking than I had imagined. She didn't look all that witchy, and she didn't look one bit evil. She smiled, seeming a little shy or embarrassed, so I tried to act like I knew nothing of what had been going on. I picked up weird vibes from her, though, as if part of her aura was under a sheet.

"Hello, Morgan," she murmured, holding out a strong, dry hand. "I feel like I've heard your name mentioned before."

"Hi," I said, shaking her hand and still wondering what I was doing here.

"Hunter said you'd like to meet my son," Patrice said,

increasing my curiosity. "He's down this way." She gestured down a hall that led toward the back of the house. I looked behind me and shot Hunter a what's-going-on look, but he only raised his eyebrows at me.

We went through a large, homey kitchen that looked fresh and pristine but like it hadn't been updated in sixty years. Old-fashioned sink, antique stove. Patrice opened a small door off the kitchen, and I stopped in my tracks.

My senses picked up on illness and pain, fatigue and hope-lessness. Hunter had mentioned Patrice had a son but hadn't said any more than that.

I followed Patrice into the room, Hunter behind me. The room was small and looked like it might have been a sunroom at one time. Cheerful posters hung on the walls, and the bed linens were printed with race cars in primary colors. There was a large TV and a DVD player and a stack of videos nearby. But everything else about the room screamed hospi-tal—the hospital bed, the IV stand next to the table, the cabi-net covered with more medicines than I could count. And of course, the little boy, thin and listless, with a tube running under his sheet. He didn't even look up when we entered the room. The TV was turned to some kind of nature show fea-turing alligators and getting right up close to them. His eyes watched the picture, but they were dull, lifeless. He wasn't really seeing anything. His body looked emaciated beneath the sheet, but his face was round and swollen looking.

Patrice seemed unbearably tense in here and with good reason. "Joshua, this is Hunter Niall and Morgan Rowlands," she said, unnaturally cheerfully. "Morgan wanted to meet you. She heard how brave you've been." She looked at me, and I saw that she wasn't entirely sure why I was here, either. But now I was beginning to understand. I smiled at Joshua and then turned to Hunter.

His gaze was measured, questioning.

I hesitated, then gave a tiny shrug and nodded.

"Oh, Patrice," he said now, turning to her. "Would you mind showing me that book on New York gardening I saw in your living room?"

They left me alone in the room with Joshua.

Now he looked at me with suspicion. "Are you a doctor?"

"No, no," I assured him. "I go to high school. I thought I'd just hang out for a while, that's all. So, you've got a lot of equipment here. What's this thing for?" I touched the IV stand. Over the next ten minutes Joshua and I talked about his leukemia, his graft-versus-host disease, how his mom took care of him, and how tired he was. It was all I could do not to just hang my head and burst into tears. But I didn't.

Instead, as Joshua talked, I very gently put my hand on his arm, picking up on his vibrations, his aura, his life essence. I felt his bony little shoulder through the sheet, and it reminded me of my own injured shoulder, which still throbbed painfully. I gently traced the side of his head, grinned and tapped his chin, and then pretended to tickle the bottoms of his feet. He gave a halfhearted grin.

I sat down in my chair again. "Joshua, is it okay if I just put my hands here for a few minutes?" I asked, putting one hand on his upper leg and one on his chest. He nodded warily.

"Gosh, what is that crazy guy doing with that alligator?" I said, and he turned his gaze back to the TV.

I closed my eyes and relaxed everything, letting go of my

tension, my distaste for the smells of disinfectant and illness, the scent of plastic and medicine and clean sheets. The faint noise of the TV faded. I sank into a midlevel meditation, where I consciously dissolved any barriers I felt between the outside world and me. After several minutes I felt that I was one with everything in the universe and it was one with me. There were no beginnings, no endings, only a calm, joyful communion among all things. And between Joshua and me. I let myself sink into him, into his tortured and weakened body. I let myself flow over him and inside him and through him. I felt his pain, artificially dulled by strong drugs; I felt his system being weakened yet also helped by other powerful and toxic medicines. I saw the normal white blood cells in his bloodstream but also cells swollen with fluid, about to burst; I saw Joshua's body being attacked from inside by his new marrow's immune system. His feelings became mine, and I swallowed down the nausea, the pain, the feelings of despair and hopelessness, the guilt he felt for upsetting his mother, the anger he felt, but didn't show, that this was happening to him.

I saw and felt it all, as if it was a Chinese puzzle knot, made up of countless ribbons twisted and knotted together in an incomprehensible way. I let myself sink deeper. The battle with Selene, and the resulting physical and emotional toll it had taken on me, had left me not at full power. But I thought I had enough to do something.

I felt like a universal solvent, able to go anywhere, see everything, unravel anything. One by one I teased out ribbons and followed them. I traced them back to his bone marrow. I traced ribbons back to each of his drugs. There was a ribbon for pain, a ribbon for anger, a ribbon for his original leukemia.

I have no idea how long I sat there. I was dimly aware of my hands growing warm, but Joshua didn't seem to notice or care. I thought at one point Hunter came back to check on me, but I didn't look up, and he didn't say anything. A tiny bit at a time I unraveled the puzzle knot. I eased his new marrow into working harmoniously with his body. I eased his body into a joyful balance within itself. I soothed blood vessels, irritated tissue, muscles taut with pain. I brought Joshua more into balance with the Goddess, with nature, with life. As things became more normal, more recognizable, I felt a general lightening, as if Joshua and I were free, soaring in the air, nothing weighing us down, no cares. As usual it was beautiful, mesmerizing, and everything in me wanted to stay in that magickal place forever.

But of course I couldn't.

When at last I raised my head and blinked, I saw that Joshua was deeply asleep in front of me. I shook my head as if trying to wake up and looked around to see Hunter and Patrice both sitting on chairs, watching me with solemn eyes. I looked back at Joshua. He looked different. His skin tone seemed more natural to me, his eyes less sunken. His sleep was restful and calm, his face unlined and free of pain. I quickly cast my senses and picked up on a balance, for lack of a better word. He felt more balanced.

I, however, felt like I was made out of Silly Putty. I didn't know if I could stand.

"Uh," I said, looking at Hunter. He immediately came over to help me stand up. My legs felt wobbly, rubbery. I felt hungry and tired. Patrice was watching me with a mix of emotions on her face. I straightened up with difficulty, then forced back my shoulders and took a deep breath. I gave Patrice what I hoped was a reassuring smile.

She looked from me to Joshua, then stepped past me to her son. She took one of his hands and held it against her cheek. He moved a little in his sleep, but to me it seemed like his puffy face was looking more normal, his limbs less stiff, his movements freer. I smiled at him.

Hunter put his arm around my waist, and I looked up to see a world of love and trust and awe in his green eyes.

Patrice turned back to me, looking grateful and scared and amazed all at the same time. She could tell he was better—anyone could. I didn't know how much I had done, but I knew I had helped somehow, to some degree.

"Who are you?" she breathed.

I thought of who I was, of everything that had gone into making me what I was, the long line of witches and women who had lent me their strength—it was mine to use, in this lifetime.

I smiled at her. "I'm Morgan," I said. "Daughter of Maeve of Belwicket."

"Morgan, you look incredibly beautiful," Hunter said for the fifth time.

I looked up at him, flushed with pleasure. This was pretty much the most effort I had ever made with my appearance, and by all accounts it was paying off. I was wearing a clingy top of a soft sage green. It had a deeply scooped square neck and three-quarter sleeves. I wore a silver chain with a piece of amber on it around my neck.

The skirt I had ordered from a costume shop. It was

made of layers of tulle, different shades of green, a layer of maroon, a layer of pink—seven layers in all, all sewn to a tight-fitting waistband. The bad thing about being built like a boy was that I usually looked like a boy. The good thing, if there was one, was that my waist actually looked small and kind of girlie if I wore a big, poufy skirt like this.

On my feet I had dark green ballet slippers, real ballet slippers, which were like wearing nothing. I had bought white ones and dyed them three times.

I had given Mary K. free rein with my makeup, and I had to admit that she had a promising future as a makeup artist. My eyes had never looked so big or luminous, my mouth looked lush and feminine, and my skin looked dewy and fresh. Not only that, but I had actually submitted to having my long hair turned into soft, fat ringlets that hung past my shoulders. I had been afraid of looking like Little Orphan Annie, but instead my hair just looked kind of wild and natural and sexy.

This was one of the very few times in my life when I felt actually feminine and strong and beautiful. And the effect it had on Hunter had cheered me up to no end. His eyes had been on me ever since he picked me up. Now he was looking deeply into my eyes over the top of his sparkling cider, and I was feeling incredibly attractive and womanly, as if I had bewitched him. It was a great feeling.

"Morgan! Fabulous!" said Bethany, sweeping past. I called hi after her, but she was already whirling away.

"How many people are here?" I asked, edging closer to a table.

Hunter glanced around. "Close to eighty, I would guess. I think all of us ended up asking everybody we knew."

It was twilight on Beltane Eve, and we were in the same

woods close to the spot where Hunter and I had had our picnics with Bree and Robbie. Tonight it looked enchanted —tiny glass lanterns with votive lights were everywhere, and there were tables covered with all sorts of food and drink. Sky and Raven, the organizing committee, had outdone themselves. Garlands of fresh flowers swooped from tree to tree. A tall, beautiful maypole stood in the center of the clearing, and it was hung with long, silken ribbons in rainbow colors. Sky had recruited musicians from various covens, and the haunting, lilting strains of magickal Irish music were weaving their own spell over everyone.

"Where did Sky get the maypole?" I asked.

Hunter grinned, moving closer to put his arm around my waist. "It's a mast, from a boat shop. She and Raven picked it up and had to transport it here, sticking out of Raven's back window."

I laughed, picturing it. My eyes automatically sought out Sky, and, sure enough, she and Raven were together by a food table, their heads bent together, talking earnestly. Hunter and I glanced at each other. They did care about each other, I knew. I hoped their relationship would work itself out.

"They did a great job," I said. I picked up some slices of fruit, admiring the platters of oatcakes, bowls of honey, herbed tea with flowers floating in it, cakes decorated with edible flowers—pansies, Johnny-jump-ups, marigolds, nasturtiums.

"Sister! Hello!" I smiled and groaned at the same time, turning to see Killian coming toward me, a glass of wine in his hand. As usual he looked cheerful and irreverent, his longish hair streaked with shades of auburn and caramel.

"Hi, Killian," I said, and Hunter greeted him, too, as civilly as he could manage.

"Niall," Killian said, then turned back to me. "Super party! Great eats, music—you went all out. What hand did you play in this?"

"I showed up."

"Sky and Raven organized everything," Hunter said evenly, and I made an effort not to grin.

"Ah." Killian gave a quick glance around, and of course, there were Sky and Raven, about twenty feet away, shooting looks at him that, if they didn't kill him, might certainly maim him. But it took more than that to upset my half brother. He smiled at them hugely, raised his wineglass in a toast, and then prudently headed in another direction.

"Ciao!" he called back to me, and I waved.

"Maypole! Maypole!" someone cried, and the musicians came closer. Sky organized volunteers, male-female, male-female, and handed them each a ribbon. Then, as the music started, the dancers began to move in opposite circles, weaving in and under, over and under each other, and as we watched, the colorful ribbons were woven around the may-pole in an even pattern of diamonds. It was beautiful, and I was glad we were continuing this old tradition.

Without speaking, Hunter and I linked hands, keeping one hand each free so we could eat and drink. When night fell, a huge bonfire was lit, and Hunter took me around, introducing me to people I didn't know. Everyone seemed to have a distinct reaction on hearing my name. I was about to ask Hunter about it, but then he pointed out where the star cluster Pleiades would rise, right before dawn the next day. At Samhain, six months from now, Pleiades would rise right at sunset. Beltane and Samhain marked the two halves of the year.

Hunter and I wandered away from the light and noise and music, talking about everything, huge, tiny, sad, funny. I had seen Patrice earlier for just a minute, and she had told me that Joshua no longer needed a feeding tube. His doctors were mystified, but he seemed to be shedding his illnesses like a snake's skin. She held my hand tightly and thanked me several times with an intensity that brought tears to my eyes.

"So Da and I are off to England in a month," Hunter said. We were far enough away so that we didn't need to speak loudly anymore.

I sighed.

"Your folks still haven't made up their minds about Scotland?" he asked.

I shook my head. "They've spoken to Eoife, but they really don't understand why there aren't any brochures for them to look at or a Web site."

Hunter laced my fingers with both his hands. "I want you to go," he said seriously.

"I feel I need to," I agreed. "They haven't shot it down—at least not yet. They want to see my end-of-year grades, et cetera. I've actually been carrying good-luck stones in my pockets. The thing is, if you're in England and I'm here, I just don't know if I can bear how far away you'll be. If I'm in Scotland, you won't be so far away, and I won't feel so panicky."

"I know what you mean," he said. "I hate the thought of being separated from you, by any kind of distance or time. But I know I have to go home for a while to see people. Da is doing a bunch of workshops about the dark wave spell, and I'm going to join him for some lectures about this new bubble spell."

"I'm so proud of you," I said, squeezing his hand.

He grinned. "It feels good to do something of real use. To possibly prevent witches from having their powers stripped— witches who have just made bad decisions or are about to. And this could effectively lessen the council's power. Which might pave the way for a new council or an adjunct council."

We stopped then and looked around, realizing we had been walking and talking, so caught up in each other that we had gone farther than we'd meant to. I couldn't hear the music or laughter at all anymore, couldn't see the light from the bonfire.

We were in a tiny clearing, no more than ten feet across, with a perfect overhead view of the indigo night sky and stars. Around the edges of the clearing was an unusual ring of violets—the last violets of the season. It looked magickal, like fairies had created this place. And we had ended up here. It felt like fate, not coincidence, that we were here.

Then I looked at Hunter, and he looked at me. My heart fluttered, and Hunter led me to the center of the violet ring. He sank down on the fine moss and pulled me down next to him. The delicate, sweet scent of the violets perfumed the air around us as we lay side by side, and when I looked up, I felt like I could see all of the sky before me, as if I were flying.

"Morgan."

I looked in his face. He looked unusually solemn, the dancing light in his eyes strangely absent. Slowly he traced one finger down my arm, and I watched as his touch left a tiny trail of sparkling shimmer wherever it touched. Smaller and finer than sparks, lacking heat and leaving only the very faintest tingle, the shimmer continued down my side and onto my skirt, wherever he touched.

I held him to me and touched his face, his angular, carved cheekbones. To me right now in the moonlight, he seemed heartbreakingly beautiful—strong and masculine, familiar and intimately trusted. He had seen me at my absolute worst and still loved me. He had seen me sick, angry, making mistakes, being stupid—and he still loved me. He had been patient and kind, demanding and true. I loved him with all my heart and believed that he absolutely loved me—not because he said so, but because he showed me he did, every single day.

I took his hand and pressed it to my chest. I could feel him shiver a little, which made me smile. I loved the fact that this calm, cool ex-Seeker—a witch who was in control in virtually every situation—consistently lost control when it came to me. Then I coiled my hand around his neck and pulled his face closer to mine. He seemed hesitant, waiting, and to dispel any doubt I opened my mouth and kissed his, hard. I suddenly felt like I had opened a dam and was now being swept away by torrents of water much stronger than I was.

We moved together, our mouths locked, our arms and legs clinging to each other as tightly as they could. Hunter paused and kissed me gently, then pulled back and looked in my eyes, lifting his hand and making a slight motion toward the sky. Immediately I saw movement above, and then we were covered in a soft wave of flowers, flowers raining from the sky—roses, peonies, daisies, too many to count. I laughed. This was the joy of Beltane—this pure love of nature, of life, of love itself.

I looked into the deep green of Hunter's eyes, moved by the intensity of the love I saw there and stunned by the intensity of the love I felt for him. Was it possible for one person to care this much about another? I felt like I couldn't get close enough to him.

Hunter kissed me again, and legs and hands got tangled in my skirt. We were gasping in the cool night air, rolling together so that first he was on top and then I was. I loved having him under me, being able to hold his face in my hands, to feel like what happened was up to me. Which it was.

There, on Beltane Eve, celebration of fertility, life, and love, Hunter and I made our own celebration, our own timeless commitment to each other, our wordless promise to be true to our love, to protect each other, to revere and respect each other always, as long as we lived.

Epilogue

"You are going to miss me so much," Hunter said confidently. Another scratchy announcement said the flight to Cleveland was now boarding.

Morgan laughed. "You think so, huh?" She put her arms around his waist, aware that the flight to London was going to start boarding any minute.

"I know so," he said. Then he lowered his voice and pushed her hair off her neck. "And I know I'm going to miss you, so much."

"It won't be for that long," Morgan reminded him, feeling the telltale prickle of tears at the edges of her eyes. Do not cry, she told herself. Do not waste time crying.

"It will feel like a long time," he said. A man dragging a suitcase big enough to hold a dead bear pushed past them on his way to Gate 17. Hunter moved them a bit to the side. "I have something for you." He pulled a small box out of his pocket, and her eyes flared. Speechless, she opened it. Inside was a silver claddagh ring, two hands holding a heart between them and a crown on top of the heart. On the heart was the rune Beorc, for new beginnings.

"It's beautiful," Morgan breathed, her fingers clumsily trying to get it out of the box. He helped her slip it on.

"I'm so proud of you, Morgan," he said softly. "I'm just incredibly proud. And incredibly happy. And incredibly in love."

Her eyes definitely felt watery now, but she swallowed hard. "I know exactly how you feel."

She threw herself at him one last time, the silver ring a comforting weight on her right hand. They hugged and kissed until they heard the boarding call for the flight to London. Then she let go of him and went over to her family. Her parents looked mildly uncomfortable at the public display of affection, but now they smiled and hugged her hard. Morgan's mom had tears in her eyes, and so did Mary K.

"I'll be back before you know it," she said. "And Mary K., feel free to borrow any of my clothes while I'm gone."

Mary K. rolled her eyes. "Like that will get me anything," she said. Laughing, Morgan hugged her tight.

Morgan stepped back next to Hunter, who touched her cheek gently, as if for the last time. "We'll see each other soon, you know," she said as she slipped into his arms.

Suddenly the noise of the airport ceased to exist and time stopped moving altogether. "I love you, Morgan," Hunter said, and the words surrounded them both in a warm and colorful flow of magick. For one final moment they were alone, together, in a world that held no one else. Then time began to move forward again, and the people around them regained their voices and resumed their movements. "I wanted a perfect moment with you," he said, his green eyes sparkling with magick or tears—she couldn't tell which.

"You'd better get going, sweetie," her mother said, and gave her a final hug. Morgan picked up Dagda's carrier, made sure she had her tickets and carry-on, and headed down the gate to the waiting plane. She turned back one last time and waved.

The future was opening up for her like the petals of a flower. She would be the strong witch she had always wanted to be.

Book Fifteen

SWEEP
Night's Child

All quoted materials in this work were created by the author.
Any resemblance to existing works is accidental.

Night's Child

SPEAK
Published by the Penguin Group
Penguin Group (USA) Inc., 345 Hudson Street, New York, New York 10014, U.S.A.
Penguin Group (Canada), 90 Eglinton Avenue East, Suite 700, Toronto, Ontario, Canada M4P 2Y3
(a division of Pearson Penguin Canada Inc.)
Penguin Books Ltd, 80 Strand, London WC2R 0RL, England
Penguin Ireland, 25 St Stephen's Green, Dublin 2, Ireland (a division of Penguin Books Ltd)
Penguin Group (Australia), 250 Camberwell Road, Camberwell, Victoria 3124, Australia
(a division of Pearson Australia Group Pty Ltd)
Penguin Books India Pvt Ltd, 11 Community Centre, Panchsheel Park, New Delhi - 110 017, India
Penguin Group (NZ), 67 Apollo Drive, Rosedale, Auckland 0632, New Zealand
(a division of Pearson New Zealand Ltd)
Penguin Books (South Africa) (Pty) Ltd, 24 Sturdee Avenue, Rosebank, Johannesburg 2196, South Africa

Registered Offices: Penguin Books Ltd, 80 Strand, London WC2R 0RL, England

Published by Puffin Books, a division of Penguin Young Readers Group, 2003
Published by Speak, an imprint of Penguin Group (USA) Inc., 2009
This omnibus edition published by Speak, an imprint of Penguin Group (USA) Inc., 2011

1 3 5 7 9 10 8 6 4 2

Copyright © 2003 17th Street Productions, an Alloy company,
and Gabrielle Charbonnet
All rights reserved

Produced by 17th Street Productions,
an Alloy company
151 West 26th Street
New York, NY 10001

17th Street Productions and associated logos
are trademarks and/or registered trademarks of Alloy, Inc.

Speak ISBN 978-0-14-241030-1
This omnibus ISBN 978-0-14-242011-9

Printed in the United States of America

*With much appreciation to all the
generous and dedicated fans of Sweep*

Prologue

Three minutes to five. In three minutes it will all begin, Morgan Rowlands thought, wrapping her hands around her heavy mug of steaming tea. She swallowed hard, refusing to start crying until later, when she knew she wouldn't be able to help it. "Cool the fire," she whispered, circling her left hand widdershins, counterclockwise, over her tea. She took an experimental sip, trying to wash down the lump in her throat.

She gazed out the plate-glass window of the small tea shop in Aberystwyth, Wales, where she and Hunter Niall had agreed to meet. It was darkening outside, though it was barely five o'clock. After living in Ireland for three years, Morgan was used to the early darkness from heavy clouds, but she sometimes missed the stark cold and thick, glittering snow of upstate New York, where she had grown up.

Heavy raindrops began to smack against the window. Morgan took a deep breath, the weather outside reflecting her emotions inside. Usually she welcomed the rain as the main reason that Ireland and Wales both were so incredibly lush and green. Tonight it seemed dreary, dismal, depressing because of what she was about to do—break up with the person she loved most in the world, her *mùirn beatha dàn*. Her soul mate.

Her stomach was tight, her hands tense on the table. Hunter. *Oh, Goddess, Hunter.* It had been almost four months since they'd been able to meet in the airport in Toronto—for only six hours. And three months before that, in Germany. They'd had two whole days together then.

Morgan shook her head, consciously releasing her breath in a long, controlled sigh. *Relax. If I relax and let thoughts go, the Goddess shows me where to go. If I relax and let things be, all of life is clear to see.*

She closed her eyes and deliberately uncoiled every muscle, from her head on down to her icy toes in her damp boots. Soon a soothing sense of warmth expanded inside her, and she felt some of the tension leave her body.

The brass bell over the shop door jangled and was followed almost instantly by a blast of frigid air. Morgan opened her eyes in time to have her light blocked by a tall, heartbreakingly familiar figure. Despite everything, her heart expanded with joy and a smile rose to her face. She stood as he came closer, his angular face lighting up when he saw her. He smiled, and the sight of his open, welcoming expression sliced right through her.

"Hey, Morgan. Sorry I'm late," Hunter said, his English accent blunted by fatigue.

She took him in her arms, holding him tightly, not caring that his long tweed overcoat was soaked with icy rain. Hunter leaned down, Morgan went on tiptoe, and their mouths met perfectly in the middle, the way they always did.

When they separated, Morgan stroked a finger down his cheek. "Long time no see," she said, her voice catching. Hunter's eyes instantly narrowed—even aside from his powers of sensing emotion as a blood witch, he knew Morgan more intimately than anyone. Morgan cleared her throat and sat down. Still watching her, Hunter sat also, his coat sprinkling raindrops onto the linoleum floor around his chair. He swept his old-fashioned tweed cap off his head and ran a hand through his fine, white-blond hair.

Morgan drank in his appearance, her gaze roaming over every detail. His face was pale with winter, his eyes as icy green as the Irish Sea not three blocks away. His hair was longer than Morgan had ever seen it and looked choppy, uneven.

"It's good to see you," Hunter said, smiling at the obvious understatement. Under the table he edged his knee over until it rested against hers.

"You too," Morgan said. Did her anguish already show on her face? She felt as if the pain of her decision must surround her like an aura, visible to anyone who knew her. "I got tea for two—want some?"

"Please," he said, and Morgan poured the spare mug full of tea.

Hunter stood up and dropped his wet coat over the back of his chair. He took a sip of tea, stretched, and rolled his shoulders. Morgan knew he had just come in from Norway.

What to say? How to say it? She had rehearsed this scene for the last two weeks, but now that she was here, going through with it felt like revolting against her very being. And in a sense, it was true. To end a relationship with her *mùirn beatha dàn* was fighting destiny.

It had been four years since she had first met Hunter,

Morgan mused. She absently turned her silver claddagh ring, on the ring finger of her right hand. Hunter had given her this ring when she was seventeen, he nineteen. Now he was twenty-three and a man, tall and broad-shouldered—no longer a lanky teenager, the "boy genius" witch hired as the youngest Seeker for the International Council of Witches.

And she was no longer the naive, love-struck high schooler who had just discovered her legacy as a blood witch and was struggling to learn to control her incredible powers. She'd come a long way in the few years since the summer after her junior year of high school, when she'd first learned there were actually a few surviving members of her mother's coven, Belwicket. She'd been spending the summer studying in Scotland when they came to her, finally able to reveal themselves after the dark wave was defeated and— more importantly—Ciaran MacEwan was stripped of his powers. They'd told her how they'd survived the destruction of their coven by escaping to Scotland, where they'd been hiding for decades. When they'd heard of Morgan's existence, they'd come to enlist her help in rebuilding the coven that had shaped their families for hundreds of years. And she'd been doing just that since moving to Ireland a year after her graduation from high school, and loving every moment—except for the fact that being in Cobh meant being apart from Hunter.

Hunter reached across the table and took her hand. Morgan felt desperate, torn, yet she knew what she had to do, what had to happen. She had gone over this a thousand times. It was the only decision that made sense.

"What's the matter?" he asked gently. "What's wrong?"

Morgan looked at him, this person who was both intimately familiar and oddly mysterious. There had been a time when she'd seen him every single day, when she'd been close enough to know if he'd cut himself shaving or had a sleepless night. Now he had the thin pink line of a healed wound on the curve of his jaw, and Morgan had no idea where or when or how he had gotten it.

She shook her head, knowing she couldn't be a coward, knowing that in the end, with the way things were, they had to pursue their separate destinies. In a minute she would tell him. As soon as she could talk without crying.

As if making a conscious decision to let it go for a moment, Hunter ran his hand through his hair again and looked into Morgan's eyes. "So I spoke to Alwyn about her engagement," he said, refilling his mug from the pot on the table.

"Yes, she seems happy," Morgan said. "But you—"

"I told her about my concerns," Hunter jumped in. "She's barely nineteen. I talked to her about waiting, but what do I know? I'm only her brother." He gave the wry smile that Morgan knew so well.

"He's a Wyndenkell, at least," Morgan said with a straight face. "We can all thank the Goddess for that."

Hunter grinned. "Uncle Beck is so pleased." Hunter's uncle, Beck Eventide, had raised Hunter, his younger brother, Linden, and Alwyn after their parents had disappeared when Hunter was eight. Hunter was sure that Uncle Beck had always blamed Hunter's father, a Woodbane, for his troubles.

"Anything but a Woodbane," Morgan managed to tease. She herself was a full-blood Woodbane and knew firsthand the kind of prejudice most Wiccans had against her ancestral clan.

"Right," said Hunter, his eyes still on her.

They were silent for a moment, each lost in their own thoughts. Then Hunter finally said, "Please tell me what's wrong. You feel weird."

He knows me too well, Morgan thought. Hunter was feeling her uneasiness, her sadness, her regret.

"Are you ill?"

Morgan shook her head and tucked a few bangs behind one ear. "No—I'm okay. It's just—I needed to see you. To talk to you."

"It's always too long between times," Hunter said. "Sometimes I go crazy with it."

Morgan looked into his eyes, saw the flare of passion and longing that made her throat close and her stomach flutter.

"Me too," Morgan said, seizing the opening. "But even though it's making us crazy, we seem to be able to see each other less and less."

"Too true," Hunter said, rubbing his hand over his chin and the days' worth of stubble there. "This has not been a good year for us."

"Well, it's been good for us separately," Morgan said. "You're practically running the New Charter yourself, setting up offices all over the world, working with the others on guidelines. What you're doing is incredibly important. It's going to change how witches interact with each other, with their communities. . . ." She shook her head. The old council was now barely more than a symbolic tradition. Too many witches had objected to its increasingly autonomous and even secretive programs to search out witches who were misusing magickal power. In response to that, Hunter and a handful of other witches had created the New Charter. It was less a policing organization than a support system to rehabilitate errant witches without having their powers stripped. It now included improving witches' standings in their communities, education, public relations, help with historical research. Wicca was being pulled into the twenty-first century, thanks in large part to Hunter.

"There's no way you could stop now," Morgan said. "And me . . . Belwicket is becoming more and more important to me. I really see my future as being there. It supports the work I want to do with healing, and maybe someday I could become high priestess—a Riordan leading Belwicket again."

Morgan's birth mother, Maeve Riordan, had died when Morgan was a baby. If she had lived, she would have been high priestess of her clan's ancestral coven, Belwicket, just as her mother, Mackenna, had, and her mother before her.

"Is that what you'll be happy doing?" Hunter asked.

"It seems to be my destiny," Morgan responded, her fingers absently rubbing the cuff of his sweater. Just as you are, she thought. What did it mean to face two destinies that led in opposite directions? "And yes, it makes me happy. It's incredibly fulfilling, being part of the coven that my birth mother would have led. Even though we're now on the other side of Ireland from the original one, the whole experience is full of my family's history, my relatives, people I never had a chance to know. But it means I stay there, commit myself to staying in Cobh, commit myself to making my life there for the foreseeable future."

"Uh-huh," Hunter said, a wariness coming into his eyes.

Now that she had gotten this far, Morgan forced herself to

press on. "So I'm there. And you're . . . everywhere. All over. Meanwhile we're seeing each other every four months for six hours. In an airport." She looked around. "Or a tea shop."

"You're leading up to something," Hunter said dryly.

Over the last four years she and Hunter had talked about the distance between them many times. Each conversation had been horrible and heartbreaking, but they had never managed to resolve anything. They were soul mates; they were meant to love each other. But how could they do that when they were usually a continent apart? And how could that change when each of them was dedicated, and rightfully so, to their life's work?

Morgan didn't see any way to make it work. Not without one of them giving up their chosen path. She *could* give up Belwicket and follow Hunter around the world while he worked for the New Charter. But she feared that the joy of being with him would be tempered by her frustration of not pursuing her own dream and her guilt that she was letting down her coven—and even her birth mother, whom she'd never known. And then what good would she be to Hunter? She didn't want to make his life miserable. And if she asked him to give up the New Charter and stay with her in Ireland, he would be in the same position—thrilled to be with her, torn that he couldn't be true to a meaningful calling of his own. She couldn't ask him to do that.

Breaking up—for good—seemed like the fairest thing for both of them. She wanted Hunter to be happy above all else. If she set him free, he would have the best chance of that. Even though the idea of never holding him, kissing him, laughing with him, even just sitting and looking at him again seemed almost like a living death, still, Morgan believed it was for the best, ultimately. There seemed to be no way for them to be together; they had to do the best they could on their own.

Back at home Colm Byrne, a member of Belwicket, had confessed he was in love with her. She liked him and he was a great guy, but he wasn't her *mùirn beatha dàn*. There was no way he would ever touch what she felt for Hunter, and she wasn't breaking up with Hunter to be with Colm or anyone else, for that matter. This wasn't about that. This was about freeing herself and Hunter to give all of themselves to their work and freeing them from the pain of constantly longing for these achingly brief reunions.

"Hunter—I just can't go on like this. *We* can't go on like this." Her throat tightened and she released his hand. "We need to—just end it. Us."

Hunter blinked. "I don't understand," he said. "We can't end us. *Us* is a fact of life."

"But not for the lives we're living now." Morgan couldn't even look at him.

"Morgan, breaking up isn't the answer. We love each other too much. You're my *mùirn beatha dàn*—we're *soul mates*."

That did it. A single tear escaped Morgan's eye and rolled down her cheek. She sniffled.

"I know," she said in frustration. "But trying to be together isn't working either. We never see each other, our lives are going in two different directions—how can we have a future? Trying to pretend there *is* one is bogging us both down. If we really, really say this is it, then we'll both be free to do what we want, without even pretending that we have to take the other one into consideration."

Hunter was silent, looking first at Morgan, then around at

the little tea shop, then out the black window with the rain streaking down.

"Is that what you want?" he asked slowly. "For us to go our own separate ways without even pretending we have to think of each other?"

"It's what we're already doing," Morgan said, feeling as if she was going to break apart from grief. "I'm not saying we don't love each other. We do—we always will. I just can't take hoping or wishing for something different. It's not *going* to be different." That was when her voice broke. She leaned her head against her hand and took some deep breaths.

Hunter's finger absently traced a pattern on the tabletop, and after a moment Morgan recognized it as a rune. The rune for strength. "So we'll make lives without each other, we'll commit to other people, we won't ever be lovers again."

His quiet, deliberate words felt like nails piercing her heart, her mind. Goddess, just get me through this. Get me through this, she thought. Morgan nodded, blinking in an unsuccessful attempt to keep more tears from coming to her eyes.

"That's what you want." His voice was very neutral, and Morgan, knowing him so well, knew that meant huge emotions were battling inside him.

"That's what we have already," she whispered. "This is not being lovers. I don't know what this is."

"All right," Hunter said. "All right. So you want me to settle down, is that it? In Cobh? Make a garden with you? Get a cat?" His voice didn't sound harsh—more despairing, as if he were truly trying to understand.

"That's not what I'm saying," Morgan said, barely audibly. "I want you to do what you want to do, what you *need* to do. I want you to be happy, to be fulfilled. I'm saying that I *know* that won't be with me in Cobh, with a garden and a cat." She brushed the sleeve of her sweater over her eyes.

Hunter was quiet. Morgan pulled the long ends of her sweater sleeves over her hands and leaned her face against them. Once this was over, she would breathe again. She would go back to the bed-and-breakfast, get in the shower, and cry.

"What if . . . things were different?" Hunter said at last.

Morgan drew a pained breath. "But things *aren't* different."

"*Things* are up to you and me," Hunter said. "You act like this is beyond our control. But we can make choices. We can change our priorities."

"What are you talking about?" Morgan wiped her eyes, then forced herself to take a sip of tea. It was thin and bitter.

Quickly Hunter reached across the table and took her hands in his, his grip like stone. "I think we need to change our priorities. Both of us."

"To what?" How could he manage to always keep her so off-kilter, even after four years?

"To each other," Hunter said.

Morgan stared at him, speechless.

"Morgan," Hunter went on, lowering his voice and leaning closer to her, "I've been doing a lot of thinking, too. I love what I'm doing with the New Charter, but I've realized it just doesn't mean much without you there to share it with me. I know we're two very different people. We have different dreams, different goals. Our backgrounds are very different, our families . . . But you *know* we belong together. *I* know we belong together—I always have. You're my soul mate—my *mùirn beatha dàn*."

Morgan started crying silently. Oh, Goddess, she loved him so much.

"I knew when I met you that you were the one for me," Hunter said, his voice reaching only her ears. "I knew it when I disliked you, when I didn't trust you, when I feared your power and your inability to control it. I knew it when you learned Ciaran MacEwan was your father. I knew it when you were in love with my bastard half brother, Cal. I've always known it: you are the one for me."

"I don't understand. What are you saying?" It was frightening, how much she still wanted to hope they could be together. It was such a painful hope. She felt his hands holding hers like a vise—as strong as the hold he had on her heart.

"You came here to break up with me forever," Hunter answered. "I won't stop you, if that's what you want. I want you to be happy. But if there's any way you think you can be happy *with* me, as opposed to without me, then I'm asking you to try."

"But how? We've been over this." Morgan said, completely confused.

"No, not *this*," said Hunter. "*This* definitely needs to change. But I can change. I can change whatever I need to if it means that you'll be with me."

Morgan could do nothing but stare. "With you in what way?"

Hunter turned her hand over and traced the carvings of her claddagh ring. "In every way. As my partner, the mother of my children. Every way there is. I need you. You're my life, wherever you are, whatever you're doing."

Morgan quit breathing.

"Look, the one constant in our lives is our love," he said. "It seems like we're squandering our most precious gift— having a soul mate. If we let that slip away, nothing else will make sense." Morgan gaped at him, a splinter of sunlight seeming to enter her heart. *Oh, Goddess, please. Please.*

He went on. "I can phase out the field work I'm doing for the New Charter. There's any number of things I can do based out of Cobh. We could live together, make a life together, wake up with each other more often than *not* with each other. I want to see you grow old, I want us to grow old together. I want to have a family with you. There can be cats involved, if you like."

Could this possibly be true? Could this really be happening? After her despair of the last two weeks the sudden, overwhelming joy Morgan felt seemed almost scary.

"I still have Dagda," was all that Morgan could think of to say. Her once-tiny gray kitten was now a hulking sixteen-pounder who had developed a distinct fondness for Irish mice. "But—can you do this? Do you really mean it?"

Hunter grinned. It was the most beautiful thing that Morgan had ever seen. He moved his chair till they were close, side by side. His arm went around her waist, and she leaned against his warmth, his comfort, his promise. The faded half life she had resigned herself to had just burst into brilliant colors. It was almost too much. It was everything.

"Do you want to be with me, Morgan?" he said softly. "You're my heart's love, my heart's ease. Will you join me in handfasting—will you be my wife?"

"Oh, yes. Yes," Morgan whispered, then rested her head against his shoulder.

Dawn. Dawn is the most magickal time of day, followed of course by sunset, Morgan thought dreamily. She stretched her feet toward Hunter's warmth and let sheer happiness, hopefulness, and contentment wash over her like a wave of comfort. From her bed Morgan could see a small rectangle of sky, pale gray, streaked with pink. It was the dawn of a whole new life, Morgan exulted. The life where she and Hunter would always be together. They would have a hand-fasting, she thought with a shiver of mixed awe and delight. They might have children. Goddess, Goddess, had anyone ever been so happy? Her eyes drifted closed, a smile still on her face.

"Sweet," Hunter whispered, kissing her ear. Morgan reluctantly opened her eyes, then frowned as she realized Hunter was out of bed and already dressed.

"What are you doing?" she demanded sleepily. "Come back here." Hunter laughed and kissed a line of warmth beneath her ear.

"My last New Charter meeting, over in Wexford," he explained. "I'm taking the eight-oh-five ferry. I'll do my meeting, tell them to get a replacement, and be back by dinnertime at the latest. We can go get some of that fried stuff you love, all right?"

"All right," Morgan said, stretching luxuriously.

She saw a familiar roguish gleam in his eyes as he watched her stretch, then curl up again under the covers. He looked at his watch, and she laughed. "You don't have time," she told him.

"Love you," he said, grinning, opening the door.

"Love you, too," Morgan replied. "Forever."

Morgan felt as if she'd closed her eyes for only a moment when she was awoken by a loud banging. Frowning, she looked at her watch. Eight-twenty. So Hunter had been gone only half an hour. What was all that noise? She sat up. The lash of rain made her look over at the window. It was pouring outside, thundering and lightning. So odd after the clear dawn.

Downstairs, people were shouting and running, and doors were banging. What could possibly be the matter? A fire? There was no alarm. Had the roof sprung a leak? That wouldn't cause this much commotion.

In a minute Morgan had pulled on her jeans and sweater and shoved her feet into her boots. She put her head out the doorway and sniffed. No smell of fire. She cast her senses, sending her consciousness out around her. She picked up only choppy, confused feelings—panic, fear. She grabbed her coat and trotted downstairs.

"Help!" someone was shouting. "Help! If you've got a boat, we need it! Every able-bodied seaman! Get to the harbor!"

A man in a burly coat brushed past Morgan and ran out the door, following the man who had shouted the alarm.

"What's going on?" Morgan asked the desk clerk. The woman's lined face was drawn taut with worry, her black hair making her face look even paler. "What's happened?"

Outside the front door two more men ran past, their hats pulled low against the driving rain. Morgan heard one shout, "Get to the harbor!"

"The ferry," said the woman, starting to tie a scarf around her head. "The ferry's gone down in the storm."

The icy rain felt like needles pelting her face as Morgan tore down the cobbled road toward the harbor. The three blocks seemed to take half an hour to run, and with every second an endless stream of thoughts raced through Morgan's head. *Please let Hunter have been late, for once in his life. Please let it be a different ferry. Please let no one be hurt. Please let Hunter be late. He's missed the ferry, he's missed the ferry, he's missed the ferry. . . .*

Down at the harbor the driving rain obscured vision, and at first Morgan could see only people running around and men starting the engines in their fishing boats. Then the local fire truck screamed up, looking ridiculously small and inadequate for this disaster. Morgan grabbed an older man's arm, hard, and hung on. "What happened?" she shouted, the wind tearing her voice away.

"The ferry went down!" he shouted back, trying to tug his arm free so he could go help.

"Which ferry?" An icy hand was slowly closing around Morgan's heart. She forced herself to have hope.

The man stared at her. "The only ferry! The eight-oh-five to Wexford!" Then he yanked his arm free, and Morgan watched numbly as he ran down a pier and jumped onto a fishing boat that was just pulling out into the choppy, white-capped waves.

This isn't happening. I'm going to wake up any minute. I know I'll wake up soon. Slowly Morgan turned in a circle, the rough wet stones beneath her feet making her feel off balance. Silently she begged for Hunter to come running toward her, a bag in his hand, having missed the ferry because he'd stopped to get a muffin, or tea, or anything. She cast out her senses. Nothing. She sent a witch message. *Hunter, Hunter, come to me, come to me, I'm here, waiting.* Nothing.

Rain soaked her hair, and the harsh wind whipped strands of it across her face. Morgan stood at the edge of the concrete pier, a heavy, rusty chain making a bone-chilling scraping sound as the wind pushed it to and fro. She closed her eyes and let her hands fall open at her sides. With experience born of years of practice, she sank quickly into a meditative state, going beneath the now, the outside, time itself, going deep to where time and thought and energy and magick blended to become one.

Giomanach. Her whole being focused on Hunter's name, his eyes, his scent, the feel of his skin, his smile, his laugh, his anger, his passion. In seconds she relived years of memories with him —Hunter fighting Cal, herself throwing an athame at Hunter's neck, him toppling over the cliff to the cold river below. Hunter placing sigils of protection around her parents' house, his fair hair glinting in the moonlight. Hunter holding her, wrapping his coat around her after she had shape-shifted. She had lain weeping in his arms, feeling as if her bones had snapped their joints, her muscles ripped in half. His voice, murmuring soothing spells to take away her pain and fear. She and Hunter, making love for the first time, the wonder of it, the beauty, the shock of pain and discomfort as they joined their bodies and their hearts. His eyes, wide and green above her. Other snatches of memories flew past, image after image; a remembered laugh, an emotion; a scent; the phase of the moon; circles of magick; witches wearing robes; Hunter's glowing aura; Hunter arguing, angry; Hunter crying silently as Morgan broke down.

"*An nall nathrac,*" Morgan whispered into the rain. "*An di allaigh, nall nithben, holleigh rac bier. . . .*" And on the spell went, the strongest spell she could weave with no preparation. She called on the wind and the rain and the clouds. She opened her hands and the clouds lightened and began to part. She threw up her hands and the rain lessened, backing off as if chastised. Morgan didn't care if anyone was watching or not. Everything in her wrought a spell that would snatch Hunter back from the very brink of his grave.

When she opened her eyes, the rain had slowed to a repentant drizzle; the seas had begun to calm. Morgan felt weak, nauseated, from working such powerful magick. Slowly she forced her legs to take her to the crowd of people huddling on the dock. Voices floated to her over the sounds of sobbing, like chunks of debris on water.

"Never seen nothing like it."

"Unnatural, that's what it was."

"Wave reached up and pulled them down."

"And then like that, the storm stopped."

Morgan froze when she saw the line of sheet-covered bodies on the ground. Men and women were crying, arguing, denying what had happened. Some ferry passengers had been saved, and they sat huddled, looking shocked and afraid.

Hunter wasn't among them. Nor among the dead, lying on the ground.

Morgan gathered every ounce of strength and power within her and sent it out in the world. *If Hunter is alive, I will feel it. If any part of his spirit is there, I will feel it. I will know.* She stayed perfectly still, eyes closed, hands out. Her chest expanded and was aching with her effort. Never had she cast her senses, her powers with so much strength before. Never had everything in her striven to sense someone. She almost cried out with the strain of it, feeling as if she would fly apart. *Hunter, are you alive? Where are you?*

Suddenly Morgan dropped to her knees on the sharp cobblestones, feeling as if she'd been knocked to the ground. She saw the dock, the rain, the covered bodies, but the scene seemed muted, all sounds muffled, all objects leached of color. It was like the whole world had lost something, some element that made it clear and rich and full. And then she understood.

Oh my God. Oh my God. He's really gone. Hunter's gone.

She stared unseeingly at the churning, gray-green water. How could the sea dare to take the one she loved, her soul mate, her *mùirn beatha dàn?* Anguish poured out of her, and she howled, *"Give him back!"* She flung her arms wide, and then, to her astonishment, her silver claddagh ring— Hunter's ring—flew off her rain-slick finger and sailed through the air. Unbelieving, Morgan watched the silver shine dully in the thin gray sunlight, then drop into the sea without a sound. It disappeared in an instant, sinking quickly and silently into the opaque water.

Her ring, Hunter's ring. It, too, was now gone forever. *No, no.*

Her world collapsed around her in a furious whirl of gray despair. Hands out, Morgan fell forward onto her face, not caring if she ever got up again.

1

Moira

"So I said, 'Oh, Mum, don't get your knickers in a twist,'"
Moira Byrne said, licking the steamed milk of her latte off
the spoon. She smiled angelically at her friends and took
a big, slurping sip. Finally the long "regular" school day
was over, and she, Tess, and Vita had headed to Margath's
Faire, on the outskirts of Cobh. The first floor was an
occult book and supplies shop; the second floor was a
café, where they sometimes had readings or music; and
the third floor was for various Wiccan classes or study
groups. The three girls had grabbed a table in the café, in
the back corner.

"Away with ya," said Tess Summerall, laughing in disbelief.

"Right, I can see you being cheeky to Morgan of Belwicket,
mum or no," Vita O'Shaunessy agreed, grinning. "Are you
grounded, then?"

Moira took another sip and shook her head. Her light,
reddish-gold hair, with its three green streaks on the left side,
swung over her shoulders. "Amazingly, no," she admitted. "I

turned on the famous Moira Byrne charm and convinced her it was for my spellcraft class."

Tess's blue eyes widened. "I can't believe your charm works on your own *mum*, and you know, spelling your initials with *ladybugs* on the garden wall was *not* what Keady meant for spellcraft class."

Moira laughed, remembering again how astonished she had been when her spell had worked. It had been the most complicated one she had ever tried, and watching the tiny, red-winged ladybugs slowly spell out *MB* had been incredibly satisfying. Until her mother had come home and caught her. "It was brilliant," she said. "I really should get top marks for it."

Vita rolled her eyes. "You probably will. Especially if you use the *famous* Moira Byrne charm."

Moira giggled. Keady Dove, their spellcraft teacher, was as traditional as her own mother. Admitting that she had toyed with the wills of ladybugs just for a lark would not go over well.

Standing, Tess asked, "Anyone want anything? I'm getting another espresso." At her full height, Tess was five feet two, six inches shorter than Moira and with all the fine-boned daintiness Moira felt she lacked. Tess's naturally black hair was cut short and spiky, with magenta-dyed tips. Much more daring than Moira's three green stripes, which were supposed to have been wash-out dye for St. Patrick's Day but had turned out to be permanent. She'd asked her mum to take them out with magick, and her mum had refused. Her dad had just laughed and hugged her. "It's not so bad, Daisy. It'll probably only take six or seven years to grow out."

Moira had moaned, allowing herself to be held by her

dad, even though she was fifteen—too old to be cuddled or called Daisy, the pet name her father had always used.

"Think of it as character building," her mum had suggested, and her dad had laughed again. Her dad and mum had met eyes and smiled at each other, and Moira had known it was a lost cause. She'd called Tess and complained about the permanent dye being the "worst thing" to happen to her.

That had been seven months ago. One month later her dad had been killed in a car wreck in London, where he'd gone on business. Now she wished more than anything that the green streaks could really have been her worst problem—and that Colm Byrne was still waiting at home to back up her mum in a lecture about the latest trouble Moira had gotten into.

"Moira?" Tess asked, waiting for an answer.

"Oh, no thanks. I'm fine." Moira forced a thin smile.

"All right, then?" Vita asked once Tess had left. Her round face looked concerned.

"Oh, you know," Moira said vaguely. Vita nodded sympathetically and patted Moira's hand in an old-fashioned gesture Moira found touching.

"I know. I'm here, whenever you want to talk."

Moira nodded. "I'd rather be distracted, really," she said.

"Well, good," Vita said. "Because I was wondering if you could help me study for herbology. I got all the nightshades mixed up on the last test, and Christa was *very disappointed*." Vita lowered her voice to sound like Christa Ryan, one of their initiation-class teachers.

"Sure," Moira said. "Come over tonight or tomorrow and we'll go over everything. I'll share all the Moira Byrne wisdom with you."

Vita threw a paper napkin at her, and Moira laughed.

"You mean the Moira Byrne wisdom that had you spelling your initials with bugs?" Vita asked dryly.

"Right! That wisdom!"

Tess came back and sat down, curling one leg neatly beneath her.

"You're so dainty," Moira said with a sigh, wishing the same could be said about her. Then she froze in her seat, her hazel eyes wide. One hand reached out to grab Tess's arm. "Goddess—I think he's here, downstairs," she whispered. She hadn't deliberately been casting her senses, but her neck had prickled, and when she concentrated, she thought she felt Ian's vibrations.

Vita fluttered her eyelids. "Oh, no—I don't think I can take the excitement of seeing Ian Delaney. Someone help me. Fetch a cold cloth." She swayed in her chair while Tess broke up with laughter. Moira looked at her.

"I'll fetch you a cold cloth," she said, "for your *mouth*."

Vita and Tess laughed harder, and Moira narrowed her eyes. "Could we have more sympathy, please?" she asked. "How often do I fancy a lad?"

"Not often," Tess agreed, sobering. "Everyone, be casual."

This made Vita laugh again. Moira turned her attention to her latte as though it were all-absorbing. *Come up here,* she thought. *Come upstairs. You're thirsty.*

She wasn't putting a spell on Ian or sending him a witch message. She was just wishing hard. Ian Delaney had transferred to her regular school two years ago, and Moira had immediately developed a crush on him. He was gorgeous in a rough-cut kind of way, with thick brown hair that never looked quite tidy enough, deep blue eyes, and one dimple in his right cheek when he smiled. He'd been such a refreshing change from some of the more upper-class snobs who went to Moira's school—outspoken, funny in a cheeky way, and completely unable to be intimidated, either by teachers or students.

Best of all, he was a witch.

Unfortunately, all last year Moira had been invisible to him—not that she had even tried to get his attention. But this year . . . he had sat next to her in study hall. Lent her some graph paper in math class. Borrowed a quid from her—*and* paid her back. And just in the last month Moira had actually started trying to flirt with him, in a lame, inexperienced way, she admitted. But he seemed to be responding.

"I can't feel him," said Vita. "Is he coming up?"

"Not yet," said Moira. "He's still downstairs."

Tess grinned. "Shall I fetch him up here? I'll stand at the top of the stairs and yell, 'Oy! You there, boy. Up here!'"

Moira's chest tightened. "If you do . . ." she breathed in warning, shaking her head. Tess was so much more confident about lads. It wasn't that Moira didn't have confidence—she knew that she was good at magick and that she had an ability to learn anything if she put her mind to it. She never questioned how much her family loved her. But where she did fall apart was with the whole world of boys, dating, and flirting.

Come upstairs, Ian. You're thirsty. Or hungry. Or you're looking for me.

"Does your mum know about Ian?" Tess asked.

Moira shook her head. "No. We're not dating—it's not like I've had him home to tea."

Two pairs of blue eyes looked at her. Tess's were expectant, shrewd. Vita's were politely disbelieving.

"So you've not mentioned your unquenchable love for Ian Delaney, son of Lilith Delaney, high priestess of Ealltuinn," Vita stated. "Ealltuinn, who's been getting members of Belwicket up in arms because they don't seem to know the boundary of when it's not right to use magick?"

"It's not unquenchable love, and no, I've not mentioned it," Moira said pointedly. "Am I supposed to only date Belwicket lads, then? There's precious few. Or should I try a nonwitch?"

Half smiling, Tess held up her hands as if to say she gave up.

"Just wanted to ask," Vita murmured, shrugging. "I mean, everything aside, Ian's deadly hot. No one says he isn't."

Moira paused. "Wait—he's coming up!" She bent over her latte, face carefully expressionless. Out of the corner of her eye she saw Ian the second he passed the top step into the café. She looked anywhere but at him, shooting subtle but threatening looks at Tess and Vita, each of whom was trying to smother a smile.

"So," said Tess brightly. "You want to take in a film this weekend, then?"

Moira nodded as if it were a serious question. "Yeah, maybe so." Her eyes widened as she realized Ian was coming straight at their table, a mug in his hand.

"Moira!" he said.

She looked up with an Oscar-worthy expression of surprise. "Oh, hey there, Ian."

He smiled down at her, and she felt her heart give a little flip. That smile . . .

"'Lo, Ian," said Tess, and Vita smiled at him.

"Hi," he said, and Moira loved the fact that his gaze didn't linger on either of her (she thought) prettier or more feminine friends. Instead he looked right at her, his chestnut brown hair flecked with mist, his eyes dark blue and smiling. "I don't want to interrupt—I was just downstairs and fancied a drink. It's wet outside."

"Do you want to sit down?" Moira asked, mentally patting herself on the back for her boldness.

"Aye, sure," he said, pleased. He asked a neighboring table if he could take a chair, then pulled it over and wedged it right next to Moira's. She could hardly keep herself from wiggling with happiness. Cool. I'm very cool, she thought, feeling almost glad about her green-streaked hair.

"Oh! Look at the time!" Tess said in a non-Oscar-worthy performance, complete with wide eyes and O-shaped mouth. "I have to be getting off. Mum'll slay me if I'm late again." She stood and pulled on her suede jacket.

"I didn't mean to interrupt anything," Ian said again, concerned.

"Not at all," Tess assured him. "Pure coincidence. Come on, then, Vi."

"Why?" Vita frowned. "Your mum won't slay me if I'm late."

Tess just stared at her, and then Vita got it.

"Right. I'm late, too." She stood up and pulled on her plaid trench coat. "Later on, Moira. Nice seeing you, Ian."

"You too," he said.

Then they were gone, and Moira and Ian were sharing a table alone for the first time. Moira felt all quivery inside, happy and anxious at once. Her latte was ice-cold, and she quickly circled her hand over it, deasil, and murmured, "Heat within." Ian sipped his mug of tea. Just as Moira was starting to feel alarmed by the lingering silence, Ian said, "I was looking at books downstairs."

"Oh?" *Yes, that was witty. You go, Moira.* "I've always liked the illustrated books—the ones with old-fashioned pictures of witches. Or the really pretty flower ones." *Do I really sound this stupid?*

Ian didn't seem to think so. He only said, "Yeah. I love the plant ones. I'm still taking private herbology lessons."

"But you got initiated last year, right?"

"Yeah, they usually do it at fourteen in my coven," he replied. "You're not initiated yet?"

"No. I'm aiming for next Beltane. Me and Tess and Vita."

"Well, you've got some time, then."

Moira nodded. "We're all taking classes—spellcraft, herbology, astrology, animal work. The usuals."

"What's your favorite?"

He's interested in me! "I like spellcraft." She couldn't help smiling, remembering her ladybug triumph. "Last weekend I wrote a new spell by myself. I spelled ladybugs to form my initials on my garden wall."

Ian laughed. "Did it work? Or did you just get a bunch of confused, ready-to-hibernate ladybugs? Or maybe bees?"

Grinning, Moira knocked her side against him, then was thrilled at the warm contact. "*Yes,* it worked." The truth was, she'd been pretty amazed herself—but she didn't want Ian to know that.

"Yeah? Ladybugs spelled out your initials? That's very cool," said Ian, looking impressed. "And you're not even initiated yet. But I guess you've got your mother's power, then."

Self-consciously Moira shrugged, although by now she was used to having a mother who was famous in Wiccan circles. All of Moira's life, she'd heard people speaking respectfully about Morgan Byrne of Belwicket—her powers, her incredibly strong healing gifts, the promise of her craft. Moira was proud of her mum, but at the same time it was hard, always wondering if she would ever measure up.

"With your powers, why weren't you initiated earlier?" Ian asked. "It seems like you would be amazing by now."

"You don't think I'm amazing?" Moira said teasingly, feeling incredibly daring. She had a moment of anxiety when Ian quit smiling and just looked at her thoughtfully. *I went too far, I went too far—*

"No," he said quietly. "I do think you're amazing."

Her face lit up, and she forgot to be cool. "I think you're amazing, too."

"Oh, yes, me," Ian said. "I can move forks. Look."

As Moira watched, Tess's leftover fork slid slowly toward her, about an inch. Moira grinned and raised her eyebrows at him, and he looked pleased.

"Pretty good," she said, an idea popping into her mind. Hopefully she could pull it off. "Watch this," she said boldly. "Look at everyone in the room who's reading"—which was three-quarters of the people there. Most tables seemed to have an open book or magazine or paper on them. Moira closed her eyes and pictured what she wanted to do, tamping down the mote of conscience that warned her it was probably not a good idea. *Right, then, I hope this works.*

All the pages move as one, as if the story's just begun. I flip the pages lightly so, and my will tells them where to go.

Then, seeing it in her mind, Moira turned one page in each paper, book, or magazine throughout the café at Margath's Faire. In perfect unison, every piece of reading material in the room had one page turned.

Most people noticed, and the witches in the room instantly looked up to see who had done it. Hearing that it had worked, Moira opened her eyes and carefully looked at no one besides Ian. She finished the last bit of her latte and gave Ian a private smile, thrilled that she'd really done it.

"That was bloody beautiful," Ian breathed, looking at her in a way that made her feel shivery. "So delicate and simple, yet so awesome." He took her hand, and Moira loved the feel of his warmth, their fingers intertwining. His hand was larger than hers, which made her feel better, because in fact Ian was only the same height she was.

I'm holding hands with Ian Delaney, Moira thought, letting happiness wash over her.

"I'm impressed, Moira of Belwicket," he said quietly, looking at her. "You are your mother's daughter."

2

Morgan

"Thank you for coming." A man with a weathered face and brown hair gone mostly gray stepped forward and took one of Morgan's hands in his.

"Hello," she said quietly, giving him a smile. Automatically Morgan sent out waves of reassurance and calm, trying to soothe nerves stretched taut by fear and worry. Since she'd lost her husband, Colm, six months ago, it had been a struggle to continue her work without her emotions interfering. But she needed the salary from the New Charter to support herself and her daughter, and also, she needed the relief from her own sadness that came from helping others. Luckily Morgan had been honing her skills as a healer for years now, and the routine of easing someone's concern was second nature.

"You must be Andrew Moffitt," she said. She was in the county hospital in Youghal, a town not far from where she lived, right outside of Cobh, Ireland. The Moffitts' daughter was in the last bed in a long, old-fashioned ward that housed eight patients.

"Aye," he said with a quick bob of his head. "And this is my missus, Irene."

A small woman wearing an inexpensive calico dress nodded nervously. Her large green eyes were etched with sadness, the lines around her mouth deep and tight. Her hair was pulled back into a simple braid, practical for a farmer's wife.

"Hello, Irene," Morgan said. She reached out and took one of Irene's hands, sending her a quick bit of strength and peace. Irene gave her a questioning glance, then shot an anxious look at her husband. "Irene, you seem unsure." Morgan's voice was gentle and compassionate.

Irene's eyes darted around the room, pausing to linger on the pale, thin girl lying in the hospital bed. The hushed *whoosh, whoosh* of machines filled the small room, with a steady beeping of the heart monitor keeping time.

"I don't hold with this," Irene said in a low voice. "We're Catholics, we are. I don't want to lose my Amy, but maybe it's the Lord's will." Her face crumpled slightly.

Morgan put down her large canvas carryall and deliberately sent out more general calming waves. "I understand," she said. "As much as you desperately love your daughter and pray for her recovery, you might not want it if it means endangering her soul. Or yours."

"Yes," Irene said, sounding relieved and surprised that Morgan understood. Of course Irene couldn't know that Morgan had been raised by devout Catholics, Sean and Mary Grace Rowlands, and knew better than many the fears Catholics had about witchcraft. "Yes, that's it exactly. I mean, she's my baby, but . . ." Again, withheld sobs choked her. "It's just—Eileen Crannach, from church—she told us what you'd done for her nephew, Davy. Said it was a miracle, it was. And we're so desperate—the doctors can't do much for her."

"I understand," Morgan said again. "Here, sit down." She led Irene to one of the two nearby plastic visitor chairs and sat down in the other one. Looking up, she beckoned Andrew to come closer. In a low voice she said, "I can promise you that anything I do would never have evil intent. I seem to have a gift for healing. My using that gift feels, to me, what you would describe as the Lord's will. Here's another way of looking at it: maybe it was the Lord's will that brought me to you. Maybe your Lord wants to do his work through me."

Irene gaped. "But you're not Catholic," she whispered. "You're a . . . witch!" The word itself seemed to frighten her, and she looked around to make sure no one else had heard.

Morgan smiled, thinking of her adoptive mother. "Even so. He works in mysterious ways."

An unspoken consultation passed between Andrew and Irene, looking into each other's eyes. Morgan sat quietly, using the time to cast her senses toward Amy. Amy was in a coma. From what Andrew Moffitt had gruffly told Morgan on the phone, Amy's brother had been practicing fancy skateboard moves, and in one of them he'd shot the board out from under his feet. Amy had been playing nearby, and the edge of the board caught her right in the neck, cracking her spine. But they hadn't realized the extent of her injuries, and over the next several days the swelling and injury had been worsened by her everyday activities. They hadn't even known anything was wrong until Amy had collapsed on the school playground.

She'd had surgery six days ago and hadn't come out of it.

"Do what you can for Amy," Andrew said, calling Morgan back to the present.

"All right," said Morgan, and that was all.

Because she was in a county hospital, with people coming and going constantly, Morgan couldn't use any of her more obvious tools, like candles and incense and her four silver cups. However, she did slip a large, uncut garnet beneath Amy's pillow to help her in her healing rite.

"If you could just try to keep anyone from touching me or talking to me," she whispered, and wide-eyed, the Moffitts nodded.

Morgan stood at Amy's bedside, opening her senses and picking up as much as she could. Right now Amy was on a respirator, but her heart was beating on its own and every-thing else seemed to be working. There was an incision on her neck with a thin plastic drain running out of it. That was where she could start.

First things first. Morgan rolled her shoulders and tilted her head back and forth, releasing any tension or stiffness. She breathed in and out, deep cleansing breaths that helped relax and center her. Then, closing her eyes, she silently and without moving her lips began her power chant, the one that reached out into the world and drew magick to her, the one that helped raise her own powers within her. It came to her, floating toward her like colored ribbons on the mildest of spring breezes. Feeling the magick bloom inside her, Morgan felt a fierce love and joy flood her. She was ready.

As lightly as a feather, Morgan placed two fingers on Amy's incision. At once she picked up the drug-dulled sensations of pain, the swollen sponginess of inflamed cells, the cascading dominoes of injuries that had escalated, unchecked, until Amy lost consciousness. Slowly Morgan traced the injuries until she reached the last and mildest one. Then, following them like a thread, she did what she could to heal them. Clots dissolved with a steady barrage of spells. Muscles soothed, tendons eased, veins gently reopened. Morgan's mind traced new pathways, delicate, fernlike branches of energy, and soon felt the rapid fire of neuron impulses racing across them. Love, she thought. Love and hope, joy and life. The blessing of being able to give. How blessed I am. These feelings she let flow into Amy's consciousness.

The injury itself was complicated, but Morgan broke it down into tiny steps, like the different layers of a spell, the different steps one had to learn, all throughout Wicca. As with anything else, it was the tiny steps that added up to create a wondrous whole. Morgan banished the excess fluid at the site, dispersing it through now-open paths. She calmed swollen muscles and helped the skin heal more rapidly. The final step of this first stage was the actual crack in the spinal column, where a minute shift of bone had compressed the nerves. The bone was edged back into place, and Morgan felt the instantaneous rightness and perfect fit of it. She encouraged the bone to start knitting together. The crushed nerves were slowly, painstakingly restored, with new routes being created where necessary. Then she waited and listened to the overall response of Amy's body. It was sluggish, but functioning. With every beat of Amy's heart it got stronger, worked better, flowed more smoothly. It would take longer to heal completely, Morgan knew. Maybe months. But this was a great start.

Her own strength was flagging. Healing took so much energy and concentration that Morgan always felt completely drained afterward. This was the most difficult case she'd had in months, and it would leave Morgan herself weak for several days.

But it wasn't over. Amy's body was functioning. Now she had to find Amy. Ignoring her fatigue, Morgan concentrated even deeper, silently using spells that would link Amy's consciousness with hers in a *tàth meànma*, a joining of their minds. Amy wasn't a blood witch, so it wouldn't feel good for either one of them, and Amy's ability to either receive or send energy was going to be very limited. Amy's spirit was sleeping. It had shut down and withdrawn to escape the horror of paralysis, the pain of the injury and the surgery, and the flood of nerve-shattering emotions that everyone around Amy was releasing.

Amy? Are you there?

Who—who are you?

I'm here to help. It's time to come back now. Morgan was firm and kind.

No. It's too yucky.

It's not so yucky anymore. It's time to come back. Come back and see your mum and dad. They're waiting for you.

They're still here?

They would never leave you. Come back now.

Will it hurt? Her voice was young and afraid.

A little bit. You have to be strong and brave. But it won't be as bad as it was before, I promise.

Very slowly and gently Morgan eased her consciousness back, then swayed on her feet as a wave of exhaustion washed over her. But she backtracked quickly to herself, sent a last, strong healing spell, and opened her eyes. She blinked several times and swallowed, feeling as if she were about to fall over. Slowly she took her hand away from Amy's neck.

With difficulty, she turned to Andrew and Irene and smiled

weakly. Then, knowing Amy could breathe on her own, she carefully disconnected the mouthpiece from the respirator.

"No!" Amy's mother cried, lunging forward to stop her. Her husband grabbed her, and in the next moment Amy coughed and gagged, then drew a deep, whistling breath around the tube that was still in her throat.

Her parents stared.

"You need to get a nurse to take out the tube," Morgan said softly, still feeling only half there. She swallowed again and glanced at the clock. It was three in the afternoon. She'd arrived at nine that morning. Time hadn't made an impression on her during the healing.

Then Andrew seemed to notice her, and his heavy eyebrows drew together in concern. "Here, miss. Let me get you some tea." Awkwardly Morgan moved to a chair and dropped into it. Andrew pressed a hot Styrofoam cup into her hand and appeared not to notice her quickly circling her hand over her tea. She drank down half of it at once. It helped.

Irene's anxious calls had alerted a nurse, who, faced with the undeniable fact that Amy was breathing on her own, removed the respirator tube. She watched in shock as Amy gagged again and took several convulsive breaths. Andrew and Irene gripped each other's hands tightly as they stared down at their daughter. Then Irene tentatively reached out and took her daughter's hand.

"Amy, darling. Amy, it's Mum. I'm right here, love, and so is Da. We're right here, lass."

Morgan sipped her tea. There was nothing more she could do. Amy had to choose to come back.

In the hospital bed the pale, still figure seemed small and

fragile. She was breathing more regularly now, with only the occasional cough. Suddenly her eyelids fluttered open for a moment, revealing a pair of green eyes just like her mum's. Her parents gasped and leaned closer.

"Amy!" Irene cried as a doctor strode quickly toward them. "Amy! Love!"

Amy licked her lips slightly, and her eyes fluttered again. Her mouth seemed to form the word *Mum*, and her pinkie finger on her left hand raised slightly.

"Good Lord," the doctor breathed.

Irene was crying now, kissing Amy's hand, and Andrew was sniffing, his worn face crinkled into a leathery smile. Morgan finished her tea and got to her feet. Very quietly she picked up her canvas bag. It seemed to weigh three times as much as it had that morning. And she still had an hour's drive to Wicklow. She was suffused with the happiness that always came from healing, an intense feeling of accomplishment and satisfaction. But the happiness was tinged bittersweet, as it had been every time she'd healed someone since Colm's death—because when her husband had needed her most, she hadn't been there to heal *him*.

She was almost out the door when Irene noticed she was leaving. "Wait!" she cried, and hurried over to Morgan. Her face was wet with tears, her smile seeming like a rainbow. "I don't know what you did," she said in barely more than a whisper. "I told the nurses you were praying for her. But it's a miracle you've done here, and as long as I live, I'll never be able to thank you enough."

Morgan gave her a brief hug. "Amy getting better is all the thanks I need."

*   *   *

"You're working too hard, lass," Katrina Byrne said as Morgan came up the front walk.

Morgan shifted her heavy tote to her other shoulder. It was almost five o'clock. Luckily she'd had the foresight to ask her mother-in-law to be here this afternoon in case she didn't get back before dinner.

"Hi. What are you doing? Pulling up the carrots? Is Moira home?"

"No, she's not back yet," said Katrina, sitting back stiffly on her little stool. "I would have expected her by now. How was your day?"

"Hard. But in the end, good. The girl opened her eyes, and she recognized her mum."

"Good." Katrina's brown eyes looked her up and down. The older woman was heavyset, more so now than when Morgan had met her, so long ago. Katrina and her husband, Pawel, and her sister, Susan Best, had been among the handful of survivors of the original Belwicket, on the western coast of Ireland. Morgan had known her first as the temporary leader of Belwicket, then as her mother-in-law, and the two women had an understated closeness—especially now that they were both widows.

"You're all in, Morgan," Katrina said.

"I'm beat," Morgan agreed. "I need a hot bath and a sit-down."

"Sit down for just a moment here." Katrina pointed with her dirt-crusted trowel at the low stone wall that bordered Morgan's front yard. Morgan lowered her bag to the damp grass and rested on the cool stones. The afternoon light was rapidly fading, but the last pale rays of sunlight shone on

Katrina's gray hair, twisted up into a bun in back. She wore brown cords and a brown sweater she'd knit herself, before her arthritis had gotten too bad.

"Where's Moira, then?" Morgan asked, looking up the narrow country road as if she expected to see her daughter running down it.

"Don't know," Katrina said, picking up a three-pronged hand rake and scraping it among the carrots. "With her gang."

Morgan smiled to herself: Moira's "gang" consisted of her friends Tess and Vita. She let out a deep breath, hoping she would have the energy to get back up when she needed to. Lately it seemed she'd been working harder than ever. She was often gone, leaving Katrina to come look after Moira, though Moira had started protesting that she could stay by herself. Last week Katrina had accused her of running away from grief, and Morgan hadn't denied it. It was just too painful to be here sometimes—to see the woodwork that Colm had painted, the garden he'd helped her create. She felt his loss a thousand times a day here. In a hotel in some unknown city, with work to distract her, it was easier to bear. Now she waited for her outspoken mother-in-law— her friend—to get something off her chest.

"When were you thinking of accepting the role of high priestess?" Katrina asked bluntly. Her trowel moved slowly through the rich black soil. She looked focused on her gardening, but Morgan knew better.

She let out a deep breath. "I was thinking maybe next spring. Imbolc. Moira's to be initiated on Beltane, and it would be lovely for me to lead it."

"Aye," agreed Katrina. "So maybe you need to cut back

on your traveling and start preparing more to be high priest-ess." She looked up at Morgan shrewdly. "Meaning you'll have to be home more."

Morgan pressed her lips together. It was pointless to pre-tend not to know what Katrina was talking about. She scraped the toe of her shoe against a clump of grass. "It's hard being here."

"Hard things have to be faced, Morgan. You've a daughter here who needs you. You've missed two of the last five cir-cles. And not least, your garden's going to hell." Katrina pulled up a group of late carrots, and Morgan was startled to see that below their lush green tops, their roots were gnarled, twisted, and half rotted away.

"What . . . ?"

Katrina clawed her hand rake through the dirt: The whole row of carrots was rotten. Morgan and Katrina's eyes met.

"You did all the usual spells, of course," Katrina said.

"Of course. I've never had anything like this." Morgan knelt down and took the small rake from Katrina. She dug through the soil, pulling up the ruined carrots, then went deeper. In a minute she had found it: a small pouch of sodden, dirt-stained leather, tied at the top with string. Morgan scratched runes of protection quickly around her, then untied the string. A piece of slate fell out, covered with sigils—magickal symbols that worked spells. Some of them Morgan didn't know, but she rec-ognized a few, for general destruction (plants), for the attrac-tion of darkness (also for plants), and for the halting of growth (modified to pertain to plants).

"Oh my God," she breathed, sitting back on her heels. It had been so long since anyone had wished her harm—a lifetime ago. To find this in her own garden . . . it was unbelievable.

"What are you thinking?" Katrina asked.

Morgan paused, considering. "I really can't imagine who would do this," she said. "No one in our coven works magick to harm. . . ." She trailed off as something occurred to her. "Of course, there is another coven whose members don't share our respect for what's right."

"Ealltuinn," Katrina said.

Morgan nodded. "I never would have thought they'd do something like this," she murmured, almost to herself. It wasn't unusual for more than one coven to be in a certain area; sometimes they coexisted peacefully, sometimes less so. Belwicket had been in the town of Wicklow, right outside Cobh, for over twenty years now; they were a Woodbane coven who had renounced dark magick. Ealltuinn, a mixed coven, had started in Hewick, a small town slightly to the north, about eight years ago. There hadn't been any problems until about two years ago, when Lilith Delaney had become high priestess of Ealltuinn.

Morgan had never liked Lilith—she was one of those witches who always pushed things a little too far and didn't understand why it was a problem. But it was more that she'd work minor spells out of self-interest, nothing dangerous, so Morgan hadn't been too concerned. She'd spoken with Lilith several times, warned her that she didn't agree with the direction Lilith was taking her coven in, and Lilith hadn't been too pleased with that. But would she really have shown her anger like this? By ruining Morgan's garden? The spell was minor, petty, but it was working harm against someone—which was always wrong.

Morgan looked around her yard, distressed. This home had always been a haven for her. Suddenly she felt isolated and vulnerable in a way she hadn't for decades. A ruined garden wasn't the worst thing that had ever happened to Morgan, but that someone was actively working to harm her . . . She didn't believe Lilith would want to hurt her—but who else could it be?

"When was the last time you saw Lilith Delaney?" Katrina asked, as if sensing Morgan's thoughts.

Morgan thought back. "Two weeks ago, in Margath's Faire. Hartwell Moss and I were there, having a cup after shopping. Lilith was sitting with another member of Ealltuinn, and they looked deep into something together."

"Do they know where the power leys are?" Katrina asked, her eyes narrowing.

Morgan felt a flash of fear. Why was Katrina asking that—was she worried that Ealltuinn was more of a threat than Morgan had thought? "Not that I know of," Morgan replied, her throat feeling tight. "Now that I think of it, though, every once in a while I see someone from Ealltuinn out on the headlands, crisscrossing them, like they're looking for something."

The two women looked at each other. In fact, Morgan's very house was built on an ancient power ley, or line, as was Katrina's house and the old grocery store that she and Pawel had run in the early days of their marriage. The building was now empty, and Belwicket held many of their circles there. But Ealltuinn must have heard the legends of the power leys, the unseen and often unfelt ancient lines of energy and magick that crisscrossed the earth, like rubber bands wrapped around a tennis ball. Those who worked magick on or around a power ley saw their powers increased. The town where Morgan had grown up in America, Widow's Vale, had had a power ley also, in an old Methodist cemetery.

Morgan dropped the rotten carrots in disgust and retied the little pouch. She would have to dismantle it, purify the pieces of it with salt, and bury it down by the sea, where the sand and salt water would further dissolve its negative energy.

"Morgan, I'm concerned about Ealltuinn," Katrina said seriously. "With Lilith Delaney at their head, what if they become bolder in their darkness? I'll be honest with you, lass: I wish I were strong enough to take them on. I've got some righteous anger to show them. But I'm not. I'm fine, but I'm not you."

"I don't know," Morgan said. "It's been a long time. . . . I'm different now."

"Morgan, you could still pull the moon from the sky. In you is the combined strength of Maeve Riordan and Ciaran MacEwan, Goddess have mercy on them both. You alone are powerful enough to stop Lilith in her tracks, to keep Belwicket safe. Twenty years ago you saved your town from a dark wave—you stopped a dark wave when no one dreamed it was possible."

"It was Daniel Niall and another witch," Morgan corrected her. "I just helped. And besides, this is hardly another dark wave."

Katrina gave her a maternal look, then brushed her hands off on her corduroy pants. "It's getting late," she said. "I'd best be getting back. You know, sometimes I still expect Pawel to come home to tea, and he's been gone six years."

"I know what you mean," Morgan said, her eyes shadowed.

"Think on what I said, lass," Katrina said, getting stiffly to her feet. She gave Morgan a quick kiss, then let herself out the garden gate and headed back up the narrow road to her own cottage, less than a quarter mile away.

For another minute Morgan sat in her garden, looking

down at the row of spoiled carrots. She was torn between feeling that Katrina had to be overreacting and her own instinct to believe the worst after everything she had experienced in Widow's Vale. But that was all far in her past, and she hadn't seen anyone practice true dark magick in ages. Of course, she also hadn't seen anyone use magick for harm at all, even on such a small scale as hurting some vegetables. But Lilith was a small-minded person who obviously couldn't handle having someone tell her she was wrong.

Morgan looked up at the sky, realizing that it was getting dark and Moira wasn't home yet. It wasn't that unusual for her to be late, though usually she called. Maybe Morgan was being foolish, but this little pouch had really spooked her, and she wanted her daughter home *now*.

Six twenty-two. Exactly two minutes since the last time she'd looked.

Six twenty-two! Moira was two and half hours late and no doubt off with her friends somewhere. Morgan was sure no harm had come to her daughter. After all, Wicklow wasn't exactly Los Angeles or New York. Everybody tended to know everybody—it was hard to get away with wrongdoing or mischief.

Trying not to look at the clock, Morgan moved methodically around the small living room, kicking the rug back into place, straightening the afghan draped over Colm's leather chair. Her fingers lingered on the cool leather and she swallowed, hit once again with the pain of missing him. Sometimes Morgan would get through part of a day with moments of amusement or joy, and she would grow hopeful about starting to heal. Then, with no warning, something would remind her of Colm's laugh, his voice, his warm, reassuring presence, and it was like a physical blow, leaving Morgan gasping with loss.

Even Moira being so late would have seemed okay if Colm were here with her. He would have been calm and matter-of-fact, and when Moira came home, he would have known exactly what to say. He and Moira were so much alike, both outgoing and cheerful, friendly and affectionate. Morgan had always been on the shyer side, a bit more insecure, needing to have the *t*'s crossed and the *i*'s dotted. Since Colm had died, it seemed that Morgan had developed a gift for saying the wrong thing to Moira, for flying off the handle, for botching what should have been the time for mother and daughter to grow closer. If she were home enough for them to grow closer, she thought with a pang of guilt. She had to quit running. Hard things had to be faced, as Katrina said. Still, how many hard things was she going to have to face in this life? Too many, so far.

Morgan glanced around the already tidy room and caught sight of her reflection in the windowpane, the dark night outside turning the glass into a mirror. Was that her? In the window Morgan looked sad and alone, young and slightly worried. Her hair was still brown and straight, parted in the middle and worn a few inches below her shoulders. It had been much longer in high school.

Morgan gazed solemnly at the window Morgan, then froze when a second face suddenly appeared beside hers. She startled and whirled to look behind her, but she was alone. Eyes wide, heart already thumping with the first rush of adrenaline, Morgan looked closer at the window—was the person outside? She looked around—her dog, Finnegan, was sleeping by the fireplace. Casting her senses told her she was alone, inside the house and out. But next to her own reflection was a thin, ghostly face, with hollow cheeks and haunted eyes, but so pale and blurry that she had no clue who it could be. She stared for another ten seconds, trying to make out the person, but as she looked, the image became even less distinct and then faded completely.

Goddess, Morgan thought, sitting abruptly at the table. She realized her hands were shaking and her heart beating erratically. Goddess. What had that been? Visions were strong magick. Where had that come from? What did it mean? Had it been just a glamour, thrown on the window by . . . whom? Or something darker, more serious? Feeling prickly anxiety creeping up her back, Morgan took a few breaths and tried to calm down. This, on top of the hex she'd found in the garden. What if Katrina was right? What if Lilith and Ealltuinn were up to something? Morgan hadn't experienced anything like these things in so long.

Standing up, Morgan walked back and forth in the living room, casting her senses strongly. She felt nothing except the sleeping aura of Finnegan, the deeply sleeping aura of Bixby, her cat, and silence. Outside she felt nothing except the occasional bird or bat or field mouse, vole, or rabbit, skittering here and there. She felt completely rattled, shaken, and afraid in a way she hadn't felt in years. Was this part of missing Colm? Feeling afraid and alone? But the pouch and the image in the window—they were real and definitely involved magick. Dark magick. Morgan shivered. And where is Moira?

Morgan looked at Moira's cold, untouched dinner on the worn wooden table and felt a sudden surge of anxiety. Even though moments ago she'd been certain Moira was fine, now she needed her daughter home, needed to see her face, to know she was all right. She even felt an impulse to scry for her but knew that it wasn't right to abuse Moira's trust and use magick to spy on her daughter. Still, if much more time passed, she might have to push that boundary.

Try to calm down. Worrying never helped anything, that was what Colm always said. *If you can change things, change them, but don't waste time worrying about things you can't change.* Tomorrow she would talk to Katrina, tell her about the face in the window. For now, there wasn't much she could do. Sighing, Morgan began to stack dishes in the sink. She couldn't help turning around every few seconds to glance at the windows. Conveniently, she could see the whole downstairs from the small kitchen tucked into one corner. A dark blue curtain covered the doorway to the pantry. Off the fireplace was a small, tacked-on room for Wicca work. Upstairs were three tiny bedrooms and one antiquated bathroom. When Colm was alive, Morgan had chafed at the smallness of their cottage—he'd seemed to fill the place with his breadth and his laugh and his steady presence. Along with Moira, two dogs (though Seamus was buried in the north field now), two cats (Dagda was now also buried in the north field), and Morgan, the cottage had almost seemed to split at the seams.

Now there were days when Moira was at school and the cottage felt overwhelmingly large, empty, and quiet. On those days Morgan threw open the shutters to let in more light, swept the floor vigorously both to clean and to stir up energy, and sang loudly as she went about the day's chores. But when her voice was silent, so was the cottage, and so was her heart. That was when she looked for an opportunity to go somewhere, work someplace else, for just a while.

What a horrible irony. Morgan traveled constantly on

business—her work as a healer had grown steadily in the last ten years, and she was away at least every month. Colm had been a midlevel chemical researcher for a lab in Cork and never needed to travel or work late or miss vacations. The one time his company had decided to send him on a business trip to London, he'd been killed in a car accident on his second day there. Morgan, the powerful witch, the healer, had not been able to heal or help or be with her husband when he died. Now she wondered if anything would ever feel normal again, if the gaping hole left in her life could possibly be filled.

She had to be strong for Moira—and for the rest of the coven, too. But there were times, sitting crying on the floor in her shower, when she wished with all her heart that she was a teenager again, home in Widow's Vale, and that she could come out of the shower and see her adoptive mother and have everything be all right.

Her adoptive parents, Sean and Mary Grace Rowlands, still lived in Widow's Vale. They'd been crushed when she'd moved to Ireland—especially since it had been clear she was going to fulfill her heritage as a blood witch of Belwicket, her birth mother's ancestral clan. But now they were getting older. How much longer would she have them? She hadn't been to America in ten months. Morgan's younger sister, Mary K., had married two years ago and was now expecting twins at the age of thirty-four. Morgan would have loved to have been closer to her during this exciting time, to be more involved in her family's lives. But they were there, and she was here. This was the life she'd made for herself.

Her senses prickled and Morgan stood still, focusing. Moira was coming up the front walk. Quickly Morgan dried her hands on a dish towel and went to the front door. She opened it just as Moira reached the house and ushered her in fast, shutting and locking the door after her. Suddenly everything outside seemed unknown and scary, unpredictable.

"Where were you?" she said, holding Moira's shoulders, making sure she was fine. "I've been so worried. Why didn't you call?"

Moira's long, strawberry-blond hair was tangled by the night wind, there were roses in her cheeks, and she was rubbing her hands together and blowing on them.

"I'm sorry, Mum," Moira said. "I completely forgot. But I was just down in Cobh. Caught the bus back." Her hazel eyes were lit with excitement, and Morgan could feel a mixture of emotions coming from her. Moira eased out of Morgan's grip and dumped her book bag onto the rocking chair. "I went out to tea after school, and I guess I lost track of time."

"It took you three hours to have tea?" Morgan asked.

"No," Moira said, her face losing some of its happy glow. "I was just at Margath's Faire." She casually flipped through the day's mail, pushing aside a few seed catalogs and not finding anything of interest.

Morgan began to do a slow burn, her fear turning to irritation. "Moira, look at me." Moira did, her face stiff and impatient. "I don't want to be your jail keeper," Morgan said, trying to keep her voice soft. "But I get very worried if you're not here when I expect you to be. I know we don't live in a dangerous town, but I can't help imagining all sorts of awful things happening." She tried to smile. "It's what a mother does. I need you to call me if you're going to be late. Unless you want me to start scrying to find you. Or send a witch message."

Moira's eyes narrowed. Clearly she didn't like the idea. Taking a different tack, Morgan thought back to her own parents being upset with her and then tried to do something different. "I need to know where you are and who you're with," she said calmly. "I need you to contact me if you're going to be late so I don't worry. I need to know when to expect you home."

What would Colm have done? How would he have handled this? "Were you with Tess or Vita?" Morgan asked, trying to sound less accusing and more interested. "Their folks don't mind if they're late?"

"No, I wasn't with them," Moira admitted, starting to pick at the upholstery of the rocking-chair cushion. "At least, I was at first, but then they went."

After a moment of silence Morgan was forced to ask, "So who were you with?"

Moira tilted her head and looked up at the small window over the sink. Her face was angular where Colm's had been rounder, but Morgan expected Moira to fill out as she got older. As it was, she'd been surprised when Moira had reached her own height last year, when she was only fourteen. Now her daughter was actually taller than she was. At least she had Colm's straight, small nose instead of hers.

"A guy from my class."

Light began to dawn. Despite her natural prettiness, boys seemed to find Moira intimidating. Morgan knew that Moira's friends had been dating for at least a year already. So now a boy had finally asked Moira out, and she'd gone, not wanting to blow her first chance. Morgan remembered only too well how it had felt to be a girl without a boyfriend after everyone else in class had paired up. It made one feel almost desperate, willing to listen to the first person who paid attention to her . . . like Cal.

"Oh. A boy," Morgan said, careful not to make too big a show of it. "So a boy asks you to tea, and you forget the call-your-mom rule?" As an American, Morgan still said Mom, though Moira had always copied Colm and called her Mum, or Mummy, when she was little.

"Yeah. We were just talking and hanging out, and I got so caught up. . . ." Moira sounded less combative. "Is it really almost seven?"

"Yes. Do you have a lot of homework?"

Moira rolled her eyes and nodded.

"Well, sit down and get to it," said Morgan. "I'll make you some tea." She stood up and put the kettle on, lighting the burner with a match. Crossing her arms over her chest, she said, "So who's the lucky guy? Do I know him?" She tried to picture some of the boys from Moira's class.

"Yeah, I think you do," Moira said offhandedly, pulling notebooks out of her book bag. "It was Ian Delaney, from Hewick, one town over."

Delaney. Morgan was speechless, her mind kicking into gear. Every alarm inside her began clanging. "Ian Delaney?" she finally got out. "From Ealltuinn?"

Moira shrugged.

Behind her, the teakettle whistled piercingly. Morgan jumped, then turned off the fire and moved the kettle.

"What are you *thinking*?" she asked Moira slowly, facing her daughter. In her mind she could picture Ian, a good-looking boy Moira's age, with clear, dark blue eyes and brown hair shot through with russet. Lilith Delaney, who was maybe ten years older than Morgan, had the same brown hair, streaked with gray, and the same dark blue eyes.

"You know the problems Belwicket's had with Ealltuinn,"

Morgan said. "They abuse their powers—they don't respect magick. And Ian is their leader's son." *Their leader, who very possibly left that pouch in my garden,* she added inwardly. She didn't want to tell Moira that part, though, without being sure.

Moira shrugged again, not looking at her. "I thought no one's sure about Ealltuinn," she said. "I mean, I've never seen anything about Ian that makes me think he's into dark magick or anything."

Morgan's breath came more shallowly. When she'd been barely older than Moira, she had fallen for Cal Blaire, the good-looking son of Selene Belltower, a witch who worked dark magick. Morgan would do anything to protect Moira from making the same mistake. Lilith was no Selene, but still, if that pouch *had* come from her . . .

"Moira, when a coven celebrates power rather than life, when they strive to hold others down instead of uplifting themselves, when they don't live within the rhythm of the seasons but instead bend the seasons to their will, we call that 'dark,'" said Morgan. "Ealltuinn does all that and more since Lilith became their high priestess."

Moira looked uneasy, but then Colm's expression of stubbornness settled over her face, and Morgan braced herself for a long haul.

"But Ian seems different," Moira said, sounding reasonable. "He never mentions any of that stuff. He's been in my school for two years. People like him—he's never done anything mean to anyone. I've seen him be nice to the shop cat at Margath's Faire when no one's even looking." She stopped, a faint blush coming to her cheeks. "He doesn't talk badly about anyone, and especially not about Belwicket. I've talked to him a few times, and it seems like if he was working dark magick, it would come out somehow. I would sense it. Don't you think?"

Morgan had to bite her lips. Moira was so naive. She'd grown up in a content coven with members who all worked hard to live in harmony with each other and the world. She had never seen the things Morgan had seen, had never had to face true dark magick, had never had to fight for her life or the lives of people she loved. Morgan had—and it had all started when Cal had promised he loved her. He had really loved her power, her potential. Moira showed the same power and potential, and Ian could very well be pursuing her at his mother's command.

But Morgan would never allow Moira to be used the way Cal and Selene had wanted to use her. Moira was her only child, Colm's daughter, all she had left of the husband she had loved.

"Moira, I know you don't want to hear this, and you might not totally understand it right now, but I forbid you to see Ian Delaney again," Morgan said. She almost never came down hard on her daughter, but in this case she would do anything to prevent disaster. "I don't care if he has a halo glowing around his head. He's Lilith's son, and it's just too risky right now."

Moira looked dismayed, then angry. "What?" she cried. "You can't just tell me who I can or can't see!"

"*Au contraire,*" Morgan said firmly. "That's exactly what I'm doing." Then her face softened a bit. "Moira—I know what it's like when you like someone or you really want someone to like you. But it's so easy to get hurt. It's so easy not to see the big picture because all you're doing is looking into someone's eyes. But looking only into someone's eyes can blind you."

"Mum, I can't live in a—a—a *snow globe*," Moira said. "You can't just decide everything I'm going to do without even knowing Ian or totally knowing Ealltuinn. Some things I have to decide for myself. I'm fifteen, not a little kid. I'm not being stupid about Ian—if he was evil, I'd drop him. But you have to let me find out for myself. You might be really powerful and a great healer, but you don't know *everything*. Do you?"

Moira was a much better arguer than Morgan had been at that age, Morgan realized.

"Do you, Mum? Do you know Ian? Have you talked to him or done a *tàth meànma*? Can you *definitely* say that Ian works dark magick and I should never speak to him again?"

Morgan raised her eyebrows, choppy images from the past careening across her consciousness. Cal, seducing Morgan with his love, his kisses, his touch. How desperately she had wanted to believe him. The sincere joy of learning magick from him. Then—Cal locking Morgan into his *seòmar*, his secret room, and setting it on fire.

"No," Morgan admitted. "I can't say that definitely. But I *can* say that life experience has shown me that it's very hard for children not to be like their parents." With sickening quickness she remembered that she was the daughter of Ciaran MacEwan. But that was different. "I think that Ealltuinn might be dark, and I think that Ian probably won't be able to help being part of it. And I don't want you to be hurt because of it. Do you understand? Can you see where I'm coming from? Do you think it's wrong for me to try to protect you? I'm not saying I want you to be alone and unhappy. I'm just saying that choosing the son of the evil leader of a rival coven is a mistake that you can avoid. Choose someone else."

"Like who?" Moira cried. "They have to like me, too, you know."

"Someone else will like you," Morgan promised. "Just leave Ian to Ealltuinn."

"I don't want someone else," Moira said. "I want Ian. He makes me laugh. He's really smart, he thinks I'm smart. He thinks I'm *amazing*. It's just—real. How we feel about each other is real."

"How can you know?" Morgan responded. "How would you know if anything he told you was real?"

Moira's face set. She picked up her mug of tea and her book bag and walked stiffly over to the stairs. "I just do."

Morgan watched her daughter walk upstairs, feeling as if she had lost another battle but not sure how it could have gone differently. Goddess, Ian Delaney! Anyone but Ian Delaney. Slowly Morgan lowered her head onto her arms, crossed on the tabletop. Breathe, breathe, she reminded herself. *Colm, I could really use your help right now.*

It was just eerie, the similarity between what was happening now to Moira with Ian and what had happened to her so long ago with Cal. She had never told Moira about Cal and Selene—only briefly skimmed over finding out she was a witch, then studying in Scotland for a summer, then how Katrina had asked her to come to Ireland. Moira had read Colin's Books of Shadows, and some of Morgan's, but none from that tumultuous period in Morgan's life. Cal and Selene were still Morgan's secret. As was Hunter. As was the fact that Morgan was Ciaran MacEwan's daughter. She'd never actually lied to Moira—but when Moira had assumed that Angus Bramson was her natural grandfather, Morgan had let her. It was so much better than telling her that her grandfather was one of the most evil witches in generations and that he had locked Morgan's birth mother, Maeve, in a barn and burned her to death.

Likewise with Hunter. What would be the good of telling Moira that Colm wasn't the only man Morgan had loved and lost? After Hunter had drowned in the ferry accident, Morgan hardly remembered what happened—losing Hunter had snapped her soul in half. She remembered being in a hospital. Her parents had come over from America, with Mary K. They'd wanted to take her home to New York, but Katrina and Pawel had convinced them that her best healing would be done in Ireland and that it would be dangerous to move her. There followed a time when she lived in Katrina and Pawel's house, and the coven had performed one healing rite after another.

Then Colm had asked her to marry him. Morgan had hardly been able to think, but she cared for Colm and in desperation saw it as a fresh start. Two months later she was expecting a baby and was just starting to come out of the fog.

It had almost been a shock when it had finally sunk in that she married Colm, but the awful thing had been how grateful she'd felt for his comfort. She was terrified of being alone, afraid of what might happen while she was asleep, and with Colm she'd thought she would never be alone again. She'd struggled for years with the twin feelings of searing guilt and humbling gratitude, but as time passed and Moira grew, Morgan began to accept that this had been her life's destiny all along. She'd never been madly in love with Colm, and she felt that in some way he'd known it. But she'd always cared for him as a friend, and over the years her caring had deepened into a true and sincere love. She'd tried hard to be a good wife, and she hoped she'd made Colm happy. She hoped that before he'd died, he'd known that he had made her happy, too, in a calm, joyful way.

She'd also found fulfillment in the rest of her life. Gifted teachers had worked with her to increase her natural healing abilities, and as Moira had gotten older and needed less attention, Morgan had begun traveling all over the world teaching others and performing healing rites. When she was home, life was peaceful and contented. Time was marked by sabbats and celebrations, the turning of the seasons, the waxing and waning of the moon. It wasn't the flash fire of passion that she'd felt with Hunter, the desperate, bone-deep joining of soul and body that they'd shared, but instead it was like the gentle crackle of a fireplace, a place to soothe and comfort. Which was fine, good, better than she could have hoped.

And until this moment she'd never thought of her life in any other way. She loved her husband, adored her daughter, enjoyed her work. She felt embraced by her community and had made several good friends. In fact, the last sixteen years, at least until Colm's death, had been a kind of victory for Morgan. In the first year of discovering her heritage she'd undergone more pain—both physical and emotional—felt more freezing fear, had higher highs and lower lows than she could have possibly imagined a human being experiencing. She'd had her heart broken ruthlessly, had made murderous enemies, had been forced to make soul-destroying choices, choosing the greater good over the individual's life—even when that individual was her own father. And all before she was eighteen.

So to have had sixteen years of study and practice, of

having no one try to kill her and not being forced to kill anyone else, well, that had seemed like a victory, a triumph of good over evil.

Until today, when she'd found a hex pouch in her garden and seen a vision in her window. Now she couldn't shake the feeling that not only was she at risk, but so was her daughter.

Morgan sighed. Was she overreacting because of her past? Getting up, Morgan made sure Bixby was in and that the front door was locked—an old habit from living in America. In Wicklow many people rarely bothered to lock their doors. Then she turned off the downstairs lights and cast her senses strongly all around her house. Nothing out of the ordinary. Later, writing in her Book of Shadows in bed, she heard Moira in the bathroom. Long after the house was quiet, after Morgan sensed that Moira was sleeping and that Bixby and Finnegan had passed into cat and dog versions of dreaming, Morgan lay dry-eyed in the night, staring up at the ceiling.

3

Moira

"Tell us all," Tess commanded the instant Moira walked up. Vita was eating a bag of crisps, but she nodded eagerly.

Moira grinned. Finally she had a lad of her own for *them* to ask about! After the last six months it was so great to have this huge, fun thing to be happy about. "Well," she said dramatically as the three of them started to walk down High Street. "What do you want to know?"

"Everything," Vita said. "What was said. What was done. Who kissed who."

Feeling her face flush, Moira laughed self-consciously. Tess had called that morning to arrange to meet early, before spellcraft class, so Moira could give them a rundown of her time with Ian. Today was unusually sunny and warm, with only fat, puffy clouds in the sky. It was hard to believe it would be Samhain in a few weeks.

"Well, we were there until almost six-thirty," Moira said. "I got home brutally late and Mum had forty fits."

"Enough about Mum," said Tess. "More about Ian. Six-thirty? All at Margath's Faire?"

They turned down Merchant Street, staying on the sunny side.

"Yeah," said Moira. "We just sat there and talked and talked. I looked up and almost two hours had gone by."

"Holding hands?" Vita pressed.

"After a while," Moira said, feeling pleased and embarrassed at the same time. "He took my hand and told me I was amazing."

Tess and Vita gave each other wide-eyed looks.

"*Amazing*," Tess said approvingly. "Very good word. One point for Ian. What else?"

Wrinkling her nose, Moira thought back. She remembered a lot of staring into each other's eyes. "Um, we talked about music—he's learning the bodhran. Initiation classes—he was initiated last year but is still studying herbology. Books. Movies—he said maybe we could go see a film next week."

"Yes!" said Vita. "Well done."

They turned into a narrow side street called Printer's Alley. Only a bare strip of sunlight lit the very center of the slanted cobbled road. Buildings on either side rose three stories in the air, their gray stucco chipped in places and exposing stones and bricks. A few tiny shops, barely more than closets with open doors, dotted the street like colorful flowers growing out of concrete.

"It was just really brilliant," Moira said. "He's so great—so funny. We looked around the café and made up life stories about everyone who sat there. I thought I was going to fall out of my chair." She didn't mention the magick they had done. It seemed private, a secret between her and Ian.

Vita laughed. "Sounds like a good time was had by all. Do

you think he could be your—" She paused, exchanging a glance with Tess. "Your *mùirn beatha dàn?*"

Moira's cheeks flushed. The truth was, she'd been wondering the same thing for a while now and especially after yesterday. Ever since she'd first learned what a *mùirn beatha dàn* was, she'd been dreaming of what it would feel like to meet hers. A true soul mate—it was just incredible. And what if Ian really was her MBD? It would be so amazing if she'd already found him. "I don't know," she admitted. "But . . . maybe."

"So did you talk about your covens at all?" Tess asked. "What's his take on Belwicket?"

"We only talked about it a little bit," said Moira. "Like about being initiated. And how he was a high priestess's son, and what that meant, and how my mum would probably be high priestess someday. It's something we have in common, trying to live up to powerful parents."

"I don't know, Moira," said Vita. "Your powers are wicked. The ladybug thing . . ."

Moira laughed, enjoying the remembered triumph. "Anyway," she said, "enough about me. Are you going to circle tonight, then?"

"Sure," said Vita. They were almost at the home of their spellcraft teacher, and unconsciously the three girls slowed down, reluctant to spend a rare sunny day inside studying.

Tess heaved a long-suffering breath. "Yeah, kicking and screaming," she said. "It's bad enough I have to spend part of my Saturday day at initiation class when I don't care about being initiated, but to give up Saturday night, too . . . It's just brutal."

"You still don't want to get initiated?" Vita asked her, brushing her feathery blond hair out of her face. "Ten years from now you'll be the only adult who still can't work the harder spells."

"I don't care." Tess scuffed her black suede boots against the uneven cobbles of the street. "It just isn't for me. It's so old-fashioned. The other day I had a splitting headache, and Mum was like, let me brew some herbs. I just wanted to go to the chemist's and get some proper drugs." She frowned and played with the magenta tips of her dark hair.

Moira gave her a sympathetic look, then realized they were at their teacher's stoop, a single concrete block in front of a red-painted door.

Tess sighed in resignation, and then the door opened and Keady Dove smiled out at them. "Hello, ladies," she said. "Come in. What a beautiful day, nae? I won't keep you too long."

Inside the small house the three girls went automatically to the back room that overlooked the garden. The sun overhead shone on the neat rows of herbs and flowers; there was a tiny patch for vegetables in the southern corner. Everything was tidy, the roses deadheaded, the cosmos tied up, the parsley trimmed. Moira thought it looked soothing and restful, like a good witch's garden should. She saw Tess looking at it also, an expression of disinterest on her face. Moira was torn—she admired Tess's outspokenness and could sympathize with her not wanting automatically to continue on a path she herself hadn't chosen. Still, to Moira, Wicca seemed as natural and omnipresent as the sea.

"Right," said Keady, rolling up her sleeves. She sat down at the tall table, and the three girls sat on the tall stools across from her. "Let me see what you've done since Monday. You were supposed to craft one spell using a phase of the moon and one that would affect some kind of insect."

Moira handed hers over. She'd gone ahead and written up the ladybug spell, planning to emphasize its excellent spellcraft and skim over the fact that it was frivolous and purposeless. She waited silently while Keady looked at it, keeping her face expressionless when her teacher frowned slightly and looked at her. Keady closed Moira's book and slid it back across the table.

"I remember how proud your dad was when you took first place in junior spellcraft," Keady said, her casual mention of Colm making Moira press her lips together. "Your dad didn't make spells often, but when he did, they were lovely, clean, well-crafted. As yours are. However, his had more use and were less self-centered. Have you looked at his old Books of Shadows?"

Moira nodded, embarrassed. "A bit. He didn't do many spells."

"No," Keady agreed. "How about your mother, then? She's been crafting rites and spells along with your gran for years. Have you looked at her books?"

"A few. Some of the recent ones."

"It would also be interesting to look at the ones she started keeping right at the beginning, even before she was initiated." Keady looked at her pupils. "That's how we learn, from the past, from the witches who went before us. The books of our families are always particularly helpful because different forms and patterns of spells often run in families and clans. Sometimes that's due to tradition, sometimes to little quirks in our heritage that make one type of spell more effective for us. My mum always crafted terrific spells with gems, rocks, and crystals." Keady grinned, her smooth tan face creasing with humor. "However, we ran like hell when she tried to get us to sample her herbal concoctions."

Moira and Vita laughed, and even Tess cracked a smile.

The class turned to business as their teacher critiqued their homework in more detail and assigned them work for next Wednesday. Then she led them to her circle room for practice.

Quickly and accurately, Keady drew an open circle on the smooth wooden floor. Its once-dark boards were irrevocably stained white from years of making chalk circles. Keady actually made her own chalk sticks, and they were part of her rituals. There were natural chalk pits not far from Cobh, and for a fee one could go and hack bits out of a wall. Keady did this, then carefully carved the hard white chalk into shapes, wands, figures of people or animals, short staffs topped with runes or sigils. She kept Margath's Faire stocked with special chalks and made some extra money this way.

"Everyone in," she directed. The three girls walked through the opening of the circle and sat down, one at each of the corners of the compass, with Keady to the east. "We're going to practice transferring energy," Keady said. "Each of us will meditate alone for five minutes, drawing energy to us, using the spell I taught you. At the end of five minutes, after you've opened yourself to receive energy from the universe, we'll join hands. Going deasil, we'll pass energy to each other through our hands. If we do it right," she said with a grin, "you should be able to feel something."

What a waste of time.

Moira jerked her head toward Tess, shocked that her friend would actually say this out loud, in front of their teacher. Tess sat cross-legged, her eyes closed, her hands in a loose, upward pinch on her knees. Her face was blank. Quickly Moira looked at Keady, then at Vita, and weirdly, neither of them seemed to have had any reaction. *Oh, wow, I picked up on it. Cool.* Witches of a certain power could send or receive witch messages—Moira, Tess, and Vita had been practicing for the past year, with varying degrees of success. Moira and her mum could definitely send messages to each other. But to pick up on someone's strong thoughts without their meaning to send them was something else. Moira smiled to herself, pleased at this demonstration that her own powers were slowly increasing.

Moira closed her eyes and straightened her spine, resting her hands lightly on her knees as the others were doing. *Right. Concentrate.* Her trousers were itching her, right in back where the tag was. She wondered if she looked like a scarecrow in them. Vita had soft, feminine curves, with actual hips and boobs. When a dip at school had tried to tell her she was fat, Vita had just laughed. "I think I look good," she had said. "And so does *your* boyfriend." Moira smiled at the memory. Vita was really comfortable with herself, her body. Unlike Moira, who was so tall and thin. Not slender, not petite, not in shape, just thin. Mum kept telling her she would fill out, but—

Moira's all over the place.

Moira's eyes snapped open at Keady's voice, ready to deny it. But again, everyone's eyes were closed, and her teacher gave no indication that she had spoken. Moira felt a jolt of excitement. Wow—this was amazing. She was definitely getting stronger. *Now concentrate, concentrate. Focus. Breathe.*

For as far back as Moira could remember, her mother had said those words. In the small room tacked onto the living room, where the family worked their magick, Moira had witnessed her parents, and especially her mother, meditating, focusing, breathing. She had allowed Moira to join her when Moira was three. Moira thought sadly on those days, when she had felt so close to her mum. She'd always felt really close to her until just last year, when suddenly Dad had seemed more understanding. It was when she had begun to prepare for her initiation, she realized. The whole thing seemed to make Mum tense, anxious that Moira do well.

Breathe. Focus. Quit thinking. Moira imagined a candle in front of her, a white pillar on the floor, glowing with a single flame. She focused on its flickering, on the ebb and flow of the flame growing and dying, one second at a time. In a few moments she became the flame, inhaling its heat and light and releasing its energy with her breath. *I am the flame. I am burning. I am white-hot. I am made of fire.*

"Right," said Keady's quiet voice, floating gently through the air. "Slowly, slowly, open your eyes, as if they were fine linen being lifted by a breeze."

Moira opened her eyes, and it seemed that the room had changed somehow. Maybe the sun had shifted. Something felt different. Looked different. Moira blinked. Things looked a little hazy. No, wait—it was just around their heads. There was a bright glow around Tess's, Vita's, and Keady's heads.

"Now," Keady said, "let's hold out our hands. When I tell you to, join hands. One person will send, one will receive. Repeat after me: A force of life I draw to me. It fills me with its light. I use this light to help me see. And in my spells I use its might."

Moira repeated the words, and they seemed to sink deep within her, as if they were smooth stones dropping gently through water to land silently on a bed of silt.

"Tess, receive my energy," said Keady, holding out her hand. Tess reached out and clasped her hand, then gave a small but visible jump. Her eyes opened a bit wider, and she lost her bored demeanor for a second.

"Now, Tess, give your energy to me and to Vita."

Tess clasped hands with both Vita and Keady, and though Vita seemed expectant, her expression didn't change. "I don't feel much of anything," she whispered.

"That's all right," Keady said. "Now, Vita, give your energy to Moira and Tess."

Moira held out her hand and took hold of Vita's smooth, soft palm. Vita's hand was smaller than hers and much less muscular. Moira let her eyes close halfway and focused on what she was receiving from Vita. Was that a faint tingling sensation? Yes, she thought it was. So Vita was actually sending her energy? Cool. She opened her eyes and nodded at Vita, who grinned and looked pleased.

"Good, Vita," Keady said encouragingly. "I can see your extra practicing has paid off. Right, then, now Moira. Give your energy to me and Vita."

Moira closed her eyes. *Focus. Breathe.* Silently she repeated the words: *A force of life I draw to me. It fills me with its light. I use this light to help me see. And in my spells I use its might.*

She breathed in, and with that breath she seemed to draw the whole room in with her. Holding her breath, she felt energy rise within her—something she'd never felt so strongly before. It was a bit scary, actually, but Keady was here and would keep her safe. Power and energy and magick and joy seemed about to explode inside her. Slowly she held out her hands, unsure if she was doing anything correctly or if she had gotten it all wrong.

Energy, I send you out. Moira imagined herself as a glowing flame, pouring energy out through her hands like sunbeams.

Keady took her hand first, and Moira felt an electrifying contact, like pure heat was pouring through her hand. Suddenly Moira knew a kind of exhilaration she'd never imagined existed. In the next second Vita took her other hand, and Moira felt it all again, but only for a second. Vita gasped and dropped her hand quickly, and Moira's eyes snapped open.

Vita looked startled and a little afraid. She stared first at Moira and then at her own hand. Moira quickly glanced at Keady and saw that the older woman was gripping her hand firmly, easily taking the sent energy and measuring it. As soon as Moira's concentration broke, everything shut down, and within a minute she felt almost totally normal. Almost.

Self-conscious, and a mite dizzy, Moira drew her hands back and folded them in her lap.

"What did you do?" asked Vita.

"What happened?" Tess asked, having seen nothing except Vita dropping Moira's hand.

"Very good, Moira," said Keady quietly, looking at Moira's face. "Have you been practicing?"

"A little. Not a whole lot," Moira admitted. "But I remembered seeing my mum call energy. She talked about how it can increase the power of spells and so on." Moira shrugged and began to trace a random pattern on her knee.

"I see," said Keady. She got to her feet and opened the circle, murmuring words to dispel magick and restore calm to the room's own energy. "I think that's enough for today. You have your assignments for next Wednesday. Go home and work on your spells and your Books of Shadows, and I'll see you at the circle tonight."

Moira started to pull on her jacket, but Keady put out a hand to detain her. Tess and Vita left without her, looking back with raised brows. Moira shrugged a silent "I don't know" and pantomimed calling them later.

Keady put the kettle on for tea, glancing thoughtfully at Moira.

"That was both unexpected and expected," she said, putting out their cups. "It was unexpected because I haven't seen that level of power from you before, and we've been working together for eight months now. It was also expected because you're Morgan Byrne's daughter. I couldn't help wondering if you had inherited her power."

Moira looked into Keady's clear eyes, the color of fog. "I feel like my powers are growing, getting stronger," she said. "But I don't know if it's like my mum's power—I don't even know what her power's *like*. I mean, I know she's a strong healer. People call her from all over the world for help. The spells she works look effortless, smooth and perfect. And I know everyone speaks of her power and her magick. But I don't think *I've* seen her work too much really big magick."

For a minute her teacher was quiet. She swirled the loose tea leaves in the steamy water. The sweet smell of tea filled Moira's nose, and she inhaled.

"If you have the power of a huge, rushing river, sometimes it's most effective to harness it and dole it out, as with a dam," her teacher said finally. "Sometimes if you let the river run free, it can destroy more than it can build."

Moira looked at her. It seemed a quality of witches to never answer questions directly. "It's just strange—I *know* she's powerful, she's Morgan of Belwicket. But that kind of big 'rushing river' stuff doesn't come up in the day-to-day." She laughed a little, and Keady smiled.

"How much do you know about your mum's life before she came here and helped revive Belwicket?"

Moira frowned. "Well, she's American. She was adopted. She found out she was a blood witch when she was sixteen. After high school she went to Scotland for a summer to study with the Gray Witches. When Gran found out Maeve Riordan's daughter was alive, she tracked Mum down and asked her to move here and help re-form the original Belwicket. Then Mum married Dad, and I was born. Now she's become an important healer, and she travels a lot." Moira let out a breath, releasing the tension she felt about how much her mum worked. "Now Mum's getting ready to become high priestess of Belwicket."

"It isn't my place to tell you any more about your own mother," said Keady. "But I can tell you that the fact that you've not witnessed anything that would strike fear into your soul is a good thing." She smiled dryly when Moira frowned. "The true strength of a witch can be measured by how much she or he does *not* resort to big magick, how much they can give themselves over to study, reflection, peace. The fact that someone can work big magick is an accomplishment. The fact that someone can work big magick but chooses not to unless strictly necessary is a greater accomplishment. Do you see?"

This was a picture of her mother that Moira was having trouble imagining. "Are you saying that Mum could strike fear into someone's soul?" she asked.

"I'm saying that yes, your mother is a witch of unusual, and even fearsome, powers," Keady said solemnly. The words gave Moira a slight chill. "There have been very few witches within recorded history who could equal Morgan," her teacher went on. "A power that great is a beautiful and also a frightening thing. And Moira? There are very few happy uses for a power such as that, do you understand? It isn't your mother's place to bring springtime or end war, or make everyone fall in love, or keep a whole village healthy. And your mother would never use her magick for dark purposes, we know. Can you think of a purpose that is left, that is both true and on the side of right, yet would allow the expression of an almost inconceivably great power?"

Moira frowned at Keady, realizing what she was getting at.

"It would be for defense," Keady said, her voice very quiet and deliberate. "To fight evil. It would be used in a battle of good against evil on a scale that's difficult for you to comprehend. And it's difficult for you to comprehend because . . . your mother, and your father, too, worked very hard their whole lives to make sure that you, their daughter, lived in a world where the most appropriate expression of power . . . is to heal people."

Moira felt as if she had stepped out of her normal Saturday spellcraft lesson and into a comic book about superheroes.

"To be fifteen years old, the daughter of Morgan Byrne, and to have no idea of such matters—it's a blessing, a gift. One that you will be thankful for, again and again, in the future." Keady looked at Moira steadily, then seemed to think she had said enough.

In silence Moira finished her tea, mumbled good-bye, took her things, and left.

"Keady says it would be helpful to read your and Dad's Books of Shadows," Moira said that afternoon.

"I think I gave them to you," her mother said, stirring the pot on the stove. She sniffed its scent and then looked at her watch.

"You gave me most of them, but I think it would be good to read your very first ones, even before you were initiated, when you were first learning about spells," said Moira. An odd expression crossed her mum's face for just a moment and then passed.

"Gosh, that was so long ago," her mother murmured. "I'm not sure where they are."

"Didn't Dad say once that all of both of your old stuff was in those crates down in the cellar?" Moira persisted.

Her mother looked thoughtful. "I'm not sure."

"Well, I could really use them," Moira said. "It would help me for my initiation. Can I try to find them?"

Her mum looked distinctly uncomfortable, but Moira wasn't going to back down, not after the things Keady had said.

"I guess," was her mum's unenthusiastic reply. "But I'll get them for you when I have a minute."

"Brilliant," said Moira, standing up and putting her dishes in the sink. As she was heading upstairs, her mom said, "Don't forget—circle in an hour."

"Right," Moira called back.

"I miss having circles outside, like in summer," Moira said. She and her mum were walking briskly down the road toward Katrina's. The sun had set, and with no streetlights the night was a solid velvety black. With magesight, kind of like a witch's night vision, Moira stepped surely on the rutted, uneven road.

"Yes," said her mother. "Being outside is always good. But it's nice to have a place to be warm and dry as well."

Soon they had almost caught up to Brett and Lacey Hawkstone and their daughter, Lizzie, who was fourteen and would start her initiation classes at Yule. Ahead of them Michelle Moore walked with her partner, Fillipa Gregg.

"Today at class I sent some energy to Keady," Moira said.

"Really?" Her mother smiled at her and seemed glad but neither surprised nor ecstatic. "Good for you. I'm sure Keady was pleased. Oh, look, Fillipa needs help carrying that bag. Let's hurry."

As the group approached the store, Moira's gran appeared in the doorway of her cottage. "Hello! Come in," said Gran, smiling. She closed the front door to her house and met them by the store's entrance. Her house was a small, thick-walled cottage, and the old store was attached directly to it. It had been a tiny country store, just one large room. Five years ago the coven had joined together and whitewashed the inside, sanded the floor, and painted good luck charms and symbols all around the room's perimeter. There were four small windows, high up on the thick walls, and a double-wide front door. The only other door led into Gran's back pantry in her house.

"Hi, Gran," said Moira, kissing her. She sniffed, then wiggled her eyebrows expectantly.

"Yes, those are gingersnaps you smell," Katrina told her with a laugh. "I felt like baking this afternoon. We'll have them after circle."

"Morgan," said Hartwell Moss, coming over to hug Moira's mum. "How are you? Rough week?"

"Not too bad," said Moira's mum, but something in her voice made Moira look at her more closely. Were those lines of tension around her eyes? Was her mouth tight? Moira tried casting her senses and picked up on a lot of anxiety. Was it just because Moira had been late last night, or was something else going on?

"Hello!" Gran called, opening her arms wide. "Hello, everyone, and good evening to you. Welcome. Is everyone here, then?" Though she was heavyset and walked slowly because of arthritis, Moira thought her grandmother still made a wonderful high priestess for their coven. Her gray hair was pulled back with silver combs and her long, dove-gray linen robe was imprinted in black with simple images of the sea.

"Hello, good evening," people answered in various forms. Moira counted: twenty-one people here tonight, a good number. In the winter it often drifted down to eight or nine, when the weather made some of the higher roads risky; in spring the number could swell to over twenty. Even their coven obeyed the law of wax and wane, the turn of the wheel.

Standing at the head of the room, Katrina clasped her hands and smiled. "The sun has gone down, and we are embraced by the harvest moon, nae? There's a crispness in the air that tells us leaves will soon fall, days will grow shorter, and we'll be staying more by our firesides. What a joyful time is autumn! We gather in our harvest, collecting Mother Earth's bounty, her gifts to us. We till the soil, and the soil feeds us. Or, for some of us, we think fondly of our soil but buy our veggies from the market!"

People laughed. Moira felt proud of her grandmother.

"Lammas is behind us: we look ahead to Mabon," Katrina went on. "We're planning a special Mabon feast, of course, so please talk to Susan if you'd like to contribute food, drink, candles, decorations, or just your time. Thank you very much. Now, I've already drawn our circle here, you can see, but if you'll forgive me, I'd like to ask Morgan to lead us tonight. Maybe I've overdone things a little lately."

Moira glanced at her mother, who was looking at Katrina

with affection. Morgan nodded slightly, and, looking relieved, Katrina moved to the side.

"Can you all please come into the circle?" asked Morgan, and the coven members filed in through the opening that Gran had left. Quickly Morgan went around the circle and sketched the rune Eolh at the east, Tyr at the north, Thorn at the west, and Ur at the south. Moira silently recited their meanings: protection, victory in battle, overcoming adversity, and strength. Powerful runes, runes of protection. As if the coven were under siege. Moira remembered what Keady had said about Morgan's power being used for defense and wondered what was this was about.

Next Morgan lit a stick of incense and placed it behind the rune Tyr. She set a silver cup of water next to Thorn and a silver cup of smooth pebbles at Ur. Next to Eolh she lit a tall orange candle. Finally Morgan took her place in the circle, between Katrina and Lacey Hawkstone. Everyone clasped hands and raised them overhead. Moira had moved till she was between Vita and Tess, who had also edged away from their parents. Tess squeezed her hand—Moira knew she'd rather be home watching television. Across the room Keady Dove smiled at her.

"I welcome the Goddess and the God to tonight's circle, and I hope they find favor with our gathering," Morgan began. "I dedicate this circle to our coming harvest, to our safe passage into winter, and to our spirit of community. We're a chain, all of us connected and entwined. We help each other, we support each other. Our links form a strong fence, and within it we can protect our own."

Moira saw that a few people were glancing at each other.

They were probably wondering what was going on, with the runes of protection and Morgan talking about being a fence. Moira hoped she wouldn't start talking about Ealltuinn. Maybe Ealltuinn wasn't as particular about following the Wiccan Rede as Belwicket was. There were lots of covens that weren't. But that didn't make them evil.

"Since we're in the middle of our harvest season," Morgan said, "let's give thanks now for things that we have drawn to us, for our times of fruitfulness, for the gifts of the land. Life has given us each incomparable riches."

"I'm thankful for my new pony," said Lizzie Hawkstone. "He's beautiful and smart."

"I'm thankful my mum recovered from her illness," said Michelle.

"I bless the Goddess for my garden's bounty," said Christa Ryan, who was Moira's herbology teacher.

"I'm thankful for the wonderful gift of my daughter-in-law and for my beautiful granddaughter," said Katrina. She smiled at Moira, and Moira smiled back.

"I'm grateful for family and friends," Moira said, falling back on an old standard.

"Thanks to the Goddess for the rains and the wind, for they've kept me cozy inside," said Fillipa. "Thanks also to the library in town—they just got in a shipment of new books."

"I thank the Goddess for my daughter," Morgan said quietly. "I thank time for passing, however slowly. I thank the wheel for turning and for helping grief to ease someday."

That was about Moira's dad, and she felt people glancing at her in sympathy. She nodded, looking at her feet, acknowledging her mother's words.

The circle went around, each person contributing something or not as they wished. Then Morgan lifted her left foot and leaned to the left, and the group began a sort of half-walking, half-skipping circle, where it felt like dancing. Moira felt her heart lifting, her blood circulating, and knew that her mum had chosen this to increase the positive, lighthearted energy.

Morgan started singing, one of the ancient songs with words that had lost their definitions but not their meanings. Her rich alto wove a melody around the circle, and Katrina took it up, singing different words but layering her melody above and beneath Morgan's. Soon Will Fereston joined in, and Keady, and then most of the coven members were singing. Some were singing songs they'd learned as children or been taught recently. Some were simply making sounds that blended with the others. Moira was trying to copy Morgan, singing the same notes at the same time. She'd never learned this song formally but had heard her mother sing it often—she called it one of her "power-draw" chants.

People were smiling, the circle was moving more quickly, and Moira could feel a joy, a lightness, enter the room. Even Katrina's arthritis didn't seem to be bothering her. People who had looked tired or stressed when they came in soon lost those expressions. Instead, faces were alight with the pleasure of sharing, with the gift of dancing. Moira laughed, holding tightly to Vita and Tess, hoping she wouldn't trip.

Then slowly Moira started to see a haze in the room—like everyone around her had grown fuzzy. This wasn't like the energy she'd seen with Keady, Tess, and Vita. She squinted, confused, as the haze grew heavier, darker, blurring her vision.

Just then Will, Michelle, and Susan started coughing. Then Moira coughed, not quite gagging, and an oily, bitter scent filled the air. Now a thick black smoke was creeping beneath the doors and around the shut windows, slipping in like tendrils of poison. One tendril began to coil around Katrina's foot.

Katrina flinched and started barking out ward-evil spells. Her sister, Susan, tried to help her but was coughing too much. The circle was broken; several people were on their knees, on the floor. Lizzie was trying not to cry, and old Hamish Murphy looked confused and frightened. Moira felt the panic grow.

"Mum!" Moira cried, dropping Tess's and Vita's hands. Morgan was standing stiffly, turning slowly to see every single thing that was happening in the room. Her face was white, her eyes wide. She looked both frightened and appalled, staring almost in disbelief at the smoke. Moira saw her lips start moving but couldn't hear her words.

"Mum!" Moira said again, reaching Morgan and taking her arm. Her mother gently shook her off, freeing herself without speaking.

While Moira watched, coughing, Morgan closed her eyes and held out her arms. Slowly she raised them in the air, and now Moira could hear her mother's words, low and intense and frightening. They were harsh words in a language that Moira didn't recognize, and they sounded dark, spiky—words without forgiveness or explanation.

Michelle had reached the door, but it wouldn't open, and people began to panic as they realized they were trapped. Vita was huddled with her parents and younger brother, and Tess was standing by her folks. Keady and Christa were trying to help others, but they were coughing and red faced across the room. Aunt Susan looked as if she were about to faint. Moira stood alone, next to her mother. Once, Morgan opened her eyes and stared straight through Moira, and

Moira almost cried out—her mother's normally brown eyes were glowing red, as if reflecting fire, and her face was changed, stronger. Moira could hardly recognize her, and that was perhaps even scarier than the smoke.

Closing her eyes again, Morgan began to draw runes and sigils in the air around her. Moira recognized more runes of protection but soon lost the shapes of the other, more complicated sigils. It was as if her mother were writing a story in the air, line after line. And still she muttered whatever chant had come to her.

Moira felt fear take over her body. The roiling smoke was choking everyone. She'd never seen her mother work magick like this, never seen her so consumed and practically glowing with power. Moira's eyes were stinging, her lungs burning. Coughing, she sank to her knees on the floor and suddenly thought of how she had sent energy to Keady. Could she do it again? Could it help somehow? She closed her eyes and automatically drew the symbol Eolh in the air in front of her. There was no time to draw circles of protection, overlain with different runes.

"*An de allaigh*," Moira began chanting under her breath, coughing at each word. She knew this power-draw chant well and closed her eyes while she chanted it as best she could. *Focus. Focus and concentrate.*

I open myself to the Goddess's power, Moira thought, trying to ignore the foul stench, the gagging smoke. She shut out the sounds of the room. *I open myself to the power of the universe.* She remembered Morgan's orange candle, set in the east. The smoke had snuffed it a minute ago, but Moira recalled its flame and pictured it in her mind.

Fire, fire, burning bright, she thought, everything else

fading away. *I call power to me. I am power. I'm made of fire.* She felt it rise within her, as if a flower were blooming inside her chest. She inhaled through her nose, the acrid smell making her shudder. Holding her arms out at her sides, Moira felt power coming to her as if she were a lightning rod, being struck again and again with tiny, pinlike bolts of lightning.

The room was silent. Moira opened her eyes. People were moving, crying, shouting, trying to break a window. Her mother was standing in front of her, her arms coiled over her chest, her face contorted with effort. Her cheeks were flushed, and her brown hair was sticking to her forehead. Her fists were clenched.

Moira felt as if she were moving through gelatin, slowly and without sound, making ripples of movement all around her. She stood and leaned close to her mother, seeing power radiating from Morgan in a kind of unearthly glow.

I send my power to you. Moira reached out and covered Morgan's fists with her own. *I give my power to you.* And she truly did feel it leave her, a slipcase of white light sliding from her, through her hands, and draping lightly over the hands of her mother. Slowly, slowly, Morgan's hands opened, and Moira's cupped them, a two-layered flower of flesh, bones, and a pure, glorious, glowing light.

Then Morgan threw her arms up and open, her head snapped back, and a final shout tore from her throat. She sounded wolflike, Moira thought, startled, as strong as a wild animal, and at that instant a window exploded in a shower of glass.

Instantly the black smoke was sucked out of the room,

as if the room had depressurized at a high altitude. Shiny shards of broken glass rained down like crystals, like ice. Moira's hands still touched Morgan's arms, below the elbows, and suddenly cool, damp air washed over her, fresh and clean and smelling of night. She could breathe now and heard sounds of choking and gasps of relief. Around her she felt the warm release of the most desperate fear, the worst of the tension.

Moira inhaled deeply, feeling that nothing had ever smelled so wonderful, so life-giving, as the wet-dirt smell of autumn night air. Her mother opened her eyes, and Moira was relieved to see that they were the mixed shades of brown, green, and gold that she knew. Maybe she had just imagined the glowy redness.

Morgan's arms lowered, and she took Moira's hands. She looked solemn but also brightly curious. "You gave me power," she said very softly, her voice hoarse.

Moira nodded, wide-eyed. "Like I did Keady," she whispered back.

"You helped save us," said her mother, and hugged her, and Moira hugged her back.

"Where did it come from?" Moira asked as they walked home along the country road. The moon was shining brightly, lighting their way. After the smoke had left, people had sat for an hour, recovering. Wine and water had washed the taste from their mouths, but no one had been able to eat anything. Finally, when her mum had been sure they were safe, the coven had disbanded.

"I'm not positive, but I think it was from Ealltuinn,"

answered her mother. She sighed. Moira waited for her to say something about Ian, but she didn't.

"That smoke—I was so scared," Moira said in a rush. "I was glad you had so much power. And at the same time, it was scary—I've never seen you like that."

Her mother licked her lips and brushed her bangs off her forehead. "Magick transforms everyone," she said.

Moira followed her mother home through the darkness, not sure what to say.

4

Morgan

Morgan looked up as Keady Dove let herself in through the green wooden gate that bordered Morgan's front yard.

" 'Lo," she said, brushing some hair out of her eyes. This morning, after Moira had left for her animal-work class in town, Morgan had paced the house restlessly. Last night it had taken all of her will not to show Moira how shocked and disturbed she had been by the black smoke. They had walked home in the darkness, with Morgan casting her senses, silently repeating ward-evil spells, trying to sound normal as her daughter asked her difficult questions to which she had no answers. She'd been awake all night thinking about what had happened and trying to make sense of everything. She was almost positive the smoke had come from Ealltuinn—she just couldn't think of any other possibility. And very likely it was connected to the pouch and to the vision. She had underestimated Lilith Delaney. Lilith was practicing dark magick against Belwicket, and Morgan had to find out why—and soon.

Thankfully at least Moira had been able to sleep last night and hadn't been awoken by nightmares. Part of Morgan had wanted to keep Moira home with her today, not let her go to class. But Tess and Vita had met her at the bus stop, and it was broad daylight. . . .

Morgan smiled as Keady sat cross-legged on the sun-warmed bricks of the front path. She and Keady had been friends at least ten years, and in the six months since Colm's death Keady had been popping in to tutor Moira more regularly. Morgan was glad Moira had such a gifted teacher.

"I'm interrupting," said Keady, watching as Morgan pulled some small weeds from around her mums. They were starting to bloom; she would have some perfect orange, yellow, and rust-colored blooms by Samhain.

"Not at all. I wanted to talk to you after last night."

"Yes. Your garden's looking lovely, by the way."

"Thank you," said Morgan. She paused and sat back on her heels, knowing Keady hadn't come to discuss her garden. "Moira gave me energy last night."

"I saw, just barely," said Keady. "I was helping Will, who was really in a bad way. But I thought I saw her. She's showing quite a lot of promise."

Morgan nodded, quietly proud, then turned back to business. "I couldn't trace the spell last night. It had to have been Ealltuinn, though." She shook her head. "It's been so peaceful here for twenty years. Now to have an enemy who would go this far—" She couldn't express how furious she was at having her quiet life, her innocent daughter, her coven attacked in this way. Hadn't she already been through all that? Why was this happening again? She looked up at Keady. "How bad do you think it was?"

"It was bad," Keady said bluntly. "Another minute or two and Will, maybe Susan, maybe Lizzie Hawkstone, wouldn't have recovered. That stuff was foul, poisonous."

"It was terrible," Morgan agreed. "Thank the Goddess I was able to fight it." She met Keady's even gaze. "Is this about Belwicket or about me?"

Keady knew what Morgan meant. "You're a big stumbling block," she pointed out calmly. "Lilith's been pushing Ealltuinn, trying to become more and more powerful. She can't have a bunch of goody-goody Woodbanes getting in the way."

"I'm not the high priestess," Morgan pointed out, standing up and brushing off her knees.

"No, but it's common knowledge that the coven leaders want you to be. And you're Morgan Byrne! Everyone knows yours is the power to reckon with."

Morgan shook her head, about to howl with frustration. "Why can't power be a good thing? Long ago my power made me a target. Now it seems to be happening again. I can't bear it." Her fist clenched her trowel at her side, small clumps of earth dropping onto her shoe.

"What has a front has a back," said Keady. "And the bigger the front, the bigger the back. Everything must be balanced, good and evil, light and dark. Even if we don't want it to be."

Morgan looked at the sky, clear blue and sunny. So normal looking. This same sun was shining on someone who even now might be planning how best to defeat her, destroy her coven. A weight settled on her shoulders, the dread of what might be in store for her already taking its toll. She turned to Keady. "By that logic, if I turned dark and started doing terrible things, the world would be a better place because of the good that would erupt to balance it."

Keady gave a wry smile. "Let's not test that theory."

"No. Let's decide what we're going to do," Morgan said. "We need a plan. If the coven is under siege, we need to know how to protect it. Come on in and have some tea." She started walking toward the back, and Keady followed. "You know, on Friday, Katrina and I found a hex pouch in the garden."

"Really? Goddess. Had it harmed anything?"

"All the car—" Morgan stopped dead, staring at what lay smack in the middle of the path. Her mouth went dry in an instant.

"Oops, sorry," Keady said, bumping into her. "Problem?"

Morgan felt her friend leaning around to see. She didn't know what to think, what to do. "Uh . . ."

"What's that, then? Is that a chunk of quartz?"

"It's, uh . . ." It was like drowning, drowning in a sea of emotions.

Frowning slightly, Keady moved around Morgan and bent to pick it up.

"Wait!" Morgan put out a hand to stop Keady. Slowly she knelt and reached out to the stone. It was the size of a small apple, pale pink, translucent, clouded, and shot through with flaws. "It's morganite," she said, her voice sounding strangled.

Reluctantly, as if trying not to be burned, Morgan turned the stone this way and that until she found a flat side. Then she felt faint as her world swam and shifted sideways. The morganite had an image on it. *Oh, Goddess, oh, Goddess.* Morgan squinted, but the image was unrecognizable, just as that face in the window had been the other night. It was a person, maybe even a man. But who, dammit? She studied the face, her heart pounding, trying to make out the features, but they were too indistinct. She rubbed her finger over the image as if to clear away dirt, but it made no difference.

"Who is that?" Keady asked quietly.

"You see it, too?"

"Not clearly—oh, wait—it's gone."

It was true. As Morgan watched, the image faded from the stone, leaving Morgan holding an empty piece of quartz. Morganite quartz. One of the first gifts Hunter had ever given her had been a beautiful piece of morganite, and inside it Hunter had spelled a picture of his heart's desire: a picture of Morgan. That was how he had told her he loved her. Now here she was, sixteen years after his death, finding morganite on her garden path. And not just morganite— *spelled* morganite. Horrified, Morgan felt a sob rise in her throat, but she held it back. Her hands were shaking, and she felt every nerve in her body come alive. What was happening to her? Who was taunting her? Was it really Lilith? Why would she go to such lengths just because Morgan had disagreed with her publicly about a few spells?

"Morgan?" Keady touched the back of her hand gently, and when Morgan didn't respond, Keady took the piece of morganite out of her hand.

"It's morganite," Morgan said again, her voice cracking. "A kind of quartz. Not native to Ireland. A long time ago a different piece of morganite had a lot of significance for me. Someone put this here, on my path. Someone who knows me well. Someone who knows my past." She felt a spurt of fear and anger rise in her. She'd thought that her days of battle were over, that she was safe and free to live a peaceful life. Over the last three days that illusion had been stripped from her, and it was devastating.

Keady took Morgan's elbow and led her into the back-yard. "Let's get that tea."

"The garden tools," Morgan said in a near whisper. She gestured to the shed, and Keady obediently detoured there. Morgan opened the shed door and mechanically hung up her few gardening tools. Something felt different. Her extra-sensitive senses picked up on something, alerting her con-sciousness, and Morgan looked around. Now wasn't the time to ignore signals like this. What was different? Her nerves were frayed and shot; she felt trembly and nauseated. All she wanted to do was sit down and have a hot cup of strong tea.

Then she saw it. The cellar door. It had been opened—there was a new scrape in the dirt where it had swung out, and the spiderweb had been recently broken. Cautiously Morgan turned the handle of the door. With everything that had been going on lately, she had no idea what to expect. Inside, Morgan tugged the light string, but nothing happened.

"One second, Keady," Morgan said, starting to descend the cellar steps. *Thank the Goddess for magesight,* Morgan thought. Even without the light she could see perfectly well. She pulled the downstairs light cord, but it didn't work either. Morgan didn't pick up on any vibrations . . . but there, in the corner, some old crates had been disturbed. In a second, her conversation with Moira came back to her—Moira asking for Morgan's old Books of Shadows, Morgan being vague. *Oh, no.*

The crate was open, and all her Books of Shadows were gone. Moira must have gotten them this morning before class. Her first Books of Shadows, with their entries about Cal, about Hunter. Moira might be reading them right now. She might be discovering the magnitude of what her mother had kept from her. Why did this have to happen now, when so much else was going wrong?

Morgan rubbed her forehead with one hand, trying to ease her tension headache. It had been good having Keady here for a while. Morgan had spilled about everything: the ruined carrots, the face in the window, the significance of the morganite, Moira being late, Moira apparently taking all of Morgan's early Books of Shadows. The poisonous smoke.

"It all seems to be building up to something," Morgan had told Keady.

Keady had frowned. "I agree, but what? It's no secret that Lilith isn't a fan of yours, but would she really go this far? This kind of coven infighting just doesn't happen that often. And simple disagreements and bickering wouldn't lead to out-and-out attacks, would they? Maybe we should contact the New Charter."

"Yeah, maybe so." Morgan couldn't help feeling a familiar twinge at the mention of the New Charter. Even after all these years she couldn't hear the words without thinking of Hunter.

Keady had stayed until she was sure Morgan felt better. Since she had left, Morgan had been lying on the couch downstairs, Bixby on her lap and Finnegan draped across her feet like a very heavy hot water bottle. She'd been thinking hard, trying to see some kind of pattern. Okay, assuming this was Ealltuinn, going after Belwicket and more specifically Morgan, why were they doing it now? Was this autumn significant in some way? Besides being the first autumn since Colm had died? *Oh, Colm.* Her heart ached for him, and she could almost see the appeal of creating a *bith dearc*, a window to the netherworld, in order to contact a loved one who had passed on. Almost, but not quite. After seeing the damage it had done to Daniel Niall, Morgan had no desire to mess with dark magick like that.

"Bixby, you're such a good boy," Morgan murmured, rubbing him behind his ears. He purred deeply, his orange eyes at half-mast.

Think, think. That piece of morganite. The face in the window. The hex pouch. The smoke. Even Moira and Ian—maybe Ian's very presence in Moira's life was itself a clue.

Cal, Morgan couldn't help thinking.

Morgan and Finnegan both sensed Moira at the same time. Thank the Goddess she wasn't late, hadn't gone anywhere after class. Finnegan cocked one ear, opened one eye, then lay back down. Morgan braced herself to confront Moira.

Her daughter came in just as the sunlight faded and the wind started kicking up. She looked surprised to see Morgan lying on the couch during the day.

"Hi. What's wrong? Are you sick?"

"Not really," said Morgan. In an instant she remembered the awful fights she'd had with her own parents when she'd first discovered Wicca. They'd been not only offended, but truly afraid for her soul. They were still unhappy about it after all these years. Morgan remembered how she'd wished that they could try to be more understanding and thought now that their fears had made everything seem worse. She could try to do it differently.

"I saw that you found some of my old Books of Shadows in the cellar," she said, striving for a casual tone. "Have you been reading them?"

Moira looked at her, seeming to weigh her answer. "I went and got them this morning," she finally admitted. "I know you wanted me to wait till you got them, but . . . after the smoke and then everything Keady said Saturday—I'm just curious. I need to see how it all started." She shook her head. "I just feel like I need to know everything."

Morgan groaned inwardly at the idea of her daughter knowing everything about her life.

"I've only just started the first one," Moira said. She came to stand by the couch, looking down at Morgan. Moira's hazel eyes were full of secrets, worries, and concerns, but her face was closed, private.

"Do you have any questions?" Morgan's stomach was tight and her jaw ached from trying to keep her face relatively calm.

"I've not read much, like I said," Moira answered, sitting down in the rocking chair. "Just the beginning of the first one—it was where you had met Cal Blaire. I got as far as you discovering you were a blood witch, and then you thought you loved Cal. I've never heard you mention Cal, have I? Was he just a high school crush kind of thing?"

A startled laugh escaped Morgan. Jagged memories of Cal and what he had been to her flashed across her mind. In some ways the beginning of her involvement with Wicca had been so painful, so dangerous and huge, that Morgan had tried hard to live it down ever since. Maybe the truth was that she hadn't just kept those stories from Moira for Moira's sake—she hadn't wanted to relive that time herself.

At Moira's confused expression, Morgan coughed and said, "No, not exactly." She got up and took a Diet Coke from the fridge, then sat back down on the couch and pulled Bixby into her lap for comfort.

"It's stuff I never told you," she said. "I wanted to protect you, in a way." Moira's eyebrows raised. "Your dad knew some of it, but not all. The thing is, when I first found out about being a witch, being adopted, and being from the Belwicket clan—it was exciting and good because it answered a lot of questions and explained things about myself and my family. But it also introduced me to a world I didn't know existed. That world was not always good or kind or safe. And because of who I was—Maeve Riordan's daughter—people, other witches, were interested in me and whatever powers I might have. And on top of all that, Nana and Poppy were so horrified and unhappy and were so afraid I was going to burn in hell forever because I wasn't a good Catholic anymore. It wasn't like your experience here, the daughter of two witches, always knowing you were a witch, growing up in a community that accepts witches, our religion and powers. Just finding out I was a blood witch caused all sorts of pain and unhappiness, mostly for my family and some of my friends, but also sometimes for me."

Morgan was very conscious that she hadn't mentioned Ciaran MacEwan yet. She figured she could handle telling Moira only one difficult thing at a time.

"What do you mean?" Moira asked, pulling one knee up onto the seat of the chair.

"Well. Let me see." Even after nearly twenty years Morgan still felt a pang of embarrassment, of betrayal. "In high school I felt kind of like an ugly duckling. And Aunt Bree was my best friend. You remember Aunt Bree, from New York?"

"The one with the big house and three daughters?" Moira asked.

"Yes. Bree is still gorgeous, but she looked like that in high school. Imagine being best friends with her."

"Ugh. Tess and Vita are bad enough, in their own ways."

"Right. So no guy ever noticed me—I had guy friends but didn't go on dates or anything. And I was almost seventeen. Then a new guy came to school, and he was drop-dead gorgeous." Morgan swallowed hard.

"Yeah?" Moira said with interest.

"Yeah," Morgan said, sighing. "That was Cal Blaire. He was really good-looking, and all the girls fell in love with him, including Bree and me. His mom was a witch, a dark Woodbane, but I didn't know about any of that at the time. She'd come to my town, Widow's Vale, to start a new coven and uncover any bent witches who would join in her dark magick or to flush out any strong witches so she could take their powers. She was a member of Amyranth."

Moira's eyes widened. Amyranth had been a coven dedicated to working dark magick and accumulating power, by any means neccessary. It had been disbanded for almost ten years, but they would be notorious for generations to come. "Amyranth," she breathed. "The real Amyranth?"

"Yes. But I didn't know about Woodbanes or Amyranth or any of that. I met Cal, and he wanted to start a coven, just kids, where we would celebrate the sabbats and stuff. And he was also supposed to find out if any of us had any real powers. He was surprised when I turned out to be a blood witch without even knowing it."

"I can't believe you were sixteen before you knew that." Moira shook her head. "Were you knocked over?"

"That's an understatement," Morgan said dryly. "But even then, untaught and uninitiated . . . well, I could do stuff. Not well, and not safely, but things just came to me. Spells. Scrying. It was a little scary sometimes but also really fun. Mostly it was like—here was something special about me that none of my friends had. I was good in math, but so were lots of kids. I wasn't ugly but not really pretty. My family was fine but not rich or important. But learning Wicca and having a blood witch's powers—that was all me and only me. It was incredibly thrilling and satisfying for me to be very, very good at something so unexpectedly."

Moira looked thoughtful. "I can see how it would be—and then you fell for Cal. Did he like you back?"

"Yes," Morgan said, letting out a breath. "Amazingly. Despite every other girl who wanted him, he wanted to be with me. That freaked Bree out, and she and I had a terrible fight. A bunch of terrible fights. And became enemies."

"You and Aunt Bree? Goddess. How awful."

"It *was* awful, losing my best friend. But it felt like Cal was the only person in the world who understood me or accepted me the way I was. And he seemed to really love me."

"What do you mean, seemed?"

Morgan made a face. "I guess, looking back on it, he did love me, in his own way." She looked down at her knees and absently played with a frayed thread. Bixby stretched, arching his back and yawning wide to show his fangs. "The thing is, Moira," she went on slowly, "Cal was the son of a powerful, dark witch. Once his mother realized who I was, she compelled Cal to get close to me so that she could convince me to join her or, if I didn't want to join willingly, so that she could take hold of me, take my powers, and use them for her own."

Moira frowned slightly, obviously starting to see the parallels with Lilith and Ian.

"Cal was very convincing," Morgan said. "I absolutely believed he loved me. But at the same time, some things about him made me uneasy—I didn't know why. Then a Seeker from the council showed up to investigate Cal and his mother, Selene Belltower. I thought the Seeker was wrong about Cal and Selene—I thought he just wanted to destroy Cal out of jealousy or vengeance. You see, he was also Cal's half brother." Morgan paused to let out another long, slow breath, easing pain out of her chest. "One night he tried to put a *braigh* on Cal, to capture him, and they fought. I threw my athame at the Seeker and hit him in the neck. He went over a cliff into the Hudson River."

Moira was staring at her as if she had just revealed that their cottage was an elaborate hologram.

Morgan sighed and looked at her daughter. She forced herself to continue. "I thought I had killed him. Killed someone to save Cal. Everything started unraveling. It was a horrible, desperate time—I can't even describe how tortured I felt. Then, thank the Goddess, the Seeker didn't die. But he started trying hard to convince me that Cal and Selene were evil. I didn't know what to believe. All the while Selene was putting more and more pressure on Cal, insisting that he get me to join them. So Cal was putting more and more pressure on me, telling me we were *mùirn beatha dàns*, trying to get me to go to bed with him, telling me that everyone else was lying to me."

"I can't believe it," Moira said, wide-eyed. She shook her head, glancing away, then looked back at Morgan. "I mean, I can't imagine this—any of it. What happened? What did you do?"

"Finally Selene decided to just get me herself and take my

powers from me so she could combine them with her powers and be that much stronger. Cal found out about it, and the only thing he could think of to do to save me . . . was to kill me before she got to me."

Moira's jaw dropped open.

"So he locked me in his *seòmar*—his special, secret room—and set it on fire." Nearly twenty years of distance made the words a bit easier to say, the memory almost bearable. "But I managed to send a witch message to Bree, of all people, and in the end she and our friend Robbie drove my car into the wall of the room and got me out. They saved my life. Bree and I were friends again. But Cal and his mother disappeared."

Several emotions crossed Moira's face—concern, sympathy, fear. "What do you mean, disappeared? He tried to *kill* you! And nothing even happened to them?" Her cheeks were turning red with obvious shock and outrage.

"Not even the Seeker could find them. Cal and Selene resurfaced, of course." Morgan's voice cracked a little, but she went on. These were things she had naively hoped her daughter would never have to know. Secrets she'd planned on sharing later, when Moira was older. "Cal turned against his mother and came to find me. Selene came back also to find me. Selene kidnapped Aunt Mary K., who was only fourteen. I had to find her and ended up in Selene and Cal's old house. The Seeker and I went there to save Mary K., and we got into a terrible magickal battle with Selene. I had no idea what would happen—she was so strong, and I wasn't even initiated. It was—there just aren't words to describe how it was. At one point Selene aimed a bolt of power at me that would have struck me dead. But Cal jumped in front of me at the last minute, and it hit him instead. He did it to save me, and it killed him. That's what makes me think he did love me, in his own way. Then it was just me and Selene, and a spell came to me—I think it was from my mother, Maeve. It trapped Selene, and she died. I caused her to die."

"Mum, I can't believe you never told me any of this," Moira said, strain evident in her voice. She looked distressed, and Morgan hated the fact that even after so many years, Cal and Selene still had the power to hurt someone she loved. "Did Dad know?"

Morgan nodded. "Yes—I told him about it."

"Then Selene was dead forever? You won?"

Morgan sighed again. "No, not exactly. A witch that powerful—her body had died, but her spirit had escaped and moved into another physical form. She took over the body of a hawk and continued to live that way. And later she came back again, to try to kill me once and for all."

"Goddess, Mum. She came back *again*?"

Thoughtfully, Morgan said, "I think . . . I think I reminded her of herself, of her own potential. I was powerful because I'd been born that way. She was powerful because she had used dark magick to increase her powers. She had fed off others. She saw me as a threat because I wouldn't join her. And if I grew up, increased my strength, became initiated—I could only be her enemy. In the end she knew that if I went against her as a grown-up, I would defeat her. So she went against me as a teenager, but I defeated her anyway. And of course after her only son died trying to save me, she hated me more than ever. She killed Cal, and she knew it. But she blamed me."

"She's not still around, is she?" Moira looked worried, pinching her bottom lip between two fingers, the way she had when she was young.

"No," Morgan said, looking out through the small living room window. Outside, it had clouded over and the first drops of rain began to hit the ancient, wavy panes of glass. "No, she's dead. She came after me for the third time, and that time she was finished."

"Finished how?" Moira's voice squeaked.

"I killed her," Morgan said sadly, watching the heavy gray clouds outside.

"When she was a hawk?"

"Yes."

Silence. Morgan still had very faint, thin white lines on one shoulder where Selene the hawk had ripped her skin with razor-sharp talons. She would always have those scars, but compared to the scars inside, which no one could see, they were nothing.

"How?" Her daughter's voice sounded fearful, as if she needed to know for sure that Morgan's old enemy was truly no longer a threat.

Morgan wondered if she had already said far too much and knew there was so much more her daughter didn't know. "I shape-shifted," she said. "I became a hawk, and I caught her, and I . . . trapped her spirit inside the hawk so that it couldn't escape again. And then she was really dead forever."

Moira was staring at her as if seeing her for the first time, and Morgan knew that it wasn't only because of her terrible story. It was also about knowing the depth and extent of Morgan's own powers. Morgan cast out her senses—Moira was both horrified by and afraid of her own mother. It felt like an athame piercing her heart to know she'd inspired her only child to feel this way. But there was something else. Awe.

Moira was quiet for a moment; then, unexpectedly, she rose and came over to hug Morgan. "I'm so sorry, Mum," she whispered, tears in her voice. "I'm so sorry you had to go through all that. I had no idea." Feeling a warm rush of love, Morgan hugged her tightly back.

"I can't believe you shape-shifted," Moira said, pulling back and looking into Morgan's eyes. "I thought shape-shifting was just in folktales. I didn't think anyone could do that."

"It isn't that common," Morgan acknowledged. "Moira, listen: I would do anything to make sure that you never had to go through anything like that. Do you understand?"

"You mean Ian. And Lilith Delaney."

"Yes," Morgan said pleadingly, wishing she could get through. "It's like watching my life flash before my eyes— only it's worse because it's you and I need to protect you. Just knowing you're seeing him makes me feel panicky, sick."

"But Mum, Lilith isn't Selene, and Ian definitely isn't Cal," Moira said earnestly, and Morgan's heart sank. "I see the parallels. I see why they would make you feel scared. But I still feel that I need to give Ian a chance. I need to give *me* a chance with him. If it's a mistake, I'll find out. But *I* need to find out—I can't just take your word for it, even though you lived through that nightmare when you were young, with another son and another witch. Ian and Lilith aren't Cal and Selene. And I'm not you." Her face looked open, concerned, eager for Morgan to understand.

Morgan sighed, mentally draping a cloak of protection over Moira. Everyone had to make her own mistakes. But did that mean Morgan had to let Moira walk into disaster?

"I'll be more on my guard, Mum," Moira promised. "I understand now why you're so worried, and I don't want you to be afraid for me. Can I see Ian if I always tell you where and when I'm meeting him?"

It wasn't a bad compromise. "Yes," Morgan said reluctantly, and Moira's face lit up. "But I can't promise I won't scry to find you if I feel you're in danger. And if I find out definitely that Ian is involved in dark magick, you have to promise me you won't see him."

"All right," Moira said, somewhat unenthusiastically. She glanced at the clock. "I was hoping to see him this afternoon. I was going to send him a witch message to meet at Margath's Faire. All right?"

Morgan nodded, not trusting herself to speak. She wanted to ground Moira, to keep her home. She wanted to follow her, to make sure she was safe. In the end she could do neither: if she tried to protect her daughter in those ways, she would only ensure losing her forever. She watched as Moira put on a jacket.

"I won't be too late, all right?"

Morgan nodded again and cleared her throat. "All right."

Then her daughter was gone, and Morgan was left with her memories.

5

Moira

Moira realized she had shredded her paper napkin into unrecognizable strips. She swept them into a little pile and walked up to the counter to throw them away. As she was turning back to her table, her senses prickled, and she saw Ian at the top of the stairs. He was smiling at her, and she gave him a wide smile in return. She pointed to her table, and he met her there.

"I'm so glad you suggested meeting," he said, sitting down. "It was a bit of a wiggle to get away—Mum wants me to gather some moss for her. What's that, an iced coffee?"

"Yes," Moira said. She felt just the faintest bit of unease when he mentioned his mum. Looking into his blue eyes, full of light, she wondered if there was some way of testing him or if she simply had to trust her instincts and wait. She'd meant it when she'd assured her mother that she was convinced of his innocence, but at the same time . . . maybe those stories about Selene and Cal had gotten to her more than she'd realized. She *had* promised she'd be careful, and she intended to be just that. "Do you want to order something?"

"Well . . ." Ian looked at the board. "Not really, actually. I was wondering if you wanted to get out of here. Do you want to come help me collect plants by the copper beeches, down by Elise's Brook?"

Moira knew Elise's Brook—it was one of dozens of tiny waterways that feathered through the southeastern part of Ireland. This particular one was just outside of town and bordered on both sides by woodlands. Since it was halfway between Cobh and Wicklow, Moira and her parents had often gone there for picnics or herb gathering. Besides the copper beeches, there were willows, sloes, furze, and hazel. She'd had to learn their Gaelic names for herbology class: *faibhille rua*, *sáileach*, *áirne*, *aitheann*, and *coll*.

"All right," Moira said slowly. "Is it raining yet?"

"Not yet," Ian told her as they got up. "I'm hoping it'll hold off. We should have almost an hour if we're lucky."

It took almost twenty-five minutes to walk to the brook. The late-afternoon sun was hidden behind thick gray clouds, and Moira wished the fleeting sunshine had lasted longer. As they walked, Moira took a moment to send a witch message to her mum, telling her where they were going, as she had promised.

As soon as they were out of eyesight of the town, Ian took her hand and held it as they walked. His hand was warm and strong and gave Moira a pleasant tingle. Their eyes were level with each other since they were the same height, and it was both comfortable and exciting walking along as if they were officially boyfriend and girlfriend.

"Does your coven have circles on Saturdays, then?" Ian asked. Instantly Moira was overtaken by memories of what had happened just last night. Why was he asking? Did he know something? She glanced at him quickly, but his face seemed open, with no hidden meanings.

"Yes," she said.

"Us too," said Ian. "Mum has what I call power circles, where she and a bunch of the older members try to work a kind of intense magick. Twelve of us younger ones often meet by ourselves and do our own thing."

"What do you mean, intense magick?" Moira asked, feeling her pulse quicken.

He didn't answer at first, and for a moment Moira wondered if he regretted bringing it up. "Oh, lots of chants and rants, I call it. You know. Superstars of Wicca." He laughed self-consciously. "I'm not so much into that—me and my mates mostly do tree-hugging stuff, you know, working with the moon, that kind of thing."

Okay, that didn't sound so bad. Tree hugging certainly wasn't dark magick.

They were approaching the small woodland grove, and Moira almost didn't want to step into the dimly lit thicket of trees, remembering her mother's terrifying stories about Selene and Cal. She glanced over at Ian, thinking, Do I trust him or not? Yes, she did.

Inside the woods it was still, and the air seemed warmer because they were out of the wind. It felt hushed inside, as if even the birds and animals were trying to be extra quiet. Moira cast her senses and picked up vague impressions of squirrels and birds and some small things she couldn't identify.

If her mum were here, she'd have been able to identify every kind of bird and animal and even most of the insects. *I want to be as strong as that one day.*

"Let's see," Ian murmured, pulling a slip of paper from his pocket. "I've got a shopping list." He read the paper, then pulled a handful of little plastic bags from his jeans pocket. "Dog's mercury, for one," he said. "And it's going to be bloody hard to find it this time of year." He looked over at Moira and frowned slightly. "Are you sure you're on for this? I know it's boring. It's just, I really should do it, and I wanted to spend time with you."

"It's all right," Moira said. "I can help you look."

He grinned at her, and her heart did a little flip. She loved his smile, the light in his eyes.

"No," he said. "You sit down there. I have to start collecting some of this stuff, but you can keep me company. Tell me what you've been doing."

"Studying for classes. I submitted my ladybug spell to my spellcraft teacher."

"Really?" Ian laughed. "How'd it go over?"

"She thought the construction was elegant and clean but that the spell was frivolous and self-centered," Moira admitted. The comments had stung a bit, but she'd half expected them. "She said to read back in my parents' Books of Shadows, so I dug my mum's up and started reading them."

Ian stilled, crouched on the ground, and looked up at her. "Really? You hadn't read them before now? What were they like?"

"I'd read some, but not early ones," Moira said carefully. Why was he so interested in her parents' Books of Shadows? Maybe he's just trying to be nice, she chided herself.

"I haven't got far in these," she said, sitting down on a thick fallen log. "But I'm reading about how my mum didn't even know she was a blood witch till she was sixteen years old. She'd been adopted, and no one had told her."

Ian shook his head. "I can't imagine not growing up with Wicca. That would be too strange. How did she find out?"

Moira hesitated. How much could she trust Ian? What if he *was* like Mum thought? No, she had to stop—this was Ian. "A blood witch moved to town and realized it and told her. It caused big problems, because my grandparents are Catholic and they didn't want anything to do with Wicca."

"These are your mum's adopted parents?"

"Yeah. Even now—I know they love her, and they love me and loved my dad, but our being Wiccan and practicing the craft still upsets them. They're worried about our souls."

Ian clawed at some dirt at the base of a tree. Gently he unearthed a small plant that already looked dormant for autumn. He sealed it inside a plastic bag and set it on the ground. "Well, they're trying to show they love you," he said, looking off into the distance. "Sometimes people can do amazingly hurtful things, trying to show they love you." It sounded as if he were talking more to himself than her, but then he shook his head and gave her a little smile.

"Anyway, it sounds like your mum's Books of Shadows are wicked interesting. You should keep reading them."

"Yeah, I'm going to." She wished she could just trust what he said, but she still couldn't help wondering—did he have another reason to want her to read the Books of Shadows? Was his mum using him to get to her like Selene had done with Cal and her mum?

The sun had almost set, and now Moira realized it was

almost dark. "Are you finding what you need?" she asked, doing her best to push away her doubts.

"I can't find a couple of things, but at least I got some of the most important ones," he said, collecting his bags. "I've done my good-son deed for the day. It feels like it's getting colder. Are you chilly?"

"I'm all right," Moira said, but her hands were rubbing her arms. Ian came to sit next to her and put his arm around her. They were alone in a deserted wood, and his warmth felt so good next to her. When he held her like this and looked into her eyes, she couldn't believe that he could ever deceive her. It was as if she could see his whole soul in his eyes and saw only good. Not angelic good, but regular good.

"I've got an idea," he said. "Let's go down and look in the water—scry."

"Scry? What for?"

"Just for fun." Ian shrugged. "For practice."

Moira bit her lip. She could almost hear her mother, warning her that Ian only wanted her to scry with him so he could test just how strong her powers were. Goddess, she wished she could stop questioning every little thing Ian said and did and just *trust* him. "Okay," she said. "Let's go."

Holding hands, they stepped carefully down the rocky banks to where the brook, barely six feet wide at this point, trickled past. There was a flattish boulder half in the water, and they knelt on it, then lay on their stomachs, their faces close to the water. At this spot a natural sinkhole created a barely shimmering circle of water maybe eighteen inches across. It was as smooth and flat as a mirror.

"Do you scry much?" Ian asked, looking down at his reflection.

"No—I'm not that good at it. I practice it, of course."

"In water?"

"Yeah—it's the easiest. My mum uses fire."

Ian looked up, interested. "Really? Fire's very difficult— harder than stone or crystal. But it's reliable. Is she good at it?"

"Very good." Moira stopped, uncomfortable talking about her mother with Ian. She leaned closer to the water. On a bright day she'd have been able to see snips and bits of sky through the treetops overhead. Today, at this hour, she could see only darkness around the reflection of her face.

"Let's try," Ian said softly. He edged closer to her so that they were lying next to each other, their chins on their hands, heads hanging over the water.

When her mother or anyone else from Belwicket scried, they used a short, simple rhyme in English, tailoring the words to fit the medium or the occasion. Moira was trying to recall one when Ian started chanting very softly in Gaelic. She met his eyes in the water, their two reflections overlapping slightly at this angle. Gaelic wasn't Moira's strong point, though she'd studied it and knew enough to have simple conversations. And of course many of the more traditional chants and songs were in old Gaelic. In Ian's chant she recognized the modern words *an t'sùil,* "the eye," and *tha sinn,* "we are." There were many more that she couldn't get.

Her gaze focused on her reflection in the water, but her ears strained to understand Ian's chant. So far she hadn't heard any of the basic words or phrases that she knew could be used as frames to surround a spell and turn its intention dark.

Was she being paranoid? Was she just trying to be safe? Had her mother ruined her ability to just be with Ian, relaxed and happy? Silently Moira groaned to herself, but as she did, their reflections in the water began changing. Automatically Moira slowed her breathing and focused her entire energy on seeing what the water wanted her to see. Water was notoriously unreliable—not that it was never right, but it was so fickle in whether it would show the truth or not.

As they watched, their bodies pressed close, the chill of the boulder seeping through Moira's clothes, their two reflected faces seemed to split apart, like atoms dividing. Their images had overlapped, but now they separated. Then Ian's reflection seemed to split apart again, dividing into two other images. From Moira's angle she thought one of the images was a man, with dark hair and blue eyes. He was older and looked sad but vaguely familiar. But the other half of the image made her breath catch in her throat—it was a shadow, the shadow of a person, with blurred features. Its mouth opened and it laughed, with water showing through where the mouth was. It was just a shadow, not in the shape of a monster, yet the sight filled Moira with dread. She felt clammy and cold, and a chilly trickle of sweat eased down the nape of her neck. It was just a shadow—why did it seem so terrible?

Gulping, Moira looked away, down at her own reflection. It too had separated into two images. One image was a fire—in the shape of a face. The fire was smoldering, red-hot coals but seemed to offer warmth and comfort rather than destruction. Tiny flames licked at the edges, like strands of hair being blown in the wind. The other image was a person, just as Ian's had been. At first Moira thought it was her, but then she realized the person was a man. She frowned, trying to see closer.

Splash! Moira jumped back as a small stone dropped into the water, destroying the reflections. Startled, she looked up at Ian and wiped a few drops of water off her face. "What did you do? There was something . . . something else there."

Ian got to his knees, looking unhappy. "I thought I'd seen enough."

Moira also scrambled up, her limbs feeling stiff and chilled through. "Are you all right?" She took his arm and looked into his face, but his expression was blank and he wouldn't meet her gaze.

"Yeah. It was just cold there on the rock." Edging past her gently, Ian picked up his collected bags, then brushed off his clothes.

He's lying. Did he see what I saw?

"Come on, then," Ian said, trying to sound natural. He forced a smile and held out his hand to help her down from the rock. She took it, jumping down, and followed Ian as he picked their way back out of the woods. The closer they got to the edge, the cooler and fresher it seemed, and Moira could smell rain and hear it pelting the tops of the trees.

"Brilliant," Ian said, looking out at the rain and the darkness. He turned to her. "I'm sorry, Moira. We're going to get soaked."

Moira? Where are you? Moira heard her mother's voice inside her head.

She sent back, *I'm here, with Ian, at the brook. I'm on my way home.*

"It's all right," she said to Ian. "I've gotten soaked before. But are you all right? Why did you break up the reflection?"

He paused, not looking at her, absentmindedly flapping the bags against his leg. "I don't know," he said finally. "It just—I wanted to get out of there."

Moira waited, holding his arm and looking at his face, his skin flecked with raindrops. "You can tell me," she said gently. "You can trust me."

His startled gaze met hers, his dark blue eyes seeming to search her face. A sad-looking smile crossed his face, followed by a look of despair that lasted only an instant. Moira wasn't sure if she'd really seen it. Stepping closer, Ian put a hand under Moira's chin. His skin was damp and cool. "Thank you," he said quietly, and then he kissed her, there at the edge of the woods in the rain.

Moira closed her eyes and stepped closer, slanting her head to deepen the kiss. It was so good and felt so right. Her worries and suspicions fell away as they put their arms around each other and held on tightly. But she knew there was something beneath Ian's skin, something he was worried about or afraid of. Her instincts still told her that he himself wasn't bad, or *evil*, as her mother would say. I can help him, she thought dizzily as they broke away from their kiss and stared at each other. Whatever it is that's upsetting him, it'll be all right.

6

Morgan

Morgan finished writing the recipe for the liver strengthener in her best handwriting. Unfortunately, her handwriting hadn't really improved over the years.

Right after Moira had left to meet Ian, Fillipa Gregg had dropped by for a quick consultation. Morgan had been glad for the distraction and, after doing some hands-on healing work, had concocted the liver cleanser for her. Tonight she needed to write up a strengthening spell and prepare a vial of flower essences for Fillipa to put in her tea for a month.

The sun was going down, but Morgan didn't need to think about dinner for an hour. It was taking all her self-control not to scry for Moira to make sure she was all right. Elise's Brook! In the middle of nowhere with Ian Delaney. Two weeks ago Morgan's life had been sad, unbalanced, but not threatening. Now danger threatened; it was almost as if she and the coven were under siege. Morgan knew she had to keep her guard up, watch her back, the way she had back in Widow's Vale so many years ago. She was keeping the animals inside more and locking all the doors and windows. Not that physical barriers would do any good if serious magick was being worked against her.

Do something. Idle hands are the devil's workshop.

Morgan smiled as she remembered her adoptive mother's words. Of course, Wiccans didn't believe in the devil, or Satan, in any form. But it wouldn't hurt to keep busy. Keeping busy helped her think. And maybe she could gather some ingredients for more, stronger ward-evil spells.

On one wall of Morgan's workroom were floor-to-ceiling shelves. All of her magickal supplies were there, from an assortment of crystals and gems to oil essences, dried flowers, powdered barks, spelled candles and runes, and incense. Maeve's four silver cups were there, polished and shiny from use. The Riordan athame rested in the velvet-lined box that Morgan had bought for it years ago. Maeve's green silk robe was folded carefully and wrapped in tissue paper.

It had been hard talking to Moira this afternoon about Cal. Maybe not as hard as she'd feared, but still difficult to talk about. And as bad as her past with Cal was, it was going to be much, much harder to tell Moira about Ciaran or Hunter. Colm had known about Ciaran and some of her history with Hunter. Telling Moira about her past—her story—was much more daunting, more painful. Morgan had thought it would get easier with time. That at some point she would know when Moira was ready to hear about her past. But waiting hadn't made facing the truth any easier. Morgan remembered what it had felt like, learning that she was the illegitimate daughter of Ciaran MacEwan. It had shaken her to the core, made her question herself like nothing else ever had. If she was the daughter of an incredibly evil witch, did that make her own darkness inevitable? She had known even then that it was going to be a constant struggle to stay on the side of goodness.

It had been, but not only because she was Ciaran's daughter. Every single person, every day, had to choose goodness over and over again. Every person, every day, could take one of two paths. It was up to that person to choose well. Choosing to work with bright magick wasn't a choice one made at the beginning of her career and then just forgot about. The temptation was constant. It was a choice that must be made continuously, despite need or anger or desire. There had been times when Morgan had known she could truly help someone, truly make a difference in someone's life, but it would have meant working the wrong kind of magick. And there had been times when Morgan could see how her own power would be increased substantially if she worked a certain spell or created certain rituals. If she were that much stronger, she could do that much more good. She always used her powers for good. She could protect her family that much more. She herself could be that much safer. But to get that power, she would have to pay the price of working dark magick, even if it were only for a short amount of time. And that price was too high. The memory of Daniel Niall, collapsed and broken after working with a *bith dearc*—a portal to the dead—flashed through Morgan's mind.

She had been tempted by dark magick. She couldn't hold her head high and say that she had never even considered it, that following the Wiccan Rede and minding the threefold law had come easily. Morgan was only too aware of the humbling effect of temptation, of the realization that she had such a desire in her, to be brought to the point of having to fight it.

Was that because she was human or because she was Ciaran's daughter? How easily had Ciaran slipped into darkness all those years ago?

There was more of Ciaran in Morgan than she ever wanted anyone to know. The only way to overcome that side of her was to look hard at it and face it head-on. The moment she pretended she was better than Ciaran, more immune to temptation than he was, that was when she would fall.

Morgan had to stop for a moment. Ciaran. She rested her head in one hand and rubbed her forehead. She took a sip of juice.

He had died four years after Morgan had put a binding spell on him and called Hunter to strip him of his powers. Thinking back on that grotesque scene still made Morgan's stomach turn. It was never clean or easy to strip a witch of his or her powers. Fifteen years ago it had been more common—now the New Charter stressed rehabilitation, reteaching, limited bindings. But to strip a witch of Ciaran's strength of his powers against his will—it was like watching a human being be turned inside out. Ciaran had never recovered from the trauma—not many witches did. For a blood witch to live without powers, without the blessing of that extra connection to the world, to oneself—most witches preferred death. Some members of the New Charter were only now trying to develop rituals and spells that could possibly restore at least some limited magick to a witch who had been stripped.

As for Ciaran—to say that he had never recovered was a

gross understatement. After he had been tried and sentenced and sent to Borach Mean, a sort of rest home in southern Ireland for witches without powers, he had simply ceased to be.

Morgan had gone to visit Ciaran only once, about eight months after he'd arrived at Borach Mean. The memory made her cringe, and she almost dropped the small bottle of rosewater she was holding. She'd had so many torn and confused feelings about what she'd done, about Ciaran himself. She recognized herself in him; she was undeniably drawn to him, her handsome, powerful father. He'd been charming and complimentary—when he'd wanted something. He'd loved her and been proud of her, had seen more potential in her than in any of his other children. But to truly earn his total love, Morgan would have had to step out of light and into darkness forever.

At Borach Mean the witch in charge had led Morgan to Ciaran, in an enclosed courtyard. The pale peach–colored stucco walls had sheltered plants of all kinds, each chosen for its scent or beauty. Herbs and roses all grew lushly, basking in the sun, releasing their scents to the warm air. They had all been spelled to be without power, of no use in any kind of spell. Just in case.

Her feet quiet on the dusty paving stones, Morgan had walked up to him, and he'd jumped: one sad effect of witches losing powers was that they could no longer sense people approaching them, and they ended up being startled frequently. It had taken him several moments to recognize her. She'd been shocked and sickened by his appearance. He'd lost an incredible amount of weight and looked sunken and hollow, even frail. His hair was almost completely white, where before it had been a rich, dark brown with just a few silver threads. But it was his eyes that had changed the most. Their hazel color, once so like Morgan's, had faded to a pale, mottled shade that seemed strangely lit from within.

"You." Morgan had felt rather than heard the word, his uncomprehending stare, the odd glitter of his almost colorless eyes.

"I'm sorry," Morgan had managed to choke out. Those pathetically inadequate words were supposed to cover so much—sorry you were so evil. Sorry you were my dad. Sorry you killed my mother. Sorry I helped bring you to this. Sorry that someone who could have been beautiful and strong and wise instead chose to be corrupt and destructive. And despite everything, sorry we couldn't have been the father and daughter that each of us would have wanted.

In the next moment Ciaran had lunged off his bench, fingers clenched like talons, and Morgan, startled, had taken a big step back. He had started spitting hateful words at her, words of revenge, accusation: "Traitor! Betrayer! Dog-witch! Nemesis! Foul, faithless daughter!" He had tried to throw spells at her, spells that, had he had his powers, would have flayed the flesh from her bones. As it was, his attempt to create magick only made him crumple in pain, retching, his fingers clawing at the light red dust on the ground.

"Ciaran, stop," Morgan had cried, raw pain squeezing her heart. And still he had spewed awful words at her. She had burst into tears, shaken by the horror of it all, and then, unbearably, Ciaran had started crying, too, as an attendant ran up. One witch had led Morgan inside, while two others had picked Ciaran up and taken him back to his room. The last thing Morgan had heard was his voice, a shattered, hollow croak, choking out her name.

Morgan could still smell the heated dust of Borach Mean, still feel the warm wind in her hair. Not long after that, she had moved to Ireland for good. Four years later, when she heard that Ciaran had died, she had gone to his funeral.

Moving the step stool, she continued to search for the ingredients she needed.

Ciaran's funeral had been in Scotland, where his wife, Grania, had lived with their three children: Kyle, Iona, and Killian. Her half siblings. Grania had finally divorced Ciaran after he'd been stripped. Morgan had heard about it from Killian, the only one of her half siblings she had any relationship with. He hadn't asked her to come, had advised against it, in fact, but she'd told him that she needed to and that he didn't have to let on who she was when she was there.

So she'd shown up at the small and ancient burial ground that the MacEwan Woodbanes had used for centuries. She'd worn a scarf and dark glasses to hide her hair and eyes. Almost two hundred people had been there: dark witches, come to mourn their betrayed and fallen leader, and others, his enemies, come to make sure he was dead at last. It had been very odd. Killian had spotted her but made no sign of recognition. Morgan hadn't known anyone else there except for a few council members, like Eoife MacNabb. Eoife also gave no sign of recognition.

Yet Grania, Ciaran's ex-wife, the one he had betrayed to become Morgan's mother's lover, had suddenly spotted her across the crowd and let loose a spine-cracking banshee howl.

"You!" she had cried. "How dare you show your face here?

You, his bastard daughter!" Her face had contorted in resentment. "You and he deserved each other! How I wish you could join him in his grave right now!"

Everyone had turned to look. Morgan had stared at Grania, not saying a word, just knowing what she could have said. Grania had once perhaps been pretty, but thirty years of frustration and anger had twisted her face, made it seem lumpy and asymmetrical. Her hair was a harsh blond that ill suited her red, windburned face and pale, gooseberry eyes. She and Ciaran had had a rocky relationship. But clearly, even after all Ciaran had done to her, she still felt something for him, something that made it impossible to bear the reminder Morgan provided of his affair with Maeve.

Next to Grania, Killian had worn a pained expression—he hadn't joined in his mother's accusations, but neither would he defend Morgan against her. Killian mostly just took care of Killian. But Iona and Kyle—Ciaran's other children—had been another matter. Iona resembled Grania in looks—she was pale, dumpy, and had none of Ciaran's handsomeness, charisma, or grace. She'd stared at Morgan with plain hatred, but then her expression had turned to something else, something sly and knowing, almost like satisfaction: a smug, triumphant look that Morgan didn't understand. Could Iona have been glad that Ciaran was dead? He hadn't made her life easy, but she had professed to love him.

Then Kyle had surged toward her, hissing a spell. He looked more like Ciaran, but where Ciaran's features had been classical and chiseled, Kyle's were softer, more doughy. He had Ciaran's coloring, as Morgan did, and Killian.

His attack had been useless. Morgan had been initiated—she

was far from an untrained teenager, unaware of her powers. Not only that, but she had already lost Hunter. Life had honed her, made her harder. Morgan, sitting there at her father's funeral, had been as hard and sharp and deadly as an athame. Kyle's power was undisciplined, unfocused, and Morgan had flicked his spells aside with a wave of her hand as if they were gnats.

This wasn't what she had come for. It gave her no pleasure to antagonize or hurt her father's other family. Sighing, Morgan had gathered her things and threaded her way through the crowd. She'd walked back toward the village and caught the next train out. Since then she'd heard about Kyle or Iona only seldom, usually from Killian, whom she continued to see maybe once a year or so, whenever she was in his area on business. Killian had changed little, despite a surprisingly early marriage and, at last count, three children. He was still happy-go-lucky, held no grudges, and managed to skip through life like an autumn leaf, tossed here and there by the wind.

Killian had told her of the political marriages of both Kyle and Iona, who had each chosen to ally themselves with powerful Woodbane families. Iona had taken her father's legacy seriously and had been studying intensively—though whether she could ever come close to filling Ciaran's shoes was unknown. Kyle had continued to soften, like an overripe cheese, and now it sounded as if he mostly played the role of country gentleman, managing extensive estates in western Scotland, supported by his wealthy wife.

Morgan sighed to herself. Okay, well, now she had managed to thoroughly depress herself. But at least she'd gathered everything she needed for the spell.

Back in the living room she lay down on the couch. It was

dark outside now, and the rain had just started. Moira still wasn't back. Morgan was tempted to scry for her daughter but instead sent a witch message to Moira, asking her where she was. Thankfully, Moira sent back that she was on her way home.

Rubbing her forehead again, Morgan lay in the shadowed room, trying to keep a lid on her anxiety. Moira was safe. She was coming home. And tomorrow Morgan and Keady would ask Christa, Katrina, and Will Fereston to join them in performing a spell to trace the black smoke from last night. Morgan was also considering taking the hex pouch and confronting Lilith with it, possibly making some ambiguous counterthreats. Maybe she could scare Lilith into leaving her alone.

Yawning, Morgan stretched, then went "oof!" as Bixby jumped up on her. Absently she stroked his orange fur, watching his eyes drift lazily shut. With Bixby purring comfortably on her stomach, Morgan gradually let herself be taken by sleep.

She and Hunter were making love. It felt oddly unfamiliar and at the same time as easy and regular as breathing. She could smell his skin, his hair, feel his short, white-blond bangs brush her forehead. It was as if he had been on a long trip and had just gotten home. Maybe this was one of their infrequent meetings: they were coming together in some city, somewhere, whenever they could.

"I thought you were going to settle down, come live with me," Morgan *murmured against his shoulder, holding him tight. The sheer delicious joy of being with him, the feeling of connection, of rightness. This was where home was: wherever they could be together, for however long.*

"I am," he whispered back, kissing her neck. "Just not as soon as I thought."

Morgan smiled against him, closing her eyes, relishing the moment, feeling gratitude for how much she loved him, that one person was able to love another person so completely. "Make it soon," she told him. "I need you with me."

"Soon," he promised. "I'm sorry it's taken me so long."

"I forgive you." Morgan sighed, kissing his shoulder.

He grinned at her, the edges of his eyes crinkling. His eyes were so green, so pure and full of light. "Ta," he said. "And I forgive you."

"For what?" Morgan demanded, and the light faded from his eyes.

"For believing I've been dead all this while."

Morgan woke up crying.

Finnegan came over to the couch and gave her hand a tentative lick. Still sobbing, Morgan patted his head and tried to sit up, dislodging Bixby. *Oh, Goddess, oh, Goddess.* With a rough movement she pushed her hair out of her eyes. She coughed, tried to hold back a sob, and wiped her eyes with the back of her sleeve.

What time was it? Only five-twenty. She'd been asleep twenty minutes. Morgan quickly cast out her senses. Moira wasn't home yet but surely would be soon. Standing shakily, Morgan went to the hearth and threw some small logs sloppily onto the andirons. Her nerves were jangled by the dream, but kindling fire with magick was almost second nature by now. She huddled by the fire for several minutes, and she could feel the first tongues of flame trying to break through her intense coldness, the coldness that seemed to crack her bones.

What had that dream meant? she wondered miserably. She'd just had a startling, realistic dream about Hunter the same day someone had left a piece of spelled morganite on her garden path. There were no coincidences.

In the days, weeks, months, years after his death, night-marish Hunter dreams had haunted Morgan so that she'd often been afraid to sleep. How many times had she dreamed he was alive, only missing, not dead? How many times had she dreamed he had simply left her for another woman—then woken up with tears of happiness on her face because even his leaving her to be with someone else was infinitely preferable to his being dead?

But it had been ages since she'd dreamed of him so vividly, dreamed that he was still alive. This, the morganite, the face in the window, the black smoke—it was all adding up to something. Someone was haunting her with her past—someone who knew her well enough to know about Hunter. She needed to find out who, and how, and, most importantly, *why*.

Morgan looked down at her shaking hands almost with detachment, as if she were in the middle of a science experiment and this was a side effect. She swallowed. Her mouth was dry. She hadn't felt this way in twenty years. *My world is no longer safe.*

I need help.

Standing, Morgan walked over to the phone. She flipped through her address book and found Sky Eventide's latest number. Sky was Hunter's cousin and, after Morgan, had probably known him better than anyone. All these years she and Sky had kept in touch, some years more than others. They'd never had a close or comfortable relationship, but they'd been united in their mutual love of and grief over Hunter and made an effort to keep track of each other. Sky had never married, though she and Raven Meltzer had gotten back together for a stretch and shared an apartment in London for several years before Raven moved to New York when her career as a fashion designer took off. These days it seemed like Sky usually had some cute guy or girl hanging around adoring her, until they annoyed the crap out of her and she cut them loose.

Sky answered at once, her clipped tone suggesting that Morgan had just disturbed something important.

"Sky? It's Morgan. I'm sorry—are you in the middle of something?"

"Just trying to get my bloody toaster to turn out one decent slice, the bugger. Have you noticed how hard it is to spell appliances?"

Just hearing Sky's voice stopped Morgan's nerves from dumping adrenaline into her system. It was so familiar, from so long ago, when Morgan had just been discovering magick and love and sadness all at once.

"Uh, isn't that *a-p-p-l-i*—"

"Oh, very funny," Sky growled, and Morgan actually smiled. "Smart ass. You know what I mean. They're impossible. Hell, even rocks are easier to control."

"I know what you mean," Morgan agreed. "I'm pretty low-tech."

On Sky's end Morgan heard the scrape of metal and a slight thud, as if Sky had given her toaster a blow.

"Anyway, what's going on?" Sky asked.

Morgan hesitated. Sky had gone through almost the same pain that she had so many years ago, when Hunter had died. She hated raking it all up for her. But she needed help.

"I'm . . . afraid," she admitted. She could almost feel Sky sit up, her interest sharpen.

"Tell me what's going on."

"Weird things. I was looking out the window at night, and

I had a vision. A face appeared next to mine in the window. I couldn't tell who it was, but it was someone fair. Then just this morning I found a big chunk of morganite right in my yard, on the path. *Morganite*. And it had been spelled to hold a person's image. Again, I couldn't make out who it was. It was blurry and the stone was full of flaws, cloudy."

"That *is* odd," Sky said slowly. "Is someone working against you? Or your coven?"

"That's not all." Morgan quickly described the black smoke at the circle and filled Sky in on her history with Lilith and Ealltuinn. "But those things don't explain who the person is that I keep seeing. Why send me images? What would that do?"

"Maybe just unnerve you?"

"Well, yes, but the images themselves aren't scary. It's the idea that someone's doing this on purpose, you know? And there's more—just now I fell asleep, and I had a dream. It was . . . it was about Hunter, about me and Hunter." She paused, swallowing. "And I said I forgave him for something, and he said he forgave me, too. I asked what for, and he said, 'For believing I've been dead all this while.'"

After almost a minute Sky said, *"Really."* Her voice was concerned, thoughtful—and held a twinge of sadness as well.

"Yes," Morgan said, hearing a slight crack in her voice.

"Who around there knows about Hunter?"

Morgan thought. "My mother-in-law knows. You know I was a mess afterward, and she took me in. Colm knew about him. Some members of my coven."

"Do you think it could be one of them, trying to work on you?" Sky asked. "Maybe they've been resenting Hunter all these years? Either Colm doing this from the other side or maybe his mum, now that he's gone and can't protect you?"

Morgan took a minute to work through those ideas. Her automatic response was, *Of course not*, but she had to think through all possibilities.

"I don't think it's Colm," she said. "Colm knew about Hunter but never seemed that jealous of him. Hunter was gone, and Colm had me, and we had Moira."

"Did he wonder if you loved him as much as Hunter?"

Morgan sighed. Sky had a knack for asking the tough questions.

"He probably did," Morgan answered with unflinching honesty. "I mean, no one could replace Hunter—he was my *mùirn beatha dàn*, and Colm knew that. But once I was married to Colm, I did my best not to let him down or make him think he was second best. And I did truly love him."

"And Katrina?"

"No, Katrina is more the in-your-face type," Morgan said. "She wouldn't bother resorting to anything this subtle."

"Which leaves who?"

"Well, the leader of Ealltuinn, as I mentioned. But how could she know about Hunter? I mean, the morganite. Who could possibly know about that? Only Bree and Robbie. And they're not blood witches. And of course wouldn't want to do this to me."

Robbie was living in Boston, a partner in a law firm, married to a woman he'd met in law school. He and Bree had dated through high school and broken up in college, but both of them and Morgan were still good friends and kept in touch regularly.

"Who else?" Sky said. "Someone who would *want* to hurt you?"

Morgan thought. "Well, there's Grania," she said. "But it's

been so many years since I last saw her, at the funeral . . . it doesn't make sense that she'd be doing all of this now. And I don't think she's all that powerful, frankly. Neither is her son Kyle. I'm not sure about Iona—but I do think Killian would have warned me if he knew I was in danger from any of his family."

"Right." Sky said. "Then we're still stuck."

"Sky," Morgan said hesitantly, "you don't think—there's no way—I mean—" She heard Sky draw in a deep breath, then let it out.

"I think we'd be able to feel it somehow if he were still alive, don't you?" Sky's voice was rough-edged but gentle. "We've both tried, with small means and powerful ones, to track him through the years. But since the day that ferry went down, I haven't felt his presence. I haven't felt him anywhere in this world. And I really think that I would. Not because I'm so powerful or even because he was, but because of our connection."

"You're right. I haven't felt him either. And I'm sure I would have as well," Morgan said. At that moment she realized that deep down she'd somehow been hoping Sky would say, Maybe he's still alive! Let's find him! *How sad, after all these years, to have that hope.*

"You're much, much more powerful than I am," Sky went on. "More powerful than Hunter. And your connection to him was stronger than mine—I'm only his cousin. I think you would have felt something if he were still alive."

"I would have," Morgan said, feeling deflated. "It was all just so horrible. Because I didn't see it happen—that seems to make it less real. They never found him. I never had that final proof. When it happened, I felt nothing. I didn't feel his living presence, and I didn't feel his definite death. I just felt nothing."

"Maybe that's what death feels like."

"I guess it feels different every time," Morgan said hollowly, thinking back to Cal, Hunter, Ciaran . . . Colm.

"I'm sorry, Morgan." Very few people saw this softer side of Sky, and Morgan was deeply grateful. She and Sky had practically hated each other when they'd met, and it had taken years for them to achieve this understated friendship. "I could come down," Sky said casually. "I'm between jobs." Sky traveled around and had most recently worked as a translator for the Medieval Studies Department at the University of Dublin.

Yes! Morgan cried inside, but she forced herself to say, "Thanks, Sky. I should probably figure things out here first. I've got some good people around me. We'll scry. Maybe we can uncover more information. How about I'll call if things get worse or I need your help?"

"Are you sure?"

No. "Yeah—I'll definitely call you if things get worse."

"Well, keep your eyes open. If someone's really doing this, it sounds a bit scary. Be careful—protect yourself, all right?"

"All right. Thanks. I'll talk to you soon."

7

Moira

I have to write this down before I forget. I want to forget, but I know it's important to remember. Who said, "If man doesn't learn from history, he's doomed to repeat it?" Or something like that. That's what this is like.

I don't know how to explain it, how to talk about it, even to my Book of Shadows. Oh, Goddess, I walked the fine edge between light and darkness tonight, and even now I don't know if I chose right.

Selene is dead at last. I saw the life fade from the eyes of her hawk, and I know her spirit couldn't escape. I didn't kill a person in a human body, but I crushed the spirit of someone who was once human, someone who was incredibly evil, who had tried to kill me, had hurt my sister.

Does that count?

Does it matter if I myself wasn't human when I did it? If I shape-shifted into a hawk, then was it one hawk killing another, and does that make it less bad?

Goddess, I don't know. Maybe I am on the dark side now. I don't want to be. I want to work for goodness. Do I get to try again? Goddess, I need answers. I'm only seventeen.

"Free!" Tess cried, throwing her arms in the air. Moira, sitting on the school steps, closed her mother's Book of Shadows and smiled.

"Mondays are always so long," she said as students from their school streamed past them. She kept a watch out for Ian—they'd had barely any time to talk today between classes.

"Is your mom still freaked about Saturday?" Vita asked in a low voice. "My folks were uptight all yesterday. It was the worst thing I've ever seen."

"Me too," Moira said. "Yeah, Mum seems really rattled. She hates to let me out of her sight. Yesterday I met Ian in town, but I'd told Mum where I was and all."

"Iiiiaaaannn," Tess sang under her breath. "Did you tell him about the black smoke?"

"No." Moira shrugged. She still couldn't shake the uneasiness she'd felt since scrying with him.

"How are things going with him, then?" Tess asked.

"Good," Moira said, nodding. She saw Tess and Vita look at each other. "What?"

"What's wrong?" Vita asked. "You're all distracted. Like you're not really here."

That got Moira's attention. "I'm sorry." She leaned closer so only they could hear her. "Actually, I'm totally weirded out about my mum."

Tess and Vita looked at her questioningly.

Moira hesitated. But if she couldn't tell her two best

friends, who could she tell? "My mum shape-shifted," she breathed. "Into a hawk." Her friends' eyes went wide.

"No," Tess whispered. Vita's mouth was open in shock.

Moira nodded solemnly. "Mum told me yesterday, and then I found it in her second Book of Shadows. These books have been something else," she said softly. "It's a whole different picture of my mum. Like she had a completely different life that I didn't know anything about. It's kind of mad."

"Do you know what happened?" Vita asked.

"Not completely," said Moira. "I mean, she told me about it, and I was like, oh, Goddess. But then I read that bit in her second Book of Shadows this morning and again just now. And for some reason, reading about it got to me in a way her telling me about it didn't. Like it was more real. But I've been freaked out about it all day."

"Don't blame you," said Tess, looking worried. "I don't know what I'd do if I found out something like that. I mean, shape-shifted! That's some wicked magick."

Moira nodded, her tension feeling like a knot in her chest.

"Did you mention it to your mum?" Vita asked.

"No. Not yet. But we've been having big talks." Moira sighed. "About her. Her past. I mean, it's good and all, but . . ."

"Come on over and get it off your chest," Vita offered. "My folks are at work still, and Seanie won't bother us." Seanie was Vita's twelve-year-old brother.

"Moira?"

Ian. Moira turned and there he was, standing on the step above her. He gave her a slight smile, as if unsure how she would be today. Last night he'd insisted on walking with her all the way to her house in the rain because he hadn't wanted her to have to walk by herself. They'd held hands, and he'd kissed her again, in the road, right before the light from Moira's house had hit them. All day they'd been exchanging glances between classes and during math, the one class they shared.

"Hi," she said, feeling shy in front of her friends.

"I'll come, then, Vi," Tess said, straightening up and acting normal. "Moira, you want to come, or maybe another time?"

Tess was giving her an easy out. Moira glanced at Ian, at the expression in his eyes, and she nodded gratefully at her friends.

"Another time?"

"Sure." Tess and Vita waved good-bye. For a moment Moira wanted to change her mind and run after them. It had been such a relief to confide in them, and she wanted to talk about it more. On the other hand, this was *Ian*.

"Are you all right?" he asked after the two girls had left.

"Yes. You?" Could he see all the emotion in her eyes?

"All right. I'm amazed we didn't catch our death of cold," he said, trying for a light tone.

"Must be all that echinacea and goldenseal Mum pumps into me," Moira said, and Ian grinned. There. Now he looked like himself.

"Want to go sit in the park for a while?" he asked, and she nodded happily. The doubts were still there, but somehow being with Ian made everything else feel all right.

"What does that look like?" Ian asked.

Moira tilted her head and squinted at the pile of leaves on the ground. "Nothing. A fat mouse?"

Ian grinned at her. They were sitting side by side on a bench in the tiny park two blocks from school. The wind was picking up, and it was getting chillier as the sun started to think about going down. But Moira wasn't going to be the first to move— not when Ian had his arm around her and they were alone. Not even her mum's worrying could budge her. Moira sent her a quick witch message letting her know where she was.

"Cair a bèth na mill náth ra," Ian sang very softly under his breath. He chanted more words so quietly that Moira couldn't hear them.

The leaves on the ground shifted and overlapped and rearranged, separating and drawing together. Soon they had formed the initials *MB,* there on the brick walk.

Moira grinned with delight. "Next thing you know, you'll be doing it with ladybugs," she said, and Ian laughed.

The wind scattered her initials, and she leaned closer to him, feeling cozy.

"No, not ladybugs," he said, still smiling. "But maybe something a little bigger." He began to murmur some words, and Moira thought she recognized their form as being a weather-working spell. She raised her eyebrows. Weather working was considered taboo unless you had a very good reason. Of course, so was turning pages in people's books without their permission and writing one's initials in ladybugs . . . but it wasn't as if any of it actually *hurt* anyone.

"Oh my gosh . . . ," Moira breathed, staring at the sky. Almost imperceptibly, Ian was sculpting the clouds above and had gently morphed them into a huge, puffy *M* and a huge, puffy *B.* She laughed, but he wasn't finished, and soon a large plus sign floated next to her *B,* followed by a capital *I* and a *D. MB + ID.*

Laughing, Moira gently smacked his knee with her hand. "Lovely—the world's largest graffiti." They smiled at each other, and then Moira said, "That's amazing—thank you. But maybe you shouldn't risk working weather magick."

"There's no risk in playing with clouds," Ian said reasonably. "I've always done it. It can be so cool." In the sky the letters were already wisping away. It *had* seemed harmless, Moira thought.

"You try it," Ian urged her. "You know how."

Moira hesitated for a second. Members of Belwicket—especially uninitiated ones—were not allowed to work weather charms. *Belwicket has such a narrow view of things sometimes.* Anyway, she probably wouldn't be able to do it—she wasn't initiated and had no practice.

"Right, then. Here goes," she said, closing her eyes and thinking about what she wanted to do. She thought about the clouds, their heavy grayness and the letters Ian had formed. Then she began to chant her coven's basic form of weather-working spells, adding in a ribbon of allowing the clouds to be whatever they wanted to be. She was proud of herself for remembering to weave in a time limitation and a place limitation. Instead of forcing the clouds into a picture she wanted, she would let them create one of their own, using their own essences. Frankly, she thought her idea was really cool.

Crack! Moira's eyes flew open as lightning bleached the world. Moments later a huge rumble of thunder shook their bench.

Her startled eyes met Ian's. "What did you do?" he asked with a mixture of amusement and concern.

"I let them be what they wanted?" Moira said uncertainly.

Another huge crack of lightning split the air not far away. Moira smelled the sizzle of ozone and felt her hair fill with static electricity. The enormous clap of thunder that followed the lightning sounded like a cannon going off right beside her ear.

"I think it wants to be a mother of a storm," Ian said, standing up and taking her hand. "Please tell me it won't last long."

"Four minutes," Moira said, then gasped as the sky opened and sheets of chilly rain dumped onto the streets. All around them people scurried for shelter. Dogs whined and barked, shoppers ducked back into stores they'd just come out of, and the whole world looked as if someone had turned off the light.

"Teatime," Ian said as another wave of thunder crashed down around them. He pulled Moira quickly up the block, then turned and ran down another street. By now they were soaked and Moira's teeth were chattering. Two more blocks seemed to take hours, with the frigid rain pelting their faces and clothes, their wet backpacks becoming heavier by the second. Finally they could see the sign for Margath's Faire, and Moira leaped through the door after Ian.

Oh, warmth, blessed warmth, she thought, shivering. Light. The smells of cinnamon and tea and something baking and candle wax.

For a minute Ian and Moira stood inside the door, silently dripping. Then they headed upstairs to the café, where Ian spotted an empty table. They grabbed it, shrugging out of their sodden jackets and dropping into seats still warm from the last customers. Ian shook his head, and fine droplets of water hit the table. Moira held up her hand. "Hey! I'm wet enough."

He grinned and took a paper napkin from the dispenser. Leaning over, he gently patted her face dry, which made Moira practically glow. "I can see why you were concerned about playing with clouds," he said low, so no one could hear.

Moira made an embarrassed face. "Sorry," she said. "I

thought the clouds would just make themselves into a nice picture."

"Your clouds seem to have had delusions of grandeur," Ian told her, and she giggled.

Privately, Moira was unnerved that she had worked such powerful magick. She just prayed her mum or gran never found out. They would have her hide.

Ian fetched them both hot tea and a plate of scones with cream and jam. You are wonderful, Moira thought, suddenly ravenous. She checked her watch—an hour before dinner.

"I better let my mum know where I am again," she said apologetically, feeling like a baby. But she had promised. Moira looked off into the distance, concentrating but not closing her eyes. She formed her thoughts and sent them out into the world, aimed at her mother.

I'm at Margath's Faire with Ian. I'll be home when the rain stops.

All right. See you soon. Be careful.

Blinking, Moira came back to the moment and smiled ruefully at Ian. He was looking at her curiously.

"Did you send a witch message to your mum?"

"Uh-huh. She likes to know where I am. She worries."

"You can send witch messages, and you're not initiated yet?"

Moira looked up in surprise from where she was spreading jam on her scone. "Well, mostly just to Mum. Tess and Vita and I practice, but it's not so reliable."

"That's amazing," said Ian, warming Moira inside. She shrugged self-consciously and took a bite of scone. "And you always let your mum know where you are? Like yesterday, at Elise's Brook?"

Now she was embarrassed. He must think she was a total git.

"Yeah," she mumbled, looking at her plate.

"No, no, don't get me wrong," he said, leaning over and putting his hand on her knee. "I'm not trying to tease you. I just think it's amazing you can do that. All right?"

Moira looked at him, at his earnest face, his eyes, the lips that had kissed her so many times yesterday. He meant it.

"All right," she said, but she still felt self-conscious.

"Anyway—everything okay?" Ian asked lightly. "Did Morgan of Belwicket suspect you had anything to do with the storm?"

"I don't think so," Moira said, just as a man from the next table turned toward them.

Moira glanced over and found him looking at her. She frowned slightly and met Ian's eyes, then looked back at her scone. The man seemed familiar—did she know him from somewhere?

"Excuse me," he said, in a strong Scottish brogue. "Did you say Morgan of Belwicket?"

"Why do you ask?" Ian said, a touch of coolness entering his voice.

The man shrugged. "I'm on my way to see her. Passing through town. On my way to Dublin. Thought I'd drop in." He took a sip of his tea, and Moira looked at him more closely. He looked very familiar. He was maybe a little older than her mum, with dark auburn hair and dark eyes. Moira didn't think she'd ever met him—she would have remembered. His face was very alive, very knowing, with laugh lines etched around his eyes and a half smile lingering on his lips.

"What do you want with her?" Moira asked. Things had been tense lately, with the attack on the coven and all. But she didn't want to sound overly rude in case he really was a friend of Mum's.

"Dropping in, like I told you. Usually she comes to see me—she travels a lot. This time I thought I'd save her a trip."

Moira's eyes narrowed. So he knew her mum traveled a lot. "Really? Who are you?"

The man smiled charmingly, and if Moira hadn't been on guard, her defenses would have melted. He was very attractive, she realized, startled to think that way about someone so many years older. But at that moment he radiated good will, humor, benevolence. Ian took her hand under the table and squeezed her fingers.

"I'm her brother, dear heart," the man said. "And who are you?"

Moira's eyes widened for a second before a look of suspicion came over her face. "She doesn't have a brother. She only has a sister."

"Actually, no," said the man with a friendly smile. "She has her American sister, the delightful Mary K., and then she also has me and two other siblings. Or half siblings, I should say."

"No," said Moira.

"How do you know?" the man asked playfully.

Ian squeezed Moira's fingers again, but not before she said, "I'm her daughter."

"Her daughter?" said the man, his eyes lighting up. "You're Moira, then. But I thought you were barely twelve or so. How time flies. Say hello to your Uncle Killian. Killian MacEwan."

Moira frowned. Why did that name sound familiar? Ian's hand had tightened on hers almost painfully, and she shook her fingers free before he cut off the circulation. Had her mum ever mentioned that name? Had she ever mentioned a half brother? No. But then, Mum hadn't mentioned Cal Blaire or

Selene Belltower or shape-shifting into a bloody *hawk*, either.

"How could you be her half brother?"

"We had the same da, sweetheart, though your mum didn't know it till she was practically full grown."

Moira thought back. "Angus Bramson? Maeve Riordan's husband?"

"Angus wasn't her da. It was Ciaran MacEwan, my father."

He spoke softly, so probably no one else in the tea shop heard them. Still, to Moira it seemed as though the world stopped for a moment, all conversation ceased, every movement stilled.

She knew the name Ciaran MacEwan. Everyone knew it. It was right up there with other historical mass murderers.

"I don't understand," Moira said. "Ciaran MacEwan was your father? My *mother's* father?" A chill of fear went down her still-damp back, as if she expected him to whip out a wand and put curses on everyone in the room. Especially her.

Killian gave a long-suffering sigh that managed to convey his own personal regret that he hadn't chosen his parents better. "Aye, that he was, I'm afraid. And Morgan's, too. But if you're her daughter, why don't you know that?" He cocked his head and looked at her.

Across the table, Ian looked frozen. Moira immediately felt horrified that he was here, listening to this stuff. It couldn't possibly be true. If it were true . . .

"Because it isn't true," Moira said firmly. "You're making it up. Why in the world would you think Ciaran MacEwan could be my mum's father? This is nonsense. I'm going." She stood up abruptly and grabbed her book bag. Ian got up also, moving his chair so she could get out.

"Come on," he said. "I'll see you home." He glanced at the stranger, but it wasn't a glance of revulsion or distrust. More like awe, Moira thought, and that upset her even more. *How could Ian be so stupid? Ciaran MacEwan was evil personified. That's his son!* She was so overwhelmed right now, she couldn't handle worrying about Ian and his motives. She had to be able to trust him, at least.

She pushed out of Margath's Faire into the street, to see that the rain had stopped and the sun had gone down and she had a long bicycle ride in the dark. Dammit. She'd just leave her bike at school and take the bus home.

"Hi, Morgan's daughter," came a voice from behind them: Killian's. "Can I offer you a lift? I'm going to your mother's now."

He had to be kidding. Like she hadn't heard enough horror stories about strangers in general and the MacEwans in particular. This guy's dad had helped develop the dark wave that had killed hundreds and hundreds of innocent witches and nonwitches.

"No," she said firmly, glancing back. "I can get home myself, thank you."

8

Morgan

Morgan answered Katrina's gentle tap on the door. Rain and wind gusted in with her mother-in-law.

"Hi," Morgan said. "Where did this storm come from? Moira's caught in it in Cobh."

"It's not a natural storm," said Katrina, sitting stiffly in a chair at the dining table. "You didn't work it, did you?"

"Me?" Morgan looked at her in surprise as she put the teakettle on the stove. "No, of course not. Why?"

Katrina shrugged. "Someone did. No one I recognize. But it is magickal."

Uneasy, Morgan filled the teapot and fetched two mugs. She'd been so deep in her thoughts she hadn't even sensed the magick behind the storm. Now someone was working weather magick. Was it Ealltuinn? Were they behind all of the things that had been happening? "I didn't sense it," she murmered

"You could, if you were outside for a minute," said Katrina.

Something in the older woman's voice made Morgan look up. "What is it, Katrina?" She slid into a chair and started to pour the tea.

"Morgan—have you been working magick I don't know about?" Katrina looked uncomfortable and concerned. "I don't mean herb spells and practice rites. I mean big magick, dangerous magick, that none of us know about."

"Goddess, no, Katrina! How can you ask that?"

Katrina's blue eyes met Morgan's over the table. She hesitated, circling her hand widdershins over her mug to cool the tea. "I don't know," she said finally. "I just feel . . . off. I feel like something is off somewhere. Out of balance. And then that black smoke."

Nodding, Morgan said, "Keady Dove and I are trying to trace it. We need more people, though. Perhaps tomorrow you, Christa, and Will can help us."

"Yes, of course," said Katrina. "That's a good idea." She fidgeted in her chair, looking around. "I just feel—off balance." She seemed frustrated about not being able to explain it better.

"It isn't because of anything I've been doing," Morgan said. "But there's been some odd stuff happening, that's a fact."

She told Katrina about the face in the window, the chunk of morganite, and even her dream. "Plus there was the hex pouch and the black smoke. Now a worked storm." She listened and realized that the storm had already blown over.

"Odd, odd." Katrina shook her head. "Let's try to scry now. Maybe if we join our powers, we can begin to figure out what's going on. It doesn't seem like we can afford to wait until tomorrow."

Morgan glanced at the clock. It was almost six, but when Moira was with Ian, time seemed to have no meaning. She nodded.

Morgan generally scryed with fire, which spoke the truth and could be very powerful, but often showed only what it wanted you to see. Colm had only rarely scried—it didn't work well for him. Some people used water or stone. Hunter had used stone. It was difficult and gave up its knowledge only reluctantly, but what it told you could be relied upon.

Morgan fetched a short pillar candle from her workroom. It was a deep cream color, and Morgan had carved runes into it and laid spells upon it to help clarify its visions.

Morgan set the candle in the center of the table, dimmed the room's lights, and sat down across from Katrina. They linked hands across the table.

"Goddess, we call on thee to help us see what we should know," Morgan said. "We open ourselves to the knowledge of the universe. Please help us receive your messages. Someone is working against us—please show us their face and their reasoning."

"We ask it in the name of goodness," Katrina murmured.

Morgan looked at the candle's blackened, curled wick. *Fire,* she thought, and pictured the first spark igniting. With a tiny crackle the wick burst into flame, coiling more tightly in the fire's heat. A thin spire of joy rose steadily in Morgan's chest: magick. It was the life force inside her.

Breathe in, breathe out. Relax each muscle. Relax your eyelids, your hands, your calves, your spine. Release everything. Release tension, release emotion of all kinds. Release your tenacious grip on this world, this time, to free yourself to receive information from all worlds, from all times.

Scrying was a journey taken within. The fire called to her, beckoned. The candle released a slow, steady scent of beeswax and heat. *Show me,* Morgan whispered silently. *Show me.*

A tannish blotch formed before her, blotting out some of the candle's light. Morgan squinted, and the splotch widened and narrowed. It looked like a . . . beach. The image pulled back a bit, and Morgan could see a thin rim of blue-green water, cloudy and cold-looking, pelted by rain, crashing against the narrow spit of sand that flowed horizontally across her vision. The coastline was dotted with gray-blue rocks, pebbles, boulders, thick, sharp shards of shale pushing upward through the beach, thrust there by some prehistoric earthquake, now clawing the sky like clumsy fingers of stone.

A beach. A beach with cold gray water and stones. Where was it? It was impossible to say. But there was no southern sunshine, no pure white sand, no clear water showing rays and corals. It was a northern beach, maybe at the top of Ireland or off the coast of Scotland?

A dim, slight figure started wandering toward the water. Morgan knew better than to look directly at it: like many optical illusions, if you stared straight at a vision, it often disappeared. She kept her gaze focused on the center, feeling the slight warmth of the candle on her face. The figure became clearer. It, too, was the color of bleached sand, tan and cream, and it had splotches of crimson on its chest, the top of its head. It was tall, thin, and it was staggering. A man.

Breathe in, breathe out. Expect nothing: accept what comes. Show me.

The man approached the water, then dropped to his hands and knees, his head hanging low. *Who?* Morgan didn't ask the question, just let the word float gently out of her consciousness. Soon the figure seemed larger, closer. Morgan tried not to look, tried only to see without looking.

The man raised his head and looked into Morgan's eyes, and her heart stopped with one last, icy beat.

Hunter.

A much older, ragged Hunter. His hair was long and wispy and so was his darker beard. His eyes were dark, haunted, like an animal's, full of pain. His rag of a shirt was tannish, the color of the beach, except for a rust-colored stain sprayed across the chest—blood. His head, too, was marked with blood, old blood, from an old wound, and in that instant Morgan saw in her mind a jagged chunk of shale clipping Hunter across the head, leaving that blood, that wound. Scents rushed toward her: the bitter saltiness of the waves, the coldness of the wind, the metallic tang of blood, the heat of Hunter's skin. Seaweed, wet stone. Illness.

I can't breathe, Morgan thought, shock actually making her feel faint. As she stared, jaw clenched, the image of Hunter faded slowly. She gulped convulsively, trying to get air to her lungs. It was all she could do not to scream, *Bring him back!* But another image slid forward: a woman. She was dark, the light was behind her, and though Morgan peered desperately, she could make out no details. It was a woman, standing before a huge fire that was spitting and smoking into the air. The woman raised her hand, and in it was an athame. In her other hand she held a writhing black snake, its triangular head whipping back and forth as it tried to bite her. Morgan winced as the woman brought athame and snake together, and then she threw the serpent into the fire.

A huge, stinking cloud of smoke rose up, billowed over, and filled the cave. Cave? The smoke roiled poisonously and blotted out the woman's image. Morgan recoiled.

Suddenly the front door burst open and Moira rushed in. "Mum!" she cried. "Mum!"

Startled, Morgan dropped Katrina's hands and pulled back. A gust of cold, wet air swirled in and doused the scrying candle. Morgan blinked, trying to make sense of reality. She'd just seen *Hunter*. Had Katrina seen him, too?

Moira was there, followed by Ian Delaney, followed by . . . Killian?

"Mum!" Moira cried again.

Morgan's brain wasn't functioning properly. Katrina was blinking, too, obviously shaken by what they had seen. Morgan felt her heart slowly begin to thud.

"Honey, what is it?" she managed, her voice a croak.

Moira motioned back over her shoulder to Killian. "Mum, who was your dad? Your real father. Wasn't it Angus?"

Oh, no. Not this, not yet. She'd known this was coming—Moira was reading her Books of Shadows. And perhaps it should have come a long time ago. But right now, on top of everything else, it just felt like too much. Morgan's shoulders tensed as she looked at Killian. He shrugged again, an unrepentant look on his face. *If you can't tell your own daughter the truth* . . . he seemed to say.

"It's . . . it's complicated," Morgan said lamely.

Moira's eyes widened, and she gestured to Killian. "So you *know* him?" Obviously she hoped that Morgan would deny all knowledge of him, but it was too late for that.

"Yes," Morgan said, wishing with all she had that this

wasn't how Moira was finding out. "He's my half brother. Killian, come in."

Killian stood a moment, glancing back and forth between Morgan and Moira. "Cute cottage you've got here," he finally said, a bit awkwardly, and then came over and sat at the table. "Is that tea?"

"Yes," Morgan said. "Moira, why don't you sit down, too." She looked over at where Ian was standing, just inside the door. "Ian, I'm sorry—this is kind of a bad time for us."

"I understand," he said, and he went up a notch in Morgan's opinion. He looked like a nice kid. Unfortunately, so had Cal. Ian squeezed Moira's hand, and she let him out the front door. Once he was gone, Morgan pulled out a chair for Moira, who sat down reluctantly.

"I'm so sorry, Moira," Morgan said.

Moira looked from Killian to her mother, her face pale. "I met him in the village," she said. "He says he's your half brother. He says Ciaran MacEwan was your father. Your father! What is he talking about?"

Morgan took a deep breath. Colm, be with me, she thought.

"You know that I was sixteen when I first found out I was adopted," she began. "I've told you about how shocking it was, how weird it made things in my family. And over the next several months I found out more about my birth mother, Maeve Riordan, and Angus Bramson."

"You've told me all this," Moira said. She picked up a paper napkin and twisted it in her hands.

"Later that same fall I discovered that Angus wasn't actually my real father," Morgan went on. She looked at Katrina, who shook her head sadly. "I found out that in fact another witch, Ciaran MacEwan, had had an affair with Maeve, and that was when she got pregnant with me. They were *mùirn beatha dàns*, but Ciaran was already married—they couldn't be together. I know Maeve loved him very much." Morgan refused to look at Killian, who was sitting quietly.

"And I think in his own way, he loved Maeve," Morgan went on. "But as I said, he was married, and he already had three children. Killian was his youngest child. I met Killian a long time ago, in New York, and we realized we were half siblings. Since then he and I have kept in touch."

Moira looked stunned and angry. "Ciaran MacEwan! One of the most evil witches in history was your father!" She looked at Killian. "You don't care?"

Killian shook his head slowly. "I wish many things had been different, lass," he said seriously. "I wish Ciaran had not been evil. I wish my parents had loved each other, I wish my dad had been different, I wish my mother could have done better for herself. But it's not Morgan's fault for having been born, and it's not my place to judge anyone. None of us are without stains. I'm happy to have Morgan for a half sister, no matter how we happened to get here."

It was times like these that made up for all the times Killian drove Morgan crazy. As close as she had always been to her sister, Mary K., she was still happy to have a sibling with whom she shared a blood bond. She smiled at him sadly, her half brother.

"But Ciaran MacEwan." The horror in Moira's voice was an eerie echo of Morgan's own reaction, so many years ago, to the revelation about her relation to Ciaran. Moira's napkin was in shreds and she started tapping her fingers nervously on a fork. "Did you ever meet him?"

"Yes," Morgan said. "I did. He was . . . already dark by then. He knew I was his daughter. He wanted me to join him, but I wouldn't. So he tried to kill me and take my powers. But all the same, in his own way, I know he loved me. He was proud of me. He saw something of himself in me."

"Goddess, I hope not!" Moira said.

"It's true," Killian said. "Not that your mum is evil, not at all. But of all of his children, Morgan inherited Da's greatness, his strength, and his ruthlessness. Your mum can be very ruthless." He smiled as he said it, and Morgan knew he didn't consider it an insult.

"Did Ciaran know about you before Maeve died?" Moira asked.

Morgan shook her head. "No. She had me and gave me up for adoption because she didn't want Ciaran to know. But he still came for her, and when she refused to be with him, because he was married and she was with Angus, he locked her and Angus in a barn and set it on fire." How bizarre to state the facts so calmly, Morgan thought.

Moira's eyes were huge and round. "Goddess," she whispered. "He killed them?"

"Yes." Morgan felt a familiar sadness. "He loved her so much, and he killed her. And he loved me and tried to kill me. And I loved him, and in the end I trapped him and bound him so his powers could be stripped. And he died because of it."

"You trapped him and bound his powers?" Moira whispered. "You bound Ciaran MacEwan?"

Morgan nodded, looking down at the table. "And he had

his powers stripped. And he was never the same after that, and he hated me for it. And then he died." She swallowed hard and felt that Killian was feeling the same ache.

"And Ciaran is part of you, and you're part of me. . . ." Moira trailed off, her eyes full of anguish and confusion. Morgan felt herself being torn apart all over again, watching her daughter suffer the same shock and betrayal she had once experienced. Only it was even worse this time, because Morgan would have taken on a world of pain to spare her daughter an ounce.

"I'm so sorry," Morgan said again, her voice cracking. "I should have told you earlier. It's just—I remember how horrified I was when I realized who my father had been. I would have given anything for it not to be true. And—for you not to have to live with that knowledge as well."

"So Ciaran loved your mum and then killed her, and Ciaran loved you and tried to kill you, and then you bound him and had his powers stripped." Moira shook her head. "And this is my family," she murmured. "This is who you are—who I am."

Morgan jumped up and went to Moira, gripping her shoulders firmly and looking deep into her eyes. "There's more to your family than that," she said. "Maeve was a good, strong witch. She didn't know Ciaran was married when she got involved with him. She loved me so much, she gave me away rather than see harm come to me. You have your gran and Poppy and Nana. You had your dad. I loved your dad, and he loved me, and it was good. Good and safe and true."

"Gran—did you know all this, all about Mum's past?" Moira's voice trembled.

Katrina nodded evenly. "As Killian said, it isn't Morgan's

fault who her parents were and what they did. Morgan is a good witch and a good person. The best daughter-in-law one could hope for. One's heritage is important, but one's own choices are more so. Morgan's got nothing to be ashamed of, and neither have you."

Moira just sat and stared at Morgan. "If you've got noth-ing to be ashamed of," she said, "why haven't you told me any of this? Why am I finding out about it from strangers in tea shops? How could you have lied to me all this time? What's next?" She looked away. "I don't know who you are anymore," she told Morgan, and Morgan felt tears come to her eyes. "I—I need some air." She strode to the front door and pulled it open, pushing through it into the night outside.

"Moira, wait!" Morgan cried, immediately heading after her.

Katrina stopped her, holding her by the shoulders, as Morgan had just held Moira. Morgan started crying, hanging her head. "I'll go after her," Katrina said. "You're both too upset. You stay here. We'll be back soon." She moved toward the door, her arthritis making her limp slightly.

"No, she's my daughter. I need to go," Morgan insisted.

Katrina fixed Morgan with a calm, steady gaze. "If you want what's best for her, you'll let me go," she said. "Moira needs a bit of space right now if she's going to come back to you. Do you understand?"

It went against her every instinct not to go after Moira herself, but Katrina was right—Moira didn't want to see her right now, and if Morgan chased her, Moira would keep run-ning. There was too much danger out there now, danger Morgan didn't yet understand. Moira trusted her grand-mother, and Morgan would have to do the same.

"Just . . . keep her safe," Morgan told Katrina.

Katrina nodded and headed out.

When the door closed behind her, Morgan sat down weakly. She wiped a napkin across her eyes, then dropped her head into her hands. "How many stupid mistakes can I make with her?"

"Quite a few, I should imagine," Killian said, not unkindly. "You'll see . . . things will be all right in the end."

If only things were that easy, Morgan thought dully.

9

Moira

Once outside, Moira stared around blankly, realizing there wasn't really anywhere to go. She had no car, and Vita and Tess both lived a good distance away.

The front door opened, and Gran came out. She walked over to Moira, limping slightly, and Moira realized that her grandmother was getting older. In fact, she'd seemed a lot older since Dad had died.

"Come sit here with me," Katrina said, patting the small iron bench that stood next to the front gate. Moira paused, then sat. Everything was wet out here from the rain, but neither of them said anything about their pants getting soaked.

"Did Dad know?" Moira asked. "About . . . about Mum's family?"

Gran smiled at her kindly. "Yes, your dad knew," she said. "He loved Morgan for who she is, not for who her people were. Tell me . . . what would you think of someone who married a man just because his family was rich and powerful and she was poor? She didn't love him, she just loved who his people were, what he had."

"I'd think she was awful," Moira said, frowning.

"What about the opposite, to *not* marry someone just because their people weren't who you wanted them to be? To think that someone's family is beneath them, not good enough?"

Moira sighed. "That's not good either, I guess."

"Morgan is Morgan," her gran said. "We searched her out years ago because she was Maeve's daughter, a Riordan, and we hoped she'd have the Riordan powers. But if she hadn't been a good person, we never would have invited her to help us rebuild Belwicket, no matter how powerful she was."

"But she's been lying to me all these years," Moira said, her feelings still raw and hurt. "Or at least not bothering to tell me the truth."

"You don't have to know every detail of your mother's past," Gran said reasonably. "No child does. It's your mother's job to love you and try to do the best she can to bring you up well. She isn't obligated to tell you every secret and make sure it's fine with you. All she can do is her best. If she makes mistakes, well, everyone does."

"But not everyone has *Ciaran MacEwan* for a father," Moira cried. "He's my grandfather! How am I supposed to live with that? What will people think about me when they find out?" A terrible thought occurred to her. "Oh, Goddess—tell me no one else knows about this. Does anyone in the village know?"

"Some of the coven. I'm sure others as well," Katrina said gently.

Moira moaned and put her face in her hands. "I'm Ciaran's granddaughter. I have his blood. What does that mean?"

"It means you face choices every day, like everyone else," Katrina said. "You will have to choose goodness over and over again your whole life. And you'd have to do that even if all your relatives were saints who had led blameless lives."

"When you first met Mum, did you know who she was?"

"Yes, of course. I sought her out, remember? When I found out a child of Maeve's existed, I learned all I could about her. I knew about Ciaran and everything else. When I met Morgan, I knew she was for Belwicket."

"You didn't mind her marrying Dad?"

"Heavens, no." Katrina paused for a moment, thinking. "I was thankful when she agreed to marry Colm, grateful that she would stay among us and help bring Belwicket back up to speed. I was grateful I was able to help her."

"Help her?" Moira looked at her gran. "How did you help her?"

"Your mum went through a bad time," Gran said, weighing her words carefully. "A friend of hers had died in an accident, and she was very, very upset. She'd already done so much to invigorate Belwicket. I knew that with her strength and positive energy, our coven could be strong once again. We could triumph over those who'd tried to destroy us. We needed Morgan, and she helped us." Gran paused and looked down. "So when I could help her, I was happy to smooth her troubles away," she said softly. "To help her adjust to her new life."

Something feels off. Gran's uncomfortable. Moira'd had no idea that her mum had ever gone through a "bad time" and that she'd had troubles. "What kind of troubles?" she asked, intrigued. "How could you smooth them away?"

Katrina frowned, as though she regretted saying anything. "Sadness. Troubles from her life before. We all loved her so much and wanted her to be able to heal. Our love did a lot to smooth the way for her here." She stood up, slowly straightening. "The important thing is not to judge your mother, love. Try not to judge anyone. You can never know what causes another person to act, can never tell how true their motivations are. Now, I'm going in to help your mum get dinner together. Looks like Killian will be staying for it. You come in when you're ready, but don't stay out too long—your mother is quite worried about you. All right?"

"All right." Moira sat on the wet bench for a minute after her grandmother had gone inside. She couldn't shake the feeling that Gran had been keeping something back, something major. Had Mum had a nervous breakdown? Had she been in trouble with the police? Moira couldn't believe that. Had it had something to do with Ciaran? Who was the friend who'd died? She had so many questions and no answers.

Moira sighed, smelling the dampness from her storm still on the grass, her mother's herbs, the stones. She'd felt so happy with Ian today. He made her feel as though she could do anything. He thought she was amazing. If only she could see him now—feel his arms around her, hear his soothing voice. It would be so comforting, so wonderful. It would help soothe this awful pain she had inside.

She knew where he lived—across the headland, around the curve of the coast, maybe three miles away. Moira glanced at the living room window. Killian was sitting at the table. Her mum was getting out plates. Gran was slicing bread. When they realized she was missing, Mum would scry to find her. But she might still have enough time to see him. Just for two minutes. Two minutes with him would feel so perfect.

After another quick glance through the window, Moira got her bike from around the back and silently wheeled it through the garden gate.

Moira had never been to Ian's house before, but she knew which one it was. He lived in the next village over, Hewick, and once Mum had taken some herbs to a friend who lived not far from Ian. She'd pointed out Lilith Delaney's cottage.

It was dark, going across the headland. There was no road here, only a rough, rutted trail that farmers used to move their sheep. The headlamp on her bicycle made a pale beam that bobbed every time she hit a pebble. Of course, Moira had magesight. Not as much as she would have after she was initiated, but she could see enough so that she could just manage to avoid killing herself by hitting big rocks or running off the road into a ditch.

Though Ian's house wasn't far, it took Moira much longer to get there than she had expected. Once she had pulled up outside the cottage's fence, she had a wave of second thoughts. This was stupid, to show up uninvited. Mum couldn't stand Lilith Delaney—Lilith couldn't stand her mum, either. And there was still the question of the black smoke from Saturday night. What if her mother was right about Lilith having been behind that? Even if Moira was right about Ian, that didn't mean his mum was good as well. And no one knew she was here. She thought for a second about sending her mum a witch message, then thought better of it. She'd just ride home.

Quickly Moira swung her leg back over the seat of her bicycle and was about to set off when the door of the cottage opened. A rectangle of light splashed onto the lawn, and then Ian's voice called, "Moira?"

Moira winced. The first thing she would do after she had been initiated would be to learn a complete disappearing spell. What was the point of being a witch if you couldn't get yourself out of stupid, possibly even scary situations like this?

"Hi," she said lamely, getting back off her bike. "I was just out, and—"

"You're upset," Ian said. "What happened after I left? Can you come in and tell me about it?"

Moira paused, torn. Something was pulling her toward Ian—she'd come here even knowing deep down that it could be dangerous. *Witches are supposed to trust their instincts, right?* Anyway, if Ian or his mom *were* going to hurt her, they could do it now whether she came into the house or not. With a sigh Moira opened their garden gate and met Ian on the walk. "It was pretty horrible," she admitted. "I needed to get out of there for a while."

Ian smiled at her. "I'm glad you're here. I'm so glad you thought I could help." He put his arms around her and held her tightly, stroking her hair and resting his head against hers.

Moira's heart melted. Her hair and jacket were frosted with mist, but now that he was holding her, warming her, giving her all the support and comfort she had desperately needed, she barely felt the chill. It had been right for her to come here.

He released her and looked into her eyes to see how she was doing. She managed a tremulous smile, and they started toward the house. As soon as Moira crossed the threshold, she smelled slightly bitter and burned herbs. Several things caught her eye at once: the glass-fronted bookcase filled with ancient-looking leather-bound books, used candles, crumpled silk shawls, and incense bowls; a ragged, red velvet couch, pushed beneath the set of windows, their panes clouded and in need of washing; and then, to her left, an open archway leading into what had once been the dining room.

Most witches Moira knew kept their houses soothing and restful, with things put away and kept clean. This much disorder was unusual, and Moira felt the back of her neck prickle. Through the archway she finally noticed that Lilith was working at the table in there, looking into a large chunk of crystal propped up against an old book. *She's scrying.* Automatically Moira looked at the crystal. In its mottled, flawed surface Moira saw an image of a man. It was quite clear: he was middle-aged, with long, light hair and a scraggly beard. He was wearing rags, like a homeless person, and his skin was sunburned and deeply etched with wrinkles.

In the next second Lilith looked up, saw Moira, and passed her hand over the crystal. The image winked out. Moira remembered her mum talking about Lilith using dark magick and wondered what she'd been doing. It had looked like ordinary scrying, but she couldn't be sure.

Then, aware that she was meeting Ian's mother for the first time, Moira managed a shy smile. "I'm sorry," she said. "I didn't mean to disturb you."

Ian's mother came over, wiping her hands on an age-worn housekeeping apron.

"Mum, this is Moira," said Ian, coming over to stand beside her. "I told you about her. From school."

"Oh, yes," said his mother. "It's Moira Byrne, isn't it?"

"Yes," said Moira. So Ian had told his mum about her. That was either a really good sign—meaning he liked her— or a bad sign, if her mother was right that this was all part of some kind of plan.

"Welcome," said Lilith. "I'm so glad to meet you. Ian's mentioned you to me, so you must be special." She smiled, and Moira smiled back, feeling an odd sensation and not recognizing what it was. It felt as if she were in the woods and had suddenly come across an animal or an insect she didn't know: a slight twinge of fear, but also curiosity.

"What brings you out at night like this?" Lilith asked. She moved through the living room and went into the kitchen, which was through another set of doors. Their house was a good bit bigger than Moira's, but not as neat or cozy. Just big, neglected, and cluttered. Moira wondered what Ian thought about it.

"Oh, just wanted some fresh air," Moira said as Lilith put the kettle on the stove. She was surprised by how uncomfortable she was. This kitchen was a disaster, and Moira blinked at Lilith's obvious flouting of witchy habits. Her mum's kitchen was tiny but usually scrubbed clean, things put away, fresh fruit and vegetables in bowls. This kitchen was the opposite. It could have been such a nice room, large, with big windows. But there were unwashed dishes stacked everywhere, cooking pots with remains of meals from who knew how long ago, bunches of wilted herbs or vegetables lying around. Moira half expected to see a mouse sitting boldly on a counter, eating a piece of dried cheese.

Ian, too, seemed to be becoming less comfortable. "Mum, I'll do that," he said, taking some tea mugs from the cupboard. "We don't want to interrupt you."

Lilith stopped and gave her son an appraising glance. Moira couldn't tell if she was angry or hurt, but she again wished she hadn't come here uninvited.

Ian looked back at his mother steadily, and finally, with a somewhat brittle smile, she nodded good-bye to Moira and walked out of the kitchen. Ian stood silently for a moment; then the kettle hissed and he turned off the gas beneath it.

"I'm sorry, Ian," Moira said in a near whisper. "I didn't mean to barge in like this. I was so upset and just wanted to see you. I didn't mean to cause any trouble." At that moment Moira got a sudden, odd feeling, as if someone had just taken her picture. She looked around, but she and Ian were alone. Then she realized her mum was scrying for her and knew she was at Ian's. Trouble was coming. Well, as long as she was already caught, there was no use in rushing home now.

Ian got out a couple of tea bags and plopped one in each mug. "I'm *glad* you came to see me. You haven't caused any trouble," he said in a normal tone. "That's just my mom. There's just the two of us, and we don't see eye to eye about a lot of stuff." He filled the mugs with hot water and handed one to Moira. "Like this kitchen, for example. All I want to do is turn seventeen so I can get my own flat and have a decent place. All this mess makes me insane. Every once in a while I lose it and clean everything up, and then we have a big row. Mum doesn't see what the big deal is. I don't care who cleans up as long as one of us does. But she won't, and she hates it when I do, so I'm stuck."

"What about your dad?"

Ian's expression darkened. "They broke up a long time ago."

"Do you ever see him?"

Ian shook his head slowly. "Nah. Not in a couple of years. We moved here, and he didn't seem too interested in keeping in touch. I think he has a new family now."

Moira blinked. Odd—that sounded a lot like what she'd

read about Cal in her mum's Book of Shadows. But still, plenty of people had divorced parents and didn't see their dads much. It didn't mean anything.

"I'm sorry," Moira said. "It's different, I know, but I do know what it's like to lose your da." Moira sipped her tea, wondering if she should just say what had driven her here in the first place. After all, according to Katrina, people knew the truth anyway, so it wasn't like she was revealing some big secret. No, the only person it had been a secret from was *her*, the one person who deserved to know. She looked up and saw Ian looking at her, concerned.

"Are you all right?" he asked.

"Ciaran MacEwan really was my grandfather," she blurted. "Mum told me everything after you left. It was all true. I feel like I'm, well, *destined* to be bad."

Ian made a sympathetic face. "Even if Ciaran was your grandfather," he said, "that doesn't change anything about you—you never even knew him, and he's gone now."

"But my mum let me believe someone else was my grandfather my whole life," Moira went on. "I feel like I don't even know her anymore. Like I hardly even know myself. Yesterday I was Moira Byrne. Today I'm Moira Byrne, granddaughter of Ciaran MacEwan. How am I going to face anyone?"

"Look . . . I know, and I don't care," Ian said seriously, taking her hand. Moira felt her breath quicken and a tingle of awareness start at the bottom of her spine. "Anyone who thinks it's a big deal, just ignore them. And that's whether they think it's good *or* bad."

"What do you mean, *good*? How could anyone possibly think it's *good*?"

Ian looked at her.

"Oh."

Dark witches. They'd be happy to find the granddaughter of Ciaran MacEwan. Without thinking, Moira glanced at the doorway, wondering if Lilith was out there. Had Ian known all along about Ciaran? Had Lilith?

Moira sighed and rubbed her forehead. "I'd better go. They were starting dinner when I left." *And my mum might be barreling down the road right now in her rusty old banger.*

She put her mug down and left the kitchen. She looked over into the dining room as she passed by, where Lilith Delaney was still working, small, half-moon glasses perched on her nose.

"Good night, Moira," Lilith said evenly.

Had she heard what Moira had been saying to Ian? There was no way to know. "Good night, Ms. Delaney," said Moira, trying to smile normally.

Ian walked her outside. The mist had let up; some of the clouds had cleared away and the stars were beginning to assert themselves again. Most of the moon was visible, and it laid a cream-colored wash of light over the landscape. Going home would be much easier than coming.

"Thanks, Ian," Moira said. "Sorry again to barge in on you."

"Please stop apologizing," he said. "I always want you to come to me if you need help. About anything." He looked awkward for a moment, then said, "I wish I had a better place for you to come to."

Her heart went out to him. "Nobody's perfect," she said, putting her hand on his arm. "There's always something wrong with everyone's parents or house or whatever."

"Yeah. I just can't wait to be on my own."

Moira looked into his blue eyes, lighter than the night sky, and saw his impatience. He wasn't like Cal. It was so clear. *I wish he would kiss me*. And then suddenly he was, leaning over and blotting out the moon. His lips on hers were soft but exploring, as if he was trying to memorize everything about her. She put her arms around his shoulders, excitement coiling in her chest, and wished ludicrously that her stupid bike wasn't between them.

Ian slanted his head slightly and put his hands on her waist. The pedal of her bike was digging into her shin, but she ignored it. Could she just break the kiss, step around the bike, and grab him again?

Then he was drawing back, his eyes glittering. "Move your bike," he said intently, and quickly she stepped around the bike, letting it fall to the soft, muddy grass. Then they were pressed together tightly, and Ian's hand was holding the back of her neck so he could kiss her. They seemed perfectly matched, their hips pressed together, their mouths slanting against each other, their arms wrapped around each other as if they were trying to meld.

She thought she might love him.

10

Morgan

Morgan thought she was going to explode. First she and Katrina had seen Hunter when they scried. Since Killian was there, they hadn't had a chance to talk about it alone. And when she hadn't been able to sense Moira outside, she'd scried for her and found her at Ian Delaney's house. Morgan had to find her, talk to her, tell her how sorry she was. She sent her a quick witch message. *Moira, please come home. Please—or I will have to come and get you.*

I'm on my way, Moira sent back, and Morgan almost sobbed in relief.

"Moira's coming back," she told Killian and Katrina.

"Oh, good. She'll be all right, you'll see," said Killian. "You'll make up."

Morgan smiled gratefully at her half brother, who'd grown up virtually without a father himself. Now Killian had three children of his own. He seemed more thoughtful, less self-centered. He stood, clearing the table, while Morgan just sat, her stomach knotting with tension.

Just then she felt Moira coming up the front path. Leaping from the table, she ran to the front door just as Moira reached it. As soon as she saw her daughter, she burst into tears and gathered her close. *Please don't push me away.* At first Moira stood stiffly in her embrace, but she slowly loosened up and gradually put her arms around Morgan.

"I'm sorry, honey," Morgan said. "I'm so sorry. I never meant to hurt you."

"I wish . . . I wish you had just told me the truth," Moira said.

"I know. I wish I had, too." Morgan pulled back and looked at Moira, brushing some damp hair out of her face. "But you're my family, and I'm yours. And that's all that matters."

Looking a little teary-eyed herself, Moira nodded.

Morgan started to draw her into the warmth and light of the house, but Moira paused, looking at the walk.

"I stepped on something," she said.

"A stone?"

"No." Moira looked, then leaned over and picked up something shiny from the brick path. "Here," she said, handing it to Morgan. "Did you drop this?"

Squinting, Morgan turned sideways in the door so the inside light would fall on her palm. Small, silver, a bit crusty but still glinting. She brushed some of the dirt away as Moira eased past her into the house.

It was a ring—who could have dropped it? She brushed more of the dirt away. Keady, maybe? Katrina? *Oh, Goddess.*

Morgan's heart clenched, and she wondered if she were dreaming again. It was a silver claddagh ring. They weren't uncommon in Ireland—many people wore them. But no one had one with the rune Beorc, for new beginnings, engraved on the inside. This was Morgan's ring, the one Hunter had given her a lifetime ago. This was the ring that had flown off her finger that day in Wales, when the ferry went down. And now here it was, appearing on her doorstop an hour after she'd seen Hunter.

Her eyes huge, Morgan stared at Moira. There were no words to describe what she was feeling, the emotions she was being assaulted with. She was losing her mind—she felt like she was about to collapse right there, in front of all of them. Who was doing this to her? Making her heart break all over again, when it had broken so many times already?

"Is it yours?" Moira asked. "Do you recognize it?"

Morgan managed a nod. The room swam around her; her breath came shallowly.

"Mum? You don't . . . feel right." Moira sounded worried. "Maybe you should sit down."

Morgan couldn't move until Moira took her elbow and led her to a dining chair. Her ring. It had fallen into the sea, with Hunter, her love. It had been torn away from her, wrenched away just as Hunter had been. How had the ring come back here? Only Sky, Bree, and Mary K. knew how she had lost it. Goddess, why was Hunter suddenly everywhere in her life, when he'd been taken from her so many years ago? The pain was too much, too much to bear.

Someone had deliberately put the ring there for her to find. Like the morganite. And it didn't make sense that it was Lilith—this had to be someone close to Morgan. Someone who knew her well. And the ring and the morganite, the vision and the dream, the scrying—they were all pieces of a puzzle, a horrible maze closing around her, scaring her, trying to drive her mad. *I'm under siege. Goddess, I'm in danger. And Hunter—my Hunter—is the weapon.*

"Mum, what's wrong?" Moira looked frightened. "What is it? The ring? Mum, you're scaring me!"

Morgan had no idea where to begin. Goddess, she didn't know if she could handle this. How many secrets had she kept from her daughter? Cal and Selene. Ciaran. Now Hunter? How many huge confidences could Moira handle in one week? How many more could Morgan handle? It was as if the whole tapestry of her life with Moira was becoming unraveled and not slowly, thread by thread—it was being torn, rent into pieces, and the ripping was painful and unexpected, leaving Morgan bare and vulnerable.

Her ring. She slid it onto the ring finger of her right hand. It fit perfectly, the silver warming instantly to the temperature of her blood. Her ring.

"Morgan . . ." Killian looked at her with concern. "Are you all right?"

"Thank you," Morgan said, speaking as if from a great distance. "I think so."

"Perhaps we should give Morgan some time," Katrina suggested gently. "Maybe you want to return to your lodgings, Killian?"

"If you're quite sure," he said, looking at Morgan.

She nodded. "Yes, I think . . . that might be best," she said, her voice strained.

"Well, then, I'll bid you all good night," he said, standing up. "I'm staying at Armistead's if you need me. Don't hesitate to call."

"Thank you." Morgan spoke automatically.

He leaned over and pecked Moira on the cheek. "I'm glad I met you," he said. Then he and Morgan kissed each other's cheeks, and he let himself out.

"Mum, you look like you've seen a ghost," Moira said. "Are you going to tell me what is going on?"

Morgan was reluctant to speak in front of Katrina. Katrina knew all about Hunter, of course. But this was a moment that needed to happen between just mother and daughter, in private. She glanced at her mother-in-law.

As if divining her thoughts, Katrina stood. "I'd best be off," she said. "Didn't mean to stay so late."

"Let me give you a ride home—it's late," Morgan said, walking Katrina to the door.

"No, lass." Katrina shook her head. "The walk is good for me. You are needed here."

At the door Katrina paused, looking into Morgan's face. "It was Hunter we saw, wasn't it?" she said, glancing back to see if Moira could hear their conversation. "What do you make of it?"

"Yes, it was. I don't know what to make of anything anymore," Morgan said, feeling lost in a way that she hadn't felt since Colm had died.

"Call me if you want to talk," Katrina said, and Morgan nodded. They hugged quickly and Katrina began to walk down the path, her stiff leg making her gait awkward.

"Be safe, be quick, be home in a tick," Morgan murmured automatically. When she turned around, Moira was still sitting at the table, her head in her hands—someone waiting for bad news. She raised her head and glared at Morgan.

"Tell me what's going on," Moira said through clenched teeth.

Morgan sighed. Goddess give her strength. "This ring . . . was given to me by someone I knew before your dad."

Moira sat up straighter, interested. "Someone? Who? Mum, just tell me."

Morgan sat at the table beside Moira. "How far have you gotten in my old Books of Shadows?" she asked.

Moira shrugged. "I've been jumping around," she said.

Morgan nodded. "Well, then, maybe you haven't read much about him yet, or at least about what he ended up meaning to me. Moira, there was someone special to me before your father." She looked into Moira's eyes, unsure of how to go on. "He . . . he was my *mùirn beatha dàn*."

Moira flinched, pain flashing across her face. "Da wasn't?"

Morgan shook her head regretfully. "Your dad and I loved each other very much, but we weren't each other's *mùirn beatha dàns*. His name was Hunter. Hunter Niall. He was the Seeker who was sent after Cal and Selene." She stared at the worn tabletop, lost in the pain of remembering. "How I felt about him was unlike anything I had known. It was how love should be. We were made to be together, two halves of a whole."

Moira looked down at the table, shifting uncomfortably. "I always thought—I mean, that's what you and da seemed like to me."

Morgan's heart squeezed. "Moira, I'm sorry, I know this is hard. . . ."

Moira let out a harsh laugh. "What isn't, lately," she said. She stared out the window, and when she spoke again, her voice was softer. "So what happened?" she asked. "With you and this guy, Hunter?"

Morgan plunged on, just wanting to get everything out in

the open. "Well, for a while it didn't seem like we could be together—I was here in Cobh, with Belwicket, and I felt like I needed to stay here. Hunter was one of the witches who created the New Charter, and he was traveling everywhere. We hardly saw each other. I had decided we had to break up and go our separate ways—"

"Break up with your *mùirn beatha dàn?*" Moira cut in. "That's crazy."

"Yes, well," Morgan said ruefully. "That was his response, too. Instead, he asked me to marry him, to have a handfasting." After so many years, those words still made her lip tremble, and a lump formed in her throat.

Moira turned to her. "What did you say?" she asked breathlessly.

"I said yes, of course." Morgan swallowed. "He was my soul mate. My other half. It was the happiest time of my entire life. All my wishes, all my dreams, my hopes—they were all coming true because Hunter and I would be together. Then the next day he had to go to a meeting of the New Charter. It was going to be his last one—he was going to tell them he had to quit traveling so much. Then he was going to come back and be with me and move to Cobh and we were going to start our lives together."

"Your lives . . . together," Moira echoed, looking slightly ill. "Here in Cobh."

Morgan couldn't imagine what Moira had to be feeling, hearing how different Morgan's vision of her future had once been from how it turned out—how another man had been the one she saw herself living this life with, not Moira's father.

Moira swallowed. "So, what happened?" she asked.

"He got on the early-morning ferry," Morgan said slowly, tracing a rune for strength on the tabletop. The lump in her throat got bigger, and she blinked back tears. She hadn't spoken about that day in many years.

"A storm blew up out of nowhere," she finally got out. "The ferry went down, and nearly twenty people died. Including Hunter."

"Oh, Goddess," Moira breathed.

Morgan nodded sadly, feeling the familiar, heavy weight of grief in her chest. "Some people they managed to save, some bodies they managed to recover. But Hunter and twelve other people were sucked into the sea and never found. Drowned."

"Oh, Mum." Moira's eyes were full of sympathy, along with the pain and confusion. "This ring—" Morgan frowned at it, twisting it on her finger. "Hunter had given me this ring years before we got engaged. Like a promise ring. The day the ferry went down, I waited on the dock all day in the rain. When they finally said there could be no more survivors, I threw my hands out, like this"—she demonstrated, realizing that her hands were trembling—"and all of a sudden this ring flew off my finger and landed in the water. And it *sank*."

Moira frowned. "How can you be sure this is the same ring? Maybe it just looks like yours."

Morgan took it off and showed her the rune. "Beorc. For new beginnings," she explained sadly.

"But there's no way someone could have gotten your ring out of the sea, even if they had jumped right in after it. Much less after all this time. Mum, this doesn't make sense."

"You're right." Morgan met her gaze evenly.

"So where did it come from?"

"I don't know. It has to be part of something bigger. You know things have been off lately. There's . . . there's more that's happened that I haven't told you." Trying to keep her emotions under control, Morgan filled her in on everything: the hex pouch, the morganite, the visions, the dream, seeing Hunter while scrying. "Now I just need to figure out what's going on and why." *Easier said than done.*

For a minute Moira was quiet, her eyes moving back and forth as she worked things out in her head. "Did you . . . did you ever love Dad as much as Hunter?" Her face was pained, and Morgan answered carefully.

"It was different, Moira," she said. "I loved your dad so much. He was the only man I ever lived with. We married, we had you. Those experiences build up to a much richer experience of love. I trusted your dad. I was so grateful for the fact that he loved me, and he was such a good person. I was so grateful he gave you to me. I appreciated so many things about him, and I tried to make sure he knew that. Yes, I loved him. Not the same as I loved Hunter, but I truly loved your father."

Moira thought for a moment. "It . . . it *seemed* real," she said. "Your love for each other, I mean." Her voice had a note of desperation. "I remember how you used to look at him—with love in your eyes. Like when you both teased me." She lifted one of her green strands and let it fall.

Morgan's throat threatened to close. "He was my best friend, sweetie."

"He was my best dad," Moira said, her voice suddenly cracking. Then she and Morgan were hugging, tears running down their faces.

"I'm so glad I still have you," Morgan said. "You're my most precious gift. I hope you know that."

Tearfully Moira nodded.

They held each other for a few minutes, and Morgan never wanted to let go. But eventually Moira pulled back. Morgan looked at her daughter, brushing the hair from her face.

"You should get some sleep," Morgan told her. "It's been a very difficult day—and I don't know what we're up against, but it seems more and more to be something—or someone—major. We'll need our strength."

Moira got up and headed for the stairs. "Thanks for telling me about Hunter," she said, looking back. "But I don't see how anyone found the ring and put it on our walk. I don't understand why someone would do it."

Morgan sighed. "I don't understand either. But I know it doesn't bode well. It feels . . . threatening. But I just don't know what the threat *is*, exactly—or where it's coming from."

"Well, don't worry, Mum," Moira said. "We'll find out."

Morgan smiled at Moira's teenage confidence and watched her daughter climb the narrow stairs.

Holding out her hand, she looked again at the ring, and fresh tears welled up in her eyes. Who was doing this? She needed some answers.

Her workroom was small, maybe nine feet by nine. Colm had built it for her soon after their handfasting. It had two small windows, high up on the walls, and a tiny fireplace all its own. Morgan kindled a fire there, rubbing her arms impatiently as she waited for the chill to lessen. Through one of the high windows Morgan could see the half-moon, partially covered by thick, heavy clouds.

Morgan put on her green silk robe, the one embroidered with runes and sigils, that had been Maeve's, decades ago. She drew three circles of protection on the floor, each one inside the other. Twelve stones of protection marked the twelve points of the compass. Next to the stones she lit twelve red candles for power and protection. Then she sat inside the smallest circle, closed it around her, and lit a red pillar candle in the center.

"I call on the Goddess of knowledge," Morgan said. "I call on my own strength. I call on the universe to aid me in my quest for the truth. I am here, safe within the Goddess's arms. I call on the ancient power leys of Ui Liathain, the power deep within the earth beneath me." She stretched out her arms, symbolically opening herself to knowledge. "Who is focusing on me? Who is sending these objects, these images, these thoughts? What do I need to find? What lesson is here for me, waiting to be revealed? Goddess, I ask you, please help me." Then she sat cross-legged in front of the candle, rested her hands on her knees, palms up, and breathed deeply, in and out. She focused on the small, single flame, the red wax melting, the scent of beeswax and fire and the wood smoke from the fireplace. Concentrating on the flame, she chanted her personal power chant, drawing energy toward her, opening herself to receive it. And she felt it, a bud opening within her, a flower beginning to bloom. Magick was rising and swelling in her chest, accompanied by a fierce joy that Morgan clung to, seized to herself. *Oh, magick.* Sometimes it seemed as if it was the only thing that made life worthwhile. It was a blessing.

Morgan kept her gaze fastened on the candle's flame. In that one flame she could see her whole life and all of life around her. Every memory was there on the surface, every emotion. But it was also like looking down on something from above—there was sometimes a distance that allowed her to see something more clearly, see the bigger picture, put the pieces together.

Now all she asked was, What do I need to know?

And suddenly Hunter was there before her. Morgan gasped, her breath catching in her throat, her skin turning to ice. Hunter was hunched over on a beach. The air was gray and still around him. The clothing he wore was in tatters, barely more than rags, offering grossly inadequate protection from the weather. His arms were burned brown from the sun, the skin freckled and leathery. His hair was much too long, wispy and tangled, with visible knots snarling the once-fine strands.

Morgan trembled. Holding her breath, she forced herself to release tension, but she could already feel the needle-fine threads of adrenaline snaking through her veins. His cheekbones, always prominent, now looked skeletal. The skin on his face had once been beautifully smooth, fine-textured, and pale. Now it was ridged, sunburned, peeling in places. There was an unhealed wound on one cheekbone below his eye. Grains of sand stuck to blood that had only recently dried.

Hunter was writing something in the sand, gibberish, childish doodlings. Morgan expected to see the beginnings of a spell, forms, patterns, something that she could understand, that would give her clues. Instead, she saw formless meanderings, a stick drawn without purpose through the sand.

He looked up and saw her. *Hunter.* Pain clawed at Morgan's consciousness. It was so real, so vivid. If she could only reach out and touch him! His green eyes, once as dark and rich as a forest, now looked bleached by the sun and were surrounded by deep wrinkles. Slowly they widened in astonishment. His mouth opened in shock, then silently formed the word *Morgan*. He shook his head in disbelief. Morgan cried soundlessly at how tight his skin was on his bones. He was starving.

"Hunter." The word was a mere breath from Morgan, a slight release. *Oh, Hunter, where are you? What's happening?* Was it actually possible—could he have somehow survived the accident? What beach was this? The ferry had gone down in a small, populated cove. There was no way he wouldn't have been found.

He shook his head, his odd, pale eyes seeming to drink her in ravenously. *Don't help me.* Morgan heard the words silently in her mind. *Listen to me. You're in danger. Don't find me.*

Are you alive? She sent the words, as if she were sending a simple witch message across time, across death, across worlds. *Are you alive?*

His chapped and peeling lips crinkled in a grotesque mockery of a smile, and he shrugged.

If you are alive, I will find you, Morgan sent, and her power and determination were frightening and inescapable.

No, he sent back. *No. I'm lost, I'm gone forever.*

Hunter's image faded, his eyes too large for his bony face, his mouth forming words Morgan could no longer hear. Then she was alone again in her small workroom, breathing fast and shallowly, her hands trembling, clenching and unclenching. The fire in the hearth had dwindled to embers. The red pillar candle had burned down several inches. When Morgan glanced at the window, the moon was nowhere to be seen.

Had those images been real? Twice she had scried and seen Hunter—first with Katrina and again just now. Had she scried reality or simply what her innermost heart wished most to see—Hunter alive, even under such horrible circumstances? It had *felt* real. Oh, Goddess, what if it were real? What if Hunter were actually alive somewhere?

Slowly she stood and took off her robe, her hands shaking so badly, she could barely put her regular clothes back on.

She couldn't do this—she couldn't let herself believe Hunter was really out there if he wasn't, couldn't go through the pain of learning he was dead all over again. But how could she ignore these messages, coming to her one after the other? She had to know the truth. She would do whatever was in her power—which, if she pushed herself to the limit, would be intense—to find out if Hunter was alive.

Morgan moved numbly upstairs, checking to make sure everything was locked. Finnegan raised his head and growled. Automatically she glanced around: no evil spirits coming down the fireplace, nothing was on fire—then a flash outside caught her eye. In a moment she had cast her senses and picked up on a person outside, walking around the house. The living room was dark; no one could see in. But she could see out, and a tall, thin person with white-blond hair was outside her house.

Her heart stopped. *Hunter.*

Without thinking, Morgan ran to the door and flung it open, Finnegan on her heels. He growled and then barked several times sharply. Morgan stood in her doorway, and at the same moment her inner senses and her eyes informed her of the intruder: Sky Eventide came around the corner of the house just as Morgan identified her energy pattern.

"Sky!"

Sky looked up and gave a slight smile. "Sorry I didn't call first."

Morgan began to breathe again, a rush of emotions overcoming her. It wasn't Hunter. Of course it wasn't Hunter.

She hurried over to Sky, grabbing her arm. "What are you doing here? Why didn't you let me know you were coming?"

Sky shrugged as they headed back to the house. She had left her pack by the front door and scooped it up as they went inside. "I was concerned after our phone call the other night, and decided to come check things out."

"Oh, Sky, I saw Hunter," Morgan blurted. "Twice today. I saw him!"

Sky's night-dark eyes widened. "What do you mean, you *saw* him?"

"I was scrying," Morgan quickly explained. "He was . . . much older, as old as he would be today. He was on a beach, wearing rags, and he was a mess. He was all windburned and battered looking—" Morgan broke off, unable to bear the memory of how haunted Hunter had appeared, how brutalized. "His bones were showing. He was starving," she went on, struggling not to break down. "He seemed to see me, and I said, *Are you alive*, and *I will find you*. And he said, *No, I'm lost, I'm gone forever. You're in danger, don't find me*."

Morgan took a ragged breath. "It seemed so real. It didn't seem like a vision, or a dream, or just a subconscious message. I mean . . . I scried, and I saw Hunter, and he talked to me. And I can't help thinking, Oh, Goddess, what if he is alive somewhere?" It was the first time she'd said it out loud, and a shiver passed through her as the words came out.

"How could he be?" Sky's voice was higher pitched than usual—she was clearly spooked, and Morgan knew that didn't happen easily. "He was on the ferry—people saw him get on it. People saw him in the water. People saw him disappear under the water."

"They never found his body," Morgan reminded her.

"Because he sank, along with the others!" Sky sounded angry, but it seemed as if she was just afraid to hope, like Morgan.

"There's more," Morgan rushed on. She held up her hand and showed Sky the ring Moira had found.

Sky looked at the claddagh ring, not understanding.

"Sky, this is the ring. My ring," Morgan said, her voice shaking slightly. "The ring I lost that day. It went into the sea. Moira found it on my front walk this evening. See the rune?"

"Goddess," Sky breathed. "Moira found this just outside?"

"Sky . . . it means something. All the pieces. The morganite. My visions. My dream. What if he's *alive?*" This time the words came out more forcefully, and Sky met her gaze, no longer arguing.

"The one thing I can't figure out," Morgan said, "is the attack on the coven. The black smoke. And it doesn't feel right here—others have noticed as well. How could there be a connection between Belwicket and Hunter? It doesn't make sense."

"No," Sky said slowly. "Not yet. But what you said, how it doesn't feel right here—I noticed it, too, as soon as I arrived. And listen, Morgan, when's the last time you checked your house for an enemy's marks?"

Morgan sat back, surprised. "Every day since Katrina and I found the hex pouch in the garden. Why?"

"Someone around here is out to harm you."

Morgan swallowed. She'd suspected that much already, but how could Sky seem so certain?

"There are sigils on every windowsill, both door frames, and on top of your garden shed. I found three different pouches, two somewhat serious. I put them in the far corner of your yard—we'll deal with them tomorrow. There's evidence of other things buried in your yard in three different places." She shook her head, her fine, light hair flying.

Morgan's whole body went cold. She and Moira were in danger—more serious danger than she'd even realized. How could she have let things get this far? "How could I have missed the sigils, the pouches?"

"I don't know," Sky said. "I can't believe you and Moira aren't in bed with the flu or broken bones."

"I've been working protection spells regularly since the strange things started happening," Morgan said. "I had no idea those things were out there." She rubbed her forehead. Who could be working against her? *And Hunter, Hunter.* The name was running through her mind in a constant rhythm, a background for anything else she said or thought. *Hunter might be alive. After all these years Hunter could be out there somewhere. Hunter, Hunter.* "How . . . how does this all fit together?" Morgan said, frustrated that she couldn't figure it out.

"I don't know," said Sky. "But if there's even a chance that Hunter's . . ."

"We have to know for sure," Morgan agreed. "We have to find out who is trying to harm me and my family—and we have to find Hunter."

11

Moira

What had Gran been talking about tonight? Moira wondered sleepily as she lay in bed that night. What kind of troubles could she have "smoothed over"? Gran had said a friend of Mum's had died—that must have been Hunter—and Mum had been upset. Gran had smoothed her troubles over. How? Why?

Moira's mind was reeling from so much new information about herself, her mother, her family. Suddenly everything she'd believed about herself, her mum—it was all wrong. She was the granddaughter of one of the most evil witches in generations! His blood ran through her veins, Moira thought, staring down at her wrist. Her stomach contracted as she was overcome by a wave of nausea. How could her mother have kept all of this from her? She didn't even know who her mum *was* anymore. And the one thing that had still been true—the love Mum and Dad had shared, that Moira had seen for herself—even that had been a lie. Colm and Morgan hadn't been each other's *mùirn beatha dàns*.

Moira blinked back tears. How could her dad have borne

knowing he wasn't Morgan's *mùirn beatha dàn*? Moira couldn't imagine being with someone who wasn't hers.

Moira ran over all the stories she'd heard about how her parents had gotten together. Mum had fallen apart after Hunter died. And when she'd fallen apart, Gran had taken care of her, and then Mum had married Dad and they'd had her.

Still trying to sort through it all, Moira drifted off to sleep.

Moira's mother was in labor. Her brown hair, very short, was damp in tendrils around her flushed face. Mum looked very young and wide-eyed. Next to her stood Peggoty MacAdams, the village midwife, and with her June Hightown, another midwife. Peggoty was holding Mum's hand, and June was wiping her forehead with a cloth.

Morgan was breathing hard. Her eyes looked a question at Peggoty.

"It won't be long now, my dear," Peggoty said soothingly. She placed her hand on Morgan's forehead and murmured some gentle spells. Morgan's breathing slowed, and she looked less panicky. June poured some tea, pale green and fragrant, and Morgan gulped it down, wincing at the taste.

Finally Morgan was pushing, her face damp, the muscles in her neck taut and ribboned with effort.

Moira was startled to realize that this was her, being born.

Peggoty said, "Just a bit more, dear, there you go, that's right, and here's her head. . . ."

"Oh, what a lovely baby," Peggoty crooned, scooping up the infant and swathing her in a clean white blanket. "She's a big, fine baby, Morgan. She's beautiful."

"Is she okay?" Morgan asked.

"She looks perfect, just perfect," Peggoty said with approval. "Goodness—she's nine pounds even. A lovely, plump baby."

"Oh, good," Morgan said weakly, her head falling back against the pillows.

Peggoty beamed. "And now I bet the proud papa would like to hold his little girl?"

A man stepped forward hesitantly and held out his arms.

Moira's stomach tightened—it wasn't Colm.

It was a stranger. He was severe-looking, tall and fit, with light hair, the palest blond. He appeared nervous but held out his hands, glancing over at Morgan. She opened her eyes and smiled at him.

With a kind of wonder, the man held baby Moira gingerly, as if she might disappear in a puff of smoke. He looked down into her face, and her eyes opened. The two of them stared at each other solemnly, as if to say, Hello. I belong to you. I will belong to you forever.

With a gasp Moira awoke. Her room was still dark; there was a faint streak of pink coming in at the bottom of her window shade. She was breathing hard and looked around her room to make sure nothing was out of place. Quickly she cast out her senses. Everything was normal. Or about as normal as it could be, given the past few days. Goddess, what a dream. She had seen herself being born. Everything about it had seemed so real, except for her father. Who was that? Why hadn't she dreamed about her dad?

Abruptly Moira sat back in bed, thoughts swirling in her head like leaves in the wind. Goddess, think, think.

Colm was her father. Everyone knew that. But Moira knew her dream meant something. She'd taken a dream interpretation class for her initiation. So what had this dream meant? That Colm hadn't been her father?

Moira sat up again, panicked. No, of course he had been. She would have known. Mum would have known. Surely her mother couldn't have lied about *that*. No. But then what did it mean?

Moira was wide awake. She raised her window shade so the palest light of the new dawn illuminated her room. Then she fetched her parents' Books of Shadows, Colm's and Morgan's, from the year she was born. She had read other Books of Shadows, but not these. Not yet. In Colm's she read about his growing feelings for Morgan, his admiration for her, his combined awe and respect for her "significant" powers. He thought she was beautiful and friendly but not openly interested.

Then she flipped through Morgan's, skimming the pages. She had moved to Cobh. She was growing to love Katrina and Pawel and Susan and all the others. She thought she might want to stay there forever. Except she missed Hunter so much, all the time. Her heart cried out for him. She ached to be with him—nothing was as good, as right, as when they were together.

Moira couldn't help feeling a pang as she read about just how deeply her mother had loved Hunter. Hunter, who wasn't Colm. Some protective instinct made Moira turn back to Colm's Book of Shadows. His job in Cobh was going fine. He was thinking it was time to settle down. He had dated several girls but couldn't get Morgan out of his mind. He knew she was seeing someone else. His feelings for her grew, and he decided he was falling in love with her. Not that it would do him any good. But he thought she was a one-in-a-million woman. Then it happened: he heard from his mother that Morgan had lost someone she loved. She was so upset that she couldn't think straight. She'd been hospitalized in Wales.

Colm traveled there and met Morgan's American parents and sister. Morgan had had a breakdown, and his heart bled for her. In her grief she'd hacked off all her hair, the thick, shiny chestnut hair that had almost reached her waist. Now it was as short as a boy's, but it made her no less beautiful. He loved her so much; if only he could take care of her. It was all he wanted: the chance to take care of her.

On the next page Colm was elated: the unthinkable had happened. Morgan had agreed to become his wife. He knew she was heartbroken, though she wouldn't talk about it. She still seemed very ill, but he was sure she would be fine in time. She just needed warmth and love and care and good food. He knew he could make her happy.

Moira kept skimming the pages. Outside, the sun was just starting to creep over the horizon, mostly covered by clouds. Great. Just what they needed—more rain.

Shortly after their wedding Morgan was pregnant. They hadn't realized it at first because of her illness. Colm was ecstatic. He loved his wife: she seemed healthier and more beautiful every day. Slowly her grief was going under-ground—she had almost smiled the other day.

Moira swallowed hard. It was so sad to read about it— how much her dad had loved Mum, how long it had taken Mum to be able to truly return his affection.

Going back to Morgan's Book of Shadows, Moira read about how Morgan was waiting for Hunter at a tea shop in Wales. There was no entry from later that night, when they had committed to being together. And no more entries for two months. Then a short one, in a weak hand, that acknowledged Morgan's marriage to Colm. And then another, two months after that: Morgan was expecting a baby. She was happy about it—it was a ray of sunlight piercing her gray shadow world. A few words about Colm—how kind he was, how gentle, how Morgan appreciated his care. There was no mention of Hunter, only a sentence about being ill and deciding to stay in Ireland.

And no magick. Before, her entries had been numerous and lengthy—a combination of daily diary, larger, philosophical thoughts, the directions her studies were taking her, spells she had tried and their results, spells she had created, different tinctures and essences she had used and their outcomes, her plans for next year's garden, and so on. But these entries were sparse, bare.

Though Moira looked, she could find no mention of Gran helping Morgan, no mention of smoothing away her troubles. The entries that mentioned her only described her kindness and caring, her constancy, her support. Morgan didn't detail any healing rites, circles held for her benefit, nothing.

Moira flipped ahead, searching for a mention of magick. A week after her birth Morgan had put some protection spells and general good-wishes spells on her new baby.

Hmmm. Something was odd. Moira skipped back and forth, looking from Colm's book to Morgan's, at earlier entries and later ones. The dates in Morgan's were messed up for a while—she simply hadn't put dates in, and it was only by her telling of events, and comparing the entries to Colm's, that Moira was able to figure out when an entry had been made.

Colm had been much steadier—virtually every entry was dated. Moira continued to flip back and forth. Hunter died, Mum got ill, Mum and Dad got married a month later. One month. Pretty fast for someone who had been so in love, for someone not marrying their soul mate. But considering how ill Mum had been, how devastated, maybe she had just really needed someone to take care of her. And from the entries it seemed she really had grown to love Colm.

Then Morgan was expecting a baby, and Moira was born . . . in December, right before Yule. Hunter had died in March. Mum and Dad had gotten married in April. Moira had been born in December. Mum's Book of Shadows mentioned that she and Colm hadn't slept together before their marriage.

So Moira had been premature by one month. A nine-pound preemie. That didn't sound right. She couldn't have weighed nine pounds.

There were sounds from downstairs. Moira realized her mum was awake and getting breakfast, and now that she was paying attention, she realized there was someone else downstairs, too, a woman. Gran? Not Gran.

Quickly Moira threw on her hated school uniform, brushed her hair and her teeth, and headed downstairs, holding the two Books of Shadows.

She froze when she spotted the back of the strange woman's head—she had the same white-blond hair as the man in her dream. Then the woman turned around. "Good morning," she said evenly. "You must be Moira."

"Yes," Moira said. She clutched the books tightly in her hands, her heart pounding.

Morgan turned from the stove. "Morning, sweetie." She looked tired, and there were dark circles under her eyes. She gestured to the woman with a dishcloth. "Moira, this is Sky Eventide. We've been friends a long time. She was Hunter's cousin."

"You were Hunter's cousin?" Moira asked, a funny feeling in her stomach. The same hair as the man in her dream . . .

"Yes," said Sky, her expression guarded. She was unusual, not like Mum's other friends. Not smiling and remarking on how tall she was and asking about school.

"Oh," Moira said inadequately. She sat down at the table and poured some cereal into a bowl, then some milk, but couldn't bring herself to start eating. Her mind was whirling. Finally, keeping her tone as calm as possible, she asked, "Mum, was I born premature?"

Morgan looked surprised. "No . . . in fact, you were late. The midwife said that nature decrees that a woman will be pregnant for exactly as long as she can absolutely bear it . . . and then another two weeks." She rolled her eyes. "Let's just say I was anxious for you to get here."

"And how much did I weigh?" Moira pressed.

"Nine pounds."

Moira's pulse raced. No, no, it couldn't be.

"What's all this about, anyway?" Morgan asked, coming to the table. She moved the teapot closer to Sky, and Sky topped up her mug.

Moira pushed the two Books of Shadows toward her mother. "I was reading these this morning, and there's something—odd. It says that you and Dad got married in April, but I was born in December."

Morgan blinked. "No, that isn't right," she said slowly. She sat back and looked at the ceiling, thinking. "We were married in . . ."

"April," Moira supplied.

Frowning, Morgan nodded. "And you were born December 15."

"Right."

Her mum looked at her, then shook her head. "No, there

has to be some mistake, something wrong with the entries. I
know you weren't premature. Goddess, you were a whale."

Moira just looked at her mother.

"Why were you up this morning so early, anyway?"
Morgan asked.

"I had a strange dream," Moira said. "It woke me, and
once I was up, I . . . I wanted to read these."

"Studying for your initiation, are you?" asked Sky, and
Moira nodded.

"What was your dream about?" Mum asked casually.
Dreams were often discussed in Wiccan households, whether
they were important, funny, meaningful, or frightening.

Don't let this dream mean anything, please, Moira pleaded
inwardly.

"Me being born," Moira said carefully. "Peggoty MacAdams
and June Hightown were there. And they said, doesn't the dad
want to hold her?" She paused, giving her mother a hard look.
"But the dad wasn't Dad. They handed me to someone else."
She turned her gaze to Sky. "He . . . well, he looked . . . like
you. His hair was very light, like yours."

Silence. Moira looked at her mom and felt her heart sink.
Her mother was pale, stricken, her eyes large. Glancing over at
Sky, she saw that the other woman also looked very solemn.

"So I was wondering," Moira went on. The words were so
thick and her mouth so dry, it was a battle to speak. "When I
was born and when you and Dad got married . . ." Her voice
trailed off. "Whether I was premature," she finished softly.

Still no one said anything. Moira looked at her mother
and saw that she and Sky were staring at each other as if the
other one would have all the answers in the world.

Morgan swallowed. "Moira, I know that you are Colm's daughter, Colm's and mine. There's never been the slightest doubt about that. There was never a question." Her mum sounded absolute.

"Must be the dates are off," Sky suggested quietly.

"Yes," Morgan said firmly, standing up. "This is one thing you don't have to worry about, Moira, I promise you. You're definitely Colm's daughter." Her mother kissed her and smiled into her eyes. "I'm sorry. I know you've had a lot of shocks lately. But believe me, you were Colm's daughter and mine, and you made our lives complete. Your dad loved you more than anything. Okay?"

Moira forced a nod, but she felt as if her internal organs were collapsing in on themselves, as if, in moments, she would be a puddle on the floor. Her mother sounded so sure, so confident—but Moira had a terrible, horrifying feeling that she was wrong.

12

Morgan

After Moira left, Morgan sat at the table, her tea getting cold. It was as if someone had taken her life, put it in a kaleidoscope, and given it a quick shake. Everything was skewed, changed, *off*. There were so many questions piling up inside her that soon enough they would start to spill out. Was Hunter really alive? Was he sending her messages from the dead or was someone else? Hunter would never, ever hurt her—that black smoke couldn't have been from him. But it had happened at the same time as all the other signs, so there had to be a connection, didn't there?

And then there was everything Moira had just said. Goddess, was there any possibility that Moira was Hunter's . . .

No, she's Colm's daughter, Morgan told herself. Colm's and mine. Moira's dream . . . it had to mean something else. It had to be connected to all these other strange visions and dreams.

"I know what you're thinking," Sky finally said, breaking the silence that hung between them. "But Morgan, we can't just sit and wait for answers. We have to act. And I think the first thing we need to do is clean up your house. Having all those sigils and hexes around here can't be helping any of us think clearly. They were probably spelled so that *you*—or members of your coven, specifically—couldn't find them, because when *I* looked, they were popping out at me without too much trouble."

"That would make sense," Morgan said. She shook her head. "It's what I would do."

"If you were the type of person who went around spelling people to break their necks," Sky agreed. "Let's sort it all out right now."

"Yes," said Morgan, trying to shake off the weighty grayness that made her shoulders and neck ache. She needed to think clearly. "That would be a start."

Morgan fetched the Riordan athame, the ancient knife carved with generations of her family's initials. When she became high priestess, her initials would be added. She and Sky went outside, and one by one Sky showed her the hexes, spells, and sigils that she'd found sprinkled liberally everywhere. Working with Sky, Morgan passed the athame over the sigils and saw the sigils glow faintly silver or red. It was off alone that she saw nothing, but as she and Sky worked, Morgan began to sense the spells more easily.

"This is unbelievable," Morgan breathed as their number grew. "I just went over the house. I can't believe this is happening." A wave of nausea overcame her, and she had to sit down. So many years she'd lived peacefully, without the thought of dark magick. And now it was surrounding her and Moira, with someone out there waiting to use it to strangle them both.

"Like I said, they were spelled to keep you from finding them. Someone wishes you harm," Sky said with characteristic understatement. She held up a small glass bottle full of nails, pins, needles, and vinegar. "How's your stomach been lately? Any ulcers?"

"No," Morgan said, shaking her head in disbelief. "Goddess. I'm just so grateful that Moira hasn't been hurt."

"These people must be just astounded every day," Sky said, "when they read the paper and don't find an article about how your roof caved in or your brakes gave out or you slipped on your walk and broke your hip. You're stronger than they think. Or else their magick is pathetic." She looked at the pouch with distaste, then added it to the small pile in the corner of the yard.

"Katrina and I have been doing a lot of protection spells," said Morgan. "This house itself is built on an ancient power ley, and we tap into that."

"Oh, yes, the legend about the local power ley. Didn't know anyone knew where it was. Good. That's the only explanation I have for the fact that you're still standing. That and you're Morgan of Belwicket," Sky said. "Some of this stuff has been nasty."

All of a sudden Morgan felt as if she couldn't bear it. She collapsed to the ground. "Sky," she began. "I thought I was done with all this."

"I know," Sky said. "And you should be. You've been through enough." Her black eyes became thoughtful. "But you're no ordinary witch. You're Morgan of Belwicket. Maeve's daughter. Ciaran's daughter. You are the *sgiùrs dàn*."

Morgan's eyes opened wider. The sgiùrs dàn—*the Destroyer.*

Ciaran had told her that years ago, as part of his explanation for wanting her dead. Every several generations within the Woodbane clan a Destroyer was born. A witch who would change the course of Woodbane history. "But didn't I already change Woodbane history, by helping to destroy Amyranth? By removing Ciaran from power? And now by leading Belwicket in a new direction?"

"I certainly thought so," Sky said wryly. "But maybe the wheel has something more for you to do."

The wheel of life. Fate. Karma. Morgan felt oddly inadequate for what the wheel kept dishing out. "Sky . . . I just don't know if I can fight anymore, not like I did back then."

Sky's gaze was calm and sure. "Morgan. You are stronger than you know. How strange that you still don't realize that."

Then she turned and began to set up what they would need to undo all the dark spells. It was harder to undo magick than to do it. They had to work backward, unraveling what had been wrought. It was easier working together, Morgan thought. If she'd had to do this alone, one step at a time, it would have taken so much longer. And unspoken between them was the same constant thought of where this could all lead, a reason to work as quickly and thoroughly as possible—*Hunter.*

By two o'clock that afternoon the house and yard had been cleared. The actual physical embodiments of the hexes and spells would be buried in the sand, down by the sea, where time and salt water would slowly purify them. Morgan and Sky began to relay new circles of protection. It was a shame there wouldn't be a full moon that night, but they had to work with what they had. They couldn't afford to wait even a moment.

They worked from the inside out. Starting in the northeast corner, which was in the guest room, Morgan and Sky lit small brushes of dried sage. These they waved in every corner, in the closet, around the windows. Their smudgy, herbal smoke would help purify the energy and rid the house of evil intentions. They chanted protection spells in each room, sprinkled salt on every floor, and washed each window so that evil would be reflected and healing energy could flow through. Morgan drew sigils of protection on the walls above every door frame and window frame. In each corner of every room she put a small chunk of pure iron, surrounded by a circle of salt.

Outside, Morgan and Sky walked the perimeter of the property, carrying lit candles and burning sagebrush. They gathered handfuls of willow twigs and lightly slapped them all around the low stone walls that surrounded the house and yard. Again Morgan drew sigils of protection above every door and window, drawing them first with silver paint, then overlaying them with invisible lines, marked with her own witch's sign.

They traced Xs across each door and window with Morgan's athame and sprinkled salt in a solid line on the inside of the stone walls.

"You're going to look out your window and find your yard full of deer," Sky said dryly as they sprinkled salt.

"As long as they're not evil Ealltuinn deer, that's okay," Morgan said.

"So you still think this is coming from them?"

"I don't know anymore," Morgan answered. "I can't see how any of them would know about Hunter. . . ."

Sky met her gaze, and neither said anything. But Sky's

eyes were filled with the same mixture of hope, desperation, and fear that Morgan felt. And Morgan even noticed Sky's hands trembling slightly. It was all either could do not to break down from the torture of needing to know if Hunter was really alive.

"We're almost finished," Sky said quietly, resuming her work.

In front of each of the garden gates they drew seven lines of protection so anyone entering with harmful intentions would find themselves slowed and perhaps even too confused to follow the path. Last but not least, the two women stood together and chanted the strongest power chants they knew, overlaying them with ribbons of protection, of ward evil, of warning, of reflection of harm. They went around the whole yard, all around the house and the back garden, singing and chanting, dispelling the last of the negative energy and replacing it with strong positive energy.

"Whew. That's done, and done well," Sky said, glancing at the sun's position when they were through. "Must be almost four."

"Moira will be home soon," Morgan agreed.

Inside the house, Morgan made a pot of strong tea. While they waited for Moira, she and Sky exchanged small talk, avoiding the one topic Morgan knew was all either could really think about.

"Alwyn's expecting a baby," Sky told her.

"So's Mary K.," Morgan said. "Twins, in fact. I'm going to be an aunt. I can't believe it's taken her so long. I thought she'd have nine kids by now."

Sky grinned, then seemed to listen for a moment. "Someone's coming."

"It's Katrina," said Morgan, casting her senses. She got up to let her mother-in-law in, then introduced her to Sky.

"Hello," said Katrina. "Morgan's mentioned you to me."

"Pleasure," Sky said with her natural reserve.

"Sit down," Morgan said. "I'll get you a cup."

Katrina took a chair, resting her walking stick against the side cupboard.

"Don't get old," she advised Morgan and Sky. "Christa Ryan tells me to walk two miles each day or become as stiff as an old board, so I do, but I'd rather be home working crosswords in front of the fire."

"Do you want me to try to help?" Morgan offered.

"Nae, lass. It's just these old bones. Don't trouble yourself," Katrina said, taking a sip of tea. Morgan had made the suggestion before that she try to heal Katrina's arthritis, but Katrina always shrugged her off.

Nodding, Morgan glanced at the clock. It was hard not to want Moira by her side every minute. She sent her daughter a witch message. *Don't be late. Not today.*

13

Moira

Moira was torn as she approached her house that afternoon. Sitting through classes had been torture, when all she could think about was all the questions she still had about Ciaran, her mum's past, and . . . Colm and Hunter. But she didn't want to face her mother yet, either. Still, she'd received the witch message from Morgan just as school had ended, warning her to come straight home—that it was important.

What now?

Moira took a deep breath, then opened the front door and saw her mum, Gran, and Sky sitting at the kitchen table.

"Hi, sweetie," Mum said.

"Hi." Moira dumped her book bag and sweater on the chair. "Hi, Gran. Sky."

"How was your day, love?" Katrina asked.

Moira frowned. She didn't want to talk about her day—she wanted to know why she'd had to come home so quickly. She tried to read her mother's face, but Morgan wouldn't meet her gaze. Then she sniffed the air. "Sage?"

"Yes," Sky said, when Morgan didn't answer. "We had to do some purification on the house."

"What do you mean?" Moira asked.

"Someone had put some bad-luck sigils around the yard," Sky said. "Your mum and I cleared them out."

Looking first at her mother, then at Sky, Moira said, "Bad-luck sigils . . . who would do that?"

"Perhaps someone from Ealltuinn," Katrina said. "But we're not sure. It's not safe for you. For any of us. We need you to stay here, where we can protect you."

Not Lilith, Moira thought in dismay as she sank into a chair at the table. Not Ian.

Finally Morgan looked into Moira's eyes. "Do you understand?" she said. "This is very serious, Moira. The coven is in danger. We are in danger."

"Okay," Moira said. She'd never seen her mum and Gran like this before. "I'll be careful." She glanced back and forth between Morgan and Gran. They looked scared but determined. Especially her mother. This morning's conversation had done little to erase her doubts. Now might not be the best time, but Moira had to know the truth about her father, about her birth, and she sensed somehow that the only way to get it was to ask her questions now, with Mum and Gran here.

Moira cleared her throat. "So, Mum, did you tell Gran about my dream? About this morning?" she asked.

Morgan blinked, surprised at Moira's question. "No, I . . . there's a lot going on right now, a lot—"

"I had this dream," Moira said slowly to Gran, cutting off her mum. "And in the dream my dad, he . . . he wasn't my dad. He was someone else."

"We've talked about this," Morgan said firmly. "Colm is your father, Moira."

Moira kept her gaze on Gran, focusing her powers on trying to feel Gran's response to her description of the dream. She's uncomfortable, Moira realized, feeling a growing dread. Just like she was the other day, when I kept asking her what she meant about helping my mother heal.

"Remember what you were saying to me?" Moira continued, surprised at how calm she sounded with the turmoil of emotions inside her. "About how you helped to soothe my mother's troubles after Hunter's accident?"

"Katrina, what's Moira talking about?" Morgan asked curiously.

Gran looked down at her teacup. "Yes, well . . ." Her voice trailed off.

"I just want to understand it," Moira said earnestly, leaning forward. "I've been reading Mum's and Dad's old Books of Shadows, so I have it from their view. But what do you remember about it?"

"It was a hard time," Gran said slowly. "We all do what we think is best."

Moira looked at Morgan, who seemed concerned.

"Katrina, are you all right?" Morgan asked.

"The weird thing is," Moira went on, wishing she could let this whole thing drop—wishing she weren't feeling more and more certain that this would lead to an answer she didn't want to hear. "The dates don't match up in the Books of Shadows. The dates when Mum and Da got married and when I was born."

Gran shook her head and gazed into her tea. "It's about time it all caught up with me," she said.

"What are you talking about? Are you sure you're all right?" Mum's face was pale, even paler than it had been when Moira had first walked in.

Gran looked up and met Morgan's eyes. "You don't remember much about that time, do you?"

Mum let out a breath, the way she did when she was tense. "Well," she said slowly, "not a lot. I was . . . so upset. Upset and sick. I hardly remember coming back to Ireland. I was in the hospital, in Wales. I had pneumonia."

It was almost as if Moira could see a wave of sadness settle on Morgan like a shawl.

"Yes, you had pneumonia, and you were beside yourself with grief," Gran told her. "Your love had died in that storm, and it was like most of you died with him."

Moira had never heard Gran talk like this—talking about Mum's past. No one ever had mentioned Hunter until this past week. It was as if a ghost had been living in their house all these years, silent and unacknowledged.

Gran looked directly at Moira. "Your mother was the descendant of our ancestral high priestesses," she said. "You know that. You know how Grandda and I found out your mum was alive and went to find her to help us restore Belwicket."

Moira nodded.

"We grew to love Morgan," Gran went on. "We could see that with her power, we could perhaps one day re-create the coven that we had grown up in, that our parents had grown up in. Your mum was the key. Not just because of her power—it was her instincts, her curiosity, the experiences that had shaped her. I grew to care for her as for a daughter. And my Colm, I saw that he loved her as well, though he didn't say anything to me. But we knew her heart wasn't whole. I wondered what would happen between her and her young man. Every so often she would go off and meet him somewhere, France or Scotland or Wales. When she came back, she would be both happier and sadder, if you can understand that."

The only sound in the kitchen was Finnegan's light snoring and the beginning of a slow, steady rain outside. Moira felt as if time itself had slowed, as if she were in a dream again.

If only this were a dream, a dream she could wake up from and hear another explanation for from her gran. Why hadn't Gran been as quick as her mum was to assure her that Colm was indeed her father? Why hadn't she said that right off? Moira's stomach was locked in a million knots as she waited to hear more.

"I didn't ask about him, and she didn't volunteer anything," Gran went on, speaking as if Morgan weren't right there. "Then your mum didn't come back from a short trip, and a hospital in Wales finally called us. Morgan was incredibly ill with pneumonia. I contacted your grandparents in America, and they flew over. We all talked about what we should do, and in the end your mum said she wanted to come back to her little flat in Wicklow. So Pawel and Colm and I collected her, but she couldn't be on her own. I put her up in our guest room, and many of us took turns nursing her. The whole coven—there were ten of us back then—performed healing rites."

Gran paused, glancing around the room. "Anyway. Colm hardly left her side—I thought he'd become ill himself. In Wales we had learned of the tragedy, and the little bit that your mum managed to tell us confirmed the worst—she had lost her young man." Gran sighed, the lines on her face seeming to deepen with remembered pain.

Moira glanced at Morgan, who was listening with the same worry and dread in her eyes that Moira felt.

"Several weeks after the accident I was holding your hand," Gran said, once more directing the story to Morgan, "focusing on sending you healing energy, and I realized something felt different. I concentrated, and it came to me—you were going to have a baby."

Moira and Morgan drew in deep, sharp breaths in unison as the truth became real for both of them. As strong as her suspicions had been growing every moment, Moira still felt like she'd been punched in the stomach. She couldn't even respond, and neither could her mum.

"I felt so sorry for you, Morgan, but I was glad for you, too. You had a reason to keep going. I knew that you hadn't sensed the baby yet. Most witches would, if they were at all in tune with themselves, but in your state you barely knew if you were awake or asleep. I worried for you, Morgan. And I worried for your child. I worried that as ill as you were, as lost, you would never recover on your own. I talked to Pawel about it and to Susan, and we all talked to Colm. Today I don't know if I would have made the same decision. At the time it seemed like the best thing to do. Colm loved you, we loved you, and we wanted you to be whole again. You were the hereditary priestess of Belwicket. It was right that you stay here and regain the strength to use your powers for good, as you have."

"Katrina . . . what did you do?" Morgan asked in a voice that was nearly a whisper yet chilled Moira to the bone.

Gran sighed. "Susan and I created a spell that would heal

you, bring you back from the brink of despair. To keep you alive, to keep your *daughter* safe and alive . . . to protect you both," she finished, looking at Moira. "The spell . . . I took your pain onto myself in order to help you. It was only intended to bring you some peace, Morgan."

There was silence in the room as her words sank in. Moira started to shake her head, slowly. She reached out to hold the edge of the table, feeling dizzy. *No, no, this isn't happening.*

Gran continued. "We were waiting to tell you about the baby until you were healthier. But then . . . Colm came to me one afternoon, when you were beginning to recover, and told me that he had asked you to marry him—and that you had said yes. He knew about the baby, and he accepted it and wanted to be with you anyway. When he shared his news, I felt I understood. You wanted to die, Morgan, but knew that taking your own life was a direct violation of all Wiccan laws. And since you had to go on living anyway, you would make the best of it, with someone you cared for. My son."

"I loved Colm." Mum's voice sounded as if it were coming from far away.

"My dear." Gran reached out and took her hand. "I know you did. I'm not saying that. Believe me, if I hadn't thought that from the very beginning, we wouldn't all be sitting here today. I knew you. You never would have agreed to marry him if you hadn't had every intention of being a good and loving wife. And you were. You were the best thing that ever happened to him. I knew that, and he knew that."

Morgan looked stricken, deep in shock. Moira was beyond shock—beyond any identifiable emotion. It was all just too much.

"The spell was working, and you continued to heal. But

there was a side effect we hadn't realized—that the spell would blur your memories and cause your senses to be off for a time. Yes, you moved on. You married. But you believed the baby was Colm's. And we—we never told you otherwise. I don't know what to say, except that it just seemed right at the time for all of you. We believed the Goddess was having her way, that you were meant to have your daughter with Colm."

Morgan covered her mouth with her hand, gasping, and tears started flowing down her face. Sky's face was like stone, alabaster, unreadable.

Blinking, Moira tried to think—the room was going in and out of focus. She gripped her chair seat, wondering dimly if she were going to fall over.

"Gran," she said faintly, "Da wasn't really my father?"

"Your da was Colm Byrne," Gran said, her voice shaky. "And no father ever loved a daughter more. He was your real father in every way that counted, your whole life. He took joy in you, he joined his heart with yours. You belonged to him and he to you."

"Oh my God, Katrina," Mum finally said hoarsely, her hand to her mouth. "Oh, Goddess." Her eyes widened. "You said you *took* my pain. Your arthritis . . . that's how it began, isn't it?"

Gran stared down at the table, not answering.

"It's why you never wanted me to heal you," Morgan breathed. "Because it wouldn't have worked, not when your pain had been taken from me to begin with . . ."

"Because it's my burden to bear. I only wanted to help you live your life," Gran said. "And raise your daughter."

"I don't understand," Moira said helplessly. "Da knew, all this time? And Aunt Susan? Everyone knew?"

"Just me, Pawel, Susan, and Colm," Gran said. "It never made a difference to any of us."

"It makes a difference to *me*!" Moira cried, the knowledge overwhelming her, stripping her of reason. She jumped up so quickly that her chair tipped over onto the floor with a crash. Finnegan leaped up and barked. "Don't you get it? You've traded in my whole life! How could you do that? Who gave you permission? Now you're not even my grandmother!"

Gran looked as if she had been slapped, but Moira was too upset to care. Instead, she grabbed her jacket off its hook and rushed out the front door. Finnegan leaped after her, bounding across the yard and just managing to squeak through the garden gate before it slammed against him. Moira didn't care where she ran—she just ran, even after her breaths were searing in her lungs, after her leg muscles felt numb. Still her feet pounded against the rain-soaked headland lining the coast of the sea, the cliffs to one side of her dropping thirty feet downward to the rocks below.

Oh, Goddess, oh, Goddess, she had no father. Colm was dead, but he wasn't her father, had never been her father. Yet she had loved him so much! He had been warm and loving and funny. He'd helped her build things, helped her learn to ride a bike, to skate, to ride a horse. It had always been him and Mum, him and Mum, at school things, at circles, at sabbats. She needed him so much to have been her father! He was her dad! Her dad! Oh, Goddess, it all just hurt too much! Her whole life her dad had been living a lie, pretending. He hadn't been able to tell her the truth—or to tell Mum. How could he have not told Mum? How could Gran have done this? It felt so wrong!

At last Moira lost her footing, sliding and tumbling against the wet grass. Fresh dirt smeared her hands and face, but she lay where she had fallen, gasping in cold, painful breaths. Her hair soon felt wet. Overhead, the sky was darkening, the clouds blotting out any sunset there might have been. In this one afternoon her whole life, her whole past, had been ripped away, to be left just a blank.

Finnegan flopped next to her, whining, pressing his soft brown, white, and black side against her, licking her face. Moira burst into sobs, putting her arms around him, holding him to her. He licked her face and lay next to her, and she cried and cried against him, the way she had when she was a little girl. She wished she were dead. She couldn't bear the fact that her dad had known all along she wasn't really his, yet he'd loved her *so much* anyway. That seemed so sad and pathetic and unselfish that she simply couldn't stand it.

"Oh, Finn, Finn," she sobbed against him. "It hurts too much."

Her school clothes were sodden and muddied, her hair was wet, her face was tearstained and mud-streaked. But she lay against Finnegan and sobbed, trying to let out the emotional pain that threatened to dislodge her soul from her body.

She didn't know how long she lay there, but gradually exhaustion overcame her and her sobs slowed, then quieted. She felt completely spent, utterly drained of emotion. Blinking, she realized vaguely that it was quite dark outside. Finnegan was resting by her side, taking the occasional gentle lick of her face, as if promising to stay as long as she needed him. Her chest hurt, and the ground was hard, and she was cold, freezing, and soaked through. But she couldn't get up, couldn't move, had no idea where she was. She would just lie here forever, she decided, almost dreamily. She would never move again.

"There you are," said a gentle voice, and Moira jerked in surprise. Finnegan hadn't growled, but he sat up alertly, his eyes locked on . . . Ian.

Moira felt frozen, stiff. Ian dropped lightly to sit next to her, seeming to neither notice nor care that he was going to ruin his clothes. Moira's first insane thought was that she probably looked like the Bride of Frankenstein. Then she thought fiercely, So what? My whole life just got ripped away from me—I don't care what I look like!

Slowly Ian put out his hand and stroked the light hair away from her chilled, wet face. "I felt you get upset this afternoon while I was being tutored," he said. "It was strange, like you were sending waves of upsetness. Then later I was putting up shelves in my mom's pantry—it's a disaster in there—and I pictured you running over the grass, with the sea in the back-ground. It's taken me a while to find you."

"Thanks," Moira said, her voice small and broken. She struggled to sit up and felt Ian's arm around her shoulders.

"Brought a tissue," Ian said with a grin, handing it to her. Moira wiped her eyes and nose, knowing it was just a drop in the bucket in terms of what she needed. She crumpled the tissue and put it in her jacket pocket, feeling cold and miserable and self-conscious. What time was it? She glanced at the sky, but there was no moon. What in the world was she supposed to say?

Gently Ian pulled her against him so that her face was on his shoulder, his arms around her back. He stroked her hair and let her cry, and she felt the warmth of his body and his arms surrounding her.

14

Morgan

The second Moira ran out the door, Morgan jumped up after her, but Sky grabbed her arm, hard.

"Let her go," she said. "She needs some space. Finnegan's with her—and we can keep an eye on her in other ways, without just chasing her farther away."

Morgan hated using her powers to spy on her daughter, but she realized Sky was right—it was the only way to keep Moira safe right now without upsetting her even more. Through the window Morgan watched in despair as her daughter raced through the garden gate and flew up the road, her long straight hair whipping in back of her.

She felt numb. No, that wasn't true. It was just that the huge, varied emotions she was feeling were working to cancel each other out. Anger, disbelief, despair, sadness, regret. And all the while the hope that Hunter was really alive was in there, too, mixed in with everything else.

Katrina got heavily to her feet. "I'll be going, lass," she said, her voice subdued. "Now, looking back, I don't know how I could have thought this wouldn't rebound on us all like a hand grenade."

"How could you *not* have thought that?" Morgan exploded. "How could you have possibly thought this was a good thing for *anybody*? You wanted me for *Belwicket*? So you lied to me about my child for sixteen *years*? It's crazy! Not even about Moira . . . but about Colm, too. I believed he was her *father*. That had a huge impact on our marriage, our lives. Every time I looked at Moira, I saw Colm's daughter. Now you tell me all those thoughts were a *lie*. What were you *thinking*?"

The older woman's shoulders bowed, and she sighed. "We didn't know the side effects. I thought it was for the best. You were dying. I'm sorry." She sounded beaten and sad, and Morgan couldn't help feeling an instinctive sympathy for the woman she'd loved like a second mother for years now. But nothing gave Katrina the right to do what she'd done.

"You did this to my life, Colm's life, Moira's life, so your *coven* would be strong," Morgan said. "How dare you? How *dare* you?" Morgan was shaking—she couldn't remember the last time she had been so angry.

"Belwicket is more than that, Morgan," Katrina said, pleading with her to understand. "It's our lives, the lives of our ancestors. It's our power. It's our heritage, yours and mine. And please understand, I didn't do it just for the coven. I did it out of love, too—for you and for your unborn child. You have to know that."

"Just leave, please," Morgan said quietly. She had no way to make sense of any of this at the moment, but she couldn't have even if she'd wanted to—she had something far more important to deal with.

"If that's what you want," Katrina said. "But please

remember how much I love you." There were tears on her face as she closed the door behind her.

After Katrina left, Morgan paced the room nervously, emotions threatening to explode out of her like fireworks. She couldn't believe it—it was just too big, too huge, too amazing. On top of everything else, today she'd found out that her only child was Hunter's daughter.

"Oh, Goddess," she cried, turning to Sky. "Hunter's daughter!" She threw herself into Sky's arms and finally allowed herself to cry.

"Moira is Hunter's daughter," Sky said, repeating the words as if they were a miracle.

"I had Hunter's daughter," Morgan said, pulling back to look at Sky. "Hunter and I had a child." And then she thought of her marriage, of Colm, who had been so good, so accepting, and she felt terrible and furious all over again.

"They lied to me!" she said, letting go of Sky and starting to pace again. "More than that! They spelled me! *Spelled me!* All this time I've been living a lie! Every day of my life Colm knew our life was a lie, and he said nothing! He and Katrina and Pawel—I thought they were my family. They were deceiving me! For almost sixteen years—I can't believe it."

Sky nodded soberly.

"I still don't understand how it's even possible," Morgan said. "Hunter and I . . . we did all the appropriate spells. It's why I never even considered Moira could be his."

Sky gave a helpless shrug. "I don't know," she said.

"Well, right now I just need to be with my daughter. Maybe I should send her a witch message," Morgan said, sniffling and wiping her nose on her sleeve. Hunter's daughter. Moira was Hunter's daughter. She glanced outside, hoping to see Moira running back to the house. Now that she knew, she was dying to look at Moira carefully, to see where she left off and Hunter began. *Oh, Colm. Goddess, Colm, what were you thinking? How could you do this to me? I trusted you.*

"I think she needs time alone," Sky said, always straightforward. "I don't feel her in the area. If she's not back in ten more minutes, we'll scry and go find her."

"She probably went to Ian's house," Morgan said, frowning with this fresh worry. "Like last night."

"Maybe not. She might just want to be alone."

"They did us such an injustice," said Morgan, and Sky nodded. "It's incredibly sad that Colm died, leaving no children."

"Moira was his daughter," Sky said gently. "She mourns him like a daughter. You know from your own experience about the bonds between parents and adoptive children."

"Yes, I do." Morgan thought of the parents who'd raised her, whom she loved so much. "But I also know there can be a special bond between blood relatives. In a way, it's like Moira has lost two fathers."

She sat down in Colm's leather chair. What would Hunter have been like as a father? Her heart constricted painfully, imagining how it might have been. His face, surprised at Moira's strong, tiny grip. Hunter changing a diaper with the same intense concentration with which he did everything else. Baby Moira sleeping between her and Hunter in bed. More tears rolled down her cheeks. How precious those moments would have been.

Sky crossed the room and sank down on the couch, leaning back. "He would have loved to have had a daughter," she said, echoing Morgan's thoughts.

Morgan nodded, crying silently. After a few minutes she

got up and washed her face and drank some water. "I'm going to scry for her," she told Sky. "I just need to know she's okay."

Then she lit the candle on the table and sat down, losing herself instantly to the peace of meditation. Scrying, she saw Moira, in the dark, sitting on wet grass. Ian was with her. He had his arm around her, and her head was resting on his shoulder. Finnegan lay nearby, panting and relaxed. She saw Moira nod, then both she and Ian straightened up slightly, awareness coming over them. They'd felt her scrying. Morgan sent a quick witch message to Moira, and Moira replied—curtly—that she was fine. Morgan warned that if she didn't return soon, she would have to come find her, then pulled out of the image and blew out the candle.

"Moira's okay," she said. "She and Ian are in a field some-where—maybe up on the headland, by the sea. But she'll be on her way home now, I believe."

"Good," said Sky.

"I just wish . . . ," Morgan began hesitantly, then decided to go on. "I just wish I could see now who Ian is underneath. Maybe he's Cal all over again. Maybe he's not. I can't let him hurt my daughter."

"We could pin him down and do a *tàth meànma*."

"And have the New Charter all over us? No thanks. But it is tempting."

"Well, then, listen—there is something else we could do while we're waiting for Moira."

Morgan looked at her, knowing exactly what Sky meant.

"You said you scried and you saw Hunter. Tell me about that again."

Morgan did, describing what he'd looked like, how he hadn't appeared youthful, as he had in all her previous dreams over the years, but instead had aged. Not only aged, but had gone through some shocking physical changes. When she finished, Sky was silent, and Morgan asked, "What are you thinking? What can we do to know the truth?"

"I have Hunter's athame," Sky said thoughtfully. "It's out in the car. Daniel once told me about a spell where you focus intently on someone's energy, using one of their tools to help focus on them. It finds them whether they're alive or dead. I've been thinking all day—it's risky, but it's what we need to try. The thing is, you need three witches for it."

Morgan was quiet for a moment. Daniel Niall, Hunter's father, had almost killed himself trying to contact his wife in the netherworld. Contacting the dead was dark magick, ill-advised, and often ended tragically.

But this is Hunter.

She didn't have to think twice. "Let's do it," Morgan said. Sky went to the car. The only question was who to enlist to help. Hartwell? Keady? In other times, when she had a difficult question about magick, she would have turned to Katrina. Not now. She wished she could call up Alyce Fernbrake, who had worked at Practical Magick back in Widow's Vale so long ago. Alyce was almost eighty now and living quietly over the store she still owned but no longer managed. Morgan hadn't seen her in eight years. It would be presumptuous to call her for advice now.

The front door opened, startling Morgan. "Look what the cat dragged in," Sky said, coming back in.

Moira looked like she had been hauled through a hedge backward. Several times.

Morgan stood up and ran to her. It was clear that she'd

been crying hard, and it looked as if she had fallen. Finnegan was right behind her, panting, wet, and muddy. Sky grabbed his collar and a dish towel and started rubbing him down.

For a minute Morgan just looked at Moira. She saw her height and slenderness. And her hair, that fine, straight, light hair—it was more Hunter than Morgan. But the pain in Moira's eyes was a reflection of Morgan's pain.

Morgan drew her daughter to her. Selfishly, Morgan was grateful that Moira couldn't be angry with her about this the way she had been about Ciaran. This hadn't been Morgan's decision, Morgan's fault.

"I was worried about you," Morgan said.

"I just ran and ran and ended up on the headland, above the cliffs. Ian came and found me there."

"Oh." How had he managed to find her? "Did he . . . help you feel better?"

A nod. "I told him everything," Moira said, sounding both defiant and tired.

"Oh, Moira," said Morgan sympathetically. "I wish you hadn't. It's family business, our business."

Moira sniffled and shrugged helplessly. "I'm sorry . . . it all just came out. I had told him about Ciaran, too, and then afterward wished I hadn't. But I was so upset . . . I'm sorry. I know you're not sure about him and his mother, but he's been so good to me."

Morgan knew the last thing Moira needed right now was to be pushed on the subject of Ian—and his family. "Well, why don't you go take a hot shower," she suggested. "Then we'll talk."

Moira nodded and headed upstairs.

"Morgan," Sky said when Moira was out of earshot, "I think I know who our third witch should be."

Morgan met Sky's gaze uncertainly. "Moira," she said simply.

An hour later the three of them went into Morgan's workroom. It was impossible for Morgan to keep her eyes off Moira—she kept examining every aspect of her daughter in order to find traces of Hunter, which now seemed so evident. And even her personality—she too kept much inside, like Hunter. They shared a similar dry humor. And Moira was tenacious, like Hunter—she couldn't let go of things.

"You don't have to do this," Morgan told Moira as she got out her own tools. "Usually it would be for three initiated witches. It's almost certain that Hunter is, in fact, dead—has been dead all these years. If he's dead and we contact him, we could all be in danger."

"I want to do it," Moira said.

"Right, then," said Sky. "Everyone take off every bit of metal. No jeans, Moira—they have rivets and a zipper."

Morgan hadn't taken off her wedding ring in sixteen years. It was hard to set it aside. Once Sky and Moira had changed into loose cotton pants and sweatshirts and Morgan was in her silk robe, Morgan and Sky drew seven circles of protection. Then Morgan drew three more circles of power. She gestured to the others to enter the circles, and she closed each circle.

Seated on the floor, they made a natural triangle, their knees touching. Sky took out Hunter's athame and Morgan's heart ached, seeing it after all this time.

A trident-shaped candleholder stood in the center

between them; its black iron cups held three candles. Sky braced the knife across the middle bar of the candleholder so that the athame's blade was licked by one flame.

Sky had shown Morgan the written form of the spell, and together they had read it through in the kitchen. Now Morgan closed her eyes, and each of the three slowed her breathing, her heartbeat, and they pooled their power so that it could be used.

Sky began the spell. Like every spell, it was a combination of basic forms overlain with instance-specific designations: the quest-for-knowledge form was in virtually every spell ever crafted. Sky wrought other delicate patterns around the basic structure, tailoring the spell with elegance and precision to search for a person, to promise to cause the person living or dead no harm, and to ward any harm from coming to him by cause of this. As a Wyndenkell, Sky was a natural spell-crafter, and she adapted this one gracefully and elegantly.

Then Morgan took up the chant, chanting first in her head, then softly aloud. She repeated Sky's basic form but wove her knowledge of Hunter into it, irretrievably chaining his image, his patterns, his essence to the spell. Using ancient words learned during years of study, she called on Hunter's energy as she knew it. If she had known his true name, this would have been a thousand times easier. Every thing—plants, rocks, crystals, animals, people—had a true name that was a song, a color, a rune, an emotion all at once. In the craft many witches went through a Great Trial, during which they learned their true name. Morgan still didn't know hers, and she'd never known Hunter's. As far as Morgan knew, no one had known his true name except for him. Instead, she recalled all her memories of him and then sent those memories out into the universe, riding along the lines of inquiry Sky had formed.

"Moira?" Morgan whispered, and then they took each other's hands and held them, combining their energies, their knowledge.

Together they sent their energies out along the lines of the spell that radiated from them like spokes from a wheel. Moira was chanting her call-power spell and continuously sending her power to Sky and Morgan. Sky was repeating her quest spell, and Morgan continued to send out images of Hunter.

It was unclear how long they worked. They wove their words, their thoughts, their energies together until it felt as if they had created a tight, complex basket of silver. In her mind's eye Morgan could see it shimmering before her, becoming more and more complete, spinning and glowing. She focused on breathing in and out, smoothly, constantly, like waves, like the sea, her life force waxing and waning without effort.

Then she saw him. Hunter's face appeared in the silver ball in front of her, life-size, close enough for her to count every wrinkle, every scratch, every bruise. Her heart clenched with the mingled joy of seeing him and the torment of seeing him hurt. But what a gift, to be able to see him at all. He was sitting on a rough, sea-wet rock, his head in his hands. He looked up and seemed to see her.

His mouth made the shape "Morgan."

A shudder passed through Morgan at the sight of him, but she had to stay strong, had to find out the truth.

Giomanach. Hunter. Are you alive or are you dead? Are you of this world or are you gone from this world? Her words felt desperate, screamed, though she made no sound.

His face seemed to crumple then, his scraped, bony hand passing over his mouth as if to help him swallow pain.

I am alive but not living. I am in neither your world nor another. I am nowhere.

Who took you from me?

I can never return.

That's not good enough! You are somewhere because we found you! Tell me where and I will come to you! Please—you have to tell me where you are.

Morgan's breath was snatched away as Hunter bent over, shielding his face from her. His too-thin shoulders shook, his matted hair fell forward on his face. It was more torturous than anything she had witnessed in uncounted years. In her chest she felt a searing pain, then a damp warmth made her glance down. Her eyes widened as a ragged splotch of blood spread slowly across her robe, right over her heart. The shock of it broke her concentration, and when she raised her head, her eyes wide, the silver ball was gone, Hunter's image was gone, and all she could see were Sky's and Moira's stunned and afraid faces.

"Mum!" Moira gasped. "What's happening to you?"

Like a snake striking, Sky knocked Hunter's athame off the candleholder. It lay on the wooden floor, showing no glowing signs of heat but searing a charred pattern into the floor. Sky kicked it over onto the stone hearth, then moved the candleholder and took hold of Morgan's robe.

"Morgan!"

It sounded as if her voice were coming from far away, and Morgan stared at her stupidly, then looked down at her robe again. The splotch of blood was the size of her palm now. Moving slowly, as if in a dream, Morgan pulled her silk robe away from her skin.

"My heart is bleeding," she whispered. "My heart is bleeding." A thin thread of panic threatened to coil through her veins, but Sky took her arm firmly.

"Moira, dismantle the circles, quickly." Sky's voice was commanding. Morgan watched with an odd, distant confusion as her daughter dismantled and erased circle after circle as fast as she could. When the last one was opened, Sky got to her feet and pulled Morgan up. "Let's go," she said briskly, and Morgan floated dreamily after her as Sky took her upstairs into the small bathroom. There Sky pulled off Morgan's silk robe and grabbed a faded tartan one, wrapping it around her. It was infinitely soft and cozy, and Morgan wanted to lie down in it and sleep forever.

Then Sky took a wet washcloth and began to dab gently at the dark red blood pulsing at the center of Morgan's chest. Moira stood in the doorway, her face pale.

"What is it, Sky?" she said softly.

"Her heart is bleeding," Sky said somewhat brusquely. "Get me some adder's tongue and some amaranth. Morgan should have some dried in her herb store."

As Moira ran down the steps, Sky helped Morgan into her bedroom. Soon Moira came back with two small, neatly labeled glass vials. Sky soaked the adder's tongue and the dried amaranth leaves in cold water, then pressed them into a flat poultice and placed it on Morgan's chest. She covered it with a clean white cloth folded into a square.

"Moira," Sky said, "go outside and pick the last of the rose geranium petals. Mix them with a pinch of dried jasmine flowers and some fresh grated ginger. Make a tea and bring it up. Can you do that?"

Moira nodded quickly but lingered.

"Now, Moira," Sky said firmly. "Your mum will be all right," she added, more gently. "It was an unexpected reaction to the spell."

"My chest is throbbing less," Morgan said in a muted voice.

Moira left but soon came back holding a tray with a mug on it. Sky propped Morgan up with pillows so she could drink. Moira sat gingerly on the edge of the bed, careful not to disturb Morgan. Morgan looked at her and smiled, starting to feel more normal.

"Okay, note to self," she said. "When I do that spell, my heart bleeds. Have help available."

Her daughter smiled weakly, and Sky cracked a smile.

"A *most* unusual side effect," Sky said. "What do you think about it?"

Morgan met her eyes, black as jet, as onyx. "I think he's still alive."

Unblinking, Sky said, "I think so, too."

"But I don't know where. Sky, we have to find him." Morgan propped herself up on her elbows. "He's on a beach, which narrows it down to tens of thousands of miles of shorelines around the world."

Sky was silent, thinking. Morgan racked her brain, still muddled from the shock. What could they do?

Then Moira took a deep breath and said, "I have an idea."

It was as if Finnegan had started talking. Morgan and Sky just stared at her.

"What?" Morgan asked.

15

Moira

With Sky driving and Moira navigating, the three reached Lilith Delaney's cottage in fifteen minutes.

"What exactly did you see?" Morgan asked for the third time.

"It was him," said Moira, from the backseat. "Turn left up here, at the second lane. I didn't recognize him before because the Hunter in my dream was young and looked really different. But the one I saw in Lilith's crystal was the same person I saw in the silver ball."

"Are you quite sure?" Sky asked, her long, bony fingers tight on the steering wheel.

Moira nodded to herself and said, "Yes. If that was Hunter we saw tonight, then I saw him in Lilith's crystal last night. Do you . . . do you really think he's alive?" Hunter had looked horrible. Moira thought about Colm, how neat and cheerful and ordinary he had looked. So comforting, reassuring. Like a dad.

"If it's the same person from the silver ball, then yes," Moira's mum said, her voice constrained.

Moira had been trying to suppress her fear this whole

time, but now it was threatening to break through. She had no idea what to expect from Lilith Delaney now that it seemed like her mum had been right about her all along. "Here!" she said, peering into the darkness, recognizing the huge oak trees that lined the small road where Ian's cottage was.

Just six hours ago he had been so comforting on the headland, when she'd felt like she was losing her mind. Had all of that really been an act? Was he using her, trying to gain her trust the way Cal had used her mum? It seemed hard to believe he wasn't now.

But something in her was still praying that *somehow* Ian had nothing to do with his mother. She just couldn't reconcile her image of him, so kind, so caring, with another image of him actively working with his mother to harm them. *Please let it not be true. Not Ian. Please, please, just not Ian.*

The house wasn't dark, despite the late hour. A light was on in one upstairs room, and several rooms were lit downstairs. The three witches got out of the car, and Moira noticed that Sky was watching Morgan intently. A wave of light fell on her mother's face as they approached the house, and Moira almost gasped aloud. Her mum looked older, harder—stronger, and almost nothing like her mother the softhearted healer. Was this what she had looked like long ago, when she'd had to fight Ciaran and the dark wave?

They strode toward the house, and about ten feet from the front door Moira suddenly felt like she was trying to walk through gelatin. The air itself felt thick: it had weight and a heavy texture.

"What is this?" she asked in a low tone.

"Spells to keep unfriendly people out," Morgan said grimly,

pushing through it as if it were wet tissue paper. Next to her Sky was murmuring under her breath, and Moira saw that her mum was tracing sigils in the air in front of her.

The door opened before they got to it. Ian stood there, still in his muddy clothes from before. "Moira?" he asked, astonished. "Are you all right? What's going on?" He sounded sincere. Moira would have given anything for him to really care, but she couldn't risk him fooling her for another minute. She turned away, not meeting his gaze.

"Where's your mother, Ian?" Morgan asked in a voice like a brick.

"What's wrong?" he answered, his voice sounding formal, less friendly. Just hearing the change of his tone made Moira's heart sink. What had she been thinking? Lilith was his mother. *Moira, Moira, how stupid are you?*

"What's this about?" Ian crossed his arms and stood in the doorway. They were on opposite sides, had been all along, but she had refused to see it. Her heart felt crushed, bruised. "Moira?" Ian asked, looking over their heads at her, standing behind them in the dark. "Are you okay?"

"Yes," she said shortly, more confused than ever.

Then a thickset figure appeared behind him, outlined by the light spilling out onto the lawn. "Morgan Byrne," Lilith Delaney said. "I confess to surprise. What could possibly make you think you have the right to show up here and harass my son?"

"For your sake, I hope Ian isn't involved," Morgan replied sharply. A shiver crept up Moira's spine at her mother's tone. Morgan's voice conjured up images of glaciers, scraping their way inexorably across a landscape of rock. "Let me see," her mum continued. "I could have come to return a boxful of pathetic, amateurish hexes, ill-luck charms, and injury fetishes that you've littered about my house and yard."

Lilith Delaney blinked and pushed ahead of Ian. "I don't know what you're talking about," she said, sounding bored.

Morgan laughed thinly, and Moira winced. "Please," her mum said. "Bottles full of nails, needles, and vinegar? Let's see . . . I think most children learn that in about the third form. Not very impressive—for a high priestess."

Moira knew that the hexes and spells put on the house and yard had been much more serious than that, with dangerously dark intentions and a great deal of thought and power put into them. Mum was obviously trying to goad Lilith by making it sound like a slow-witted child had created them. Moira could feel the coil of anger starting in Lilith's stomach.

"Are you done?" Lilith asked. "It's late, and the children have school tomorrow. Moira's already interrupted Ian's studies enough for one day."

Ian frowned and glanced at his mother.

"But then I guess she was upset, finding out she was a bastard daughter, just like her mother," Lilith continued.

Oh, Goddess. Ian had told Lilith about Ciaran and Hunter and everything. Moira took in a breath, then let it out, trying to release the raw sting of betrayal. She deliberately refused to look at Ian.

"You are so mistaken, Morgan," Lilith sneered. "You're ashamed of your father, who was one of the greatest witches to ever live. But you ought to be ashamed of yourself. You are weak, uncommitted, unfocused—you belong to a coven of dog-witches who have milquetoast circles where you all celebrate someone having a good day. Ciaran

MacEwan! His blood should be celebrated, his memory revered, his lessons learned by every witch! But no—you think him evil. Your vision, your knowledge, is so small, so pedestrian, that you can't begin to encompass what a leader he was! You shouldn't be allowed to live, much less work your pointless and juvenile magick."

"We have different views," Morgan said, her face like stone. "But we have some things in common. Hunter Niall. I want to know what you know."

"Never heard of him," Lilith said, shrugging. "Now quit wasting my time." She stepped back into the doorway.

"You do know him!" Moira cried, rushing forward. "You were looking at him in your crystal the first day I came by!"

Lilith's eyebrows raised slightly, then she rolled her eyes and started to shut the door, refusing even to acknowledge Moira's words. In the next second she froze almost comically, as if suddenly pretending to be a statue. Her hand was on the door, but her back stiffened and the only thing she moved were her eyes, which widened and focused on Morgan.

Moira saw that her mother's right hand was stretched out, palm facing Lilith, and as Moira watched, Morgan slowly began to close the fingers of that hand.

Lilith Delaney whimpered, and Moira stepped back and brought her hand up to her mouth. She'd never seen anything like this. Never seen her *mother* do anything like this. Morgan kept her hand outstretched, but the more she closed her fingers, the more Lilith seemed to crumple against the door. It was clear that Lilith was striving not to look afraid, but Moira could feel the prickles of fear emanating from her, the way she had felt her anger a minute ago.

"You will tell me," Morgan said, her voice low and terrible to hear, hardly human. *Mum?* It was hard to keep from panicking—things were spinning out of control so fast that nothing made sense anymore. How could her mum be so cruel, so deadly? Moira's legs felt weak, and she struggled not to fall to the ground.

Lilith's eyes were still wide, but they shot a momentary glance at Ian, who was standing to her side. He reached out to touch her. "Mother?" he asked, concern in his voice. He turned to Morgan, angry. "Stop it! What are you doing?"

"It's a binding spell, Ian," Sky said, her voice as dry and calm as a desert rock. "Morgan's always been particularly good at them. Must be Ciaran's blood."

There was a spike in the fear that Moira felt coming from Lilith, fear and disbelief.

Lilith hadn't thought Mum was so strong, Moira realized. She'd had no idea who she was up against. Even after everything Moira had heard about her mum, even after the stories about the dark wave, it was hard for Moira herself to believe.

"Hunter Niall," Morgan said again. "Tell me everything you know." Her voice was like thunder, felt but unheard, deep tremors rolling through the five of them.

"I know nothing," Lilith spit through stiff lips. Morgan made an almost imperceptible movement, and Lilith whimpered again.

"Stop it!" Ian cried, trying to step between his mother and Morgan. "Moira! Make her stop!"

Moira ignored him, feeling her heart rip apart. She hated to hear the pain in his voice, but she couldn't give in. He had lied to her, betrayed her. She was so ashamed of how stupid, how naive she had been. Even after her mum had warned her about

Cal, had tried to make her see the parallels, Moira had refused to believe it. She'd thought Ian was different. She'd been wrong.

"Where is Hunter Niall?" Morgan pressed, and when Lilith didn't answer, she closed her fingers a bit more. Lilith seemed to shrink against the door, her knuckles white, as if someone were wrapping her in a cloth of pain and twisting it. Her knees bent slightly, and Moira could see tiny beads of sweat appear on her upper lip.

"The thing about binding spells," Sky added conversationally, "is that they can do quite a bit of damage without leaving a mark." She let these words sink in, and then she looked at Lilith and said, an edge of steel in her voice, "The other interesting thing is that you're not the only one at stake here." She glanced first at Ian, then looked back to Lilith, making her intentions clear.

Moira bit her lips, tension making her muscles feel like knotted wood. *Tell Morgan what she wants to know. Do not force her to harm your son.*

Feeling ill, Moira started to sink to her knees in the wet grass, giving in, but instantly stood when Sky's eyes flicked to her. She could not show weakness. She could not become a liability in this desperate situation. She was Moira of Belwicket, Morgan's daughter, and she would show that she had her mother's strength. Locking her knees, she clenched her hands at her sides and pressed her lips firmly together. Only now was she beginning to understand what it must have been like for her mother when she'd found out she was a blood witch, when she'd realized that Cal was using her, when she'd had to fight the darkest forces Wicca had seen in generations. She'd never be able to look at her mum in the same way again.

"Moira saw you looking at an image of Hunter Niall in a

crystal," said Morgan. "Tell me what you know. Don't make this worse than it has to be."

"You don't know who you're dealing with," Lilith snarled.

"Neither do you. You would be hard-pressed to come up with someone who could scare me," Morgan said coldly. "Not after my father. I've felt the foul wind of a dark wave against my face. I've gone face-to-face against Ciaran and defeated him. I've been hard to impress since then. Now, for the *last* time, you will tell me what you know, or after tonight *you* will know what it's like to be hard to impress."

With that she clenched her hand into a fist, then twisted it sideways, and Lilith crumpled like a puppet with cut strings. She slumped to the ground, curled around the door, her face contorted into a mask of pain and rage. Ian dropped to his knees next to her and put his hand on her shoulder, then shot Morgan a look of anger.

"Stop it! Stop it!" he said harshly, and Moira closed her eyes for a moment and stepped back, still unable to bear seeing Ian frightened, angry, hurt.

Flecks of blood appeared at Lilith's lips, but she could not speak. Morgan made the tiniest gesture with her closed hand, and a high keening escaped from Lilith and split the night air, a howl of agony.

Morgan leaned closer, not looking at Ian. "I can do this all night," she said slowly. "Can you?"

Lilith's face deformed one last time, then suddenly she spit out, "It was Iona! Iona MacEwan!"

Moira saw her mother step back, visibly shocked. "Iona. What about her?" she demanded.

Iona? Moira thought. Ciaran's other daughter?

"She'll know the answers you want," Lilith said.

"And where's Iona?" Sky said, her voice sounding like a dry knife on leather. "Where is she now?"

Lilith seemed to wrestle with this answer. Her short, heavy body was still frozen on the ground, and Moira thought that if she could move, she would be writhing and screaming. Then she burst out, "Arsdeth."

"Where is Arsdeth?" Sky snapped.

With an effort Lilith gasped, "North. North, by the sea."

Morgan looked at Ian. "Get a map."

He clearly wanted to refuse: his face was red with anger and overlain with worry for his mother. But Morgan's voice was a force field, and Ian stood and disappeared into the house. A few moments later he returned, a much-used and faded map of Ireland in his hand. He threw it on the ground between Morgan and Sky, and Sky picked it up.

"Arsdeth," she said. "In the north."

Moira swallowed hard as she saw a dark red drop of blood slide from Lilith's nose to sink onto the worn stone step under her head. Goddess, this was a bloody night. She understood now what Keady had meant when she'd told Moira it would truly be better never to understand what Morgan was capable of. So much pain and terror already. Did she have enough of her mother's strength in her to bear it?

"Arsdeth," Sky murmured again, tracing the map with her finger. "Oh, Goddess, here it is. Arsdeth, way the hell up north in County Donegal, by the ocean."

Morgan looked at her, and Sky nodded. Then Morgan said to Lilith, "What will happen to you if we go there and find you've been lying to us?" Morgan let Lilith have a minute to think about it. "What will happen to your son? Your house?

Your coven? You do know you'd never escape me." Her tone was conversational, mildly curious.

There was no response, and Morgan rocked her fist from side to side slightly. A crumpled sound of agony came from Lilith, and once again Moira had to look away. "You know that I'll track you to the ends of the earth if you flee, if you've lied to us?"

Lilith nodded. Ian looked as though he was trying not to cry. Goddess, how could she turn off her feelings for him? How could he have betrayed her to his mother? Nothing would ever seem normal again. In one short week, one long night, her life had changed dramatically forever.

"Lilith," Morgan said, her voice sounding horribly gentle, "think about this. Do you believe I'm my father's daughter?"

A flash of fury sparked from Lilith's eyes. Her lips, stained with blood flecks, pressed even more tightly together. Her nod was unwilling, but it was there.

"You are right," Morgan whispered, and straightened. She nodded to Sky, who was looking at her curiously. Sky folded the map and put it on the ground next to Ian. Ian angrily scraped his sweater sleeve across his eyes. Moira couldn't resist meeting his gaze one last time. To her surprise, the look he gave her was anguished, but not full of hatred.

Morgan had already left Lilith and was walking to the car when Sky said softly, "Morgan?"

Morgan turned to look at her, and Sky met her gaze, then flicked her glance over to Lilith, still on the ground. Quickly Morgan turned and strode back to the high priestess of Ealltuinn. "I release you," she said, her voice low and steady. Her hand sprang open, and with an audible gasp Lilith seemed to melt onto her doorstep.

"Mother?" Ian said, his hand on her shoulder. He gave the three of them a last glance, then went inside to return moments later with a blanket, which he pulled over his mother. Her face was waxen, and the blood from her nose shone dark and red against her skin.

Morgan turned again and walked to the car, her back stiff, hands hanging like claws from her sides.

Moira followed her quickly, sliding into the backseat as Sky started the car. She still couldn't believe what she'd just seen— her own mother had hurt someone on purpose. Had frightened and threatened someone. *Bound* someone. Miserably Moira leaned her head against the window, wishing she could just shut down and stop thinking, stop feeling.

In the front seat she saw Sky glance quickly at Morgan, saw her mother's shoulders bend and her head droop—and then she heard her mother start to cry. Not just smothered sniffles, but huge, heaving sobs.

Then Moira remembered one of the most basic Wiccan teachings, the threefold rule—*What you send out comes back to you—times three.* Morgan had just sent horrible pain to Lilith—what would be returned to her or to Moira and Sky for participating?

Sky shifted the car into a higher gear, and Moira saw that they were going back toward town, where Sky could get on the highway going north. "Morgan, it's all right," Sky said. "You need to be strong now. You had to do it. For Hunter."

"Oh, Goddess," Morgan sobbed. "What have I become? Who am I?" And she cried harder. Those were the only words Moira heard her mother say the rest of the night.

16

Morgan

In the end it took almost seven hours of driving to get to County Donegal. There was little traffic, but the roads were small and often curvy or hilly. Dawn was starting to break when Sky stopped the car not far from Arsdeth.

Morgan looked back at her daughter, sleeping in the back-seat. What had she been thinking, dragging Moira into this? Moira ought to be at home, just waking up to go to school. Some mother she was. *Oh, Colm, help.* Colm had been her rock, her anchor, all those years. It was his steady presence that had allowed her to put her painful past behind her. His gentle insistence that she live in the present, that she continue to find joy and meaning in her life was what had enabled her to fulfill her dream of becoming a healer.

Nearly twenty years ago she'd thought she'd seen the last of truly dark magick. For all these years in Ireland with Colm, it had been a triumph to live a quiet, satisfying life, filled with healing rites, study, school, and Saturday night circles. Now *this*, plunging back into strong, hurtful magick, dealing with people who reveled in darkness and pain—it was so deeply wrong. That outside forces were causing her to sink back into darkness and fear, rage and revenge, filled her with fury. She was the Destroyer. She would end this, here and now.

Next to her Sky was looking fatigued. She had worked a couple of keep-awake spells during the night but hadn't let Morgan share the driving. Morgan had cried for an hour, and by then they had been on the highway and Moira had fallen asleep. They had thrown a blanket over her when Sky had stopped for gas, and when they got back in the car, Sky had glanced over at Morgan and said, "Bloody hell."

There had been blood on the front of Morgan's sweatshirt.

When the bleeding had abated, Sky had convinced Morgan to rest for a while.

Now, with dawn approaching, Morgan was feeling better. At least she wasn't crying anymore or oozing blood.

"We don't have a plan," said Morgan, and Sky made a noise like a bitter chuckle.

"Let's turn around and go back home, then," she said.

"You know—we could be walking into a trap here," Morgan said. If Hunter was alive, why was Iona just now letting Morgan glimpse the truth? Could they even trust Lilith's information? These signs that had been coming to her . . . they had a purpose behind them. Had Lilith set Moira up to "catch" her scrying for Hunter? She certainly hadn't been very careful about hiding the image from Moira, and if she was behind those hexes and spells at Morgan's house, then she was capable of more secretive magick. Then there was Hunter's warning, too, not to come. It all pointed to the fact that this was a trap. Iona *wanted* Morgan to search for Hunter—but why?

Trap or no, Morgan couldn't stop now. She had to find Hunter.

"I know," Sky said. "But what choice do we have?"

"I should have left Moira at home," Morgan said.

Sky shrugged. "This is her life, her father. She would never have allowed us to leave her behind."

"Maybe so."

"And Morgan . . . you need her right now. Hunter needs her."

Morgan swallowed hard, thinking about this.

Behind them Moira stirred, then sat up, yawning. "Where are we?" she asked, and then Morgan watched the memories of the night before cross her face.

"Almost to Iona's," Sky answered her. Turning, she said, "I have a friend who lives not far from here. Maybe I should call her and you could stay there, just for today. Your mum and I don't know what's going to happen."

Morgan was grateful the suggestion came from Sky, but not unexpectedly, Moira's reaction was an instant furrowing of the brow, a determined expression on her face. "No, thank you."

Morgan turned to face her daughter. "Moira, last night was terrible. But it was nothing compared to what we might be facing. I can't guarantee that Iona won't be expecting us, that we're not heading into a trap. In fact, I'm sure we are." Morgan shook her head, thinking with dread of what might lie before them. "All my instincts are telling me to run a thousand miles from this situation, but I can't—not if Hunter's still alive. That's my choice, but it doesn't have to be yours." She looked deeply into Moira's hazel eyes, like her own, but with slightly less brown, slightly more green.

"We lost your dad six months ago. I can't risk anything happening to you. I can't let it. Iona could be much worse than Lilith ever was. Please, go to Sky's friend's house."

"No."

"I wonder where she gets that from?" Sky murmured.

Sky had the foresight to begin casting pathfinding spells while they were still almost twenty kilometers—a good half hour or forty-five minutes—away. Even with the spells, they took wrong turns and got lost twice. Without them, they never would have found their way at all.

Arsdeth itself was a small, unremarkable village, not as quaint as some more southern towns, but with an older feel to it. It was rougher, less civilized in a way, with bits and pieces of ancient castles visible in the distance.

On a side street in Arsdeth they stopped the car and Morgan scried. She closed her eyes, lit a candle she placed carefully on the dashboard, and called images of fire to her, building her own power and strength. She pictured Iona as she remembered her from Ciaran's funeral, then asked the Goddess to show her the way to her. In her mind she wandered down roads, turning, heading north, then east, then north again. Eventually she saw the house, an ugly redbrick saltbox, with white-painted window frames and doorway.

"Okay, head north." She consulted their map. "We'll hit it up at this intersection. Then I'll tell you where to turn."

"Right, then," Sky said, shifting into a higher gear. "Let's go wring some information out of this woman."

Morgan knew that what was ahead of them was going to be very dangerous. There was no way to turn back now. Not when Hunter might be at the end of the trail. Not while there was still the slightest shred of hope. She still couldn't believe all of this was really coming from Iona. Iona wasn't strong enough—but then, Killian had told her that since their father's funeral, Iona had vowed to become stronger.

Ciaran's funeral. Morgan sat up. "Sky. Ciaran's funeral! At Ciaran's funeral Grania, Kyle, and Iona were furious I had come. Kyle tried to put a spell on me. But then Iona—Iona smiled. As though she had a secret." Morgan shook her head, remembering. "She knew she had taken Hunter from me."

They finally found Iona's house. Sky carefully turned the car and parked it facing outward, back toward the road, in case they had to leave in a hurry. Morgan pulled a windbreaker over her sweatshirt to conceal the bloodstain in front. As calmly as they could, Morgan and Sky took several minutes to lay new and stronger ward-evil spells on the car.

Looking behind her, Morgan made sure Moira was beside her. She paused for a moment, casting out her senses. Frowning, she walked to the edge of the driveway and looked past the house.

"She's up there," she said, pointing. There was a low hill behind Iona's house, and on the hill were the battered remains of what had once been a Celtic stronghold.

"Up in the castle ruins?" Moira asked.

"Yes." She looked at the two of them. "Are we ready?"

Moira nodded, though she was unsuccessful in keeping the fear out of her eyes. Sky's face was grim, resolute. They pushed through the hedge bordering the driveway and headed toward the hill.

There was no path, and the turf was spongy with rain. Soon their shoes and pants bottoms were soaked through and flecked with grass. They'd reached the first gentle slope of the hill when an unearthly baying sent chills down their spines. The next thing Morgan saw was four large Rottweilers, tearing down the hill at them, barking ferociously. Their jaws gaped, showing large white fangs that seemed ready to snap a tree limb in half. Suddenly the dogs were almost upon them, and Morgan felt Moira freeze with fear.

"Stop there," Morgan said softly when the dogs were ten feet away. Holding her hand out flat, she sent out a sensation of running up against a wall and a calm, quiet, happy feeling, where life was good, bellies were full, and there was a raw steak waiting back at the house.

Gentle things, Morgan crooned in her mind. *Sweet and calm. We're friends, friends to you, we mean no harm.*

The four dogs stopped with almost comical suddenness, their front paws backpedaling and screeching to a halt on the wet grass. From snarling, vicious, out-to-kill man-eaters, they became almost bashful giants, bobbing their heads and pulling their lips back in apologetic grins. Muscular tails began wagging as they stood in a confused group, wondering what to do next.

Morgan walked up to them, held out her hand for them all to smell. Sky did the same, and Morgan made sure Moira did also.

"We're your friends," Morgan said gently. "Remember us. Remember us." She traced the rune Wynn on each silky black forehead, writing happiness and harmony on them.

The huge black-and-tan dogs stood aside, cheerful puppies wishing they had a tennis ball. They watched the three witches walk past them up the hill, unconcerned.

Every muscle in Morgan's body was coiled and ready for anything. Her blood was singing with tension, adrenaline flowing through her veins like wine. Each breath took in more oxygen than she needed, each sense was hyperaware: the clouded blue of the sky, the scent of the wet grass. No birds sang here; there was no other life than the four dogs they'd just left.

They were maybe thirty feet away from the ancient stones when Morgan became more aware of Iona's presence. In a gaping window hole, where she had looked only a moment before, stood Iona.

Iona looked nothing like Morgan remembered. At Ciaran's funeral Iona had been plump, doughy, with a heavily made-up face. This Iona was thin to the point of being skeletal, with burning, overlarge eyes. Her skin was chalk white, as if she spent too much time indoors, and her hair was stringy, wispy, and prematurely gray. This was her half sister, but as unlike her as if they shared not one chromosome, not even the ones that made them inherently human.

With no warning Iona's hand snapped forward and a crackling, spitting blue ball of witchfire shot toward Morgan. Instinctively she raised her own hand to deflect it, but the fire grazed her skin, causing a stinging burn.

Iona laughed, showing a gaping mouth, the skin of her jaw stretching grotesquely. "That was a welcome, sister," she said. "I've been expecting you, of course. Ever since that idiot Lilith told me you'd be coming. Pity about Lilith—she was a blubbering mess after you finished with her. She hasn't held up quite as well as I'd hoped. But she played her part well: you are here. I can only imagine what you had to do to get her to admit where I was."

Morgan kept her face expressionless. "I started crushing her capillaries, from the outside in. They're very, very small and very delicate. If you damage enough of them, you bleed to death."

Morgan's senses prickled as everyone's tension level ratcheted up a notch.

For an instant a wary, speculative look crossed Iona's face but disappeared at once. "Sounds nasty," she said dismissively.

Morgan narrowed her eyes, wondering if Iona had ever believed the rumors about Morgan's power all these years. Whatever it took, Morgan had to convince Iona that she was no match for her. If she could frighten Iona, Morgan might not be forced to do things that would diminish her own soul.

"It was," Morgan was surprised to hear Moira say.

Iona looked at Moira, and Morgan forced herself not to panic. *Moira, stay back, be invisible,* she sent.

"It was very ugly," Morgan said evenly. "I was sorry to do it. But it's only a fraction of what I will do to you." This wasn't her true self, who she was inside. It was a warrior Morgan—one who came out only in times of need.

"Ooh, stop, you're scaring me," Iona said in a bored tone, leaning against the crumbling stone window. "By the way, where are my dogs?" Her tone was casual, but Morgan picked up on her true emotion—fear.

"They were in my way," she said, and Iona's eyes darted around, searching. Her jaw, with its tissue-thin skin, tightened.

Slowly Morgan realized that she felt no fear and surprisingly little anger. She was icy and unstoppable. She was Morgan of Belwicket. This pathetic excuse for a witch was just someone in her way. The feeling simultaneously thrilled and terrified her.

"Where is Hunter Niall?" Morgan asked. "Lilith told me everything she knew. I'm sure she would have preferred to be loyal to you, whatever your hold on her is. But in the end she crumbled. She had no choice. But you do. I recommend you choose wisely."

"Why, I heard Hunter Niall drowned in a ferry accident almost sixteen years ago," Iona said lightly.

"Iona," Morgan said, her voice glacial, "tell me where he is." She was becoming more and more tightly wound, a rubber band about to snap. She didn't want to cause harm here. She didn't want to. But she would.

"Tell me!" she shouted, flinging out her hand. An ancient stone burst apart next to Iona's head, shooting ragged shards of rock in a starburst. Iona flinched and turned away, but Morgan saw scrapes on Iona's cheek and flakes of stone in her thin hair.

Morgan could feel Iona's fear growing—but she could also sense fear coming from next to her. From Moira. She cast a quick glance at her daughter, sending her as much warmth and reassurance as she could. Moira's face was a mask—she was fighting hard not to show her true emotions, Morgan knew. But she was terrified inside, and Morgan wished with all her heart she wasn't here to witness what Morgan was doing.

"How dare you!" Iona shouted. Morgan whipped back around to face her. Iona brushed at herself—she was covered with dust and rock flakes. She looked at Morgan, her eyes burning. "This place is sacred!"

Wordlessly Morgan snapped out her other hand, her fingers stiff and tight. Another rock exploded, on Iona's other side. This time Iona cried out and covered her eyes with her hands. Gingerly she brushed at her face, leaving pale streaks of blood where her fingers had been.

"My eye!" Iona snarled, then looked up in concern as they heard a rumbling, scraping sound. The explosion had weakened part of the wall, and a large boulder was teetering on the edge above her. Quickly Iona jumped down onto the grass in front of Morgan just as the boulder fell and crashed into the window frame, right where she had been standing.

Morgan now had Iona's full attention. Clearly her half sister was angry. Her lips were tight with annoyance, her face streaked with blood, her eye was swelling, and she was glaring at Morgan.

"You don't know who you're dealing with," Iona said in a deadly voice. "You have no idea the things I've done or who or what I've become."

"Really. Just who are you, *Iona?*" Morgan said, filling her voice with unheard waves of power like tiny seismic shocks, intended to cause discomfort and anxiety. Next to her Moira shifted on her feet. Sky stood quietly, tense and at the ready.

Iona's eyes flared slightly and again she lost her composure for a split second. "I've become my father's daughter," she said in a voice full of rage and triumph.

With a calculated force Morgan thought, *Push,* and Iona was slammed against the back of the stone wall behind her. Her breath left her lungs with an audible "oof!" and she struggled to hold on to her balance.

"Hunter Niall," Morgan reminded her in a steely voice. "Where is he? Or should I start trying to persuade you?" She latched onto the image of Iona before her, pictured her ear, and whispered some of the words she had learned from her *tàth meànma*—or Wiccan mind meld—with Ciaran all those years ago. Iona shrieked, grabbing her ear, her face screwed up with pain. Morgan imagined it felt as though a railroad spike were being driven into her brain.

Iona writhed against the wall, screaming curses at Morgan that had no weight.

Morgan took a deep breath and released her. "You see, Iona," she said, "I've *always* been my father's daughter. Now stop wasting my time. Where is Hunter?" The urgency for an answer was so great inside her, she was no longer even forcing this cold, hard anger to terrify Iona—it was real. It was everything she was right now—a great, pulsing need to find Hunter.

Iona, trying not to weep, managed to stand up and lean against the wall. With no warning she stood ramrod straight and shouted a spell. Morgan felt her knees buckle and her muscles become lax. She dropped to the ground, knowing instantly that Iona had managed to put a binding spell on her.

"You twit!" Iona screamed, standing over Morgan. "All these years you've had no idea—no idea about what I did to you—to your precious Hunter!"

Morgan saw Sky move forward, but Iona stopped her with a flex of her hand.

Stay put, Moira, don't move, Morgan sent, knowing her daughter had to be terrified. Her mind was reacting quickly, feeling her way through the invisible bond that Iona had put on her.

"You're nothing," Iona shouted at her. "You're Ciaran's bastard, his mistake, his embarrassment!"

At the same moment Sky and Moira began chanting together, softly—they must have exchanged witch messages. They were working a spell to interfere with Iona's.

Morgan concentrated and felt the binding spell weaken. Iona was powerful but not nearly as strong as Morgan. Moira and Sky had weakened Iona's spell, and now Morgan could take care of the rest. With a burst of energy Morgan pushed her way through the spell, not bothering to dismantle it piece by piece but simply breaking it altogether. She broke free just as Iona was turning her focus to Moira and Sky, realizing the meaning of their chant.

Instantly Morgan again sent the pain to Iona's ear with Ciaran's dark words. Iona shrieked even louder, curling up as if to get away from the agony. Sky moved closer to Morgan—Iona couldn't hold her back any longer. Iona was on her knees on the grass, both hands pressed to her ear.

Morgan counted to twenty slowly, then she released her. "You are a joke," she said with unnatural calmness. "Do not make me ask again. Hunter Niall."

Iona sat up again, holding and rubbing her head, her bony face marred by hatred. "Haven't you figured it out yet, Morgan of Belwicket? *I* made the ferry go down. *I* did it, made that wave. I took the ferry." Her eyes were glittering with an unnatural brightness, and Morgan began to believe that twenty years of fury and resentment had made Iona insane. "And I created a *bith dearc* that opened above the water. *I* took Hunter. Poor thing, he was actually trying to swim to shore when I sucked him through it."

Morgan shook, rocked to the core at the idea of what Hunter had gone through. "You? How could *you* possibly do that?" she got out.

Iona smiled coyly, still looking like a wreck but starting to enjoy her own story. "With his true name. I have Hunter's true name."

No! No, no, no. Morgan tried to hold back her panic, knowing Iona would sense it, but she could feel the ragged edges of fear reaching for her. To know something's true name was to have ultimate power over it. Total control, in every way. Morgan had learned Ciaran's true name and had used it to stop him for good. How could Iona have learned Hunter's?

"Years ago I met a witch named Justine Courceau," Iona went on, as if reading Morgan's question on her face.

Justine—the woman who had collected names—the woman whom Hunter had once kissed. Hunter had told Morgan that Justine had been bitter when he had made it clear nothing would never happen between them, but . . . that couldn't have been enough of a reason to go along with Iona's scheme. And besides, Justine hadn't known Hunter's true name.

"She hated Hunter and had spent years searching for his true name," Iona went on. "She finally found it using a *bith dearc* to speak to the dead. I offered to buy it from her. The silly woman wouldn't sell it." Iona's mouth crooked upward in a horrible mockery of a smile. "So I killed her. And took her soul—her power—for myself. With her power joined to mine, I was unstoppable. I was my father's daughter. And I wanted you to suffer. I wanted to cause you pain—so I created the *bith dearc* and stole Hunter from you with his true name." Iona stopped, wiping the disgusting glee from her face and attempting to look more in control. She laughed. "How does that make you feel?"

Oh, Goddess, Morgan thought in horror. Now she understood why Iona was oddly strong. She had taken someone's soul, absorbed her power. Who knew if she had even stopped at Justine? Iona was power mad, but the corruption of souls—of the power—was eating away at her, Morgan realized. Iona had gained power, but the power was killing her and destroying her. An icy hand clenched around Morgan's heart as she realized that Iona might have taken Hunter's soul, too. Morgan's knees started trembling, and she prayed it didn't show. A thin, cold line of sweat had started at the back of her neck and was snaking slowly down her spine. She felt surrounded by death and horror and hatred, and all she could think of was Hunter. *Hunter, Hunter. Please don't let that have happened to him.* She swallowed carefully and kept an iron grip on her self-control.

"Iona, where is Hunter?" she repeated flatly—staring at the shaking, weak witch huddled at her feet.

"Oh, no, he isn't dead. No, no, that would have been too quick, too easy. Hunter's been alive all this time." Iona imparted this information as if sharing a delicious secret. "Can you imagine? You grieved like a widow for all these years. And he's alive! If you call his existence living."

Oh, Goddess, she's insane. Goddess, please help me. Please get me through this. Hunter's alive.

Sky stepped forward next to Morgan. She grasped Morgan's elbow. "Where is he?" Sky demanded. Morgan was grateful—it gave her a minute to pull herself together. Finally she knew for sure. Hunter was *alive.* A dull throb started in her chest, and she felt the warm, heavy stickiness of blood flowing.

Iona cackled. "On an island," she said triumphantly. "An island cloaked in fog and rain, where no one goes. An island where nothing grows, nothing lives, and every day is exactly the same as the day before it. Hunter has been there, suffering, all this time, since I pulled him there through the *bith dearc*. Because of you and what you did to my family."

"Alone on an island?" Morgan asked, clearing her throat and strengthening her voice. Alone for sixteen years on an island. Surely he was mad by now. The thought of her beloved Hunter, her *mùirn beatha dàn*, going through such unimaginable torment for sixteen years almost knocked her to the ground.

"No," Iona said, surprising her. "There are a few other witches there, those who had angered the MacEwans through the years. I don't keep track of them. Why bother? They are nothing."

"Tell us how to get there," Sky said, her voice like stone. "Or I will gouge your eyes out and feed them to what's left of your dogs." Her tall, slender frame was rigid with tension, her hands clenched at her sides. Her face was inscrutable, still, her black eyes piercing.

Iona blinked. Morgan felt Moira step back.

Iona seemed to think for a few moments. "North," she said, then smirked. "In the ocean."

Morgan let every ounce of menace rise up in her. She gave full rein to every hateful thought, every desire she'd ever had for retribution. Malignancy welled up inside her, and she let it flow outward toward Iona. It was grotesque, the antithesis of everything she had worked toward in her life. It was darkness, it was against the Wiccan Rede, it was power and threat and bleakness and a complete absence of love or life or hope.

When it reached Iona, an invisible miasma of the worst of human expression, she recoiled and started to gag, grabbing her throat with one hand, bracing herself against the stone wall. Her burning eyes seemed to start from her head; her tongue looked swollen.

Morgan watched her writhe in pain. *How far am I willing to go?* She would go as far as it took.

Sky took Morgan's arm and shook her gently, and Morgan swallowed hard and with effort squashed the feelings rushing deep inside her and crumpled them into a tight, dark ball, scratchy and painful, that she pushed to the bottom of her consciousness. Looking into Sky's troubled eyes, she nodded.

Iona coughed and sank to the ground, gasping. She was shaking, her eyes wide and frightened.

"Where is the island?" Sky repeated with quiet menace.

"Between North Ulst," Iona said, her voice sounding strangled and thin. Her white hands were shaking, fluttering around her uncontrollably. "And the Isle of Lewis." She choked on a sob and turned her face away, one hand clutching at the grass.

"Are we just leaving her here?" Sky asked Morgan as they turned away.

Morgan paused. They didn't have a *braigh*—a chain used to bind witches. There was no time to deal with bringing Iona with them, constantly having to watch over her. "We'll send a witch message to the New Charter," she decided. "Have them send someone to come get her right away." Morgan glanced back at Iona, who was bent over, moaning. "She's in no shape to do much anytime soon," she said.

They walked to the car, and Moira was silent and sad next to Morgan. Morgan knew she had changed her daughter's image of her forever. What would that mean in the coming years? What would it do to Moira's ideas about magick and about love? As they headed down the hill, Morgan heard Iona moaning. But she kept walking forward, always forward, toward the car. To turn back would be to set in motion something beyond reconciliation.

They passed the four Rottweilers on their way to the car. Morgan walked past them and got into the car, pressing her hand over her still-bleeding chest. She leaned her head against the window as Sky and Moira got in. Casting her senses, she realized that they were both on the edge of breaking down: frightened, sad, upset, anxious.

After they flew through Arsdeth, some color returned to Sky's pale face. "Hunter's alive," she said, looking at Morgan. "We're going to find him. That's what matters."

17

Moira

By the end of that day they had reached the Isle of Lewis. The drive had been tense, with no one speaking much until now. Moira's hands were still trembling, and no matter how many deep breaths she took, she couldn't seem to get her heart rate to slow down. She'd thought what she'd seen with Lilith had been incredible, but that fight between her mum and Iona . . . she'd never felt such sheer terror in her life.

And worse, she'd felt helpless. She knew she and Sky had helped a little, when they'd worked together to weaken Iona's binding spell on her mum. But that had probably been mostly Sky. What if Moira was just holding them back? Her power was nothing next to that of Morgan of Belwicket.

Morgan of Belwicket. Moira finally understood the awe she'd always heard in people's voices when they said those words. Her mum was a stronger witch than she'd even believed existed in the world. She'd thought the stories had to be exaggerated, but now . . . it was all so unbelievable. Had that really been her mum, whirling spells at Iona that had reduced her to a whimpering mess on the ground?

"Let's just go now," Morgan said.

"No." Sky's voice was final. "It's dark. No one will rent us a boat at this time of night. And we're all exhausted—we need to be prepared for what's ahead."

Curled up in the backseat, Moira listened to them argue, torn between a strong desire to find Hunter as soon as possible so she could come face-to-face with the man she'd just learned was her father—and a terrible fear of it at the same time. There had been so many shocks, so many terrors in the past twenty-four hours alone. She was still consumed with the grief of learning that she wasn't really Colm's daughter, the horror of knowing that her mother was *Ciaran's* daughter, the intense disbelief of seeing for real what Morgan of Belwicket was capable of. And underneath it all—a fresh, piercing pain over Ian's betrayal. How could she deal with meeting Hunter now, in the middle of all of this? But how could she *not* yearn to see him, to know him? To save him from whatever that terrifying woman, Iona, was doing to him?

Iona. Just thinking the name brought a bitter taste to Moira's mouth. She'd always known evil existed, but today she had seen it close up, alive. She shivered, pulling her jacket more tightly around herself.

"He's *alive*," Morgan was saying sharply. "We have to go *now*! Hunter's out there and he's alive, and we're going, right now!"

"Morgan," Sky said, her voice just as sharp. "We *don't* know what's waiting for us out in the middle of the bloody ocean. We *don't* know what kind of power or magick we're going to need to use out there. But I *do* know that I couldn't light a damn candle right now! And neither could you!"

"But—" Morgan began.

"You're Morgan of Belwicket! You may be one of the

most powerful witches to walk the earth, but you're not a goddess!" Sky said, raising her voice. "You're not totally invincible, even if you think you are!"

Moira's eyes got larger. She propped herself on one elbow to see better. Her mother was looking at Sky with a shocked expression on her face.

"Is that how you think I see myself?" Morgan asked in a small voice.

Impatiently Sky shook her head and ran a hand through her fine, light hair. "No. I'm sorry. I didn't mean that. I'm saying that we all have limits. Look, Morgan, Hunter was—is—my cousin. I grew up with him. He's like my brother. We were best friends. Don't you think I want to find him? Don't you think I'm desperate to see if he's truly alive? Don't you think I'm desperate to get to him as soon as possible?"

Morgan didn't say anything, just looked at Sky. Her face was scraped and her hands still had dirt on them. She looked pale and wrung out and like she was about to cry.

"Iona's waited sixteen years to do this," Sky went on patiently. "She knows we're going to the island. She gave us just enough information to possibly find it. Lilith was a plant of hers. Don't you see? All of this is her *plan*."

Morgan looked away, then looked back and nodded.

"If Iona has been consuming souls and increasing her power through dark methods, we're going to need to be in better shape to fight her," Sky said. "Everything in me is telling me to jump into the ocean right now and *swim* out there to get Hunter. But I know that if we are going to try to save him, if we're going to go up against Iona on *her* terms, on *her* ground, we need to be able to pull out all the stops. Do you follow me?"

Morgan sighed.

"A few hours," Sky said, sounding weary and beaten. "That's all I'm asking for."

Morgan nodded again. "You're right," she said quietly. "I hate it, but you're right."

Moira sat up, brushed the hair out of her eyes, and wiped away the tears that had slipped out. She looked down at her hands, which were still shaking. *Be still,* she thought, focusing her energy and shutting out all of her fear and confusion. As she watched, the trembling began to stop. Moira felt a small jolt of triumph.

"Right. Good," said Sky. She started the car again and drove off. Two minutes later she said, "Look, there's a bed-and-breakfast. Tomorrow morning we'll rent a boat. All right?"

"Yes," Morgan said, sounding exhausted.

Moira gathered her coat and put it on. Dread welled up in her, and she swallowed back her nausea. She could do this. She could be strong, too. Her mum needed her. And he—Hunter—needed her, too.

The sky was barely streaked with pink and orange when Moira, her mother, and Sky got up the next morning.

Moira had slept like the dead, closing her eyes as soon as her head hit the pillow. She'd had many dreams, but the only one she remembered was of Hunter. In it he had said, "Don't find me, I am lost forever," and Moira had responded, "I must find you. I'm your daughter." Tears on her cheeks, she'd sat bolt upright in her narrow bed. She'd lost one father six months ago. Today would show whether she would gain another one or lose him as well. But how could she see a stranger, Hunter, as her father?

Down at the harbor Sky was negotiating to rent a

twenty-foot fishing boat for the day. It was big and clunky, with an outboard engine and a canvas tarp on aluminum poles as the only cover. To Moira it looked ancient and only vaguely seaworthy. Its name was *Carrachan:* "Rockfish."

Moira's mum turned to look at her. "You're staying here," she said in a no-nonsense tone. Moira's mouth dropped open in shock. After all this—after facing Iona without flinching and seeing her mum become another person, she was being asked to stop *now?* Her mother went on: "You're fifteen, you're not initiated, and you're my only child. I cannot lose you. You're going to stay in the bed-and-breakfast until we get back. Don't wander around. Stay in the room and don't open the door."

"What?" Moira cried, staring at her mother. "You can't be serious! After all this?" She waved her arms in a completely inadequate description of the last three days. "You need me!"

"No discussion," her mum said firmly. "You're staying here. Sky and I will do what we have to out there, but I won't be able to think if you're not safe."

"I am not staying here," Moira said, setting her jaw and looking down at her mother. "I want to be with you. I want to be there if—when you find Hunter."

Her mother's face softened. "Moira—I've lost so many people I've loved. If I lost you, too, I couldn't go on. Do you understand? I couldn't go on." Her brown eyes looked searchingly into Moira's. For a moment Moira felt a twinge of guilt. Her mum *had* lost a lost of people: Cal, then Hunter, then Dad. Her birth parents.

But none of that changed the fact that Moira had to do this. "I'm going," she said firmly.

In the small boat Sky had pulled on an ill-fitting life vest. Her pale hair was already being tossed by the wind.

Wordlessly Morgan pointed back to the bed-and-breakfast.

Moira felt a spark of anger. "I'm part of this!" she cried. "He's my bloody real father!" It didn't sound right, coming out of her mouth—Colm was her father. But she knew it was still the truth, and stranger or not, if Hunter needed help, she wasn't going to sit by and do nothing.

Morgan shook her head, her eyes full of pain. "No." Then she turned from Moira and climbed down to where the boat was tied. She stepped into the boat and pulled on a life vest. At Sky's word she pulled up on the rope tying the boat to the pier, and Sky pulled back on the throttle. The small engine roared to life. Without a backward look Sky sat back and took the old-fashioned tiller under her arm. There was no steering wheel, no console—only battered vinyl seats, ripped and smelling of fish.

Moira stared unbelievingly. Were they really going to leave her here, on an island a thousand kilometers from home, with strangers? Were they really going to make her sit out this final stage when they were looking for her birth father?

She didn't think so.

The boat was slowly pulling away from the pier, its engine already sounding asthmatic. Without allowing herself time to think about whether it was a good idea or not—she knew it wasn't, but she was way past caring—she sprinted forward and threw herself off the pier as hard as she could.

Whoosh! She hit the surface of the water hard, going under before swimming back up. The plan had actually been to land *in* the boat, even if it was headfirst. Morgan and Sky both turned at the splash, and in an instant Morgan was grabbing her arm and hauling her upward.

"What were you thinking, Moira!" Morgan shouted.

Air, breathe, air. "You're not leaving me!" Moira shouted back when she'd finally gotten her wind.

Sky had slowed the engine and was looking at Morgan inquisitively. Moira looked at Sky, then at her mum. Total exasperation crossed Morgan's face, but finally she shook her head. They wouldn't turn back—they'd wasted too much time as it was.

Her mother took off her life vest and handed it to Moira.

"What will you wear?" Moira asked.

"There are only two," her mother said shortly.

Moira looked around. They'd left the harbor behind and were passing slower-moving fishing boats. It had been sunny, with just a few puffy, cotton-ball clouds in the sky when they'd set off. The sea had looked a rich blue-green, full of life.

Now, only minutes later, Moira could scarcely see any blue in the sky at all. An endless, heavy-looking mass of gray clouds was sweeping across the sky as if pushed there by a huge, invisible hand. Moira moved forward to sit on one of the vinyl side benches up front. The sea was the color of lead. Instead of perky little white-capped waves, it was churning, uncomfortable, roiling with some deep disturbance. There were no birds overhead, Moira noticed. Seagulls had been thick by the harbor, bright white and gray, raucous cries filling the air. Now it was as if they had been erased from the picture.

She looked up to see her mum looking solemnly at Sky.

"Come into my parlor," Sky said dryly.

Said the spider to the fly. Iona had sent this weather. There would be more, Moira knew. They were going forward, even if this was a trap.

Moira sat shivering. Her shirt, jacket, jeans, socks, and sneakers were soaked, and she was freezing. The temperature had dropped about fifteen degrees and the wind had gotten brisker.

Salty spray occasionally flew up into her face, feeling like needles hitting her skin.

Sky turned the boat slightly, aiming for a gap between two big islands. The ride became much rougher as the boat cut across the current. Moira sneaked a glance at her mum, who was staring straight ahead, white-faced and determined. Morgan looked over at her, and her eyes were so sad and solemn that Moira felt a touch of panic.

Crunch, crunch, crunch. Her hands were white-knuckled from gripping the handhold on the side of the boat. Her face stung from salt spray and wind.

Oh, no. A familiar sensation began in the pit of her stomach. She swallowed convulsively. Then her mouth flooded with saliva, and with her last few working brain cells she realized she needed to hang over the edge of the boat *now*, because she was going to vomit.

More salt spray hit her face—she was closer to the water. She started to cry, her body suddenly racked by sobs. She'd never felt so lost in her whole life.

Then her mother was there, scooping her long hair back, her hand on Moira's neck. When Moira's stomach finally seemed not only empty but inside out, Morgan pulled Moira back up. She'd taken a bandanna out of her back pocket, and she wiped Moira's stinging face. Moira was sobbing now, knowing she had to stop right away, knowing she looked like a baby, knowing her mother had been only too right about wanting her to stay.

"I'm sorry," she sobbed. "I'm sorry."

"Shhh, shhh," said her mother. "It's hard. That's why I didn't want you to come."

"I'm sorry," Moira repeated, shivering again.

Morgan studied her for a second, then closed her eyes.

She spread out the fingers of her right hand and placed them over Moira's face, touching her temple, her forehead, a vein in her neck. Then she started to murmur words in Gaelic, a few of which Moira recognized from class, but most unknown. Within moments Moira breathed a sigh of relief. Her pounding head, racking nausea, fatigue, and fear were easing.

Within a minute Moira tentatively let out her breath. Oh, Goddess, she could breathe without pain. She took in slow, deep breaths, feeling pain and tension leave her with every exhale. She opened her eyes just as her mum opened hers.

"Thanks," Moira said, feeling a new sense of awe. Her mum had healed her before, but now Moira truly understood where the ability came from—a source of power deeper than she'd ever imagined. "That's so much better."

"We need you in good shape," Morgan said, and hugged her.

It was right then, at that moment, that Moira realized that her mother's powers as a healer were probably exactly equal to her power to destroy. It was almost blinding, this huge example of how everything in life was both black and white, good and bad, healing and destructive. Mum always called it the thorn on the rose, and Moira marveled at how complete everything felt, how reassuring it was, in some way, that the wheel always turned unbroken.

Morgan took her hands away and shook off any magickal energy that was left over. There were pale violet circles under her eyes; she looked sad and weary and oddly expectant, as though she were waiting for bad news.

Within Moira's next breath, the whole world went gray.

Blinking wildly, Moira could still see her mother, less than three feet away, and could still see Sky, three feet in back of her. Everything else was gone.

"What is this?" she cried as Sky slowed the engine to a crawl.

"Fog," Sky called back. She cut the engine and swung the tiller all the way to one side and fastened it there; now they would go in slow, tight circles for a while. She stood and came to the midsection of the boat, where Morgan and Moira were. The three of them peered uselessly out, but it was as if they were surrounded by a thick, gray wool blanket.

"Well, I can't see a bloody thing," Sky remarked. "Goddess only knows if we're about to beach up on some rocks—I thought we were still pretty far away, but who knows? We're in the middle of bloody *nowhere*. Goddess, Iona's much more than a pain in the arse."

"So we need to get rid of the fog," Moira said, trying to think.

"Well, yes," said her mum, running her hand through her hair and getting stuck almost immediately in a tangle. "It's just that we have no way of knowing how much is there, how wide it is, where to move it to."

Fog. Fog was made of water vapor. "Can we make all the tiny water drops in the fog sort of stick together, be attracted to each other?" Moira asked. "Then they would turn into rain and fall. Rain would be miserable, but you can see through it."

Her mother looked at her, blinked, then looked over at Sky. A slow smile split Sky's usually solemn, thin face, and she nodded.

Moira felt a spark of pride—maybe she *could* hold her own with these two strong witches. She was Morgan's daughter after all, and she had to remember that.

Moira, Morgan, and Sky held hands and concentrated. Sky worked the main part of the spell. They concentrated on feeling each infinitely small atom of moisture floating in air, boundless numbers of them. One tiny particle joined another and was joined by a third. Slowly a chain reaction started where each water molecule joined with others and still others. They became heavy, too heavy to float in the air, and began to drift downward, pulling others down with them as they went. Within minutes a frigid rain pelted down, soaking them instantly. The small canvas roof didn't cover where Sky sat by the tiller and offered little in the way of protection for the other two. Rain slanted at them sideways, stinging their faces, drenching their salt-sticky hair.

It was miserable. But they could see.

Sky cranked up the engine and took hold of the tiller. They were through the two islands of North Ulst and Lewis, headed out to open sea. The rain followed them. The waves were still spine-jolting. Time ceased to register as they made their way across the leaden sea. It seemed as if they would be crossing this water forever. They passed a smaller island on the left. Ahead of it, slightly east, was another, even smaller island.

"We should be able to spot another one soon," Sky said, raising her voice over the waves.

The whole world lit up with the biggest bolt of lightning Moira had ever seen. Her hair stood on end with the electricity, and every detail of the horizon was blotted out. *Boom!* It was followed immediately by an enormous, rolling peal of thunder that shook Moira right through her body into her bones.

"We must be getting close," Sky said, grim determination on her face. Her eyes were dark, like obsidian, her skin pale and leached of color. Her wet clothes stuck to her tall, graceful figure, and she gripped the tiller hard with both hands.

Morgan turned to Moira. "Don't touch anything metal," she instructed, then lifted her arms to the sky.

"Morgan! Don't!" Sky shouted. Startled, Morgan turned to look at her.

"Save your strength," said Sky. "Don't waste it here. I can see the island ahead. We'll need you more later."

Morgan nodded and sat down. Sometimes Moira thought she could see the island, but mostly she could see nothing but rain, highlighted by huge, spiky lightning bolts. The booms of thunder rolled through them incessantly, one merging with another.

The wind picked up. Waves doubled in size and crashed against the boat like wrecking balls, jarring Moira, making her teeth rattle, almost pulling her hands from where they clenched the torn seat cover. When she looked in one direction, she saw a wall of sullen gray water. When she turned her head to look over the other side of the boat, she saw another wall of water. The sea itself seemed to have come alive, awakened by the uneven chortlings of their motor, angry at their presence. It seemed to well up around them, eager to drag them to the bottom of the sea.

No sinking, Moira told the universe. *We are not going to sink. This is not the ferry. We are in control. We are protected.*

"I see it!" Morgan shouted, pointing off to the right. They had almost passed it—if they'd kept going, they'd have headed out into open sea.

Sky tried to turn the tiller but strained—it was stuck. Morgan joined her, and the two women pulled the long wooden bar with all their strength. The boat creaked ominously—it didn't want to turn—and Moira refused to think about their fate if the tiller should break and they had no way to steer. *Iona isn't going to win this,* she thought fiercely. *She will not win.* Just as she was about to go help, the tiller finally budged, working against the waves, the wind, the rain.

The island itself looked like a row of giant, black, moss-grown teeth, sticking up out of the water like some huge, decayed jaw. Lightning flashed every other second, and the thunder was so constant it was impossible to tell where one clap ended and another began. Every jagged streak of lightning highlighted this rocky wasteland, and the closer they got, the more uninhabitable the island seemed.

What if this has all been a wild-goose chase? What if Iona was lying? What if we came all this way for nothing? What if Hunter's really been dead for years?

Moira felt a blanket of despair settle over her and knew it was futile to battle it. She looked at her mother and Sky and saw the same gray feeling of helplessness cover their faces like a shade.

Her mother frowned and rubbed a hand over her wet forehead. Then light dawned in her eyes. "It's a spell!"

Why was Mum bothering? It was pointless to struggle, to hope, Moira thought with weak despair. They were all going to die.

Morgan drew runes in the air: Eolh, for protection, Thorn, for overcoming adversity, Tyr, victory in battle, Ur, strength, and Peorth, hidden things revealed.

Slowly Moira realized what was happening. Her head began to clear, and she stood up and joined Morgan. Together they repeated them. At the tiller Sky joined them, and as the three drew Peorth in the air, there was a tremendous bolt of lightning, and suddenly the island was upon them, rearing up like a dragon from the sea, so close they were about to be dashed on the rocks. The sea, the despair, and even the distance had been an illusion.

Frantically Sky grabbed the tiller. Moira sat next to her and pulled also. Morgan scanned the shore magickally and then with one hand shielding her eyes from the rain.

There was no place to land a boat. The shore was rocky and jagged, sharp, broken boulders protecting the island at every turn. They kept on, and finally, just as Moira was afraid that she had no strength left in her arms, her mother spotted a tiny inlet, just a small stretch of sand barely big enough for their boat. Sky and Moira steered the boat into it, wincing as they bashed against rocks with an unholy scraping sound. They beached, the V-shaped hull of their fishing boat completely unsuited to being pulled up onshore. Morgan jumped off the boat, looking wobbly on land, and managed to secure a rope to a twisted and deformed tree that grew out of a crack in one rock.

Then Moira jumped down into the sand. Sky leaped down after her, and they looked at the boat, tilting dangerously sideways on the beach. The propeller was halfway out of the water, long, slimy strands of seaweed twisted around it. It was amazing that it had worked at all.

As far as they could see, there were only rain-slicked black rocks, sodden sand, stunted and gnarled trees, and storm. There was no sign of any human existence. Moira kept blinking against the onslaught of rain, trying to peer into the distance. She cast out her senses. There was nothing.

Her mother reached out and took her wet hand. Sky took her other hand. The three of them walked forward, their feet leaving squishy footprints in the slippery sand. Moira tried casting her senses again and felt a dull ache in her head, but nothing else.

The sand weighed her feet down. Her chest felt odd, tight, and the pain in her ribs was sliding slowly back. The idea that they had to get back in that boat and somehow get off the island filled her with a gray, hopeless fog—and this, she was sure, was no spell.

They walked literally across the island, a distance of maybe half a kilometer. It tapered to an arrowhead shape, rounded at the tip, maybe sixty meters across. The wall of rock ended, too, cutting off the beach at its other side. Moira searched the land, looking for anything that would indicate that any other human had been here. There was nothing. Only a dead feeling, a numbing of her senses, a dulling of her emotions. This place was spelled, created to be a mindless prison. Hunter's not here, Moira thought frantically. This had all been a trap; Iona had lured them here to capture them. She had to get out of here— she had to get her mum and Sky out of here.

But before she could speak, Morgan squeezed her hand and strained forward. Moira followed her mother's gaze, and her mouth dropped open. In the face of the tall rocks was a cave opening, barely visible. But they could see the outline of a person, a human, shuffling toward them from the entrance.

18

Morgan

He had to be here—he had to, Morgan thought in despair. But she could feel nothing, pick up on nothing. She had risked her daughter's life to try to save her *mùirn beatha dàn*'s. But there seemed to be nothing here—only grotesque, deformed trees and sharp bits of rock that stabbed at her feet through her shoes. She gripped Moira's hand more tightly. *Hunter is here somewhere. He simply has to be.*

Then she saw it—an opening in the wet, black rock face. A cave. Visible only because of a faint, flickering light deep inside the rock. The light was blocked, and slowly an outline appeared, a person. A human being was walking toward them.

Morgan's heart constricted painfully, her eyes straining to see into the cave's darkness. Holding hands, she, Moira, and Sky hurried toward the cave. There was no need for words. Their hearts and minds were too full to speak.

They were almost upon the cave when the figure shuffled awkwardly out into the storm, into the palest, most fractured bit of light available. It was not Hunter.

"Oh, Goddess!" Morgan whispered, staring in dismay at the wizened old woman. The woman had wild, tangled gray hair, large, vacant eyes, and sunburned skin crinkled in folds over a face that scarcely looked human. A woman. A leftover witch, put here by some MacEwan, possibly Ciaran, for all Morgan knew. Put here and forgotten for who knew how long.

The woman's faded gray eyes fastened on them blankly. "You're not real," she muttered indistinctly, shaking her head and looking away. "You're not real. They never are." She turned around and began to head back into the cave.

"We're real," Morgan called strongly, starting to follow her. "We're real. We're looking for—"

Her words wisped away into the wind. A second figure was blocking the cave entrance. This one was tall, thin, gaunt. He had long, pale blond hair and a darker blond beard. His eyes were deep set and an odd, light green, as if bleached by the sun and sea.

Morgan could do nothing but stare silently, desperately praying that this wasn't an apparition, that what she was seeing was real. She was shaky, unsteady on her feet as the figure stepped slowly closer.

Oh, Goddess, it's Hunter! Hunter, after all these years! He stared at them, first Morgan, then Moira, then Sky, as if recognition was taking a long time to seep into his brain.

"Do you see him?" Morgan asked Sky, not taking her eyes off him.

"Yes," Sky croaked, her voice broken. "Yes, I see him."

"Hunter. Hunter," Morgan said inadequately, tears springing to her eyes.

"Morgan," he whispered in disbelief. Frowning, he shook

his head, not seeming to make sense of what he was seeing.

A few quick steps brought Morgan right up to him, where she had to tilt back her head to meet his eyes. He looked so different—it had been so long. Goddess only knew what atrocities he'd lived through these past sixteen years. But deep within his oddly light eyes, Morgan saw the Hunter she loved.

He raised one shaky, bony hand, the knuckles bruised and scraped, and ever so gently brushed a strand of wet hair off her cheek. Bursting into tears, Morgan threw her arms around his waist, clasping her hands in back of him as if she'd never let go.

"Hunter, Hunter!" she cried, her tears mingling with the rain. Sixteen years fell away as she closed her eyes and pressed her face hard against his ribs. Then his arms came around her, pulling her even closer as he rested his head on hers. Here was Hunter, her love, back from the dead. It was a miracle, a blessing. "I thought I'd never hold you again," she sobbed. "I thought I'd never, ever see you."

"Morgan," he said, his voice a raspy croak, ruined, but definitely Hunter's voice. "Morgan, my love. You're life itself, you're my life."

"And you are mine. Always." Morgan's heart had stopped when she saw him; now it seemed to thump slowly once, twice, and more. A damp warmth seeped through her sweatshirt: her heart was bleeding again. This was Hunter, and he was speaking to her. He was alive, and she had found him. As she held him, she felt him start to tremble and realized that he, too, was crying. Pulling back, she looked up at him, at his tears, at his dear, beloved face, now broken and battered and much too thin. She blinked, then glanced at the sky to see if the sun had come out. It hadn't—the clouds still hung heavy and low, deep gray and sullen. Quickly she looked from Hunter to the rocks to the sea to Sky, who was weeping silently, a smile on her face, to Moira, who stared solemnly at this stranger who had fathered her.

Everything was brighter, the colors deeper, richer, as if a filter had been taken off her eyes. Every sound seemed clear and precise and exact—she could hear each small wave breaking, each twisted tree branch creaking in the wind. Moira and Sky looked so bright and alive. All those years ago, on the dock in Wales, when she'd felt nothing of Hunter's spirit, everything had dimmed. Everything had become dull, every sight and sound had seemed as if a fine, thin wall of cotton separated it from Morgan. Now the wall was gone, torn away by the indescribable joy of seeing Hunter again.

"She told me you had died," Hunter said hoarsely. "She told me you had died, trying to save me when the ferry went down. Then I saw you, days ago, saw you scrying for me."

"I don't know why I couldn't find you before," Morgan said. "I tried, so many times."

Hunter looked down at her sadly. "You found me now because Iona wanted you to find me," he said. "I told you not to come. Iona wanted you to come here, to get you here."

A dull dread sank over the joy in her heart. She and Sky had feared this, and they'd been right. Now they were here, as Iona had planned, and would have to face whatever she had in store for them—whatever she'd set up.

In the next second Morgan's breath left her in a harsh gasp, and she froze, unable to move. *Iona.* Morgan recognized it as the same binding spell that Iona had used—was it only yesterday?—

at the ruined castle. The New Charter had promised to send someone right away—and no one had warned Morgan that they hadn't successfully taken Iona into custody. Iona's powers must be much stronger than Morgan had realized. Who knew what she had done to the people who had come for her? Morgan felt a pang of guilt that she hadn't done something more to Iona when she'd had the chance. She focused her energy, trying to break through the binding spell . . . but nothing. Stunned, her mind clouded by emotion, Morgan looked to Hunter.

"Morgan!" Hunter said next to her as Sky and Moira ran over.

"Mum, Mum, are you okay?" Moira asked, her eyes wide with horror. Sky took a moment to reach out and grab Hunter's arm, as if to reassure herself that he was real, then turned her attention to Morgan.

"Don't touch her!" Iona said, appearing between two tall black rocks. "What I have is for her alone." Slowly Morgan edged her eyes over to see her half sister standing above them, holding a dark stick in one hand.

"Hello, all," Iona said, giving them her disturbing, skeletal smile that seemed to unhinge her jaws. Her thin, graying hair was plastered to her skull with rain, and Morgan wondered again why Iona seemed so old, so ill, yet burning with such an odd energy.

"Sixteen years of hard work have finally paid off," Iona said, her voice sly and satisfied. "Poor Morgan. Haven't you figured it out yet? Lilith Delaney's been keeping tabs on you for years, but I didn't decide to move on you till this year."

That was important, Morgan thought dimly, trying to think, trying to fight her way through the spell as she had before.

Why now? With her mind she examined the edges of the binding spell, testing its strength. It was stronger than yesterday's. She had to focus and concentrate on getting free, on fighting Iona. If she thought about anything else—Hunter, Moira, Sky—all would be lost.

"Me. The visions, the dreams. I sent the morganite—I even sent the ring," Iona gloated. "That was a brilliant touch, I must say. The actual ring! And now you finally find your heart's true love, only to watch him die! You get to suffer twice!" She threw back her head and laughed.

"I can't help you," Hunter whispered to Morgan. He sounded like he was near tears. "I have no powers. Over time this island binds powers."

"It's all right," Sky told her cousin kindly. "It's all right."

"Mum?" Moira said. She had edged closer and was standing very still, trembling.

Stay back and be invisible, Morgan sent.

You need me, Moira sent back.

Think, think, Morgan told herself fiercely. Unravel the spell. Figure out why now? Iona had mentioned the ring, the morganite, the visions, the dreams . . . but not the hexes and spells around Morgan's home. Had those been an extra touch from Lilith—her own personal vendetta?

Focus. It didn't matter right now. What mattered was learning Iona's intentions and uncovering the best way to defeat her. She had gotten her power from taking the souls of other, more powerful witches. Would that make her vulnerable somehow? She looked up at Sky, whose dark eyes watched her, worried. Taking in very slow, shallow breaths, Morgan visualized herself to be strong, whole, powerful. I can break out of this binding spell, she told herself. I'm Ciaran's daughter. But more important, I'm Maeve's daughter, Maeve of Belwicket. I have her blood, her power in me. I am the *sgiùrs dàn*—the Destroyer.

Morgan raised her hand.

A look of fleeting surprise crossed Iona's face and she frowned. She raised her stick, and Morgan felt the force of Iona's rage crash against her mind, pushing into her consciousness. Buckling over onto the sand, Morgan frantically slammed up every mind block she could think of, remembering the last time she'd had to fight this hard, two decades ago. But she was no longer an uninitiated teenager. She was stronger, with a wealth of power and knowledge. Wincing, she felt Iona pressing harder. If Iona managed to get inside, Morgan would have no chance.

"Let her go!" Morgan heard Hunter's splintered voice dimly, from far away. "You have me! Isn't that enough?"

"No," Iona said, her voice tight. "I want you both."

Think, Morgan! How integrated were Iona's souls? How hard was it for Iona to keep them focused? To control their power? What kind of power would it take just to use them?

A throaty chuckle of triumph reached Morgan's ears. Iona was enjoying watching Morgan bent to her will. Morgan knew that, given the opportunity, Iona would kill them all. Kill Moira. Her daughter. The very thought filled Morgan's blood with anger.

Then suddenly, with no warning, Iona was gone, no longer pushing against Morgan's mind. Morgan keeled over, her face hitting the wet sand. Immediately she pulled her shaking arms under her, rising to her hands and knees. She spit wet sand out of her mouth and stood up.

"I want you to have the chance to fight," Iona said. "And

lose. I want Moira to watch you die, as I watched my father die," she went on, stepping carefully down the rocks. "And then I'm going to take your souls. Well, yours and your daughter's and Sky's. Hunter's isn't worth much at this point."

Watch Ciaran die? Morgan thought hazily. They said he died alone at Borach Mean.

"Can you imagine what I can do with your power?" Iona asked, already looking awed by the thought. "I'll have your power inside me." She shook her head, pleasure showing on her sunken face.

"Why now?" Morgan asked. "Why wait sixteen years?" Her mind raced as she tried to think clearly, desperate to protect her daughter. The beginning of an idea started to form. But to try it could cost her her life.

"I wanted you to have a child," Iona answered, as if it were obvious. "I wanted her to be old enough to suffer, losing you, the way *I* suffered. I wanted your loss to be greater. See?" She flicked her stick over at Moira, and Morgan's stomach clenched as her daughter cried out in pain, wrapping her arms around her chest. Morgan lunged to protect her, but Iona flung out her hand. Gasping, Morgan dropped to the sand, feeling as if knives were cutting into her lungs with each breath; she was being flayed slowly from the inside out. She prayed it was only an illusion. Struggling, she tried to put up a wall between her and the pain.

Moira was whimpering now, curling up.

"It makes it so much worse," Iona observed calmly. In that moment Sky suddenly took out her athame, which she'd been concealing in her pocket. She held it out toward Iona, focusing on the tool as her lips moved silently to form a spell. Rocks flew up from around them and launched at Iona.

Astonished, Iona whirled and at the last second managed to deflect most of them, with a few only grazing her neck. A thin band of blood appeared, dark red against her white skin.

"How dare you?" Iona cried angrily, raising her stick again. The athame fell from Sky's grasp and thunked into the wet sand, buried up to the hilt. Sky dodged as Iona fired crackling, spitting balls of furious blue witchfire at her. One careened off a boulder and slid past Morgan, singeing her face and making her flinch. Sky reached for her athame, but Iona held out her hand and drew the athame to her. She gave Sky a malicious smile, then tossed the athame into the air, away from Sky. It whizzed above her to bury itself in a twisted tree, right over Moira.

Quickly Morgan gathered her strength and choked out a laugh. "A child? That's pathetic, Iona, even for you. Was that really it? Or did it take that long to amass enough power to fight me? We all know that I'm so much stronger than you."

Anger flushed Iona's ghastly face and her eyes sparked. Yes, Morgan thought. She was getting to her—just a few more well chosen words and Iona would be pushing her way into Morgan's consciousness. Iona raised her stick again—but didn't use it. She seemed to sense something. Morgan watched, breathing shallowly, as Iona slowly looked around her.

Sky was crouching behind a dark, wet boulder. Moira had edged up against the tree. Her face was contorted with pain, and tears ran down her cheeks. The old woman Morgan had seen, plus two more forgotten witches, were milling around, watching this happen but with no comprehension on their blank, childish faces. Clearly they were also powerless to help and beyond caring what happened to them.

Come on, Iona, try to get into my mind. "You know it's true. I am strong and you are weak," Morgan went on recklessly. "Father said so."

That did it. With a snarl of rage Iona threw both of her hands out, and instantly Morgan felt it, her furious, barbed consciousness, crashing against Morgan's mind like a burning battering ram. Once inside, she would wipe Morgan's mind clean, steal her power, drain her soul. It was a chance Morgan had to take. For an instant Morgan dropped her mind blocks, and Iona was inside her head, twisted with hatred, power starved, greedy, clutching at Morgan's powers. Morgan steeled herself, ignored her terror, and scanned what she could of Iona's mind.

The soul of the witch Justine Courceau, insane with rage and a frenzied desire to escape; another, lesser soul of a faded witch who had crossed Iona without even realizing it. *And Ciaran.* Morgan gasped as she recognized the soul of her father, the soul she had joined with once before in a *tàth meànma. Ciaran! Oh, God, no wonder Iona is so powerful now! No wonder she could hold me in a binding spell.* Somehow she had reached Ciaran's soul when she'd killed him and pulled out the knowledge and strength that had been crushed when he was stripped of his ability to use magick.

Gritting her teeth, Morgan drew on every bit of power she had within her and once again slammed up her mind block, forcing Iona out. Iona fought her viciously, but Morgan squeezed harder and harder, and then her mind was free again, and Iona was just pressing against her.

It had taken just a moment.

"Why do you even try to fight?" Iona snarled, coming closer. "We all know how this will end."

We need to join our powers! Morgan sent a witch message to Moira and Sky, wincing with each word. *Ciaran's soul is inside Iona! She must have killed him and taken it.*

What should we do? Moira sent, and Morgan was surprised at how steady her daughter felt. Anyone looking at Moira would have dismissed her as out of the fight, but she was strong—stronger than Morgan had realized. Stronger than she herself knew.

Bind her.

Iona was circling them now, keeping an eye on Sky but ignoring both Hunter and Moira.

Iona was still pressing against Morgan's mind, still holding the razorlike spell of pain on her. In Morgan's haze of agony, words floated toward her: "You have the power to devastate anything in your path—or to create unimaginable beauty." Ciaran had told her that, right before she had bound him. He'd said, "You're the *sgiùrs dàn*." The Destroyer. The one who would change the course of the Woodbane clan.

It had been so many years since she'd needed to call on the very depths of her power. Yet as a teenager, she had bound one of the most powerful witches of all time. She had helped stop a dark wave, a thing that had regularly killed hundreds of people, whole villages.

It had been a blessing, all these years, not to have to work magick like that, magick that made one touch the edge of darkness. Now she was soaked through, cold, and shot through with an unholy pain. The man she loved was powerless, in desperate need of help. Her only daughter was in danger. And they needed her to save them.

Morgan sank back on the sand and closed her eyes. She

called on the very depths of her power, every aspect of her history—of her ancestors. She was the Destroyer, and she would defeat her enemies. She let every muscle go limp, from her eyelids to her toes. Every single feeling flowed out of her and onto the sand. Caring, anger, pain, panic, joy, longing, all seeped out of her motionless body. She felt dead, numb, and with it came a kind of freedom. She imagined herself rising, dressed in white, a shining aura around her. She imagined her small silver athame to be a mighty sword. She pictured herself able to deflect any spell, crush any attack, triumph over any foe. Even her half sister. True, Ciaran's soul was in Iona, but without him Iona was weak. It was Morgan who had inherited Ciaran's strength, out of all his children. It was Morgan who had inherited Maeve's strength, her mother who had loved her so much, she had let strangers adopt her so she would be safe. Morgan was the *sgiùrs dàn*.

Be ready, she sent to Moira and Sky. *Gather your power—everything you have. I will tell you when to send it to me. It will be harder without touching. But it's our only chance.*

Her eyes opened. She got to her feet, pain held at bay for now.

Iona stopped and stared at her. She raised her stick, but with a harsh phrase Morgan deflected it. Iona's face twisted into an ugly mask of rage. She shouted out something, and Morgan instantly knew it was Hunter's true name. Iona sketched a rune in the air, called a color to her, and then turned to sneer at Morgan.

"He is mine," she snarled. "He's nothing but a walking puppet." She slashed one clawlike hand through the air, and Morgan watched in horror as identical slashes appeared across Hunter's face and chest, as though a tiger had raked him. In his state it was enough to make him stagger backward, lose his balance, and fall heavily against a low rock. He lay still where he fell.

My love! My love! Morgan's eyes blazed with the pain of seeing her soul mate attacked. And then the realization came to her. Iona was doing all of this to Hunter because she knew his true name.

And I know Ciaran's true name. All those years ago, she'd learned Ciaran's true name the night she first shape-shifted. Stepping forward, her hands clenched into fists, Morgan faced Iona. Iona turned her sights to Moira, who was standing now, her young face resolute. *No!* Morgan thought, but Iona swept her hand again, and Moira crumpled to her knees, welts across her face.

It was time. Her face anguished, Morgan met Sky's eyes. *Yes,* Sky sent. *Do it, no matter what. It's why you're here.*

Moira, Morgan sent. *It's time. I need you—I need you to fight through the pain and send me your power.*

Morgan closed her eyes, took in a deep breath, and felt waves of power come to her from both Sky and Moira. She was amazed at the strength she could feel from her daughter, even injured.

"An nal nithrac," Morgan began. *"Bis crag teragh. Bis nog, nal benteg."*

"How pointless," Iona said, her voice angry. "Amusing, but pointless."

Morgan opened her arms wide. She was full of power, the power of generations of her ancestors. She was made of power, she was power itself.

"I am the *sgiùrs dàn!*" Morgan cried, and her voice, clear and strong, pierced the air, pierced the fog of Iona's power.

Iona looked startled and took a step backward, then straight-ened her shoulders and strode forward.

"You're nobody!" Iona cried. "You're nothing! You're going to be the first to die!" She held out her stick, about to begin a new spell.

Morgan felt Moira drawing some of her power back and whirled to see what her daughter was doing. In one move Moira was back on her feet and lunging for Sky's athame. She pulled it from the tree and whispered something, then threw it at Iona, hard, furious power showing in her eyes. Iona tried to deflect the athame, but Moira must have spelled it with a ward-evil spell, and it hit her shoulder, knocking her off bal-ance. Iona clapped one hand to her shoulder, where dark blood was oozing sullenly through her robe. Morgan whirled to see Moira standing by her tree, angry red marks on her face, furious power showing in her eyes.

With one hand Morgan flashed the shape of a rune through the air, even as she began to sing the first notes of Ciaran's true name. Iona gaped at her, but Morgan continued as swiftly as she could, calling a color from the air, singing the tight, hard song that defined who her father was to the entire universe. In seconds she was finished.

"You are going to die!" Iona shrieked. She raised both arms and started to swing her stick in a huge arc over her head.

"I know your true name!" Morgan commanded. "Enough!"

Iona wavered, her arms jerking as she tried to keep her balance. The major part of her strength, Ciaran's soul, was now under Morgan's command. Iona fought against her, her bony jaw clenched until Morgan thought it would snap.

"I am the Destroyer, Iona," Morgan shouted. "Didn't your

father ever tell you that?" She felt tall and terrible, and even as Iona struggled against her internal force, Morgan's power swelled and rose. She was the conduit for power that had been held deep within the earth for centuries. It was gathering now, rising, and pouring out from her. Sky grabbed one hand, sending her power to Morgan.

"Ciaran is powerless. You are powerless!" Morgan cried, pointing at Iona.

Iona stood there, shocked and with the first glint of fear on her face. But she wasn't beaten yet. Harsh, dark words were pouring from her lips, and her arms moved, writing sigils in the air. A slow rumbling shook the sand beneath their feet, and Morgan whirled to see its source. The cliff above the cave was spitting, the rocks being rent with the last bit of Iona's stolen power. Even with Ciaran bound, she had enough power to craft a spell that was rending thousands of tons of black basalt, fracturing a hill of stone. Rocks and pebbles, boulders and shards, began to rain down on them.

Morgan hurried toward the sea, with Sky following close behind. Morgan grabbed Moira's hand and yanked her backward. Hunter was looking up at the wall of rock, then at Iona, and Morgan rushed forward to drag him into the water.

"It won't be enough!" Iona shouted, laughing.

Huge waves of stone tumbled down the side of the hill, thudding into the sand, bouncing off one another. In a split second Morgan had made her decision. *Scaoil,* she thought, and she sent her power out in a tightly coiled knot that knocked Iona squarely on the chest. Her back hit the rough wall by the cave, and in the next instant a huge boulder tumbled down, sweeping her thin body to the ground like a stick puppet.

Moira cried out and covered her face, looking away. Morgan gathered Moira to her, still urging everyone backward. They were up to their necks in the frigid, salty water, and still cannon-ball-size rocks were striking the water all around them. Morgan treaded water, keeping Moira, Hunter, and Sky in sight. Her face crumpled as she saw two of the withered witches pinned beneath a house of rock. The cave had been crushed, no doubt killing any who had been inside.

Eventually the hill was nothing more than a crumbled rock pile, half as tall as it had once been. There was only a small area of sand still visible, and slowly, all holding hands, the four of them made their way through it, shivering uncontrollably as the cold air hit their wet bodies.

Teeth chattering, Morgan turned to look at her family, all of them.

"It's over," she said wonderingly. "It's over." Tears of joy washed the salt from her eyes, and then they were all hugging, crying, laughing.

"Thank the Goddess." Morgan felt completely and utterly drained but so thankful.

"Blessed be," Sky said, smiling and shaking her head.

Morgan.

Morgan froze, blood draining from her face. Hunter, Sky, and Moira all looked at her quizzically, and she held up one finger.

Iona's voice was surprisingly strong in Morgan's thoughts. How had she survived the rock slide in her weakened state?

Morgan. This isn't over, Iona said. *At this moment Lilith and Ealltuinn are making their final move—on Belwicket. You're not home to protect it. By the time you get back, everything you knew and loved will be a black, smoking plain. You see, I am my father's daughter.*

A dark wave. As soon as Morgan thought the words, her whole body shook, as though a shock of ice water moved through her veins. She felt dizzy. *No. It can't be.* Not Belwicket. Not her coven, her home!

"You're lying!" Morgan shouted desperately, looking back at the stunned faces of her family. "You haven't the power! You haven't the skill!"

"Perhaps not," Iona's voice replied from behind Morgan. Stunned, Morgan spotted Iona crawling weakly from a small space beneath several fallen rocks. She was battered—a huge cut bled fiercely on her arm, and she limped, scarcely able to stand—but she was alive. Iona reached the sand and cackled, enjoying Morgan's stunned expression. "You bound Ciaran," she said. "But you didn't bind me. And what you don't realize is that I am not relying only on my own power"—her voice was weakened now, no better than a desperate hiss—"but also that of my ally, Lilith Delaney. It's *Lilith* who cast the dark wave spell. That was what she truly wanted all along—to rid her country of the so-called good Woodbanes, like Belwicket. It was just a fortunate coincidence that I wanted their future high priestess dead."

As Morgan opened her mouth to reply, Iona suddenly extended her hand and spat out a chain of ugly words. *"Feic thar spionnadh! Thèid seòltachd thar spionnadh!"*

Morgan barely had time to react as a sharp spear of energy, glinting silvery blue in the sunlight, sped toward her. Automatically she threw up a blocking spell. She was shocked that Iona would try to hurt her in her weakened state—what possible good could it do her? But then her thoughts turned darker. Iona was clearly beyond reason. She was crawling blindly toward a single purpose—hurting Morgan.

As Iona's attack reached Morgan, something unexpected happened. Morgan had long known that her element was fire, and so she called on the power of fire to add strength to even her most basic spells. But as Iona's sharp spear of light reached Morgan, it bounced off the shield she'd created and turned to roaring orange flame. Before Morgan could take in a breath, the flame turned upon Iona and consumed her.

"No!" Iona wailed as the flame overcame her body. The fire grew, and soon an oily, roiling black smoke—eerily like the smoke that had invaded Belwicket's circle—emerged from the fire. Morgan gasped. In a matter of seconds the flame burned to nothing and winked out. No evidence of Iona's body remained on the beach. No smoke, no charred earth, nothing. Morgan stared, disbelieving, at the spot where Iona had stood. She's dead, she thought finally. Evil serves no purpose. It consumes you. But before she could react further, she remembered Iona's final promise.

"We have to get home as soon as possible," she cried, turning back to her family and running for the crude boat they had rented only hours before. "There's a dark wave coming for Belwicket!"

19

Moira

They had to swim back to the beach where they had left their boat, since rock slides had destroyed most of the original path. Sky, Morgan, and Moira held on to Hunter, helping him along. They climbed on board with difficulty, and Morgan and Sky pushed the boat off the sandbar. Sky started the motor, and then the island was in back of them and they were headed out to sea. Moira shivered, not only because she was freezing and wet and her face burned where Iona had raked it: what had happened on the island had been far worse than anything she could have expected. All those poor people—dead. That horrible witch, Mum's half sister—dead. Not just dead, Moira thought. Burned to death by her mum's own deflection spell. She'd thought she couldn't be any more horrified by what her mum was capable of, but she'd been wrong. There wasn't even time to react, though. Because the four of them were heading back home, where another, even bigger disaster awaited them

Moira had heard about dark waves, of course, but during her lifetime nobody had seen one. When she'd asked her mum about it, she'd explained as best she could—it was a huge, sweeping cloud of evil, made up of tortured souls who were hungry for new energy. A dark wave could kill any number of people, it could level houses, it could leave a village as nothing more than a black, greasy field. Moira was torn between her terror of what they'd find when they reached Cobh and the many other emotions battling inside her at the sight of Hunter, real and alive in front of her.

Hunter shook his head, the slashes on his face covered with dried blood. "I still can't believe it," he said hoarsely. His eyes looked so large in contrast with his gaunt face. "I'm so afraid I'll wake up and find this was a dream."

Morgan laid her hand on his arm. "No," she said. "This is real. We're alive, and you'll never be back there again. Of course, it will be a long road back after . . . after everything you've been through. And unfortunately, there's no time to start healing just yet. We still have something else to face."

Nodding, Hunter wiped the sleeve of his shirt against his eyes. Then Morgan looked at Hunter's shirt and frowned. In the center of his chest were dark stains, one on top of the other, that had happened in the same place again and again. She looked down at her own dark sweatshirt, then again at Hunter's. Hunter's heart had been bleeding, just as Morgan's had.

Moira couldn't keep her eyes off Hunter. This was her biological father. Colm, gentle, warm, loving Colm, was her da, but this man . . . he was half of who she was. And while Colm was gone, Hunter was here. But she was still as lost as ever about what that actually meant. Could she ever know this man as her father? Was it a betrayal to Colm, who had loved her with everything he had?

The sea had calmed, and it wasn't difficult to speak over the sound of the overtaxed engine. The four of them were solemn, beaten physically and emotionally and facing a dark wave.

"So this is your daughter," Hunter said, nodding at Moira. Moira shot her mum a meaningful glance and saw Sky do the same. Hunter's eyes took it all in.

"Yes, this is Moira," her mum said, then cleared her throat. "Moira Byrne."

"Byrne." Hunter looked at Moira again, speculatively, and she blushed.

"I'm a widow," Morgan said awkwardly. "Colm, my husband, died six months ago."

"I'm sorry, Morgan," Hunter said, and he seemed sincere. He loves her, Moira thought. She could sense the emotion coming from him in waves, despite his obvious weakness. Raising her eyebrows slightly, Moira looked again at her mum.

"What?" Hunter asked, noticing Moira's look, a slight frown on his face. "What are you not saying?"

Morgan started picking at a loose thread on her soggy jeans. Moira knew she did that when she was nervous. Actually, Moira did it, too. "I have something to tell you," her mum said, not looking up. "At first I thought it should wait. This must all be so much for you to take after . . ." She stopped and took a deep breath. "But you need to know. Perhaps it will even help somehow. The truth is, I found out only—oh, Goddess, only a couple of days ago—that Moira is . . . I was pregnant with Moira already, before I got married. Before I was with Colm."

Confusion crossed Hunter's battered, exhausted face. It was

clear he was struggling even to speak at all and to understand the meaning of words he hadn't needed to use in so long.

"I'm your daughter," Moira burst out, surprising even herself. "From when you and Mum were in Wales. Before you died. I mean, I'm sorry, you didn't . . ."

Hunter's green eyes grew even wider, taking over his too-thin face. His mouth opened slightly, almost hidden beneath his scruffy beard. Looking from Morgan to Moira and then to Sky, he didn't seem to know what to say.

"We didn't know," Moira went on more strongly. "Mum had been spelled—by my grandmother. She hadn't meant to make her forget the truth, but it happened, and then she and Dad just—" Moira stopped, seeing the growing confusion on Hunter's face. "It's a long story. But it just came out—the same time we learned you were alive."

Hunter stared at Moira blankly, as if his mind was working too slowly for him to comprehend what she was saying. He looked over at his cousin for confirmation, and Sky nodded gently.

"Oh my God, Morgan," Hunter said in his scratchy voice. "We have a daughter." He looked at Morgan again, and Moira could see his love for her shining on his face.

"Yes," Morgan said, her eyes bright with tears. "We do. But—but I still can't figure out how."

"What?" Moira asked. "What do you mean?"

"I shouldn't have been able to get pregnant." Her mum looked a little embarrassed. "We took precautions." She turned to Moira. "That was another reason I had no idea you were Hunter's."

Moira knew about pregnancy prevention spells and how a blood witch would be pregnant only if she consciously skipped them. Somehow in all the chaos of learning Hunter was her father, she hadn't stopped to think how that didn't make sense. "But you got pregnant anyway," Moira said.

"I think I might know why," Sky said slowly, and the others turned to look at her. "Remember what I already said, Morgan, about the Goddess having her way? Well, you are the *sgiùrs dàn*, fated to change the course of the Woodbanes. Maybe you were fated to have Moira. Maybe your precautions didn't mean anything in the face of fate."

Morgan blinked. "But . . . that means that fate has something important in store for Moira."

"Like what?" Moira asked nervously, a chill going down her spine.

"I don't know," said Morgan. "But I do know that after what I saw you do on the island, you'll be up to handling whatever comes your way." She gave Moira a proud smile, and it warmed Moira deep inside.

"My daughter," Hunter said wonderingly. "I have a daughter." He gazed at Moira, drinking her in with wonder until she looked away, feeling suddenly shy. Yes, she was his daughter—but she'd been raised by another man. And she wasn't ready to make sense of all of it yet.

What if Sky was right—what if her birth had been fated? Her own mother had played such a huge role in the Wiccan world. If she was meant for something similar, then she couldn't let anyone down. Moira pictured Tess, Vita, and her gran—all back in Cobh, unprepared for the danger coming at them. A week ago it wouldn't have occurred to her that she would help fight a dark wave. Now it was unthinkable not to. She tried to sit up straighter, ignoring her aches and pains and cuts and bruises. "We need a plan," she said firmly. "To beat the dark wave."

*　　　*　　　*

Back on land, Morgan and Sky rented a small charter plane to take them directly back to Cobh. It would take only three hours, compared to two days of driving. The flight had cost pretty much everything Morgan and Sky had in their combined accounts, but that didn't matter.

Now that they were on the plane, headed for home, any lingering joy at finding Hunter had been put on hold. As horrific as the island had been, Moira knew she was facing something far worse. Part of her wanted to run and keep running. But there was no way she could leave her coven, her house, her town to face a dark wave without her.

"Da made a . . . a simpler spell before I . . . left," Hunter said. He spoke slowly and not very smoothly after not having had to talk in years. Sometimes he had to pause to think of a word. "I knew it well once, but it's . . . gone." He frowned in frustration, his sunburned face wrinkling. "I haven't been able to work magick for sixteen years . . ." he said; then he looked out the window, his voice trailing off, as if even admitting that was too painful to bear.

"How long did the long version take?" Sky asked Morgan.

"A little more than an hour, I think," Morgan said. "I have it all written in my Book of Shadows, but I remember that we coached Alisa for days before and even then had to help her during it." She shook her head. "I don't see how we could do it. And anyway, Alisa was able to survive performing the spell because she was only half blood witch. The spell would destroy a full blood witch. I don't see how any of us . . ."

Hunter started to speak, then coughed. It took him a

moment, and finally he was able to get the words out. "The spell Da worked, it could be performed by full blood witches," he said. "If only I could remember it, or—"

"I'm just not sure where Uncle Daniel is," Sky said. "I haven't spoken to him in a couple of months. He still travels a lot."

"Da's all right, then?" Hunter said cautiously.

"Yes," Sky said, a slight smile on her face. "He's doing well. Seeing you again will give him another fifteen years at least. But I don't know where he is, and we don't have time to track him down."

"As soon as we get home, we'll go to Katrina's," said Morgan, her face set. "Most likely the coven will be there. Maybe they'll have come up with something."

It would be hard seeing Gran again, Moira thought, for both her and Mum. But again, it was a small consideration compared to the dark wave. Right now they all had to focus on that.

By the time they landed at the small commuter airport in Cork, the weather had turned nasty. To Moira, it felt as if she hadn't seen sunshine for years. The minute she stepped off the plane, she frowned. When she touched the ground, she felt a jolt of nausea that made her swallow quickly.

Morgan narrowed her eyes. "Do you feel bad?"

"I'm going to throw up," said Moira, looking for a trash can.

"It's the dark wave," her mother explained. "It makes blood witches feel awful, hours before it arrives."

They were all tired and hungry and ill. Moira's face was killing her. Now her mum stopped, looked at the sky.

"How much time?" she asked Sky.

"Three hours? Four?" Sky said, and Hunter nodded.

"At best."

Home! Moira thought with relief when they reached the cottage. She would never take it for granted again—there had been more than one time in the last twenty-four hours when she'd believed she'd never see it again. Now she was going to do her utmost to protect it.

"This is where we live," Moira heard her mum explain to Hunter. He still seemed dazed, half there. He kept touching things, running the tips of his long, thin fingers over objects, textures, as if he had to reidentify everything.

Inside, Bixby was hiding under the couch, his pupils wide and his tail fluffed. Finnegan barely greeted them, sniffing Hunter before he slouched under the dining room table, an occasional low growl coming from his throat. Hartwell Moss had been taking care of them, but she wasn't here now.

"They know," said Moira's mum, referring to the animals. She sounded ill.

Ten minutes later Morgan and Sky were poring over Morgan's old Books of Shadows. "See, it took the combination of the four of us," Mum was explaining in a low voice. "Daniel, me, Hunter, and most importantly—Alisa. And it took hours. I don't see how we can possibly . . ." She shook her head.

"What if we each take a part?" Moira suggested, resting her head in her hands. Her skin felt clammy and cold, her head felt as if it would soon explode, and she never wanted to see food again.

"With this version of the spell, we'd all be in great danger," Morgan said in distress.

"And I won't be of any use," Hunter said, sounding at the end of his rope. Morgan had immediately fixed them all an herbal concoction to help give them energy and take away the nausea, but so far it hadn't been doing very much. Hunter took a sip of his and grimaced.

"I feel like death," Morgan said. "Hunter has no power. Let's just get to the coven and see if they know anything."

The short walk to Katrina's seemed to test their limits. Moira was dizzy and bone tired, and everything seemed to smell awful. Hunter especially looked bad, dragging his feet, swaying sometimes. His face was an unhealthy white beneath the sunburn, and his eyes kept closing as if he could barely go on. Morgan put her arm around his waist, supporting him. As soon as they were within sight of the old store, its door opened and Katrina hurried out.

"Morgan!" she cried. "Thank the Goddess you're here. You know about the dark wave?"

"Yes," Morgan said, letting Katrina usher her into the coven's meeting room. By unspoken agreement, they would deal first with the dark wave—later with their personal matters, if they had the chance. Inside, Moira saw most of the initiated members of the coven. They were obviously suffering the dark wave's effects. Pale and hollow eyed, they came forward to greet Morgan, hugging her, and Tess and Vita ran forward to greet Moira.

"Where were you?" Tess asked, looking frightened.

"I'll have to tell you later," Moira said. "But it's good to see you." She pushed her way through the crowd of people surrounding her mother and saw that the coven was looking at Hunter with undisguised interest.

"This is Hunter Niall," Morgan said shortly. "He created the New Charter." That seemed to be all the explanation she was going to offer for his presence, his extraordinary appearance.

"I haven't asked this yet because it seems too easy," Moira said. "But why can't we all just leave here now? Let the dark wave have the buildings but save the people?"

Morgan shook her head wearily. "That doesn't do any good. It's too close. The wave would follow us."

A sudden pounding on the door startled them—no one had felt anyone approach. Katrina answered it, and Ian stood there, breathing hard. Moira's heart slammed against her chest as all the horrible events of two nights ago—three?— came back to her, and she looked away.

"I'm not sure," he began, trying to catch his breath. Through the doorway Moira could see his mud-spattered bicycle dropped on the ground behind him. "But I think we're all in danger."

Morgan put her hand on his shoulder. Moira saw her look at Sky, as if to ask, Is he being honest?

Sky looked over his head and nodded at Morgan, and she nodded back. Moira guessed they weren't picking up on any hidden agenda or falseness from him. She wasn't either. The night they had visited Lilith, she'd thought he'd betrayed her—he'd participated in Lilith's work. But was he here now, going against his mother? Moira was so afraid to let herself believe in him again.

"My mother's coven left this morning before dawn," Ian said, nervously looking around. "In her workroom I found— stuff to work dark magick with. Really dark magick. I hadn't really known it before." His voice was sad. Moira closed her eyes briefly and cast her senses, reaching for Ian's emotions. She blinked her eyes back open, her heartbeat quickening. It was genuine, Ian's pain—genuine and overwhelming. She was almost sure he was telling the truth, and doing so was ripping him up inside. "I didn't want to know what they were doing. But now there's something awful in the air."

"We're pretty sure Ealltuinn has created a dark wave," Morgan said, and Ian flinched in shock. "It will destroy everything around, all of us. Everything."

Ian looked nauseous. "A dark wave? I didn't think anyone could do those anymore."

"Ealltuinn has found a way," Morgan said. "Now we have to stop it." She turned to Hunter. "Do you remember *any* of your dad's simplified spell?"

Hunter looked at the ceiling, concentrating hard. Silent words came to his lips.

Outside, the wind kicked up, blowing a small branch against a window. The light coming in had a sickly greenish tinge to it, like the light before a tornado.

"No!" he said finally, his fists clenched in frustration.

Morgan's face fell.

Oh, Goddess, Moira thought. What now? We need a plan. There must be some way to fight this!

"It's still in there," Sky said to him, gripping the back of a chair. "She didn't wipe your mind, just bound your magick."

The other coven members stood around, listening. Some smaller groups were discussing ways to act, but no one seemed to be coming up with much.

"I don't know what she did," Hunter said, his cracked lips tight with tension. "I just know I can't remember . . . a lot. I don't have any power."

Moira could hear his frustration and could hardly imagine

what he must be feeling. Would she ever get to know him, even close to as well as she'd known Colm? Would she ever see him healed and happy? Or would this, today, be her only memory of him? Her heart ached at the thought.

"Dammit!" Morgan said suddenly, smacking her hand on the table. "She can't win, not now! We have to stop this."

Katrina and some others nodded, but they all looked uncertain and afraid.

"Can we all just join together and use the strongest protection spells we know?" Christa Ryan asked, rubbing her temples.

"A dark wave isn't just fought," Morgan explained. "It has to be dismantled."

We have to stop it, Moira thought desperately. We're all going to die—none of the past two days will have meant anything. Iona's defeat will mean nothing. The four of us together defeated her—surely we can defeat this now. That was when it came to Moira: *The four of us together . . .*

"Mum?" said Moira, swallowing down her nausea. "I have an idea. I think Sky's right—that Hunter still has the spell locked up inside his brain. He just can't remember it. You could do a *tàth meànma* with Hunter, getting the spell from deep inside, where he doesn't remember."

"I thought about that," Morgan said. "But . . ." She paused, looking at Hunter. "I don't know how well he could stand it right now," she finished softly.

Hunter's eyes hardened. "I can stand it," he said, clearly using every ounce of strength left in him to make the words sound firm and believable.

Moira glanced down at the floor, overcome by the power of his feelings for Morgan, how much he would do for her. And

. . . for Moira, too. She could feel concern for herself in him as well, even though he'd only just learned she was his daughter.

"Still, I'm not in great shape myself," Morgan said. "Iona drained so much power from me."

"I know," Moira said. "Get the simplified spell from Hunter, then send it to me. I'm not initiated yet, but I have power. You said it yourself—how strong I am. And Sky can help, joining her power with mine."

"No," Morgan said flatly.

"Mum, it's the only way," Moira said urgently, leaning forward. "None of us, no one in this room, has what it takes to do this alone. You and Hunter at least have some experience with a dark wave. You know both me and Sky, you know how to work with us. We have to do it. And what happens if we don't try anything? Are we all just going to sit here and die? *After everything?*" Moira met her mother's eyes, pleading with her.

"Moira may be right," Sky said reluctantly. "We have maybe an hour before the dark wave gets here. One person working the spell alone might not make it, even with the shortened version. If both of us are working simultaneously . . ." She looked up. "We just might pull it off."

"We've no other good plans anyway," said Hunter. "None of us are thinking clearly—we've all been through too much. We can either stay here and die, or we can go fight it."

"I hate all of these options," said Morgan, looking from face to face.

"We all do," said Sky. "But there is one problem. We need more than one witch to work the spell, and my powers are still quite weak. I don't know if I . . ."

"Please let me help," Ian said. His face was solemn and grim. "For years I've not asked questions about my mother's work—even though deep down I always felt something wasn't right. I've gone on and done my own thing and tried not to see what she was doing, she and the new members she recruited to Ealltuinn. But now I see what a coward I've been." His voice dropped so that they had to lean in to hear him. "I need to help make this right if I can. Please let me help. I'm initiated, and I have a fair amount of power."

Moira knew—in every fiber of her being—that he was telling the truth. She'd been right about him all along. Maybe Lilith *was* like Selene Belltower, but Ian was *not* Cal. And she hadn't been a fool for trusting him after all. Even with all the danger they still faced, knowing that helped.

Morgan looked at Sky, who looked at Hunter and Moira. Moira waited anxiously, thinking, *Please, please, please.*

It was only after her mother hesitantly said, "All right. We have no choice," that Moira allowed herself to realize she would be going up against a dark wave. But there was no time to be afraid or to panic. If the dark wave killed her, she would go down fighting, trying to save her family, her coven, her town. Her mum had made the same decision, when she was barely seventeen. Moira was an ancestral Riordan. She was Moira of Belwicket, with her mother's strength, her grandmother's, her great-grandmother's. And Ciaran's strength also. He'd used his power for evil. Moira would use hers for good.

Nodding, she said, "Let's go."

They decided to meet the wave as it approached the village, on the high road by the headland and the cliffs. It was hard to walk fast, with how awful everyone felt, but they tried to hurry, going over the plan as they went. The twelve strongest members of the coven would station themselves in a circle of protection around Moira and Ian. They might not help, but they couldn't hurt, and everyone had agreed to stay together. The rest of the coven would be nearby, sending whatever power they could to Moira, Ian, Morgan, Sky, and Hunter.

"Moira," her mum said, easing closer to her. Her voice was low, confidential. "I have to tell you: dying by a dark wave is much worse than dying almost any other way. And by far the worst thing about it is that your soul then joins the collection, and you become one of the hungry, desperate for energy, for life. That's what we're facing today. I want you to understand just what you're going up against."

Moira tried to ignore the aching, hollow feeling in her chest. "I understand, Mum," she said, keeping her voice as strong as she could. "But as long as we're together, it will be all right. You and Hunter and me and you, all together."

Her mother's eyes grew bright with tears, but she just nodded and squeezed Moira's hand. "I love you," she said. "More than life itself."

"I know," Moira said. "Me too."

"Looks like here," Sky said, a few feet in front of them. They slowed, and Sky looked up at the clouds, then down the road. The air itself felt foul, a mixture of oily fumes, smoke, depression, illness. On the farthest horizon Moira could just barely make out an eggplant-colored line.

Her heart sank down into the pit of her stomach. "Is that it?" she asked faintly.

"Yes," Hunter said grimly.

Moira met Ian's eyes, which were solemn and wide. He gave her a quick nod.

"Yes, I think you're right," Morgan said, sounding tired down to her bones. Moira saw her watching Hunter, as if to make sure that he was miraculously still alive. Desperately Moira hoped they would have more time together. They deserved it. Moira was sad for Colm, sad that he hadn't been her mum's *mùirn beatha dàn*, and still devastated that he hadn't been her own biological father. But it didn't change the fact that Hunter *was* both of those things—and Morgan and Moira deserved the chance to be with him. To know him, even, in Moira's case.

"Right, then," said Sky. She sounded tired also, cranky, but she seemed in better shape than Morgan. "Looks like it's going to sweep right on through here. I think Moira and Ian should be in the middle of the road. We three should be over there, maybe. There's a copse of shale—it looks like there's a crevice in it. It won't save us, should it make it here, but it'll shelter us from the worst effects before it does." She looked up at the small crowd of anxious but grimly determined coven members.

"Twelve of you, take your posts," Sky said. Katrina, her sister, Susan Best, Keady Dove, Christa Ryan, and Sebastian Cleary broke away from the group and began positioning themselves. They were followed by Hartwell Moss, Fillipa Gregg, and Michelle Moore, and then Brant Tucker and Brett and Lacey Hawkstone moved to the other side. Lastly, Will Fereston took his place.

"Good," said Sky, looking tense and pale. "Now, are we clear on what's going to happen? Morgan's going to get the spell from Hunter."

"We hope," Morgan muttered.

"Yes, we hope," Sky said somberly. "Morgan will pass it on to me and to Moira. I will pass it on to Ian, then join my power with Moira's. Moira, you're going to work on the first and third parts of the spell. Ian will work on the second part, which is long. At the right moment Moira will ignite it. Got that?"

Moira cleared her throat. "Yes. Got it." Inside she was quaking with fear and a kind of bleak, private admission that this might all very well be for nothing. Her head was pounding, she felt queasy and shaky. But she wasn't going to show it.

Ian nodded, his jaw tight.

"We'd better move," Hunter said, his voice sounding like rocks scraping metal.

Moira forced a smile at her mum, who was slowly walking backward away from her with a desperate look on her face. Her mum looked stricken, as if she would give anything not to leave Moira right now. And every part of Moira longed to reach out and grab her, to hold on and never let go. She was terrified to face the dark wave without her mum at her side. Her mum, who she understood would do anything to protect her. But now it was her turn to protect her mum.

"Go on," Moira urged softly, working to keep her turbulent emotions cloaked. Her mum nodded stiffly. Then Morgan, Hunter, and Sky disappeared below the shallow copse. Now Moira had to wait till Morgan contacted her with the spell.

"I'm sorry," Ian muttered, looking down. He looked as bad as Moira felt.

"It isn't your fault," Moira said. "I'm sorry . . . about the other night."

Ian nodded. "That was awful. But it wasn't *your* fault."

Then he reached out and took her hand. Both their hands were cold, trembling, but Moira seized his as if it were her lifeline. She wouldn't have to go through this alone.

The sky to the east was sickly green, tinged with purple. There was a foul stench in the air. Anxiously squawking birds of all types were flying past as fast as they could, escaping in the way that wild animals have of knowing.

It was very near.

Moira. Mum was ready. Moira quickly closed her eyes, trying to blank her mind for the *tàth meànma* with her mother. It would be extremely difficult, since they wouldn't be able to touch. She had to have absolute concentration. Then her mother's consciousness was there, pressing on her brain, and Moira immediately opened her mind to let her in. Surprisingly it hurt, and Moira winced and tensed up at the pain of it. *I forgot to warn you this would hurt. We didn't have time to prepare properly with fasting, meditating, and so on.*

It's okay, Moira sent back, gritting her teeth. Then, with Morgan guiding her, Moira opened her eyes and created a circle with purified salt around her and Ian. She put out Morgan's four silver cups, carved with ancient Celtic symbols and representing the four elements: earth, air, fire, and water.

On this day, at this hour, I invoke the Goddess, Morgan told her, and Moira repeated the words. "You who are pure in intent, aid me in this spell."

And on it went, the first part of the spell. It had been greatly simplified, but Moira still needed to define it, clarify her intentions, and identify all the players and parts.

Next to her Moira heard Ian start to speak as he received his part of the spell from Sky. He moved in a carefully crafted pattern that would define the spell's limitations: exactly where, when, why, and for how long the spell would ignite. The things it would affect, the things it wouldn't. Looking tense and frightened, he knelt and drew sigils on the ground and in the air. Finally Moira finished the first part, and she waited anxiously for Ian to finish the second part before her mum would coach her through the third.

Okay, now Ian's done, Morgan sent, and Moira nodded. *This third part is the actual spell.*

Slowly and carefully her mum fed Moira the words to say, the words that defined for all time exactly what this spell would do. Moira needed to move at certain times, to trace runes in the air or on the ground, to rub salt on her hands, to spill water on the ground. She started feeling really terrible about halfway through, when the throbbing pain of the *tàth meànma,* her rising nausea, and the abhorrent stench in the air all combined to make her sway on her feet. *What next?* she thought, forcing herself to concentrate. Her mother repeated what she was supposed to do, and, almost in tears, Moira began it. Then her head started spinning and Moira seemed to lose all her peripheral vision. An acrid taste rose in the back of her throat and her stomach heaved. Clapping her hand to her mouth, she fought it down, then fell to her hands and knees in the mud of the road.

Moira! Mum sent urgently. *Moira, get up! You have to get up! Get up NOW!* Panting slightly, Moira raised her head and blinked. She was shaking, every muscle trembling uncontrollably. Oh, no, she thought in despair. *They're all going to die because of me.* It was too much, this responsibility. What had she been thinking, promising everyone that she could do this?

She had been too bold, too arrogant—and everyone she loved would pay the price. She took in another shallow breath.

Around her the twelve coven members were watching her with desperate expressions. She met Katrina's eyes, saw the fear and horror in them, the love and regret. Her gran's lips were moving silently; all this time the coven members had been chanting protection spells, ward-evil spells, spells to try to limit the sickness Moira and Ian felt.

Go on! Morgan sent urgently. *You can do this, Moira—you're almost done!*

Moira stared down the road. The dark wave was almost upon them. Birds who hadn't escaped were dropping dead from the sky. She could see bits of shredded tree, pulverized rock, wisps of burned grass blowing ahead of the wave. Moira gagged with every breath, covering her mouth. Death was coming. Death was here.

"Now!" Sky yelled out loud, then coughed. "All of you twelve, send your powers to Moira and Ian! Chant your protection spells! All of us together!"

Then her mum shouted, *"Ignite it!"*

Her mum believed in her. She believed Moira could stop the dark wave. Now it was time for Moira to believe in herself. She reached into the very deepest reserve she had, summoned her last bit of strength, and slowly, slowly staggered to her feet. *I call on you,* she thought, imagining her strong and powerful ancestors—her mother, her grandmother, Maeve, and everyone before them. *I call on your power.* It was amazing, the rush of energy that suddenly flowed through her. She *could* do this. She was Moira of Belwicket, daughter of the *sgiùrs dàn, fated* to be born. Today, this moment, she would prove her birthright.

Yes. I must. It's up to me. With a huge effort Moira threw up her hands. With her last breath she shouted the ancient Gaelic words that would ignite the spell. Her hair was blowing backward, she was struggling to keep her balance, but again she shouted it, louder this time. Next to Moira, Ian also shouted, his arms out from his sides. A third time they shouted the words.

What's wrong? Moira wondered hysterically. *It should have stopped! What's wrong? What did we do wrong? We missed something, we skipped something, Hunter misremembered. The spell was wrong.*

She watched in horror as the people forming the line of protection scattered, running to the sides of the road and flinging themselves down face-first. Then the cloud was upon them, barely licking the place where Moira and Ian stood.

I'm going to die, Moira thought with one last moment of clarity.

Then suddenly a rip appeared in the fabric of the universe, an odd, eye-shaped nether place. A *bith dearc*, Moira realized. In a split second the dark cloud was sucked into the rip with more force than one could imagine, like a plane suddenly becoming depressurized at thirty thousand feet. The wave, large enough to cover a field, was pulled through the *bith dearc* in a matter of seconds. Moira fell to the ground, her hands sinking into the soft mud. It seemed to root her to the earth, and she grabbed a tough clump of muddy grass and held on to it. She saw Ian fall. He'd been standing a fraction of an inch closer to the *bith dearc*, and he was being pulled inexorably toward the opening. In another second he would be through.

"Moira!" Morgan shouted, racing toward them. "Moira!"

Ian was on his stomach, clawing at the ground, his eyes wide. Without hesitation Moira reached out and grabbed his hands, the mud making them slick. There was a half-buried rock in the ground and she braced her sneakers against it, leaning back and pulling with all her might. Feeling as if she were in slow motion, Moira gave a huge heave, her teeth gritted, eyes screwed shut, veins popping on her neck. Then all at once Ian was free and the *bith dearc* sealed seamlessly, leaving no trace of ever having been there.

Moira's mum dropped down next to her, grabbing her and holding on tightly, tightly. Sky skidded to a halt next to her, grabbing Ian's leg, anxiously making sure he was all right. Behind them Hunter knelt down awkwardly, breathing lightly and shallowly, a clammy sweat dewing his skeletal face.

Moira put her muddy arms around her mum and hugged her back. Then she pulled away and turned around. "Is Ian all right?" she asked shakily.

Ian nodded. He was sitting back in the dirt of the road, looking stunned, sweat only now breaking out on his forehead. "You saved my life," he whispered.

Morgan laughed, brushing Moira's hair off her face, "You saved us," she said, her eyes shining with obvious relief, joy, and pride.

Moira smiled. Then, with no warning, she covered her eyes with one hand and started to weep.

20

Morgan

"I see," Morgan murmured into the phone. "Yes, yes, I think that would be best. When? Tomorrow. I think we can do that. It will be late tomorrow, though."

Hanging up, she looked over at the table to see four pairs of eyes watching her inquisitively. Morgan sat down and put her hand on Ian's arm. "The New Charter has found your mother and eight of her followers at the border between England and Scotland. They wanted to know if I could come up to identify Lilith and file formal charges against her."

Ian looked down at his bowl, a slight flush rising to his cheeks. Sky, Hunter, and Moira waited sympathetically. They'd all been gingerly hunched over bowls of soup for lunch. It had been only two days since the dark wave, and everyone still felt awful. Morgan was drained but had been busy creating teas and herbal concoctions for everyone in the area. She'd also tried to work some magickal healing but found it strained her still-weak powers. Right now they had to let time do its work.

"What are you going to do?" Ian asked quietly.

"I'm going to go identify her," Morgan said gently. "And file formal charges against her."

He nodded, still looking at his bowl. "Can I go with you?"

"Of course."

Only Morgan and Ian went. Sky had wanted to be there to see for herself that Lilith was being punished, but they agreed it was better for her to stay home and watch Hunter while Moira was in school. He was still unsteady on his feet sometimes, weak, and also just absentminded and foggy. He looked slightly more normal, with short hair and no beard, and his bruises and face slashes were healing well. But he couldn't eat very much, and his nightmares would take a long time to work through. He had settled into the guest room at Morgan's house, and Sky had moved down to the couch.

There was no reason for Moira to go. She, too, was still healing both physically and mentally and wouldn't add much to Morgan's testimony. She and Hunter were getting to know each other, and one of the first times he'd smiled was when she had cracked a dry joke. Morgan and Sky had looked blank, and Hunter had been the only one to get it. Morgan smiled, remembering it.

Sky hadn't been in America twenty years ago when they'd battled the last dark wave, and this had been her first experience with one. It had left her as shaken and drained as the others. Morgan envied her these few days alone with Hunter, getting to know each other again, picking up where they had left off. But as soon as her obligation with Lilith was over, she would rush back. Despite having the rest of her life to spend with him, she felt a need to seize every minute.

She looked over at Ian, pretending to read in the train seat next to her. After the wave had gone, the coven had met back at Katrina's store to comfort and help each other. Katrina had come forward and offered to let Ian stay with her, and he had agreed, at least for a while. He knew his mother would probably never come back to share their house again.

"This is going to be hard," Morgan said sympathetically.

Ian nodded, then sighed. "She was all I had," he said. "I've no idea where my dad is. Don't really want to find him, anyway. Mum had been getting worse and worse, and I just didn't want to see it. Our house—" He shrugged. "Maybe in a while I can go back to it."

"Take your time," Morgan said.

For a moment Ian looked as if he wanted to say something, then thought better of it.

"What?" Morgan prompted him.

"You're Ciaran's MacEwan's daughter," Ian said hesitantly. "You . . . you know. Did you . . . did you love him?"

Morgan hesitated, understanding Ian's pain all too well. "I didn't really know Ciaran," Morgan said. "Actually I only saw him a handful of times before he died." *Before Iona killed him.* "But there's something between a parent and child—you want, or maybe need, to love a parent. I have the best adoptive parents anyone could hope for. Really good, caring people who did their best by me. I never knew Maeve. I knew Ciaran was evil, I knew he would betray me or use me or kill me if I didn't join him. Yet what I felt for him was very much like love, despite everything. Something deep inside me felt good that he was proud of me, proud of my powers, that he wanted me to join him when he didn't want his other children. I almost wanted his approval. It crushed me to have to bind him, to have his powers stripped. It was the worst thing, the worst decision I ever had to make. But he was my father. And he loved me, in his way." She paused. "Does that help?"

"Yes," Ian said softly, looking out the train window. "It does, a bit."

Lilith and her followers were being held at a New Charter building not far from Scotland's southern border. When Morgan and Ian arrived, they were led into the manager's office. Matilda Bracken was tall, gray-haired, and severe-looking but smiled warmly when she saw them. Rising, she came to meet them.

"Morgan Byrne of Belwicket," she said. "How very good to meet you. Well done, down in Ireland."

"Thank you," Morgan said. "It took all of us, including Ian Delaney here."

"Yes, Ian." Matilda took both his hands in hers. "I'm sorry to meet you under these circumstances, my dear."

Ian nodded uncomfortably.

"Morgan, first I need you to identify Lilith Delaney and then to fill out a form about your charges. Then, Ian, you'll have a chance to see your mother."

Lilith was being held in a small room. The doorway was spelled so no one could enter or leave, but Morgan could see Lilith through the open door. She pressed her lips together as she saw that Lilith's face still bore signs of the bruising that Morgan's attack had caused. What a terrible night that had been.

"Yes, that's her," Morgan said.

Lilith rose from her narrow bed and literally spit at Morgan through the doorway. "It still isn't over," she said, her eyes glittering. "It will never be over."

The prime emotion Morgan felt was sadness. "No, Lilith," she said. "It *is* over. Iona is dead. You're here, and unless you're rehabilitated, you'll be in the care of the New Charter for the rest of your life. Your house and workroom are being cleared and purified."

Lilith actually looked surprised. "No."

"Yes." Morgan paused. Certain questions still gnawed at her. "Tell me, why did you agree to work with Iona? What was in it for you?"

"Power," Lilith said, as if this were obvious. "She helped me gain control of Ealltuinn. She sent strong people to work with me. We're going to find the power leys of Ui Laithain and use them to become the most powerful witches this world has ever seen. Once I get out of here, you're just going to be a memory." She smiled at the thought, her eyes taking on a crazed gleam.

Lilith's hold on reality was clearly slipping. She had no comprehension of her situation, what her future held.

"That's why you kept an eye on me and reported on me to Iona?"

"Yes. Little enough, for all she did for me."

"What about all the hexes this past month? Why bother? Iona never mentioned them—they weren't part of her plan, were they?"

"I can think for myself just fine," Lilith retorted, her voice rising. "Those were intended to harm you. To show you you're not welcome." She frowned. "They should have worked better. You or your brat should have had accidents, hurt yourselves."

"I guess you underestimated us—both of us," Morgan said, feeling a spark of pride in her daughter. "You know that it was Moira in the end who defeated your dark wave?" Lilith's frown deepened. "How did you learn to create a dark wave, anyway? It's clearly beyond *your* strength."

Lilith's face grew tight with fury, and the answer was right there.

Iona. It had been in Ciaran's knowledge when Iona had killed him and taken his power.

"So why now?" Morgan pressed. "Iona made a point of telling me that now was the perfect time for all of this— before I defeated her, that is."

Lilith looked ready to explode. "She had to move now," she muttered, "before you became high priestess. Before Moira was initiated. And . . . she was growing desperate."

"She was dying," Morgan said. "The souls whose power she took were eating away at her. She wasn't strong enough to hold them in check for that long. She was losing control, and she had to act before they tore her apart forever."

Lilith looked contemptuous. "You can think that if you want. But Iona is strong; she'll recover from whatever you did to her. And I'm her partner. Together she and I will be able to crush the New Charter. And when we do, we're going to come after you."

There was nothing to say to that. But Morgan did have one last thing to discuss with Lilith. "Ian is here," she said.

"Ian? My boy?" Lilith looked eager, coming to the door.

"Yes. You can explain to him why you abandoned him,"

Morgan said. "Why your pursuit of power was stronger than your love."

The older woman's eyes narrowed and she stepped back. Morgan turned and headed down the way she had come.

The long train ride home was mostly quiet. When Ian had returned from seeing his mother, he'd obviously been crying, but his face was stoic.

"Time works wonders," Morgan said inadequately, even though she knew firsthand that some pain never seemed to ease.

"Yes, thank you," Ian said, then resumed looking out the window.

I'm going home, Morgan thought, joy blooming in her heart. Home to my daughter, to Hunter, to safety and calm.

Katrina was at the train station to meet Ian. It was thoughtful of her, and Morgan was glad she'd reached out to him. Despite the terrible injustice she'd done to Morgan and to Moira, Morgan believed that Katrina was a good person and would be of great help to Ian during this lost time.

Then she was home. The front door opened before she was halfway up the walk, and her family waited for her. Moira, her daughter, who had saved them all, and Hunter, her Hunter, who was home again at last.

"Welcome home," Moira said.

"Yes," Morgan sighed, reaching out to hug one after the other. "Yes."

Epilogue

"So we've set it up for me to be initiated at Yule, only six months late," Moira said to Tess. She and her mum had made the decision together to wait a little longer, give themselves some time as a family to heal from everything and for Moira to begin to get to know her birth father. "You've not changed your mind, then?"

Tess rolled her eyes. "You only ask me that once a month. Hand me that garland."

Moira handed Tess a garland of woven grapevines and autumn branches. They, along with some others, were decorating their circle room for the Mabon celebration. This year would be especially joyous, commemorating the first anniversary of the defeat of the dark wave.

"Vita's going to be initiated at Imbolc and me at Yule, and that leaves just you," Moira pointed out.

"I'm proud and happy for you both," said Tess firmly. "But it's just not for me. I need the hammer."

Moira handed her the hammer. Tess pounded some

short tacks into the wall and placed the garland on them. Across the room Vita was helping to decorate the altar with gourds, fresh vegetables, fruit, and more autumn branches.

"This place is looking fantastic," Katrina said, coming over to hug Moira. Moira smiled. It had taken a while before she had been able to forgive her grandmother, but it had been such a relief when she had. Gran had made the wrong decision, but Moira believed that she had thought she was acting for the best.

A couple of months after she and Moira had sorted things out, Gran and Morgan had gone for an all-day walk, and by the time they'd come home for dinner, they'd also been on better terms. It was so much easier this way, especially since Ian still lived at Gran's.

Hmmm, where is Ian? Moira looked around, then spotted him carrying in a large wall hanging. It was black, with a silver zodiac sign painted on it: Libra, the balance. At Mabon the day and the night would be exactly balanced, the same length, and then the next day the dark would start to dominate until spring.

It was kind of funny, Moira thought, how she still got a fluttery feeling in her chest whenever she saw Ian. They had been seeing each other for a year now. The more she'd gotten to know him, the more amazing she thought he was. For the past three months he'd been helping her study for her initiation, and she was impressed again and again by how smart he was, how quick he was to understand. They were a good team. And his kisses . . . Moira gave a pleasant shiver.

With help from Brett Hawkstone, Ian hung the wall hanging behind the altar. Ian had worked so hard to fit into Belwicket.

People in the coven had been suspicious at first, but he had steadily proved himself by taking part in circles. With Gran's continued support, Ian had become at home with Belwicket.

"What do you think?" Ian asked, coming over. He gestured at the wall hanging.

"It looks great," Morgan said. "Where did you get it?"

Ian looked surprised she didn't know. "Tess made it."

Mouth open, Moira looked up at Tess, who shrugged and smiled. "I was expressing myself artistically," she said.

"Well, it's terrific," said Moira. "I'm really impressed." Tess smiled again, seeming a bit self-conscious.

Moira glanced at her watch. "Time for me to get home, guys," she said.

"Thanks for all your hard work," Gran said, kissing her. "You must have been collecting branches for days."

"Ian helped," Moira said. Then, holding hands, they left the store and began walking to Moira's.

"Can you stay to dinner, then?" Moira asked him. As soon as they were alone on the road, their arms had gone around each other. Moira hooked her thumb in his belt loop as they matched strides.

"Not tonight," Ian said. "I think Katrina's got a shepherd's pie in the oven. Some night this week, though."

She smiled at him, then sobered as they reached the section of road where they had performed the dark wave spell a year before. Only recently had the grass started growing back on both sides—it had remained scorched and sparse for ten months afterward.

"Will we ever be able to get past this place without it feeling bad?" Moira wondered aloud.

"I don't know," Ian said.

So much had changed since then. Hunter had never left her and Mum's cottage, and the guest room had become his. In the past year there had been so much rebuilding: rebuilding Hunter's health, her mum rebuilding her relationship with Hunter. Moira and Hunter had slowly gotten to know each other, a bit shyly at first, and then more and more comfortably. She still called him Hunter, though. She couldn't bring himself to call him Da.

At Moira's garden gate Ian stopped. "I better get back," he said. He bent down and kissed her, and she smiled up into his eyes. "Can you meet me tomorrow?" he asked. "Before the circle? Take a walk or something? Or we could go to town, get tea."

"Yes," she said happily. "Come by around two, all right?"

He nodded and kissed her again. Then Moira stood and watched him walk down the road, back to Gran's.

Inside, the house smelled like baking bread and beef stew, and Moira sniffed appreciatively. Hunter was setting the dining table, and her mum was just coming in from the back garden with some fresh bay leaves.

"Hi, sweetie," she said, smiling. "How's the decorating going?"

"Good," said Moira, sitting down in the rocking chair. "It all looked really great."

"I've always liked Mabon," Hunter said. His voice had smoothed out quite a bit but would always be slightly hoarse, Moira thought. She watched him as he moved around the table. He looked very different than when she had first seen him. Over the past year he had gradually put on weight, and now she could no longer see his knobby spine through his shirts. All of his bruises were gone, but there were scars he'd always have.

His magick had come back, very slowly. It had been hard, watching his frustration as he couldn't perform the simplest spells. Then one day he'd been able to snuff a candle by thinking about it. Just that had made him so happy, Moira had almost cried. It had increased after that, and though Mum said he wasn't as strong as he had been, she thought he would continue to get better.

"Okay, supper's ready," Moira's mum said, starting to serve up the bowls.

The three of them sat down around the table. The sun had almost set, and inside the cottage it was cozy and lamplit. Moira picked up her spoon and waited while Hunter cut slices of bread.

"Thank you," said her mum as Hunter served her first. The smile she gave was so deep, so perfectly happy, that it made Moira feel warm inside.

Next he passed Moira her bread. "Thanks." Every once in a while she was still surprised that this man, living in their house, sharing every meal, was her actual father. And after a while her guilt over the feeling that she was betraying Colm by caring for Hunter had lessened. Gran had promised her that Colm would have wanted her to be happy and to have a relationship with her biological father.

And Hunter really *was* an amazing person—she could understand now why her mum loved him so much. He was funny in a really dry way, but Moira could trust him to be serious when she needed him to be. She loved talking with him about spellcraft— his mother had been a Wyndenkell and a great spellcrafter. She'd met his father, Daniel, her grandfather, who had been old and kind of crotchety but pleasant enough. Aunt Alwyn had been really nice. Sky came back every couple of months to visit.

Moira's whole life, whole family, had changed. But it was good. It had been good before, with Dad and Mum and her, and it was good now. She was so lucky, so fortunate. Tess and Vita hadn't seen it that way, when she'd first told them about Lilith, and the island, and Iona. They'd felt so sorry for her, going through that. But Moira wasn't sorry for herself. Those horrible experiences had helped her so much in learning who she really was and what was truly meaningful to her. Since they'd gotten back, she and her mum had far fewer rows about unimportant things. They'd been reminded of what was truly important.

Now she sat at the table, warm and happy, already planning what she and Ian would do tomorrow before circle.

"I've been thinking," Hunter said into the silence.

Moira and Morgan both looked up.

"Oh, good, that's coming back," Moira's mum teased, and Hunter looked at her with a pained expression. She laughed—she laughed more often now.

"Despite your attempts at wit," Hunter went on, as both Moira and her mum laughed, "I've been thinking that this is good, what we have, the three of us."

"Yes, it is," Morgan said, her eyes shining.

"I'd like to make it permanent," Hunter went on, his voice softer. Morgan's eyes widened, and Moira stopped eating, her spoon in midair. His sculpted face caught the candlelight, and Moira saw the smile gently curving his lips.

"Morgan, for the second time, will you be handfasted to me? You're my heart's love, my heart's ease, my savior in every sense of the word. Will you be my wife?" Hunter reached across the table and took her hand.

Moira held her breath. She'd known this would be coming

and hadn't been sure how she'd feel. But now she knew—it was right. It was perfect.

Morgan looked at Moira, then back at Hunter. "Yes," she said, her voice clear and firm. "Yes." She looked again at Moira, love and hope showing plainly on her face.

Moira was speechless, looking from one to the other. She felt strange and happy and surprised and excited and a tiny bit sad as well.

"I think it's a very good idea," she said, nodding. "I really do."

Morgan tilted back her head and laughed, and Hunter laughed, too. Reaching out, he took hold of Moira's hand, and she reached for her mum's, and the three of them sat around the table, joined. They had gone through pain and horrors and tests of fate to get here. But they had made it. And they were a family.

SWEEP

Cate Tiernan

BOOK OF SHADOWS

THE COVEN

BLOOD WITCH

Love. Danger. Magick.

VOLUME I

Morgan Rowlands never thought she was anything other than a typical sixteen-year-old girl. But when she meets Cal, a captivatingly handsome coven leader, she makes a discovery that turns her whole world upside down: she is a witch, descended from an ancient and powerful line. And so is Cal. Their connection is immediate and unbreakable; Cal teases out Morgan's power, her love, her magick. But Morgan discovers too soon that her powers are strong—almost too powerful to control. And she begins to suspect that Cal—her love, her soul mate—may be keeping secrets from her . . . secrets that could destroy them both.

978-0-14-241717-1

VOLUME II

Morgan Rowlands is a blood witch, the last of a long line of ancient and powerful witches and the holder of an unfathomable power. With the help of her love, her soul mate, Cal, she has realized her true self—but at a price. For Morgan and Cal share a terrible, dark secret, one that binds them together even as they are rent apart. Yet there is something about Cal's hunger for magick that frightens Morgan. . . . And now there is another, one who can bring Morgan clarity, truth . . . love. Morgan must decide who is her true love, and who is out to destroy her forever.

978-0-14-241897-0

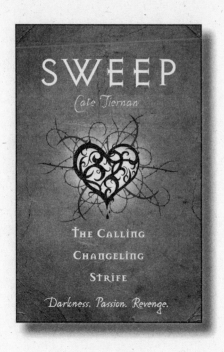

Volume III

Morgan Rowlands holds a profound magickal power . . . a power that some will stop at nothing to obtain. For Morgan is the last of an unbroken line of ancient and powerful witches. Though she still has much to learn, magick has brought her more than she could ever have imagined: the love of her soul mate. Yet her dreams uncover something else—a dark force threatening her entire world. As the darkness closes in, Morgan realizes that she must make a choice—good or evil; love or hatred. Is she strong enough to make the sacrifice and discover her true nature, or will the darkness consume all she holds dear?

978-0-14-241955-7

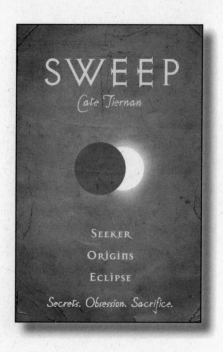

SWEEP
Cate Tiernan

SEEKER
ORIGINS
ECLIPSE

Secrets. Obsession. Sacrifice.

VOLUME IV

Morgan Rowlands has accepted her place as the most powerful blood witch of her time. Yet still, she's desperate to uncover the mystery of her heritage . . . and terrified of what she might find. Impending darkness looms as an evil wave of devastating force threatens to alter her world forever. Morgan knows she must fight against it and risk everything to preserve the life she has come to love: a life with her soul mate, Hunter. But when her past reveals astonishing truths, and destruction is a near certainty, it's up to Morgan to face the darkness.

978-0-14-242010-2